SON OF TWO FATHERS

Also by Jacqueline Park

The Secret Book of Grazia dei Rossi: Book One

The Legacy of Grazia dei Rossi: Book Two

SON
of
TWO
FATHERS

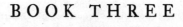

BOOK THREE

JACQUELINE PARK

WITH

GILBERT REID

ANANSI

Published in Canada in 2019 and the USA in 2019 by House of Anansi Press Inc.
www.houseofanansi.com

House of Anansi Press is committed to protecting our natural environment.
As part of our efforts, the interior of this book is printed on paper that contains
100% post-consumer recycled fibres, is acid-free, and is processed chlorine-free.

23 22 21 20 19   1 2 3 4 5

Library and Archives Canada Cataloguing in Publication

Park, Jacqueline, author
Son of two fathers / Jacqueline Park, Gilbert Reid.

Sequel to: The legacy of Grazia dei Rossi.
Issued in print and electronic formats.
ISBN 978-1-4870-0396-8 (softcover).—ISBN 978-1-4870-0397-5
(EPUB).—ISBN 978-1-4870-0398-2 (Kindle)

I. Reid, Gilbert, author II. Title.

PS8581.A7557S66 2019   C813'.54   C2018-900669-2
                                        C2018-900670-6

Library of Congress Control Number: 2018961552

Cover design: Alysia Shewchuk
Text design and typesetting: Alysia Shewchuk and Laura Brady

Canada Council   Conseil des Arts   ONTARIO ARTS COUNCIL
for the Arts   du Canada   CONSEIL DES ARTS DE L'ONTARIO

We acknowledge for their financial support of our publishing program
the Canada Council for the Arts, the Ontario Arts Council, and
the Government of Canada.

Printed and bound in Canada

MIX
Paper from
responsible sources
FSC® C004071

This book is dedicated, on behalf of Jackie and myself, to Jackie's cousin Howard Cohen and to the memory of Howard's sister, Marylin Walder

CONTENTS

CAST OF CHARACTERS

* An asterisk denotes a real historical character.

RABBI ABRAHAM HAZAN — widower, father of Miriamne Hazan

ACHILLES — boy performer, bought by Andreas Satti in Palermo, twin to Ajax

AGOSTINO CHIGI * — rich banker, financier for the Papacy, patron of Grazia dei Rossi

AJAX — boy performer, bought by Andreas Satti in Palermo, twin to Achilles

RABBI ALAMANO — rabbi in Rome

ANDREA MANTEGNA* — court painter in Mantua, great Renaissance painter, died 1506

ANDREAS SATTI — impresario working for Isabella d'Este

ANGELICA SATTI — actress, wife of Andreas, working for Isabella d'Este

ANSALDO — cook for Isabella d'Este, friend to Sappho

BARBAROSSA* — Greek admiral and pirate, maritime raider, working for Suleiman

BEATRICE DE LUNA* — New Christian, banker, head of the Mendes Bank, Jewish name Gracia Nasi

BRUNO SCAVO — Dominican friar, crusader against corruption and against Jews

BUCEPHALUS — Danilo del Medigo's horse when he was a teenager in Istanbul

CELESTE DEL VOLPE — Venetian beauty, model for Titian

CHARLES V* — Holy Roman Emperor from 1519 to 1556, persecuted Jews and New Christians

CIECHERELLA — innkeeper in Mantua, friend of Sappho

DANIEL BOMBERG* — publisher of books in Venice

DANILO DEL MEDIGO — biological son of Grazia dei Rossi and Pirro Gonzaga

DIOGO DE MELO DE CARVALHO — Portuguese aristocrat

ERCOLE II D'ESTE* — Duke of Ferrara, nephew of Isabella d'Este, son of Lucrezia Borgia

FEDERICO II GONZAGA* — Duke of Mantua, son of Isabella d'Este

FILIPPO — Christian errand boy for Vincenzo, the Christian gateman to the Ghetto Nuovo

FRANCESCO MENDES — banker, late husband of Beatrice de Luna, uncle of Samuel Mendes

FRANCESCO II GONZAGA* — husband of Isabella d'Este

FRANCESCO III GONZAGA* — Duke of Mantua, son of Federico II, grandson of Isabella d'Este

FRANCESCA ORDEASCHI* — Venetian, lover and then wife of banker Agostino Chigi

FRANÇOIS I* — King of France from 1515 to 1547

GALEAZZO BRAMBILLA — Milanese gentleman, informant to Ottomans, agent of François I

GIOVANNI SABADDIN — printer in Venice

GIULIA GONZAGA* — distant relative, by marriage, of Isabella d'Este

GRAZIA ROSSI — mother of Danilo del Medigo, wife of Judah del Medigo, died 1527

HEINRICH CORNELIUS AGRIPPA VON NETTESHEIM* — occult writer, died 1535

HÜRREM*—also known as Roxelana, former harem slave girl, wife of Suleiman

IBRAHIM PASHA OF PARGA*—Grand Vizier, Administrator of Ottoman Empire for Suleiman

ISAAC—Old Uncle Isaac, widower, friend of Miriamne Hazan

ISABELLA BOSCHETTI*—la Boschetti, mistress of Federico II Gonzaga

ISABELLA D'ESTE*—Marchesa of Mantua, wife of Francesco Gonzaga, mother of Federico Gonzaga

JACOB—young boy, protected by Miriamne Hazan

JEAN VUYSTING*—Charles V envoy in Milan, charged with capturing New Christians

JEREMIAH LEVY—Jewish banker, ally of Mordecai Hazan, wants to marry Miriamne Hazan

JESSICA—young woman, protected by Miriamne Hazan

JUDAH DEL MEDIGO—personal physician to Suleiman, legal father of Danilo del Medigo

LEONARDO BRESSAN*—Venetian naval architect, designer of warships

LUCREZIA BORGIA*—daughter of Pope Alexander VI, mother of Ercole II d'Este

MARCO—Venetian spymaster, "controller" of Danilo del Medigo and Angelica Satti

MARTINA—girl performer, bought by Angelica Satti in Naples

MEHMED II*—Ottoman Sultan, great grandfather of Suleiman, conquered Constantinople in 1453

MELANIA—Christian, niece to Vincenzo, helps out in the Ghetto

MICHELIS—stationer, works with printer Gionvanni Sabaddin

MIKA—Christian, neice to Vincenzo, helps out in the Ghetto

MIRIAMNE HAZAN—daughter of Rabbi Hazan, Venetian poet and writer

MORDECAI HAZAN—brother of Miriamne Hazan, son of Rabbi Hazan

MUHARREM KONEVI—Turkish merchant, agent of Suleiman, client of Veronica Libero

PERINA*—la Perina, a young waif, protected briefly, and much loved, by Pietro Aretino

PIETRO—manager of the Andrea Satti Acting Troupe, messenger for Angelica Satti

PIETRO ARETINO*—famous poet, playwright, polemicist, libertine

PIRRO GONZAGA—distant cousin of Isabella d'Este, biological father of Danilo del Medigo

SAIDA—Ottoman princess, daughter of Suleiman the Magnificent, former lover of Danilo del Medigo

SAMUEL MENDES—banker, nephew of Beatrice de Luna

SAPPHO—young black slave of Isabella d'Este, brilliant performer, singer

SULEIMAN THE MAGNIFICENT*—Ottoman Sultan, ruler of the Ottoman Empire 1520 to 1566, father of Saida

TITIAN DA CADORE*—leading painter of the Renaissance, friend of Pietro Aretino

TOTO—Venetian torch-boy, young lad who guides people around at night

VERONICA LIBERO—leading Venetian courtesan and poet, works for the Venetian spy service

VINCENZO—Christian gatekeeper of the Ghetto Nuovo, uncle to Mika and Melania

VITO ANSELMO—Venetian banker

SENATOR VITTORIO ALTEBRANDO—Venetian patrician, director of Venice spy service

ZARAH—Veronica Libero's young protégée, works in Veronica's salon

ZENO—wealthy Venetian patrician, politician, ally of Senator Altebrando

ZUFOLINA*—la Zufolina, androgynous girl, dresses as a pageboy, lives with Pietro Aretino

ITALY IN THE

SIXTEENTH CENTURY

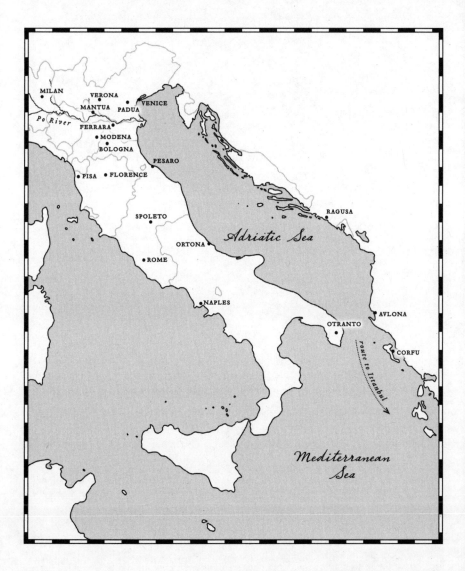

I N 1536, WHEN TWENTY-YEAR-OLD DANILO DEL MEDIGO, SON OF
Grazia dei Rossi, arrives, incognito, in Venice after ten
years in Istanbul, he is returning, without realizing it, to a
Western civilization in profound crisis.

Fear and loathing are spreading everywhere. Jews and
"New Christians"—people whose families had been forced to
convert from Judaism to Christianity in order to survive—are
threatened throughout Europe with expropriation, expulsion,
imprisonment, and death.

While persecuting others, Christendom is itself in mortal
peril, threatened from within and from without.

From without, mighty Islam looms on Europe's doorstep.
Suleiman the Magnificent, father of Danilo's great childhood
love Princess Saida, and leader of the vast and powerful Ottoman
Empire, is poised to invade Italy, conquer Rome, and seize much
of Europe for Islam.

And within Europe, Christendom is ripping itself apart in
ferocious political and religious strife. François I, King of France,
is continually at war with the Spanish King and Holy Roman
Emperor, Charles V. Protestantism, in open revolt, has begun

its century-long life-and-death struggle with Catholicism, while Catholicism and the Papacy mobilize for a vast counterattack against Protestants, heretics, and freethinkers of all kinds.

Caught in these titanic battles, the great maritime Republic of Venice, and the small city states of Italy, fight to defend their independence. The freethinking libertine energies of the Renaissance are threatened by suspicion, dogmatism, and intolerance, and by the spreading terror of a horrible new sexual disease — syphilis.

As panic spreads, in April 1536, an inquisition, modeled on the Spanish Inquisition, is about to be introduced into Portugal and the Portuguese Empire. Jewish converts to Christianity — New Christians — must flee, or they must die.

PROLOGUE

Lisbon, Portugal, April 15, 1536, the Eve of Passover

DIOGO DE MELO DE CARVALHO SWEPT THE CURTAINS aside and peered out of the second-story window of his mansion overlooking the river Tagus and Lisbon's port. A woman, dressed all in black, was just alighting from her sumptuous carriage. Beautiful and unbelievably rich, she was a widow who controlled half of the famous Mendes Bank.

Diogo frowned. She was also a Jewess, pretending to be Christian. In a few months, when the Portuguese Inquisition began, she would be judged, and burned at the stake, along with others of her kind.

She disappeared into the entrance of his mansion. He imagined her gathering up her skirts and nervously hurrying up the broad marble staircase towards him, alone and vulnerable, anxious as to why he had summoned her.

He turned from the window as the woman was ushered into his office.

Diogo bowed but remained behind his desk, favoring her

with a thin smile. She was what they called a "New Christian," or a *Conversa*. Whatever term you cared to use—it was all the same blasphemous charade—an obscenity, really, which she attempted to mask with a beautiful Christian name—Beatrice De Luna.

She was twenty-six years old and recently widowed. Her banking fortune was built on a monopoly in financing the spice trade, a monopoly granted by the Portuguese king to her late husband, Francesco Mendes, whose bank, based primarily in Lisbon and Antwerp, was renowned throughout Europe.

He motioned to the woman to sit down.

She did, in front of his desk, and gazed at him.

Diogo de Melo de Carvalho was fifty-eight years old and known to be powerful and dangerous. By reputation, he was quick-tempered, violent, and occasionally sadistic. He possessed large estates in Portugal, interests in the New World, and in the spice trade. He was also an influential confidant of the Portuguese king. And, perhaps even more important, at this precise moment Don Diogo had enormous debts, debts soon coming due.

Diogo remained standing. The light from the tall second-floor windows was at his back, throwing his face into shadow, so that the Jewess, sitting in front him, brightly illuminated and totally exposed, had to concentrate, narrowing her eyes to read the shifts in his expression. The gold crucifix that hung from the woman's neck caught the sunlight.

Diogo spread his strong dark hands on the surface of the desk and leaned forward. "You know what people call you—you New Christians, you *Conversos*?"

She held his gaze.

"They call you pigs, they call you swine." He bared his teeth and took his time pronouncing the words. "They call you *Marranos*—pigs—something unclean."

Beatrice lowered her eyes. In Spain and Portugal many of her ancestors, like thousands of others, had been murdered in riots, in massacres. Some had been burned alive. Many more

Jews and New Christians, the wealthiest and most powerful, even the counselors of kings, had been insulted, humiliated, stripped bare and reduced to rags and barefoot beggary. If they had not been murdered, they were sent into exile. She stared at her hands clasped in her lap, at her gloves, the finest leather and craftsmanship money could buy.

She looked up. "It is not clear whether Old Christians originally called us *Marranos*, swine, because they believed that our families—converted from Judaism—had not truly embraced our new faith, and that we were hypocrites and secretly still Jews, or whether it was the Jews—our former coreligionists—who invented the expression *Marranos* because they despised our families since we had abandoned the religion of our forefathers."

Diogo laughed. "You New Christians—you *Conversos*—are despised by all." He lowered himself into his chair, toyed with a quill on his desk. The glare from outside shone on his shoulders and on his white hair. He was a handsome man, with broad shoulders and an amiable smile. Only his hands betrayed the peasant-like brutality, the edgy, fidgety coarseness.

Diogo sighed and stood, turning his back to her. Letting the tension build could be useful. He stroked his beard and gazed out of the large window. It gave him a fine view of the river Tagus and Lisbon's port. Less than fifty years ago, Christopher Columbus and Vasco da Gama had sailed off to discover new worlds—the Americas—and new routes to old worlds, Asia and the Indies. This meant new sources of wealth, even for Diogo and his family. But competing with the new wealth for status and glory was expensive for an aristocrat like Diogo; it meant vast new outlays for balls, dowries, sumptuous entertainments. . . . It never stopped."

He watched as one of the caravels left the quay and moved into midstream, followed by a heavier, three-masted carrack laden with high-priced goods. It had all happened so fast. Less than forty years ago, da Gama, on his twenty-thousand-mile voyage, had discovered the sea route to India and to the spices—black pepper, cinnamon, ginger, cassia, cardamom, and turmeric—that grew in those distant exotic lands. Europe, particularly northern Europe, had an insatiable appetite for these strong, mysterious tastes and aromas, and their food-preserving and medicinal qualities. That unbridled appetite made merchants, adventurers, and nations rich. It had made the bankers who financed the trade, such as the late Francesco Mendes, even richer. And much of that wealth was concentrated, right now, in the person of the slender young Jewess sitting behind him.

Even now on the quays, carracks and caravels were preparing to leave for the Indies and other destinations. Some would sail around Africa towards India, the land of spices, and come back, with luck, in a year or less, laden with that new-found wealth; others were about to set off westwards, across the Atlantic, for the recently discovered New World and all its treasures and promise. Still others, heavily laden, were departing for Antwerp in the Netherlands, where all the spices and exotic goods imported from distant non-European lands would be sold into the huge markets of northern Europe, where the real wealth lay. The Mendes Bank, with its monopoly over spice-trade finance, captured much of that wealth, money that Diogo desperately needed.

He slid his hand along the windowsill. Only a few decades ago, Portugal had been a small, poor country, barren and stuck on the edge of the world. Now it was an empire and Lisbon was the center of vast trading networks. It was a dizzying new world of glory and plunder; a new world in which to spread the faith in Christ, the faith of the Savior, the Messiah. But to keep their power, prestige, and dignity, Diogo and many of the old aristocratic families had to shine ever brighter in the face of the new wealth. This meant Diogo's expenses—like those of the Portuguese king—always outran his revenues. He tapped his fingers on the windowsill: He had to provide for his family—the most fashionable ball gowns, the most elegant carriages, the newest furniture, the greatest homes—he had to give to charities . . . Diogo needed money, and he needed it now. If this woman were to be arrested by the upcoming inquisition, her assets would be frozen, all that wealth would go to the crown; it would be lost.

"I believe, Dona Beatrice, that we might do business together," Diogo said, still staring at the port, where the carrack was just now unfurling its sails. "I have a foundation. And I thought you might make an investment."

"I see." She paused. "I am honored you thought of me."

Diogo turned away from the window and gazed at her. Like everyone at court, he knew her background: Her family, originally from Aragon in Spain, had been forced to convert, generations back, to Catholicism to protect their fortune and their lives. Her father, Alvaro de Luna, had traded in silver. She came from *Converso* wealth, had married into *Converso* wealth. And she had celebrated her wedding to the New Christian Francisco Mendes — of the old Spanish Jewish Beneviste family — by putting on display the couple's Catholicism in a grandiose ceremony in Lisbon's great Cathedral. Francisco was also her uncle and twice her age. To preserve their wealth and power, the rich *Converso* families intermarried, like aristocracy and royalty. Now, with Francisco dead, Beatrice had somehow managed to keep control of the family fortune. So far.

"I do think an investment would be advisable." Diogo leaned forward, his hands flat on the desk, staring at her. Her beauty was so fresh and seemingly composed, even when faced with possible imminent torture and death.

"We can discuss details, if you wish." Her dark eyes gazed steadily back at him. She understood what he wanted — money, right away, and lots of it.

He sighed. This Beatrice de Luna would make a wonderful lover. With her, he could play some exquisite, brutal games. He imagined her naked — her shapely legs, white as ivory, and as they must be now, damp and sheathed in suave black silk. However rich she might be, she was vulnerable. She was a woman, a widow. She was prey.

And soon she would serve as an example. The Inquisition would reveal the New Christians for what they truly were—secret Jews—traitors, hypocrites who defiled the Catholic faith by their pretense, who mocked all the sacred and warrior traditions that ran so deep in his family's blood. For centuries his ancestors had fought to free Spain and Portugal from the Muslims, to defend the faith, to make the peninsula pure, purely Catholic. But with the Muslims finally defeated, the *Conversos* remained: the enemy within—unfinished business. The Inquisition would solve that problem and reveal this woman, too, as a liar and heretic. Yes, she would burn.

"I do not wish to be impolite, Dona Beatrice, but just how Catholic are you?"

"As Catholic as you." She raised an eyebrow. "As Catholic as I need to be."

"You are so clever!"

"I'm not at all clever."

"Once a Jew, always a Jew."

Her lips tightened, her gaze flickered and narrowed. She cleared her throat. "I thought we were speaking of religion, of beliefs and loyalty, not of race. Belief does not run in the blood."

"How cunning you are!" Diogo smiled. He loved this little game of cat and mouse. He had his spies. In an instant, he could denounce her as a secret Jewess. The proofs lay close to hand—Hebrew books in her household, Hebrew rituals performed behind shuttered windows, and he knew she observed the Jewish festivals. Merely denounce her as a secret Jewess and it would be done. He could destroy her, reduce her to rags. He clenched his fist. The swift cruelty of it tempted him; but first, he needed to use her.

He clasped his hands, gently, piously. "The Pope has, unwisely I would say, been resisting our requests."

"Your requests?"

"The King's requests. John III wishes to begin a Holy Inquisition here in Portugal, modeled on that of Spain."

"Ah, yes, of course." She smiled daintily. The Inquisition in Spain had driven her ancestors from that kingdom; soon, as she well knew, perhaps within a month, a similar fiery and cruel inquisition would begin in Portugal.

"The inquisition will quickly uncover who the heretics are, and who among the otherwise honorable New Christians are, in reality, secret Jews." He leaned forward. "I do believe some people—I shall not name names—have been lobbying his Holiness. Perhaps they have even been paying bribes to influential men in Rome, in an effort to delay the Portuguese inquisition." He smiled.

"Really! Someone has been greasing palms in Rome?" Again, she held his gaze. "I find that hard to believe."

Diogo laughed. "We must ferret out heresy, and crush those who secretly practice Judaism."

"Of course." Her gaze did not flicker.

"The time has come. The Pope will shortly announce the opening of the Inquisition in Portugal."

Beatrice clasped her hands in her lap. "Well. That is fine, then. That is splendid."

BEATRICE DE LUNA LEFT Don Diogo's office.

She hurried down the broad marble staircase. Her two-year-old daughter, Ana, was at home with only the servants to guard her. Would Diogo have sent his thugs to seize Ana as a hostage? Would she herself be arrested, thrown in prison?

The doorman opened the door with a little bow.

Emerging into the light of day, she stopped to breathe. The sun shone, a few bright clouds drifted lazily in the deep blue sky; a warm breeze came up the river Tagus. The light on the water broke into a myriad of sparkling ripples.

Three sleek, low-slung caravels were edging in towards their quayside berths, their triangular sails, fluttering brightly, each marked with a huge cross. They were elegantly designed ships, swift and easy to maneuver; ships that had allowed

Portugal and Spain to conquer worlds and within two generations become immensely rich. Such ships were the source of her own fortune, but the giant, fluttering cross was also a curse and a warning—believe or die! She fingered the gold cross hanging from her neck. It was a symbol of servitude, embodying an inner darkness, a life of constant betrayals and painful charades, an imminent and deadly menace. She shivered.

Beside the carriage, Aleixo, her manservant, patient always, with his understanding smile, his neatly trimmed beard and impeccable white ruff, bowed. Then, seeing she was distracted, he whispered, "Dona Beatrice . . .?"

She shook her head, looked away, and then climbed into the carriage, her stiff skirts rustling against the warm leather of the seat.

As she sat back, she took off her gloves, looked at her hands. Diogo's foundation was of course a front, a pious fraud. The money would go directly to Diogo and not to any widows or orphans. He had asked for a bribe. If she were already in prison, under investigation by the Inquisition with all her assets frozen, it would be too late. He had acted before the curtain came down. She sighed. Rather clever of him, really.

The carriage rattled over the cobblestones, the horses trotting gaily. First, she had to make sure Ana was safe. The girl had already lost her father; what if she lost her mother too? If orphaned, Ana would become a helpless pawn in power games: either a penniless waif or forcibly married to some cruel aged Christian aristocrat so that King John III and his friends could, by controlling Ana, seize control of the Mendes Bank and all its wealth.

Beatrice squeezed her hands until the knuckles turned white. The blackmail and bribery never stopped. The Mendes Bank and others had bribed influential churchmen in Rome, and that had delayed the onset of the Inquisition in Portugal. But the reprieve was at an end.

Forever in exile and forever on the run—that was the destiny of the Jews, even the secret Jews, everywhere and forever.

How to escape this infernal cycle of repression, expulsion, exile, torture, and death? Where could she and the others—Jews and *Conversos*—find refuge?

She knew one thing: if she ever did find refuge, she would throw off the Catholic disguise, go by her real name, her secret name, her Jewish name, Gracia Nasi. At last, she would be herself. She closed her eyes and took a deep breath as the carriage rumbled up the street towards Ana, who would be watching for her, as she always did.

It was the Eve of Passover, April 15, 1536.

VENICE LA SERENISSIMA

I

THE GATEWAY

THE SUN WAS LOW, HIDDEN BEHIND THE FOUR AND FIVE-story buildings that lined the narrow, placid rio del Ghetto, the little canal that separated the Jewish Ghetto Nuovo from the rest of Venice. It was almost dusk, April 15, 1536, the Eve of Passover. A lone figure stood on the footbridge before the wooden gate that barred the way to the Ghetto.

Danilo del Medigo presented all the appearance of a fashionable Venetian man-about-town, an athletic aristocrat, a gentleman warrior. His white shirt was of the finest linen and trimmed at the neck with a ruff of white ermine; his black peaked cap set at a jaunty angle above a darkly tanned face with startling blue eyes and blond hair. He had noticed that his looks drew attention. Just walking in the city, he had caught the eye of more than one young woman. Having spent a decade, all of his adolescence, in Istanbul, he was not used to European manners. And this was the Most Serene Republic of Venice, *la Serenissima*, famous for its wealth, its art, its diplomacy, its ships and trade, its courtesans, its prostitutes, and for its worldly, unrestrained, pagan joie de vivre. The friendly glances reflected his appearance. He looked Venetian and could easily be taken for the son of a wealthy Venetian patrician, or a Norman aristocrat. Only the carpetbag slung over his shoulder indicated that he was a wanderer.

He glanced cautiously behind him. The alleyway was empty. No sign of the assassins who had almost certainly followed him from Istanbul. The footpath beside the canal was empty too, except for a workman trudging along head down, carrying a few bricks on a wooden plank on his shoulder. Danilo watched the man approach. He could not be too careful. Danger could be hidden behind any face, any façade. But as the workman neared Danilo saw the man was elderly, too frail for his precarious burden, and so late in the day. Venice was, he had been told, a nonstop building site, magnificent new splendors being added every day.

The workman nodded. "Beautiful evening, sir."

"Indeed it is," Danilo answered, with a slight inclination of his head. "Where are you headed with that load? Might I give you a hand?"

"Not far now, sir," he said, grinning toothlessly, "and I'm stronger than I look."

"No offense intended," Danilo said.

"And none taken," the old man answered. "Good day to you."

He watched the workman head down the *calle*, one of the multitudes of labyrinthine walkways that made Venice so delightful and so confusing. He shifted his carpetbag and glanced once more behind him. Even here in Venice, he wasn't safe. He had to be aware of every movement, every person and every possible ambush point. The Men in Black, professional assassins, had orders from the Ottoman Sultan's wife, Hürrem, to kill him. Ottoman assassins were known to be persistent and very good at their job.

He imagined the dagger strike, anticipating how he would parry it. The killers would be quick; he would be quicker. Escaping from Istanbul, he had already killed one of the Men in Black. They were an elite corps of hundreds, and they protected their own. If they knew he had killed one of them, their determination to kill him would be even greater.

Who else knew he was in Venice? The spies of Venice— and Venice had spies everywhere—would surely know that a lone young man had arrived from Istanbul; and, if they knew he was the son of the Sultan's personal physician, they would certainly be eager to "question" him, a polite euphemism for torture. The Ottoman Empire was a trading partner, but it was also the greatest rival and enemy Venice faced. In the war of civilizations, Venice was in the front line, facing the mighty Islamic threat that hung over all of Christian Europe. So the Venetians would be suspicious of any undocumented stranger arriving from the Ottoman capital. They would want to know all about him.

Only a few hours ago, down near the Rialto bridge, Samuel Mendes of the Mendes Bank, who had sold him his present splendid suit of clothes, had warned him of the dangers: "A great storm is coming, Danilo. It will sweep all the Jews and New Christians before it. We must prepare."

As they stood together, watching a sea squall approach from the Adriatic, Mendes had also hinted that, with his warrior skills, familiarity with the Ottoman Empire, contacts in Istanbul, and knowledge of languages—Arabic, Persian, Turkish, Italian, and French—Danilo might be useful to the bank.

As they talked, the storm dissipated before reaching land. The evening sky was untroubled and clear.

"A good omen?" Danilo had ventured.

"I doubt it," Mendes said.

Danilo stared now at the entry before him, his gateway to the Ghetto, first established twenty years before. The low-ceilinged passageway was closed by a stout wooden gate from sunset to sunrise, and it was guarded, always, by a Christian watchman. The gate had already been closed for the night. He glanced at the high walls, at the barred, bricked-up windows. It looked like a prison.

Danilo had been born in the Ghetto; he was, in fact, the first male child born there, the moment the Ghetto was established with all the Jews, barges laden with their possessions, streaming into their inner exile. His mother had often described it to him, a searing, tragic moment. But what did he really know of that? Was he a Jew, did he want to be a Jew? Did he belong in the Ghetto?

Who are you, Danilo del Medigo? A Jew? Or a gentile? He had been asking himself this question all his life.

The sun disappeared below the rooftops; the canals and alleyways were suddenly shrouded in a luminous blue Venetian penumbra. High up, roofs and elaborately shaped chimney pots were tinged a bright blood-red, reflecting the light of the setting sun.

The gathering bluish shadows recalled those in the stable where he and Saida—his Muslim princess, his first love, and the favorite daughter of Suleiman the Magnificent—had made love for the first and only time; even now, he could see her—how she had come to him through the shadows and slowly, elegantly, shed her clothes, one diaphanous item at a time. Saida, ingenious and enterprising as always, had arranged for his departure from Istanbul, and the ship she had chosen had sailed for Venice. She knew, from the tales he had told her, that this was the city in Italy he dreamed of. So here he was.

His mother was a Jew, so by the laws of Judaism, he was a Jew. But he was only half a Jew. His legal father was Judah del Medigo, a scholarly Jewish doctor, personal physician to Suleiman the Magnificent. But his real father, his blood father, was a Christian aristocrat, Pirro Gonzaga of Mantua, a blond, blue-eyed warrior and gallant adventurer, and the great love of his mother's life. He must seek out Pirro, it was what his mother, Grazia, would have wished. It would be his act of filial fidelity towards her, finally setting things right, explaining to Pirro . . . what had happened, what Grazia felt, why she had died . . .

He glanced back down the narrow street that led to the bridge to the Ghetto. Two women were gossiping at a corner, one carrying a basket of vegetables against her hip. A man stopped to talk with them. They were sketched silhouettes in the twilight. The murmur of their conversation and laughter echoed down the *calle*.

If he stayed outside the Ghetto, where would he sleep? People would ask questions. If the Men in Black found him, he would be out in the open, with no friends and no protection. He would be vulnerable.

There, on the Ghetto side of the canal, the windows were barred and bricked up; the walls were blank. On the Christian side, brightly colored flowers overflowed from window boxes, and curtains gently drifted from open windows. Beyond those buildings, away from the Ghetto, lay all of Venice, with its freedom and promise of adventure, with all its invisible but infinite variety, a tangle of canals, footpaths, alleyways, arches, footbridges, courtyards, workshops, taverns, and then the Grand Canal, with the great houses, the mansions of the patrician and merchant families of Venice, gondolas and barges everywhere plying the waters.

A gondola moved down the rio del Ghetto, stirring up little patterns and reflections as a fresh breeze wafted along the canal, bringing smells of the lagoon, the vast open space, clayey water, ozone, the sun and earth mingling in a dying shimmer. He breathed it all in.

Twilight. From the minarets in Istanbul, the muezzins would have just called for the evening prayer. The sweet evening breeze off the Golden Horn and the Bosphorus would rustle the leaves in the splendid open courtyards and among the many pavilions of the Sultan's immense Topkapi Palace. His father, Judah del Medigo, would be sitting down to dinner, perhaps with some guests, young apprentice doctors, or elders from the Jewish community. Saida would be dining with the other women of the harem, or perhaps she would be assisting the Sultan's wife in the kitchen, flattering Hürrem and listening to the woman's clever advice on how to make the Sultan's favorite meals.

All of this now was lost in the distance; it was a world to which he could never return. The moment he had been accused of planning an attempt on the Sultan's life, his lover, Saida, and his father were in mortal danger. Danilo had to flee to keep them out of danger. The more invisible he became, the better for all of them. If he was to protect them, and if, for his mother's sake, he was to find his blood father, Pirro Gonzaga, he had to stay alive, he had to avoid the assassins Hürrem had sent to kill him. The safest, most discreet place for him to be in Venice would be the Ghetto.

Was this his home, within these walls? Or was his life to be in the vast adventurous world beyond the Ghetto?

Either was possible.

The sky was darkening, soon it would be night.

It was the Eve of Passover. If he wished to enter the Ghetto, Jewish law stipulated that the community must take him in — a Jewish traveler stranded far from home.

Danilo shifted the weight of his carpetbag and approached the gate.

He rang the bell.

"WHO GOES THERE?" THE voice echoed from behind the gate.

"A traveler, far from home, seeking a place at a Seder table." Danilo shifted his carpetbag and stepped forward. Everything he owned, he carried with him. Andrea Mantegna's portrait of his mother, his mother's *Secret Book*, a small pouch full of ducats, and the jeweled dagger and string of pearls given to him — as a cash reserve — by Princess Saida.

The gate swung open.

The gatekeeper looked Danilo up and down with dark, quick, mischievous eyes. The man had a short, neatly trimmed salt-and-pepper beard; his gray hair combed carefully over his forehead. The tangled eyebrows gave him an air of quirky wisdom. He wore a simple leather jacket, white blouse, tan trousers, and black leather boots.

Danilo smiled and bowed.

The gatekeeper stroked his beard and narrowed his eyes. "Well, well, traveler far from home, you look like the fellow those two chaps were looking for earlier this afternoon. Handsome gentleman, they said—blue eyes, blond, charming smile, they said, high forehead, and a jaunty cavalier attitude, probably tanned from a sea voyage."

"Someone was looking for me?"

"Two dark gentlemen. Seemed like Turks to me. In fact, now that I think about it, I am sure they were. Said they were your friends, and were eager to see you."

Danilo nervously glanced behind him.

"Not your friends, eh?" The gatekeeper nodded. "Lean and hungry fellows. Not long in Venice, I think, and the Turks in Venice tend to gamble. Perhaps you owe them money? Gambling debts?"

"I assure you not."

"Problems with a woman . . . jealousy? Crime of honor sort of thing?"

"No."

"Well, they didn't look quite . . . how shall I put it? Not quite kosher. They didn't smell right. Looking around, suspicious folk. Their Italian was not good and they had not a single word of Venetian. I had to work hard to explain myself to them— spell it out, you know."

"So, you told them . . ."

"That I had not seen you. But I promised that if they came again, I would tell them if I saw you. They advised me not to tell you they were looking for you—it was to be a surprise, they said. I didn't like the look of it. But no business of mine, is it?"

"Thank you."

"Good! I didn't see you. Didn't hear you! Didn't smell you! In any case, I believe you will be safe in the Ghetto. I will close the gate again. Snug as a bug in a rug, you'll be, among your own folk. Mind you . . ."

"Yes?"

"There are spies everywhere—Ottoman spies, Venetian spies. It is even said some Jews are spies. Dreadful thought. Hard to credit! They spy on each other. Paid for it, or threatened, or offered something in exchange—some protection, or favor. Jews often need protection, as I'm sure you know, often subject to blackmail too. Some of them work for Venice—for the Council of Ten. *Quid pro quo*. I scratch your back, you scratch mine."

"The Council of Ten?"

"The committee in charge of security for the Republic—internal and external. More than ten members, I believe. The Doge is an additional member, and some senators or some such. They change membership every three months or so, so nobody gets too uppity. The Council of Ten keeps files on everything and everybody. Big filing system, lots of clerks and scribes, beavering away day and night in the Doge's Palace. But the Ghetto is as safe as you'll get, I'd say. Safer than being outside, on your own."

"I will be locked in?"

"Sundown to sunrise. Only exceptions are for Jewish doctors who tend to patients outside the Ghetto, and for musicians who often perform in the houses of courtesans and rich merchants. They come and go. As for the rest, the gates open when the call-to-work bell in the *Campanile* tower rings. It's the bell we call the *Marangona*—named for the carpenters, but it calls all the workers to work. It's the morning bell. Then it rings again when it's time for the workers to stop. It is a beautiful sound, sir, the *Marangona*, most melodious and sublime and ancient."

"Melodious. Yes, I'm sure." Danilo glanced around. This man talked too much. The Men in Black had already tracked him to the Ghetto. A dagger needs only an instant to do its work. One path led here, to the gate, and another along the edge of the canal. No danger in sight, not now. But the Men in Black specialized in surprises.

"Since you have come from far, you may not know this, sir,

but we have bells and chimes all over Venice. The *Campanile* is a most beautiful building, just on the Piazza San Marco. It collapsed and was built, all new, in 1513."

"I see." Danilo shifted the carpetbag. What if the killers came back now? What would happen then? What if he had to fight and kill them? And if Hürrem got wind of it—she could take revenge on his father. Any misstep and Judah would be in danger—perhaps Saida as well.

"Not all the bells are as benign, sir, as the *Marangona*. There's the *Malefico*, which announces an execution. A rather somber bell makes you think, it does, of death and of crime and punishment; and *La Trottiera*, which calls the magistrates to the Ducal Palace, gets them to trot along so they get to their meetings on time. Ah, San Marco, sir, it is a beautiful place, truly. And there's lots of construction. A new architect came up, escaping after the Sack of Rome when Charles V's troops went crazy and destroyed the city."

Danilo winced. Mention of the Sack of Rome brought back that horrible, searing memory—the flight from the city and the death of his mother. He blinked it away.

"Jacopo Sansovino, he is, and doing wonderful work. Many artists and writers fled Rome after the disaster, sir. It emptied out the Eternal City, so they say, broke its spirit. So now they are working on turning Piazza San Marco into even more of a thing of beauty, sir. You will find it fascinating."

"I'm sure I will."

"And there's *La Nona*. It sounds at midday, sir."

"La Nona. I see."

"And, finally, there's the *Pregadi*. That tells us the Senate is about to meet. They are prayed, as it were, to attend."

Danilo shifted his weight. "Very interesting."

"Then, here in Venice, as a Jew, since you are a Jew, though you don't look like a Jew—mind you, lots of Jews don't look like Jews, if you know what I mean—you must wear the yellow cap when you are outside the Ghetto. If you are a woman, a yellow veil."

Danilo frowned. In Istanbul, he went about dressed according to his station, like anyone else. In fact, as a page to the Sultan and a warrior, he was part of the elite; people just had to glance at him and they knew he was someone. Here in Venice he was to be branded. People would look at him and think, "There goes the Jew!"

"It's not so bad, sir, you'll get used to it. If you go to the mainland, to the town of Mestre, where many Jewish bankers still do business—financing the grain harvest, and canal improvements, and agriculture, and such like—there are many places where you don't have to wear the yellow cap. Each place, sir, has its own vexations."

"But, being closed in . . ."

"It's unpleasant, but . . ."

"It is the Eve of Passover . . ."

"They will invite you to a Seder, sir, whether you are a Jew or not." The gatekeeper's face was lit by reflected bluish light from the narrow little canal. A woman walked by, and the gatekeeper tipped his hat in her direction, "Good evening, Maria!"

The woman smiled, "And a good evening to you, Vincenzo, and my best wishes to your wife!" She shifted her basket of vegetables and, inclining her head in the gatekeeper's direction, gave him what looked like a sly smile.

The gatekeeper waved, and turned back to Danilo. "I am sure you will find a welcome in the Ghetto, sir. Jews are hospitable. 'A stranger at the table is the best thing,' people say."

At the mention of a table, Danilo could smell cooking, roast lamb, perhaps, and fish being grilled. His mouth watered. His stomach rumbled. "But which . . . do I attend?" Danilo shifted his carpetbag.

"I have a solution to that!" The gatekeeper tore up four bits of paper and wrote something quickly on each before tossing them into his hat. "Destiny is decided here!"

The guard thrust out the hat. Danilo closed his eyes, and his fingers found a slip of paper. He pulled it out and handed it to Vincenzo.

"Ah! You have won a seat at the Seder table of the healing rabbi—Rabbi Abraham Hazan!"

Vincenzo cupped his hands around his mouth and hollered into the entry tunnel, his voice echoing in the dark, squared-off passageway that led under the buildings and into the heart of the Ghetto. "A Passover traveler is coming to Rabbi Hazan's Seder!"

He turned back to Danilo. "Just follow the walkway under the building. It will take you directly into the central square of the Ghetto, the *Campo del Ghetto Nuovo*. That is where Rabbi Hazan conducts his Seder, in the open air, in a sort of curtained pavilion, as many of them will do tonight, under the stars. It's a good night for it, warm."

"Thank you, Vincenzo!" Danilo, with his carpetbag slung over his shoulder, strode forward, crossed the little bridge, and entered the passageway.

The tunnel-like passageway caught and echoed all the sounds—the lapping of the water in the canal, the stroke and swish of a gondolier's oar, and whispering and shouting voices. From somewhere beyond the Ghetto came a song, a melancholy romantic voice, a man—perhaps a gondolier—singing in pure Venetian. And, from farther away, a sound Danilo hadn't heard in many years—church bells; some of them deeper and some lighter; some mournful, some gay. They contrasted with one another and, in his mind, with the solemn, austere melancholy of the muezzin's call to prayer in Istanbul. The bells echoed down the narrow canals and alleyways, and in the *sotoportego*. This truly was no longer Istanbul and Islam, this was Christendom!

Had he exchanged freedom for a prison? Had he escaped from one danger only to plunge into another—the spy-infested prison of the Ghetto?

The heavy gate slammed shut, was bolted and locked behind him. In an instant, the church bells, the melancholy gondolier's song, all the sounds of Venice, and of the whole world, vanished.

2

THE SEDER

THE *sotoportego* LED DIRECTLY INTO THE CAMPO. APARTMENT buildings soared up on all sides. The Campo itself, a large irregular-shaped space, was plunged into the deep blue shadows of evening. The crowd jostled among the tents and tables set up everywhere. Lamps and candles burned in the windows of all the buildings. It looked like a fairground.

Young women and old were setting the tables, already laden with food and lit by candles. Excited children ran everywhere, shouting and laughing. The smell of roast meat and grilled fish drifted across the Campo, and the perfume of vegetables, and unleavened bread. Torches cast flickering reflections on the façades of the buildings. Voices echoed from windows and narrow staircases, from under the porticos and tents and pavilions. As Danilo stood there, the high-pitched ritual Passover Seder question began to echo in the Campo. Children's singsong voices, asking the ancient question repeated down through the ages: "Why is this night different from all other nights?"

The question echoed from the different Seders. It was a mysterious and mystical chorus, rising out of the mists of time. Torches perfumed the air. Shimmering columns of amber light ascended into the branches of the trees.

Only a few years ago in Istanbul Danilo had been that young boy, his singsong voice had asked the question during the Seders held in the cool, shadowy courtyard of his father's home in Topkapi Palace.

The Ahrida Synagogue he and his father had attended was beautiful and ornate, all in gold, and situated in the Balat neighborhood, on the southern shore of the Golden Horn. Sitting with all the girls and boys and adults under the shade of the tree, and listening to the fountain in his father's courtyard as it splashed water, Danilo was eager to hear all the stories his father and his father's friends had to tell, glancing around at all the learned, torch-lit faces: old Aron Abenkual, with his gnarled hands and wise, deeply seamed face; Rabbi Leon Adoni, who always looked so stern; and young Izak Niego, who loved to tell stories and never stopped talking. The children were always so eager to see if the Prophet Elijah would turn up to drink his glass of wine and announce the imminent arrival of the Messiah.

Thinking of those nights, Danilo wondered again: Was he the son of Judah del Medigo or of Pirro Gonzaga? Was he Jew or Christian?

Life, just now, was full of mystery and promise. Cast adrift from his past, he could invent himself anew. He could never again be a warrior and page in the Sultan's service. With Hürrem's Men in Black on his trail, he would never be able to return to Istanbul. He must forget all that—all his training, all his schooling, his whole life. He must even forget his horse, loyal, fierce Bucephalus! He must create his own destiny! After all, his mother had invented herself—she had educated herself, had broken free of the limits of family and community, become the great love of a Christian aristocrat and the aide to the famous Isabella d'Este. She had become a writer. The destiny Grazia had forged was truly extraordinary. And Danilo was aware he must walk in her footsteps also.

The leaves rustled in the warm breeze above the curtained pavilions. Danilo hesitated—which one belonged to Rabbi Hazan? Danilo was a stranger in a strange land.

A man pushed past him violently. Danilo reached for his dagger. But the man was rushing to embrace a child. He lifted the laughing girl up in the air. Danilo removed his hand from the dagger. A moment of inattention and he would be dead; too quick a reaction and he would disembowel some innocent.

But he had to be wary—of everything and everyone. Was his life to be haunted like this to the end of time? Would he always be looking over his shoulder, always waiting for, anticipating, the fatal thrust of steel?

At his elbow, a curtain of one of the little pavilions was pulled abruptly aside.

A young woman stood before him, framed by the open curtain. He had been warned that the women of the Venetian Ghetto were beautiful. Her blouse, half off her shoulders in the Venetian manner, shone brilliant white in the bluish shadows; her jet-black hair, escaping a tiny hairnet, tumbled down to her shoulders. "Sir, I am the daughter of Rabbi Hazan. My name is Miriamne. Please join us!" Her smile, quivering at the very corner of her lips, sparkled with mischief. She glanced around the darkening Campo. "There are dangers everywhere, sir, but here, with us, you will be safe." She held the curtain open. "Please step in!"

Danilo bowed and entered. In the candlelit tent stretched a long table cloaked in pristine white damask and lined with celebrants. At the far end was a raised lectern and behind the lectern stood a distinguished-looking man with sad, intelligent eyes. He was dressed all in black, with a black cap and a full salt-and-pepper beard. He cast at Danilo a quick, penetrating, questioning glance. He must be Rabbi Hazan.

At the table, old faces and young faces of men, women, and children shone in the candlelight. The Seder plates and dishes were set out in a colorful pattern: the covered plates of unleavened bread and bitter herbs; platters of hard-boiled eggs, and of *charoset*, the sweet, dark-brown paste made of fruit and nuts. The cups of wine and beakers of water all glinted in exquisite, colored Venetian glass. The place settings gleamed — gold and silver. Two blond female servants, wearing aprons, stood behind Rabbi Hazan.

The rabbi directed his speech towards a young boy.

"On all other nights we eat both leavened and unleavened bread." Rabbi Hazan's voice resonated in the small tented space. "But on this night, we eat only unleavened bread." The rabbi smiled at the child. "When the Jews were fleeing Egypt towards freedom, they had to leave quickly, so there was no time to let the bread rise; and so on this night we eat unleavened bread to remind us of freedom, to remind us of our flight from Egypt, when we escaped from slavery."

"Rabbi Hazan, what's the difference between leavened and unleavened bread?"

The question came from a beautiful little girl. She had long black hair, porcelain-white skin, and startlingly large eyes. The sparkle in her eyes and her bright smile were just like Saida's when she was a girl. How Saida loved to laugh! To her, everything was amusing; everything was a game, an adventure. Caught in some mischief, she would cover her mouth, blinking flirtatiously at him. How she had loved to tease! So curious about everything, and so impertinent. Danilo wondered at it — the bright, unspoiled loveliness and intelligence of children, so inquisitive and so free, their minds open to everything, and so alike, all over the world, in their magical curiosity.

Rabbi Hazan smiled. "Dear Jessica, the difference lies in yeast or some form of fermentation. This creates little bubbles in the bread and the bubbles lift the bread up. 'Leavened' means lifted up. It comes from the Latin, *levare*, to lift. It takes time for the yeast to act, to leaven, or lift the bread."

He returned to his deeper, more formal voice. "At this time, we remember the words 'Blessed art thou, Lord, our God, King of the Universe, who hast chosen us above all peoples, and hast exalted us above all tongues.' Uncover the bread." He paused while the cloth was removed from the dishes of matzah. "You see, my child, this is the poor bread, the unleavened matzah, which our fathers ate in the land of Egypt. During the Passover Seder, we give thanks to God, who has stood with the children of Israel against those who in each generation attempt to annihilate us."

The rabbi's conversational tone was quite unlike the singsong chant Danilo had been used to hearing from rabbis in most synagogues he had known. In Istanbul, Rabbi Hassan, so tall and skinny and serious, chanted everything. It was hard to follow or even understand the words. Danilo got restless and bored. But Rabbi Hazan made the words meaningful. Was this bringing back to him part of his mother's world? Was it bringing back the Jewish Italian world that had been hers and that had been torn away from him, with everything else, when she died? And she had died because of him! It was one of the things he had to explain to Pirro. . . . But of this he did not wish to think.

The rabbi gazed at the faces of the children, one after the other. "On all nights, on normal nights, we need not dip the bitter greens even once; but on this night we dip them *twice.* The salt water into which we dip the *karpas* — or green parsley — stands for the salty tears we Jews shed while in slavery in Egypt."

The rabbi dipped a sprig of parsley into the salty water.

"The act of dipping the *karpas* is, too, a symbol of freedom. The poor and the slaves had nothing to dip their food into. So they ate dry food. When we were slaves in Egypt, we ate dry food. So, dipping the parsley, the *karpas,* into the salt water tells us we are free; and dipping it twice means we have leisure and time, like our rulers, and leisure is an expression of freedom."

At this humble table, a great and heroic tale was being told. For the first time, Danilo understood the grandeur of the moment. Somehow, after so many centuries in exile, after

centuries wandering, always strangers in strange lands, after centuries of persecution and hatred, the Jewish people had maintained their covenant with God. How many exiles had there been? The Egyptian, the Assyrian, the Babylonian, and the Roman, all these empires had been places of exile.

Through it all, the Jews had not forgotten their forefathers. They had not forsaken themselves. They had never lost the memory of Israel, of their homeland. For the first time, the sublime story of struggle and survival and holiness flooded, with all its drama and heroism, into Danilo's heart. This little community of the Ghetto Nuovo was a caravan of nomads, moving through the desert, wandering in exile. They had to be kept safe. They had to survive. They had to pass on the faith. They had to keep their sacred covenant with God. They had to be true to themselves. Each detail of the Passover Seder echoed this basic fact. This was as heroic in its own way as all the gallantry of Pirro Gonzaga or Suleiman the Magnificient.

Rabbi Hazan lifted up a small round plate. "The *charoset* symbolizes the mortar we slaves used to build bricks for the pyramids in Egypt." His eyes shone with a dark, melancholy light. "On this night we eat bitter herbs—the *maror*—that bring back the bitter taste of slavery. Remembering slavery, once again we learn to treasure our freedom.

"How is this night different from all other nights?"

Rabbi Hazan smiled upon each one of them in turn. "On all nights we eat sitting upright, on this night we eat reclining—like royalty—and thus we remember and celebrate our freedom. When we are free, we can lounge, we can recline, we are like royalty."

The rabbi seemed to glow. He freighted each word with the whole glorious history of Judaism and of the Jewish people.

Danilo thought with a pang of guilt of his father, celebrating Passover in Istanbul without him. He must be in anguish, celebrating Passover for the first time in almost ten years without his son, and not knowing what had happened to him. Had he been kidnapped? Was he dead?

Little Jacob lifted a glass of wine. "Wine, joy in freedom, and in life."

"Yes, yes! Wine gladdens the heart of man . . . and bread sustains the heart of man," shouted an old man sitting halfway down the table. He raised his glass and held it out.

"But why four cups?" young Jessica asked. "Why not three or five?" The girl, Danilo guessed, must be ten or eleven, probably Jacob's older sister.

Rabbi Hazan stroked his beard. "This is complicated, Jessica. God used four different expressions when he freed us from slavery in Egypt. So we drink the four glasses of wine to experience these four different moments of redemption—God saved us from *harsh labor* when the plagues descended upon Egypt, He saved us from *servitude* when we fled from our masters, and He *redeemed* us when He parted the waters of the Red Sea and *allowed us to pass*, but not the Pharaoh's army, which was pursuing us. So those are the four aspects of our liberation."

The children nodded solemnly. Miriamne winked at them and their faces broke into big smiles. Danilo thought they might begin to giggle, but they resisted. The little girl, Jessica, glanced at Danilo and then down at her plate, and covered her mouth with her hand, a secret little girl's smile.

MIRIAMNE LED DANILO ALONG the table to her father as the two blond waitresses—handsome girls—carried in more food—plates of lamb and grilled fish and more boiled eggs. "Don't be intimidated," Miriamne whispered, "Father can look awfully serious and terribly sublime. Sometimes he even frightens me!"

Rabbi Hazan was deep in conversation with a sleek-looking older man sitting next to him. Miriamne tapped her father on the shoulder. "Look what has been sent to adorn our Seder table, Father—a solitary wanderer, seeking refuge from all the mortal dangers that lie beyond our gates."

Her father, still in animated conversation with the older

man, didn't seem to hear her. The other guests were talking noisily among themselves.

Miriamne winked at Danilo, and again tapped Rabbi Hazan on the shoulder.

The rabbi turned and blinked, as if waking from a dream. Miriamne gave Danilo a little shove, pushing him forward. "We must have won him in the lottery, father. Is he not a pretty fellow?"

Rabbi Hazan frowned and looked Danilo up and down, and then looked him straight in the eyes. Danilo held the rabbi's gaze. Even sitting, Rabbi Hazan was an impressive man, grand in the Old Testament style, tall, slightly stooped, with a long, jet-black beard streaked with white. His eyes penetrated with a fiery intensity.

"He's handsome enough, I suppose," the rabbi said, and then putting on a more friendly expression, he swung his chair around so he could talk more confidentially. "What is your name, son?"

Danilo hesitated. "My name is . . . Forgive me, sir, my status is, ah, problematic."

"Oh, how so?"

"Well . . ."

Rabbi Hazan smiled. "Go on! Say what you have to say! I'm sure it can't be so horrible! You seem an honest fellow."

"My documents say I am David dei Rossi, the son of a merchant from Mantua."

"That sounds reasonable. And so . . ."

"In truth, sir, my real name is . . ." Danilo bowed his head. "My real name is Danilo del Medigo. I am the son of the Ottoman Sultan's personal doctor, Judah del Medigo."

"Judah del Medigo . . . He was personal physician to the Pope, I believe. Well, then . . . this is . . . interesting . . ."

"But it is not the whole truth, sir."

Rabbi Hazan glanced at his daughter. She grinned and shrugged.

"You see, Judah del Medigo is my *legal* father." At the

thought of his father, he felt a pang of guilt, having left Judah without warning, without explanation. What must the poor man be thinking, feeling?

"*Legal* father. I see . . ."

"But my blood father is a Christian knight."

"How fascinating!" Miriamne tilted her head to one side, and, half closing her eyes, directed a bright mischievous smile at Danilo. "A Christian knight, an aristocrat warrior!"

Glancing at his daughter, Rabbi Hazan frowned. "So you, a wanderer, have come here, among us, because . . . ?"

"I grew up in Istanbul, sir, in Topkapi Palace."

"The palace of the Sultan." The rabbi nodded.

"The palace of the Sultan? Now that is impressive!" Miriamne's eyes sparkled. "That's where the harem is, isn't it?"

"Yes, it is." Danilo gave her a hesitant smile.

"How extraordinarily intriguing. I would like to know as much as I can about such things. You must have many tales to tell!"

Rabbi Hazan frowned at Miriamne. "Go on, young man."

"I was trained in the Sultan's School for Pages. And, on graduation, was drafted into the Ottoman legions for service in the Sultan's Baghdad campaign."

"A warrior too!" Miriamne clasped her hands together.

The rabbi blinked at his daughter. His brow furrowed, his tangled eyebrows rose, almost in wonder. "You must forgive us, young man; my daughter is rather like her late mother—impetuous, and quick, and occasionally given to irony, I'm afraid."

Danilo glanced at Miriamne. "I'm not exactly a warrior. And then, for stupid reasons, I fell out of favor with an important member of the Sultan's court."

"Who was that?"

"The Grand Vizier, Ibrahim Pasha of Parga."

"The most powerful man in the empire. That was not convenient."

"No, sir, it wasn't."

"And so . . ."

"The Sultan's Men in Black have orders to kill me. The orders did not come from the Sultan or from Ibrahim Pasha. They came from Hürrem, the wife of the Sultan."

"That makes two enemies!" Miriamne's eyes sparkled.

"Hürrem is a bad enemy to have," the rabbi said. "She was, Miriamne, a slave girl, a harem girl, who managed to entrance Suleiman—and now she is the wife of the Sultan, something quite unheard of. Sultans do not marry their concubines."

"It's like a fairy tale," said Miriamne, "or a French romance."

"Hürrem is remarkable, sir. She rose from nothing to become everything; she is wilful, clever, and powerful. It is said she makes the Sultan laugh. Ibrahim Pasha, who was away on campaign with the Sultan, sent Hürrem a letter claiming that I planned to poison the Sultan; the accusation was false, of course. But Hürrem believed it. Her assassins have traced my steps all the way from Istanbul. I have been told they are in Venice. Their orders are to kill me on sight."

"The Men in Black! This is dangerous, young man!"

Danilo glanced down. Perhaps he had confided too much.

"Father, we surely cannot refuse hospitality to . . ."

The rabbi raised his hand.

"To such a splendid . . ."

The rabbi raised his hand again.

". . . such a splendid young man . . ."

"Welcome to our Seder, young man." Rabbi Hazan held out his hand. "Miriamne, make a place beside you for our guest. You can tell him about our friends, and our little community."

"Yes, Father." Miriamne bowed her head, only half hiding her smile.

The rabbi put his hand on Danilo's shoulder. "And one thing—it is perhaps wise, Danilo, that you be known, in our little community, as David dei Rossi. We would not want the Ottoman killers to catch wind of the fugitive Danilo del Medigo's presence among us."

· 33 ·

"ONE DAY THEY WILL kill us all—every single Jew," said Jeremiah, a heavyset, bearded, middle-aged man.

It was almost midnight. Danilo patted his stomach and leaned back in his seat; he had rarely eaten so much. He glanced at Miriamne. She returned his gaze and smiled.

He lifted his glass. It seemed so safe here. But death hovered just outside the gates of the Ghetto. And perhaps inside the Ghetto. He drank and he looked around.

The candles fluttered, the breeze gently stirred the curtains. The table was still heavily laden with food, such abundance! All through the Seder, the two blond waitresses came and went, discreetly, efficiently, silently clearing away plates and bringing more.

Glancing at one of the waitresses, Danilo raised a quizzical eyebrow. Miriamne smiled, leaned close, and whispered. "They are Christians, Mika and Melania, nieces of Vincenzo, the gatekeeper. We prepare the food, but they serve us so we do not have to carry things or work, as it is Passover. This way everyone can partake of the meal. They are always in the Ghetto and always very helpful."

"Ah," said Danilo. He couldn't help but admire how efficient and silent the two Christian girls were. Mika and Melania—he would try to remember their names.

"Yes, one day they will kill us all," said Jeremiah as he lifted his glass and took a long drink. "Europe is less and less friendly to Jews." He wiped his lips, and gazed into space. "The Muslims are our only friends."

"That's ridiculous! The Muslims are not our friends!" Old Isaac coughed and hawked away some phlegm; he was a bearded old man, seated directly across from Danilo. His black kippah was tilted sideways on his head. His curly beard was salt and pepper, his hands and knuckles gnarled, and his eyes were clouded over—white cataracts. He groped for his glass. "In truth, we Jews have no friends. We have been enslaved many times." Isaac made a face. "And driven into exile so many, many times."

"Yes, yes."

Miriamne's eyes lit up. "Yes, let us count the times! Who has enslaved us? Who has driven us into exile? We Jews are not very popular! Everybody goes after us! The Egyptians, the Assyrians, the Babylonians, the Romans, the Spaniards, the Portuguese, the English, the Germans, the French. . . . Have I left anyone out? Is the whole world always against us?"

"Now, now, Miriamne," said Jeremiah softly, gazing at her with a sad but covetous and lustful smile. He licked his lips, and his eyes took on a crafty, narrow look. He was a heavy-featured, distinguished-looking man who sat two seats down from Isaac. He leaned forward, turned, and wagged a thick finger at the old man. "Venice gives us shelter."

"Ah, Jeremiah, you may be good at business, but you are naive!" Isaac coughed, his voice thick with phlegm. "You don't understand our real situation. The Venetians act out of interest—not charity, not goodness. Is that not so, David?"

"Everyone, I think, acts out of self-interest," said Danilo cautiously. Living in Istanbul, he had not realized how dangerous, how precarious the situation of the Jews had become in Europe; perils were everywhere for them—and also for those who had converted from Judaism, the so-called *Conversos*.

At the beginning of the meal, just before they sat down, Miriamne had introduced Danilo to everyone as David Rossi, and sat him down next to her and the two children, Jessica and Jacob. Across the table were Isaac and, farther down, the banker, Jeremiah.

Miriamne had leaned towards Danilo and whispered, "Jessica and Jacob are often in my care; their father is dead and their mother is too sickly to take them anywhere. They are like my own children. Old Isaac, across from you, is a widower; he is almost totally blind and rather deaf. He's a fine fellow—but he has a weakness."

"What would that be?" Danilo leaned close.

"He gambled. Once he was rich. Now the community has to look after him."

"That's a horrible vice, gambling." Danilo stared at his plate.

His grandfather, his mother's father—a brilliant, handsome, charming man—had ruined himself and his family through his addiction to gambling. His vice had almost brought the deadly wrath of the ruling d'Este family down on the whole Jewish community of Ferrara.

"Isaac doesn't gamble anymore—he has no money and no credit. Nobody will gamble with him, not even the sharks. And being blind and a bit deaf, it is hard to gamble."

The old man's whey-colored eyes stared into empty space slightly to Danilo's right. When Isaac reached for his wine glass, his skinny, mottled hand trembled and groped.

The candles flickered lower. One of the blond waitresses appeared beside Miriamne and put another full jug of wine on the table, and an extra plate of sweets. "Thank you, Melania," Miriamne said with a smile and received a dazzling smile in return. It was clear everyone loved Miriamne. The two children, Jessica and Jacob, were entranced by her, and Jeremiah kept glancing sneakily in her direction.

Earlier, while Isaac was teasing Jessica about her school work, Miriamne had nodded towards Jeremiah and whispered, "Jeremiah is a banker. He is wealthy; he reeks of money, and—alas—he is a friend of my brother Mordecai's."

Danilo followed Miriamne's glance. Jeremiah was gazing into space and nervously breaking bits of the unleavened bread into fragments. There were bread crumbs in his salt-and-pepper beard. He suddenly focused, turned, and eyed Danilo with what looked like intense suspicion and hostility. Danilo returned his gaze. Was this Jeremiah one of the Jewish spies Vincenzo had mentioned? And if so, who would he be spying for, Venice or the Ottomans?

"Why 'alas' that he is a friend of your brother's?"

Miriamne looked down. Melania was again at her shoulder, exchanging a new candle for a burnt-out one.

"Thank you, Melania." Miriamne turned to Danilo and whispered, "My brother Mordecai wants me to marry Jeremiah, and I . . . well, I have other ideas."

"Other ideas? How old are you?"

"I am seventeen. But I shall one day, God willing, be eighteen. In any case, dear David dei Rossi, I am much older than my seventeen years."

"And what does your father think of this marriage idea?"

"Father lives inside his head. He is an idealist, a thinker, and, in his own way, a mystic. He is fascinated by the Kabbalah, the symbolisms that can lead to knowledge of God and of the eternal source of our being. Father sees deep meaning in even the most minuscule events. And he is also, in a way, the captain of this little ship, the Ghetto Nuovo, the leader of our community. He worries all the time. He has too much to worry about. I don't think he contemplates a marriage for me at all, although the other elders bother him about it. They certainly think I should be married. And . . ."

"And . . . ?"

"And Father knows that I don't want to marry. For the moment, he respects my wishes. And then, there is a small practical problem, insignificant, really. I don't have a large enough dowry to be a good match. So, I shall probably end up a cranky old maid. This will be very sinful of me, I know! The community insists I should marry, be fruitful, and multiply; but I am stubborn. If I were a Christian I might become a nun!"

"Perhaps not having a dowry will be a good defense, for a time. It will keep undesirable matches at bay." While Danilo spoke to Miriamne, he was aware that Jeremiah was glaring at him. Such a woman would be a prize for any man! What account would a dowry — or no dowry — be, measured against such gracious loveliness, such lively intelligence?

"A good defense — well said, Signor David dei Rossi!" Miriamne laughed. "You really are a military man, a warrior. You think in terms of defense, of sieges, and battles, and entrenchments, and flanking movements, and thrust and parry."

Jeremiah coughed. "Miriamne, you must not monopolize this charming young man!" His thick lips moved as he chewed a piece of the unleavened bread. The candlelight deepened the creases on either side of his nose, and the pores of his skin. Underneath the man's beard, Danilo noticed a triple or quadruple chin. This Jeremiah must be about fifty or fifty-five years old, perhaps older; his jowls fought with his beard for dominance, his lips glowed with oil and perhaps with wine. His eyes, though, were lively and quick. He was a crafty fellow, clearly. Could he be a spy? He was certainly jealous. And he'd naturally be an enemy for any man who was, even for a moment, close to Miriamne. He could be both: a spy—and jealous! Not a good combination.

"I am sorry, Signor Jeremiah." Miriamne inclined her head, hiding a sly little inward smile. "David is all yours."

"And where have you come from, then, David, to invade our Seder this fine April evening?"

"I have come from Istanbul, sir," said Danilo, deciding in that instant that it would be easier to cleave as close as possible to the truth; a simple deception—or lie—would be easier to maintain than a complex multi-layered one.

"Ah, Istanbul," Jeremiah exclaimed. "All of Europe trembles before Suleiman and his Ottoman armies!" Jeremiah poured himself more wine, and then launched into a long, complicated, and learned monologue on banking and the Ottoman Empire; on how the Venetians and the Ottomans had a love-hate relationship involving commerce and trade, and even fashion and art, all the strands mingled together; they fought each other, and traded with each other, and imitated each other; they went to war with each other and sued for peace; on how the Venetian and Ottoman fleets would soon face off in a final showdown that would decide the fate of the Mediterranean; and on how as the Christians turned against one another—Catholics against Protestants—and increasingly against the Jews, the Ottoman Empire might one day become the only safe refuge for all the Jews in Europe, who might have to flee for their lives. "Europe is becoming our enemy. One day they will kill us all—every single Jew. The Muslims now are our only friends."

It was then that Old Isaac said that the Sultan and the Muslims were no friends to the Jews; that the Jews had no friends; and that Venice, in giving shelter to the Jews, acted only out of self-interest.

Jeremiah laughed. "I don't care a fig if the Venetians act out of interest. They are practical people, business people, and profit-and-loss people. They are not fanatics, not mystics. Take Anselmo—he is working out of Mestre now and trading mostly in silk and wool. He has just bought—in partnership with a Christian—space on the next Venetian merchant convoy to Istanbul. Money is money, whether Jewish, Christian, or Muslim. The Venetians don't care. Those convoys are like Venice. They are practical devices: The Venetian government owns the fleets, it designs and builds the ships, it organizes the trading convoys—so we can get our goods and our persons safely to Syria and Greece and Istanbul. If you are a merchant, Jew or not, and if you have an entrée or possibly a Christian partner, you can rent space on one of the ships. You get protection, safety in numbers, and with Venetian war galleys and galleons accompanying the convoy, it's safer and it reduces the cost of risk. North African Muslim pirates sailing out of Tunis and Algiers are the big danger and, occasionally, enemy ships like the Sultan's or roaming privateers. So Venice is our partner. We can depend on Venetian self-interest to do the right thing."

Isaac grinned blindly around the table. "You see! You see what a businessman Jeremiah is! Risk, partners, shipping schedules, and working with Christians!"

There was a moment of silence. The curtains drifted inward, stirred by the breeze coming across the Campo. The moving air made a feathery, rustling sound in the leaves of the trees. The candle flames flickered. Voices and laughter echoed, here and there, softly, closer and farther away, all contained by the soaring walls of the Campo.

"And who is that fellow?" Danilo whispered to Miriamne. He raised his glass to his lips and glanced farther down, towards the end of the table.

"The lean, handsome, hungry-looking one, down there at the end?"

"Yes. The one who looks like he wants to kill me."

"That's Abel. He's a tailor. He makes new clothes, but puts a small invisible flaw in each item. That means he can sell the new clothes he has made, but claim they are old, second-hand clothes. He has to keep within the rules, you know. Only Christian tailors can make new clothes. Venetian craft guilds protect their members, so we Jews—who are considered foreigners or migrants—are only allowed to practice certain crafts. Customers turn a blind eye. Abel is another suitor—well, I think he is. He looks angry all the time and he acts like he hates me and wants to kill me. Whenever he sees me, he lowers his head and glowers like a bull. So I have naturally concluded that he likes me." She laughed. "But . . ."

"But . . . ?

"I don't like him." Miriamne gazed straight into Danilo's eyes. "He has a temper, or so I have been told. So you see, dear Signor David, I am surrounded by vexations and difficulties, and navigate in perilous waters. I shall remain an old maid forever."

"That would be . . . a tragedy."

"In any case, I am sure no man could handle me."

"Any man, I think, would be honored to try."

"Do they teach flattery in the Sultan's court? Or did you learn this talent in the harem?"

Danilo laughed.

Jeremiah was still crumbling bits of bread, and still talking, his voice lower now. "We are safe here, Isaac. The Ghetto Nuovo is not a prison, it's a village. It's ours. The mainland is not safe. Jews have been accused of killing children there, and it served as an excuse to kill Jews. Venice is an island, like the Ghetto. The Venetians need us, so they accept us."

"Then there are the friars," Abel said, staring fixedly at Danilo. Danilo held his gaze and then casually looked away. Yes, that man wanted him dead.

"Oh! The friars!" cackled Isaac. He raised his glass.

"Ah, yes, the friars," mumbled Jeremiah. He took a piece of bread and ripped it in half.

"Ah, the friars!" shouted Isaac, almost gleefully. "Dominicans! Franciscans! They hate us! Ha, ha, ha!" He laughed and choked on his own laughter, spluttering.

Jessica, following Isaac's lead, laughed and stared at Isaac and then covered her mouth and turned her bright dark eyes on Miriamne and Danilo. Miriamne took the girl's hand.

Isaac wiped his mouth and took another sip. Danilo wondered at the old man's fragility and his passion. Were the friars really so dangerous? He had heard stories — fiery preachers wandering up and down Italy, stirring up mobs, and the mobs murdering Jews, chasing them through the streets, cutting them down, burning houses and shops.

Jeremiah picked up a piece of bread and dipped it in the sauce. "The friars, Franciscans and Dominicans, they hate us. We Jews do the work of the Devil, or so they claim."

"The Devil?" Jessica looked up, startled.

Jeremiah glanced at the little girl. "Yes, the Devil," he said. He frowned. "The friars claim it is the work of the Devil if the poor depend on Jews for cash, for loans. The friars try to compete with our pawnbrokers and moneylenders. They mean to drive the Jews out of business. They set up the so-called *Monte di Pietà*, their own pawnbrokers, meant to operate as charities. Those friars are dangerous. When they fail, they fall into a rage. They are purists, true believers, and purists are dangerous; and often they are not very hygienic, not very clean."

Rabbi Hazan said from down the table, "We must not speak ill of people, not even of those who hate us."

Jeremiah turned his heavy face towards the rabbi. "But it is true. Dirt is part of holiness, or so the friars seem to think. They preach against everything. Everything is a sin! Everybody has to atone for everything all the time! They don't just attack us. They attack everybody! Look at Savonarola. That mad Dominican friar destroyed Florence — art, beauty, literature, he burned everything—until they revolted and burned him alive in the Piazza della Signoria. Look at the monks and friars in Spain—murderers! Madmen. They even preach against nuns. Convents are brothels, they say. The Church is corrupt, they say, sodomites everywhere! The Pope is a demon. Venice is a seething pit of corruption. Licentious poets and forbidden books thrive in Venice! Ah, they make me sick, those friars." Jeremiah swallowed some more wine and picked up a piece of bread and stared at it. "According to them, we Jews are the worst, corrupting everything and everybody. The Jews bring the judgement of God down on the poor Christians!"

"And we murdered Christ!" Isaac cackled. He coughed, covered his mouth, and blinked his whey-colored eyes, looking blindly towards Danilo, as if challenging him.

"And we make blood sacrifices—we murder children." Abel was clearly enjoying himself; he pronounced the words *blood sacrifices* with relish.

"Please stop," Miriamne said. She stared at Abel. "You'll scare the children."

"The blood libel!" Abel laughed, his eyes flashing defiance. "That's an old story!"

"What does blood libel mean?" The little boy Jacob looked up at Miriamne. She smiled and brushed his hair out of his eyes. "It doesn't mean anything, Jacob."

"It means death!" said Isaac.

"Please," said Miriamne. She tapped her fingers on the table.

Isaac poured himself more wine. "And many Jews who escaped came here . . ." He was about to spill the wine when one of the blond waitresses helped steady his glass, saying, "There you are, Signor Isaac."

He looked up at her blindly. "Thank you, Mika, you are always very kind."

"One thing the Christians always wonder, how do the Jews make money?" Abel said, dipping the bread into the sauce.

"Not all Jews make money, Abel." Isaac coughed. "Jeremiah makes money. I've always wondered how he does it."

Jeremiah snorted. "You had money, Isaac. You gambled it all away. You are a learned and eloquent man! Could you not control yourself?"

"I couldn't, I couldn't, Jeremiah. It made me feel alive. It made me feel free."

"Ah, free . . ." Jeremiah let the word hang in the air. "Who, I wonder, is really free?"

"We have always known exile," said Isaac, "it is our destiny. We are wanderers."

"We have a home here." Miriamne patted her mouth with a napkin.

Danilo glanced at her. This seventeen-year-old girl was standing up to the old men as if she were a leader of the community. What did Rabbi Hazan think, having such a daughter? The rabbi was talking to one of the blond waitresses—Mika. The young woman bowed her head, smiled, and laughed.

Isaac looked down at his plate and began to mumble. "It is strange, though, how things have come to pass. There was the story of Genesis and of our people in the books of Moses. Then, in the exile, the scholars, the rabbis, commented on those stories, and then other rabbis commented on those comments, and then other rabbis commented on the comments on the comments. So we got more and more words, more and more layers, layer upon layer. We have become a nation of quibblers, of cogitators, of nitpickers. We are lost in words!"

"Now, now, Isaac," Miriamne whispered gently.

"I know, I know, Miriamne. I am old and cranky. But . . . Once we Jews were a nation of warriors, of chieftains and prophets, of builders and architects, of kings and priests, and now . . . Now we are ragpickers, seamstresses, tailors, moneylenders, bookworms, doctors; and quibblers, alchemists, clowns and jugglers and fiddlers—where is our heroism?"

Danilo looked around him. This was truly a different world from Istanbul. There he had grown up in the military and the masculine camaraderie of the Sultan's school. His companions and friends were all young lads, all Muslim. He was used to the rough-and-tumble masculinity of hundreds of thousands of men on the march in the Sultan's army; he was used to dealing with the Sultan himself on campaign, to the dignity, the taciturn reserve of the man, and to his mystical intensity.

Danilo had grown into manhood surrounded by the airy grandeur and glamor of the Sultan's court, with its gardens and fountains, and he had been the childhood friend and then the secret lover of the Sultan's favorite daughter, Saida — wonderful, funny, glorious Saida. And here, next to him, was a woman that reminded him of Saida, and of his mother, Grazia, also: Miriamne was clearly a strong, wonderful woman.

Melania filled his glass.

"Thank you," he said.

Danilo began to realize how deeply the rituals of Judaism were in the very fiber of his being. Now, perhaps for the first time, he clearly understood why his mother had been so reluctant to give up her faith. He saw her, bent over her books, a quill in hand, and recalled how, hearing him enter the room, she would look up, gaze into his eyes, and her smile would light up the whole world.

He glanced around the table: Isaac, Jeremiah, Rebecca, Abel, Rabbi Hazan, Jessica, Jacob, and, above all, Miriamne. They seemed, already, to be family.

Isaac said, "It will be Easter in a few days: Maundy Thursday, Good Friday, and then — Easter Sunday."

"Yes," said Rabbi Hazan.

"That means trouble." Miriamne picked up her glass of wine and stared at it.

"Trouble?" Danilo raised an eyebrow.

"Why will there be trouble?" Jessica turned her bright gaze on Miriamne. The stiff little ruff at Jessica's neck set off her glowing complexion. Her teeth gleamed white; her dark eyes wide open, intense.

"Oh, I shouldn't worry about trouble, Jessica. We are safe here," Rabbi Hazan said in his deep voice and winked at the little girl.

Isaac coughed. "There will be some of those preaching friars we were talking about, Dominicans and Franciscans—preaching hate as usual! They come at Easter. They will inflame the populace."

"The Venetian government has assured me . . ." Rabbi Hazan held up his hand.

"Oh, the government . . ." Isaac coughed again, and covered his mouth.

"They do the best they can," Rabbi Hazan sighed.

"But why will we be in trouble?" Jessica looked frightened.

Isaac turned his cloudy eyes towards her. "Well, at Easter, the Christians celebrate their Messiah."

"What's a Messiah?" Jacob was struggling to eat a boiled egg. A young woman sitting on his right helped him.

Rabbi Hazan cleared his throat. "The Messiah is one anointed—chosen—by God. He is a king who will come and deliver the Jews. He will unite the twelve tribes of Israel, and rebuild the temple, and he will bring about peace in the world."

"And the Christians have a Messiah?"

"Yes, Jessica. His name was Jesus, as you certainly know. Jesus was a Jewish rabbi or teacher in Israel. He was a beautiful speaker and a wise teacher. The Christians believe he was—is—the Messiah. At Passover, he held a supper with some of his friends—men who followed his teaching. This was in Jerusalem. He was accused of causing trouble, and was arrested and tried and crucified by the Romans, who governed at the time. His Passover Seder, which Christians call the Last Supper, is remembered on what the Christians call Maundy Thursday. His crucifixion and death are remembered on what the Christians call Good Friday. Then, so they believe, he rose from the dead . . . and that is what they celebrate on what they call Easter Sunday."

Jessica gazed at Rabbi Hazan, her dark eyes intense and serious. "This rabbi came back from the dead?"

"That is what Christians believe. And so for the Christians, he is the Messiah. They believe he died to cleanse humans—all humans, not just Jews—of their sins. To wipe away the sins of humankind, to save people—to save those who believe in him, at least. On many points the Christians disagree among themselves."

"But if the Romans crucified him—why do the Christians hate us? We didn't kill him. Why don't they hate the Romans?"

Rabbi Hazan sighed and looked around the table. Danilo followed his gaze, considering all the faces—bright, eager, and lit up by the candles. Each face, however ragged, however old, was beautiful. This little vessel of humanity, crowded into the Ghetto Nuovo, was, in a sense, entrusted to Rabbi Hazan.

Rabbi Hazan glanced at Danilo. "Miriamne thinks we are, some of us, too negative, dwelling only on disasters, whereas we have great moments of exaltation and joy."

"Yes, joy, and even simple happiness," said Miriamne. She stroked Jessica's hair; the girl leaned close against her. "We must seize what we can. *Carpe diem.*"

Isaac gazed around at all of them. "And we Jews are mysterious, are we not? To the Christians, I mean. What goes on in a synagogue? What goes on at a Passover Seder? What is Purim? Why are the boys circumcised? What are all our taboos about? Why do we insist on unleavened bread? Mystery makes people suspicious." He glanced at Mika and Melania. "Are we mysterious to you, Mika? Are we mysterious to you, Melania? You are Christians, after all."

"You are not that mysterious, Signor Isaac," said Melania. "You are a fine gentleman."

"Signor Isaac sometimes talks in riddles, but other than that . . ." Mika smiled as she refilled Isaac's glass.

Rabbi Hazan nodded. "We are not that mysterious. Passover is not so mysterious. It is about who we are. It is our history. In the end, it is human history—the history of everyman. Exile, in the end, is everyone's lot."

3

THE INTERVIEW

W HEN THE CANDLES AND TORCHES HAD BURNED LOW and the food had been eaten and the guests had left, Mika and Melania washed and put away the dishes. Rabbi Hazan motioned to Danilo. "Now, Danilo del Medigo, tell me your story."

"Yes, sir, what would you like to know?"

"Did you learn any languages at the Sultan's School for Pages? Or was everything taught in Turkish?"

"Every member of the Sultan's entourage is required to master Arabic, the language of the Koran; Persian, which is the language of poetry; and Turkish—the language of administration and everyday life."

"No Western languages? No Latin? No Greek? No French?"

"No, sir. In the Sultan's school, Latin and Greek are considered irrelevant, barbaric western tongues, beneath the notice of scholars and students."

"Barbaric? Latin and Greek? That is too bad. French and Latin and Greek would be useful, particularly French."

"I learned French from my mother."

"Your mother?"

"Grazia dei Rossi. She was a scribe and translator—and author—and private secretary to Isabella d'Este."

"Really? Isabella d'Este? I have heard her husband, Francesco Gonzaga II, never forgave her for being better at tactics and diplomacy than he. A strong woman: when Francesco was a prisoner in Venice, she refused to ransom him if it meant turning over her son Federico to the Venetians. I've been told Francesco never forgave her for that either. And she promotes artists—Venetian artists in particular. She has patronized all of the best modern artists: Giorgione, Giovanni Bellini, Titian, Michelangelo, Leonardo da Vinci, and of course the great Andrea Mantegna."

"Isabella also pioneered the plunging neckline, Father." Miriamne flashed a bright, innocent smile at both Danilo and the rabbi.

Rabbi Hazan gave his daughter an indulgent look.

"Isabella d'Este loved French romances. So my mother read them to her. I listened, and I learned. My French has been useful. In tricky situations."

"How so?"

"During the Baghdad campaign, when Sultan Suleiman's army was pursuing the Persians, an emissary from the French king, François I, arrived at our camp."

Rabbi Hazan stroked his beard. "Ah, yes, François wants to make France the most powerful country in Europe. He needs the Ottomans as an ally to outflank their common enemy, the Spanish Holy Roman Emperor, Charles V. François believes he is encircled—to the south, to the north, and to the east—by Charles V, who rules in Spain, in the Netherlands, and in much of Germany. So to encircle his encircler, as it were, François has made an alliance with Islam."

"You put it much more clearly than anyone I have listened to."

"Father is brilliant." Miriamne's eyes flashed. "And he is much, much too modest."

The rabbi gave her a smile. "By allying himself with Suleiman, François has become a traitor, many think, to Christendom, and to Europe. If you are meddling in these things, this is dangerous territory, my son. Working with the Ottomans can be fatal. People are hung and drawn and quartered for less, even here in Venice."

"I really don't know much about politics, sir." Danilo looked down and frowned. What sort of trouble had he gotten himself into? He swallowed. "In any case, the French emissary had come to confirm the terms of a trade treaty being negotiated between France and the Sultan. On the final day of negotiations, the Sultan's interpreter collapsed."

"How unfortunate!" The rabbi stroked his beard, raised an eyebrow, and glanced at Miriamne. She kept her gaze steady.

Danilo looked back and forth. Unspoken messages were being passed back and forth between father and daughter. Did they know something he didn't? It suddenly occurred to him that perhaps the interpreter had been poisoned. Maybe the Venetians had done it—to stop the treaty from being signed. "The interpreter died. It turned out that without him the treaty could not be confirmed."

Rabbi Hazan sighed. "Small events often have huge consequences." He tapped his fingers on the table edge. "So this interpreter suddenly, unexpectedly, died . . ."

"Yes, and so, with no interpreter, the treaty was in jeopardy." Danilo paused. Should he continue? "The whole French-Ottoman alliance was up in the air."

The rabbi frowned. "But how does this concern you?"

"My role was a small one. The Sultan, Suleiman the Magnificent . . ."

"All of Europe, all of Christendom, trembles before Suleiman. The Pope, people say, is terrified. Suleiman, it is said, plans to seize Rome, turn Saint Peter's into a mosque, and impose Islam on Italy—and perhaps on all of Europe."

Danilo said nothing. He had had no inkling of all of this. How could he have been so stupid, so naive? He had been too far away from Europe and too close to events in Istanbul to understand their meaning for other people. For him, Suleiman the Magnificent, the ruler of perhaps the greatest empire in the world, though certainly grandiose, was just a man—a man to whom he read a translation of the *Life of Alexander the Great*, a man whom he had, by chance, saved from a wild boar; a man who was the father of Saida, the first love of his life. He had not seen things from the European or Christian or Venetian point of view; in fact, he was hardly aware such points of view existed.

Rabbi Hazan turned his large, sad eyes on Danilo. "Great events are afoot. Some say Suleiman's invasion of Italy is imminent. All of Europe might become Muslim. This could spell the end of Christianity."

Danilo looked down. Had he, by helping the Sultan, imperilled the whole of Christendom? Had he made enemies on all sides? The Sultan's Men in Black intended to kill him. Now in the whole of Christendom, including Venice, he would be considered a traitor, an enemy to be imprisoned, tortured, and executed.

He glanced at up at Miriamne.

She was gazing at him with an indulgent, forgiving smile. She seemed to be enjoying this conversation, and his embarrassment.

Danilo cleared his throat. "I was just a page in the Sultan's suite. The Sultan asked if there was anyone who knew enough French to verify that the treaty reflected what had been negotiated and promised."

"And who did he find? You?"

"Of course he found Danilo, Father, who else could he find?"

Danilo swallowed and glanced away from Miriamne. Her gaze was just a bit too intense. Laughter hovered on her bright lips and sparkled in her eyes. Did this girl find him funny? Did she find him ridiculous? He focused on Rabbi Hazan. "Yes, sir, it was I. The treaty was signed, so now there is a commercial treaty between François I and Suleiman the Magnificent. So that was my role."

"Son, you are too modest." Rabbi Hazan smiled. "The

Sultan is greatly indebted to you. Though perhaps the rulers of Christendom — aside from François, of course — will not be so happy with the role you played. Nor, frankly, will Venice. Venice has been fighting a duel with the Ottomans on and off for over 150 years. Perhaps, by helping Suleiman, you have facilitated the invasion of Italy, the collapse of Rome. These are dangerous times, Danilo. You must be careful."

"I see that now."

"This French-Ottoman commercial treaty is probably a front for another, more dangerous kind of agreement."

"Oh?"

"Perhaps a military agreement." Rabbi Hazan drummed with his fingers on the table.

Danilo looked down. This was getting worse and worse! How could he have been so stupid?

"Most likely François and Suleiman have agreed to invade Italy. The French will attack from the north, the Ottomans from the south. The Pope is terrified. Such is the talk down on the Rialto."

"Down on the Rialto they know absolutely everything!" Miriamne gave Danilo a bright smile.

Melania had appeared beside them. "A last glass of water, Rabbi Hazan? Miriamne? Young gentleman?"

Melania filled their glasses and carried off the beaker of water, disappearing through the curtains of the pavilion. By now the table was bare; just a few candles burning, their flames wavering in the breeze that still smelled of cooking fires and meat.

Miriamne put her hand on her father's. "Perhaps this was all meant to happen."

Danilo turned to the young woman. Miriamne's beauty was painfully intense. He felt a catch in his throat. He swallowed. Saida was lost to him and he knew in his heart she was lost forever. Miriamne radiated sensuality and grace, just as Saida had, as he last saw her, when they made love in the stables. The tenderness, the playfulness, the pure explosion of desire, had been overwhelming—and so had the sudden reversal of his fortune. The feelings flooded back. Saida had declared that they must never again see each other; he must leave Istanbul and never return; she must marry the man her father, the Sultan, would choose for her.

Danilo cleared his throat. "This was meant to happen? What do you mean?"

Miriamne tilted her head to one side, mischievous lights dancing in her eyes. "A few days ago, I had a vision. A lone traveler was about to enter our lives, and he would do our family a great service. And here you are, just as predicted in my vision!"

Rabbi Hazan glanced at his daughter. "Miriamne possesses visionary talents which I, unfortunately, do not share. What are you going to do now that you are in Italy? What are your plans?"

Danilo took a deep breath. What was he going to do next? Since the instant he had left Saida, he had acted instinctively, from moment to moment—with no plan, no thought for tomorrow. Just surviving. Now, he must decide. It was up to him to determine just who he was.

But now, tonight, he had to find a place to stay, and he had to make money. "My father—my legal father—Judah del Medigo—wanted me to go to the University of Padua, study medicine, and become a doctor, like him. But, then I also have the blood of . . ."

". . . of your Christian father, your blood father."

"Yes, I feel the warrior's blood of my Christian father running in my veins. I am rather good with the Turkish lance."

"Rather good with the Turkish lance!" Miriamne favored Danilo with a roguish grin. "So you ride? And you can use a lance?" Her eyes sparkled. The candlelight reflected on the smooth curves of her shoulders and collarbone. "This is just like in the tales of knights in olden times, jousting and fighting for the honor of their fair demoiselles. How romantic! I'll bet Danilo can swing a sword and throw a javelin, use the crossbow, and handle a dagger too."

Danilo looked down. This girl was a trickster, high-spirited, worse than Saida. She could drive a fellow mad!

"Well," the rabbi cleared his throat. "I'm afraid we have little use for champion swordsmen and warriors here in the Ghetto. We are a peaceful people."

"Yes, but . . ." Miriamne glanced at her father. "But Father, you do need someone to translate from French. That book that you just acquired . . ."

"Miriamne oversees my intellectual interests—and almost everything else!"

Miriamne bowed her head. Her eyelashes were lowered, a shade on her cheeks. Was she blushing?

"Are you familiar with the works of Heinrich Cornelius Agrippa?"

"I am not, sir."

"He died last year. He was a scholar at the Court of the Holy Roman Emperor Charles V. He has written a number of volumes. Some of them were placed on the Pope's index of forbidden books . . ."

"Forbidden books!" Miriamne shuddered in horror; she rolled her eyes, and then grinned.

"I have managed to acquire the original manuscript of Agrippa's volume *Occult Philosophy*. It is much in demand among a certain class of . . . special connoisseurs. The book is in Burgundian French. I need a linguist who can translate this text into a civilized language. Where are you staying in Venice?"

"I'm afraid I haven't found a place yet."

"What about here, Father?"

"Here?"

"Upstairs. Mordecai's room is free." Miriamne turned to Danilo. "My brother Mordecai is an alchemist. He is always off on mysterious missions. Right now he is roaming the countryside, on the Italian mainland, looking for materials for his experiments. At least, that's what he tells us." She blinked innocently, her head tilted to one side, a skeptical smile hovering on her lips.

"But, Miriamne," Rabbi Hazan raised an eyebrow, "what if your brother does not want a stranger sleeping in his room?"

"It's Passover Eve, Father." Miriamne glanced at her father and then at Danilo. "Danilo del Medigo is a Jew stranded far from home. We were obliged to give him a Seder meal—and we are obliged to give him a place to lay his head. We have given him the meal, and now we must give him a night's rest. I am certain Mordecai would not object. It's only for the one night."

The rabbi nodded. "Yes, daughter—well said, as usual. It would certainly be a sin against God if we were to turn this wandering stranger, a fugitive pursued by assassins, away."

"Perhaps," Miriamne said, eyes sparkling, "by the clarity of the morning's light, we may even discover that Danilo is indeed the traveler in my vision, and that he has been sent to us, just as was foretold, for a reason."

4

A DIVIDED SOUL

HOLDING A TORCH, MIRIAMNE LED DANILO UP A NARROW, crooked staircase. "We are crowded in the Ghetto. The rooms are small and we have sometimes put two floors, or stories, and several rooms where there used to be one floor and one room. Watch you don't bang your head."

Danilo promptly bumped his head. He stooped down to avoid another wooden strut that went up at a steep angle.

"Did it hurt?"

"No." He was not going to admit to any weakness. This girl had too sharp a wit; like Saida, she knew how to mock and make fun of a fellow. Like Saida, she was a girl warrior. He must handle her with care.

"You must remember to stoop. It is such a pretty head. I do not want it to come to any harm."

She held the torch aloft, casting flickering shadows on the walls. She turned to look at him. Her smile was bright, her hair shone, her shoulder glowed in the torchlight like the smoothest silk.

The passage twisted back on itself. "And right here, it's all higgledy-piggledy." She turned away. "The building and adapting never stop. You will hear sawing and hammering where people are working to make space. Christian carpenters and workmen from the guilds do all the work. In most trades, Jews are not allowed to compete with Venetians."

"How old are you?"

"As I told you, just barely seventeen."

"Young."

"I am an old spirit. When he is annoyed with me my father sometimes tells me I should already be married. Be fruitful and multiply, we are told, thus the tribes of Israel survive even the worst of our tribulations. Some of the elders are scandalized that I am still single; they go tut-tut and occasionally make a fuss. But Father controls them all and he doesn't insist upon marriage."

"Ah."

"And as I said, there is not a sufficient dowry for a decent match, and . . ." She turned away from him, the torch reflecting off the wall, throwing shadows. The delicacy of her back was striking, neatly arched and plunging to the fine, narrow, supple waist—again, like Saida; and, again, he felt the exquisite, tender, heartrending pang of loss.

"And . . ."

"I dislike all the contenders, and . . ."

"And . . ."

"And I don't want to get married—not yet."

"Ah."

"I am, I suppose, waiting for the right man. Most men are . . ."

"Yes?"

"Idiots." She swirled around to face him, a fierce fire in her eyes.

"You think most men are idiots?"

"Yes! They are pretentious and silly and overbearing, and unwilling to give a woman a chance to be herself. And then . . ."

"Then . . ."

"Father would not survive without me. Who would wash things, who would cook, who would remind him to eat? More and more, he is absent-minded. He floats in the clouds. He cares for ideas and for other people, but not for himself."

"Ah . . ."

Her eyes flashed. "I am curious. I want to learn all I can. It is not easy for a woman. We are supposed to remain ignorant. Men want us to remain like silly, trivial children."

"My mother was a scholar. It was hard for her. In many ways, her family opposed her every step of the way."

"She was a brave woman, a heroine."

"Yes."

"She is no longer alive?"

"No."

"I am sorry. When did she die?"

"Ten years ago—we were escaping from the Sack of Rome, we were on a ship, sailing from Ostia, north along the coast, transporting some of Isabella d'Este's treasures. We were captured by pirates."

"Pirates?"

"Yes."

"You and your mother?"

"Yes. My mother was shot. She died protecting me. The pirates murdered everyone. I was the only survivor. They thought I might be worth ransom—or, if there was no ransom, they could sell me as a slave."

"Oh, that is horrible. I am so sorry! It must be awful for you! You must miss her!"

"Every single day."

"That is cruel, so cruel, to lose one's mother . . . and so young and . . ." Her eyes were wet, gold flames dancing, sparkles on her eyelashes. She turned away. "The stairs can be steep. Our synagogue is on top of one of the buildings. There was no space in the Campo for it. The synagogue must be open to the sky so that at the beginning of Shabbat on a Friday night we can see the first stars from the synagogue itself. So it is on the top floor, above people's flats, with the Holy Ark facing Jerusalem." She pushed open a curtained door. "Well, here is the room. It is small, as you can see."

Danilo put down his carpetbag. The room, lit by Miriamne's torch, was flickering and shadowy. In a corner was a thin mattress on a small wooden platform. The room had one window — with bars — looking out on the Campo. On the walls were engravings of instruments for alchemy — an alembic, a crucible, a mortar and pestle. Against one wall was a table; under the table was a chamber pot, and on the table was a washing bowl, and standing beside the washing bowl a pitcher of water, and even a bar of soap! There was a small bookshelf with a few books on alchemy, and astrology, and suchlike.

Miriamne pointed at the table. "Here is a bowl and some water to wash with. We live in a lagoon, but water — drinking water and washing water — is precious. It comes from wells. Here in the Ghetto, on the Campo, there are only three wells." She used her torch to light two candles, and turned towards him. "So, my dear friend, what are you, really?"

Danilo thought for a moment. "I'm a naïve warrior who is tired of war."

She placed the candles close to the washing bowl. "And why, my naive warrior friend, are you tired of war?"

Danilo held her gaze. It was too intense. He looked down. How much should he confide in this young woman? What could he tell her? What should he tell her? He would evade the big questions, leave them for later. "I wanted to fight and I didn't do any fighting."

Miriamne mimed a sad pout, and then flashed that diabolical mocking smile. "The man wanted to fight, and he didn't do any fighting! And so he is bored with war! When people go to war, they come back without a nose, without eyes, without arms or legs. It is not very pretty, your war." She looked away and knelt by the bed, fluffed the meagre mattress, and patted it down. "At one point during the Seder you told me you were a rationalist, a sort of Neoplatonist."

"Yes," said Danilo, frowning: now she might ask him to explain philosophy; how horrible! He was going to get into trouble.

"So, Mr. Neoplatonist, what is a Neoplatonist?"

"I'm not a philosopher."

"You just said you were—you believe in rationalism, and rational ideas and methods."

"Well . . ." Danilo sighed. He was tired. How had he gotten himself into this dreadful tangle? Why was he tempted to confess his deepest feelings—about Saida, about Grazia, about his two fathers, Pirro and Judah—to this beautiful young woman? He should be thinking about how to protect himself from the killers, how to avoid the Venetian magistrates, if they were looking for him, not about philosophy, and . . .

"Don't be shy, sir."

Danilo took a deep breath and steeled himself. He'd rather be in the midst of the blazing thunder of cannon fire, surrounded by smoke and flame, astride his gallant warhorse, Bucephalus, charging a fierce Persian warrior, than try to explain philosophy. "My father is a doctor, as I told you. He is careful and methodical. He tries to test his cures to see if they work. He taught me some philosophy."

"How marvelous—you were lucky!"

"Well," Danilo swallowed, "the Neoplatonists believe the world is organized by ideas, by concepts; and they believe that reason—thinking—can discover those ideas. Everything, they believe, comes from—is caused by—one idea, a first cause, a simple first cause, and that this first idea that causes everything is the origin of everything. Some people say the first cause is God, others say it is an idea, or that it is the Idea of the Good. They also believe that mathematics, numbers, manifest the ideas, and underlie everything, and can give access to this invisible world of ideas, and can explain everything."

"So, somehow, this one thing—the Idea—gave birth to the many things we see around us, including us."

"Yes."

"How did the one thing become many things if it was only one in the beginning? How did the one thing—or idea—become chickens and eggs and cows and rocks and trees, the city of Venice, the paintings of Titian and Leonardo, and you and me?"

"It's a mystery." Danilo sighed. His head ached. This woman was beautiful and kind, but . . . she was too intelligent. Maybe it was a blessing she didn't have a dowry. Her headstrong wit, sense of fun, and curiosity would drive a normal fellow mad! Of course, his mother was rather like that—headstrong, intelligent, curious about all things, and so was Saida. Why did he always end up confronting high-spirited, challenging women—women who had a sense of irony, who laughed so easily, and who knew how, with a glance or a word, to put a fellow in his place?

"It's a mystery?" Miriamne raised an eyebrow.

"I told you. I'm a warrior, not a philosopher."

"Oh, beautiful man, you are many things—let us see what you are! Have you ever had your palm read?"

"Why? Are you going to try to read my future in my hand?"

"Your future is not written in your hand, but your character certainly is. And some people do have visions that give them hints as to what might lie ahead."

"Are you one of them? Do you have visions?"

"Sometimes," she answered airily, with a charming grin.

Danilo raised an eyebrow. His father, Judah del Medigo, was an observant Jew, but he was not particularly a believer, and he had indeed taught Danilo the need for rationality; his mother had also cultivated rational thought. Witch-like visions of the future and palm reading, and such like mumbo-jumbo—sorcerers and magicians—didn't enter into their worldview; nor did wild-eyed messiahs or fanatical friars. But Miriamne was generous, high-spirited, and certainly intelligent. And she was providing him with shelter, and food. Perhaps a fairy tale was just what he needed.

"You don't believe me!" Her eyes flashed; her lips curled.

"Of course I believe you!" He gave her his best reassuring smile.

"Do not mock me! When I am provoked, I am a vengeful spirit!"

Danilo sighed. She did look so very tempting. The instant he had that thought, the image of Saida, laughing, twirling around, and making fun of him, rose before his eyes, a mocking, chiding, amorous spirit, bubbling laughter. How interesting! Miriamne, the Jewess and daughter of a rabbi, and Saida, the Muslim princess, daughter of Suleiman, could be sisters. "I surrender, Miriamne!" He grinned and held out his right hand. "Read on!"

She beamed at him. "Are you right-handed or left-handed?"

"My right arm is my sword arm."

"The right hand it shall be!" She bent over to examine his palm. The candlelight lit up in a warm golden glow half her face, her cheek, the shadow of her lashes, her bare outstretched arm, and the delicacy of her wrist. She took his hand in hers. Her grasp was firm, but gentle and warm. It was, he realized, the first human touch he had felt since — since Saida.

"Being a right-handed person," she looked up at him, "you have a natural gift for leadership."

"I do?"

"Yes. That characteristic can be seen in the lines and mounts on your palm."

"What lines? What mounts?"

"Well, my dear skeptic! Let me show you. If you follow the path my finger is tracing across your palm . . ."

"I'm following it." Danilo took a deep breath. Her hand was delicate, her touch was smooth and slow, soft and warm. This was a dangerous thrill; a young gentleman was not built to withstand such sensations.

She looked up at him. The candlelight danced in her eyes, and reflected on the delicate line of her cheek, on the ripeness of her lips. "You will find that under your first finger, there is a mound of flesh that palm readers call the Mount of Jupiter."

She touched it with the very tip of her finger, with its carefully trimmed, slightly pointed nail. "It is right here. It's this sweet little bulge at the base of your index finger. The name goes back to Greek mythology, to the god Zeus, who was called Jupiter by the Romans. If the Mount of Jupiter is too prominent, it may mean that you are overbearing and a bully."

Danilo felt that, at this point, he'd better say something intelligent and display—perhaps—some scraps of erudition, and avoid giving the impression of being merely a flat-spirited, disabused, and naive warrior. He cleared his throat. "Of course, Zeus is an interesting god; the god of the sky and of thunder and storms, like Baal, the old thunder god of the Phoenicians, and Zeus is King of the Gods on Mount Olympus, the home of the Greek gods. So Jupiter is very similar, the Roman version of Zeus."

A smile hovered on her lips. "You are an encyclopedia— a gallant knight, a disabused, exhausted naive warrior, and a Platonic philosopher."

Danilo stared at her. This Miriamne was diabolical; at every turn, she laid a trap for a fellow. "I wouldn't go so far . . ." He sighed. Anything he said would just offer her a new angle of attack. "So what does this Mount of Jupiter tell you about me?"

"The Mount of Jupiter indicates how you see the world, and how you want the world—other people—to see you. How you want to be considered. Right-handed people like you are natural-born leaders, but . . ."

". . . but?"

"Your Mount of Jupiter is telling me that you may be one of those who lack the persistence to see things through. You may be a divided soul. That might mean you are indecisive, with a tendency to shilly-shally. You may not know what you are going to do with your life, what cause or ideals you want to fight for—if any."

"Really?"

"Yes."

Danilo shifted uneasily. "Maybe there is nothing worth fighting for."

"Really?'

"Yes."

She frowned. "That is a very cynical and detached point of view, my dear disabused naive warrior. It is as if, behind your beauty and strength and many talents, you are determined to be Mr. Nobody. It's as if you don't want to grow up at all."

"Maybe it's better to sit out other people's battles, to stand aside."

"In the end, you will not do that, my dear beautiful warrior. I am quite sure you will make a choice, you will become a hero, even if you don't want to."

He had to challenge her. "Explain."

"I somehow have the impression I already know you." A flush appeared on her cheeks. She lowered her gaze and concentrated on his palm. "Everything interacts with everything else. Character interacts with events, and with opportunities — and, most important, with choices. Occasions are to be seized. Choices define the man."

"Choices . . ."

"Yes, choices." She narrowed her eyes. The candlelight reflected on her thick, long lashes. "Now, as to your palm, there are a number of these bumps, as you call them, seven to be exact. We have the Mount of Saturn, right below your middle finger; the Mount of Apollo, under your third finger; the Mount of Venus, snuggled in right here, under your thumb; the Mount of Mars, and the Mount of the Moon. And you will notice that each mount corresponds, not only to a god or goddess, but to a planet or to the moon; thus they are related to the heavenly spheres, so that in the end everything connects to everything else, all the symbols overlap and have correspondences. And you know that the astrologers will say there is destiny written in the —"

"Enough! Enough!" Danilo exclaimed, laughing. This beautiful woman was a bubbling fountain of crazy knowledge!

"I thought you were a thinker. But if you are not curious, if your mind is so closed, if your thirst for knowledge is so limited, if your prejudices are so rooted, well then . . ." She withdrew her hand, turned away, and, in profile, displayed a deliciously angry pout.

"I *am* curious. I am totally, totally consumed with curiosity!" He seized her hand. He must redeem himself! What had he done? How cruel could he be? He could not allow himself to insult, to wound, this generous creature. "My thirst for knowledge is infinite, dear Miriamne! Just tell me, what do all these interacting bumps and lines and mountains and valleys and constellations and stars have to say about me?"

"They say many things." She paused, her gaze far away. She was not seeing him. He had disappeared. Then, she lowered her gaze, concentrating on the lines that criss-crossed his palm. "Right-handed people trust their brains more than their muscles."

"Well, that's certainly not me!" Danilo laughed. "I never think about what I'm going to do. I just do it."

She looked up sharply. "Oh, yes, it *is* you! You may mock and flatter yourself by denying it, but you are *very* brainy." She held his right hand up to the light, "This palm is a perfect image of what a right-handed palm looks like."

"I may not share your gift for palm reading, but I know who I am, and no matter what you see in my right hand, I am sure I am more a man of action than of thought."

"That is strange." She bit her lip. "This hand does not appear to belong to the man you describe, to the man you believe yourself to be."

"Maybe you should look at my other hand."

"As you wish." She reached across his chest, took his left hand in hers, and raised it to the light. "This is strange." She pursed her lips. "This hand tells a very different story from your right hand. Here I see ambition, courage, and honesty. But I also see that your heart line runs dangerously close to your lifeline. If you are mistaken about your right-handedness, watch out! Your impulsive nature could be your undoing."

"I have been known on occasion to make a rash decision or two, or three." He frowned. This palm reading was nonsense of course, but there was something intriguing in her speculations. Perhaps she had spotted a civil war going on in his soul between his scholarly, scrupulously intellectual Jewish legal father, Judah del Medigo, and his real blood father, the dashing, romantic, and foolhardy warrior-aristocrat Pirro Gonzaga. She was an acute observer and keen-eyed psychologist; she saw into a fellow's heart; the palm reading was a mask for her real talent—instant, penetrating intuition. "What else do you see?"

"I see a life of travel and adventure. Does that sound like you?"

"Well, I did volunteer to go on the Sultan's Baghdad campaign." He looked down—and he had done it against Judah's wishes, dreaming of the sort of warlike life that Pirro led. Oh, what an idiot he had been and how divided he was!

"That's more like it! War, adventure, volunteering! Wonderful! Look here!" Her smile lit up. She pointed to his palm. "There is a branch in your lifeline that takes you on a long journey. You will wander here, there, and everywhere. That line could be Baghdad! Or it could be predictive of vagabond and itinerant adventures to come—of your chivalrous romantic side."

"Anything else?"

"There is a conflict in your past between love and duty. It has caused you great pain, and it will continue to cause pain until it is resolved. So you have regrets."

"Only one."

"And what is that?"

"I told you I am on the run from the Sultan's assassins. But there is more to it."

Danilo hesitated. Should he confess everything? Miriamne was so astute, so attentive, and so kind. But he could not mention his love for Saida—not to anyone. Even to breathe her name would put the Princess in mortal danger. If it was discovered that she had a lover—and that her lover was a Jew— it would mean instant execution. The secret must be shared with no one. He looked straight into Miriamne's beautiful eyes. "When I escaped from the Men in Black, I had to move fast—I didn't have time to say goodbye to my father, Judah del Medigo."

"Is he still alive?"

"Yes."

"And living in Istanbul?"

"Yes, certainly."

"So you could go back and pay him a visit."

"No."

"Why?"

"If the Sultana—Hürrem—or the Grand Vizier thought my father was in contact with me . . . they would have him killed."

"I see. Of course."

"Hürrem, the Sultana, never forgives and never forgets."

"Yes, she is a remarkable woman."

"Yes. That's what everybody says—she is a remarkable woman! I don't know how many times I've heard it!"

From Saida, Danilo had learned more than he wanted to know about Hürrem, her charm, her cleverness, her cooking skills, and her almost magical influence over Suleiman.

Miriamne glowed with enthusiasm. "I was told Hürrem was captured as a young girl by a Tartar raiding party somewhere up on the steppes north of the Black Sea, and the Tartars put her on sale on the slave market in the Crimea, and she was given as a gift by Suleiman's mother, Valide Sultan, to Suleiman; and so Hürrem became a harem girl and then quickly became the Sultan's preferred concubine. Suleiman fell in love with her and broke all the rules and married her. She must have enchanted him, I suppose, or cast a spell. Her other name is Roxelana."

"You know a lot about it."

"I may be a Jew, Signor Disenchanted Warrior, but I am a Venetian too. We want to know everything." She was almost breathless with enthusiasm. "I love it here. This is a city of gossips and spies. Venetians love to talk, and they have very loose tongues. They love to listen too. They loiter around the market, and in the alleyways and public squares, and in taverns, and pick up tidbits every way they can. Merchants have to know things, like prices, supplies, risks—where the pirates are, which crops are about to fail, where drought is likely, who is who at court, who is in, who is out!" She paused for breath. "Venice is a trading empire, an emporium—and we trade a lot with Istanbul and the Ottoman Empire, and we have colonies, trading posts, and ports, all through the Eastern Mediterranean, though your friend the Sultan wants to take them away from us."

"He's not my friend!"

"And so we fight with the Sultan as well as trade with him. That means we have to know what he's up to. Down on the Rialto, at the central market, it is the business of the merchants and moneylenders to know everything—the price of grain in Alexandria or Anatolia or Milan, the next military campaign the Sultan or the Emperor Charles V are planning, the price of spices and timber in Antwerp or Ragusa, and how the shipbuilders are doing—the newest ideas and machines. And we Jews have to know everything too—what the Council of Ten is discussing, what horrible new inquisition the Pope is mulling, what the Portuguese king wants, what the French are up to—otherwise we would not survive or do business and make money!" She stopped, covered her mouth. "I talk too much, I really do. Father says so!"

Danilo had lived, in the last few years, in a world of men. How did one deal with a woman like Miriamne? Except for Saida, and, in the distant past, his mother, Grazia, he didn't have much practice dealing with women. Both Saida and Grazia were exceptional. Now he was up against another exceptional woman.

Miriamne tilted her head to one side. "So the Sultana is dangerous for you. You see, that is an interesting piece of information."

"Dangerous and clever. Hürrem means 'the cheerful one' in Persian. She keeps the Sultan amused. That is her power over him. She is playful, witty, sensual, and dangerous. And she believes I am a threat to the Sultan."

"And she will defend her Sultan like a tiger defending its young." Miriamne arched her eyebrows and frowned. Then she brightened. "But you are young and alive. And I see a long life in your palm."

"If one can believe what you think you see in my left hand."

"I see what I see." She favored him with a lofty smile and then allowed it to soften. "Now, my disillusioned warrior, close your eyes and get some sleep! It has been a long day. Sleep well, Danilo. Sweet dreams."

Danilo watched the curtain door shut behind her. She was gone. Her image lingered — the way she held up the torch, the delicacy of her wrists, the slender beauty of her hands, the way the light shone on her skin and on her eyes, the way her pout instantly changed to a smile, the way her hair tumbled, glossy, full, and jet-black, her high clear forehead, her . . .

What was he thinking? He stood up and walked around the room. Her voice, too, was beautiful, even when she was making fun of him. She . . .

He stopped himself.

Her image, now, was superimposed on that of Saida, beautiful, wilful Saida. Saida too could be bossy — and ironic — and make fun of him.

Danilo stopped pacing. He stood by the small barred window. A gentle spring breeze moved through it. There was a scattering of stars about the rooftops on the opposite side of the Campo. Was Miriamne right? Did he lack resolution? Was he destined to drift through life?

He laid his hand against the wall; he glanced at the drawings of alchemic instruments, a few charts too, drawn in ink. Was there anything to this mystical mumbo jumbo — alchemy, astrology, palm reading? All of this nonsense left him cold and skeptical.

Still, when Miriamne's hand touched his, when her fingers . . . She was so delicate, so quick; she had probed deep. He bit his lip. She was . . . Enough!

He sat down on the bed. His heart was racing, his palms

were sweaty. He clenched his fists. He had to prove he was a man of action! Where to start? He stared at the wall opposite, at the little work table.

With the Men in Black on his trail, he was not the only one in danger. He was a danger to others—to Miriamne and to Rabbi Hazan. And if the Venetian authorities found out about him, well, that too could be a danger, not only to him, but also to the Ghetto, and to his father, and to Saida. The Venetians might make a fuss, they would want to know so many things; and, if he was known to have helped Suleiman conclude his treaty with François . . .

Yes, he was a danger to everybody. He must leave. Now! No, that would be impossible—not tonight. Where would he go? Stepping out of the Ghetto now would raise more questions and dangers—for everybody—than just staying put and lying low. He blew out the candles and lay down on the bed and stared at the ceiling. Pirro, Pirro Gonzaga . . .

He knew what he would do. Tomorrow he would leave Venice, he would head for Mantua, he would search out Pirro, he would explain to Pirro what had happened to Grazia, he would redeem her last minutes, her strongest desires, her great love for Pirro, and he would claim Pirro as his father. And then, perhaps with Pirro, he would set off to explore some far corner of the world—far from Suleiman, from Venice, from Saida—and even from Miriamne.

He took a deep breath. He listened to the quiet, to the peace and serenity of the Ghetto.

The past is dead, he thought. Let the future begin—and the future would be with Pirro Gonzaga. To sweet Miriamne, he must say goodbye.

5

"NOTHING BAD WILL
HAPPEN!"

MIRIAMNE STEPPED OUTSIDE AND TOOK A DEEP BREATH. Two or three torches still flickered in the Campo. In a few windows, lamps and candelabra burned low, shimmering gently. High-pitched voices of children could be heard; after the excitement of the Seder, they were often restless and didn't want to go to sleep.

Two old men—Samuel, a tailor, and Saul, a printer's assistant who translated Hebrew into Italian—were sitting under one of the arcades talking. Bits and pieces of their conversation drifted across to her. A gentle breeze touched the top of the trees, a sweet rustling sound. Miriamne looked up. Above her were bright diamond-like stars. It was an exceptionally clear, dry night. Venice was usually humid, the colors and silhouettes muted by a gentle haze, giving everything a misty, dreamy quality, like in those pictures by Venetian painters who specialized in subtle gradations of color and nuances of shade, paintings that she had seen in the guilds and churches.

An old man was coughing. It must be Mr. Selig, the pawn-broker. He had a bad chest. A baby was crying. It was Claudia Frankel's youngest. Miriamne crossed the Campo. She entered an adjacent building, climbed up a narrow dark staircase, and knocked on a low wooden door.

"Come in."

Miriamne bent low and entered. The room was tiny and candlelit.

Claudia, who was sitting in a corner, looked up, "Oh, Miriamne!"

Miriamne took the baby into her arms, sat and hummed a lullaby. The baby stopped crying and fell asleep.

Claudia put her hand on Miriamne's arm. "You are the only person who can make her sleep. Your touch is magic."

"Not magic," Miriamne said, looking down at the baby and rocking him slowly. The movement, the simple rhythm, back-and-forth, was rather like singing a lullaby.

"I'm so afraid," whispered Claudia.

"Afraid?"

"Of what will happen. I'm afraid for the children, and I'm afraid for you."

"Afraid for me?"

"Mordecai, your brother—he is a dangerous man . . ."

"Now, now."

"I know you don't like to talk about it, Miriamne. He is family. But he is associated with some dark forces, and he has debts . . . I have heard he is a spy, working for some very bad people . . ."

Miriamne raised a warning hand and smiled. "You know I don't want to talk about it. I'm afraid that—"

"Yes, forgive me. But you know, I think about you all the time. You are fearless—you go everywhere in Venice. I know, I know—people love you, but there are those itinerant preach-ers and the friars. They don't respect women, they don't even respect children. And they hate us; they hate Jews."

"Now, now . . ."

"Mika brought me a plate of food. She told me she had heard there was a friar, a dangerous man, who had been seen in Venice. She said all of us—all Jews—should be extra careful—with the approach of Easter."

"I'm very careful." Miriamne smiled. "We are safe. You are safe. I am safe. And he is safe." She looked down at the sleeping baby. "Nothing bad will happen. I'm sure of it."

6

VENETIAN
NOCTURNE

AND SO THE MOST SERENE REPUBLIC OF VENICE—*la Serenissima*—a vessel of one hundred thousand souls—slept on the waters; but in a few places it was wide awake.

In Venice's giant shipyard, known as the Arsenal, behind high, fortified walls, night workers toiled without stop, tending hungry, glowing forges. Warships had to be built, and fast.

Along the Grand Canal, which snaked through Venice like a giant S, a few gondolas and barges moved silently, carrying late-night revellers, or great bales of goods and crates of produce, while laughter and music tinkled from the tall, brightly lit windows of the magnificent mansions that lined both sides of the canal.

Outside Venice, on the vast, placid lagoon that protected the city, war galleys and merchant galleys, barges, and even the occasional gondola, moved through the dark water, carefully following invisible channels of deep, navigable water, the only sounds being the rhythmic splash of oars, the gentle snap of a sail, fragments of laughing conversation, or the occasional shout of command.

Farther out still, beyond the sandbars that protected the lagoon from the Adriatic Sea, fishing boats were returning, slipping through gaps in the long, straight, sandy Lido, bringing fresh fish, the night's catch, to the markets of the city.

In Venice itself, on quays and in warehouses, merchants and stevedores busied themselves sorting and stacking goods, preparing them for the next day's sale or for shipment to markets far inland in Italy, up the great rivers, or farther, across the Alps, to northern Europe, or for export to the Orient— Istanbul, Alexandria, and Syria.

In narrow *calles* and alleyways, on *fondamenti* along the canals, prostitutes, young and old, waited for a lonely traveler or sailor heading to his lodgings after a night in the tavern.

More than one hundred thousand souls, each about his or her business, or sleeping and dreaming, in a labyrinth of buildings—churches, warehouses, and workshops—on a tiny archipelago of mud banks, shoals, and islands in the middle of a vast, placid lagoon, a miracle of human ingenuity and labor: *la Serenissima*, the Most Serene Republic, Venice.

7

THE FRIAR

"AND THE LORD SHALL JUDGE THEM, DOWN TO THE VERY last one!"

Brother Bruno Scavo stared up at the stars, tiny brightly shining silver pinpoints in a strip of blue-black sky above the *calle*. He rubbed his chin, looked down, stared at the paving stones, and spat a globule of yellow-silver sputum that landed with a splat and shone in the starlight.

Bruno had arrived in Venice on a barge just twelve hours before; since then he had wandered the streets, sniffing the air, the sweat of indignation and fiery hate pearling on his skin.

Bruno was twenty-eight years old. Since the age of sixteen, he had been a Dominican friar. The calling towards holiness and sainthood had been irresistible. He wore sandals and the distinctive white robe and black cloak of the Dominicans. Asceticism and self-denial were integral to holiness. Bruno ate as little as he could and drank wine only at Holy Mass. His body was thin, hardened by self-abnegation, by months alone on the road, by frugal habits, and by tortured, sleepless nights spent in prayer on his knees in mystical exaltation.

Bruno's dark eyes shone with the bright flame of spiritual intensity. His thirst for justice knew no bounds. The fever of holiness was within him. God had given him a gift of eloquence. It was a terrifying power. Even he was in awe of it. Men and women fell at his feet. With a few words, he could whip a mob into a pitiless frenzy of exaltation and hate. Instinctively, he knew which themes to touch, which feelings to arouse, which images to deploy. In his quest for holiness and purity, he burned with barely contained fury.

Bruno abhorred Venice. Sin was everywhere. The city's enthusiastic embrace of evil was contagious, insidious like the plague. The Republic of Venice was a dangerous cesspit and miasma of pollution, a profanation and perversion of all that was holy, with all its pagan glories and obscenities.

The so-called new art and architecture of the last three generations was filth, a collection of idolatrous abominations. Some fools had labeled these sinful horrors a "rebirth" of civilization. These so-called artists and architects and writers, Botticelli, Michelangelo, Raphael, Leonardo, Titian, and that miserable scribbler, Pietro Aretino, they and their kind were emanations of Satan. Savonarola—a fellow Dominican—had been right to ban their work in Florence—books, fine costumes, paintings, music, sculpture, and other horrors! All had been heaped upon the purifying fire.

Venice was even more evil than Rome; an emporium of whores and money changers, usurers, heretics, pagans, hedonists, libertines, Turks, and Jews. But worst of all were the Jews! Those evil parasites were a stain on Christendom, murderers of Christ, and practitioners of secret abominations and atrocities.

In Venice, books were printed, instruments of the Devil. The printed word was poison for the spirit, utter spiritual pollution. And Venice printed books in profusion—Latin books, French books, Italian books, Greek books, even German and—worst of all—Hebrew books. The voice of Satan spoke in Venice. Whoremonger Venice sheltered the most evil scoundrels, fornicators, atheists, sodomites, and personifications of evil incarnate, like that Pietro Aretino. But amongst all the abominations sheltering in Venice, the Jews were the worst. They were all the abominations in one package, and of Jews, the world must be cleansed.

Bruno Scavo turned his face to the breeze. It came up the canal, from the lagoon. It smelled of the sea, of the earth, of the mingling of the two, water and soil, fecund, fertile, and vaguely arousing—sexual.

He shook himself, sniffed the wind, wiped his nose, and turned away. Then there were the secret Jews, the so-called *Conversos*. The *Conversos* were even worse—more insidious than Jews who were openly Jews. Many of the *Conversos* in Spain had already been exposed, jailed, tortured, despoiled of all their worldly goods, their children taken from them. And then the parents—as was only just—were burned at the stake in an *auto-da-fé*, a true Act of Faith. Soon the Inquisition would extend its cleansing fires to Portugal and the Portuguese Empire. Now was the moment for judgement. The cleansing fire would spread everywhere, and it would come soon, even to Venice. Evil would be swept from the world!

Bruno turned into a narrow alleyway and headed towards the house where he would be welcomed for the night. He refused to depend on priests for hospitality. The priests in Venice were worse than the laypeople—corrupt hedonists, fornicators, and sodomites, more Venetian than Christian. He came to the low doorway, the rough-hewn bricks, the familiar worn stone lintel, and the weathered oak door. He had been here before. These were good people, humble people. In each city he and his brothers had their secret contacts, their network of friends, brothers and sisters in the struggle for justice and salvation. He knocked. These were poverty-stricken people. Poverty was pure and purifying. The poor were the true Christians, the salt of the earth, oppressed, exploited, despised. They would inherit the Kingdom of Heaven.

The door opened. The young woman—cursed with the saintly beauty of a Madonna—fell to her knees. She kissed Bruno's hand. He smiled down on her and said, "No, no, Agnes, get up! I cannot let you kneel before me. You are the saint, and I am the sinner."

He helped her to her feet and smiled upon her. Yes, he would hunt down the whores, the money changers, the pawnbrokers, the sinners, and above all, the Jews. He would preach to the simple people, the true people. The people then would exact justice; the people in their righteous fury would become instruments of divine judgment, pitiless, mindless instruments. "I have come to drive them out, Agnes." He smiled at this beautiful and innocent woman, "I shall drive them out, every last one!"

8

THE COURTESAN

NOT FAR AWAY, NEAR THE RIALTO BRIDGE, THE BREEZE briefly quickened as it came down the Grand Canal, rippling the water with reflections from the lamps, torches, and candles that shone in the windows of some of the stately homes that lined the canal.

Inside a prestigious and ancient mansion, behind the gothic façade with its arched windows and slender fluted columns, Veronica Libero pulled the heavy velvet curtains shut, closing out the Grand Canal, and turned to her guests. Lamps shone in every corner of the vast room, the suave velvets and satins and richly woven tapestries reflected the light. The divans, the side tables, the paintings—by Titian, Giorgione, and Carpaccio—everything was of the richest and most stylish quality.

"You were saying, Senator?" Veronica approached her most honored guest and handed him a glass of wine. The Senator, a tall, thin, ancient and distinguished-looking member of one of the great patrician families of Venice, accepted the wine with a slight bow, took a sip, and nodded his approval. "I was saying this alliance between François I of France and the Sultan is extremely worrying. We suspect that, behind the so-called commercial treaty, there is a secret military agreement and that the two of them—the Muslims and the French—intend to invade Italy."

"Italy is a choice morsel, is it not?" Veronica allowed her dazzling gaze to rest on the Senator, then turned to Signor Zeno, whom she knew was presently on the Council of Ten—in charge of state security—and one of its most capable members.

Veronica was twenty-five years old, an accomplished poet and linguist, fluent in French and Spanish and even the German of the trading cities, as well as Italian and varieties of Venetian. She was almost certainly the most famous courtesan in Venice and her clientele consisted of the richest and most powerful men in the city. Her list also included, on the suggestion of the Council of Ten, a sprinkling of important foreign merchants and diplomats.

Zeno bowed slightly, recognizing Veronica's beauty and her status as their hostess. "It is worrisome. Italy is too divided to defend itself. Perhaps Rome will be lost to Islam; the consequences of such an event are too horrible to contemplate. Suleiman is developing a new, stronger navy, and he has the largest army in the known world, with the best artillery, and perhaps the best cavalry. His great-grandfather, Sultan Mehmed, after conquering Constantinople and destroying the last remnants of the Byzantine Empire, dreamed of conquering Rome, capturing the Pope, and turning Saint Peter's into a mosque."

"At first Mehmed intended to turn it into a stable," said Veronica.

Zeno laughed. "So it is said!"

"But then he had a dream . . ." Veronica let the phrase trail off.

Zeno turned to the Senator. "You see, Senator, dear Veronica knows everything. We have no need for spies! Or for the Council of Ten!" He turned back to the courtesan. "Yes, you are quite right, Veronica. But then Mehmed had a dream. When he had conquered Rome he would turn Saint Peter's not into a stable, but into a mosque, the flag of Islam would be raised over the ruins of the Papacy, and, in the name of the Prophet and in service to Allah, he would tear the heart out of Christendom."

"And now Suleiman wants to realize Mehmed's dream," said the Senator.

"So it would seem, Senator, so it would seem."

"And Venice?" Veronica raised her eyebrows and nodded at a bare-breasted young woman who advanced to refill the two gentlemen's glasses.

"Venice will maneuver, Veronica, Venice will maneuver; like the lightly armed ship of state we are, we shall try to avoid this war." Zeno reached out his glass and the girl filled it. "We shall try to buy time. Thank you, Miranda." He nodded to the girl.

"But . . ." Veronica let her gaze linger.

"Yes, but . . . Zeno, what is your best guess?" said the Senator as he reached out his glass and Miranda filled it.

Zeno paused, took a sip, licked his lips, and gazed down at the splendid rug, one of Veronica's recent, brilliantly stylish and tasteful acquisitions. "Yes . . . but . . . I fear Suleiman's war will come to us, whether we wish it or not."

The Senator sighed. "Many of our colonies — vulnerable little outposts stretched out in the eastern Mediterranean — are ripe for the plucking . . ." He made a plucking gesture as if seizing grapes from a vine.

"That is so, Senator! If Suleiman fails to take Naples and Rome, he will want to pluck the low-hanging fruit. He will go after us."

"It is important, I imagine, to know what is going on in the Sultan's mind." Veronica inclined her head and blinked at the Senator.

"The more we know, the easier it will be to avoid war. So we certainly do want a window into Suleiman's mind. Anyone who can tell us what Suleiman is thinking would be very valuable indeed — a priceless catch!"

"War is such a dreadful thing." Veronica said with a sigh. "But gentlemen, let us be less somber. I have a fetching new friend you will be delighted to meet, and she is expert with the mandolin, and with many other things. Her fingers are deft, her eyes sparkle, her mind is lively and poetic, and she has . . . well, you shall see for yourselves!"

THE LIBERTINE

NOT FAR AWAY, OPPOSITE THE RIALTO MARKET, WAS
where the notorious poet, playwright, and polemicist Pietro Aretino rented his splendid lodgings.
Men were carousing, shirts open, jackets off, hair tousled,
plunged deep into arguments, poking fingers into each
other's chests.

Two women perched on a divan reciting naughty verses,
while several men and women sat at their feet. One girl, her
dark hair cut very short, was naked except for a scarlet and
gold veil she had tied around her waist. She was serving wine.
Another girl, petite, slender, impertinent-looking—her nickname was *la Zufolina*—was dressed as a pageboy. She too was
serving wine and fetching food from the heavily laden buffet
table.

In a corner, two bearded men were in earnest conversation. They were Titian da Cadore, one of the leading painters
of Venice and of Europe, and his host, the infamous Pietro
Aretino, now living in exile in Venice.

"My Lewd Sonnets did get me into trouble." Aretino plucked a grape from a plate. "They were too physical, too frank." He popped the grape into his mouth. "I use all the evil little words for the parts of the body that are veiled in shame! But why should we be shameful, I ask you? Why? Life is life; the body is the body; sex is sex; shit is shit; piss is piss. What is, is; that's it, there is no more. So—enjoy it while you can."

"Yes, *carpe diem!* Pluck the rosebuds!" Titian looked up as the girl dressed as a pageboy offered him wine from an elegant beaker of Murano glass. "You, my dear, are so beautiful you almost look like a boy."

"Why, thank you, Maestro!"

"Here, let us have more of that wine!" Aretino gazed upon the girl as if she were a fine piece of porcelain.

The girl filled both their glasses. Then, as she turned away, Aretino slapped her on the bottom; she looked over her shoulder and smirked. "Thank you again, Maestro!"

Aretino laughed. "That's the way I like them, impertinent, you know, alive with fire and spark. The fires go out soon enough, alas." He took a deep breath and a long slow drink of the wine, savoring the texture, the taste, the bouquet. "You know, Titian, we live in censorious, joyless times. If you like boys you get into trouble. If you like men you get into trouble. If you like girls or women you get into trouble."

"Terrible times, trouble all around!" Titian murmured. He grinned. His former mistress, Celeste Del Volpe, a wonderful artist's model, was now in what looked like deep conversation with the impertinent girl who was dressed as a pageboy. Celeste was nodding and listening intently.

Aretino leaned forward. "The big secret, my dear Titian, is that people are hypocrites. Everyone, without exception. In Rome, they are the biggest hypocrites of all. They commit every sin conceivable, and invent new ones. Not for nothing do those Protestants call Rome the Whore of Babylon. And then, when these Roman fornicators have finished fornicating and sodomizing and profaning everything that is holy;

then, when they are dying or old, and can't get it up anymore; when they have forgotten what lust is and have no nose any longer, nor eye, for beauty, no tingling, overwhelming, irresistible desires; when they can't pee when they want to pee, and pee when they don't want to; with sagging bellies, drooping wrinkled bottoms, and flaccid penises, then suddenly—as if overnight—they forget their former selves, deny their former lives, turn away from their former friends. They become pious, censorious prudes, thundering against anyone who is having fun, cursing all laughter, casting anathemas on all delight and joy and youthful energy, and then—poof!—they die, and then of course they are canonized and become saints and sit at the right hand—or somewhere—of God, singing god knows what ditties of infinite praise! And incense is waved about, and hosannas are sung."

"And expensive and lavish paintings will be commissioned for these truly holy men, which is a good and fine thing!" Titian said with a sigh of pleasure.

"And eulogies will be written and paid for. We scribblers go to work! We turn dross into gold, rascals into saints. And so we have a cornucopia of commissions! People will believe any rubbish you tell them, and they'll pay you for it too!"

Titian was watching the pageboy girl, la Zufolina, flirting with Celeste. Well, that was splendid; it made a nice contrast. The girl was a slender slip of a thing with a pert boyish figure and saucy attitude—a mischievous putto—while Celeste, with her long elegant body and sublimely refined features, was languorously seductive, wise, and patient, drawing the girl in, smoothly responding to her charm, drawing her ever closer. It might become quite interesting. They were clearly enjoying each other's company. He stroked his beard. There were several pictorial ideas lurking there.

Pietro turned to face him. "By the way, Titian, King François is eager for some more of your paintings for some new project in Paris or in the Loire Valley, some chateau or other he is building. I can negotiate, for my usual commission. You don't want to kowtow and bow and scrape! I love being a pimp for genius. And I adore bowing before majesty. I love to perform. Life is all a comedy, don't you agree?"

Titian laughed. "And François is a good customer. You look after him. You don't have to exercise your wiles and charm on me, Pietro, you know that. We are old friends and you are the best of agents, among your many other talents of course."

Aretino glanced across the room and lowered his voice. "Now, look at that young chap, a smooth-skinned ephebe he is, a warrior I'm told, but he looks like a girl, and blushes so easily." Aretino raised his voice. "Come here, my dear, come, let me chuck you under the chin, let me slap you on the bum."

The young man's smile was bright and quick, Titian noticed, as if flirting were second nature to him. The lad's eyes were large and dark; his cheeks showed no sign of a beard, just the faintest suggestion of gold down on his upper lip. His thick curls, catching the light, spilled down over his shoulders, and were of a coppery gold. Yes, he too could be an interesting subject, supple, promisingly effeminate—an interesting complement to, or contrast with, Celeste. The lad's shirt was unbuttoned halfway down his chest, which was milk-white and smooth as alabaster. Titian took note of the bluish shadows cast on the skin by the open shirt—an intriguing, subtle visual trick of the eye, and of the light; he could use that.

The young man licked his lips, and smiled again. He came over and allowed himself to be caressed and toyed with by the famous poet;. Then, when Aretino had tired of the game, the young man drifted off towards the buffet, where a rich array of food and drink glittered in the candlelight. Various pastas were heaped up, and coils of marinated meats, and sticks of bread; thick stuffed tubes of pasta, maccheroni with cream sauces, and jugs of olive oil; mounds of olives and aubergines and grilled mozzarella; salted fish, sardines, grilled sea bass, mackerel, and bream. The girl with the golden veil around her waist came up to the young man and, pointing, began to explain the various dishes and the choice of wines.

Aretino sighed, and turned to Titian. "Pleasant fellow, beautiful skin, but he's rather bland. Youth sometimes lacks salt, you know. Wrinkles and scars are the thing!" Aretino sat down heavily next to Titian. "I feel old!" He stroked his beard, which flowed down his chest. "We have such full beards, we look like prophets." He caught Titian's smile. "And yes, Titian, we *are* prophets, you say, of times to come! To freedom and to fucking! '*Fuck me, fuck me quickly, oh, soul of mine,*' that was one of the best sonnets of the lot, you know. My quill is my sword! I call a spade a spade. Not like Petrarch—he was from Arezzo too—he turned every sordid little lustful thought into something lofty, every little itchy desire into a singing angel. Dante, too, turned his lust for Beatrice into sublimity, an embrace of everything—Paradise, Purgatory, and Hell. He encompassed the whole world! Well, people need illusions, do they not? Let us drink to that."

"Most certainly, Pietro, most certainly." Titian examined his friend, the notorious libertine and writer, the deadliest quill in Italy, perhaps in Europe. Kings and popes trembled before the man, and yet he had been born in a small Tuscan town, and, though he didn't like to admit it, into humble beginnings. "So, Pietro, this Arezzo side of you, what do you make of it? As for me, I was born in Pieve di Cadore, a little town nestled under the mountains, northeast, in the Venetian territories, near where the Slavs begin. My family was a family of lawyers. My father served from time to time as a soldier—and in times of peace he oversaw the local castle and managed the local mines. It's dirty and dangerous work down in the mines."

Aretino nodded and leaned back. He began to speak with a loud voice. People gathered around, eager to hear the performance. "Well, my dear Titian, my lineage is ancient and lofty. In Arezzo, we were Etruscans. We were civilized before there was civilization, I tell you. Have you seen any of those Etruscan goblets? Those people knew how to drink, they knew how to live. Have you seen those Etruscan statues and tombs? Women and men portrayed as equals. The Romans were bores. They built big, but no delicacy, just engineers, all of them! Obsessed with bricks! Didn't always treat their women very well either!"

Titian laughed. Others joined in. The naked girl, the veil knotted at her waist, standing by the buffet with the pale young warrior, giggled, covered her mouth.

Aretino stood up and looked them over—his people, his flock. "Now our friend here, Titian Vecellio, Titian da Cadore, he is a true giant, aren't you, Titian?"

"Pietro is too kind," said Titian, rising to his feet. "I paint, that's all I do."

"You see! Modesty itself!" Aretino bowed, and moved with Titian to the windows. They were still close friends, but Titian had sobered up and become more serious and more domestic after his first wife died; he had settled down in his splendid but rather isolated house in the Cannaregio district, not far from the Jewish Ghetto. And Titian had acquired a new wife, though no one ever saw her or even knew her name.

Celeste and la Zufolina, the girl pageboy, joined them.

"Did you know, Titian?" Aretino went on. "François I and Charles V are competing for my favors? Did you know that?" He fingered a chain of heavy gold, his favorite medallion. "This neck chain is a gift from François I, and now Emperor Charles V has offered me a salary of 200 scudi a year, and so, hearing that Charles offered 200, François has upped the ante, offering 400 scudi! Empires vying for my favor! Ah, the quill is as mighty as the sword. They fear my quill, they fear my wit! They pay me, and handsomely, not to write. Call it blackmail, if you will!"

"Indeed they do fear your quill, Pietro, but you must be careful." Titian laid his hand on his friend's shoulder. "Your tongue will be clipped, Pietro. They will cut off your quill! The Inquisition is coming our way, even to Venice. And with the rise of this new religion, Protestantism, with the rise of these so-called Lutherans, this revolt against Catholicism, the priests will become desperate and afraid, and less understanding and broadminded and patient, less forgiving, than they have been. I fear we are entering a new period of fear, anger, and hate. Free spirits will be banned. Thinking will be branded an abomination. Books will be burned. Scapegoats will be sought out. Outsiders—freethinkers, libertines, heretics, Jews, immigrants, New Christians—will be strung up or burned alive. The stranger will be the enemy. Subtlety and irony and joy will be strung up by the neck and strangled."

"Yes, Maestro, do be careful." Celeste Del Volpe, holding the girl pageboy close, leaned against Titian. He put his arm around her. She let her all-forgiving Madonna-like gaze rest on their scandalous poet friend.

"I shall do my best!" Aretino bowed gallantly, a sparkle in his eyes. "But I make no guarantees!"

They all laughed, and then turned to look out the window at the Grand Canal. On the opposite side was the fish market. Soon it would throb with activity.

"Ah, this is life." Aretino breathed the air. "In the morning, early, the fishmongers are already here. The boats bring in the catch along the canal. And then you have the smell of fish, the smell of life, and all the hawkers shouting their wares: the squid, calamari, white fish, tuna, fennel, cabbage, lettuce. Give me life! Give me life by the handful!"

"Ah, life," sighed Celeste Del Volpe.

"Do not be melancholy, fair maid," whispered the girl pageboy.

Celeste smiled and tousled the girl's hair.

From the splendid mansions on both sides of the Grand Canal came various tunes and melodies, mingling with laughter and shouts, and with the murmur of voices and the gentle splash of a gondolier's oar. Venice was displaying its superb, proud, and insolent joie de vivre, its insouciance before priestly madness and fanaticism, its disdain for rumors of war, its defiance of the Ottoman Sultan and of the shifting winds of destiny, all those threatening clouds building up on the horizon.

"Sublime, is it not?" Aretino said with a sigh.

Lights shone, reflecting in the water. A woman, silhouetted by lamps, appeared in a full-length window opposite. A man appeared next to her. They kissed. The woman turned and pulled the curtain shut.

Aretino clapped. "Did you see that? Eros is not dead! It is life! It is life!" He took a deep breath, inhaling the air that drifted down the Grand Canal. "In the morning, even before dawn, this place will come alive. The market will be abuzz with people, goods, buyers and sellers, hawkers, merchants, moneylenders, fishmongers, vegetable vendors, servants, and slaves." He glanced up at the glass dome overhead that was one of the central features of his reception room. "And inside, here in my little nest, from up there, ah, with dawn, the light comes in, multicolored, through the dome; it is marvelous." He looked around. "And down here, in this room, what an abundance there is! Look around, I clutter and I collect. I heap up all things—a cornucopia."

"A gondola! No! Three of them!" La Zufolina pointed. Usually she was a nonstop chatterbox, but tonight she was unusually quiet—awestruck, Aretino reckoned, by Titian and Celeste. One of the gondoliers was singing a vague and melancholy song. His oar made a swirling pattern of darkness and light on the water.

Aretino watched la Zufolina, taking her in—she was a gem! Not more than twelve or thirteen years old, though she really didn't know her own age. "The gondola, dear lad, is a divine means of conveyance—silent, discrete, private, it moves like a whisper upon the waters, and takes you to and from the most indiscreet assignations with the greatest of discretion."

"And the gondoliers?" Titian asked, glancing at Celeste. They both knew Pietro's routine speeches, his virtuoso performances, by heart, though he did vary them, so there was always a surprise and extra pleasure to be had. His friends liked to encourage him and set him off. His enthusiasms, exuberance, and generosity knew no bounds; they were like life itself.

Aretino took the bait. "The gondoliers are rascals of high principle. They never betray a betrayer. Their scruples are of the highest order, pure poetry!"

But then, his mood changed, as it tended to do, like an unfurled sail, sensitive to the slightest shift in the breeze. Suddenly the world was somber. He turned back to the room. "But you know, friends, I am set upon, I am infested, I mean with visitors."

"Oh, dear! Shall we leave?" Titian put his hand to his mouth, displaying mock horror. He was familiar with Pietro's problem; the man was so warm-hearted, so impulsive, so generous, and so open, that every sort of character came to him for help, people in genuine need and a few rascals too. And Pietro was always running short of money, earning a great deal but always too generous, too lavish, spending too much, always treading a fine line.

Aretino laughed. "I do not mean you, fair friends, or the girl in the veil. But that thickset fellow over there, lounging by the buffet, stuffing himself, he's an amusing rascal. He was hurt in the fish market, so they brought him here. And here he still is! And they also brought one of those Germans, so drunk he tumbled into the canal, had to be fished out by the light of the moon. He caught the death of a cold. So they bring him here, I look after him. He's still in bed, grumpy and spoiled rotten! La Zufolina makes him hot broth, and takes him plates of grilled fish, don't you darling? My servants nurse him to health. My purse and my house are so open, they think I run a hospice or a hospital. I am not rich. I am not a lord. I am not one of the patricians! I am a poor man, a simple writer!"

"Kiss me, Maestro," whispered la Zufolina, turning her sublime face up to him. Her youth shone with the brightest, most fragile, of flames.

Aretino laughed and, bending over, with all the passion and tenderness of which he was capable, the famous Pietro Aretino kissed the beautiful orphaned girl.

I O

THE BANKER

S AMUEL MENDES SHIVERED AND PULLED THE COLLAR OF HIS
jacket closer. The breeze rose as the eight oarsmen of
the open, low-slung boat rowed harder, cutting even
more quickly through the dark water. It was cool and damp
out on the lagoon, a remarkably clear night. The constellations
shone forth in all their ancient and eternal splendor — the Great
Bear, the Lion, and Libra. He leaned back, closed his eyes, and
listened. The sounds were peaceful, soothing. The oars rose
and fell, rose and fell, now settling into an even rhythm. He
ran his hand over the smooth varnished surface of the wooden
gunwale and opened his eyes. A large bird lifted off the dark
water, slowly beating its way upwards, its wide wings making
a slow, low flapping sound, and then it was skimming silently,
gliding, heading for land; a second bird followed, close behind,
exactly the same path. "So," Samuel thought, "you and I, my
dears, are setting out on the same route." Samuel's destination
was the mainland port of Mestre, where he had to meet with
the local representative of the Mendes Bank.

As a New Christian, Samuel could do business during the days of Passover, though he would have much preferred not to. But it was important that he be seen to be doing business on days when business was forbidden to Jews; it was essential to reinforce his credentials as a New Christian.

Samuel had adopted a jaunty, superficial cynicism to hide his split personality as a public Christian and secret Jew, but increasingly, he was growing tired of the charade, the hypocrisy, and the many masks he had to wear.

In reality, his life was a deadly serious nonstop game of cat and mouse. There was no respite. In his inner pocket was a letter from his aunt, Beatrice de Luna. The Inquisition would soon be declared in Portugal. Preparing for the worst, Beatrice was shifting her money and treasure—and soon most of the Mendes Bank's operations—from Lisbon to Antwerp. She asked him for details of the bank's situation in Italy. How much money was available? How safe was it? Who were his most trusted correspondents and agents? Did he think an escape network could be established so that Jews and *Conversos* could flee the Inquisition and find safe haven? And where would such a safe haven be?

Samuel sighed. Life was getting more complicated. Beatrice was right. New forms of fanaticism were rising everywhere. The Mendes Bank, originally based in Portugal, had agents and correspondents throughout Europe, and now it had an urgent and secret task, promoted by Beatrice: to set up an underground network to save New Christians and Jews from persecution and from the Inquisition. Samuel smiled. Beatrice de Luna was a remarkable woman—and she was even younger than he was!

"Shallows coming up, sir," said the chief oarsman, nodding towards a thick, dark pole that stuck up at an angle out of the water, indicating where dangerous shoals began and where the deeper channel, the safe passage, was to be found.

"Yes, I see. Thank you, Giovanni," said Samuel. When he could, he always hired the same crew and the same boat, men he paid well, men he could trust.

The rhythm of the oars, a gentle thrusting, was restful; the sky offered a panoply of stars, with the great swath of the Milky Way arching across the firmament, all this celestial glory reflecting in the calm lagoon. There was a gentle, smooth swell on the water; the tide was just turning.

Samuel closed his eyes. His wife and two daughters were in Antwerp. Were they safe? When would he see them again? Would he ever see them again?

He pressed his fingers into his palm and squeezed his fist until it hurt. Keeping everything straight was a deadly challenge. The most sensitive information could not be written down. Bribes had to be paid. The fiction that the Mendes Bank was a Christian institution had to be maintained. It was an unending tightrope act. There was no safety net.

The bank spanned Portugal and Spain, as well as the Netherlands, England, and Italy. It lent to the governments of Italian city states and dukedoms; it lent to the Papacy; it lent to farmers and landowners and merchants, mariners and warriors, spice dealers and miners. It lent money to the Spanish Holy Roman Emperor Charles V—who was fanatically Catholic and hated the Jews—and it lent money to Charles' deadliest enemy aside from the Protestants: the French King François I, who, for reasons of strategy, had made an alliance with the leader of the Islamic world, Suleiman the Magnificent. The whole world, it seemed, consisted of a series of balancing acts. Indeed, it might be possible to reduce it to a series of mathematical equations. Well, that was a fanciful thought!

He had once, years ago, seen a juggler at a fair, dressed in motley, bells on little jiggly horns on his head, bells on the turned-up points of his shoes, dancing around, first on one foot, then on the other, keeping all those balls—at least eight of them—bouncing in the air. Samuel frowned. That's what we Jews and New Christians are. We are clowns in motley, dancing to survive, keeping all those balls in the air. One slip can be fatal.

Even just at the level of pure business, there was an immense amount to keep in mind: scheduling payments and repayments, calculating interest and risk, speculating on the exchange rates of multiple currencies, and price differentials between one market and another, and the fluctuating prices of gold and silver. And then there were the risks of crop failures and of wars. Even sovereigns could go bankrupt, or be overthrown, or suddenly renege on their debts. Danger lurked on all sides.

The Holy Roman Emperor Charles V, amiable as he could be, was always ready to pounce. Charles would have burned all the Mendeses at the stake long ago, but, poor man, he needed their money—their loans—to wage his wars against François and against Protestants. The Old Christians could turn on the New Christians at any moment. The preferred instrument of destruction was the Inquisition, and it was spreading like the plague. If Beatrice de Luna's information was accurate, Portugal would be hit next, and soon.

The horizon shimmered with starlight. Mestre was a dark, crouching silhouette. It was long past midnight. There were hardly any lights on land. Beyond the low, indistinct shore lay the great plain of northern Italy, the breadbasket of much of the peninsula. The Mendes Bank—along with other banks and some local Jewish moneylenders—had lent heavily this spring to the farmers and peasants and landlords; it was an advance against the wheat crop. Everything now depended on the weather—too much rain, too little rain, too much heat, too much cold, and the crop could be ruined. Then there was the political factor—the possibility of a French invasion. If troops go wild, they can endanger everything—rape the women, murder the peasants, burn the crops, farms, and barns. Samuel had to make sure the local branch of the bank was covered for these risks. You needed people you could trust.

Might that Danilo del Medigo be useful? The young man had turned up at the tailor's booth on the Rialto in Oriental Turkish garb, standing out like an eyesore, fresh off the boat and looking like it, abashed and a bit confused. But he was a handsome, quick fellow, with a wry sense of humor twinkling in his eyes, and acutely aware of what was going on around him, watching for enemies and assassins. Samuel, who was lingering in the tailor's booth, his usual spot when he was in Venice, had sold Danilo a suit of clothes, the very best, outfitting him like a gentleman. Then he had accompanied him to the gates of the Ghetto. Danilo knew languages; he knew Istanbul and the Sultan's circle; he was handsome and presentable. But he was also strangely naive, seemingly unaware of the bigger picture of politics and the plots and counter-plots of the great powers. He was also disengaged, detached, and in a very superficial, adolescent way, he was cynical. Was del Medigo's cynicism a pose, or was it real? Well, he had been away in Istanbul and with the Sultan—and the grandiose Islamic world of the Ottomans was quite different from the petty internecine squabbles of European power games and politics.

A barge surged out of the darkness, and the bargeman hailed the chief oarsman. Greetings were exchanged and voices echoed over the dark water; the rhythm of the oars went on, and on, and on.

Samuel closed his eyes. Perhaps someday he would find a use for Danilo del Medigo, but that moment had not yet come. He must discuss the matter with Beatrice. When the time was ripe, they would need to recruit talented people, outsiders who knew the Ottoman Empire. Yes, he would write to Beatrice.

In the meantime, what would become of Danilo del Medigo?

I I

THE SENATOR

THE SENATOR AND ZENO LEFT VERONICA LIBERO'S GRAND Canal mansion together. They parted on the quayside, Zeno taking a gondola back to his palatial home farther down the canal, just where it angled around and headed east towards Saint Mark's Basin and the customs house.

The Senator watched the gondola glide off, gently rippling the starlit water. He stood for a moment contemplating the slowly moving currents, and then he walked down a narrow alleyway, came out into a broader walkway, strolled along and finally, looking left and right, slipped into a narrow entryway to a small courtyard. He knocked softly on a door and whistled, a short melodious fragment. Within a minute a young man emerged, rubbing his eyes, and glanced at the Senator.

The Senator was in his eighties, but as fit and quick as a much younger man. Unlike many Venetians, he kept his beard carefully trimmed and short. He was lean and muscular. His face, creased with lines and bronzed by the sun, made one think of a sea captain, or perhaps of a statue of one of those austere, ancient Roman republicans from before Caesar's time.

The Senator shook the young man's hand and said softly, "Marco, good evening."

"Good evening, Senator."

"What news?" The Senator sat down on a stone bench and patted the space beside him. Marco sat down. Again he rubbed his eyes and yawned.

"I do apologize for waking you, Marco."

"No apologies needed, Senator!"

"Always on service, are we not?"

The two spoke softly, though they both knew the little courtyard was secure; the only person nearby was Marco's wife, Letizia, a sprightly young woman who also worked for the service, the Council of Ten, and she undoubtedly had gone right back to sleep; she knew Marco would tell her anything she needed to know.

Marco rubbed his chin. "Your information was correct: A young man did disembark this morning at San Marco on the quay. He'd been traveling incognito on the *San Domenico*. He came from Istanbul. And he was dressed in Ottoman garb, a disguise. He took a curtained gondola down to the Rialto and bought some fine clothes from Samuel Mendes. This young man is very handsome, according to Livia, the fishmonger's wife."

"Samuel Mendes of the Mendes Bank, I presume."

"Yes, that's him. When in Venice, Mendes sometimes helps out in a tailor's shop on the Rialto. It's a base for him, a way to test the wind, to blend in and gather information and gossip. Then, after the young man had changed suits, he and Mendes were seen walking together."

"Mendes is a Jew, a New Christian. So the young man is a Jew, then. What do you know about him?"

"He is traveling under an alias, David dei Rossi. His real name is Danilo del Medigo. He is the son of Judah del Medigo, who is personal physician to Suleiman the Magnificent."

"Ah . . . Now, that is even more than interesting."

"Danilo's mother was Grazia del Medigo, née Grazia dei Rossi. Grazia dei Rossi was a scribe and assistant to Isabella d'Este, rather a close friend of Isabella's."

"In so far as one can be a friend to a ruler. So this Jewess, Grazia dei Rossi, frequented Christian aristocrats . . ."

"Yes, particularly Isabella and the Gonzaga family. A bit of a history there. The dei Rossi family had a bank, active in Mantua and Ferrara, with a branch in Bologna. They provided loans for the Gonzaga family."

"So this Danilo del Medigo comes from a privileged but vulnerable background; they are insiders, but, as Jews, also very much outsiders. Their allies and benefactors can turn against them at any time." The Senator stared off into space, he frowned. Destiny was pitiless.

Knowing that even when he seemed absent, the Senator was an attentive listener, Marco continued. "Grazia dei Rossi wore her Judaism rather lightly, I believe. She was a cultivated, beautiful woman, lots of character; she wrote a book about famous women. She was close—I believe through her brother—to the Chigi banking family."

"Ah, yes, Agostino Chigi. He was the richest man in Rome and used his money lavishly to keep the Papacy afloat. The Chigi family are Tuscan bankers from Siena. And Agostino's mistress was Venetian, was she not?" The Senator often pretended to forget details. Marco knew it was a feint. When the Senator pretended to forget or not to know something, it often meant he knew a great deal—it was, perhaps, a test. Marco tried always to be ready to provide the missing tidbit.

"Yes, she was Venetian: Francesca Ordeaschi, the 'jewel of Rome'—she had many admirers."

The Senator turned to Marco with a smile and half-closed his eyes; it was as if he was remembering past pleasures. "They built that little pleasure dome in Trastevere. They called it the 'Pleasure Garden,' just on the Tiber."

"Yes."

"And Agostino and Francesca protected that charming rascal, Pietro Aretino, and they also sponsored some splendid artists."

"Yes, Senator—Chigi and his mistress were the toast of the town, typical of the splendor of Rome before Charlies V." Marco paused. "I don't know if its vitality and joie de vivre will ever recover." Marco hated violence of all kinds unless absolutely necessary, and he hated the enemies of the good life. One of his cousins—a beautiful, high-spirited young girl with dark eyes and jet-black hair, a splendid dancer, witty, funny, affectionate, and kind, full of infinite promise—had been raped and murdered by Spanish mercenaries during those horrible days in Rome.

"The year 1527 was horrible, just horrible! Rome has not yet recovered. The population was reduced by half. Less than ten years ago. Hard to imagine!"

"Danilo's mother was one of the victims. Murdered by pirates while escaping the city and protecting some of the treasures of her patroness. Tapestries by Raphael, I believe. Grazia sacrificed herself. Dead ten years now."

"You know, just the other day, pirates were seen off Ostia, close to Rome itself. Imagine! The gall of it! They rush ashore, ransack, and rob, kill everybody they don't think would make a good slave, and pick up a few hundred poor souls—particularly children—to be sold into servitude in North Africa. It is a scandal. These North Africans—with Muslim and Greek crews—often sponsored and backed by Suleiman—have been ranging up and down the coasts of Italy kidnapping thousands. The Pope of course is incompetent and has no navy worthy of the name! Naples—ruled by Charles V and his Spanish viceroy—is a shambles. The Inquisition and expulsion of the Jews did great damage there!"

Marco leaned forward. "Grazia dei Rossi was, as I said, very close to Isabella. Her son, Danilo, was with Grazia when she died. Isabella had entrusted Grazia with the artistic treasures she was trying to smuggle out of Rome. The idea was to get them away from the looters. So as far as I know, Isabella believes that Danilo died with his mother. Everyone thinks Danilo, who was ten at the time, is dead."

"Dead . . . That might be useful." The Senator half-closed his eyes.

Marco nodded: dead men often proved very useful.

"The d'Este family has always been partial to Jews." The Senator paused. "It's a clever policy. Jews are good for business. They bring capital. They know how to make money, and they know how to lend it. Also, many of the Jewish craftsmen and women are very talented. Clever of the d'Estes to welcome them! The d'Este fiefdom of Ferrara is perhaps the safest place for Jews in Italy."

"Ferrara, Mantua, and Venice."

The Senator sighed. "For the time being, that is. We have enemies here in Venice, Marco, and our enemies are also, for the moment, enemies of the Jews, the respectable Jews at least. Some of the Jews, alas, are playing another game. And as you know, there are many in the Senate who think we are too free, too easygoing. We have to be careful."

Marco took a deep breath. He didn't want to upset the Senator, but he had to tell him. "That reminds me—that Dominican friar, Bruno Scavo . . ."

"Yes?"

"Scavo has been seen in the San Polo neighborhood."

"What?" The Senator started up, then sat down again. He must control his temper. "How did I not know this?" Like many practitioners of *realpolitik*, the Senator abhorred fanaticism, no matter what form it took. Fanaticism was an insult to the intelligence; it was unpredictable and uncontrollable; it made rational calculation, reasonable negotiations, and compromise impossible. And fanaticism spread. It was catching, like the plague; there was no reasoning with it. "The Devil! Damn! The last time Scavo was here he stirred up a mob and attacked one of the poor prostitutes—a slip of a girl, an orphan, who worked down from the Rialto fish market. They chased her, stripped her bare, beat her. She barely got away alive. She wouldn't have, if the guards hadn't arrived. Took her weeks to recover. She was only fifteen. I could strangle the man! Bruno Scavo. Here for Easter, I imagine — and to stir up trouble."

Marco looked down, clenched his fist until his fingers hurt, opened the hand, and looked at his fingers. He had known the girl; Letizia had befriended her, an innocent little thing, so naive, so hopeful, wanting to learn to read. Letizia had given her lessons.

"It is too bad we cannot draw and quarter the rascal and throw his limbs to the dogs." The Senator took a deep breath. Fanatics like Scavo stirred up violent emotions, and therefore created fanaticism in those who were opposed to them. It was insidious. Fanaticism bred fanaticism.

The starlight made a faint pattern on the opposite wall. A vine, winding its way up from a pot, was held to the wall by a simple trellis. Beauty, however transient, was calming, a consolation.

"Let us get back to this young Danilo del Medigo."

"Yes, Senator. His father is, as I said, personal physician to Suleiman the Magnificent."

The Senator laughed bitterly. "The most feared man in the world, and rightly so. Among the many enemies of Venice, Suleiman is undoubtedly the most intelligent and the deadliest. If he were to succeed in his grand design, it would be fatal for us. He has already advanced deep into the Balkans, he has conquered Hungary, he has knocked at the gates of Vienna, and now he has taken Egypt. And the clever devil is working with the pirates of North Africa. He wants to be master in the Mediterranean, to replace us — to replace Venice, in other words."

"And so he must be stopped by all means possible. Not only for Venice, but all of Europe."

"Precisely. Suleiman's grand ambition is to subdue and destroy Christian Europe. For Suleiman, Christianity is an insult to God. He is pious, a true believer, and I think, perhaps a bit of a mystic. He is of great interest to us, his sense of his own destiny. What does he think he has been put on earth to accomplish?"

Marco nodded. "And how can he be stopped?"

"Too bad the good doctor, Danilo del Medigo's father, cannot slip some poison into his food!"

"Judah del Medigo is apparently not for sale, a model of professional integrity. His son, though, would be a great catch; he was close to the Sultan." There were other details that Marco would not share with the Senator unless they became useful. Some tidbits were too explosive, too dangerous to be shared. A forceful interrogation of Danilo del Medigo might reveal quite a bit in the way of essential information and insights into the Sultan's personality and intentions. "Shall we arrest this young del Medigo?"

"No, but perhaps a chat with him would be useful."

"He has made enemies at the Sultan's court."

"Ah, how so?"

"The Grand Vizier Ibrahim Pasha is jealous of young del Medigo's influence with the Sultan. Ibrahim has accused him of being involved in a plot to poison the Sultan. And the Sultan's wife, Hürrem, has put the Men in Black on the young man's trail."

"Ah, Hürrem, an interesting woman, the power behind the throne. A dangerous person."

"Interesting and dangerous, yes . . . a clever schemer; I wouldn't want her for an enemy."

The Senator closed his eyes and rubbed the bridge of his nose. "So this young del Medigo is a fugitive. Can you make contact with him?"

"He is staying in the Ghetto Nuovo. He was a guest at the Passover Seder hosted by Rabbi Hazan. He will, I imagine, be staying the night there. In any case, the gates to the Ghetto are of course closed. If he leaves, I will know."

"And do you have means to persuade him to be useful?" The Senator opened his eyes.

"I believe I do."

"I shall not ask, then. I suppose we can keep him in reserve. See what he knows."

"By the way, Senator, two Turks were looking for him."

"Men in Black?"

"Yes."

"And?"

"Our agents intercepted them. The Turks have been placed on a galley headed back to Istanbul."

"Good. No trouble, I hope. We don't want an incident, or diplomatic problems with Istanbul. Remember—we are trying to stay out of their damned war, whenever and however it begins."

"It was all very polite and gracious. They are traveling first class. At our expense, paid for out of the Council of Ten's special fund."

"Good then. You will tell me what happens with del Medigo." The Senator stood up. "You know, Marco, there was a sad ending to the story of Agostino Chigi and his great love, Francesca."

Marco smiled. The Senator knew more secrets about Venice and Italy than perhaps any other living person.

"Agostino married her in the last year of his life. I imagine he sensed he was going to die. He wanted to make her, and the children he'd had by her, legitimate."

"True love . . ."

"Yes, true love." The Senator cleared his throat. There was a glaze on his eyes. "But the Chigi family was not happy with the marriage. After Agostino died, they got rid of Francesca, possibly poisoned her." There was rare anger in his tone. "And they made sure her memory was smeared. They slandered her and buried her body somewhere far away from Agostino's grave, defying his wish that they be interred together. She was the great love of his life. And he the great love of hers. Raphael adored her. As for her children by Agostino, they were tossed away, deprived of any share in Agostino's fortune, exiled, and mostly lived in poverty until they disappeared."

"I don't like unhappy endings." Marco rubbed his right knee, which had been aching these last few days.

"Neither do I, Marco, neither do I." The Senator inclined his head in a parting salutation, then turned and went out of the courtyard and down the walkway. His footsteps faded.

Marco waited a minute, breathing the night air. Then he stood, opened the narrow little door, and climbed up the stairs to the third floor. He slipped out of the few clothes he had put on and slid into bed next to Letizia, whose body was warm and welcoming. The bed smelled of Letizia and of warm, freshly baked bread. Letizia groaned and turned towards him. "Well?"

"The Senator has an idea — a new project."

"Do I have to do anything?"

"Not for now."

"Good. Now kiss me. The night is warm but this bed was getting chilly without you."

Marco kissed her and held her tight and, as he did so, a thought dawned. How stupid! Why hadn't he seen it? Agostino Chigi's lover, Francesca Ordeaschi, was Venetian, she was of humble origins, and yet she had become the lover and the confidante of the richest man in Rome, the man who knew all of its secrets, and all the ins and outs of Vatican finance. And finally she became his wife. When the Senator spoke of her there had been a catch in his throat. It was as clear as day! Francesca had worked for the Senator; she had been one of his agents, one of his protégées. He had quite possibly set up the whole thing. And yet, in the end, with all his power, he could do nothing to save her.

Marco held his wife closer, kissed her again.

"Oh, that is so nice, Marco!" Letizia whispered, pressing herself against him.

An hour later Marco fell asleep.

I 2

TO SLEEP, TO
SLEEP, PERCHANCE
TO DREAM

MOST OF VENICE SLEPT.

Veronica Libero had just slipped into bed with one of her most prized clients—a rich French merchant who visited Venice only once a year. He was a talented lover, with just the right mixture of cruelty and tenderness, and willing to give as well as receive. He was witty, an acute observer who frequented the court of the French king, and a well-informed gossip too, which was almost equally pleasurable—and even more useful. The Senator and Signor Zeno would be pleased.

ACROSS TOWN, TITIAN HAD disembarked from a gondola on the Grand Canal and was walking home through a labyrinth of *calles* and alleyways to his house in Cannaregio. In his mind he was sketching a new nude portrait of Celeste, lying on her side, perhaps with la Zufolina frolicking in the background, or teasing Celeste with a bouquet of flowers or beckoning or . . . He might fit in the effete, pale young man too . . .

He climbed the stairs to his second-floor lodgings and discovered that his young wife was asleep. He was careful not to wake her. A simple country girl, she was so young, she was like a child.

IN HIS LODGINGS ON the Rialto, Pietro Aretino snoozed fitfully on a divan while la Zufolina giggled and chattered with two of the other women who lived in his apartments. He snorted, woke, and shook himself. "Go to bed, ladies, go to bed!" And to la Zufolina, he said, "Off with you, you mischief-maker. Scamper! Scatter! Skadoodle! All of you!"

"Yes, Maestro." La Zufolina giggled and disappeared with the others, all of them laughing at the old man; he was so funny!

"I am too patient, really," Aretino mumbled.

Only one lamp was burning. Soon it would be dawn. Oh, well, he could sleep in! He stood up and yawned and stretched. Should he sleep with one of the girls or leave them to their own devices? Decisions, decisions!

THE SPY

13

THE RENDEZVOUS

DANILO HAD JUST EMERGED FROM THE MORNING Passover service in the synagogue. The other men were gathered around in small clusters, talking. He looked around — so this, in the brilliant light of day, was the Campo, the center of Ghetto life. Soon he would be gone. He would leave, without telling anyone — for Mantua, to find his mother's sponsor, Isabella d'Este, and his own father, Pirro Gonzaga.

The Ghetto, in any case, was a trap, and he had to escape — to freedom, and adventure, and to find his own destiny. He must leave beautiful and charming Miriamne, Rabbi Hazan, and all the others behind.

The sun was overhead; it was almost noon.

Miriamne, who was crossing the Campo, came up to him, smiling. Happiness was written in her bright smile and her sparkling eyes. "Let me accompany you. I'll show you the Ghetto. The tour will be quickly done. The Ghetto is quite small."

Danilo returned her smile, knowing full well that his

own was utterly false. The morning had not brought a change to his resolution; all through the long Passover service, he thought about it. He was going to leave Venice today. He would head to Mantua to find Pirro, tell him of Grazia's love, and of her last days and her death, and stake his claim to his identity as a Gonzaga. He had to tell Miriamne. But how could he? Dangers were everywhere; sharing his plans with her was impossible. She was so innocent, so happy . . . and so vulnerable.

Even now, even in the Ghetto, he had to be on his guard—he'd noticed one or two suspicious-looking fellows, one thick-set young man loitering near one of the wells, and another, tall and thin and swarthy, lingering in the shadowy arches that ran along one side of the Campo. If they attacked him here, he would have to kill them. And he did not want to put Miriamne in danger.

He and Miriamne were standing in the middle of the Campo near one of the wells. Since it was the first day of Passover, no one was working except a few outsiders, Christians who came to do necessary tasks Jews were forbidden to do on the holy days of Passover.

The buildings, brightly painted, soared up around them. The breeze rustled the leaves. Miriamne opened her arms, presenting her kingdom. "So this is our little empire. The housing is, as you can see, crowded. Eight hundred, maybe a thousand people live in these buildings huddled around the Campo. As you know, we have had to divide the apartments up. The work never stops. Now that we have added floors on top, the buildings are higher than most in Venice. I just hope they don't fall down!"

"They look solid." Danilo glanced around, assessing by instinct. If the Men in Black attacked him here, they would find it difficult to escape—there were only one or two exits, and they were guarded. But if there was trouble, a hostile mob, could the Ghetto be defended? And for how long? Around the Campo the buildings were like a wall, continuous without a break on all sides, with an alleyway going off under a building

towards the bridge. On the other side of the wall of buildings two canals ran around the Ghetto and turned it into an
island. The Ghetto was a prison or a fortress, a trap or a refuge,
depending on how you viewed it. Danilo narrowed his eyes.
There he was again, that shadowy individual loitering near the
arcade. The fellow was staring at Miriamne. Was he alone, did
he have an accomplice — and, if so, where was he?

"Miriamne . . ." Danilo began, "I —"

"It's so quiet!" Miriamne swirled around, her pleated burgundy skirt flaring, her white blouse bright in the morning
light. "The windows on the exterior side of the buildings, facing
over the rio del Ghetto, have, as you've probably noticed, been
bricked up, most of them." She laughed. "That's so we Jews
can't peek out and infect our neighbors with our terribly dangerous Jewishness."

Danilo nodded. Miriamne was like a bright bird trapped in
a small cage. He did not want to break her heart. He had to go,
the sooner the better. He would tell her later, perhaps.

"Good morning, Claudia!" Miriamne saluted a woman
carrying a basket.

"And good morning to you, my dear Miriamne. And to
your handsome companion!"

Miriamne laughed and turned to Danilo. "You see, you
make conquests wherever you go, even among Christians."

Danilo bowed. He remembered his mother telling him
how new floors and new rooms had been added when, twenty
years ago in 1516, hundreds of people had been forced to crowd
into the Ghetto almost overnight. They had been given only
ten days to uproot and move everything. He blinked up at the
buildings.

As if following his thought, Miriamne turned. "And more
people come all the time, fleeing this problem or that, so, as I
said, the building and adapting never stop."

"It's amazing it works at all."

"Yes, it is," she said. She looked up at him with those beautiful dark eyes.

"And yet, people survive."

She was walking beside him now, talking quietly. "Yes, people survive. We are not allowed to own the buildings, or any property in Venice. But the rents are controlled and the owners cannot just kick us out. Families are allowed to inherit their spots in the building. Everything is regulated. That hut in the corner of the Campo is the home of a teacher, Elias. He's rather eccentric, and lonely, I think."

"No family?"

"His wife and child died in the same moment, in childbirth."

"Ah, that is tragic."

"His wife was young. She helped my father teach me how to read and write and do my sums. My father insisted that I be educated. Elias was hopelessly in love with his wife. It broke him when she died. Love is dangerous." She paused. "The banker, Vito Anselmo, lives up there. Lazaro is a doctor; he lives there. Gilad is a butcher and he has the ground floor apartment there, on the corner."

"It is crowded."

"Higgledy-piggledy, we are all tossed together." She blinked at him. "The upper floors are usually for the good flats. As you come downwards, things are more crowded; the lowest floors are usually the worst. As you can see, there are three wells. The water vendor controls access, and he charges for the water and the service. One of the wellheads is faced Istrian stone, and two are Verona marble." She paused and stroked the stone with the flat of her hand. "Venice picks up its pebbles and stones — marble and granite and limestone — where it can. We live on mud banks, in the middle of the water, so we have no stone of our own. Everything is imported. As you can see, someone has carved the Lion of Judah into the stone on the fountains. We are making our mark."

They lingered at the edge of the fountain beneath the tender fluttering green leaves and a high metallic blue sky. A few feathery strands of pure white cloud sailed slowly by. Danilo glanced sideways — the shadowy fellow had disappeared.

"Some of the people, like the bankers, are quite rich. Some are very poor. There are German Jews, Spanish and Portuguese Jews, even a few Jews from Palestine and Syria, and Italian Jews from the mainland."

Danilo's nostrils twitched. He made a face. "What's that. . . ?"

"That smell? Oh, yes, that's fabrics being washed and treated, and old rags. We have many tailors and seamstresses. They are not working today but the smell lingers. And last night it was masked by the perfumed torches and lamps. The poor girls work long hours. They ruin their eyes, stitching and washing and dyeing." She pointed. "Up there, that is our German synagogue, left of the *sotoportego*, where you entered the Ghetto. It has five arched windows. They represent the five books of the Torah, the five books God gave to Moses—Genesis, Exodus, Leviticus, Numbers, and Deuteronomy." She numbered the books off on her fingers, then grinned. "I keep forgetting you are Jewish. You surely know all of this better than I. Christians come here every day and I've gotten into the habit of giving little lectures."

"I like to listen to you explain things." He said it in spite of himself. He was encouraging her; that was dangerous. Truth be told, Miriamne was irresistible. Saida, his vanishing Muslim princess, immediately came to mind—a fluttering, glamorous presence, already ghostly, already a shadow.

He found it hard to take his eyes off Miriamne—the fluid, quick way she moved, the ironic, playful, enthusiastic way she talked. In this she was so very similar to Saida. Could two such women ever meet? It was an absurd thought.

He shifted his stance so he could also keep an eye on where the shadowy fellow had been loitering by the entrance to the Ghetto. But there was still no one.

"Over there, next to those arches and under the overhang, the money changers and pawnbrokers set up their stands. We have a lot of stands on a normal day. Today, because of Passover, it is very quiet, sort of spooky. Usually there are crowds of Christians here, doing business."

"So, relations are good."

"On the whole, yes. We Jews are useful—we are pawnbrokers, moneylenders, tailors, seamstresses, doctors, musicians, entertainers . . . The Venetians try to keep out troublemakers, people who would harm us. The Venetians don't like troublemakers. Business first is the motto, and Venice first, and Venetians first. Trouble is bad for business."

"That approach has served Venice well."

"It has." Miriamne gazed up at the arches of the synagogue. "The Jews from Germany came earlier than most of the Jews here. They fled the persecutions north of the Alps."

"So, people came in waves—fleeing from this or that. Immigrants."

"Yes, we Jews are considered immigrants, though I don't feel like an immigrant. I was born here. Since we are immigrants, we are not allowed to compete with Venetian craftsmen, so Christian Venetians—carpenters, painters, sculptors and glass-workers—did the work on the synagogue. I can show you if you wish. The Venetian guilds are very protective of their own crafts and members. Christians do most of the work on the apartments too, and on the new stairs that we need. And for the Seder, Mika and Melania, the girls who served the food and cleaned up afterwards, are, as I told you, Christian, a couple of very nice girls from Dalmatia."

"Not slaves?"

She laughed. "They are not slaves and they are not servants. We Jews are not allowed to have slaves. Mika and Melania are cousins of Vincenzo, the gatekeeper."

"They are pretty girls."

"Yes, those handsome Slavs—Vincenzo's family was originally from Dalmatia, across the Adriatic, in pirate country."

"But Vincenzo seems so Venetian."

"He's the perfect Venetian—gossipy, knows everything, knows everybody. Somehow Vincenzo managed to get permission for Mika and Melania to live in Venice, and even to work in the Ghetto."

Danilo caught sight then of the shadowy fellow, who had reappeared near the *sotoportego*. Was he trying to box Danilo in?

"You seem distracted." Miriamne gazed at him, her expression serious.

"I was just appreciating the architecture. So solid . . ." He gave her his most reassuring smile.

She smiled. "I can be boring, I know."

"You are the opposite of boring, dear Miriamne. Go on." He kept his gaze fixed on her, but over her shoulder he could see the shifty fellow turn and greet a young woman who was holding a child by the hand. He sighed. So this was what life would be like for him now. Suspecting everyone, always looking over his shoulder.

"Dalmatia was a source for slaves, as well as for pirates and slave dealers. There is a slave market in Venice, and most of the patrician families and even some of the rich commoners have slaves. There are even a few black slaves from Africa. They are very fashionable. Did you know that great ladies, when they are married, think it the ultimate in chic to have a beautiful black girl carry the train of their wedding gown? Most of the black girls are domestic servants, and there are some black gondoliers who belong to the rich and patrician families. And there are a few Muslim slaves; but most come from beyond the Balkans or farther east, from the steppes of Asia. In the old days, slaves were bought in the Crimea and shipped from the Black Sea. But that route is largely closed since—"

"Since the Ottomans conquered Constantinople in 1453, transformed it into Istanbul, and took control of the Bosphorus and the Dardanelles."

"Yes, the Turks have changed many things for Venice. They are probably the biggest threat Venice faces. Everybody here is terrified of your friend Suleiman."

"So I understand."

A church bell rang in the distance. A young boy, perhaps twelve years old, spurted out of the *sotoportego* and galloped towards them, his tousled blond hair catching the light. Danilo's hand moved to his dagger, hidden under his tunic. The boy certainly didn't look like an Ottoman assassin, but you never knew. . . sometimes young boys were recruited as killers.

"Greetings, Filippo!" Miriamne smiled at the boy. "Why in such a hurry?"

"Signorina Miriamne!" The boy doffed his cap and bowed. "Signor Vincenzo sends his greetings and salutations. He must speak with your friend immediately. Signor Vincenzo told me it is urgent! Signor David must follow me — and now!"

"That sounds very exciting!" Miriamne turned to Danilo, eyebrows raised in concern. "I wonder what it is about."

"Just give me a few minutes." Danilo thought he would go up to his room, grab his carpetbag and few possessions, and go, just be gone. In fact, he might have fallen into a trap coming into the Ghetto. There was no way out. How could he sneak past the gatekeeper? They would be waiting for him outside, either the assassins or the Venetians, ready to arrest him. That Vincenzo fellow must be a spy.

"No, you must come with me now, Signor David."

Danilo smiled and glanced at Miriamne; there was clearly no choice. "I will see you later," he said.

"If you are delayed, tonight's Seder begins just after nightfall." Miriamne smiled brightly, but she was clearly puzzled and worried. "I will save a place for you. And tonight, you sleep here, in my brother's room. You must not run away and disappear."

Danilo stared back — had she somehow guessed his intentions? Did she know he planned to flee? No, he was being overly suspicious. He recovered his aplomb and saluted her with a bow, before following Filippo towards the exit from the Ghetto. Miriamne really was a marvelous, fascinating girl. He glanced back. She stood watching him, her smile lingering, doubtful. She waved and then turned quickly away, her skirt swirling on the pavement, and her shoulders and hair catching splashes of sunlight reflected off a window high up in one of the Ghetto's apartment buildings.

VINCENZO WAS PACING UP and down just outside the gate, next to the bridge over the rio del Ghetto. "Ah, there you are! Listen. There is a gentleman who wants to talk to you. No, don't worry—it's not your two dangerous Turkish friends! It's a Venetian gentleman. You must meet him, now. It is important."

Danilo instinctively looked around. "Why?"

"I can't tell you. But it's for the good of everybody." Vincenzo nodded towards the Ghetto. "I mean, everybody . . ."

Danilo frowned. It sounded like blackmail. No, it *was* blackmail. Jews were vulnerable, Miriamne was vulnerable, and so . . .

"Where do I meet this gentleman?"

"That's a good fellow! Off down that way," Vincenzo pointed. "Follow the directions on this piece of paper. Don't show the paper to anyone. Burn it. The directions will take you out to open water, to the edge of the lagoon, and the gentleman will be there at the *Fondamenta Giurati*. Make sure you are not followed. That is very important. Ah, and if you have your yellow cap stashed away somewhere on your person, don't show it and don't wear it."

"Why?"

"You don't want to draw attention. If you have it, keep the cap handy but invisible. Don't let it be seen. You'll understand. All will become clear. Again, don't mention any of this to anyone. You and I did not have this conversation. Go now, go— and quickly!"

DANILO WALKED QUICKLY DOWN the first walkway. He glanced behind him, and seeing nobody following, he turned left, down another narrow *calle*, just as Vincenzo and the scribbled little map indicated. Who was he going to meet? What did this mysterious "Venetian gentleman" want? Was it a trap? He'd find out soon enough.

Again glancing behind him, he crossed the bridge over the rio della Misericordia. It was a much wider canal than the rio del Ghetto Nuovo. The breeze smelled of the lagoon and the open sea. The sun shone brightly, seeming to be almost directly overhead, making a myriad of sparkling reflections on the choppy, slate-green water, and sharp dark shadows on the walkways, only slightly smudged by the humidity that hung in the Venetian air even on the clearest of days.

Danilo looked behind him. Had anyone followed him across the bridge? The best thing might be simply to run for it, leave all his things behind, get lost in Venice and then head for the mainland.

He glanced at the paper map and pictured his route in his mind. It was indirect, twisting through the Cannaregio district, a busy place on this first day of Passover. A killer could easily lurk in these crowds.

As he hurried along, he was intensely aware of everything and everybody. A woman wearing a red kerchief leaned out of a second-story window. A little girl rushed, laughing, out of a doorway. A grizzled worker nodded as he trundled past with tools over his shoulder; two handcarts followed with bricks and stones. Three girls skipped with a rope on the crooked paving stones. A man was painting a doorframe red. It was a noisy, chattering place. Craftspeople worked out in the street in front of their workshops, or stood in doorways hawking their wares, gossiping, polishing, and carving.

He glanced back. Yes, he'd been right. Through the last two alleyways a tall, skinny fellow dressed in black had been walking behind him, about one hundred feet back. Danilo ducked into a dead-end alleyway, where there were three little shops and windows with bright flowers in boxes; he pretended to watch a cabinetmaker polishing a small ornate table. The smell of varnish was overpowering. "It is delicate work, sir," said the cabinetmaker, looking up. "It certainly is," said Danilo, peering back at the main alleyway. His fingers caressed the handle of his dagger. He waited. Then the mysterious gentleman, who seemed to have been following him, walked past, framed by the end of the cul-de-sac. He didn't even glance in Danilo's direction.

Danilo waited. "That is very fine work," he said, nodding at the craftsman. Then, glancing left and right, he left the little dead end and continued on his way through the throng. For the Christians, it was a normal working day. People hurried to and fro; shops were open, displaying clothing, household goods, vegetables, and fish.

Smells of cooking, of charcoal, of burning wood, of frying fish; smells of woodcuttings, sawdust, and fresh paint and varnish; and smells of the canals, of water and hemp, and rope and canvas and stucco, drifted across his path.

People nodded as he passed. Some doffed their hats and murmured, "Good day" or "Fine morning." The women glanced at him and often their glances lingered.

Every little while, he looked back or lingered, pretending to examine some merchandise. He saw no one. The tall, skinny fellow dressed in black had disappeared.

A young woman hanging baskets on hooks turned, stared at him, and for some reason giggled, covered her mouth, and looked away. It was clear. When he was not wearing the yellow cap, he was just an ordinary young gentleman. As in Istanbul, he was not marked as a Jew.

DANILO STOOD ON THE quay Fondamenta Giurati, facing the lagoon, a vast, shimmering watery flatness with a low brown and green line at the horizon that must be the mainland; and to his right, a small cemetery island; and next to it, the silhouette of Murano, a whole island specializing in glasswork, reputed to be the best in the world. Four seagulls swooped in close, screeching, and then swooped away, low over the water.

Where was the mysterious Venetian who wanted to meet him? He didn't see anybody. Was this just a trick to get him away from the Ghetto, in an out-of-the-way spot, where his body could be dumped into the lagoon? Or where he could be kidnapped? And if there really was a gentleman waiting for him somewhere, what the devil did he want?

He leaned on the parapet and sniffed the air. It had that peculiar Venetian smell, fecund and yielding, earth, water, and air all mingled softly together, and it aroused somewhere in his soul a half-buried, uncanny yearning. It seemed to take him back. But what did it take him back to? He couldn't remember, it was just an aching sense of nostalgia, a void, a ghost of a feeling. Did it remind him of his mother? He had been born in the Ghetto Nuovo. And Grazia had spoken of it often and told the story of her flight to the Ghetto and his birth in her *Secret Book*.

But of course, of their life in Venice he remembered nothing, just stories she had told him and the descriptions in the *Secret Book*. Her book was her gift to him, one of her many gifts, aside from life itself. In the book, the story of her life written just for him, she had distilled all the lessons she had learned, so that he could know how best to live his own life. And she had spoken of her passion for Pirro Gonzaga, and how his love was the great transcendent experience of her life. Could the lagoon and its smell have evoked memories and feelings that he didn't even know he had?

Church bells began to ring. It was noon. He was still not used to church bells; part of him missed the ghostly, unearthly call of the muezzin, calling the faithful to prayer from the minarets of the mosques of Istanbul.

He looked around. No one. He paced up and down. The sun was warm on his face. It was pleasant, like a lazy, sleepy day in summer. Whatever happened, he didn't want to die, not yet. And, if he was honest with himself, Miriamne Hazan had given him a new taste for living and for . . .

But, no, he would not think of that, of her. He must depart and leave Miriamne behind. It was the only way he could protect her from the dangers that he was sure would follow him everywhere. He leaned on the parapet and stared at the water. The lagoon beckoned and, misty in the distance, the mainland called to him, all of the cities of northern Italy, the cities of his mother's youth—Modena, Ferrara, Bologna, Mantua . . . This afternoon he would leave for Mantua.

An athletic young gentleman stepped out of the shadow of a nearby doorway. He was tanned, but dressed as he was, he did not look like an Ottoman.

"Danilo del Medigo?"

Danilo slipped his hand towards his dagger. The man knew his real name. That was not good.

The man was perhaps twenty-five or thirty years old. He had a short, neatly trimmed beard, dark hair, a simple black cap and cloak and trousers, and good boots. He was fit and muscular, and he had a handsome, pleasant face—an open face, a mariner's face with very blue eyes, a face you felt you could trust. That was probably not a good sign. Danilo tightened his grip on the dagger and looked around. If it came to a fight, was he a match for the gentleman? Was the gentleman alone? Or did he have companions hiding out of sight? Maybe he shouldn't have trusted Vincenzo.

"I am alone." The man said with a smile.

"You want to talk to me?"

"I think we might do business together."

"Business?"

"You have people you would like to protect and I have things I need."

"What do you need?"

"Information—and perhaps a few other services."

"And . . . ?"

"What do I have to offer?" The gentleman smiled his warm, open smile. He half-closed his eyes against the flickering reflections from the water. "I too have information. Your father is personal physician to the sultan, Suleiman the Magnificent."

"Yes. So . . ."

"It is an important but vulnerable position."

Danilo held the man's gaze; there was no use denying it, his father's position was vulnerable, more than vulnerable—dangerous. Any hint of disloyalty, any . . .

The man looked away towards the shimmering silver flatness of the lagoon, sleepy in the midday sun. "I speak not for myself, I speak for Venice."

Danilo stroked his beard. So, perhaps this was not personal blackmail. In any case, he didn't have a fortune to ransom his father's safety.

"And then, there is a certain princess, a beautiful and high-spirited woman."

Danilo stiffened. How did this man know so much? He knew about Saida, and he knew about Danilo's father. How much did he know? And what else did he know? If the Sultan were to suspect Judah of anything, anything at all, it would be Judah's death warrant. If the Sultan or Hürrem were to learn of Danilo's love affair with Saida, it would be Saida's instantaneous death sentence; there would be no appeal. This man knew so much, he was certainly not acting alone. To strike him down now would serve no purpose and would endanger everybody. He stared steadily at the man. "I would kill anyone who harms the Princess, or my father."

"I am sure you would." The man smiled. "I would do the same. No one wants any harm to come to them, least of all me." The man leaned on the balustrade and gazed at the sparkling water.

Danilo swallowed.

The man turned towards him. "Venice, you know, is a sort of miracle. Here we are, on a few low-lying mudflats and sandbanks in the middle of a swampy lagoon, and out of this, a thousand years of labor and ingenuity has created a jewel of a city, a powerful empire, and the greatest trading and industrial emporium in the Mediterranean. A rich and independent republic, alone in the midst of empires, monarchies, and dukedoms, a republic that values its freedom, its culture, its art, its wealth. It is unique, is it not?"

"Every successful civilization thinks it is exceptional and unique—an exception to the rules, unique in history. And then comes the crisis, and the fall."

"That is so, my friend. That is so. We all cling to our myths. Once an old woman saved Venice, it is said, from Pepin, the son of the Holy Roman Emperor Charlemagne, when he invaded in the year 810. The old woman, who had been left behind on the Lido, gave Pepin directions on how to cross the lagoon and reach Venice and slay all the Venetians. But her directions were a trap. Pepin's cavalry and soldiers floundered in the lagoon, plunging deep into the mud, and drowned. So the story goes. And Pepin had to give up his idea of taking Venice. It's rather like the story of Moses and the sea closing over the Pharaoh's army, isn't it?"

"Every nation has its stories." Danilo kept his gaze steady, studying the man.

"You know a great many things, Danilo. You are intelligent—and you speak several useful languages."

Danilo shrugged.

"Danilo, you are not in the happiest of situations. Your father thinks you are dead. You betrayed his patron, the Sultan. So they all believe. And you abandoned your father, left him in danger."

"My only way to protect my father was to abandon him," Danilo said evenly. Inwardly, he shuddered. What must Judah think? It was too painful. Even in Istanbul, he had been neglectful of his father. He was a child, an adolescent—too enamored of the Sultan's school, too obsessed with war and competitions, and obsessed, too, with Saida. Judah must have suffered greatly, and he would be suffering now, not knowing; not knowing can be the worst thing. He banished the thought of Judah and turned away from it.

The man held his gaze. "You know that. I know that. The Princess knows that. But your father doesn't know that. Your father is a lonely man. His wife, of course, is dead. And now you have disappeared. Your father, a great man, a famous man in his own right, is in a foreign land, isolated and far from what he once considered home: Italy."

Danilo looked away. Beyond the lagoon the distant shore of Italy shimmered in the heat like an illusion, a mirage — the lure of Mantua, Pirro . . . This man was threatening him, threatening his father, threatening Saida; but at the same time he seemed to know everything about them, and he was putting into words Danilo's own unspoken thoughts and fears and anguish: his father betrayed and in danger; Saida, possibly betrayed and in danger.

"Danilo, come, let us take a stroll."

"If you insist."

"Call me Marco."

"If you wish — Marco."

"We will be great friends, Danilo, I am sure of it."

"I am not so sure."

Marco smiled amiably and they began to walk along the quayside.

"You do realize, Danilo, that the treaty between François I and the Sultan is a problem for Venice and for all the states in Italy, even for Christendom in its entirety. If Suleiman were to conquer Rome, he could bring the whole edifice of Christendom crashing down. Islam would unfurl its flags over Rome, Milan, Vienna, perhaps even Paris and London. A catastrophe."

"Yes, I see that now."

"It is strange, is it not?"

"What is strange?"

Marco turned to Danilo and smiled. "That the translator suddenly fell ill and died, just as he was needed most, just when Suleiman was about to sign his vital treaty with France."

Danilo almost blushed. What an idiot he had been! Rabbi Hazan had understood, Miriamne almost certainly understood, and he . . . The translator must have been poisoned, possibly by the Venetians, possibly by the Spanish, and he, Danilo, naive idiot that he was, had foiled their plot. No wonder the Venetians wanted him dead! And probably not only the Venetians!

"Just think, Danilo, if you had not been there to take the place of the translator and, with your skills and knowledge of

French, to verify for Suleiman the contents of the treaty—who knows what would have happened? Perhaps there would have been no commercial treaty at all. And no alliance between mighty France and mighty Islam . . ."

"Yes, who knows."

"Sometimes, Danilo, great events hang by a single thread. A man falls sick and history changes. An old lady misdirects Pepin and Venice is saved. All of Europe, it is said, gained a last-minute reprieve from in 1241 when, back in Mongolia, Ögedei Khan, the Mongol leader, drank too much while out hunting and dropped dead; and so Batu Khan, who had devastated Eastern Europe and was about to seize the West, called a halt to his invasion of Europe—where virtually nothing stood in his way—and galloped back to Asia to seize the throne for himself. So Europe and Christendom, which might easily have been obliterated in that one military campaign, survived to fight another day. All because a silly fellow back in Mongolia drank and ate too much on a hunting trip, and dropped dead."

Danilo was still smarting: how incredibly stupid he had been! The Venetians had almost certainly poisoned the translator. And then he, Danilo del Medigo, stepped in and destroyed their plans. They certainly must wish him dead; they must think that he . . .

"In truth, Danilo, the treaty between François I and Suleiman was not just a commercial treaty. It had a secret military clause, for military cooperation: France and the Ottomans against the rest, particularly against the Holy Roman Emperor, Charles V, the enemy of both."

Danilo knew about the Sultan's campaigns in Europe. He had studied them at the Sultan's school. He cleared his throat. "Charles V blocked Suleiman's entry into Vienna and central Europe."

"Yes." Marco nodded. "And Charles V rules territories that surround France. And he wants to rip France into pieces, and swallow some of those pieces."

"Which does not make François I particularly happy."

"So the result is that Suleiman, the paladin of Islam, and François I, his Most Catholic Majesty, have celebrated a marriage of convenience. And the principal victim of this flirtation is to be the Papacy, Christendom—and, above all, Italy." A shadow passed over Marco's eyes. He looked down and clenched his fist. "Italy is divided, it cannot defend itself, and it is rich. It is a tasty morsel. It will be destroyed."

They both stared out at the Mestre shore, the mainland in the distance, and at the island of Murano.

"You Jews are survivors, Danilo. Well, Venice too is a survivor."

"I am aware of that," said Danilo.

"And I understand you saved Suleiman from a wild boar, or so I have heard."

"Well, I . . ." Danilo frowned. As usual, in saving the Sultan, he had acted without thinking. But he would do the same, even now, even knowing what he now knew. Whatever the Sultan's plans and ambitions, Suleiman was a great man, a formidable leader, and Saida's father. But, now, above all, Danilo had to think of protecting his father and Saida; he must humor this Marco fellow.

"You see, Danilo, I think this. It is just my own opinion, mind you. If Suleiman the Magnificent—admirable fellow that he is—conquers Italy, then the bright, sparkling, cut-throat competitive chaos that is Italy will die. All the little dukedoms and fiefdoms, and even the Papacy, even Rome, are competing for artists and for wealth and for the latest in ideas. If Suleiman conquered Italy, all that sparkling creative variety would end. We are living through a rebirth of civilization, Danilo, whether people realize it or not. After the dark ages, rationalism has returned. Philosophy, the arts, architecture—everything is being invented anew, and new worlds are being discovered every day—the Indies, Africa, the Americas; new continents, new fruits, new vegetables and plants, new animals . . . whole new worlds."

"And new diseases," said Danilo.

"Yes," Marco said with a laugh. "Sex is more dangerous than it has ever been. Syphilis—which many insist on calling the "French disease"—is moving like a scythe through the land. But generally, Danilo, we are just at the beginning of a great rebirth. Your mother knew that. Your father must know that. He is a rational man, a new man for the new age. But if Islam is triumphant, if Suleiman plants his flag over Saint Peter's, then I fear all that new creative fervor will be lost."

Danilo frowned. He had never thought about it. What, in fact, would happen if Suleiman and Islam conquered Italy and Rome, and then moved north?

Marco gazed at him. "So, Suleiman intends to outflank Europe from the south, along North Africa, and in Italy, and from the East."

Danilo nodded. "A sort of giant pincer movement, yes; it is an ambitious plan. But Suleiman has a cautious and reasonable side too."

"Cautious?" Marco's gaze flickered.

"He cuts his losses. Suleiman studied the campaigns of Alexander the Great, and he took note of Alexander's over-reach—how Alexander tended to go too far, to go beyond his supply lines, to overstep his limits. Suleiman knows too much ambition can be fatal. He is torn—he wants to conquer the world for his empire and for his own renown, and for Islam, but he is aware of the danger of overreach. At the end of the Baghdad campaign, he could have attacked Persia. He chose not to."

"So, if rebuffed, if he suffered a setback, he might retreat."

"Yes."

"Who influences him?"

"The Grand Vizier, Pargali Ibrahim Pasha."

"And . . . ?"

"I know Pasha well; he is not a pleasant man. He is Christian, born in the Balkans, probably spoke as a child some Slavic language, and also Greek and Albanian, but he was captured and became a slave. They call him 'the Westerner' or 'the Favorite.' His bedroom is next to the Sultan's. Pasha is jealous and overweening and dangerous. He is handsome and charming, and too proud. He has made himself very rich, and he is contemptuous of Islam and expresses his contempt openly."

"That is dangerous, I would imagine."

"It is tactless and dangerous, above all for a man in his position. He already has many enemies. And as he tries to monopolize power, he makes more. I suspect he has made one enemy in particular, the most dangerous of all."

"Who?"

"The Sultan's great love—Hürrem."

"Ah, Hürrem, the famous—"

"Suleiman is deeply, passionately in love with Hürrem. She has great influence over him."

Marco narrowed his eyes and nodded. "So this Slavic woman from the steppes of Asia, this former slave girl, this girl from the harem, has conquered the Sultan's heart and made him take her as his wife. She must be intelligent."

"She is astute and crafty. She was a gift to the Sultan from his mother, the beautiful Hafsa Sultan, who died only two years ago. Hafsa had great influence over Suleiman. The harem is a kind of school. The women learn about politics, about seduction, about sex. Hürrem is bold. She is opinionated, hugely ambitious, and stubborn and fiercely protective of the Sultan. And she is amusing."

"Amusing . . ."

"Playful, she is playful, Marco, so I have been told."

"Ah, playful . . . Of course . . . Well, a man involved in great affairs like Suleiman does need moments of relaxation. As to tactics and strategy, what did you observe?"

"He moves with a huge army. The wagon trains are endless. Just to feed the men and the horses involves thousands of foragers. It is slow and cumbersome. Supply and logistics are the big esential problems: how to keep the army moving and how to keep it and its animals fed. But the cavalry is fast."

"So the logistics—the supply lines—are cumbersome, heavy, and perhaps vulnerable. And the artillery? Their gunners are famous."

"The siege guns are enormous." Danilo thought back on his adventures accompanying the great guns back from the Baghdad campaign. "They move slowly, though; it takes time, and can move only on very solid ground. They can destroy anything, once they are in position."

Marco stroked his beard. "Thank you for this. I may call on your services, Danilo, if you agree."

"What services?"

"A man such as you can do many things. You are handy with a dagger and a lance, and you understand languages. You have seen many things."

"You want me to be a spy."

"Perhaps, among other things."

"An assassin?"

"You have killed before, I believe."

"Yes, I have."

"You see, you are a man of many talents!" Marco looked away, and then back again. "There's one other thing. I believe you have a certain relationship with Isabella d'Este, and with the House of Gonzaga, in Mantua. Your mother was secretary to Isabella, I believe, and your mother was also . . . close to Pirro Gonzaga, a distant cousin by marriage of Isabella's."

"Yes . . ." Danilo held Marco's gaze. The damned man seemed to know everything.

"I would advise you very strongly not to contact Isabella or Pirro Gonzaga."

"Why?" Danilo asked.

"Mantua is a complicated place. It is alive with spies. Both Pirro and Isabella have enemies. People watch Isabella. If you contact her or Pirro, we would not be the only ones to know. You would lose your value to us, to Venice, and it would put everyone you love in danger."

"I see."

"So if you will agree to work with us, we can help protect you and those you love."

Danilo looked down.

"The arrangement will have advantages. Protection for you—and, as I said, protection for those you love. Nothing is guaranteed, of course. There will be risks, big risks. But you will know you are not alone."

Danilo gazed at the rippling water, and then at the distant shoreline—Italy, his mother's land, the land of his first childhood, the land of his Christian blood father, Pirro Gonzaga. But he didn't have a choice. If he made a wrong move, everybody would be in danger. He had thought, in leaving Istanbul, that he would at least be forced to choose life and freedom, but he was imprisoned all over again.

If he left Venice to go to Mantua to see Pirro and explain everything to the man Grazia loved; and to see Isabella to claim his aristocratic heritage, his warrior culture, if he made that move, he would put everyone he loved in mortal danger. His father's and Saida's safety, and Rabbi Hazan's and Miriamne's too, and perhaps the safety of all the people who had welcomed him into the Ghetto, depended on what he did now.

He leaned against the balustrade. A barge was slowly making its way towards Venice, passing close to Murano. Behind the barge came other barges, dark and low, brown smudges on the shimmering water—their sails pale, creamy triangles and squares. Venice was a giant machine, taking in goods and ideas from everywhere, exporting goods and ideas to everywhere, and transforming everything into wealth. It was powerful, mysterious, and ancient.

"Yes," he said, turning to Marco.

"Good." Marco held out his hand.

Danilo hesitated, only for an instant, and then shook it.

"By the way . . ."

"Yes?"

"I may have been followed to Venice."

"Men in Black? Agents of Hürrem?" Marco asked. Danilo

nodded. "They have been escorted out of Venice. But they will come back, or others like them. Thousands of people come and go every day. If you see them, tell Vincenzo. Not the other gatekeeper, only Vincenzo. In the meantime, be careful. Do not mention this to anyone, not even Rabbi Hazan, not even Miriamne. And don't talk about it with Vincenzo. He will be my conduit to you and, in emergencies, yours to me, but neither of you should talk about what you are doing or allude to it in any way. Tell Vincenzo only what he absolutely needs to know. This is for everyone's safety."

"I understand."

"Goodbye then. Ah, one thing . . ." Marco turned back to Danilo. "There is a Dominican friar in Venice. Bruno Salvo. He arrived the other night. He is a brilliant rabble-rouser. He will try to create trouble. He is against everything and everybody, but he has a particular hatred for Jews and New Christians. He exploits Easter, using the memory of Christ's crucifixion to stir up people against the Jews and against anybody he disapproves of—courtesans, prostitutes, the Venetian government, Venetian patricians, and even priests. If it were up to me, Bruno's tongue would be cut out. Be on the watch. We try to discourage this sort of thing, but it is difficult. The Church is divided and the various orders—the Dominicans and Franciscans in particular—have a great deal of influence. Hatred of Jews slumbers, but the monster can easily be woken. Even the Council of Ten must proceed with caution. Even the Pope is terrified of such men."

"I understand."

Marco gave Danilo a long look. "Easter is coming up. Bruno will be preaching. The next few days will be dangerous for Jews—and not only for them."

When Marco left, Danilo leaned against the balustrade and gazed at the distant mirage of Italy. So he was to become a spy and an assassin! It had happened so fast, and he'd had no choice but to agree. This new life would be complicated and he would not be able to share it with Miriamne or with Rabbi Hazan.

Being a prisoner in Venice, spying for Venice, was one more division in his soul.

He was, he realized, a triple exile—from his father Judah del Medigo and Saida in Istanbul; from his blood father Pirro Gonzaga in Mantua; and, now, as a spy, he was an exile from himself.

14

MIRIAMNE'S
DOMAIN

"WELCOME TO MY DOMAIN!"

Miriamne's smile was dazzling. She was sitting at her workbench, close to a window, small jewels and stones and tools spread on the table in front of her. She stood up and offered him a glass of water. The brightness of the day spilled through the window.

"A toast!" Miriamne raised her glass. "To your new life."

Danilo looked at her sharply. *His new life!* Miriamne had an uncanny knack for brushing close to truths she could not possibly know.

"And to a new friendship," Danilo added carefully as they touched glasses.

It was his third morning in the Ghetto, and from the moment he poked his head through the curtain of his room, Danilo had noticed the change from the quiet of the last three days. The buzz of human voices echoed in the narrow stairwell that led up to Rabbi Hazan's quarters on the top floor.

Danilo had gone immediately to the bottom of the stairs and looked out. The sun shone. The Campo thronged with people. Brightly colored stalls had been set up against the walls of the buildings and under the arches. Little booths and stands packed the middle of the Campo itself. It looked like a fairground, with bustling, jostling, hawking, shouting, arguing crowds. The Christians had come back to the Ghetto. The Ghetto was open for business.

He looked upon all this activity with new eyes. He was now a spy and an informer, separated from everyone by more than one lie. He was sure the Venetians would want to make use of him—and soon—but how would they use him, and to what ends? For the time being, at least, he was their prisoner.

With all the peaceful bustle in the street, the threat of Bruno Salvo, the mad Dominican friar Marco had warned him about, seemed very far away. After a glance or two at the Campo, he shut the door and climbed up the stairs to Miriamne's room. Rabbi Hazan had given him work, and he had better start doing it; this would be his cover for his new existence as a spy.

And now here he was with Miriamne in her workroom, toasting their new friendship. How false! How hypocritical!

She reached into a drawer and pulled out a sheaf of vellum sheets bound with a velvet ribbon and handed it to him. "My father asked me to show you this philosophic manuscript. It's the text written in Burgundian French by Heinrich Cornelius Agrippa that my father spoke of that first night, when we were talking about his translation work. See what you can make of it."

He took the papers and glanced through them.

"Father told me to warn you." Miriamne gazed at him. "This manuscript is dangerous. You can refuse to have anything to do with it."

"How dangerous can it be? It's not a weapon—it's just words."

"Oh, my warrior friend, surely you know that words can be dangerous! The quill, they say, is mightier than the sword. God's Word created the world. The Torah and the Bible and the Koran are mighty indeed. They move armies and destroy nations! And these are not just any old words!" She laid her hand on the pages. "As I said, the manuscript is by Heinrich Cornelius Agrippa von Nettesheim. The title is *Occult Philosophy*. It is on the Church's List of Forbidden Books."

Danilo sighed; he did have a talent for attracting trouble. Now a forbidden book . . . What would happen next?

"Anyone suspected of owning it or even reading it risks a terrible punishment." Miriamne gazed at him from under her eyelashes and favored him with her most seductive smile. "You owe us nothing. You don't have to take the risk."

"I owe you a great deal—my room and board, for one thing, and friendship and community. I'll take my chances."

"That's the spirit!" She laughed and squeezed his arm. "Brave fellow! Just as my vision told me! I'll spread the manuscript out for you on the desk by the other window. The light is good. I'll fetch you a quill and some paper in case you want to make notes. Will you need anything else?"

"Actually, there is something. I need to go out this morning to find a place to stay here in Venice." He was feeling too comfortable. Miriamne had become his companion. She was just too enticing; and her father, though absent-minded and hardly present at all except at the synagogue, could all too easily become like a father, or a father-in-law. It was a dangerous situation. And he could best protect Miriamne by finding another lodging.

"Are you not comfortable in our house?"

"I am too comfortable."

"What does that mean?"

"What if your brother doesn't want me in his room?"

"You are being silly. Mordecai needs a companion. He needs somebody his own age. When he returns from his travels, a roommate is just what he will need. Perhaps you will be a good influence."

"He needs a good influence?"

"Perhaps. He can be difficult, and he is very opinionated. And he wants to force me to marry Jeremiah. I don't even like the man, even though he is, as you will have noted, very intelligent and well-informed. Mordecai has a few other little problems, which, being a discreet and bashfully shy young lady, I will not go into. Aside from these few faults, he's a splendid fellow. In any case, he isn't here, so he can't object. Now, come over to this table and make yourself comfortable. There are hours of work ahead! And, as for the community disapproving of your presence, my father has explained that you are indispensable to his work, and that you absolutely must work here. The elders follow father in all things."

Miriamne was an irresistible force. Danilo sat down at the table as she laid out the yellowed pages of the dangerous and forbidden manuscript. The light coming through the window illuminated the dark print.

"If there is anything else you need, I am right here, five feet away. I'm finishing up a bloodstone amulet for a soldier heading off to war. Trouble is brewing. François I and Emperor Charles V are squabbling over who will control Milan, or something silly. Men are impossible! My father and some of the elders are obsessed with all of this—politics! And in the Rialto Market people talk of nothing else. It seems the invasion of Italy is imminent."

"The wars never stop."

"Not in Italy they don't. The little states fight with one another and, in all that confusion, the big countries and empires—France and Spain and Austria—invade to grab what they can, not to mention your friend Suleiman and his Turks, who would like to eat us all up, alive or dead." She bent over her work, narrowing her eyes in concentration. "The bloodstone was very popular among Roman gladiators and centurions, you know. They wore bloodstone amulets into battle to protect themselves against loss of blood if they were wounded. I'll make one for you."

"I have no intention of going to war."

"Maybe not." She glanced over her shoulder. "But dangers lurk everywhere, even in the most unexpected places, and there are amulets with different properties and for different purposes."

"Oh? Such as?"

"Emeralds bolster the ability to love."

"Really?" Danilo raised an eyebrow.

She gave him a sly look. "Oh, you of little faith! Opals, worn close to the body, give you self-confidence. Diamonds and crystals shield the wearer from evil spirits."

"And which of these talismans do you recommend for me?"

"Oh, dear disabused warrior, I shall have to think about that. You are a complex and intriguing character, a bundle of delightful contradictions." She looked down at the bloodstone. "But now I must get to work, as must you."

Danilo bent over the manuscript and made notes, dipping his quill in the ink pot, and making a list of difficult phrases and mysterious barbaric words. From time to time, he glanced up from the dangerous manuscript of Heinrich Cornelius Agrippa von Nettesheim to watch Miriamne as she concentrated on the delicate task of etching her bloodstone with a fine-point. The golden light from the window fell on her shoulders and sparkled in her hair. Her movements were quick and deft. He closed his eyes, and then turned back to staring at the manuscript. Damn it! She was just too beautiful. Aside from Saida, he had never been so close to such a magical and womanly creature before.

Having spotted and listed some preliminary difficulties, he flipped through the pages, looking for a good place to begin his translation. Various phrases caught his eye: "How the elements are in the heavens, in the stars, in devils, in angels, and, lastly, in God himself." What on earth could that mean? What elements? Air? Fire? Water? And Earth? And how could elements be *in* anything? Didn't Aristotle say the four elements *made up* everything? If Aristotle was right—and his father had taken him several times through Aristotle—the four elements which made up earth and all terrestrial and sublunary things—fire, water, air, and earth—did not extend up to the angels and to the stars, and God forbid, to God himself. The celestial realm was the domain of unchanging perfection, of the mysterious fifth element, the ether. Agrippa's conjectures sounded heretical and dangerous.

And then there was this: "Of geomancy, hydromancy, aeromancy, and pyromancy." Hmm! Geomancy, let's see! Danilo's brow furrowed. He squirmed in his chair. What in the devil did the man mean? Geomancy apparently meant that a handful of earth thrown down on the floor or on the ground could, from the pattern of the splotches of earth, enable you to guess, or know, the future. Nonsense! This Agrippa was claiming that tossing a bit of earth around, or splashing up water by tossing in a pebble, or gazing into the patterns of a flame, or gazing at the clouds, or feeling the wind, or watching a comet, or any celestial portent—thunder, lightning—could foretell the future. This was magic! These were forbidden arts. If you meddled in such gibberish, you could get yourself burned at the stake! He turned several more pages. It was crazy, but fascinating!

Then there was this: "Of the Twenty-Eight Mansions of the Moon." The moon moves through these mansions, each mansion is a day, and there are twenty-eight mansions, since the moon's cycle, from full moon back to full moon, takes twenty-eight days. And depending on which mansion the moon is in, you can make various complex prognostications and divinations about events on earth. More obscure, nonsensical, outlawed stuff.

Danilo leaned back in his chair, glared at the manuscript, and flipped a few pages. There was a chapter entitled "Of Speech and the Occult Virtue of Words." Here Agrippa went into a great rigmarole, making a distinction between speaking out loud, with words, and speaking to oneself, with words, and he argued, it seemed—in so far as Danilo could disentangle the syntax—that these words were what distinguished man and woman from the beasts of the field, who shared most of our emotions, but not our reason, which depended, so said Agrippa, on words. In other words, words and language made reason possible, and that was what defined humans as humans. Well, that did not seem unreasonable.

Danilo scratched his head and delved deeper. Agrippa seemed to say too, in a rambling indirect way, that words, being celestial in nature, had some sort of magic power over things, and possibly over other people, just by being uttered. More magic! On every page were mysterious terms that seemed to have no meaning. This monstrosity would not be easy to translate. The prose was dense and complicated. Danilo turned over more pages: "Of Spells and Charms, Their Manner and Power." It was fascinating, grotesque, and ridiculous!

"Miriamne?"

"Mm?"

"Listen to this!"

She looked up. The light from the window caught the graceful elegance of her neck and the immaculate white lace at the edge of her blouse.

"'A cup of liquor made from the brains of a bear and drunk out of its skull makes he who drinks it as fierce and raging as a bear, and, thinking himself to be changed into a bear, he will judge all things he sees to be bears. He will continue in this madness—of being a bear—until the force of the draught shall be dissolved.'"

"Are you crazy? What in the world is that?"

"That is a passage translated from Agrippa's chapter 42. Does that sound like philosophy to you?"

"It certainly isn't Plato."

"'The tongue of a water-frog laid under a man's head makes him speak truth in his sleep. And the heart of a screech-owl laid upon the left breast of a woman that is asleep makes her utter all her secrets.'"

"Let me see that." Miriamne got up from her workbench and peered over Danilo's shoulder. She pointed at a phrase. "What does that say?"

"'The liver of a chameleon, when burned on top of the house, raises showers and lightning.'"

Miriamne frowned. "That definitely has the sulfurous odor of sorcery about it."

"Precisely my thought." Danilo turned a few pages. "There is a whole section that deals with how to use animal carcasses. Listen: 'Hang the heart of an animal upon the neck of a victim of quartan fever while the body is still warm, and the malady will be driven away.'"

"That's an interesting cure for four-day-fever."

"Four-day-fever?"

"Quartan fever. It returns every four days until it runs its course. It's a common form of sweating fever, particularly here in the lagoon."

"This Agrippa goes back all the way to the ancients. He borrows his nonsense from everywhere. I even found a quote from Pliny." Danilo rifled through his notes. "Here it is: 'When the posts of a door are touched with the blood of civet cat, all the powers of jugglers, sorcerers—even of the gods—over that household are rendered invalid.'"

Miriamne laughed.

"Where did your father get this?"

"That is not for me to know." Miriamne looked down, with something that almost looked like false modesty.

"No wonder this book is forbidden. The Church would consider it sorcery or blasphemy! The Inquisitors would love to burn somebody alive for this." Danilo turned back to the manuscript. "'Should a woman take a needle, smear it with dung, and wrap it up in the earth in which the carcass of a man is buried, no man shall be able to lie with her as long as she keeps the needle on her person'"

"What kind of dung? Horse? Cow?"

"Either, I imagine."

"This is obviously no book of philosophy! My father has to see it—and now."

She grabbed the pages, rolled them carefully into a scroll,

and led Danilo to the stairway. They pushed past the long line of supplicants that blocked the entrance to the rabbi's quarters.

"Papa!" Miriamne shouted through a slit in the curtain doorway of her father's study, "Open up. There's something you have to see."

"Can't it wait?" The rabbi's voice echoed.

"No, Papa."

The rabbi audibly sighed. "Just give me a moment."

While they waited, Danilo whispered. "What are all these people here for?"

Miriamne leaned close. "Some are for chronic fever. See that poor wretch, the trembling one? He's got it."

Leaving Danilo next to the rabbi's door, Miriamne moved down the stairs, along the line of supplicants or clients, talking to each one.

"How are you feeling, Sara?"

"Much better, Miriamne. Thank you!"

"Signora Grillo, has your daughter fully recovered?"

"She has indeed, Miriamne. Thanks to Rabbi Hazan!"

"Is Mr. Lewinsky taking his medicines every day as he should?"

"I keep reminding him, Miriamne, but it is a struggle. He is stubborn as a mule and he always pretends he's forgotten."

"Remember, Ezra, what father told you. You are to go on long walks and eat less of those fat meats!"

"Miriamne, I fight temptation, I really do. And I walked all the way to Piazza San Marco the other day."

Miriamne returned to Danilo and whispered. "Some of Papa's patients have tremors and seizures of ague. Some have dog bites, cat scratches, or cuts and bruises from working with sharp tools. I think that fellow, the fat gentleman down at the bottom of the queue, wants Father to cast a spell, probably so somebody will fall in love with him. His wife died three years ago."

"Poor fellow!" Danilo glanced at the man. He might indeed need a spell to find a wife. No, that was an uncharitable thought!

Miriamne whispered, "Some of them really just need to get out and walk around, and not sit at home and mope. Hopelessness can be paralyzing, it creates a vicious cycle. Melancholy breeds inertia, breeds more melancholy and so on . . . What was it the Greeks used to say, or was it the Romans, a healthy mind in a healthy body, *mens sana in corpore sano?*"

Danilo raised an eyebrow.

"Little Latin, and no Greek, that's me," whispered Miriamne. She poked him in the ribs.

"You are extraordinary, you know."

Miriamne looked down and blushed; she bit her lower lip, and then whispered, "That chap with the sharp chin and the narrow eyes, he has a rival in trade he wants to get rid of, or at least cause trouble for. He's come here for magic, for a spell. Some of Papa's clients want to get rid of curses their neighbors or enemies have cast upon them."

"What are the most common illnesses?" Danilo asked, smiling. She was unbearably charming; and for some reason this talk of forbidden spells and magic only made her more interesting.

"The shivering chills of quartan fever are the most common complaint."

"Are all your father's patients Jews from the Ghetto?"

"At least half are Christians. They come into the Ghetto to see the moneylenders, the pawnbrokers, the tailors and seamstresses, and the doctors. And they come too, sometimes, for dancing and entertainment, and sometimes for theater. Father is a doctor, a healer. He heals both spiritual and physical suffering. Sometimes he just listens, and that is enough."

After some mumbled conversation behind the curtain, Rabbi Hazan emerged escorting a weeping woman to the staircase. Having said goodbye to her, he ushered his daughter and Danilo into his study. The walls were lined with books and manuscripts piled pell-mell, and the desk was lit with four candles and by the daylight that filtered down through a high, crooked, barred window. The rabbi was dressed in black, with a black cap on his head. Next to his desk were two chairs, one for him and one for his patient. Along one wall were shelves filled with jugs and small vials and glasses, and different colored liquids and jars containing what looked like spices.

Miriamne thrust the scroll into her father's hands, saying, "Danilo has done some translating of this manuscript of yours, Papa. I don't think it is what you were expecting."

"And what would that be, Daughter?"

"Oh the usual, Virgil, Tacitus, Ovid . . . It does call itself a book of philosophy. But it reads like a manual of witchcraft!"

Rabbi Hazan stroked his beard and smiled. "How interesting!" He turned to Danilo. "There are those who will pay a very good price for such a volume, though it is forbidden; perhaps because it is forbidden."

"The attraction of that which is illicit," said Danilo, having read the phrase somewhere.

"I know several Christian scribes here in Venice who could translate the book." The rabbi fingered the pages and frowned. "But I don't trust them. I rather doubt they would keep our little secret."

"If they revealed it . . ."

"It could result in an accusation of witchcraft. The consequences can be torture and death. On the mainland, Jews have been murdered by mobs for accusations of witchcraft and so on. I myself have been accused of practicing magic." He gestured towards the vials and bottles of herbs. "People easily mistake science — and medicine — for witchcraft. We do have nosy neighbors; some are even spies. Venice is not without mischief-makers. I was almost torn apart by a mob myself once."

"Papa," Miriamne said, laying a hand on his arm.

"My daughter does not like me to speak of it. We must be careful. And now you are here, Danilo, a linguist with the very skills I need. Miriamne was prescient; as is so often the case, her visions and dreams have proved to be most valuable." He smiled warmly at his daughter.

She squeezed his arm, lowered her head, and smiled back.

"Danilo, as Miriamne foretold, our meeting was meant to be. You must work for me as a translator. You must stay here, where you are, in our home."

"But what if your son does not want to share his quarters with me?"

"When he understands what a help you are to me, he will be as happy as I am to welcome you. Don't worry about Mordecai. You can live and work here like a member of our family. And when I sell this manuscript you will share in our good fortune."

"You mean to sell it?"

"Papa does a small business in certain books." With a mischievous glance towards Danilo, Miriamne half-closed her eyes, "Certain *special* books." She grinned. "Venice is a printing center, we have the famous Aldine Press, and over a hundred publishing houses, and we even print books in Hebrew. The printer Daniel Bomberg, who, strange to say, is not a Jew, is bringing out a Hebrew Bible."

"Having you here to work on the manuscript will help to keep it hidden from prying eyes." The rabbi turned to Miriamne. "You will find this young man some place in the house where he can work undisturbed."

"I already have."

"Perhaps it would be best if I find another place to work . . ." Danilo began to protest, but he knew quite well that no place in the Ghetto would be as secure as being with Miriamne and her father; besides, here, he could watch over her and be sure no harm came to this delightful young woman. But what if his very presence did attract danger to them? There were no easy choices.

"I won't hear of it!" Miriamne flared up. "Besides, there is no other room, not one that is so ideal for working on a forbidden manuscript. As father said, we have nosy neighbors. And there are spies everywhere. You see, it's a question of safety."

"I . . ." Danilo began.

"Wonderful, then it's all settled." The rabbi put his arm around Danilo's shoulders. "You will live here with us, my boy, as a member of our family, and eat at our table, so you needn't concern yourself with rent or meals." Then to his daughter, "This young man has come to us as a gift from heaven."

15

HATE

"WHAT THE DEVIL DOES THIS MEAN?" DANILO WAS alone, crouched over his desk in Miriamne's workroom, squinting at a particularly confusing and annoying paragraph in *Occult Philosophy*. "What the devil can the man mean?"

At that moment, Filippo, Vincenzo's messenger boy, appeared in the doorway. "Vincenzo says you must come— and quick! It's urgent. Life and death, Vincenzo says."

"What?"

"Come, Master David!"

Danilo pulled on his jacket. "What's this about?"

"Signorina Miriamne and the children . . . They are in trouble."

Danilo's heart plunged. "Let's go!"

He and Filippo leaped down the stairs and stormed out into the sunlit Campo, where shoppers and shopkeepers, seamstresses and tailors, and pawnbrokers and moneylenders were all haggling and talking. It all seemed chaotic and normal, with buyers and sellers, shoppers and gawkers. Everything was just as it always was. He and Filippo raced, pushing their way through the crowd. Danilo was in a fever.

What could possibly have happened?

"THE JEWS, THEY ARE an abomination! Murderers of Christ!" the voice screamed.

The instant she heard the voice, Miriamne knew she was in deep trouble, maybe fatal trouble. Above all, she had to protect Jessica and Jacob, and blind Old Uncle Isaac.

The day, up to that moment, had been perfect. Danilo was tucked away in her workroom toiling at his manuscript. Getting angry with Agrippa and his *Occult Philosophy* always put Danilo in a good mood. He loved reading the most ridiculous passages to her; together they would try to figure out what the man could possibly mean by that particular tangle of words.

She had promised to take Jessica and Jacob for an outing in Venice. So she had herded her little flock — Isaac, who acted as a sort of chaperon, and Jessica and Jacob — to the Rialto, where she had a good gossip with Livia, the fishmonger's wife, and Livia's husband explained the day's catch to Isaac and the children. Then they had strolled through the market, looking at all the goods piled up on display — fish, vegetables, fruit, nuts and spices, textiles and clothes — and she and Jessica had taken turns explaining to Isaac what they were looking at. It was a good exercise for Jessica; by describing things, the girl was learning more words and perfecting her Italian and Venetian, which were already excellent. It also taught Jessica how to observe things and really see them, to be curious, and to ask questions, particularly of the merchants, men and women, who, if they had just a second of time, were always willing to explain what they were doing, especially to a charming and intelligent young girl, even if she was wearing the yellow veil.

Then they had headed towards Saint Mark's to see how the work was progressing on the new library. After a stroll down the main shopping street, le Mercerie, they had decided to explore a labyrinth of little streets near the rio di Santa Fosca.

Miriamne was wearing the yellow veil that marked her as a Jewess and Uncle Isaac had the yellow cap—tipped at a jaunty angle—that signaled he was a Jew. So far, nobody seemed to notice or care.

The people on the Rialto knew who Miriamne was, and they'd often seen Isaac and the children with her. All sorts of people thronged in the streets of Venice—Turks, Frenchmen, Spaniards, Portuguese, Italians of various kinds, Slavs from the Balkans, Egyptians, North Africans, Germans, Swiss, Englishmen, Black Africans, sometimes even Persians and people from even farther afield. When she was talking to people, Miriamne usually flipped the veil up over her hair, so there was no barrier between her and the person she was speaking to. In the Rialto, all the regulars knew her, and she was a favorite. When she was younger, she had even occasionally helped some of them out, or run messages to-and-fro, or picked up packages for people in the Ghetto. She loved the bustle and confusion and smells and clamor.

But the rio di Santa Fosca was a quieter neighborhood. Miriamne was not familiar with it, and she didn't know anybody. The little streets and alleyways were eerily calm. A chilly tremor of unease snaked down her spine, unsettling and uncanny. She glanced up and down the little alleyway.

Then she heard the voice—"Jews! Jews! Jews!"

She saw them: People gathering, not far away, in a tiny piazza. There was some commotion. It took her a second to realize somebody was pointing at her. She turned to the children, and taking them by the hand, said, "I think we'd better move on. Come on, Uncle Isaac! Let's head back towards the Grand Canal."

But by that time it was too late.

The crowd was coming from every direction.

They were trapped.

BROTHER BRUNO WAS ENGULFED by a spasm of joy. He had spotted her from afar, and he had followed her. She was wearing the yellow veil, though it didn't hide her face. A shameless Jewess, here in Venice! She was flaunting herself openly in the street, spreading the plague of unbelief, of Judaism, of foul secret rituals, of Jewish usury and exploitation of the poor. And now she had wandered away from the crowded Rialto and the cosmopolitan le Mercerie. Here, in out-of-the-way Santa Fosca, she could be taken. Here she could be broken!

Beautiful she was, too, and high-spirited. The more high-spirited such vile creatures were, the more virtuous and holy it was to bring them down, to strip them bare, to annihilate them. She would quiver at his feet, this Jewess. It was God's work! The very existence of the Jews was an affront. The work of cleansing never stopped. Two nights ago he had humiliated and stripped bare a young Venetian whore, and there had been, thanks to the Lord, no Venetian guards to intervene. Purification! Exaltation!

He rushed into the alleyway, the crowd he had gathered streaming and clamoring behind him. He stopped, pointed at Miriamne, and screamed, "Look, see, see the Devil!" He turned and glared back at the crowd. "Good people! See Evil in our midst! See the Slayers of Christ! See the Drinkers of Christian blood. See those who sacrifice our children! Oh brothers in Christ, oh sisters in Christ, let us show these foul creatures true justice!"

The crowd seethed around him, overflowing the alleyway. They came from every direction.

Brother Scavo pointed. "See! See the scarlet whore of Judah, clothed modestly to disguise her true nature. Clothed too in beauty, to disguise her true demonic ugliness! Let us see the Jewess in all her nakedness. Strip her pretense from her, good people! Strip her clothes from her, good people!"

Miriamne had put the children and Old Isaac behind her. They were backed up against a wall, next to a small shop. The crowd was pressing closer. Miriamne looked left and right— there was no escape.

Old Isaac glanced around in a daze. "What is all that shouting about?" His cloudy eyes were panes of frosted glass. Miriamne always remembered he was blind, but she had—just for a moment—forgotten he was deaf too, so deaf he couldn't make out what the crowd and the friar were screaming.

Miriamne shouted. "It's a friar, he wants the crowd to kill us or do something worse."

"Oh, oh, perhaps if I speak to him . . ." There was saliva on the old man's lips. His face turned blindly, this way and that. "I have known good men of Christ."

"No, Uncle Isaac, you are not going to speak to him."

A man grabbed Miriamne, ready to rip away her blouse. She turned and glared at him. He let go and stepped back, as if her eyes had burned into his very soul.

Miriamne wanted to run, but running would just inflame the crowd. She had to stand her ground. She and Old Isaac and the children were pinned in, surrounded on all sides. The air smelled of sweat and fear and hatred; it made her dizzy.

The friar, invisible behind the crowd, screamed, "Leave her naked, and the children with her! Let us see the foulness of Jewish sin, for such creatures as she have refused the love of our Lord Jesus Christ, they have refused salvation, they have, in their wickedness and in their foul worship of the Devil, denied the Messiah, they have turned their backs on God. This Jezebel! She has spurned God. She has turned her back on Him and on his son, our Lord Jesus Christ! And so God has turned his back on her!"

Pressed against the wall, Miriamne held herself erect, glaring at her tormentors. One of the women spat at her but missed. The ugliness of hatred was written in every face. Miriamne lifted her veil so she could look each person in the eye. A man turned to the woman who had spat, "She is just a harmless maid—and beautiful!"

"And you, Gandolfo, are a lustful sinner! I shall take no words from you! Do you wish me to denounce you for what you are—to reveal your filthy and foul deeds to the friar?"

Gandolfo shrank back into the crowd.

A woman shouted, "Jewess! Jewess! Burn in hell!"

Some in the crowd took up the cry. Sparse at first, it spread like wildfire.

"Jewess! Jewess! Burn in hell!"

"Jewess! Jewess! Burn in hell!"

Miriamne looked this way and that. The few sympathetic people were shrinking back; they didn't dare speak. They were terrified, edging away. It was dangerous to oppose the friar, and suicidal to oppose the mob.

A man came down the alley pushing a cart. "Make way, make way!" he shouted as the cart, laden with bundles of cloth, rumbled and bounced forward. It was a narrow alleyway, and the crowd gave way, making an opening.

Miriamne saw her chance. She pulled Jacob and Jessica closer and pushed into and through the crowd, following in the wake of the cart. "Come, children, let's go. Come, Uncle Isaac!"

"Jewess! Jewess! Burn in hell!"

Miriamne herded Jessica, Jacob, and Uncle Isaac behind the man pushing the cart as it plowed through the crowed. She kept as close to the carter as possible. He seemed to be ignoring the whole thing. "Make way!" he shouted. "Make way!" He had a broad back bent forward, pushing the cart, and under his neck his tunic was stained with sweat.

A rotten apple smashed against her shoulder.

Miriamne was trembling with fury and fear. She held the children close. She tried to keep moving, as close to the carter as possible. Now she tried not to look into anybody's eye. They were beyond appeals to humanity, beyond reason. "Come, Uncle Isaac. Stay close to me. Here, take my arm."

The cart turned down a side alley and the crowd surged in, blocking Miriamne's way; now she was separated from the cart, with no way forward and no way back. The man kept pushing his cart, disappearing.

The friar, who had fallen behind the crowd, herding them forward, shouted, urging the people on. The crowd had grown.

More and more people were coming down side streets, appearing at windows, leaning out on balconies, looking down to see what the fuss was about, hungry for news, eager for a catastrophe. A young woman pressed by, pushed close to Miriamne, and whispered, "Get away, Jewess! That man is a killer."

The woman managed to shield Miriamne for a moment. Using this bit of respite, Miriamne pushed forward, holding Isaac and the two children close. "Let us through, kind people. We mean no harm."

Keeping her eyes down, Miriamne pushed her way to the edge of the crowd. Then she looked each person in the eye; she smiled; she repeated, "We mean no harm, good people. Please let us through! Thank you! You are very kind!"

The humor of the crowd was darkening. Bodies, sweaty, excited, heated by the sun, worked up by the friar's words, pushed against her, almost tore her basket from her arm, touched her face, but they didn't stop her. As she looked them in the eye and smiled, and repeated, "Thank you, good folk! Thank you! You are most kind!" slowly, grudgingly, the bodies made way, and she passed through them, and then she and Jessica and Jacob and Isaac were beyond the crowd. Miriamne took a deep breath; she was trembling, but she dared not show her fear. Fear would be like the smell of blood to a pack of baying hounds.

Pushing the children ahead of her, Miriamne felt the crowd surge behind her. She didn't dare look back. She didn't dare run. A shopkeeper glanced at her and nodded. She had often exchanged pleasantries with him and even recipes with his wife. As she passed, he stepped into the alleyway and began to rearrange his merchandise, putting a large crate down right in the middle of the walkway. He was trying to slow the crowd without seeming to do so. It was a small gesture, but she was thankful.

The friar was shouting, "Jewess! Jewess! See, she runs away! She proves her guilt by her fear. She is steeped in sin, filthy with the blood of innocent Christians! She soils and pollutes the very air she breathes! She should be forced to wear a mask of yellow to hide the ugliness of her shame; she should be forced to wear gloves, as lepers do, so that no one can be infected by the touch of her pestilence. She should be forced, like lepers are, to wear bells that jingle, jangle, and bounce, warning good Christians that cursed pollution is approaching!"

Miriamne pushed forward. She had been told about such horrors, but she had never really believed that it could be so, not in Venice, that people could be so . . . so stupid, so easily swayed, so cruel.

The friar was closer now. He was hollering, but strangely, his voice was musical. With part of her mind, Miriamne realized it was a beautiful voice, such timber, such tones, yet such hatred, such evil. "Burn, burn, burn! Christ-killers!" Her heart was beating faster and faster; it thundered in her ears. Again the crowd took up his chant:

"Jewess! Jewess! Burn in hell!"

Were they all about to die? What would happen to her father if she died? She must save the children. They were terrified, huddled against her. She took a deep breath. "Everything will be fine. That man is a crazy man," she whispered. Comforting the children, concentrating on them, she had let go of Isaac. She looked around. He had wandered away. Oh, no! Alone the old man would be helpless. He was so innocent and naive he would stumble into his own slaughter. He would make some cynical or frivolous remark and get himself killed.

Miriamne shouted, "Uncle Isaac!"

Uncle Isaac had wandered, feeling his way and jostled by people, into a dead end. She could just see him at the end of the short alleyway where the greenish waters of a small side canal blocked the way, bringing the alleyway to an end.

Holding the two children close, Miriamne pushed back through the crowd and went to get Isaac. He turned his blind face to her. "What is happening, Miriamne?"

"It's a riot, Uncle Isaac. It's a friar and some people who don't like Jews."

"Ah, a friar," he said, half in a daze. "Friars are dangerous. Even the Pope says so." It was as if Isaac had forgotten everything that had just happened; he had moments like this.

When she finally had Isaac by the hand, she turned to see that the crowd had thickened and blocked the way out of the dead end. Behind her there was nothing, no escape, just the green waters of the narrow and deep side canal. Faces were blinded by hatred, faces that looked like masks, like grotesques, like gargoyles—there was not an iota of kindness or humanity left anywhere. There was nowhere to go. They were cornered.

"Filthy Jewess! Filthy Jewess!"

She would just push through them, there was no choice. They couldn't hurt her; they wouldn't dare hurt children and an old man. Surely not! She couldn't believe they could be so wicked. This was Venice. The Most Serene Republic. This was civilization. This was righteousness. This was her home.

Jessica looked up at her with giant dark eyes. "What are they going to do to us?"

Miriamne looked Jessica right in the eye. "They won't hurt us, Jessica, don't worry. Venetians are good people."

The faces screamed hatred, they foamed at the mouth in a frenzy of outrage.

"Come, Jacob. Isaac, stick close to me, will you?"

"Filthy Jewess! Filthy Jewess!"

"Why are they shouting at us?" Jessica whispered.

"A bad man has made them afraid."

"They're afraid of us?"

Just then, the friar appeared, pushing himself forward, emerging from the crowd. Miriamne took a deep breath. So this was what he looked like—handsome, gaunt, and dark, burning with righteous passion. His skin glowed. She blinked but did not look away.

"Fall to your knees, Jewess! Accept Christ as your savior, and perhaps you will be spared! As for the old man, it is too late for sinners such as he! Such creatures as he shall be consigned to Hell. And as for the children, we shall make good Christians of them! Fall to your knees, Jewess!"

And he reached out to wrench Isaac and the children away.

DANILO ARRIVED, RUNNING AND breathless, at the entrance to the Ghetto.

Vincenzo—his face beaded in sweat, cap in hand—was pacing back and forth. He put his hand on Danilo's shoulder. "Here, sir! Follow Filippo. Go now! Filippo will lead you to them."

"What's happening?"

"Bruno Scavo is stirring up a mob against the Jews. Miriamne is there, with Jessica, Jacob, and Old Isaac. They are in danger. Hurry! Hurry!"

Danilo turned to the boy. "Lead on, Filippo. Fast!"

They raced along the little alleyway leading from the Ghetto, and then into a labyrinth of alleyways. "The watch might have got there already, but we can't take any chances, sir! It's not far now!"

They plunged into a tangle of little streets, and then Danilo heard shouting and screaming.

"Hop into this gondola, sir. Otherwise we must go the long way round."

The gondolier ushered them into the gondola, saying, "A sort of riot is going on," and then following Filippo's directions, he steered them along a narrow canal.

"The trouble is over there, sir," the gondolier said. "I think a friar is haranguing the crowd. We'd better go in close. There are a lot of dead ends along here, little side alleyways that end at the water."

And sure enough, as the gondola glided in close, there were Isaac, and Jessica, and Jacob, cowering by the water's edge in a small dead-end alleyway that stopped at the water, and behind them was a furious mob, shouting and swearing.

"Filthy Jewess! Filthy Jewess!"

Somewhere behind the crowd, he could hear the mad friar shouting. But where was Miriamne?

"Let's get in close and take them into the gondola" said Danilo. "Take off your yellow cap, sir."

Danilo thought for a second. "No," he said. "I am not going to hide the fact that I am a Jew."

"As you wish, but you are a brave man, sir."

Danilo stepped out of the gondola and into the little dead end alleyway. He put himself between the children and Isaac and the mob, a wall of furious distorted faces, a wall of pure hatred. Helped by Filippo, he handed Jessica and Jacob and Isaac into the gondola. He glanced at the gondolier. "Wait for us!"

The gondolier nodded, holding the gondola steady. "We shall be here, just behind this building, out of sight. Good luck, sir!"

Danilo put his hand on Filippo's shoulder. "Stay here. Watch over the gondola."

Filippo doffed his cap. His eyes were wide, as if in shock. His forehead was beaded in sweat. "I shall be right here."

Danilo turned away from the little canal and walked steadily towards the mob. He caught a glimpse of Miriamne. The mob had surrounded her. Her veil was lifted, baring her flushed face. Her hairnet had been ripped off; her glossy jet-black hair fell, rich and glorious, over her face and shoulders. She disappeared into the surging throng.

Danilo was strong and he was fast, and he could be deadly; but here he was calm, he was deliberate. And as he pushed towards Miriamne he found that he was being excessively polite. As he elbowed and jostled people aside, he said, over and over, "Excuse me, good people; excuse me, kind sir; excuse me, dear madam."

When he pushed through the last barrier of flesh, he found Miriamne. Her eyes were flashing. Sweat beaded her forehead. She stood there, hands on her hips, looking like she was going to scold someone, the crush of people circling close around her. "Good Venetians, and friends," she was saying, "you must not listen to this friar. He has come to Venice to cause trouble."

Some were chanting, "Jewess! Jewess! Burn in hell!" Others, those who were closest, were standing agape, doing nothing to defend Miriamne, but not attacking her either. Danilo pushed his way into the middle and stood next to her.

"Ah, my guardian angel," said Miriamne, attempting a trembling smile.

Danilo knew he must control his anger. The friar was there in front of them, his sharp, handsome face ablaze, glowing with sweat. "This woman must repent. This Jewess must fall to her knees. She must accept Christ! This Jewess is a sinner, an abomination!"

Danilo put his arm around Miriamne's shoulders. "So, friar, we attack women and children and old men, now? Is that what we do? Is that what Christ would have wanted? Is that what Christ would have done?"

The friar's eyes flared. "You are an abomination!" He foamed at the mouth. "You are filth!"

Danilo calmly stared at the friar. The man was a fanatic. However intelligent, however knowledgeable, he would have no sense of honor, no decency, and no respect for persons or for truth. His self-righteousness would banish all doubt, all humanity. Such men would lie, would cheat, and would murder—all for the Cause. An appeal to reason or to charity or to justice would be useless.

Danilo raised his voice. "Venetians are honorable people. If a Venetian says he will protect the weak, he protects the weak. If a Venetian says he will shelter the stranger, he shelters the stranger. Venetian hospitality is known throughout the world! Venetian gallantry is known throughout the world!"

Many of the people mumbled, "Yes, yes, yes."

"This man is a Jew! He is a Christ-Slayer! He is filth incarnate. He sacrifices children to his foul appetites. He worships Satan!"

The crowd swayed, back and forth. Emotions were swinging one way and the other, riptides of fear and hate, of compassion and understanding.

Danilo forced himself to smile, a truly amiable smile. "Dear friar, hatred is not generous, hatred is not noble, and hatred is not Venetian. I might even say hatred is not Christian."

"Aye, aye," grumbled a man at the front of the crowd. He was a large man, broad-shouldered, missing one eye and looking like he had fought in the wars. "Venice is Venice. Venice is serene. Venice has its own justice. To attack this woman is not justice. It is not gallant. It is not Venetian!"

The mood of the crowd shifted. Both the friar and Danilo understood the tide was turning.

"Thank you, kind sir!" Miriamne directed her glance at the big man.

"It is my pleasure, madam. You have a fine man with you. Look after him!"

"She does, she does," said Danilo, determined to keep up the game.

Some of the crowd laughed. From tragedy the mood had changed to farce and to comedy. It might not last, but at least it was a respite.

The friar glared at Danilo. "I shall remember you."

"That is fine," Danilo said. "I shall remember you too, friar."

Miriamne leaned closer to Danilo and nodded and smiled at the big man who had come to their defense.

The big man tipped his cap and smiled. His grin revealed several broken teeth. A scar ran across his cheek and down over his lips.

"Thank you again, kind sir," said Miriamne.

The big man bowed towards her; he turned to the crowd. "Let us move along now, good people. It is a day of business, is it not? Venice is business, is it not? It's a day to make the ducats shine!"

Danilo backed away with Miriamne, the crowd still milling around, uncertain now of its feelings, but letting them pass, sometimes even with good humor.

"You are a brave lass."

"You were right to stand up to him."

"Those friars are mischief-makers."

"No, no, the friars do good works. The Jews are difficult, won't convert to Christ, and they persist in their wicked ways."

"Well, then we embrace them, we show them that Christianity is love, not hate."

"Are you sure, my dear, that Christianity is love? That friar didn't look too much like love."

Danilo and Miriamne got to the end of the little alleyway. The greenish water of the canal sloshed onto the mossy steps, a blank wall on the other side of the canal, and—nothing, there was no escape.

Miriamne turned and seized Danilo by the hand, panic rising. "Where is Isaac? Where are the children?" Her eyes shone, tears brimming over.

"They are safe, Miriamne."

"Safe! Oh, Danilo!"

16

THE GONDOLA

THE GONDOLA SLID INTO SIGHT FROM WHERE IT HAD BEEN hidden behind a corner of a building.

"Here we are, sir, safe and sound," said the gondolier. With a neat twist of his oar, he propelled the gondola forward, bringing it snug up against the canal bank, next to the stone steps leading down from the alleyway.

Miriamne sighed, her face lighting up in a glorious, tired smile.

Danilo tightened his grip on her hand.

Young Filippo jumped ashore and helped Danilo hand Miriamne into the gondola. Miriamne looked up at Danilo. "So you are indeed a *chevalier gallant*, a heroic knight in shining armor."

"You are the brave one," said Danilo as he helped Filippo back into the gondola. Danilo looked back—no crowd at all. Everyone seemed to have disappeared. It was just a peaceful little Venetian alleyway. He stepped into the gondola and the gondolier shoved off, moving away from the mossy steps.

"See, this is fine, Jessica and Jacob, this beautiful gondola," Miriamne said, settling in and smiling. "It's all right now."

Jessica's eyes were wide and dark. She was huddled in on herself, her fists squashed between her legs, shivering, her teeth chattering. Little Jacob was hunched up, staring at his lap, and gnawing at his knuckles.

Miriamne took the children in her arms. She stroked Jessica's hair. "Now, now. Everything is fine. We are in a gondola!"

"Why do those people hate us?'

"They don't hate us, Jessica, they were excited. They were confused."

"I want to go home," Jacob stuttered in a whisper, barely audible.

Danilo sat down, gazed at Miriamne with the children, and looked away. He yearned to take her in his arms and comfort her and the children.

"And Danilo here is our true hero." Miriamne held Jessica and Jacob close. "Him and brave young Filippo!"

"You are the true hero, Miriamne," said Danilo.

Yet she scarcely seemed to need comforting, and he realized it was his need for closeness, not hers. He wanted to promise her nothing bad would ever happen to her or to the children. He wanted to protect the two children as if they were hers and his. The image of Saida rose up before him, but she was fading, overshadowed by this new presence: Miriamne, beautiful, high-spirited, brave Miriamne. Was the heart of man so fickle? Was his heart so fickle?

He thought of the friar. He could have killed the man. He closed his eyes: his fingers gripped the friar's throat, crushed the man's windpipe; he watched as, in the man's eyes, the dawning realization appeared that he was going to die because of what he had done, or tried to do, to Miriamne.

"That's a bad man, that friar," said Filippo. "They turn up often at Easter, want to stir up trouble."

The friar was as close to evil as anything Danilo had seen. Of course the Grand Vizier was his enemy. But Ibrahim Pasha was motivated by feelings you could understand—by jealousy, by vanity, by a desire to protect his power and relationship with the Sultan. Hürrem, the Sultan's wife, was crafty and calculating, and protective of her power over the Sultan, and she was willing to sacrifice Danilo, or anyone else, to that end. But you could understand her—you could, if it came down to it, reason with her. Ibrahim and Hürrem were rational people. And the pirate who had shot Grazia—yes, it was an evil act, vicious and unforgiveable, but the man was driven by greed and perhaps by fear or even by sheer cruelty. Those were understandable feelings and motives. But with the friar . . . with men like him, you could not reason.

Danilo grabbed the gunwale and stared at his own clenched fist. Certainly the friar was driven by fear too—he feared what he did not understand; he feared Jews, he feared freedom, he feared art . . . he feared life. True, he wanted to defend and exalt the poor, but he chose his enemies badly, he chose scapegoats, the weak and the defenseless, easy victims of his wrath. And by a form of well-tried and ancient psychic alchemy, he had transmuted his fear and his ignorance into self-righteousness and hatred.

Danilo saw it all clearly. It was almost too clear. Bruno Scavo was driven by abstract rage, rage disguised as holiness. And, full of fear himself, he knew how to tap into everything fearful and hateful that was dangerous inside everybody else—fear, anguish, insecurity, self-righteousness. He perverted and misused people's natural sense of justice. He would make other people do the killing for him; he would convince them they were doing right; he would turn people into puppets. He would cause people to be burned at the stake, and what for? Not for Christ or what Christ stood for. It added up to a betrayal of his prophet, a betrayal of Christ.

"Those friars, they are strange people!" Old Isaac said, staring blindly ahead. "Strange, strange . . ."

"Where do you wish me to take you, ladies and gentlemen?" The gondolier, nattily dressed in his gondolier's tights and narrow-waisted jacket, was steering them along a brackish little side canal. It was a quiet place, fully of watery smells, a narrow, ribbon-like road of speckled, greenish water between walls of weather-worn brick and stucco that went straight up from the water. The thin corridor held the odors and the sounds suspended in the air in a strange watery intimacy. A few voices came from afar, the rattling rumble of the wheels of a cart, and nearby, a suave, rippling swish of the gondolier's oar. Farther down, at the end of the canal, was an arched wooden footbridge where in shadowy silhouette, two tradesmen leaned against the railing.

"Back towards the Ghetto," said Danilo.

With a smooth twist of his oar, the gondolier swung them around. After a few minutes they came into a wider canal. Many gondolas were going up and down, some of them public, some private. The private gondolas had coats of arms of all sorts of different colors; a few sported banners and flags and were steered by spiffy gondoliers decked out in the livery of various great patrician families.

As they passed, people saluted, "Signorina Miriamne!" Miriamne smiled and waved back.

Danilo was pleased, as if the homages were directed at him.

Miriamne leaned forward and whispered to Danilo, "I am still shaking. I don't know if I shall ever breathe easy again." She stroked Jessica's hair as the little girl huddled against her. "That was not the spirit of Venice."

Danilo nodded, but he was not so sure. Hatred was contagious. Strangers, people who were different, outsiders, made convenient scapegoats. Maybe there was no safe place, not for Jews. The gondola slid past mansions and four-story apartment buildings. Workers were seated on suspended benches, hanging from beams, repairing and replacing bricks that had been worn away by the weather and the tides.

Then he said, "Look at that gondola, Jessica, Jacob . . ."

The gondola in question was emblazoned in scarlet, with a large coat of arms, a fluttering scarlet banner, and a splendidly handsome black gondolier in a scarlet uniform. He tipped his hat to them.

"That is a beautiful gondola, a showy gondola," said their gondolier, tipping his hat back. "Certain of the grandees like to show off. Enrico's a splendid gondolier, though, one of the best."

"Some people are too proud," said Old Isaac, turning his cloudy white blind eyes towards the scarlet gondola. "All glitter and show, it's not good for morale. The poor don't like to see these displays. Bad taste, if you ask me. One of these days they'll bring in sumptuary laws against showy display, mark my words, make them paint all their bright gondolas black, like for a funeral. No more glitter and splash then—ha, ha!"

"Could well happen," said the gondolier, giving an artful twist to his oar and standing, legs slightly apart and braced, as he swung the gondola into a turn.

They were entering the Grand Canal, a wide expanse of water, little glittering wavelets. Barges and long boats and gondolas crowded towards the Rialto Bridge. People thronged the walkways and market stalls on both sides of the canal. Sounds drifted across the water—people singing, people shouting, people hawking their wares.

"Now, I don't know if you know this," said the gondolier, "but the ordinary gondola is, in fact, a miracle." He deftly steered them past two slow-moving barges. "It is a uniquely Venetian thing."

"A miracle?" Danilo said testily. He had had enough of religion today.

"A stranger to Venice, are you?"

"Not entirely."

"Well, one can always learn, sir, one can always learn. That friar is not Venetian. He brings his hatred here to us, like the plague. And that mob was not, as lady Miriamne says, Venice at its best. Now, the gondola, sir! That is Venice at its best."

Jessica was still shivering, huddled in on herself. The gondolier smiled at her. Miriamne held the girl close, stroking her hair, and whispered in her ear. The girl sat up tentatively and wiped her eyes.

"I like gondolas," said Jacob, wrinkling his nose. "I like gondolas very extremely much."

Isaac blindly ran his hand along the smooth varnished gunnel. "I remember a gondola once, black varnished it was, the gondoliers were singing, the lamps were lit, and I was with . . . Well, I was young then . . . And the lady was . . . the lady was . . ." He coughed.

"I want to be a gondolier," Jessica ventured.

"Well, a lady gondolier," said their conductor, "now that would be a thing to see! Lots of study involved. There is an art to the gondola, as to all things."

"Art—like in a painting?" Jessica watched the gondolier's every move.

"Well, I wouldn't say a gondola is like a work by Titian or Carpaccio or Leonardo. Or maybe I would say that. In fact, I will say that. A gondola is a very special boat, young lady. Now, you may well ask, 'How is it special?' First, it has a cute flat bottom so it can skim along in the shallowest of waters, slip in and out of the trickiest situations." The gondolier winked.

Jessica covered her mouth and smiled.

"The gondola flirts with danger, she does! She is a delicate, talented, skittish, special young lady, the gondola!" He steered them between two other gondolas. "The gondola—and perhaps you know this—has no keel, and no rudder, which means it can slide over the shallowest sandbank, just like that, in a whisper!"

They were slipping under the Rialto Bridge, and all the voices and the clamor of the marketplace echoed around them, and footsteps on the bridge, reverberations, and the smells of the market—fish and meat and vegetables, and cloth and wood shavings and salt.

"Boats don't whisper, people whisper," Jessica said, her eyes extra bright.

"Ah, now, there you are wrong, Signorina! Boats and ships talk all the time. Sails whisper, and sometimes oars whisper, and wood can creak and groan and snap, and sails, too, can snap and crack, and a gondola gliding along can make a soft swishing sound that you can hardly hear at all—and that is what it is, a whisper. And in the lagoon, in these foggy, treacherous waters, the captain and navigator and crew are all one, one person—and that is me, the gondolier. He stands up, so he can see what he is about, what is to come. The sandbanks and shoals and shallows and channels are always shifting in the lagoon, Signorina, so you need a keen eye and a quick hand. Some parts silt up, other parts are worn away."

"So it's always changing," said Danilo.

"That's one of the things that makes Venice safe, sir. An invading force gets lost in the shallows of the lagoon. They flounder in mud, drown in brackish water, or run aground. They get lost in the muck. About 300 years ago, crusaders, a whole deadly army of them, were out on the Lido, and they refused to pay their bills, wanted to attack us, but couldn't get at us, and we starved them out, so they had to pay their bills; then we put them on ships for Constantinople and the Holy Land.

"Our great trading rival Genova attacked us, tried to get into the lagoon and attack Venice itself, but their ships got stuck and ran aground, and then we sank them, drowned them, all those gallant men—husbands, fathers, brothers, and sons—thrashed about in the muck and then disappeared—gone, gone. The Genovese didn't know the channels, you see, they didn't know the obstacles. And only twenty years ago, everybody, even the Pope, attacked Venice, but they couldn't get at us and, in the end, we won. Our enemies were stuck on the shore, yelling at us! So, you can see, Venice is snug and safe here in its lagoon."

Danilo thought of the friar. Venice was perhaps not as safe as the gondolier wished to believe.

"You have to know the shallows and the depths, sir." The gondolier winked. "And you have to be able to swing around on a small point. The oarlock of a gondola, sir, is designed especially for that. It is called the *fórcola*. It gives the gondola its quick, supple movement. It gives you different positions, different forms of leverage. It sticks out from the side of the gondola, as you can see. That's to give the oarsman total control, sir, and it has these little twists in its shape—like a zigzag—to allow for different positions for the oar, and different maneuvers."

"So the gondola is unique to Venice."

"Yes, sir. Horses were outlawed early in the fourteenth century. They are messy things, and noisy. Best restrict them to terra firma. And they need to be fed. There is no grass to graze on here in Venice. Hay had to be imported. Manure had to be cleared away. A gondola doesn't need fodder."

"A gondola is not a horse," said Jessica, smiling up at the gondolier.

"No, Signorina, a gondola is definitely not a horse. Now, to move about in Venice, we have our feet, or litters with bearers for fine ladies, or barges and rowboats, or gondolas! Your gondola glides, Signorina, smooth like the talk of your most gallant gentleman. And now, the great families, and not so great, compete with one another in grandiose displays with the bright colors of their family gondola, just as they compete in building bigger and bigger palazzos on the Grand Canal."

Danilo nodded grimly. Gondoliers were water-borne philosophers. If you wanted to spy on people, being a gondolier would be one way to do it; they saw and knew virtually everything. Then he thought, I am the spy! I am the one betraying everyone—and Miriamne thinks I am a gallant hero. And yet tomorrow I may be asked to murder someone. If he had to assassinate Bruno Scavo, that would be satisfying, in a macabre sort of way.

Thunder echoed down the Canal.

"We had best hurry." The gondolier nodded towards the sky. Huge black clouds were piling up behind them to the southeast. A bright white flash of lightning shot brilliant against the steel-black of the clouds. The thunder rolled in, louder now.

They slid past the *Fondaco dei Tedeschi*, the House of the Germans, a massive four-story building with arches and loading docks, where German merchants living in Venice were housed and worked.

Miriamne seemed happy with the gondolier's chatter. It was a distraction. She glanced up at the stormy sky, and then she turned to Danilo. She had been deeply hurt, but Danilo could see the tense little lines around her mouth had disappeared. Her hair, freed from the net, shone in the darkening light, the yellow veil barely covering half her face.

Lightning flashed again, and thunder rolled as they approached the entrance to the Ghetto. The gondolier deposited them just a few steps away from the little bridge leading to the Ghetto.

Vincenzo was waiting anxiously just under the *sotoportego*. The sky opened and rain poured down, a clamorous wall of silver. "You are all safe and sound! Ah, Signor David, I knew we could count on you!" Vincenzo took off his cap.

"Miriamne and Isaac, and Jessica and Jacob, and your friend Filippo were the true heroes."

Vincenzo bowed to Danilo. "I would expect no less of them, Signor David, I would expect no less."

MIRIAMNE SHOOK AWAY THE raindrops that were on her dress and sat down. She put her hands flat on her work table. She picked up an amulet. It was silver. She put it down. She covered her eyes with both hands.

"I am so angry, so angry at myself."

"It wasn't your fault, Miriamne. You were brave, and calm, and perfect."

"I put Isaac and the children in danger. I was careless. I am too optimistic, too sunny. I actually believe people are good. I actually believe people are people and they will try to understand other people—Christian, Muslim, Jew, Venetian, or Turk, it doesn't matter." She stood and started to pace. "I really am an idiot."

"You are the opposite of an idiot, and no harm came to anyone." Danilo got out of his chair, moved to her, and took her in his arms.

He kissed her on the forehead. She looked up and stroked the side of his face; then she looked down and buried herself in him. He held her close. *Oh, Miriamne!* Pressed against his chest he felt the warmth of her spirit and the beating of her heart.

BROTHER BRUNO SCAVO FELL to his knees. The stone of the court-yard was cold and damp. The weather had turned chilly. For a long time, he remained there, alone.

He had managed to preach a sermon or two. His righteous-ness shone bright, his rage against the injustices of the world, against usury, against wealth, against the cruelties visited upon the poor and the humble, who were the true Children of Christ. But it was such a long and difficult struggle. Sometimes, in truth, he despaired of saving souls, of purifying the world. Sometimes, in the darkest of nights, he doubted it was possible.

A raw wind from the northeast swept in from the lagoon. The damp, rough cloth of Bruno's habit pressed against his sweating skin; the thorns and bristles wrapped around his chest created a sacred, prickly, self-conscious itchiness. Truly, it was as if he were Christ Himself. He imagined himself, jeered at by the presumptuous Jews, as he staggered barefoot under the weight of the cross towards the place of His crucifixion.

The Jews—how could they refuse the Messiah? How could they be so perverse as to refuse salvation? How could they be so blind? Surely they were the servants of the Devil! They and the Mohammadans, they were all possessed by Satan and doing the demon's work. The Jews were foul pollution, the plague, leprosy, like the whores of this sink of iniquity, this Venice. But Venice would soon be brought low.

That prostitute, just the other day, the second one he had chastised—she'd had all the beauty of innocence, and yet she was as foul in ugliness and sin as the demon himself. How old was she—fourteen, fifteen? Ah, he had made her suffer! Given more time, she would have repented. He could have packed her off to a nunnery.

But the guards had intervened. Why was he terrorizing the girl? How dare he? This was the second time in a few days, they had shouted. The guards had no respect for him or for Christ!

And then there was that Jewess! Miriamne, they'd called her. She was beautiful, and so proud and defiant, the Devil incarnate! She was the epitome, the very symbol of Judaism. Her beauty and high spirits represented all the seductions of evil, all that can lead man and woman astray towards perdition, towards Hell itself. Like an Old Testament heroine, she was Judaism in the flesh! The people were about to do her justice, strike her down; but then along came that Jew—he too would burn! They would be cast down, into the deepest depths of Hell.

Brother Bruno felt the chill wind against his face. Now he had to leave Venice. The government had hinted he would regret it if he stayed a day longer. Well, there were sinners, corrupt priests and prelates, whores and courtesans, and New Christians and Jews, on the mainland. He closed his eyes.

The burning of heretics, the purifying promise of fire—an Act of Faith—it was so tangible he could touch it. Soon the sacred fires would burn, everywhere!

WHAT I DO, I DO
FOR YOU

ONE CHILLY AFTERNOON, VINCENZO SENT WORD TO Danilo that he was wanted by "a certain gentleman in the usual spot at the usual time."

And so, wrapping a cloak around his shoulders and with his yellow cap stuffed away, Danilo set off through Cannaregio towards the quay. This time he took a different route. Head down against the breeze, he walked quickly, glancing left and right from time to time. Why did Marco want to see him? What was he going to be forced to do? Had something happened to his father, to Saida?

Horrible thoughts crowded into his mind. Danilo's heart sank. He hurried onward, ignoring the few passersby; then he thought again and paid more attention to his surroundings. The danger of assassins never went away. Such was his life.

When he arrived at the quay, a chill wind was whipping up choppy little waves on the lagoon. The island of Murano was wrapped in a shroud of white mist and the mainland was invisible behind a low bank of thick white fog.

Marco was there, gazing out at the water, huddled against the wind, a cloak whipping around his shoulders and legs. His nose was red and running. "Let us find a warmer, quieter place," he said. "The wind beats about my ears."

Marco led Danilo to a small tavern. They sat at an oaken table in the back, in a private, curtained alcove. A fire was burning bright and soon they were warm, facing each other over mugs of wine.

"So, Marco?" Danilo studied the man. It looked like Marco hadn't been getting much sleep. "Why did you want to see me?"

"Danilo, you are fluent in Persian and Turkish, I believe."

"Yes. I am."

"Good. This evening I wish you to visit this address. Veronica Libero, a well-known courtesan. She lives in a mansion on the Grand Canal, two buildings down from Ca' Dario. Dress fashionably. Enter by a side door, just off this little alleyway next to the Grand Canal. Here." Marco shoved a scribbled map in front of Danilo. "This is the alleyway. The side door is here. There is a lamp over the door, and there will be a guard. He will be expecting you. Don't wear your yellow cap; don't even take it with you. Tonight you are not a Jew. Here is a special pass. Keep it with you always."

Danilo slipped the scribbled map and the pass into his breast pocket. "What am I to do there?" He had relaxed while Marco was speaking; his father and Saida were all right, then.

"Veronica will explain. She is...ah...much-celebrated. I am sure you will find her charming."

Danilo frowned. "I suppose I must say yes."

"I would like a full report on what you hear, what you notice, what you see. Everything! Forget nothing, even little details, even things that seem irrelevant. Do not fail me, Danilo."

Danilo nodded. "I have no choice."

DANILO LEFT THE GHETTO in the evening. Vincenzo winked and tipped his hat, and said, "A very good evening to you, Signor David. And good luck!"

Danilo consulted the map. It would have been simpler to take a gondola, but Marco had told him to go by foot for the first part of his trip and to avoid the Grand Canal, where he would be too visible. He was to take a gondola for only the middle part of the journey, and then go ashore and walk the final bit. Danilo peered at the roughly drawn map. He had a good sense of direction, at least he thought he did, but Venice, like its lagoon, was a labyrinth that puzzled even the most seasoned navigators. He squinted. The light of day was dying. But there were lights reflecting from the windows of a tavern. Yes, he was on the right track. He hurried down a little laneway. Venice definitely was mysterious. Danilo felt he was surrounded by a world of secrets, and that he was part of a game, or a set of games, that he didn't understand. What would be demanded of him? Was he to interrogate someone? Or assassinate someone? Was this a trap?

He kept checking over his shoulder to see if he was being followed. Anything could be an ambush. Two men, arm in arm, were strolling along. As he watched them, they were greeted by friends coming out of a doorway. Not assassins, then. To his knowledge, when the Men in Black were sent on a mission they never gave up until it was accomplished. So, yes, they would return.

He took a gondola to well beyond the Rialto Bridge, got off, walked down an alleyway, then doubled back and followed another alleyway—a *calle*, this one parallel to the Grand Canal—until he came to the mansion that was the home of the famous courtesan.

It was an old and distinguished-looking building. Candles burned in the windows. He turned into a side alley and walked down it until he came to a door. A single small lamp, a votive offering to the Virgin Mary, burned over the entrance. A tall, broad-shouldered man stood next to the door. He looked

Danilo up and down and nodded. Danilo entered and went up a narrow wooden staircase, and when he stepped through a door he found himself on a large landing with a marble balustrade, large windows overlooking the Grand Canal, tapestries, and marble flooring. Everything was sparkling and impeccable, as if the whole setting had been installed only that morning. Several fashionable Venetian youths were hanging about on the landing gossiping and laughing, but they did not bother with him, giving him only a cursory glance and then returning to their skittish talk.

A very pretty, very young maid servant in a tight bodice with a flared skirt was coming up the stairs; she nodded at Danilo, held his gaze, and whispered, "Follow me, sir!" She led him farther up the broad, torch-lit staircase to the second floor.

When they entered the main salon, Danilo was dazzled by the sumptuous carpets, the tapestries, the paintings, the gold and silver, the opulent furniture, the gilded mirrors.

"Ah, here you are!" An elegant young woman turned away from the window and greeted him as if they were old friends. She was perhaps twenty-two or twenty-three. Her manners, self-assurance, and sophistication made her seem older; the freshness of her beauty made her seem younger. She was standing by a tall window that looked over the canal. Her red hair tumbled freely down her bare shoulders, her breasts were barely concealed, her long robe was open along one side, exposing a length of perfect leg, sparkling white, in silk. She looked at him with an amused, calculating expression.

"You are a handsome fellow, my friend. So, we are to work together."

Danilo bowed. "Madam."

"And gallant, too!" She favored him with the brightest of smiles. "I am indeed pleased. My name is Veronica Libero. My work is to give pleasure—sensual, sexual, intellectual, and cultural. The quality of the conversation is essential. People must relax. They must feel free to express themselves. My clientele is varied, but on the whole it consists, with a few necessary and unfortunate exceptions, of the very best of society. Many of Venice's leaders are my friends. I do use the word 'friend' with caution. But I think I can say that. So, among the clientele who frequent my little abode there are also foreigners, German merchants, people who deal with Charles V, some ecclesiastical figures who visit Venice from time to time, several Frenchmen who are close to the Court of François I, and of course Turks and Persians and Arabs."

"Yes, I see."

"Now, some of these gentlemen speak languages I don't understand; we would like very much to know what they are saying, what they are talking about. I understand you speak Turkish, Persian, and Arabic."

"Yes, madam, I do."

"Call me Veronica, please." Her eyes sparkled in merriment. "And who shall you be? Let's invent someone, shall we? You are . . . Daniel del Monte!" For her, Danilo realized, life was a game.

He bowed. Now he had three names: David, Daniel, and Danilo. He felt, somehow, that he should kiss her hand. She moved with the fluid ease, casualness, and feigned intimacy of royalty.

"In a few minutes, the visitors will arrive. I will entertain them, as will some of my friends and colleagues. But our guests often speak in their own languages among themselves."

"I see."

"And here, let me show you. I do apologize for the indignity of it, but you will be stowed away here, in this closed little alcove." She pressed against a small decorative detail and pulled it aside. A door—up to that point invisible—opened, and Danilo saw what looked like a padded closet, or perhaps an invisible corridor running parallel to the wall of the salon. A whiff of stale air wafted out.

"I have put in a stool to make it more comfortable," Veronica said as she turned to him. "You have a good memory, I hope."

"I believe it is fairly good, Veronica."

"Would you like a glass of wine?"

"I shall abstain, thank you."

"Very wise, Daniel. A clear head is essential in this business. Venice is like the Virgin Mary, or if you prefer classical allusions, she is like Aphrodite freshly risen from the sea. She is a gallant lady and she needs to be protected."

"Venice has many enemies."

"Yes, and many jealousies. Venice is rich and Venice is a republic; Venice is small, and she belongs to all of us. She has been around a long time—a thousand years at least—and so she deserves our care and solicitude." She smiled. Her perfume, a heady mixture of jasmine and rose, made Danilo dizzy. The lamps sparkled off the gilt and silver and glass.

Veronica put her hand on Danilo's shoulder and gazed straight into his eyes. "I must warn you, my dear Daniel. One of our guests is of a particularly violent temperament. He's quite brilliant. A Turkish gentleman, Signor Muharrem; he is excessively intelligent and cultured and charming, but he is known to have murdered many a man, and some women too."

Danilo held her gaze and nodded.

"He delights in strangling people with his bare hands, and he is adept with a dagger. He must not discover our little game. Even if there is trouble, you are not to intervene. Julian will take care of it." She nodded towards a tall, broad-shouldered man who had been standing against one wall. The man nodded at Danilo. Veronica smiled. "Silence is essential."

"Certainly."

"Here, now I shall lock you in. For a little while, my dear friend, you shall be my prisoner."

Danilo sat down on the stool in the little alcove. Veronica closed the door. He was in darkness. There was a peephole so he could, if he wished, glance out and see who was talking. The space was narrow and lined with a thick carpet and wall padding to muffle any footsteps or movement, which meant he could move along, parallel to the room, and to other rooms. The important thing now was to listen. He sat on the stool and fidgeted. If he was going to get involved in a struggle, he would have preferred, really, to be on a horse, hurling a lance; or on foot, wielding a sword or a dagger; or possibly scouting, far behind enemy lines; or perhaps manning one of the Sultan's giant guns in the midst of flame and thunder. Sitting on a stool in the perfumed dark was not his idea of heroism; but then again . . . wars were often won by stranger devices.

Danilo heard the fuss as the gentlemen arrived. Some guttural voices, a man with a Milanese accent, someone talking in Turkish. There was a girl giggling, and one man's laughter, and Veronica's suave voice, in Italian and French, greeting the gentlemen and giving instructions to the girls.

Danilo leaned forward and put his eye to the peephole. One of the girls placed drinks and sweets on a table close to Danilo's hiding place, so close he could smell the bouquet of the red wine.

The Turkish gentleman, a massively built, handsome dark-skinned man, moved close to the table. Speaking Turkish, he began asking questions, very confidentially, of a thin, sharp-featured Italian gentleman. The Turk wanted information on the Arsenal and the building program for new Venetian warships. What was the production schedule? What were the choke points—access to good quality timber? Was anyone vulnerable to blackmail? And was sabotage a possibility?

The Italian smiled. Also speaking in Turkish, he explained that, yes, timber supplies could be cut off. Sabotage could be arranged. Pirates could be used to intercept supplies.

The Turk put his hand on the Italian's shoulder and began to give details of the Sultan's accelerated shipbuilding program. "Suleiman himself visits the shipyards virtually every day. You can assure King François, everything will go according to schedule."

"So, what is the grand plan, what are you working towards?" asked the Italian. He seemed to Danilo to have a Milanese accent.

The Turk whispered, but still Danilo, his eye pressed to the peephole, could hear quite clearly. "François will invade Italy from the north, and the Sultan will invade Italy from the south, from near Otranto, on the very heel of the Italian boot. Next spring or summer is the probable date."

"Ah, Otranto," the Italian said and laughed, then wiped his mouth with a handkerchief. "Already it has been attacked, decades ago. The Sultan's army massacred 12,000 and enslaved 5,000, perhaps more. Eight hundred men were beheaded because they refused to convert to Islam, or so the story goes."

"The story is correct. It was bloody, and profitable. All praise and thanks be to Allah! We failed to keep Otranto. But this time we shall come in force and we intend to stay. The aim, you see, is to conquer Naples—to take it away from the Spanish and Charles V, and then move on to Rome."

"To Rome, you say?" The Italian took a sip of wine. He seemed to be staring straight at Danilo. Danilo held his breath. The Italian picked up a sweet and contemplated it. "That is ambitious." He popped the sweet into his mouth.

"Suleiman wants to complete the conquest of Europe, of Christendom. His great predecessor, Mehmed II, took the eastern capital of Christianity, Constantinople, in 1453. Suleiman is already at the gates of Vienna and has access to the great central plain of Europe, which will carry him into Germany and beyond. And he is expanding Ottoman suzerainty along the shores of North Africa. Suleiman wants to take Rome itself, the original Rome, the heart of Christianity. His dream is to complete the work before the centenary of the conquest of Constantinople, before 1553. All of Europe will lie at our feet. Islam will triumph."

"A grandiose project."

"Suleiman is a visionary, a great ruler. He is building the greatest fleet ever seen, much more powerful than the Venetian navy. He will complete Mehmed's work. Mehmed at first wanted to turn Saint Peter's into a stable. Suleiman is, let us say, more respectful. He will transform Saint Peter's into a mosque. In the end, the aim is to unite all of Europe under the true religion, Islam. All praise to Allah!"

Each time the gentlemen wandered away, Veronica or Zarah, one of Veronica's lightly clad and beautiful young girls, managed to gently shepherd them back close to Danilo's hiding place, and then Veronica or the girl would drift away on some pretext, leaving the gentlemen alone to discuss business. It was always Veronica or Zarah, Danilo noticed, who did the shepherding. Zarah must be special. Probably the other girls were not aware of Danilo, sweating in his hot cubbyhole.

Zarah kissed several of the guests. And then she brought the Turkish gentleman—whom Danilo had noticed had been very generously plied with drink—into a bedroom separate from the reception space. Danilo had to move along the inner corridor to follow what was happening and what was being said.

In this room there was no peephole, but from the sounds and groans and whispers, and from the man's words, Danilo concluded that Zarah must be very talented. She laughed and cooed and made witty remarks in Italian and offered the man a massage, which he accepted. Some of her remarks were extremely subtle, designed, indirectly, to elicit information, but when the Turk did not take the bait, Zarah veered off into frivolity and caressing little sounds, telling him how strong and virile and handsome he was.

The Turk began to laugh and he spoke to her in slurred Turkish, which of course she did not understand. "Ah, you Venetians think you are so clever," he said. "You aren't clever, not really. We have penetrated your secrets, my dear, just as now I shall penetrate you."

While she squealed in pleasure, he continued in a sort of rhapsodic monologue in Turkish. "And you know, in the Arsenal we have our own little spy, our very own forge master in the very heart of the Arsenal, and he tells us all. How much is being produced, when, and for what purpose. But even more interesting, he tells us how the Venetians manage to build so many ships so fast. So we can copy them."

He stopped his speech while she kissed him and she asked if he liked what she was doing. He replied, now speaking in

Italian, that he adored what she was doing, that she was as beautiful and as talented as the most talented girl in his harem, and then as both of them groaned in real or simulated pleasure, he continued, in Turkish, "All of your advantages are gone, my dear little Venetian. Let me take you just like this. You like it! Yes, you like to be taken like this!"

And she, not understanding Turkish, still got the gist of the last part, and sighed, "Oh, yes, master, more, more."

He went on in Turkish, "You are so quick, my dear Zarah, such a supple, smooth little body, just like a boy." He shifted to Italian, "I had a favorite boy, a Greek, a slave. You remind me of him. I loved him, I truly did. It was a great passion. Dead now, he is. But you are a girl — so two for the price of one."

"I am delighted, master, that I can give you pleasure. For you deserve so much pleasure and love!"

He took her again and again. Her cries were artful and exquisitely modulated, but from some of her silences and from a catch in her voice that sounded almost like a sob, Danilo guessed she was not having all that much fun. It was work — painful, dangerous, and humiliating. She was a brave girl, this Zarah.

Not much more of political import was discussed, and when the lovemaking ceased, the Turk left Zarah and returned to the salon. Danilo shuffled cautiously back to his original position, sat down on the stool, and put his eye to the peephole.

More talk between the Turk and the Italian followed — army logistics and possible contracts for supplying the Sultan's armies, ways to cut off Venice's supply of shipbuilding timber, and some speculations on how afraid people in Rome and Naples were at the idea of an Islamic Ottoman invasion, plus a few ideas on how to increase the fear. "A few spectacular raids with wholesale slaughter might accomplish the purpose," the Italian suggested.

"Yes," the Turk agreed, "Striking terror in the populace is a good idea." He moved closer to Danilo's hiding place and lowered his voice. "Pirate raids by Saracens, on the coasts of Italy, to burn villages, seize hostages, and take people to be sold into slavery—that is a tactic we are going to emphasize in the coming months, a campaign of terror."

Finally, the gentlemen left. Veronica chased away the young women and the servants, except for Zarah.

On a signal from Veronica, Danilo emerged from his hiding place. Zarah did indeed look like an exquisite boy, with dark lustrous skin, marvelous, big dark eyes, and curly black hair cut short. She blinked at Danilo and reached out and took Veronica's hand. The girl's eyes, Danilo noticed, were red, the kohl smudged, as if she'd been crying. Veronica pulled Zarah to her and caressed the girl's short, cropped hair. Zarah looked down, then glanced up, smiled shyly at Danilo and then glanced down again. "Zarah is a very brave girl," said Veronica, "aren't you, my dear?"

"It is nothing, Veronica. I do what I do for you—and for Venice."

Watching the look in the girl's eyes, Danilo was sure that Zarah was in love with Veronica and that in some sense at least, the feeling was reciprocated.

Veronica offered Danilo a glass of water in an exquisite Venetian glass. "Thank you for being so patient, my friend. I hope it was useful. Perhaps the gentlemen said nothing of interest; I can't be the judge of that, and you are not to tell us of what you heard, but you are to meet now with another of our mutual friends."

Just then, the young maid who had first met Danilo on the staircase rushed into the room. "Veronica, the Turk is coming back! He is quite drunk, and aggressive! Julian is delaying him, but—"

Veronica turned to Zarah and kissed her on the forehead. "You and Daniel go into the cubbyhole and along the secret corridor. You know how to get him out of the building. Hurry!"

"Why is he coming back?" Zarah's eyes were wide in terror.

"Because of you, darling!"

"Of course," Zarah whispered, and lowered her eyes. "I knew it!"

"Go, now! Explain to Daniel what he has to do next. And darling, wait in the secret room, on the roof under the eaves, until I or Julian come for you."

Zarah and Danilo entered the small space. Veronica closed the door behind them just in time. The Turk came storming into the room. Even from inside the cubbyhole, his voice was loud and clear.

"Divine Veronica!" he shouted, "I have an infinite favor to ask of you."

"What is that, my dear Signor Muharrem?"

"I must buy the boy-girl, your sublime Zarah. She is exquisite! How much do you want for her? I will pay anything—gold, silver! I must take her with me to Istanbul."

"Please sit down, Signor Muharrem. Zarah has gone back to her mother's."

"I must have her! She has awakened in me passions and desires I have not felt since . . ." The man's voice broke.

"Let me offer you this prosecco, Signor Muharrem. It is one of the finest in Italy. I had it especially ordered, thinking of you."

"Have you known love, Veronica, true unbridled, unlimited, passion? It has a touch of divinity, and . . . it is pure torture, like the rack . . ." Signor Muharrem stopped, apparently overcome by emotion.

Veronica sighed, theatrically. "Although I am merely a woman, Signor Muharrem, I too have known unbridled passion, love, desire, and longing. I do have an inkling of what you are suffering. You can confide in me. I am sure Zarah will be infinitely flattered by your offer, but alas, she is not my property and she is not for sale, but I do know that you are a man of exquisite taste. Tell me what you need and I am sure that, on your next visit, Zarah or one of the girls can give you some special . . ."

"Veronica has him well in hand," Zarah whispered. "Follow me, Signor Daniel."

They crept along the narrow, padded corridor and came to another padded door, which Zarah unlocked and opened carefully, silently. It was almost totally dark, but rays of dim yellowish light filtered down from openings somewhere above. They crept down a short, narrow, low-ceilinged corridor and came out onto a set of creaky wooden stairs, in a sort of interior stairwell consisting of wooden beams, crossbeams, and steeply angled struts. It smelled of varnish, wood shavings, mold, and mouse droppings. Danilo stared into the shadowy darkness. This was clearly part of the basic hidden structure that held the building up. The stairs led up two floors. At the top, a fat black-and-white cat was stalking along the edge of a wooden banister.

"This is Phoebe," Zarah whispered. "She is our chief rat and mouse hunter. We have many cats, but Phoebe is the boss cat."

"From her size, she looks like a successful hunter." Danilo put his hand on the banister. The cat turned and looked at him. It purred.

"Yes, Phoebe is talented. You are my favorite cat, aren't you, Phoebe?"

The cat meowed and leaped into the girl's arms.

They climbed up one more rickety staircase and came out on the roof, a small perch. A few stars shone overhead, but the edges of the sky were yellow and red. Dawn was breaking. Zarah pointed to wooden scaffolding that stood up against one side of the building. "That's the way down. You walk back to the main *calle* at the back of the building; you turn left into that *calle* and walk past two alleyways on your left, then turn left again into the third alleyway. That takes you to a small side canal. The man Veronica calls 'our mutual friend' will be waiting for you there."

"And you, Zarah?"

"I'll be safe." She was stroking Phoebe. "I have my own little shelter up here on the rooftop. I often come up here. Veronica or Julian will come for me."

The rising sun suddenly lit up her curly jet-black hair. Holding Phoebe in her arms, she watched as he climbed down the scaffolding.

When he looked back, she was gone.

18

DAWN

D AWN WAS BREAKING, AND DOWN BELOW, THE SUN BEGAN
to illuminate the shadowy alleyways. The Marangona,
the bell that began the work day, was tolling, its melodic
chimes echoing in the alleyways and *calles*. Workers and apprentices hurried along the *calles* and disappeared under porticos.

Following Zarah's instructions, Danilo found a glossy black
gondola, with a gondolier standing ready at the stern, waiting
for him. The gondolier beckoned him forward.

Danilo stepped down into the gondola. In the center was a
curtained cabin. Inside was Marco.

"Greetings, Danilo."

"Marco."

"I trust you enjoyed meeting Veronica."

"She is charming, more than charming."

Danilo told Marco what he had seen and heard; a Milanese
gentleman, Signor Galeazzo Brambilla, was an informant for
the Ottomans, and probably an agent for François I of France;
a Turkish merchant, Signor Muharrem Konevi, an agent for

Suleiman, was trying to find weaknesses in the Arsenal and in the Venetian fleet; Suleiman and King François intended to invade Italy at the same time, the Ottomans attacking from the south, on the heel of the boot near the city of Otranto, the French attacking from the north, towards Genova and Milan; and in the months prior to the invasion, the Ottomans intended to create panic along the coasts of Italy by a series of small and large-scale pirate raids—rampaging through the countryside, burning towns and crops, and seizing people to be sold into slavery.

Marco listened as the gondola slid smoothly out onto the Grand Canal. Finally, he spoke. "So, Danilo, how do you see Suleiman's strategy developing?"

Danilo half-closed his eyes and thought about it; he thought about the maps he had seen laid out in the Sultan's tent; he thought about the discussions he had heard between Suleiman and his officers; he thought about reading *The Life of Alexander the Great* to the Sultan, and about the Sultan's reactions and comments on Alexander's actions and tactics. "Suleiman likes simplicity. Since it will be difficult to get the bulk of his army across the sea, he will choose the narrowest passage. That would be from the port of Avlona, which is on the Adriatic coast in Albania, in Ottoman territory. He will march his army across the Balkans from near Istanbul. And his fleet will rendezvous with the army at Avlona, and transport the troops across to the heel of the Italian boot, to Apulia, near Otranto. It is, I think, about one hundred miles distance by sea."

"How big an army would you guess he'd use?"

"Suleiman does things on a grand scale. It will be two or three hundred thousand men, plus horses, plus artillery."

Marco sat back, staring. "That's monstrous. The largest European armies are barely 50,000. Charles V's army that sacked Rome totaled about 34,000 men, and it was huge. Three hundred thousand! Just think of the food and forage—they will be like locusts and the plague together; they will eat everything in their path, starve everybody, and destroy everything."

Danilo nodded. "The best thing would be that they do not land at all. You Venetians possess the island of Corfu, do you not? And you have your navy . . ."

"Yes. Corfu is just south of Avlona," said Marco.

Danilo remembered the maps he had seen. "So if Suleiman invades Italy using Avlona to embark his troops, Corfu lies just south of his communications and transport lines. His fleet will have to go past Corfu."

"As you said, Corfu is a Venetian base."

"Yes."

"Corfu also controls the entry to the Adriatic." Marco closed his eyes and rubbed his forehead. "The entry to the Adriatic is narrow, it is a bottleneck. So if Suleiman took Corfu, he could control the Adriatic—and invade anywhere along the east coast of the Italian peninsula, anytime he wanted to."

Danilo nodded. "Yes."

"So Corfu is the key," Marco said with a frown. "Suleiman will want Corfu—he will *need* Corfu—before he launches his full invasion. And he will also want to be sure his invasion coincides with the French invasion from the north. We must defend Corfu."

"That would be logical."

"The salvation of Italy and Christendom depends on Venice keeping control of Corfu."

"The stakes are indeed high."

Marco suddenly smiled. "This has been a very useful meeting, Danilo. Thank you."

"There is something more precise."

"Yes?"

"The Turks have a spy—possibly a saboteur—in the Arsenal."

"What? Who?"

"Muharrem didn't give a name." Danilo paused. "But their spy works in the forges. He is an older man, a supervisor, he has a wife who is ill, and he has six children who are mostly adults. One, a girl, is sickly and lives with the man and his wife."

"That," said Marco, "is exactly the sort of thing I need to know."

MARCO SET OFF ON foot alone towards Piazza San Marco, towards the Ducal Palace, where he wrote his notes and then dictated a more polished version to a scribe in the Venetian Intelligence Service.

The Intelligence Service reported directly to the Council of Ten, which was responsible for the internal and external security of the Republic. The Council of Ten was complicated, like all things in Venice. The Venetians feared a coup d'état, so they had created so many checks and balances in every institution that Marco wondered how anything got done at all.

The first thing he had to do was uncover the spy in the Arsenal who was working for the Ottomans. Ideally, the man should be executed, and his whole family punished. Or perhaps he should be cultivated, turned, and used for counter-espionage, so that misleading information could be fed to the Ottomans.

It would all have to be done so that the Ottomans—and in particular that rather clever Signor Muharrem—would not suspect that Veronica Libero was a spy; she and Zarah had to be protected at all costs.

He would have to discuss with the Senator how to best arrange this affair. The spy could, of course, die in an accident, a painful, fatal accident.

That might be the best, the most discreet method—yes, an accident.

DANILO HEADED BACK ON foot through the Dorsoduro neighborhood, the "Hard Ridge" district, which lay on the opposite side of the Grand Canal from San Marco and was quite far from the Ghetto.

The breeze had picked up and on the Grand Canal the water

was choppy. Barges and gondolas were moving up and down in endless procession. He turned inland.

Then, out of the corner of his eye, he noticed a familiar figure — was it that tall, skinny, shadowy fellow he'd first seen in the Cannaregio district? Danilo stopped and pretended to watch a vendor set up his stall displaying used clothes. Then he walked faster; he went down a side alley, turned a corner, sheltered behind a hanging curtain, and waited. The man was nowhere to be seen.

Danilo left his shelter and strolled casually. He went past the great buildings of the various guilds, he wandered down little alleyways, all thronging with activity. Shops, small markets, craftsmen, tailors, goldsmiths, tinsmiths, carpenters, painters, bakers . . . From time to time, carefully, he glanced back.

There he was again — the tall, skinny fellow.

The man was trying not to be seen. Sometimes he lagged behind, sometimes he was closer, and sometimes he disappeared altogether, only to reappear.

The closer Danilo got to the Rialto Market, the more crowded the alleyways became. Activity was frenetic, the smell of fish was everywhere, the high piles of vegetables and fruit, the slabs of meat, whole lambs strung up, the fowl hanging by their legs, feathers fluttering in the breeze.

The man had disappeared.

No, there he was again.

Danilo stopped, glanced at a pile of fresh calamari and octopus, sardines, and mackerel, and then he slipped between two stalls, moved into a side alley, and doubled back. This should put him behind the fellow. He stopped in a doorway and glanced around. Was the man alone, or did he have an accomplice?

Ah, there the fellow was, in the fish market. He was looking around, obviously puzzled, probably thinking Danilo had gotten ahead of him. The man headed towards the Rialto Bridge.

Danilo slipped out of his hiding place and followed. It would be best to confront the man now, in broad daylight, and find out who he was and what he wanted.

Glancing behind him to make sure the fellow wasn't a decoy, that he wasn't being stalked by another hunter, Danilo headed towards the bridge.

Colorful gondolas and heavily laden barges streamed past, going in both directions. It was so crowded on the bridge that Danilo had to elbow his way through. Rabbi Hazan had told him that the Venetians had been debating replacing the bridge for decades. "Venice mulls and Venice reflects and Venice debates, but Venice, sometimes, just cannot decide!" Rabbi Hazan had said with a laugh. "There are always too many cooks involved in preparing the Venetian broth." The bridge certainly did look rickety and ancient. It groaned under the weight of shoppers and merchants.

Once he had crossed the bridge, Danilo was free of the crowd. He could breathe. He went down a small side street. It thronged with shoppers and artisans. People worked in the street, making and repairing picture frames, cabinets, tables, chairs; the smell of wood shavings and varnish filled the air.

Nowhere did he see the man who had been on his tail.

He came out onto a walkway that went along the edge of a wide canal. Boats were tied up along the quay, and merchants were selling directly from the boats and barges or from stalls that lined the walkways. The shadowy man was nowhere to be seen. Who was he? What were his intentions? Was he an agent of the Sultan?

Shopkeepers hawked their wares, ogling each passerby, and making alluring or ironic remarks with toothy, childlike grins. "Come, you beautiful man, inspect this, you cannot possibly live, my young handsome fellow, you cannot possibly survive another day without buying this from me — and it is, I assure you, dear sir, the best of its kind. Nothing better can be found in all of Venice. What am I saying? There is nothing better to be found in all of Italy! In all of Europe, there is nothing better. Even the Sultan has not got it better than this!"

MIRIAMNE WAS SITTING AT her workbench, fitting a bright green stone into what looked like a setting of silver. The morning sun made patterns on the wall next to her; the bars of the narrow window and a fluttery, wave-like pattern reflected from something outside. Danilo was struck by how fresh and fragile she looked. The night had been so crowded with events that it seemed he had left her long ago; at the same time, it seemed to him that he had known her forever.

She glanced over her shoulder. "Well, my invisible man—it seems you have been out all night. Have you become a musician, a strolling minstrel, an entertainer for the rich and profligate?" She gave him her usual bright smile, but behind the smile lurked curiosity, disquiet, and perhaps a hint of jealousy. The hurt was clear behind the brightness. "What have you been up to?"

Danilo crouched next to her, looking her straight in the eyes. "It's probably best, dear Miriamne, if nobody talks about this, and if nobody knows that I am out, occasionally, at night. It is work, a kind of work I must do."

"You are not gambling, are you?"

"I am not gambling."

"I couldn't stand it if you were gambling."

Her eyes shone, and held just a suggestion of tears. The fullness and ripeness of her lips, and her bright, white, perfect teeth shone in the sunlight. She was achingly beautiful. She put down the amulet, swiveled around and put her hand on his shoulder. "I thought we were friends, Danilo. And then you disappear without a word. You are not in trouble, are you?"

"No, dearest Miriamne, I am not in trouble."

"I cannot believe you would betray us, Danilo."

"Never."

"So I must trust you. Whatever you are doing, or whatever you have to do, I must believe it is for the best."

A BROTHER RETURNS

"**W**HO THE HELL IS THIS?"
It was a scream loud enough to wake all the devils in hell.

Danilo had been deep in a pleasant dream. He and Miriamne were walking hand in hand on a beach on the Lido, the sea bright cobalt blue, the sky pure azure, a warm breeze wafting gently over them, Jessica and Jacob were . . .

But the dream shattered into tiny little iridescent pieces. He opened his eyes. He blinked. He was staring at a dark, handsome face that looked like it had risen, in thunderous rage, from Dante's Inferno.

The man had large, dark eyes, high cheekbones, a sallow, unhealthy complexion; his beard was neatly trimmed but sparse, letting bits of skin show through. He looked dissolute and perhaps not in the best of health; handsome but not a happy fellow. And he was holding a knife as if he were about to plunge it into Danilo's heart.

Miriamne's brother: Mordecai.

"Who the hell are you?" Mordecai said through clenched teeth.

"Ah, I am . . . Well, I am . . ." Danilo struggled to sit up. In his nightshirt he felt particularly vulnerable; it was like being naked. It would have been much better to face the man fully dressed.

Miriamne burst into the room and placed her arm around Mordecai. "Now, now, calm down, everyone!"

Rabbi Hazan appeared just behind her.

Miriamne leaned in close and crooned into the man's ear. "This is Danilo del Medigo. He has come to us from heaven to help Papa with his translation work. Papa will explain."

"Is this the truth, father? Is this fellow working for you?"

Rabbi Hazan held his son's steely gaze. "Yes, Mordecai, Danilo is a master of languages and he is being very helpful with my, ah, with my book business."

Mordecai turned to his sister. "Out of what stagnant polluted puddle did you fish him?"

Danilo, now sitting up and sufficiently awake to speak for himself, cleared his throat. "I arrived in Venice hidden on a Venetian galleon after I managed to escape from the Ottoman Sultan's Men in Black. I found myself on Passover Eve at the Ghetto gates."

"Danilo's appearance was foretold to me in a vision. I knew he would appear!" Miriamne stood there, eyes bright, hands on her hips, like a housewife ready to referee a fight between two naughty children. "And so he did!"

"And tell me, stranger, did you too have a vision from heaven?" Mordecai spat out the words; he made no effort to hide his sarcasm. "Did you have a vision that brought you directly to my father and sister?"

"Mordecai." Rabbi Hazan raised his hand. "This young man has been educated in many languages, including Burgundian French. He is brilliantly translating some of the most difficult of occult and philosophic and anatomical texts, including Agrippa's *Occult Philosophy*."

"How convenient," Mordecai sneered. "A good-looking good-for-nothing turns up out of nowhere, tells you a far-fetched story, and you both immediately entrust him with a task that, if he is not to be trusted, could do grievous harm to all of us. Agrippa's book is dangerous! Have you forgotten that? Do you want to be thrown into prison or burned at the stake? You have only his own word for who this ragtag fellow is. You don't know where he comes from. You don't know what he's really doing in Venice. Why is he here? He is a total stranger to us."

"You are so mean!" Miriamne flared up. "I know what you think of my visions, but you don't hear me making nasty comments about those useless smelly experiments you carry out in your nasty little laboratory, those crazy potions you cook up!"

Mordecai wheeled on his sister. "Useless? How dare you? Do I have to remind you, little sister, those smelly potions I mix have pacified mad dogs, healed snake bites, and made blind people see?"

"Really? I didn't see the blind people see. And where was that mad dog? Did you hide it somewhere in the mountains between Bologna and Florence? What about the magic fluid, with that weird dripping machine you built, that alembic, or whatever you call it? Remember how you promised us that would turn base metal into gold?" She sketched a little curtsey, as if performing on a stage. "That, dear people, was a big zero—a total failure!"

Mordecai clenched his fists. He was going to hit Miriamne. Danilo tensed, ready to spring up and grab the man's wrist.

"Children, children!" The rabbi raised his hand. "Stop quarrelling. My decision has been made. This young man is already translating other manuscripts for me. Mordecai—as of this day, you will recognize Danilo del Medigo as a member of our family. Understood?"

Mordecai's face was flushed. He bowed. "Your wish is my command." He turned to Danilo. "Welcome to our family, Danilo del Medigo. I wish you success in your efforts to assist my father and invite you to share my quarters. Sadly, I am too exhausted from my long journey to give you a welcome tour of Venice today. And there are a few matters I must attend to at once. But be assured, we will spend time together and soon. I shall show you the best sights in Venice."

"Danilo already knows Venice," Miriamne said.

"I wish to spend time with our new family member before I leave for Ferrara."

"You are leaving us again? So soon?"

"I found a merchant in Ferrara who deals some rare metals. I have ordered them from him and I must return to claim my purchase. Besides, I have business in Bologna, and possibly Rome. I shall be away for quite a while, perhaps a month or two, or even more."

"Well," Miriamne said, "that is a shame."

SCARCELY AN HOUR LATER, just after Miriamne and her father had stepped out on errands, Mordecai appeared at Danilo's work desk to invite him on a tour of Venice.

"What, now?"

"Do you have any objection?"

"Ah, no . . ."

And so together they headed awkwardly off to the gondola station at the foot of the Rialto Bridge. They sailed eastward, past the line of imposing palaces that rich Venetians had built on both sides of the Grand Canal.

Mordecai pointed. "That is the home of Veronica Libero. She is the most celebrated and famous courtesan in all of Venice and perhaps in Europe."

"A courtesan! Is she beautiful, do you think?"

Mordecai scowled. "I do not know how anyone could find a whore, even a celebrated and perfumed whore, beautiful. It is all putrescence and filth underneath, is it not? Purity, del Medigo, is a thing of the past. We are surrounded on all sides by corruption and decay. The world is rotten and it must be cleansed."

"The world has gotten complicated of late, or so it seems," Danilo said with a nod. The world had always been complicated, but each generation seemed to discover that fact, and others like it, as if for the first time.

He didn't trust Mordecai one iota, and he didn't like him. There was a secret corruption in Mordecai; Danilo wasn't sure what it was, but it was there.

"And over there, just opposite the Rialto Market, are the apartments of Pietro Aretino, the wickedest of writers," Mordecai sneered. "It is said the libertine holds orgies in his rooms, that he invites vagabonds and other trash to stay with him."

"How horrible!" Danilo said, grimacing. "I am shocked—a libertine and a wicked man? Here in Venice! I will be sure to avoid him, if perchance I run into the fellow."

"I do not know why Venice tolerates him. We should throw this sort of scum out! Better yet, he should be executed."

"Are you, by any chance, acquainted with the friars, the Dominicans and Franciscans?"

"What?" Mordecai asked. "Why would you ask that?"

"No reason."

They sat in silence awhile. But Mordecai could not remain still.

"These mansions," he said, "have been built, and are being built, by the patricians—the old families belonging to the elite merchant families of early Venice. And some of the new families too, who don't belong to the old elite. The new money wants to outshine the old money. The old families, and now the new, refer to their opulent mansions with typical snobbish Venetian understatement and irony as *ca'*, their designation for casa, or a simple little humble home. Here we have Ca' Loredan."

Mordecai cast Danilo a disdainful glance. It was clear to Danilo that Mordecai was making no attempt to hide his hatred, and he was just biding his time until he could strike. How would he strike—and when? That was the question.

Mordecai instructed the gondolier to drop them off near San Marco. They stepped onto the quay near the Piazzetta, the little square that separates the Doge's Palace from Piazza San Marco. They turned and looked outwards, towards Saint Mark's Basin. Facing them was the Island of Saint George, with its hulking monastery. And far off, lingering on the horizon, like a long strip of green ribbon, was the Lido, the seven-mile-long sandbar, which, with its little villages and market gardens and beaches, separated Venice's lagoon from the Adriatic and all the dangers and enemies that lingered out there in the open sea.

"Now, del Medigo, let us have a look at the heart of Venice — Piazza San Marco."

Mordecai glanced at Danilo as if calculating his reactions.

"On our right is the Doge's Palace; it is the center of government for the Republic. It is where the Doge has his offices, where the Senate meets, and where the Council of Ten meets; it also contains the Republic's archivers. It also has, I might add, a prison — well, two prisons — for traitors and other villains." As he referred to the prisons, Mordecai let his gaze rest on Danilo's face.

"Traitors and other villains," said Danilo, smiling at Mordecai. He let the smile linger. How could Miriamne be sister to such a rascal?

"There is a prison up under the roof. And there is another down in the basements. They are not very comfortable, I'm afraid. Something to keep in mind." Mordecai swung out his arm. "And on our left is the site for a new library."

Danilo tried to feign interest. All his senses were on alert. Mordecai was a truly nasty bit of business. Danilo was surprised at the violence and rapidity of his judgment. Was he jealous of anyone who might come between him and Miriamne? Could that be distorting all his perceptions?

"Look skyward, del Medigo." Mordecai pointed to the dome of the Duomo. "In 1204, Doge Enrico Dandolo sent those bronze horses back to Venice as part of the loot sacked from

Constantinople in the Fourth Crusade. If you look at the side of the building you will see what appears to be a post box. They are all over Venice. Venetians have named them Boche di Leone—the Lion's Mouth. On the face of each one is engraved a monstrous creature with gaping jaws carved into the stone; they look rather like lions. If you want to accuse a friend, neighbor, or stranger of a criminal or treasonable act against Venice, you need only slip a piece of paper containing the name of the culprit into a Lion's Mouth and within hours the suspect will be apprehended by order of the Council of Ten. Many traitors have walked into the dungeons, never to leave, forever stripped of their freedom, because of an accusation thrust down the gaping mouth of a Bocca di Leone. The reason this system works so well is because the accuser stands to earn himself a substantial reward."

"Interesting. In some places anyone who betrays a friend or relative to the police is considered the lowest form of human life. And to benefit from it financially would be even lower."

"Here it happens every day. It is good to watch one's back."

Mordecai turned and led Danilo back to the quay, and signaled for a gondola.

At the entry to the Grand Canal, where the Venetian Customs Service was located, Danilo was reminded of his arrival in Venice. He wanted to see deeper into Mordecai's mind and, if possible, sound out his intentions. "This is the route I traveled the day I arrived in Venice, down the Grand Canal."

Mordecai merely nodded. "There is a site at the far end of Venice the likes of which I'm sure you have never seen. And when I return from my travels, I will take you there."

"Why not now?"

"I still have to complete arrangements to get us full access to the site. It is a closely held Venetian secret."

"Now you've whetted my curiosity. How about a hint?" Danilo smiled easily. He had a fairly good idea what Mordecai was talking about—the Arsenal, Venice's shipyards and shipbuilding facility, the secret to Venice's power in the

Mediterranean: ships could be quickly built, and quickly launched, giving Venice a large, fast, flexible navy. Entry to the Arsenal was strictly forbidden to outsiders. Even hinting at entering it was dangerous. Any outsider who went inside the Arsenal, where Venice kept its greatest and most secret technologies, would be imprisoned or executed immediately. Danilo certainly did not want to go into the Arsenal. He would ask Marco what he must do.

Mordecai grinned. "No hints. Think of it this way, I'm giving you something to look forward to. I promised my father I would make you feel welcome and show you around, and I will. I am leaving tomorrow, but when I return I will wake you up at the crack of dawn and take you there."

Then Mordecai's tone changed.

"I was against you being left alone with my sister. I still am. Miriamne is the pride of our family. Her virtue is our most precious jewel. She and father are a pair of innocents. Father has his head in the clouds. But I know the ways of the world. Make no mistake about it, if you lay so much as a finger on Miriamne, I will see you dead."

MARCO WAS IN HIS usual spot, gazing across the lagoon at the island of Murano and the low silhouette of the Italian mainland. He and Danilo strolled along the embankment.

Marco turned to Danilo. "Mordecai has some dangerous friends and he also has some dangerous enemies. He is playing a double game, pretending to work for Venice but really working for one of the more dangerous factions in Venice, a very unprincipled and ambitious gang."

"What do they want?

"They say they want a more religious, less tolerant city. But they really just want power—personal power. The banker, Jeremiah, is also involved. He has lent Mordecai a substantial sum of money, and he would like to be paid back, as would others. If Mordecai offers to give you a tour of the Arsenal, well, you will have to accept. It will be dangerous, but it may allow us to trap him. If the time is ripe, and if he overreaches . . ."

"Give him enough rope and he will hang himself."

"Something like that, though it may take time, quite a bit of time."

"So, in the meantime, I just wait."

"Do as you have been doing, Danilo. And by the way, I have another assignment for you; this one should be pure pleasure."

LA BOHÈME

ONE WARM, SMOKY AUTUMN EVENING—FIRES WERE burning somewhere on the mainland and a smudge-like haze colored the sky—Danilo, following Marco's instructions, headed towards the Grand Canal and, after navigating a maze of small alleyways, found himself again playing the role of Daniel del Monte, as baptized by Veronica Libero, but this time in the salon of the famous libertine writer, Pietro Aretino.

It was a large room with a glass dome, and it overlooked the Grand Canal, just by the Rialto Bridge and opposite the Rialto Market. In style, everything was a contrast with Veronica's salon. Veronica's elegance was orderly, with everything in its place. Here, in Pietro's lair, there was profusion and disorder; people lounged on divans and chairs, food—breads, grilled meats and fish and fowl, sardines, anchovies, boiled eggs, piles of rice, tureens of thick soup, and aubergines—was set out pell-mell on a large buffet; books and objects—a map of the world, a sextant, a model galley, a profusion of candlesticks and candelabra—were piled up every which way, and paintings hung casually here and there.

Aretino stepped forward. "Daniel del Monte, now you are indeed a handsome specimen, so well turned-out. Here, let me introduce you. This creature is la Zufolina. La Zufolina is self-explanatory. What she is is what she displays, though what she displays may change from moment to moment."

The creature Aretino had introduced as la Zufolina gazed at Danilo and, still staring him in the eye, performed an excellent pageboy bow, then grinned at him as if they were the oldest of friends. Was this child flirting with him?

"Celeste Del Volpe is a model, one of the most famous, if not the most famous, in Venice. And this is Titian, you will know all about Titian."

Danilo accepted a flagon of thick brown ale. He sniffed its beautiful, frothy bouquet. This would provide a whole meal for some poor family. Tapestries hung from the walls, paintings leaned against them. Miriamne would be jealous. She was fascinated by the great artists—Leonardo, and Raphael, and Giorgione, and Carpaccio, and certainly Titian, the virtuoso of virtuosi. He wished he could tell her of the evening. He wished he could bring her here so she could experience it for herself.

Titian was in an expansive mood. He reminisced about studying with the Bellini family, and about his rivalry with Giorgione. "We influenced each other, I think. We spurred each other on, as if we were two thoroughbreds in a race. He is dead, now, alas, long dead. I miss him. It is good to have someone to cross swords with." Titian accepted a drink from la Zufolina, who bowed and whispered in a cute and insinuating way, "Maestro!" And as she withdrew, she cast a sideways glance at Danilo.

Titian explained to Danilo how he had been in difficult negotiations with Federico Gonzaga, Isabella d'Este's son, to do a favor for Charles V's right-hand man, Francisco de los Corbos. "I was trying to get a benefice for my son. An artist is not rich. An artist needs to arrange for his children." And he went on about how difficult and capricious these particular chaps were—kings, and emperors, and dukes, and their hangers-on. "Corbos was obsessed by a woman, Cornelia Malaspina, and so Federico Gonzaga wanted me to do a portrait of Cornelia, to curry favor with Corbos, and thus, indirectly, with Emperor Charles V, so that little Mantua could shelter safely, keeping its independence, under Charles V's wing. These diplomatic acrobatics can be quite complicated. We artists are at the mercy of politics!"

Celeste, who was flirting with la Zufolina, was heard to say, "Pirates have been seen just off Ostia once again, hunting for victims—and slaves!"

"Ah, pirates!" Aretino cried. "They are so bold." He turned to Danilo. "Now, I presume you know the story of the beautiful Giulia Gonzaga. I believe she is related by marriage to Isabella d'Este."

"No, I don't," said Danilo. He was eager to hear it. Anything pertaining to Isabella was of interest, since Isabella had been so much a part of his life, and above all, of his mother's life. If only he could speak to Isabella, he might learn so much!

Titian smiled, put his hand on Danilo's shoulder, and nodded. "Well then, Pietro will, I am sure, enlighten you!"

"Oh, yes, Maestro, tell us a story!" La Zufolina said, clapping. She was exquisitely androgynous, Danilo thought, and also really just a child. She glanced at him, a quick flash, as if she had read his thought. Maybe she was one of those creatures who didn't want to grow up, but hoped to just stay suspended forever between boy and girl, rather like Veronica's lovely Zarah.

Aretino rubbed his hands and came over to the window. "Well, the Grand Vizier Ibrahim Pasha—whom you will have known, Daniel, in Istanbul—was eager to obtain a prize for his beloved Sultan, Suleiman the Magnificent. And the Grand Vizier also wanted to undermine the influence of Hürrem, his only real rival in influence over Suleiman. And the best way to undermine Hürrem was to find another, even more brilliant, woman. So the Grand Vizier ordered Red Beard—Barbarossa, the pirate chief and admiral of the Ottoman fleet—to kidnap Giulia Gonzaga. Now Giulia was beautiful. And she was a widow. She was rich. And she was, unfortunately perhaps, excessively intelligent and extremely cultured. And she held a very cultural salon—Isabella d'Este in a minor key—in her castle in Fondi, near the coast. Lots of poets and scribblers and suchlike would frequent the place, a delicious little seaside retreat."

"Oh, this is exciting! Pirates! And a beautiful lady!" La Zufolina clapped again. Aretino ruffled her hair and smiled.

"One hot, sultry night in August two years ago, Barbarossa's pirates landed at Fondi. As we all know, it's on the Tyrrhenian coast halfway between Rome and Naples. Giulia was already sleeping, or perhaps bathing. The pirates stormed ashore, rampaged through the town, and assaulted her residence, a castle, but lightly fortified. Someone, however, raised the alarm. And so, helped by a single gallant knight, a part of her retinue (and possibly her lover, who knows? And a brave fellow he must have been), Giulia, who was twenty-one at the time, escaped by the skin of her teeth and in a state of considerable undress. It is said, in fact, that the gallant young knight seized her out of her bed, stark naked—or out of her bath, stark naked—and carried her off, flouncing and bouncing over his shoulder, down a back stairwell and out to the stables, and put her, bareback, on his horse, and then jumped on himself. And so they galloped off, the knight and the lady, romantically, into the night. So in fact, as I have said, according to our most reliable reports, Giulia was stark naked, or next to naked. It is healthier, some say, to sleep or bathe that way, naked, as nature intended."

La Zufolina giggled. Celeste put her arm around the girl and pulled her close. "Shush, now, you rascal!"

"Barbarossa was so annoyed that Giulia had escaped, he ravaged through Fondi and through the countryside. His men massacred everyone they found, except for perhaps some girls and boys they took as slaves and catamites. The boys, the prettier ones, they almost certainly castrated to turn into eunuchs. Everybody in Fondi and in the nearby town of Sperlonga was killed. But then the pirates failed to take the little town of Itri, which somehow managed to defend itself and drive them away. So Barbarossa and his men, covered in blood and gore, and herding the children they'd captured, got back on their ships and sailed away. And so it was that Suleiman would never know the pleasures of having the beautiful, talented—and difficult—Giulia Gonzaga serve as his slave for sex, conversation, and amusement."

"That is a dramatic tale."

"Indeed."

Titian coughed. "It does have an unfortunate coda, though."

"Oh, what was that?"

Aretino frowned. "Well, Giulia was rather vexed that the chivalrous, gallant young knight who had saved her life had seen her naked, and carried her off in that state. This was too much, apparently, for her dignity. She was, dear lady, of a rather exalted and mystical temperament. And she had, in spite of her adventurous, active sex life, a puritanical and modest side. So she had the poor man murdered."

"Thou shalt not gaze upon the goddess." Titian said, and emptied his glass. He held it out; a slender but buxom young woman with a golden see-through veil tied around her waist and black satin high-heeled mules immediately appeared at his elbow and filled it. "Princes and aristocrats are indeed capricious."

Celeste, still holding la Zufolina close, nodded. "I believe Giulia has become very religious and devout. I am told she has entered a convent. And she is turning out—so I am told—to have a talent for mysticism and complex new forms of theology, perhaps even for Protestantism. She is exchanging letters on lofty subjects with a number of priests and intellectuals."

Aretino laughed. "Giulia will get someone—one of her correspondents—burned at the stake for heresy. She has a talent for mischief. If you make a wrong move in interpreting Holy

Scripture . . ." He made a cutting motion across his neck.

"Another interesting woman!" Danilo exclaimed, and allowed the next-to-naked girl to fill his glass. There seemed to be just too many women like Hürrem and Giulia Gonzaga in the world—interesting, beautiful, and dangerous.

"Interesting! Yes! Aren't they all!" Titian said, smiling at Celeste and la Zufolina. The girl giggled, covered her mouth, glanced at Danilo, and lowered her eyes. Yes, it did seem she was flirting with him, but then she flirted with everybody.

Aretino took a quick sip from his glass. "So, that was one of Ibrahim Pasha's failed schemes. He wanted Giulia to displace Hürrem as the Sultan's favorite, but Giulia fled the coop."

"She was never snared."

Aretino sighed. "Ibrahim Pasha—poor man."

"Why poor?" Danilo asked, thinking of the man's handsome, jealous countenance.

"Perhaps you haven't heard."

"Heard?"

"He is dead, poor fellow. Strangled in his bedroom."

IBRAHIM PASHA WAS DEAD!

Danilo stood absolutely still. Did this make any difference to his own fate? No, it wouldn't make any difference at all. Hürrem was the one who had sent out the order to have him killed; given Hürrem's weakness for fixed ideas and her stubbornness, the order had undoubtedly been followed. And Hürrem had triumphed over Pasha as a rival for the Sultan's affections. She was a woman who always won.

Aretino lifted his glass and stared at the blood-red wine. "Ibrahim fought, apparently. The walls of his bedroom were coated in blood."

La Zufolina looked up at Aretino with her great, childlike, liquid eyes. "Just think! If beautiful Giulia had been captured, and had become the lover of Suleiman, the story might have had a happier ending for Ibrahim Pasha, Maestro."

Aretino shrugged. "History is like a toss of the dice—unforgiving; and the vagaries of human passion and desire are infinite, unpredictable and cruel!"

"You speak out of personal experience, Maestro," whispered Celeste with a sly, sad smile.

Aretino rolled his eyes. "Oh no, good friends, do not make me speak of that. I gave that girl everything. I nursed her when she was sick. I took her in when she was abandoned. I succored her when she was destitute! I nursed her when she again fell sick!"

"He is talking about Perina," whispered Celeste to Danilo. "Perina was married at fourteen, left her husband, and turned up on Aretino's doorstep. A slip of a girl, pale, blond, fragile, sickly. Pietro became—"

"I became infatuated, entranced, hypnotized, under a spell, hoodwinked, and blinded by Cupid, a dunce's cap and fool's cap set upon my head, a cuckold's horns for ornament."

"In short, Maestro, you were insane," said la Zufolina. "A waif will do that to a man, even to a genius such as you, Maestro."

"Yes, my waif, I was insane indeed."

Aretino groaned and turned to look out the window. Lamps were lit in the mansion opposite, reflecting on the water of the Grand Canal and on the façades of the Rialto Bridge.

Danilo listened to the tale of Aretino's woes with half an ear; he was wondering what exactly had happened to Pasha. Who stood to gain? Hürrem, of course. Who else had died, or was the assassination limited to Pasha. How would this affect the Sultan? How would it affect Saida? What could he do, if anything? He noticed that la Zufolina was watching him slyly, as if reading his thoughts. She had been doing so all evening. Did she suspect he was a spy? Another thought struck him then: was she a spy?

"Perina loved my apparent wealth; she loved the food, the wine, the warm bed, the shelter. But my old body could not satisfy her. And she understood nothing of my genius! My wit was deployed in vain! Pearls, pearls, cast upon dark waters . . . And so . . ."

"And so she ran off with a handsome young gondolier, all muscle, no brains," la Zufolina said softly; she reached up and caressed the side of Aretino's face.

"And with lots of Pietro's ducats, and silk, and brocade, and some very fine porcelain," said Celeste.

"I was a fool. Oh, when I think of her—Oh, the wretch, the evil little vixen, the cold, calculating little wench . . ."

"And then . . ." Celeste sipped from her glass, watching Aretino's expression.

He grimaced and nodded. "And then . . . Perina came back. Her lover, the handsome gondolier, had contracted the French disease, syphilis. He was rotting from within. Dying, useless, no more sex, no more jokes. La Perina left him. She returned, pale and sick, to me."

"Pietro cannot resist, he is too kind."

"Waifs . . ." whispered la Zufolina; she put her hand to Aretino's cheek and stroked his beard.

"Waifs," said Titian, glancing from Celeste to la Zufolina and back, "Dangerous creatures, waifs."

"I nursed her. She began to cough blood, she wouldn't eat. Then she seemed to recover, that sparkle returned to her eyes, and that crafty little smile, that silly, delightful laugh. Then suddenly, without warning, she died, Perina died!" Aretino's eyes were glossy with tears. "She was an evil little thing, and I . . . well . . . I . . ."

"Eros is blind, Maestro," said Celeste.

"Dear Aretino, it is late." Titian said, suppressing a yawn. He kissed la Zufolina's hand, which she, pert in her pageboy's uniform, and performing something between a mock curtsy and a bow, had extended.

"Ah, gallant lad, and lady, and child, you are all those things, Zufolina, you are the whole world in one precious petite person! And that is a wondrous thing!" Titan tousled her hair and, putting one finger under her chin, tilted her face up so he could look into her eyes.

"Do you wish a gondola, Maestro?"

"No, little one. I shall walk home. It will do me good." Titian pulled on his overcoat and turned up his collar. "Thank you, Pietro. This has been a splendid and entertaining evening, as always."

Danilo was leaving at the same time. La Zufolina leaned over and kissed him, and as she did so she pressed a small, folded piece of paper into his hand. He immediately hid it and stood back.

"It has been a great pleasure meeting you, Signor Daniel," la Zufolina said, making a courtly pageboy bow.

Danilo and Titian saluted Celeste, Pietro, la Zufolina, and the other guests and servants, then they went down the stairs together and came out in a little alley right next to the dock that gave onto the Grand Canal.

Titian looked up at the sky and sniffed the air. "It is the darkest of nights, with a smoky perfume in the air."

"Indeed," said Danilo, bowing, "a warm night and pleasant."

"So Daniel, you know Mantua. One of my best clients, as I was saying, is Federico, Duke of Mantua."

"Isabella's son."

"Yes. He is insatiable. He can be difficult, as I explained. He wants a special commissioned painting to please one of the courtiers of Charles V; he is besotted by a beautiful and difficult woman, I might add. Lust does move mountains. Federico wants more and more paintings. I'm always haggling with his ambassador here in Venice, Benedetto Agnello. Nice fellow, curious and inquisitive, and well-informed, as ambassadors must be, I suppose, but Benedetto knows nothing, I think, about art. He doesn't need to; he knows about money. And the d'Este family in Ferrara, they too are fine clients."

They walked down the little alleyway and came out onto a larger one.

"If you are headed towards Cannaregio," Titian said, glancing at Danilo, "we might as well walk along together."

"With pleasure."

They walked in silence for some time, down small, shadowy alleyways; along narrow, rippling canals; past little market gardens with wooden fences, private detached homes, and one or two building sites. The air was incredibly fresh, smelling like the countryside. Danilo took a deep breath—delicious!

Titian, gazing at a small garden plot, began to talk. "You know my first wife, Cecilia, the great love of my life, died six years ago. She was a barber's daughter from my hometown, Cadore. And just a few years ago, well six now, I signed a lease on a new house in Biri Grande, in Cannaregio, an isolated, nice district. To start again, you know. One can breathe, away from all the buzz and glamor." He waved towards the center of Venice, towards the Rialto and the Grand Canal. "From my windows on the second floor I can see the mountains of Cadore, where I was born. My second wife is from Cadore too. I adore sophisticated and complicated women, like la Zufolina, or Celeste, or Veronica Libero; sparkling with ideas. They are wonderful friends, and allies, and companions; but not to marry. I'm a simple, small-town fellow."

They walked down a narrow alley and came out into a more open space with a small canal running along one side. At one corner a lamp was burning above a tavern door, and beside the tavern was an open area with several trees and wooden tables. Titian nodded at the lamp and the hazy halo of light that surrounded it. "Venice is a city of gradations. It is a subtle place, and Venetians are subtle people, aware of nuances and of many points of view on any question. It is an ideal place for a painter—with the reflections, the mist, the fog, the drizzle, the watery light, the muffled sounds and echoes. It is all very suggestive and infinitely changeable. No two moments are alike."

Danilo nodded. "In some ways Venice is the antithesis of Istanbul, with its breezy clarity, on a point near the open sea."

"Ah, yes, Istanbul! Well, the Sultan is certainly an interesting subject. Lively intelligence, big vision of what to do and how to do it, insight and sharpness, that's the way I see him." They turned a corner and came to a wider *calle*, where, at the end, Danilo could see a quiet-looking quay and the watery glimmer of the lagoon.

Titian turned to him and smiled. "Now here we are at my little abode. There, you can see the lagoon; we are very close to the quay, and just opposite the mainland. An outside staircase, as you can see, takes us up to my quarters. And the garden, it has a nice high wall, as you can judge for yourself, so I can put out paintings to dry and nobody can see them; so it's very pleasant, quiet, and away from things. And that shack out there in the garden, I call it a pavilion, that is where I work. The light is splendid, we have plants and trees, and I am alone, as it should be, except for a model, when I need a model — Celeste, or one of the others. They are good company, among other things. And we are far away here from the fashionable world. Few come to visit, unless I ask them."

"So in order to work, you try to stay away from society," said Danilo.

"We all live in many worlds, Daniel. I've been at the Papal Court, I've courted various aristocratic families, and yet I work with my hands, like an artisan. And I know the wood carvers, the picture framers, the paint grinders, the butchers and bakers, and the printers and carpenters, as if I were a member of their guilds. I like people who work with their hands, creative people, people who make things, however simple those things might seem to be."

"And here is your refuge."

"Refuge is a good word. The domestic life is important, Daniel. And you can see, as I said, the quay is close by. I can order a boat, and send my paintings off with the greatest of ease, discreetly, no prying eyes. It costs me forty ducats a year, mind you! Come up and I'll show you!"

They climbed the staircase. "My wife is usually asleep by this time." Titian opened the door. It was sudden chaos — barking, yapping, sniffing, tails wagging. Dogs leaped up all around them. Danilo found himself licked and assaulted from all sides.

Titian laughed. "They are friendly. I have a project, a Venus. I'm going to use the pose Giorgione used way back, in his *Sleeping Venus*, which I dabbled with after he died; it needed a bit of finishing. But I shall make this version a touch bolder, the most sensual of paintings, a trifle wicked perhaps: a naked woman, life-sized, tempting us, drawing us in, and a little action in the background possibly, maybe a maid on her knees being punished, or two maids rummaging in a trunk, looking for clothes to drape the shameless Venus, and a dog. I want at least one dog in the painting. One can never have enough dogs." He rubbed the head of one of the jumping dogs and laughed. "Down, down, down! A dog represents virtue. So perhaps the dog should be snoozing. Virtue is asleep, you see, while the naked lady, barely covering her pudenda, flirts sleepily with us, arousing our lust, displaying beauty, temptation, and vice!"

"Aretino's specialties—beauty, temptation, and vice. He is an artist in that domain."

"Ah, yes, poor Aretino. Desire is a flame; after a certain age, it flickers. A man gets too old for wild girls! And Aretino has a particular fondness, as he boasts, for men. Poor Pietro, he no longer has the energy for what la Zufolina calls 'waifs'—and she is a waif too, but loyal. Aretino should have known better! Perina was delightful in a way. She pouted all the time. She displayed her discontent like a proud banner. She was a challenge. Aretino yearned to make her happy. But happiness was not in Perina's repertoire. An old man should learn. One cannot be young forever!"

A young woman appeared in a doorway. She was blond, pale, and wore nothing but a white smock, which went down to her knees. Her legs were bare and she was barefoot.

"Ah, this is Daniel, he just accompanied me back from Aretino's."

The girl, probably in her mid or late teens, smiled. "Good evening, Signor Daniel."

Danilo raised his cap and dipped his head in acknowledgement, and the young woman waved a little wave and disappeared back into the shadows, and through the door.

"Well, I suppose that is a signal that I must to bed. My little wife, she takes care of me," said Titian, putting his hand on Danilo's shoulder. "Thank you for accompanying me home. The walk is more amusing with a thoughtful companion."

At the door, he turned and said, as if it was an afterthought, "By the way, Daniel, la Zufolina is charming, adorable even, but she is not as simple as she seems."

Outside, by starlight, when he was alone, Danilo unfolded la Zufolina's note.

"Dear Daniel del Monte, I know you who you are. Fear not." Then, a series of numbers and letters separated by commas, followed by a last phrase: *"You will know to whom to deliver this note."*

DANILO MET MARCO BY the fire in their usual inn close to the Fondamento Giurati. Marco unfolded the note and glanced at the handwriting. He looked up at Danilo and smiled. "This is la Zufolina's list of who was there and whether anything of note was discussed. The numbers and letters are her shorthand, a sort of code. So you made contact with her."

"In a manner of speaking; she made contact with me. I thought at first she was flirting."

"Of course she was flirting!" Marco said with a laugh. "La Zufolina always flirts. She keeps an eye on things. She is very astute. She is what she seems and yet she isn't."

"That is . . . ambiguous."

"Or a paradox, yes, I'm not sure which. But then, la Zufolina is ambiguous, and a paradox. She likes it that way; it is her personality, and also her art."

"She is seductive—and makes people laugh."

"She puts people at ease; they trust her, so they talk. Waifs such as she are dangerous. But she is scrupulously honest, an idealist, really. Did you talk with her?"

"Not about anything important. Scarcely at all."

"You should. She has been useful to us. We are always interested in who attends Aretino's evenings, and which vagabonds or scribblers he is sheltering in his flat, and what is discussed during his soirées."

"It is a complicated menagerie, always shifting."

"Indeed, it is. Aretino and Titian have contacts all over Europe, at the highest and lowest levels, so savory tidbits often fall from their lips. Gossip is always useful. La Zufolina loves Aretino—worships him, really—and she serves him, but she also knows how to harvest what is relevant for us. By helping us, she knows she is helping to protect Aretino; as you know, he has many enemies who wish to see him dead. And he is our guest. Venice wants nothing untoward to happen to Aretino."

"So la Zufolina is, well, a sort of little alarm bell."

Marco laughed. "Well said."

Danilo nodded and smiled. Humans and their reasons were infinitely complex. Even children, even waifs, were spies and counter-spies. "I believe Titian knows."

"About la Zufolina? Alluded to it, did he?"

"Yes."

"He trusts you then."

"I think he does."

"Titian is part of our little cabal."

"Cabal?"

"People like la Zufolina, people like me, who conspire to keep Aretino safe. Titian recognized you as one of us. Now you are a member too."

"I am honored, I suppose." Danilo said with a frown. What a layered world of complications he had entered!

"Tonight I would like you to attend on Veronica Libero. Veronica will explain." Marco put his hand on Danilo's shoulder. "You are very good at this, you know."

Marco pulled up his collar and pulled down his hat, and slouched out into the night, leaving Danilo to finish his glass of wine and a plate of bread and cheese. But Danilo was uneasy. Surely he had done nothing to deserve Marco's praise. *Good at this?* Hardly. Was Marco just trying to pacify him? And who, after all, was Danilo to trust?

21

HYGIENE

"THERE YOU ARE, DANIEL. HOW PLEASED I AM TO SEE you."

Veronica shook Danilo's hand as if they were two gentlemen meeting on the riva degli Schiavoni. Her hair was tied up, giving the effect of a turban. Her neck was long, graceful. The neckline of her dress plunged to a bodice of embroidered black silk, tightly crisscrossed with scarlet laces, revealing her slender waist. And her skirt, slit up the side, swayed and swished each time she moved, revealing her shapely legs, gleaming in black silk. "I'm afraid the gentlemen who are our guests tonight are a bit late. I shall be giving some of my new young women a few lessons while we wait. I don't like to waste time. You can listen in, if you wish. Secretly, of course."

Danilo bowed. "That might be instructive," he said.

"Indeed, it might," she said with a laugh, handing him a glass of water. "Our guests tonight are one Frenchman who served in Istanbul and one Turkish merchant. I am not sure whether they will speak French or Turkish, and I am not sure what you might learn—but Zarah and I shall try to steer them your way."

Danilo drank the water, and glanced around the room—paintings, and tapestries, and gilded frames, and marble floors, and all that was most exquisite and expensive. And best of all, since it was a wet and chilly night, a fire brightly burning.

Danilo slipped into his little hideaway behind the wall so as not to be seen by the other young women. Only Veronica and Zarah, their bodyguard Julian, and the little maid knew he was in the building, why he was in the building, and what he was doing. "The less each person knows, and the fewer people who know, the better," Veronica had whispered as she closed the invisible door behind him.

He sat down on the stool and listened. Veronica was giving some of the new young women lessons in how to converse with and seduce men. Danilo couldn't resist peeking through the hole.

Veronica was striding up and down the room in front of four or five young women like a schoolmaster. Zarah was standing close, like an assistant.

"Gentlemen do not always bathe; a woman must. Above all, we professionals must." Veronica paused. "Filth is for friars, saints, and self-flagellants. For us, it is essential to be clean and perfumed. Zarah will give any of you who feel you need it detailed instructions on personal hygiene. You already know the basics."

Several of the girls asked questions and received detailed answers. Some of the questions, and certainly some of the answers, were about things Danilo had never even dreamed of, involving special perfumes and soaps, where and how to use them, which scents should go where and when, and how often to wash one's intimate parts; as well as how to deal with the rhythms of the moon and those special periods when a woman was "indisposed." Saida had told him that harem girls had a great deal of shared experience and knowledge of the science of the intimate workings of hygiene and the female body. It was clear Veronica and Zarah did too. He wondered if there was a secret worldwide guild of women who traded in such craft.

Veronica was holding up a bar of soap. "Julian makes sure the bathrooms are clean and ready with hot and cold water and soap, and warm towels whenever you need them. You know what you should take particular care of, and how and where to do it. If not, Zarah or I can instruct you. When in doubt, come to us. You can ask Julian too, for anything at any time, even if he is a man. He has heard and seen everything. No question, however naive, however embarrassing, is stupid. None of us were born sophisticated. Understood?"

"Yes, Veronica," they answered in chorus.

"Clothes must be immaculate. But you already know that. Signora Diana will look after any soiled linen, any problem with your clothes, or the bed clothes. If Diana is not nearby, ask Julian to find her or, if it's urgent, ask me or Zarah."

"Yes, Veronica," they repeated.

She laughed. "You are a fine and talented lot, you are doing well, and you will do well. We have already talked about illness. Watch out for any signs or symptoms upon the client. You know what to look for. Just be as diplomatic as you can, and call for Julian or me. We will look after it. Syphilis is unforgiving. This is your life and your health we are talking about. So be careful."

"Yes, Veronica!"

"Now, let us talk about the soul, about conversation. Charm and seduction and pleasure come not only from the body, but from the mind. Above all, you must be a good listener. Each man is, essentially, interested in himself. Each man lives in his own little world, or big world. So you must ask yourself: What does he fear? What does he want? What is he interested in? What are his passions—horses, ships, falconry, his family, the work of the Senate, crops on his estate, commerce, money-changing, painting, art, sculpture, or even literature? We must not judge. We must ask questions—discreet, teasing, pleasant, and flattering questions—but we must not be curious."

One girl raised her hand. She was a dark-skinned beauty, Arab or perhaps Spanish, with sleek black hair combed down around a perfectly symmetrical oval face. "How do we know what he is interested in?"

"A very good question, Cleo." Veronica paused and went up to the girl and straightened a frill on her bodice. "Before you meet the clients, I shall try to give you a thumbnail sketch of each man's background and interests, and tell you which subjects to mention, and which to avoid. Who is he? What experiences has he had? How does he conceive of himself—is he a warrior, is he bluff and rough, is he smooth and subtle, is he cultured or simple, is he quick or slow? How does he see himself? Is he a wise elder statesman or a young man on the make? You must be sensitive to the slightest shifts in his mood. If you perceive limits, do not trespass where he does not want you to go."

"But what do we do if we see warning signs?"

"If you perceive the slightest unease, veer off into lightness, or distract him by offering him a glass of wine, or a sweet. Or fiddle with your hair and clothes or ask him if he can help you lace or unlace something. Create a distraction. Men like to be useful and busy. That way they don't have to think."

"May I tell the Senator that?"

Veronica laughed. "Darling, you may tell the Senator anything. He is one of us. He knows all our tricks—and then some. And he is a good friend. Now, as for expressions, men can be charmed by certain attitudes you strike, expressions you display. For instance, you can incline your face downwards and glance up at him from under fluttering eyelashes, but do not exaggerate. Most men, the intelligent ones, do not appreciate a simpering idiot. Taken with moderation, this submissive stance will indicate you are yielding to him; that you recognize his grandeur, his superiority, his strength; that you admire him. Zarah, please demonstrate."

Zarah demonstrated, running through a whole range of submissive looks, from the subtle and the sublime to the ridiculous. Danilo had to jam his fist into his mouth to stop laughing.

"Pooh!" said one of the girls. They all laughed, and Veronica laughed with them.

"Sometimes, a more skeptical and arrogant expression is useful," Veronica said, swinging around and putting her hand on Zarah's shoulder.

"Veronica, teach us how to be arrogant!" Cleo exclaimed. She clapped and the others laughed.

"Raise your chin, half-close your eyes, smile slightly, and gaze down your nose straight at the man, as if you are short-sighted and can't really see him. As if he is a speck of dust, hardly visible. Perhaps lick your lips, let your tongue be glimpsed, just glimpsed, between your lips, its tip just touching your teeth perhaps, so that skepticism is mingled with desire and teasing lasciviousness. Skepticism, complicity, but not insolence, is the effect we are looking for here—you are teasing him very gently, you are indicating that you understand him, you are challenging but not *really* challenging him, you are only inviting him to explore his theme with you a little further."

Zarah and Cleo tried the arrogant glance out on each other, and then they all broke out in laughter.

Veronica waited until they had calmed down. "Men, like all humans, yearn to be understood, but do not want to be judged. That is one reason people go to confession. We are, often, like confessors. We brush away guilt and shame. But we never impose penance."

Zarah giggled and covered her mouth, feigning bashful shame.

Veronica glanced at the girl, circled around her, and put her hands on Zarah's shoulders, "Unless perchance, as young Zarah here has suggested, the gentleman wishes to be humiliated in some subtle or not-so-subtle way, mentally or physically. If he requires such special treatment and if you are puzzled as to what to do, then refer your perplexities to me or to Zarah, though in most cases you will probably figure it out yourself, and in most cases too, the man will help you. Such men, those who have special tastes, if they are not young and inexperienced, are usually fairly frank and forthcoming in explaining what they want. In addition to such . . . particular tastes, such penances, men do also want to be forgiven for everything, even for being alive; that is, except for the truly arrogant and monstrous men who already think they are perfect. The greatest form of forgiveness for a man is a woman's smile. Men will do anything for that."

"And we should move like dancers!" said Zarah, imitating Veronica's schoolmarm tone and sketching out a dance step.

"Absolutely, my imp, move gracefully, we must be objects of aesthetic delight. Do not unveil too much too quickly, unless desire has been aroused to a fever pitch. Then, perhaps, ripping off your clothes, or his clothes, is best."

"Oh, oh, oh!"

Veronica's smile was full of indulgence. "But try not to damage them. Our clothes are expensive, and so undoubtedly are his. Undressing the man slowly can be very exciting."

"What about . . . ?" Cleo gestured towards her pubis.

"Yes, Cleo, some men prefer soft, smooth, hairless skin, like the ancient Greeks or the Ottomans, and, as you know, we accommodate that taste. Obsessions vary. Some men, in some moods, will prefer languorous and sinuous lines, and a yielding, almost maternal embrace, or an earthy, carnal surrender. Others will prefer an androgynous look, a pert, playful glance, a teasing, flirtatious demeanor, a boyish slenderness, a quick sense of irony, and so on. Zarah can demonstrate. Well, you have seen her perform, so we probably don't need to do that now. There are infinite gradations in taste and preference and mood. So, that is it. Julian has just waved at me. I believe our guests are about to arrive. Take your positions, ladies, let the show begin!"

Danilo sat behind the wall for the next five hours wishing he had another glass of water; it got quite hot in the dark, confined, dusty space. Beneath the fragrance of perfume, it smelled of stucco, paint, and varnish. He followed a number of conversations, but heard nothing of great import.

Veronica took the Frenchman to bed in the "special room," and Danilo shuffled carefully along the narrow corridor behind the wall and listened. They spoke mostly in French and sometimes in Italian. They did whatever they were doing slowly. Danilo yawned. Actually doing it, for the man or the woman, might be quite arousing, but listening to it was definitely not thrilling. Danilo closed his eyes. On second thought, if he used a bit of imagination and envisaged the scene, it could be quite titillating. For Veronica, of course, this was work, possibly hard work. Most of what they talked about, interestingly enough, was art. François I of France was a collector and a connoisseur. He was building a whole slew of new chateaux—castles—in the Loire valley, apparently buildings of an extraordinary elegance and a unique new design. And he was filling his buildings with works of art. He had also established a national library and made it obligatory to deposit a copy of each book published in France in that library.

"That's a brilliant idea," Veronica said, and she asked how the King arranged for that to be done, in practice. "How do you make sure all the books are registered? In what order do you register them?"

The Frenchman gave a rather technical answer about registering, collecting, and cataloguing books, and about the dangers books presented. "Printing creates a whole range of new possibilities and new problems. It becomes more difficult to censor and control ideas, and for monarchs and priests that is a challenge." And then he gave more details on how the French book registration system worked.

There was no peephole here, but Danilo understood from the dialogue that followed that Veronica undressed the Frenchman and he insisted on undressing her. Then there were lots of amorous noises and Veronica cried out, "Yes, yes, yes!" and almost immediately, the Frenchman listed all the Italian artists that François I had hired, many of whom, including Leonardo da Vinci, Andrea del Sarto, and Benvenuto Cellini, he had enticed to France. "Money draws them," the Frenchman said, "and François spends an immense amount of money on artists, on art, on building, and on architects."

This was, in fact, interesting information from the spying point of view. What had Veronica said about seduction? She said that you must know what the man is interested in, what his passions are, and how he conceives of himself. Venice certainly had lots of artists, architects, and craftsmen of immense talent, as well as a lot of money, so perhaps one way to influence François I—or Charles V—was to use art. Titian was in negotiations with François I and would probably be creating a portrait on commission. And both he and Charles V were known to be interested in Titian's work.

Danilo pursed his lips. This was a new perspective. Art could be used in the service of influencing foreign governments.

THE FRENCHMAN LEFT AN hour before dawn. Danilo emerged from his hiding place. Veronica was dressed in a simple chemise, her hair was all undone, and she was barefoot. She looked ravishing. "Perhaps, Danilo, you'd like a glass of wine. I could use one."

She poured two glasses and they sat down. "I rather doubt much of that was useful," she said, taking a deep drink.

"I'm not so sure," said Danilo. Should he share his insight with her, that Titian and the others could be instruments of diplomacy, that they could be used to bring pressure upon or to seduce a king or an emperor? Perhaps not. Even if she was a fellow spy, he shouldn't share; he shouldn't trust anyone.

Veronica looked thoughtful. Now that they were sitting across from each other, he could see that her eyes were tired. She leaned forward. "Art and diplomacy and influence—all these little bits and pieces of information we pick up, I suppose we never know which may actually be of use. It's like poetry— you see a child sneezing, or a bird gathering twigs for its nest, or mist rising off a beach among the foam and scattered pebbles, and you store it away, and then, suddenly, you say, 'Yes, that's it, that's exactly the bit I need!'"

So she had understood—seemingly unconnected things could in future prove connected, and useful—and Danilo remembered that Veronica was, among many other things, a well-known poet, with a reputation that went far beyond Venice.

Zarah appeared, barefoot and in a chemise that went to her ankles. She was rubbing her eyes with her knuckles. She bowed at Danilo in her gallant pageboy style, and then turned to Veronica. "You have an important afternoon today! Come to bed! I am sorry, Signor Daniel, but Veronica is being a very bad girl. If she doesn't come straight to bed I must punish her!"

Danilo stood.

Veronica laughed and stood too. She kissed Danilo on the cheek. "I must to bed. My master calls."

2 2

BLISS

AVING FINISHED HIS TRANSLATION OF AGRIPPA'S *Occult Philosophy*, Danilo began working on other books, sometimes just providing Rabbi Hazan with a summary of the contents so the rabbi could sell the book to collectors and other book dealers.

Working for Rabbi Hazan, Danilo became a regular visitor to Daniel Bomberg's printing shop. He liked the machinery, he loved the smell of ink and metal and grease and paper, and he befriended the typographers, who set the books and worked the press. They were real craftsmen, doing real things, like carpenters who make a beautiful desk or chair, or painters and sculptors who take raw material and turn it into something entirely new.

Danilo had shown Mantegna's portrait of Grazia to Miriamne, and she had gazed at it for a long time. "Mantegna was a great painter," she said, "And your mother is very beautiful."

"Yes, she was. Mantegna was court painter to the Gonzagas in Mantua, and he painted it when Grazia was seventeen.

Lord Pirro Gonzaga, a cousin to Isabella d'Este, gave it to my mother. When she was alive, she kept it with her always."

"You must miss your mother terribly."

"I do."

"And she had such a brilliant and romantic life; she wrote books, and she had a great passionate love affair! I think that is beautiful." Miriamne turned to him and put her hand on his shoulder, and then turned again to the portrait.

"Yes. It is moving, it is real." Danilo gazed at the portrait. It did capture his mother—the light in her eyes, the intelligent expression, alive to everything, to every nuance. And he thought of Pirro, and how Pirro had worshipped Grazia, and how, with the death of Grazia, Pirro's life must have been shattered. Danilo sighed. He must, when he freed himself of his present entanglements with the Venetian spy service, go to Pirro and explain everything—Grazia's passion, and how she had died, and how she had, after all, left behind a son: Danilo, Pirro Gonzaga's son.

ONE EVENING, RABBI HAZAN lifted his glass of wine, paused, and looked thoughtful. "We don't write that many books in Venice, Danilo, but we publish a great many. We are, I think, perhaps the leaders in Europe. We publish Greek books, Latin books, Italian books, Hebrew books, and so on. Perhaps Amsterdam is close to us—or ahead. I don't know."

"And why is that, Papa?" Miriamne asked, as she piled another slice of grilled sole, along with fried rice and artichokes, onto Danilo's plate.

"Because it's business. And the Venetians adore business. A book is an object, like a table or a vase, a bag of spice, a bushel of grain. You can store it, you can market it, and you can see it. And then . . ."

"Yes?"

"Venetians are exuberant and have a great deal of personality, but displaying too much of oneself in Venice is considered in bad taste. It is somehow against the ethos of the Republic."

Danilo picked up his thought. "And writing a book means you express your individuality, you display yourself—and that is, in some ways, non-Venetian. Aretino can write because he's not Venetian, whereas if you are Titian, a painter, you are putting other people on display—foreign monarchs or anonymous models, not essentially yourself. And when Venetians do go wild, it is often behind a mask, as during carnival. They are most themselves when they are not themselves, when they are disguised."

"Indeed," said the rabbi. "That is indeed so."

They talked on, pleasantly. Then the conversation took a darker turn. Rabbi Hazan had been terribly shocked by Bruno Scavo's attack on Miriamne. He had thanked Danilo profusely for saving Miriamne and Isaac and the children, and he had talked to the Venetian authorities about the incident. He now seemed to Danilo to be more apprehensive than he had been before.

"Our people are afraid, Danilo, and they are right to be afraid," Rabbi Hazan said, glancing at Miriamne. "When people are afraid they look for a savior, a messiah."

"Or they look for scapegoats." Miriamne said as she topped up Danilo's glass. Danilo had noticed that just a hint of a new darkness had entered her soul since the incident with Brother Bruno Scavo.

"Yes, that too." Rabbi Hazan said, and sighed. "People will look for scapegoats. You now know that better than anyone, my daughter. But our people also looked for hope, for deliverance; they looked for a messiah, a Jewish messiah, or a messenger."

Miriamne filled her father's glass.

"After the Jews were chased out of the Spanish Empire, in the space of a few days despair took over. It seemed like the end of days had come. The Apocalypse had come!"

"We have been chased out of everywhere," said Miriamne. She counted off the places on her fingers. "England, France, Spain . . ." She smiled, but now there was a shadow in her smile.

"When there is a need for a messiah, then perhaps a messiah or a false prophet will appear. People, even Jews, become hysterical and welcome fakes, charlatans, and false messiahs. Have you heard of David Reubeni?"

"I remember talk," Danilo said. "Even in Istanbul people whispered about him. But I don't know much about him." In fact, he knew quite a bit about David Reubeni. His mother's brother, Uncle Jehiel, had followed the false messiah, becoming a mad fanatic. And realizing his error too late, Jehiel had ended up burned alive by the Portuguese in a public square in the city of Tavira.

"Reubeni was the Jew who claimed he came from a kingdom in Africa somewhere, from the lost tribes of Israel, and he wanted to raise an army to go fight the infidels—by which he meant the Muslims—and liberate Jerusalem. He wanted Christians and Jews to unite in this fight. He wanted arms for his kingdom, whatever it was, in Africa somewhere. He even met the Pope."

"But he was a fraud." Miriamne was staring at a flickering candle. "He faked documents. And he was caught doing it."

"Yes, Miriamne, but he was also powerful—a small, dark little man, but with fire in his veins. An artist of deception. He even convinced a fellow called Diogo Pires that he should convert to Judaism. Diogo circumcised himself to show he was serious."

"That is painful when you are an adult. It is painful anytime," Miriamne said, and grinned.

"My amazing daughter is both devout and occasionally irreverent, and often too bold, Danilo. She takes risks, and sometimes she shouldn't."

"Being alive is a risk, Papa." She looked up and made a charming face. She was still her funny self, ironic and amused, but since the episode with Brother Salvo, there was, Danilo sensed, an undercurrent of vulnerability.

"Pires changed his name to Solomon. He was a powerful speaker. He got to meet Charles V. Charles listened to him for two hours, but apparently was not impressed. Solomon was turned over to the Inquisition and burned to death. The same thing perhaps happened to David Reubeni, or maybe he just faded away. His life, in any case, ended in obscurity."

"It is dangerous being a messiah, or claiming to be what you are not," said Danilo, aware of how, in many ways, the statement applied to him. David dei Rossi, Daniel del Monte, Danilo del Medigo; wherever he was, he was continually claiming to be what he wasn't.

"Exile can drive people mad." The rabbi said as he stared at the table. "And fear can drive people mad."

"Power can drive people mad too, Papa."

"Yes, power too, I suppose," the rabbi said, considering, "if you have too much of it."

When Miriamne carried out the plates and cutlery and left them, Rabbi Hazan sat silent, tapping the tabletop with the fingers of one hand, as if plucking out a melody or contemplating a difficult decision. He looked steadily at Danilo. "I want to thank you once again for saving Miriamne."

"She was—she is—a heroine. Very calm. Brave."

"Yes, yes, she is." The rabbi looked down, and then looked up, staring straight into Danilo's eyes. "You are often out at night."

Danilo held the rabbi's gaze. "Yes, sir."

"May I ask why?"

"It would be best not to, sir."

"You do not wear the yellow cap."

"I do not."

"May I ask why?"

"It would be best not to, sir."

"I see." The rabbi kept staring at Danilo and tapping his fingers on the table. From below, Miriamne's voice could be heard. She was laughing. "Thank you, Mika!"

"It is nothing dishonest, sir. It is not gambling."

"No, not like her brother, then. Not like Mordecai."

"No, not like Mordecai."

The rabbi's gaze was far away, no longer seeing Danilo. "We Jews must do many things to survive—sometimes we must make compromises, even with ourselves. Venice has eyes everywhere."

"I am only too aware."

"Whatever you are doing, I trust it will not hurt Miriamne. She has been hurt enough. I see it in her eyes. If someone hurts her, whoever it is, I will never forgive them."

2 3

FIREWORKS

D ANILO WOKE WITH A START. HE WAS IN LOVE WITH
Miriamne. He realized it the moment he opened his
eyes.

The room was full of sunlight. He gazed at the drawings
of alchemical instruments on the wall opposite and at the
water jug. His heart was racing. Yes, he had been in love with
Miriamne for weeks, and he was sure she was in love with him.
Yes. Miriamne was in love, and so was he.

There was a wonderful symmetry about it—to come back
to the very place where he was born and to find a new life here.
He could make a life in Venice with Miriamne. He would have
to find some way of making a real living, he would have to
assuage Rabbi Hazan's doubts. He would have to negotiate
things with Marco. While being a spy, and while still being
under threat from the Men in Black, could he even dare to ask
for Miriamne's hand?

And then, Mordecai hated him and wanted to marry
Miriamne to Jeremiah or at least someone rich. Mordecai,

according to Marco, was involved in some tricky and shady political business, and he owed Jeremiah, and possibly other people, lots of money. But maybe Mordecai was just defending the honor of his sister, as would any good brother. Then again, perhaps there was more to his hostility . . . Maybe he had other motives. If Mordecai really wanted to get rid of him, then Danilo must proceed with caution; he must find the right moment to talk to Miriamne, and then to Rabbi Hazan. He leaped out of bed. He was in love! And so was Miriamne!

FIREWORKS BLAZED ABOVE SAINT Mark's Basin, great fountains of gold, yellow, and orange rising up and blossoming above a flotilla of boats — galleys and great round ships with their high forecastles and masts of sails, and fleets of gondolas. Jews had been permitted to stay out this special night to watch the spectacle of Venetian concord and Venetian power.

"Oh, that is grand," said Miriamne, gazing up, the lights sparkling in her eyes. She held Jessica by the hand, and Danilo had his hand on Jacob's shoulder.

Next to them stood Old Uncle Isaac, his blind eyes turned towards the bright night sky. "And what is happening now, Master David?"

Danilo described the yellow and orange light splashing up in the sky, and the torches everywhere, reflecting on the walls of the monastery on Saint George's Island opposite them, and on the halls and sheds of the Customs House on the point of Dorsoduro. "The light is everywhere, Uncle Isaac," he said, "on the water, on the gondolas, on the spars and masts of the great ships, and on the rows of oars of the great galleys, and it is reflecting on the water like little flashing serpents."

"That is quite poetic," said Miriamne. "You are a poet."

"Not quite." Danilo said, and grinned. He felt a bit foolish. The spectacle and the large crowd and the naval display — the might of Venice — had aroused in him a whole herd of childlike feelings and enthusiasms. There was the wonderful time his mother Grazia took him through the gardens by the side of the Tiber. Foolish, ignorant child that he was, he was excited in the horrible days of the Sack of Rome. Then, too, he was thrilled when they first boarded the doomed *Hesperion* in the Roman port of Ostia. Well, he was only ten years old—what did he understand? Then there was the first innocent thrill and magic sense of power when he first learned to ride and throw the lance and show off his prowess before all the other young cadets in Istanbul.

He turned towards Miriamne. Her eyes were glowing with excitement and happiness. This, Danilo thought, was the perfect time to declare his love, to ask for her hand . . . Yes, he would do it. He would do it now!

At that moment, only a few yards away, a beautiful woman in a gorgeously cut, revealing dress, accompanied by what looked like an extremely handsome young pageboy, inadvertently caught Danilo's eye. Just as inadvertently, she smiled, as did the stunning pageboy with the dark flashing eyes.

Danilo automatically smiled back and bowed his head in salutation. He immediately realized his mistake, as did Veronica, who spun quickly away, leaned down, and kissed Zarah on the crown of her head. Zarah, equally quick, turned her back on Danilo and followed Veronica's lead. They disappeared into the crowd. But it was too late.

Miriamne's smile had tightened. "And who is your gorgeous friend? To judge by her plumage, she is an exotic bird indeed." There was a hurt edge in Miriamne's voice.

Danilo put his arm around her waist—the first time he had dared do such a thing in public—and let his chin rest against her hair. "It is nothing, but it is also something . . . something I must not talk about."

Miriamne looked up at him, and with one finger traced a line along his cheek. "Oh, my beautiful, chivalrous warrior prince, I wonder who you are, so full of mystery and so full of secrets!" There was a catch in her voice. "All those evenings you spend far from us, out in the big world, beyond the walls of the Ghetto, all these sudden disappearances, and, so I have heard, all those times you saunter around Venice without the sign of the Jew upon you—no yellow cap, no sign you are one of us." She looked into his eyes. "Are you going to deny us, Danilo? Will you betray and abandon us?"

"What, what are you saying?" Uncle Isaac was distracted from the exploding noise of the fireworks and the shouts of admiration from the crowd. "What did you say about deny and abandon?"

"We were wondering whether we should abandon this show," said Miriamne. "This is a big crowd. It makes me uneasy."

"Who was that beautiful lady with the sweet pageboy?" asked Jessica. Her eyes, bright with excitement, reflected the parade of torches. "I should like one day to wear a dress like that!"

Miriamne knelt down to kiss the little girl. "You have a beautiful dress too, and you are even more beautiful than the beautiful lady."

They stayed a little longer, watching the processions and the flotilla, and the crowd with all the various costumes of the people of Venice—the tradesmen in their somber outfits, the senators and patricians in their black caps and robes, the society women in puffed-out shoulders and plunging necklines and platform shoes. But the mood was broken. Whenever Danilo glanced at Miriamne, she turned away; when he reached for her arm, she refused to give it; she spoke to Isaac and the children as if Danilo were not there. He kept as close to her as he could, but he did not want to insist, and he could not explain— above all not here, not now.

On the way home, heading through the milling crowds, Danilo again reached out to take Miriamne's hand, but she withdrew it.

When they arrived back at the Ghetto, Vincenzo opened the gate for them and asked if they had enjoyed the evening. Miriamne said, in an even voice, "It was very interesting."

Vincenzo glanced at Danilo. Danilo nodded, and tried to smile. "Uncle Isaac and the children had a wonderful time," he said.

And they entered the Ghetto in silence. Even Uncle Isaac and the children realized the mood had changed; something had happened that they didn't understand. All they knew was that for some reason, Miriamne, always so happy and gay, was angry with Danilo, and that being angry with Danilo made her sad. Although she didn't intend to, she communicated this sadness to all of them.

After delivering the children back to their mother and leaving Isaac at his front door, Miriamne walked silently with Danilo across the Campo. It was a warm night. Many people were outside, preferring to breathe the night air rather than remain in their small, ill-lit rooms.

"You know that woman."

"Yes, I do."

"She is a courtesan, I believe, one of the most famous, perhaps the most famous in Venice."

"Yes, she is."

"How do you know her? Why do you know her?" Miriamne stopped, swung around, and looked him straight in the eye.

Danilo was on the point of blurting it all out. He almost told Miriamne everything; he wanted to tell her all. But Marco had warned him against sharing anything, even the smallest detail, with the people he loved. "The best way to protect them, the *only* way to protect them, Danilo, is to make sure they know nothing. If they know what you are doing, they may, in all innocence, reveal something that will jeopardize you, and them, and everything we are working for. It could be a death sentence— even worse—for Rabbi Hazan and for Miriamne. This is not a threat; it is a fact. The harm would not come from Venice. It would come from others. And it would hit all of us. There are hostile spies among us, Danilo. Do be careful, very careful!"

Danilo swallowed. He wanted to seize Miriamne by the waist and lift her up, kiss her, hold her, caress her, and tell her everything. He took a deep breath. "I can't explain, Miriamne. I wish I could, but I can't." He tried to take her arm, but she shoved him away. "It is important that you forget that whole incident. Forget you saw her."

Miriamne's eyes brimmed with light. Her glance hardened. "I shall. I shall forget everything!"

And she strode away across the Campo, skirts swirling.

Danilo had just deeply wounded the person he most loved in the world. He had betrayed the trust of the woman he loved, the woman with whom he wanted to spend the rest of his life. For the first time, the full import of his actions hit him.

How could this be? It suddenly occurred to him then that he had not thought of Saida in many days. Could a man love two women? Could an honest man love two women? But he did not love Saida, not really. Not anymore. Or it was a different kind of love, a fading tenderness, a nostalgia. He stood in the crowded Campo, wondering what to do. People were talking excitedly. Some said they could see the fireworks from the highest windows in their buildings. Four children danced in a circle, holding hands. Their mother, a conservative, severely dressed young woman, tried to calm them. "No dancing, children—stop, stop!"

Danilo felt a hand on his shoulder. He reached for his dagger and turned.

Mordecai.

The man's grin seemed positively diabolical. "We meet again. I am delighted to be back! And tomorrow, you and I shall take a tour!"

Danilo wanted to say, "Go to hell," but he didn't dare. He knew he could not refuse Mordecai's offer. He must risk it—and whatever Mordecai wanted to do would be a risk, of that he was certain.

"So, del Medigo, what have you been up to while I have been away?"

"I have been working for your father."

"Translating his forbidden books? That is dangerous."

"Everything is dangerous." Danilo answered, and tried to smile.

Mordecai grinned and snapped his fingers. "One whispered word, del Medigo, and off to a dungeon you go!"

THAT NIGHT, DANILO DID not sleep. He lay on a thin bedroll against the wall in Mordecai's room, while Mordecai occupied the bed. Danilo stared at the ceiling and then at the small barred window. The night would never end.

He must talk to Miriamne, must explain to her, without putting her in danger, that knowing Veronica Libero was merely part of the work he was doing, work that was essential if he was to protect her and her family. And his father, far away, alone, vulnerable and exposed, in Istanbul under the watchful eyes of the Sultan and Hürrem.

He couldn't think of these things now. He would concentrate on something else. He had begun to translate for Rabbi Hazan a recent astronomical treatise on the celestial spheres, which explained in detail how the earth, which is a globe, stands immobile at the center of the universe while all the other components of the universe, it is said—the moon, the sun, the wandering planets, and the distant stars—rotate on crystalline celestial spheres, turning around the earth. The mathematical model—really, it was a geometric model, consisting of sets of circles—explained all the phenomena observed in the heavens.

The diagrams, consisting of cycles, and cycles circling on cycles, and cycles circling on the cycles that were circling on the cycles, were complicated and gave Danilo a headache. He had to understand the diagrams, though, and these damned cycles on cycles, if he was going to understand the French text and translate it accurately into Italian. The book, apparently, was a valuable collector's item, and represented the most advanced astronomical research. It was difficult enough that the language of the music of the spheres was . . . was . . . Danilo fell asleep.

24

PARADISE LOST

"**G**ET UP, DEL MEDIGO, IT IS TIME TO GO SIGHTSEEING."
Mordecai stood above him, already dressed,
staring down with that sneer that pretended to be
a smile. Danilo rubbed his eyes and struggled to his feet.

"No time to waste, del Medigo. You will find this day very
interesting."

Danilo splashed water on his face and hurriedly dressed.
Mordecai stood watching his every move.

They went downstairs. Miriamne was nowhere to be
seen. The building seemed deadly quiet, a ghost of itself. "Is
Miriamne . . . ?"

"Out," said Mordecai.

In a daze, Danilo allowed himself to be led by Mordecai
out of the building and across the Campo, through the *sotoportego*, and across the bridge. Oddly, Vincenzo was nowhere to
be seen.

They came out onto a walkway beside a rippling canal. Both
wore their yellow caps. An old woman standing in a doorway

spat at their feet as they passed and hissed, "Bloodsucker scum!"

Mordecai grinned. "Hatred is invigorating, is it not?"

Danilo said nothing. There was nothing at all invigorating about hatred. He had already seen too much of it—Bruno Scavo, the mob that attacked Miriamne, the campaign heading towards Baghdad, the pirates who murdered his mother. And now, the hatred in Mordecai's eyes.

As they approached the Rialto Bridge, the alleyways and walkways became crowded. Barges, their oars rising and falling in a hypnotic rhythm, and dozens of brightly colored gondolas packed the waterway. The bridge thronged with people. The smells and the sounds of the market were overpowering— mussels, octopus, raw fresh fish, and all the vendors hawking their wares; buyers haggling and the carters pushing their carts and shouting, "Make way! Make way!" The greenish-blue water of the Grand Canal sparkled, dancing with brilliant morning light.

Danilo, darkness in his heart, shielded his eyes and took a deep breath: What must Miriamne be feeling now? What did she think of him? Surely, she must realize he loved her! Surely, she must understand that whatever he did was for her good, that whatever he did he did honestly, that he would never betray her, that he cared only for her, surely . . . ?

He turned to Mordecai, both of them walking fast, taking long strides, dodging and weaving among the crowd, zigzagging, slipping past the stalls vendors had set up everywhere.

"Where are we going exactly?"

"You are interested in technology, are you not? You were fascinated by all those Ottoman cannons you talked about."

"I like to know how things work." Danilo said, and tightened his lips. Mordecai was odious and dangerous, but Danilo *was* interested in technology. Reading books in Rabbi Hazan's library, and eavesdropping on conversations in Veronica Libero's soirées, and listening to intellectuals and politicians hold forth in Pietro Aretino's salon had awaked in him an interest not only in politics and the maneuverings of the great and less-great powers, but also a fascination for all the deadly instruments of those nations and empires and dukedoms—the cannons, the ships, the wagons, the cavalry, the compasses, the astrolabes, the swords and pikes and crossbows, the harquebuses, and all the paraphernalia and equipment of power, raw power, real power. And behind the instruments of war lurked that other vital sinew of power—finance, money, gold and silver, and credit. How did you pay for 100,000 or 200,000 men? How did you feed and clothe and equip them?

"And soon you will see how things work!"

"I can hardly wait." Danilo responded. He clenched his jaw and walked quickly to keep up with the man. Why was he bothering to conceal the hostility between them, to pretend friendship and brotherhood? There was something excessive in Mordecai's hostility. It was not merely a brother defending his sister's honor, and it was not merely a brother who wanted his sister to marry a rich old man; there was something visceral. "But surely you can tell me where we're going."

He knew already where they were going, but he was hoping that by some miracle of misunderstanding he was wrong, that they were headed someplace innocent and . . .

"To the Arsenal."

Danilo quickened his pace. There must be a way out of this. Going into the Arsenal, into the top-secret heavily guarded shipyard, if that was truly where they were going, was suicidal. Anyone who tried to steal the Arsenal's secrets was executed, usually after lengthy sessions of torture.

Marco had told him there were reasons to go along with Mordecai. "There are complicated games being played here, Danilo, and to a certain extent they are beyond us." And he added that, if Mordecai proposed anything, Danilo was to let him take him wherever he would . . . even into the Arsenal, even if going into the shipyard might be equivalent to suicide.

They headed inland, away from the Grand Canal, and came to *le Mercerie*, the main shopping street, a narrow walkway crowded with shops and thronging with jostling buyers and sellers. From there they strode under the clock tower and came out onto Piazza San Marco, where just in front of them, the famous *Campanile*, with all its bells, soared into the sky. To their left was the low, cowering mass of San Marco's Cathedral, and just beyond it that glittering, cream-colored, lattice-like wedding cake, the strangely ethereal Doge's Palace. "Beautiful, is it not, this Venice of ours?" Mordecai asked, and glanced sideways at Danilo.

"It's not ours; we Jews are here on sufferance."

"You are right." Mordecai said, and grinned. "We Jews are never at home. Nowhere is home. Strange, isn't it, that a people obsessed as we are by the land, the Holy Land—the sacred places, the mountains, the deserts and towns and all those ancient hills (and we know the names of all those places, we have them engraved in our hearts)—is it not strange that we are condemned to wander the earth, and nowhere, or almost nowhere, are we allowed to own the land, or till the soil, or purchase the houses we live in?"

Danilo's stomach tightened. The intense beauty of the magnificent autumn day, with a bright blue sky and a brisk, balmy breeze that caressed the skin and tingled the appetites, made his anger at himself, and his sadness for himself and for Miriamne, even more acute. He had already been thrust into exile, inner and outer exile, and he had a terrible feeling, a premonition, that things were ending; his life had just changed—or was about to change—forever. Somehow and for some reason, he was convinced he would never again see Miriamne. He shook the thought away.

They strode across the Piazzetta and out onto the riva degli Schiavoni. Close to the buildings and along the quays were market stalls, all doing a brisk business, with hawkers touting their wares, selling meat, dried fish, fresh fruit, and vegetables to a noisy, multicolored throng of shoppers.

It was here, last night—just twelve hours ago and yet it seemed eons—that Danilo had been watching the fireworks and standing next to Miriamne as she pressed against him. He was about to declare his love, to ask for her hand . . . And now here he was, separated from her perhaps forever, in anguish in the bright sunlight, walking along with a man who behind his smiles and bonhomie most certainly meant him harm.

Mordecai pulled Danilo into a passageway. He looked around. "It's best if we take off our caps." Danilo wanted to ask why, but he decided not to. In any case, he hated the damned yellow cap; it was a stigma, a sign of servitude and exile. They took off their caps and stowed them away. Now they were no longer Jews, just two rather smart-looking young gentlemen.

"Let's go," Mordecai said, and gave Danilo a little push.

THE GATES TO THE Arsenal rose up before them, a big arch over a waterway that led into the shipyards. Glimpsed through the arch, Danilo could see the huge basin of water where new ships—long galleys, light galleys, great galleys, and round ships—built in the dry docks that ringed the basin had already been launched and, floating there, were being fitted out with rigging and sail and deck superstructures. Guards were stationed at the entry, and the walls of the Arsenal soared above them, impregnable, and studded with watchtowers.

"We will not be allowed to enter," Danilo said. He looked around. None of the buildings outside the Arsenal or close to it were tall enough to provide a view over its walls. The heart of Venice's power was indeed well protected, its shipbuilding secrets essential to the survival of the Republic.

"Oh, don't you worry, del Medigo!"

Something was definitely not right; the man was so eager, and so sure of himself. That meant he had planned it all. But Danilo couldn't openly challenge and insult his host, whose room he slept in, the brother of Miriamne, the son of his benefactor. And then there was Marco's instruction: Do whatever he wants you to do.

"Well, that is splendid then."

Mordecai slapped him on the back. "Wonderful!"

"I am sure this will be most instructive," Danilo said, in order to say something.

Mordecai favored Danilo with a wolfish smile.

Danilo forced himself to grin back. The man should play the villain in some play. How could such a character be Miriamne's brother?

"Let us enjoy ourselves!" Mordecai said, as he strode forward to the gates. He approached a guard, smiled, and held out a folded slip of paper sealed with wax.

The guard called a colleague. Together they broke the seal, opened the document, and read it. One of the guards called over another. The three men stared at the document. They turned their backs on Danilo and Mordecai and walked away, apparently arguing. Then one of the guards came back, and saluted.

"Gentlemen, you may enter!"

THEY PASSED UNDER THE gate, and Mordecai grinned and waved, as if he owned the place. "The holiest of holies. Isn't it splendid?"

And in fact it was. In front of them stretched a vast, placid body of water, enclosed and protected by the high walls; this was the basin of the Arsenal. Ships of various kinds, already afloat, were lined up—long slender galleys, larger robust galleys, and a few round ships with more elaborate and higher riggings and sails, higher decks, and higher stern and poop. All these vessels floating on the sparkling water were being completed and rigged. Workers clambered over the decks, doing the finishing work. Hammering, sawing, and shouts echoed. Small boats scurried among the ships, carrying men and supplies and equipment. The edges of the basin were lined with large open-faced hangers, some of them with dry docks containing the skeletons of ships in various stages of construction. Smoke and sparks rose from flaming forges. Mordecai turned to Danilo. "Did you know? In a single day they can build a whole ship and launch it into the water. It's top secret! The high walls surround the whole vast structure, so no one can see how the ships are built so quickly. No houses or buildings are allowed to be built high enough to look over the walls."

"How interesting," Danilo replied. And it was. The Arsenal was a fascinating, vast installation, perhaps the largest single manufacturing site in Europe, the continent's biggest, most efficient shipyard. It was legendary.

"Do you know the etymology of Arsenal?"

Danilo shook his head, though he did.

"It comes from the Arabic *dar as-sina'ah*, or workshop.

"Very interesting."

"This is all part of a plan," Mordecai was saying. "The Arsenal belongs to the government, to the Republic. The ships here are built by the government, and the great merchant convoys are owned by the government and escorted by government galleys, and the private merchants rent a ship or space in a ship in a convoy."

Danilo cleared his throat. "So," he said, still straining for civility, "traveling in convoys, the merchants are protected against pirates, against raids by other countries, and even against Ottoman warships?"

"Yes."

"Convoys of merchant ships accompanied by warships — that's a very good idea," Danilo said. "And many of the merchantmen are designed to defend themselves too, aren't they?"

Mordecai cast a quick, suspicious glance at Danilo. "Yes, that's right." Mordecai turned away, and added, "And then there are the smells and the sounds — it's not exactly a quiet place."

In fact, Danilo's ears were ringing with the sound of saws sawing and the bang, bang, bang of hammers and tongs; the heavy, hollow echoes of loads of timber being shifted; the squeal of a ship being moved in a dry dock; the hollering of men from the rigging of one of the ships; the shouts of men dragging something heavy; and the splash of oars. It was deafening. The smells, too — pitch, tar, and hemp; timber, resin, and wood shavings; charcoal and wood burning; heated metal from the forges; even the smell of baked bread and roasting meat. "It's like a special, exotic perfume," Danilo exclaimed.

Mordecai smiled, obviously very pleased with himself. "Dante Alighieri, the poet from Florence, came here a little over 200 years ago."

"Hmm," said Danilo. This too he knew; he could even quote the lines. But it was best to let Mordecai talk.

Mordecai stared out over the water at the more distant workshops. "Dante used images from what he saw in the Arsenal—the smells and the noise—to create his image of the Eighth Circle of Hell, the 'Evil Ditches.' It must have been the endless rhythm of work that impressed him, the heat, the smells, the clamor, and the shouting of workers and foremen. There was nothing like it anywhere else at the time." Mordecai recited:

> *As in the Arsenal of the Venetians*
> *Boils in winter the tenacious pitch*
> *To smear their unsound vessels over again*
> *For sail they cannot; and instead thereof*
> *One makes his vessel new, and one recaulks*
> *The ribs of that which many a voyage has made*
> *One hammers at the prow, one at the stern*
> *This one makes oars and that one cordage twists*
> *Another mends the mainsail and the mizzen.*

"Impressive," Danilo muttered, nodding.

They walked along the edge of the basin. Danilo noticed the forges burning bright, molten metal. It was dangerous, working in a forge.

"See those puffs of black smoke? That's the foundry that casts the metal to shape small parts, like those footrests for the oarsmen, and the anchors, and the chains, and the prows. That's where that poor fellow Gaudi lost his life. A cruel death—covered in molten metal, burned to death—it must have been painful."

Danilo started but said nothing. Giovanni Gaudi was the spy he had uncovered by listening to Signor Muharrem describe the man to the Milanese gentleman in Veronica's salon! Danilo had pieced that description together with some things Muharrem had said when he was making love to young Zarah. And it had led to the man's death. He had died in agony, consumed by flame. And Danilo had killed him.

"Strange it should happen to such an experienced worker. The world is full of strange events, is it not?"

"Indeed." Danilo could picture it; he had pictured it often. He just had to accept that. But did Mordecai know about his role? And if he did, how did he know? Was Mordecai a spy too?

Mordecai turned and grinned at Danilo. "A dreadful accident. Just imagine—one of the most experienced workmen, a foreman, made a mistake, and he was sprayed with molten metal. So careless . . ."

"Yes, strange . . ."

"Indeed! Strange how fate works, is it not?" Mordecai asked as he grinned at Danilo again.

Danilo turned away and glanced over the water. A galley was being outfitted as they spoke.

"Hundreds of workers," Mordecai said, "each specialized in a separate task, each working on a part of the ship, and so with all the parts pre-cut and prepared, and stored in the right place, the Arsenal can rebuild a whole Venetian fleet in a matter of weeks."

Danilo tried to concentrate on anything but the image of Gaudi scalded to death. The poor man had probably betrayed Venice just to feed his family, to look after his sick wife and sick daughter. Danilo turned away from that painful thought, and tried instead to envisage the whole building process: the ribs of the ship put together as a skeleton, the planks of the hull added, then hemp soaked in pine tar to caulk the seams and seal the hull. Once the hull was watertight and prepared, the ship was launched into the basin, where parts of the superstructure and the rigging were added.

"The hemp is used for caulking the seams of the hulls and for making rope. You know, del Medigo, the Arsenal makes its own rope, its own masts, its own iron, its own chains and anchors, its own oars. A whole ship is put together here, just like that!" He snapped his fingers. "Teams of workers lay down the keel, they put up the ribs, they attach the timbers, they prepare the canvas and sails, and they make and install all the auxiliary materials."

"So everything is self-contained, right here."

"Some of the materials are highly flammable and they too have to be kept secure; and of course, the skills and techniques are the most advanced, probably, in the world, and they have to be protected."

Danilo stopped, turned, and looked at Mordecai.

"What have you been doing all these weeks, Mordecai?"

Mordecai just gazed into the distance over the great basin. "The lagoon gives Venice time to react, because it is impossible to attack Venice from the land. And it is difficult for enemy ships to navigate safely across the shallow lagoon, because only Venetians know the safe channels and where the dangerous sandbars are."

"What were you doing all this time?"

"What I do or don't do is none of your concern." Mordecai said, and slapped Danilo on the shoulder. "Let us live in the present, shall we? Early in the morning, what is lowered into the first dock at the end of this walkway is simply a bare hull. And what sails out at sunset is a galley, fully equipped and ready for the open sea."

Danilo held the man's gaze. Yes, there was indeed something wolfish and predatory about the fellow's grin.

"There is even a bakery."

"A bakery?" Danilo pretended to be curious. "Why a bakery in a shipyard?"

"It makes the biscuits the sailors will eat at sea. It's a special kind of hardtack that never gets stale and doesn't rot."

"Hard on the teeth, perhaps."

"I have saved the best part for last. Come, follow me."

They walked towards the naval architecture office. That was the holy of holies, the place where plans for new warships and galleys were drawn up. That was where the most vital and newest secrets were held.

Mordecai led Danilo towards a slim tower at the end of the walkway and up a winding staircase. At the top in a large room behind a large desk, buried in a sea of drawings, sat a man sketching what appeared to be architectural plans.

Mordecai dug into a deep pocket and presented the man with a bright-red satin book bag. "This book is a gift for you from my father." He handed the man the bag and introduced him as Signor Bressan.

Danilo was braced for whatever would come next. But abruptly, after apologizing for interrupting the designer's work, Mordecai hustled Danilo out the door and back down the narrow staircase.

When they were back on the walkway, he explained. "The man you just met is the most important naval architect in all of Venice. He is creating a new ship design for the Venetians in order for their fleet to deal more effectively with the Ottoman Navy." Mordecai leaned against the walkway's balustrade. "It is essential that these naval developments remain secret. If the Ottomans learn of the new Venetian ships, they will have time to develop counter-measures."

Mordecai was silent as they walked back towards the entrance to the Arsenal. They passed by the two guards who had inspected them on the way in and exited the shipyard.

Danilo took a deep breath. Suddenly he felt safe. They had seen the Arsenal; now they had left it. He was out of danger. Perhaps he had misjudged Mordecai. "This has been a very instructive tour. Thank you."

"That is not all you have to thank me for," Mordecai said, as he turned and smiled.

"Oh?" Danilo said, evenly. The air suddenly felt cold.

"I am about to do you a much greater service. I am about to save your life."

"Save my life? From whom?"

"From me."

Danilo stiffened. This was not a joke.

"The Venetians are confident they have Bressan hidden away from prying eyes in the high reaches of the Arsenal tower. But this afternoon that secrecy was breached when an Ottoman spy gained access to the tower and made off with copies of the new plans."

"Did that happen?" Danilo raised his eyebrows, feigning naiveté. "I didn't see any plans being stolen. I didn't steal any plans. I don't have any plans on me."

"It makes no difference what you saw, or whether you have plans on you or not." Mordecai moved up close, bringing his face to within inches of Danilo's. "What matters is what the Venetians can be made to believe. I have witnesses who saw you enter Bressan's studio, and who saw you leave. And who will swear you made off with vital documents."

"Ah."

"The Venetians—and you know this—see a spy in every foreigner. And they know spies steal plans. There is no greater enemy for Venice, no greater threat to Venice and to the whole of Christendom, than the Ottoman Empire, than Suleiman the Magnificent and his Muslim hordes."

Danilo's instincts had been right all along. The man was going to blackmail him.

Mordecai licked his lips. "Do you know what Venetians do to spies? They hang them between two pillars in Piazza San Marco. They draw and quarter them, but only after extensive torture, weeks, months of torture. That is the fate I am saving you from."

Danilo gazed straight into Mordecai's dark eyes. "What about you? Aren't you putting yourself in danger? After all, you're the one who took me into the Arsenal, you're the one who explained the technology, you're the one who introduced me to Signor Bressan."

"True, true!" Mordecai answered, and smiled a self-satisfied smile, infinitely pleased with himself.

"Then, aren't you endangering yourself?"

"My friend, I have proven, again and again, my loyalty to the Venetians. I have powerful friends. I have protection. And I had a gift to deliver to Signor Bressan. Whereas you are a stranger, and you have served the Ottoman Sultan, and you have fought in his army, and you travel under a false name, and you have lied to everyone."

"You know why I . . ."

"No, I don't know. What I do know," he said, pausing, "is that you are a spy."

"I am not a spy!"

Danilo realized he was equivocating; he *was* a spy, but he was a spy *for* Venice, not against her.

Mordecai laughed. "Don't deny it. And don't ask for pity. I am, in fact, being very generous—I am giving you a chance to escape with your life."

"So—our visit to the Arsenal was a trap, an ambush." Danilo was furious. He took a deep breath. He was tempted to give Mordecai a lesson in manners. He could certainly kill the man with his bare hands, no need for a dagger. "Why are you doing this?"

"As I suspected from the very beginning, you are a liar and a fraud! I don't know who you are, but I do know you are not who you pretend to be. You are not Danilo del Medigo."

"Is that so?"

"That is so." Mordecai paused again, for effect. "The real Danilo del Medigo died at sea with his mother, Grazia dei Rossi, while escaping the Sack of Rome in 1527."

"Where did you hear that?"

"I've just been in Mantua. I went there to talk to Lady Isabella d'Este."

"And what did she say?"

"She said that Danilo del Medigo died when he was ten years old. She had the information from the Venetian ambassador to the Ottoman Court in Istanbul."

"And where did the ambassador get his information?"

"From the same place Venetians get all their information! Their spies."

"Then why don't you just denounce me and be done with it?"

"Because if the Venetians discover that we Jews have been harboring an Ottoman spy in the Ghetto, then many will suffer. In particular, Miriamne and my father will suffer. Everybody you know will be under suspicion, including me. But, unlike my father and Miriamne, I have protection at the very highest level; nothing can touch me. Your very presence, as a fraud and a spy, endangers my family and even the whole Ghetto. So I am telling you, gather up your possessions and be gone before the Ghetto doors are sealed for the night."

Another look into Mordecai's dark, steely eyes convinced Danilo that arguing would be useless. If he tried to defend himself, he would just create more questions, more problems. "Very well! I will do as you say. I will leave tomorrow."

"Not tomorrow! Today! Tonight! Leave behind no trace that you were ever known to us. And if you take my advice you will board a ship for Istanbul. There you can face the man you claim is your father and ask him who you are. Ships set sail every morning from the San Marco dock. If you are not on one of those by the tolling of the *Marangona*, I will turn you over to the Venetians as a spy. They will torture you and they will hang you, and you will have nobody to blame but yourself."

Danilo bowed, held Mordecai's contemptuous gaze a moment, then turned on his heel and headed off down the riva degli Schiavoni.

"And be warned!" Mordecai's voice followed him. "Not one word of this to Miriamne! If you speak to her, I will have you dead within the hour!"

IN ORDER TO AVOID meeting and compromising Rabbi Hazan and Miriamne, Danilo didn't return to the Ghetto. He wandered aimlessly in the city, trying to think what to do. He sat down on a bench and watched sea gulls swirl around in the wake of a barge that was headed across the lagoon towards the Lido. He ate — though he had no appetite — in a small inn tucked in an out-of-the-way corner of the Castello district. What could he do? What should he do? If he left Venice, he would betray Miriamne and the rabbi. If he stayed in Venice, he would put Miriamne and the rabbi in danger. If he returned to Istanbul, he would face death — and, worse, he would expose his father, and possibly even Saida, to the full wrath of Hürrem and her killers. Then too, if the Sultan knew he was a spy for Venice, the revenge and punishment would be terrible and would spare no one. After exploring all possible alternatives, he finally decided he must submit. He must leave Venice. First, he must talk to Marco. If anyone could discover a way out of this labyrinth it would be Marco. Danilo paid his bill, got up, and headed back to what, until a few hours ago, had seemed like home. When he got to the entrance to the Ghetto, he greeted Vincenzo. "I must speak to our mutual friend. It's urgent. Is that possible?"

"I shall see," said Vincenzo, narrowing his eyes. "I'm not sure."

"Thank you." Danilo nodded, went through the *sotoportego*, and crossed the Campo. Several people saluted him. "Hello, David! Beautiful day! Beautiful evening, David!"

Old Isaac was sitting in the sun, and hearing David's name, he beckoned. Danilo went over and sat on the stone bench next to the old man.

Isaac laid his hand on Danilo's thigh. "You are a good man, David," he whispered, leaning close. Isaac smelled like an old man — the urine, the moldy clothes, the dried sweat, the loneliness.

"Thank you, Uncle Isaac."

"This is something I shouldn't know, David, but an old man hears things."

"Yes, I suppose he does," said Danilo. What new horrible revelation was to come?

· 252 ·

"An old man is a useless thing, and often people forget an old man is there. An old man is invisible, David. I cannot see, and I am not seen. An old man is a thing no one sees."

"You are not invisible to me, you are not invisible to Miriamne and Jessica and Jacob—they love you."

"Ach, ach, ach," the old man mimed a mixture of a cough and a spasm of denial. With a sideways brush of his hand, he waved the very idea of love away.

"They do love you." Danilo took the old man's hand, dry and bony and cold; the cold of old flesh, dead and not yet dead.

"It is all well and fine to be loved, but . . ." Isaac turned his blind eyes to Danilo. It almost seemed as if he could see. "Miriamne was crying this morning. I don't believe she slept a wink last night."

"Ah."

"Miriamne is an angel, David. She never cries, but never. I heard Rebecca ask her, I heard her say, 'What is wrong, Miriamne? You look like a ghost. Your eyes are all red.' And Miriamne, when she answered, sniffled, and there were sobs in her voice, David, sobs! I have never heard Miriamne sniffle! Never! Not even when she has a cold! You talked about love, David. Well . . ." Isaac coughed. "You know, Miriamne loves . . . She loves . . . David . . . She is in love. David. You understand an old man when he speaks to you from his heart, David?"

"Yes, thank you, Uncle Isaac. I do understand."

"Good, I am not entirely a useless thing then, and you have been very kind, you and Miriamne and the children, taking me on our expeditions—last night, all those fireworks. I felt I saw them through your eyes, David. You and Miriamne have given me new life, David, new life. Go now, and do good works! An old man will sit here in the sun and wait for evening. It will come soon enough. Our covenant with God is divine, David." Isaac patted Danilo's sleeve. "Love," he sighed, "love is divine."

2 5

BETRAYAL

IRIAMNE TURNED TOWARDS HIM, SETTING ASIDE THE amulet she'd been working on. "Well, here he is — our prince charming! He charms even the greatest of Venetian charmers!" Her tone was light, but her eyes were red; she was paler than usual, and tense. Then her tone changed. "You look glum."

"It has been a long day. Mordecai showed me some interesting sights. He is a very good guide." Danilo didn't mention the Arsenal, though he could still hear the hammering and sawing and grinding, still smell the tar, the hot metal from the forges, the timber shavings. It was overwhelming. The sensations filled the dreadful void in his heart.

Miriamne stood. "Here, have some warm fish broth, and some fine bread, just baked an hour ago!"

Danilo sat and ate while Miriamne watched. He smiled at her. This is what life should be like! And he thought, as he smiled, that in her generosity and love she had forgiven him for the night before, that she trusted him, that their life together was still possible, and that, tragically, he was about to betray her and abandon her; his smile was a lie, his words were lies.

"I finished four amulets today, and I even found time to read some Boccaccio."

"Naughty girl," he said with a smile, "reading Boccaccio!"

"It is a classic." She said, blinking at him and feigning a pout. "And as you know, written in the very best Italian. I wish, every day, to learn something new. You are so erudite, I feel I must continually improve myself to be worthy of your friendship. I don't want you to be bored with me. If I have to compete for your attentions with women such as Veronica Libero, well, then I really will have to shine, won't I?"

"Ridiculous! You are perfect just as you are! I could never, ever, be bored with you, not for an instant. Veronica Libero cannot hold a candle to you!" In fact, Miriamne knew Boccaccio and Dante almost by heart. She had read Castiglione's *The Book of the Courtier*, and Machiavelli's *The Prince*. She had the same passion for culture that he remembered in his mother. Miriamne would have shone at Aretino's, even among the wittiest and most erudite company. La Zufolina would circle around her. Celeste would love her. Titian would adore her!

He gave her his best and warmest smile. Inwardly he grimaced. His face had become a carnival mask, everything about him was false.

"So I am not so naive after all, my dear, disabused warrior?"

"You are elegance and sophistication itself!"

"You are indeed a diplomat. Your education in the harem was excellent. Or perhaps Veronica has taught you all the suave arts of seduction."

"My greatest, my best teacher is you, dearest Miriamne."

Her color had returned. She was looking at him with brightly shining eyes and her usual intense gaze. "Tomorrow—if you have time, Danilo—we could take Jessica and Jacob to see the Doge's Palace, and perhaps the frescoes and paintings by Carpaccio in the School of Saint Giorgio degli Schiavoni. They are letting the public in to look at the paintings, all day. I know the doorman there, and he knows all about the paintings and can tell delightful stories about Carpaccio!"

"That is a wonderful idea." Danilo managed to smile; the falsity burned in his heart. That particular tomorrow would never come. And yet he yearned that it would. Jessica and Jacob had become like his own children, and Miriamne was for them a second mother. Danilo realized that he had begun to long for a family—a family with Miriamne. But right now such an idea was impossible.

He dipped the bread into the soup.

"Are you going to see the printer tomorrow, too?" Miriamne asked. She poured him some more wine.

"I might." Again, a lie. "I'm going to ask him about the new edition your father wanted to see. Bomberg is eccentric, but he is a true artist. His work is unique."

"Will you be looking at the new edition of the Hebrew Bible? Father can't wait to see the new volumes. Perhaps we can come with you, Jessica and Jacob and I. It would be wonderful for the children to see how a book is made."

Danilo gazed at Miriamne. Her hair, free of the hairnet, tumbled down around her shoulders and caught the lamplight in a tangle of shining and sparkling black, and her skin—her shoulders and her collarbone—shone like gold. Her chemise and bodice, as always, were impeccable, freshly washed. She was smiling at him with total trust, and just a touch of amusement.

And he was about to betray her, and betray her father, by abandoning them, just as he had caused his mother to die, just as he had abandoned Judah, and just as he had abandoned Saida.

But, to protect them, he must betray them.

"Danilo, you seem worried, preoccupied."

"No, I'm just tired. I shall be my old self tomorrow!"

She put her hand on his forehead. Her palm was cool and smooth, a balm to his soul. Her eyes shone. "I don't want you to catch a fever, my brave warrior friend."

"No, no, I'm absolutely fine, dear Miriamne."

She withdrew her hand and allowed her gaze to linger. "Good. Prince charming must be in splendid form when we do our tour tomorrow. Jessica and Jacob do consider you their knight in shining armor, you know."

Danilo looked down. "I'm glad. I'm honored."

"I must run to attend to Claudia and Jessica and Jacob. I suppose Mordecai will be coming in later."

"He said he had errands to run."

"Well, sleep tight. I'll see you tomorrow." She touched the side of his cheek. "Don't be sad. We'll have a wonderful time tomorrow."

He waited until he heard her exit the building, closing the door behind her. He was tempted to rush down, follow her into the Campo, embrace her, and confess everything. But the risk was too great, not only for him, but for her and her family. He went to Mordecai's room; he lay down on the bed. He stared at the ceiling and at the drawings of alchemical instruments and alchemic formulae. He almost dozed off. But then he forced himself to get up. Tonight there would be no dreamless sleep; there would be no sleep at all. Tomorrow there would be no breakfast with Miriamne, no romp through the city, no viewing the paintings of Carpaccio. There would be no stopping to eat in a little food stall.

He packed his mother's book—*The Secret Book of Grazia dei Rossi*—into his carpetbag. He wrapped Mantegna's portrait of Grazia around his waist. He stuffed all his clothes into the carpetbag. He went to Miriamne's workroom and gathered up all his papers, all the notes he had made on the books he had been translating, all the summaries he had written, so that not a single compromising trace of his presence would remain and potentially endanger Miriamne or Rabbi Hazan. He looked around the room to see if there was any sign he had ever been there. Just the quill and the inkpot remained on the little desk where he had worked, close to Miriamne, all these months.

He went back to his room—Mordecai's room—and checked. No trace of Danilo del Medigo remained. He tiptoed down the narrow staircase, carefully opened the door onto the Campo, and stepped out into the warm autumn evening. There was no sign of Miriamne; she must still be with Claudia and the children. A breeze stirred the leaves of the trees. The smells of the Ghetto—he had become so used to them that he hardly noticed them anymore—seemed sharp: the smell of freshly baked bread, the smell of grilled fish and lamb, and the bittersweet odor of the dyes and washing materials used by the tailors and seamstresses. Old Isaac was out, sitting talking with his friend Abel. A baby was crying somewhere. A man was drawing water from one of the wells. A few women were sitting gossiping under one of the trees. Danilo walked into the *sotoportego* through which he had come so many months ago. He remembered his first glimpse of Miriamne in the shadowy dusk, welcoming him, a stranger, to their Passover Seder. His coming had been foretold in a vision, she said. His coming was destiny. Perhaps she was right—perhaps some things were destined to happen; perhaps some meetings just had to take place. It was fate, as his mother used to say.

Vincenzo was still on guard. "Our mutual friend will be at the second usual place," he said, "and he would like to talk to you now, if possible."

"Good, thank you, Vincenzo."

"Also, I am to tell you, David, that some old enemies of yours have been seen in Venice."

Danilo nodded. One more problem—at least the Men in Black were a simple problem. He merely had to kill them before they killed him.

Vincenzo glanced at the carpetbag. "Are you going on a trip? Just between us, sir, it helps if I know what is what. That way I can best be of help."

"I do believe I am, Vincenzo."

"Well, good luck, sir. It has been a pleasure knowing you, and I am sure we shall meet again soon. And I presume I did not see you tonight. Nor did you see me."

"IS THERE A WAY we can neutralize this threat?" Danilo gazed at Marco. "I want to stay here. If I go, I am betraying Miriamne and Rabbi Hazan and I am betraying you too." They were in a tiny interior courtyard, with no windows, and only a stone bench for ornament.

Marco shook his head sadly and sat down on the bench. "Ah, my dear fellow, don't worry about me. This Mordecai is playing a dangerous game, I think, but he is right, in a way. You are in danger. I wish I could protect you and make the threat go away but unfortunately at this moment I can't. Mordecai has powerful allies. There are different factions fighting right now, in the Council of Ten, and in the Senate. And there is great pressure upon us here in Venice to introduce an Inquisition. We don't want an Inquisition. But the pressure is increasing. And the probability of war with the Sultan is also increasing. Anybody who seems to have compromised the security of the Arsenal will not receive the benefit of any doubt. And, unfortunately, our political protector, our patron, the Senator, has been called away from Venice. And for the moment even his situation is, let us say, delicate. He too has enemies. So, it would be better for your friends — for Rabbi Hazan and for Signorina Miriamne — if you were to disappear, and leave no trace."

"I shall do so then."

"Where will you go?"

Danilo hesitated.

"You've trusted me so far, Danilo," Marco smiled, "and I've trusted you. Honor among thieves, or spies, something like that."

"It isn't that, or it isn't just that. I think I've only just now made up my mind about where to go."

"And? Where will you go?"

"To Isabella d'Este in Mantua. To find my father, Pirro Gonzaga, and prove that I am the person I say I am. Isabella knew my mother well and she knew me when I was a boy — before the Sack of Rome."

"Well, I am in no doubt about your identity. And, as of now,

I no longer have any objections to your going to Mantua and to Isabella. As for Mordecai, as I said, he has powerful friends. And by luring you into the Arsenal, he has revealed his hand—and the hands of some of his confederates. That, for us, may be useful, and when we can act, we will."

"Good, I suppose." Danilo was both annoyed and relieved. He was a mere tool, and expendable, but there was a larger scheme of things, which might bring about a reversal of fortune.

"I have heard some other things about Mordecai. As you know, he is close to a rather reactionary, very conservative moneylender. A man who is rich, but, how shall I put it, not very kind to women—Jeremiah. He is a polished, intelligent fellow, but he does have a few rather violent vices—in particular as regards to women. I understand Mordecai is pushing a certain marriage . . . ?"

"Miriamne will not marry Jeremiah. She knows what sort of man he is."

"I see. Well, perhaps there are ways to nudge things in the right direction, without revealing ourselves or being too heavy-handed. In any case, I shall keep an eye on them all. I will do what I can to protect Rabbi Hazan and Miriamne from Mordecai's foolishness and Miriamne from her unfortunate suitor."

"Thank you."

"Mordecai has been flirting with fire, in more ways than one. He will come to a bad end." Marco looked at him sharply. "But I didn't say that and you didn't hear it."

"Quite," said Danilo. "Perfect. And there is another little point: Vincenzo mentioned that some—ah—enemies of mine have been seen in Venice."

"That is true. Some gentlemen belonging to the Sultan's Men in Black have been spotted in the city. Two of them. They have been making inquiries about you. So be careful, I would hate to lose you. Venice would hate to lose you."

"I'd hate to lose me too."

Marco laughed and put his hand on Danilo's shoulder. "Find

yourself one of the lantern boys and get on one of the barges heading across the lagoon to Chioggia. From there you can catch a barge heading up the Po to Mantua."

"Good. Yes, I shall do that."

"I have one question, Danilo: how will you earn your keep? What will you do?"

"Ah!" Danilo scratched his head. The only thing he had trained for was war, throwing a lance, managing a dagger, stabbing a man in the heart, galloping full speed against enemies. "I don't know. I have a bit of money, I speak languages. And . . ."

"And you trained for war." Marco gazed at him. "You are a warrior, a killer, a tactician."

"Yes, I trained for war."

"Well, there are mercenary armies—Charles V, and François I, and the Papacy, and . . ."

"I suppose I must put my life in the hands of fate."

"Yes, I suppose you must." Marco shrugged. "What will be, will be."

Danilo nodded and stood up. Was that what he would become—a mercenary? How could he return to Venice and present himself to Miriamne—or to Rabbi Hazan—covered in blood and as a sword for hire?

Marco got to his feet. "Good luck! If while you are in Mantua someone should quote to you—rather out of the blue—a few phrases from Dante, it will mean the person works with me and you can trust that person. That way, perhaps, if you are gone for some time, we shall find a way to stay in touch. I would very much like to continue our work together—even when you are not in Venice."

"Yes. I would too." Danilo bowed. How much he had changed in a few months!

"Good! The lines from Dante are these: *'Here it was, also, that I saw a nation of souls, lost, far more lost than existed above . . .'* Can you remember that?"

"I can remember that."

"Good luck," Marco said, shaking his hand. "I hope you find what—and who—you are looking for."

Danilo lifted his carpetbag, nodded goodbye, and went back the way he had come, again a wandering exile but now, at least, with a direction and a purpose—to find a way to survive, and to find his blood father, Pirro Gonzaga.

THE FUGITIVE

2 6

THE BOY WITH
THE TORCH

ANILO HESITATED AT A CROSSROADS — ALLEYWAYS LED off in three directions. The moon had not yet shown itself, the only lights were dim shimmerings coming from second-story windows. Which way should he go? He had to find a barge or boat of some kind that was heading towards Chioggia and then up the Po River towards Mantua, and he had to watch his back. Even with the Grand Vizier dead, Hürrem's death order certainly stood, and the two Men in Black who had been seen in Venice were certainly under her orders and coming after him.

Ahead, loitering at a corner, stood a young lad holding a torch. Danilo had seen him before. Occasionally, the lad had lit Danilo's way on dark and foggy nights back from Veronica Libero's mansion, or Aretino's.

"Toto, how are you this fine evening?"

"Feeling perky, sir."

"Perky?"

"Yes, sir, perky. Do you need a light, sir?"

"I do. How much?"

"Depends on where you are going, sir."

"Of course. How silly of me. I need to catch a barge for Chioggia, or for the Po. I'm heading for Mantua. I don't even know if there is such a barge."

"There might just be such a barge, sir, a barge with bales of cloth, silk, and cotton, and spices too, and I think some glass goods, made in Murano, best quality, leaving in about half an hour, sir, about when the bells chime eleven. They will drop in at Chioggia, pick up a few passengers and merchandise, and continue up the Po, and then I think up the Mincio, right to Mantua. They might possibly have room for a gentleman traveling alone, with only his carpetbag for company."

"Well, my lad . . . lead on!"

"Are you a Jew, sir?"

"Why do you ask?"

"The last several times I guided you it was back to the Ghetto, though you weren't wearing the yellow cap, so I was in considerable uncertainty, sir, as to the true situation."

"Yes, Toto. I am a Jew." Danilo had considered, for an instant, showing Toto his special pass, which allowed him to be out at night, and which freed him from wearing the yellow cap, but Marco had insisted it be used only under extreme circumstances.

"You don't look like a Jew sir, though some of the Jews, the German Jews, are blond and blue-eyed, like you."

"Well, yes, I am unusual in some respects."

"It costs more for a Jew, sir."

"How much, then?"

"Three soldi, sir."

"That's steep, my friend."

"I'm sorry, sir, but if we are discovered, and if they know you are a Jew and that you are out after curfew and not wearing the yellow cap, we will be in trouble."

"Then we will both suffer."

"Exactly, sir! I regret charging you extra, but the punishment can be terrible!"

"Well, lead on, Toto."

They made their way down past a little church, through a campo, along a *calle*, through a market, all the shops shuttered, carts tilted up against the walls, and they turned a corner. A woman—once she had certainly been beautiful—thrust her skeletal face out of the shadows.

"Oh, my beautiful gentleman, oh, my cute young lad, it won't cost you much, just a few soldi and I can give you pleasure such as you have never experienced in your whole lives."

"I am sorry, madam, but we don't have the time!" Danilo said, and bowed. "But thank you, thank you very much!"

They left her behind. A narrow canal ran beside the walkway, and on the opposite side of the canal were blank walls that went straight up from the water.

Toto stopped and raised a finger to his lips. "I think someone is following us, sir."

"What? Who?"

"I'd judge two men."

Danilo glanced behind him. It could be the Men in Black or Mordecai or some of his henchmen, hired killers, or other Venetian enemies aware of his spying activities and bent on murder or mischief. "How do you know someone is following us?"

"Sounds, sir."

"Sounds?"

"I know all the sounds of the night sir, I am always out at night, in all weathers and all seasons, and I know how it sounds when it's dry, when it's wet, and when it's raining. I can tell you a woman's footsteps, a man's, and sometimes how old or young they are. I can tell the sort of boots they are wearing, I can estimate weight and height, and I can tell if the path is muddy or dry, paving stones or cobblestones, and whether the stones have been laid down crooked or even. There are two men following us. They don't know Venice. They don't want to be noticed. They stop, they hesitate; sometimes they whisper to each other."

"So what do we do?"

"They are closing in, sir. We'd best confront them."

"Where are they coming from?"

"Down that way, sir. They will come out on this quay in a few seconds, and they will come down here."

"Good." Danilo spotted something that looked like a rake or a broom leaning against a vendor's little cart. A small alcove framed a shadowy doorway just beside the cart. "You go on ahead, Toto, and turn down that little alleyway so the light of your torch can still be seen reflecting out here. Bounce it around, as if you were walking onwards."

"Yes, sir."

"Is the water here deep?" Danilo nodded at the canal.

"Deep enough, sir. A man would have to know how to swim."

"Good! Go!"

Toto ran into the alleyway; his torch cast a flickering, changing light on the buildings opposite. Danilo grabbed the rake and tested it. Yes, the handle was thick and solid. There was also a shovel leaning against the little cart. Danilo took both, and slipped into the shelter of the doorway and waited.

ALONG THEY CAME, THE two men, soft footsteps, muttered querulous words in Turkish. One of them whispered, "There they are! See the torch!" and then they were opposite Danilo, between him and the canal. He saw them clearly enough. They certainly looked like Men in Black. He hoped they were not innocent Turkish merchants out for a stroll or coming back from a party or some visit to a courtesan.

He leaped out, smashed one of the men across the face with the sharp edge of the shovel, and pushed the other with the handle end of the rake. The thrust of the rake was so quick the fellow, cape billowing, arms flailing, had no time to steady himself or unsheath his dagger, but stumbled backwards in an exaggerated comic three-step, knees high in the air, and fell off the quayside, plunging with a great dark thumping splash into the canal. The other man's face was slashed wide open. One cheek and half his nose looked to be a huge black gash. He lunged. Danilo sidestepped and flattened himself against the wall. The man drew his dagger. He struck wildly at Danilo's eyes, the blade brushed Danilo's cheek. Danilo whirled around. The man, his face a mask of blood, beard dripping, plunged his dagger. It whispered past Danilo's elbow. The man crouched, gathering himself to charge. Danilo prodded him with the sharp end of the shovel, whispering, "Come, then, my friend!"

The man stood. "I kill you now."

Danilo slammed forward, the point of the shovel pushing the killer backwards. The man flailed, trying to slash Danilo. In a whirling movement, Danilo stepped aside, lifted the shovel, and whacked the man over the head, a sharp, echoing crack. The man crumpled, scrambled to get up, and stumbled back, coughing and wheezing. Danilo advanced, prodding him with the point of the shovel.

"You devil!" the assassin gasped. He backed up, blindly, groping in front of him, his face covered in blood, and then he fell, arms flailing, into the canal, where his comrade was thrashing in the water, screaming for help in Turkish. The second Turk just made a splash and floated there, inert, face down. Danilo stepped back. He put the rake and the shovel carefully back in their places and walked swiftly away to where Toto held the torch aloft.

"They are making a ruckus, sir."

"We have to get away, Toto. Where do we go?"

"Down this alley, sir, and through a little courtyard. There is a door that is always open, though it always looks closed. And, sir, the fog that is coming will help. I can smell it. This night will soon be as dark as pitch, sir, and as damp as a mug of stale beer."

They slipped through the door that looked closed but was

always open. Toto shut it behind them, gently, so it would make no noise. A woman wearing a scarlet shawl over her shoulders above a low-cut bodice was sitting in one corner of a small room; she was knitting under a lamp that cast a narrow yellowish light upon her lap and her hands, which were long and smooth and carefully manicured, and quick in the complex click-clack movements they were making and which she didn't interrupt, not even for an instant. She looked to be in her early twenties, in the full blossom of beauty. She glanced up and smiled. "Good evening, Toto. Is this your friend?"

"He is indeed a friend, Signorina Abigail. But we cannot stay."

"Bring him to see me one of these nights. He looks interesting."

They went through the lady's bedroom and through her tiny kitchen, with its pile of onions and red peppers and radishes, and a plate of olives on a wooden table under a lamp, and a tall jug of drinking water, and came into a little courtyard where leafy vines grew up a trellis on a burnt sienna wall, next to what looked like a little stone fountain dribbling water from the mouth of a gargoyle. Then they went out of the little courtyard, through another door that looked closed but was, in fact, always open, into another *calle*, which was a narrow and winding alleyway with no doors or windows, and with barely space for one person to pass. Toto, his torch held high, went first; Danilo followed.

They came out onto a wider passageway. The night had become darker; fog rolled down the alley, flooded in between the inward leaning walls like a rising tide. Toto's torch sent weird shadows up into the bank of fog. "The smells are more interesting when the fog is thick, sir. You can smell everything. I could write a book about smells, sir, about smells and sounds."

"You should write that book, Toto." This boy would certainly be useful when campaigning in the mountains and deserts—he seemed to have extra senses, like a good hunting or tracking dog, but adapted to the city. Wherever fighting or hunting was going on, you could always use a good scout. He should discuss this with Marco. Suleiman and others used light cavalry for scouting, but if you were to find yourself fighting in a city . . .

A few minutes later, Toto and Danilo stood on the edge of the Grand Canal. The broad, rippling expanse of greenish water disappeared into the fog only a few feet out. The echoing, muffled sounds were as intimate as if Toto and Danilo were in a small curtained and tapestried room. No lights were visible anywhere, no people. Venice was a ghost city. Danilo reached out his hand—it was a vague silhouette. He shifted his carpetbag. The fog pearled on his skin. He whispered, "So, Toto, what now?"

"We cross over. It will take those gentlemen some time to recover. They may catch up, if they are very clever. But they will make a dreadful squishy thumping sound, and I shall detect them long before they get close!"

Then, with a low whistle that was hardly a whisper, the boy gently called into the fog. Within seconds, a gondola glided into sight, as if conjured out of nothing. Gondola and gondolier were vague phantoms. Danilo took a deep breath. This was the ghostly magic of Venice. The whole city, so materialistic and commercial, a monument to wealth and power, built by earthy, ruthless, flesh-and-blood warrior-merchants, could in an instant dissolve. Without a word, they climbed into the gondola. The gondolier saluted and said, in a whisper, "Evening, Toto!"

"Evening, Signor Grato!"

"Out on an adventure, are we?"

"Indeed we are, Signor Grato!"

"Invisible, I imagine, Toto."

"Indeed, Signor Grato, we have not been seen."

The gondola glided like a ghost across the Grand Canal; the gondolier's oar strokes were silent. When they slid along the quay opposite, where stone steps came down to the water, Danilo paid the gondolier and whispered his thanks.

Holding his smoky torch aloft, Toto led Danilo through another foggy labyrinth under low-roofed porticos; across sleepy, misty, empty squares; through vague spaces with sketched-out trees and buildings and stone wellheads; and through one long, narrow marketplace with all the stalls already set up for the next day's business, and one or two merchants—thick, dark, muffled silhouettes settling boxes of goods next to their stalls. All the sounds and sights were muted.

"Fog will do that, sir," said Toto, as if he had read Danilo's thought. "The sounds get thicker and closer and lower in a heavy fog. You think you can touch the sound, sir."

They came out onto a wider quay—a real quay and not just a narrow path along the side of a canal—and Danilo caught a whiff of the open lagoon. It filled his lungs. The fog, clinging close to the water, trailed off into long, white, ghostly fingers of vapor. Danilo looked all around him.

"Toto," he said, his heart sinking, "there's no ship."

2 7

THE VOYAGE

PPEARING FROM BEHIND A RAGGED STRETCH OF DARK
cloud, the moon suddenly showed itself, and the flat,
peaceful lagoon shone, almost clear as day, a vast,
open expanse of watery ribbons of silver and black.

"Sir," Toto said, and pointed across Danilo's shoulder.
Danilo turned.

And miracle of miracles, the fog drifted off and there it was,
a big barge tied up at the quay. The moonlight shone silver
light on the bales of goods stacked on the deck, on the mast and
the yardarm, and on the gangplank that led to the quay. "It is
about to leave, sir."

The master, a thickset man wearing a seaman's cap, stood
at the top of the gangplank. He looked down on them, lit up
in the moonlight and with Toto still carrying his torch aloft.
Danilo glanced at the flame. It made a gentle flapping sound
and a thin column of black smoke spiraled up into the crystalline air.

"Toto, what are you doing out so late at night, you rascal?"

"Earning my keep, master."

"You are a good boy. And what have we here?"

"A merchant, master. He needs to travel to Chioggia, then to the Brent Canal or up the Po. He's headed for Mantua." Toto turned to Danilo. "Sorry, sir, but I have to say this."

"Go ahead, Toto, say it."

"He's a Jew, master."

"A Jew — well, that's extra then. But no matter, we don't have the watchmen out here on the water, do we. No enforcing the curfew out on the bobbing waves. Does the gentleman have the means to pay?"

"How much would that be, then, Captain?"

The captain named the price, which Danilo to his surprise found reasonable. He handed over the coin.

"Find a place to sit, sir, and then we can settle you in proper. You'll probably want to lie down in some corner and get some sleep before dawn."

The barge was piled with goods. Danilo found a solid wooden case, tested it — it seemed firm enough. A sailor nearby was handling a rope and he nodded and said, "As good a seat or bed as any, sir. It will hold your weight and then some."

Danilo shifted his carpetbag off his shoulder and set it next to the box and then he sat down slowly. Yes, it was as solid as a stone bench. He turned and raised a hand in salutation to Toto standing on the edge of the quay. Toto lifted his torch and waved. Seen clearly now in the moonlight and at a distance, Danilo realized Toto was even younger than he'd thought — a child, really. And there he was, out working at night, alone, exploring all the little alleyways and mysteries and secrets of Venice, the Most Serene Republic.

Toto waved a last time. Then he and his torch loped off into the darkness.

THE ROPES WERE CAST away, two men pushed against the quay with long poles, and the barge swung off, making hardly any noise at all. The big lateen sail, catching a slight breeze, billowed lazily out.

"Hardly any wind, this will be slow," said the master, coming up next to Danilo. "We must be patient. I have oarsmen, but don't often use them. Just if we're becalmed or maneuvering in close to shore."

The canvas snapped and swung around. The vast lagoon was silent. Above and below were mirror images; the heavens and the lagoon, air and water, had become one. Venice fell away behind them, reduced to a shadow—towers, domes, steeples, all crouched on the rippling darkness of the lagoon.

White fog trailed out across the water. On the northeast horizon lay the low, dark silhouette of the Lido—the long finger of sand that separated the lagoon from the Adriatic and protected Venice from the dangers that came from the sea.

Danilo gazed at the vast flat seascape. Here he was, again a wandering Jew. In that fading shadowy city, he was leaving the vital, living part of himself. Miriamne would be asleep, dreaming of tomorrow. Soon the light of dawn would show over the Adriatic to the east. If she was awake, Miriamne would be planning their day together—she and Danilo, with the children and Uncle Isaac, would inspect paintings by Carpaccio; they would visit Daniel Bomberg's printing shop and examine the Hebrew Bible; they would stroll along the riva degli Schiavoni. Then they would return with the children and Uncle Isaac to the Ghetto to dine together and they would attend service at the synagogue. But that was an imagined day in an imaginary life; it would never come. He saw his own absence as Miriamne would see it—his papers gone, his clothes gone, his carpetbag gone. Danilo del Medigo had never been there, Mordecai would insist, he had never existed. For Miriamne, Danilo del Medigo must now be a myth, a lie, an emptiness, a bitter betrayal.

Uncle Isaac would be asleep on his cot in his tiny ground-floor apartment not far from the synagogue, having wild dreams about his great gambling triumphs and the women he had known, dreams he had confessed to Danilo late one night after too many glasses of wine. Rabbi Hazan was probably awake, poring over a book, some collector's item he was planning to sell but wanted to study first; he would be reading by lamplight or by candlelight, forgetting, as he often did, to sleep at all. The rabbi was fearful for the fate of the Jewish people. "Difficult times are coming, Danilo, horrible times," he had once said, "but do not speak of this to Miriamne. We Jews will be driven out of everywhere. And, as for the so-called New Christians, it will go even harder for them. The Inquisition will tear their children from them, take everything they own, torture them, and burn them alive." Though the rabbi tried to protect her, Miriamne was quite aware of her father's fears — and she had seen the face of hate, up close, in the person of Brother Bruno Scavo.

Marco would probably be in bed now, beside his woman, if he had a woman. Danilo closed his eyes. Did any of the shadowy creatures from the world of spying have normal lives — women to sleep with, children to play with? Danilo wondered at it. And he wondered at himself. Who and what was he?

Veronica Libero would be making love to one of her more privileged clients, or perhaps she would be sleeping with Zarah, her little boy-girl. "Zarah is wise and, in the ways of the world, she is old, Danilo. But in her spirit, Zarah is young," Veronica had said. "She is, in truth, still a child."

And Aretino, perhaps drinking late into the night, collapsed on a divan, having chased his little tribe of vagabonds to bed. La Zufolina might be looking after some sick German, or curled up in bed making notes for Marco on what she had observed during the day. And Titian, in his house in Cannaregio, was almost certainly asleep, holding his young wife. But even in his dreams, he would be eager to get to work the next morning on whatever painting was on his easel, probably the one with Celeste and la Zufolina — and, possibly, with a virtuous but snoozing dog.

Jessica would be tossing in her little bed, and Jacob probably asleep, lying next to her. And, somewhere too, Mordecai would be weaving his plots. And Toto, maybe he would be waiting at a corner for a new client. In the Arsenal, workers would be toiling all night, gearing up for the wars to come. The vast panorama of Venice, resting on the waters, over one hundred thousand souls! It was a vessel containing the woman he loved—Miriamne. Danilo sighed. What magnificence. What fragility.

THE MIDDAY SUN GLARED.

Danilo walked on deck, back and forth; then, finally, he sat down on a chest beside a stack of goods bundled in great packages and piled up towards the stern. He imagined what it would be like: holding Miriamne in his arms, here, on this barge, sailing away, together. She would love it—the sense of adventure and movement. He would press her close, they would kiss, and . . .

The sail billowed out lazily. There was just enough of a breeze to push the barge along. And so they sailed up the great river Po, the pulsing heart of northern Italy, and the landscape slipped languidly past: the dykes by the side of the river, hemming in an endless, low, flat shore line; steeples and domes of little villages, just visible beyond lines of poplars and fields; and then more dykes and minor canals. They sailed slowly past Ferrara, the exquisite and cultured little city that was the fief of the d'Este family, and from which Isabella d'Este had been married into the equally brilliant—and equally violent—Gonzaga family of Mantua.

Danilo paced the deck. Before he could even dream of a life with Miriamne, he had practical problems to solve—he had to get rid of the threat from Mordecai, and he had to find his place in the world. What sort of welcome would he find in Mantua? Would Isabella recognize him? Would she remember the many services Grazia had rendered her, including sacrificing her life? And how old would Isabella be now? When was she born? He tried to remember. And what about Pirro? So much time had passed. Would Pirro remember the son he had from an old love affair? If Pirro thought he was dead, then he might have forgotten all about him—and about Grazia.

He leaned against a railing. A line of white poplars flickering in the sunlight slid by, and a heavy wagon pulled by horses glided past with the driver hunched forward, loosely holding the reins, and then it disappeared astern as the barge smoothly progressed westward. Would Isabella even remember Grazia? It was only ten years ago. Grazia had died protecting Isabella's treasures. But rulers and aristocrats are capricious; they often forget to be thankful, or even to remember what has been done for them. Everything is due, quite naturally, to the sovereign!

What would Isabella say when he confronted her? If Mordecai was to be believed, Isabella thought he was dead. How had that happened? Judah had sent a letter from Istanbul to Isabella reporting that Danilo was alive. Perhaps the letter had not arrived. In any case, in spite of pirates, kidnappers, Hürrem and Mordecai's plots, and the Men in Black, he was still very much alive. He was Grazia's son and the blood son of Pirro Gonzaga; hence, he was, in a sense, part of the Gonzaga family. And he intended to find Pirro and claim his place.

And then he would claim Miriamne. Yes, he was very much in love, which meant that, in spite of rumors, he was very much alive.

AS THE BARGE NEARED Mantua, one of the voyagers came up and stood beside Danilo. The fellow was middle-aged, with a coarse shock of gray hair sticking out from under his cap and straight down over his wrinkled forehead. He had the tanned, creased, sun-weathered skin of a man who worked the land, and the confident demeanor of a man who had money. His vest was of leather, his jacket of serge. He wore heavy fustian trousers, and leather boots stained with dry mud. "Going to Mantua, are you?"

"Yes, sir, Mantua," said Danilo.

"Ever been there before?"

"Not since I was a child," said Danilo. Involuntary memories flooded back: the endless corridors of the Ducal Palace, the huge assembly room in the Palazzo del Capitano, the exquisite little courtyard garden Isabella cultivated, the perfectly designed streets and squares, and his mother laughing gaily about something—a joke, a book, a dance—he couldn't remember. The fragments seemed more like dreams than memory. "And you?"

"Me, ah, well, I have some lands outside the city, work them myself, with my farmers and peasants and a few slaves. Our family has been here—oh, lost in the mists of time, I suppose. We might be Etruscans, for all I know, and I rather hope we are. Makes me feel rooted, tells me I have a place on this earth I can truly call my own."

"I understand."

"You have a place of your own?"

"Not exactly." Danilo blinked against the light. In fact, he had no place he could call his own. Mantua was swinging into view, the forbidding silhouette of Castello di San Giorgio and the city walls shimmering.

"Ah, Mantua," the man sighed. "A beautiful little town."

The barge moved slowly into a wide turn and, as they watched, the trees appeared to swing around and the walls of the town and the fields opposite the city drifted sideways, slipping away in the hazy golden heat of the late autumn day. It did indeed look like paradise, green fields and shimmering poplars.

The landowner squinted towards the town. "It is truly the Gonzaga town, of course, and has been since Ludovico Gonzaga overthrew his friend Rinaldo Bonacolsi more than 200 years ago. Ludovico put himself at the head of a popular revolt. A bloody affair, the Gonzagas killed everybody."

"Most revolts are bloody." Danilo gazed at Castello di San Giorgio. It looked formidable. That was where Isabella d'Este had first created her little studio, crammed with works of art, and her grotto, stacked with exquisite curiosities. Images flooded back to him now of Isabella during the Sack of Rome, protecting with her prestige Rome's Palazzo Colonna, the building piled with art and filled with refugees. The chaos, the wealth, the desperation . . . Isabella surrounded by supplicants, rich and poor, begging her to save them.

"All these little places," the landowner said, "are ruled by condottieri, soldiers by trade, professional fighters who raise armies and fight each other and then grab a principality or city and hold onto it. Then they hire architects, builders, artists, poets, writers, sculptors—all the best they can find—to make themselves glorious. Wise of them too! Artistic prestige is a protection of sorts, like walls and cannons, and alliances."

"I suppose so. It's not a big city, and yet it is famous."

The man leaned against a bale of cloth and pointed at the walls rising up as the barge edged closer. "It is strange it has survived—it really is a little speck on the map, a little splotch. You'd think Milan or Venice or the Papacy would have eaten it up by now. Or the French or Charles V. And yet the Gonzagas have parlayed it into greatness. Here it is, right on the edge of the Mincio River; the city is really an island, surrounded by the three lakes that the Mincio River forms, and by a canal. It's not natural, this position; it's artificial, made over 300 years ago. All those waterworks—the upper lake, the middle lake, the lower lake—were built by an engineer brought in for the purpose. The city wanted to discipline the water and control it and use it as protection. The location is strategic, too, just ten miles up from where the Mincio enters the Po. Still, even with all their cleverness, it's strange they've been able to keep their independence."

"Balancing one power against the other," said Danilo, remembering discussions he'd heard in Veronica Libero's salon—the balance of power an emerging idea and illuminating concept; it made politics seem a bit like acrobatics. The balance was delicate, and if disturbed, there was trouble: a tumble, and usually, war.

"That's true. They are right in the middle between the power of Milan and the power of Venice, so they have learned to do a clever tiptoe tightrope-balancing act. Also, they are between the power of the Emperor and the power of the Papacy, not to mention the power of France. It takes skill in maneuvering and dodging—and often deceit—to stay alive and keep your head with hungry monsters on every side. But she's a crafty woman, that Isabella d'Este! She talked the wolves from the door. She flattered and cajoled and temporized and delayed and talked the threats down. She was beautiful when she was young, so they say, and talented."

"So I have heard." Danilo said, and nodded. How would Isabella have changed? When he had last seen her, he was ten years old and in the chaos of their escape from the Sack of Rome.

"Isabella's husband, Francesco—well, he was not such a clever chap in some ways. Pig-headed, a bit impulsive. Handsome though, in an ugly warrior sort of way irresistible to some women; bumptious fighter, lots of paramours, and got into trouble with women." The landowner paused, took out a handkerchief, and sneezed. "He died, I believe, Francesco did, of the French disease, syphilis. An ugly thing. Had an affair with Lucrezia Borgia, Isabella's sister-in-law! Now there was a woman! Isabella hated Lucrezia with a cold rage."

"Nothing so furious as a woman wronged?"

"Indeed. Isabella is not the same, alas. Since her son, Duke Federico II, took over she has been excluded from power, pushed into a corner, a virtual prisoner. He won't listen to her. And she's getting old. She dwells in the past, doesn't understand the present, obsesses about the glories of yesterday. It is sad indeed." The man wiped his eyes with a kerchief and blinked at the rising light. "And her favorite, that Pirro Gonzaga—an adventurous, charming fellow, most charming, well . . ."

"Oh? What has become of him?" Danilo's heart sank. Was Pirro dead?

"Out of favor too, with Duke Federico. People haven't seen or heard of Pirro, not for quite some time now. He's been pushed out to the margins. If you fall out of favor, anything can happen. You can even lose your head."

This was bad news! Could Isabella be powerless, was Pirro an outcast? What did this mean? Was his trip to Mantua a mistake? If Pirro was gone, what was the point of coming to Mantua? What should he do? Where should he go? He couldn't return to Venice, not now, and he could never return to Istanbul. Whatever Pirro's situation, he would seek him out. Pirro was his father, and Pirro had loved Grazia passionately and she had loved him. He must honor the memory of his mother, and he must speak to Pirro, tell him of Grazia's last days, of her great love for him, and reveal to Pirro that his and Grazia's love had not been in vain, that he had a son—Danilo del Medigo.

But perhaps the man didn't know what he was talking about. Maybe all was well with Isabella and Pirro. After all, this fellow was just a local landowner, so it might be gossip and meaningless.

To distract himself, Danilo automatically began to analyze the position of the city from the military point of view. It was a habit from his days at the Sultan's school. Surrounded by water on almost all sides, Mantua, if well defended, would not be easy to capture, as the man had said, not with foot soldiers or cavalry alone. You'd probably need artillery—but maybe not. Suleiman would make short work of it. He'd take the city in half a day or less, probably a few hours. Danilo narrowed his eyes against the light.

"Look." The landowner pointed to the expanse of water. "The river winds around the town on three sides, widens out into those three lakes, and then all around here is marshland and swamps." He swung his arm around, encompassing the countryside. "It has good farmland, so it's a rich town. It's worth owning, but difficult to capture. Charming place to live, too—cool, with water all around it. In winter it can be chilly, mind you, and foggy, and damp as a swamp; when the wind blows down the river, ah, my God, you want to wrap yourself up, drink a deep draught, cling to your woman, and keep warm."

Danilo sighed. He knew the heritage of Mantua almost too well. Since he was half-Gonzaga, it ran in his blood. And the Gonzagas, rulers of Mantua, were warriors, mercenaries, adventurers; they put their swords and their troops at the service of others. But without Isabella and without Pirro, what would become of him?

Well, he would adopt the Gonzaga tradition! He would become a mercenary, a sword and dagger and lance for hire, a soldier of fortune, and return to Venice someday, gray and grizzled, battle-scarred and rich, and like a chivalrous knight of old, he would throw himself down on his knees and claim Miriamne's hand.

28

ISABELLA D'ESTE

T HE IMMENSE DUCAL PALACE WAS IMPOSING, ALMOST TOO imposing.

Grandiose was the word, a sprawling collection of monumental buildings, pavilions, courtyards, and gardens. Inside the vestibule, Danilo stood patiently, his (non-Jewish) cap in hand, as he presented himself to the servant, who would have to go through the doors to the inner sanctum of Isabella's apartments to transmit Danilo's request for an audience with the famous Marchesa of Mantua.

The servant, a tall, thin, distinguished-looking man with a long nose and dark eyes, curled his lip and asked, "And who are you, sir?"

"Danilo del Medigo."

"That means nothing, sir."

"It should suffice."

"Very well." The servant disappeared. The door closed.

Danilo walked up and down. He looked down at the magnificent marble pavement and up at the tapestries and art lining the walls. One window gave out onto an interior courtyard and a garden.

"The Marchesa has instructed me to inform you that she is not here."

Danilo smiled tightly. "If she says she is not here, then she clearly is here."

The man did not deign to reply. He tilted back his head and looked straight down his long nose, staring at Danilo through narrow eyes.

The impertinence of the fellow! But he was merely a servant, and undoubtedly doing his mistress's bidding.

"I shall return." Danilo bowed stiffly.

"Very good, sir," said the servant, "as you wish, sir." The man turned on his heel and disappeared. The door closed.

Danilo went out into the street and walked back and forth. This was . . . intolerable. Insulting! He stopped pacing and stared at the walls of the palace. Well, what purpose would a meeting with Isabella serve? If Isabella did not choose to remember Grazia, then she would not recognize Grazia's son; and if Pirro was in disgrace, then . . .

He strolled around the gardens, then walked down to the middle lake. He gazed out over the water and at the forbidding walls of Castello di San Giorgio, the fortress attached to the Ducal Palace that loomed over the juncture between the middle and the lower lakes. A hostile, gloomy place, and yet so much life and art had been contained, and was still contained, inside those massive walls.

He returned to the Ducal Palace. This time he would present himself as the son of Grazia dei Rossi. Again, he went through the bronze doors.

The impertinent fellow looked at him. "I told you she was not present. And she is not present. She is reposing, she is not receiving."

"If you just tell her the son of Grazia dei Rossi humbly requests an audience."

"I am not sure I can do that."

"You are not sure. Why are you not sure?"

"The Marchesa does not wish to be disturbed."

"Well, perhaps when she has ended her rest, you could tell her the son of Grazia dei Rossi requests an audience."

"I shall see, sir. Return in an hour."

Danilo did. An hour later, as he came back up the steps to the imposing doors of the palace, an elegantly dressed young black girl was about to enter. Her hair in tight braids, she was wearing a tiny white cap, and a white gown.

She bowed her head, and with a bright smile, stretched out her arm, indicating he was to enter first. He hesitated, and she tilted her head and laughed, and said, "No, sir, do go first. You must go first. I do insist!"

He entered. She followed, bowed to him and to the servants, and disappeared down a hallway.

The lofty thin servant smiled in the girl's direction and nodded pleasantly towards Danilo. "Signor del Medigo, I shall transmit your request to the Marchesa now, if you wish, sir."

"Thank you very much," Danilo said, astounded at the change in the man's demeanor.

He paced up and down.

The man returned. "You may enter, sir."

Danilo followed the man into a corridor, then through massive bronze doors thrown wide open, and into a room where tall windows let in the morning light.

And there she was: the renowned, formidable Isabella d'Este; the woman who had inspired all the great artists of her time; who had invented new forms of fashion, hats, shoes, perfumes; and who had, for a considerable period of time, ruled over the city state of Mantua.

ISABELLA D'ESTE TURNED TOWARDS Danilo as he entered. She was much changed from the imperious woman he remembered; she was older certainly, and more frail and vulnerable. Her face was less clearly delineated than it once had been; there were creases beside her nose and on her cheeks, and folds under her chin, but her eyes were lively, and quick, and intelligent—yes, inside the aging body, the old haughty and demanding Isabella was still there, still visible.

The room with its high embossed ceiling and large windows was imposing. One of the windows gave out onto an exquisite courtyard garden with a profusion of plants and trees, and vines growing up the walls.

"Well, young man, what brings you to my court?"

Isabella was perched on a gilded, throne-like chair; she tilted her head to one side, and fixed him with a penetrating gaze. She wore the high, turban-like headdress she had invented, and that had become fashionable headgear for aristocratic ladies throughout Italy and France. Around her neck was a heavy necklace, and her elaborately patterned gown had a plunging neckline and a high frilled collar. There were traces of her former beauty and energy, but the shadows under her eyes were heavy.

Danilo stepped forward, and executed a low bow. "Danilo del Medigo, at your service, Madonna Isabella."

She stared at him. The stare was not unfriendly, though it showed no sign that she recognized him. She tapped her fingers on the armrest of the chair. It was immediately clear that Lady Isabella was bored and eager to find something to amuse her and pass the time. He could see her thinking: here was a handsome, comely young fellow; whoever he was, he might prove entertaining. Since she no longer ruled Mantua, he could easily imagine her life had become dull. Old age was a curse and a disgrace. It really shouldn't be allowed.

"My Lady Isabella, an acquaintance of mine paid a visit to you recently. You told him I was dead. I have come to correct that erroneous impression."

"You are dead. Or Danilo del Medigo is. You must have a vivid imagination, whoever you are. Danilo del Medigo died at sea. I was told so by a most reputable authority, the former Venetian ambassador to Istanbul."

"You received the news of my death from an authority higher than the very Danilo del Medigo who stands before you in the flesh?"

Isabella laughed. Her eyes brightened. She looked him up and down. "You are insolent, young man, which can be an endearing quality if held within bounds. Decorum is important. Whether you are an authority on Danilo del Medigo will depend, my good fellow, on whether or not the young man who stands before me is indeed the person he claims to be— that is, the son of my great friend Grazia dei Rossi. You are certainly an imposter."

"Bear with me, Marchesa." Danilo bowed. "Allow me to take you back to the years when you spent your winters in Rome. When you engaged my mother as your confidential secretary, you also took on her young son as a page at your court. We all escaped from the Sack of Rome together."

She frowned. "There was a fair-haired young page bearing my coat of arms. He was a pretty child." She reached for a pair of gold-rimmed spectacles that hung from her girdle. "Come closer, young man. Let us see what we have got here." Squinting through the lenses, she muttered, "Pooh, pooh. I see no resemblance whatsoever."

"Well, Madonna . . ."

"Fiddlesticks! You look like a fraud to me. An adventurer, on the road, his carpetbag over his shoulder, determined to torture an old woman with made-up memories of the past. It is outrageous how every mountebank feels he can cheat and fraud someone who is old and vulnerable. There should be a law. You may be handsome, young man, and even have gracious manners, but you belong in my dungeons."

"My mother died protecting your tapestries, the tapestries of Raphael that you removed from Rome."

"What did you say? Are you accusing me of Grazia's death? Are you saying Grazia died because of me?"

"Madonna, when you left the *Hesperion* to take the land route home and chose to leave your treasures with—"

"Stop right there!" Her eyes blazed. "How dare you! That is a terrible accusation! I did not *choose* to abandon my treasures! I did not choose. I was seasick. It was horrible! I could not continue the journey by sea. There was no *choice*! I had to continue by land."

"Forgive me, I . . ."

"Go, go, be gone from my sight! To come here and accuse me — me, Isabella d'Este — of cowardice, of abandoning my people! I never . . . the gall, young man! Enrico! Enrico!"

The distinguished-looking servant with the long nose arrived and bowed. "Yes, Marchesa?"

"Take this young man out of my sight. Hold him in the vestibule until I decide what I shall do with him."

Danilo bowed sharply and exited.

"You might as well sit here, sir," said the servant, indicating a chair.

"I don't know if there is any purpose in my staying. The Marchesa's wrath can be dangerous," Danilo said doubtfully.

"You never know, sir. And at any rate, she will not allow you to leave."

Danilo sat down, his carpetbag at his feet. He clasped his hands in front of him. He was a fool. How could he convince Isabella that he was Danilo del Medigo?

Fuming, he stared at the patterns the light that came through two lofty windows made on the pavement and on the wall opposite, and on a heavy tapestry hanging on the wall, representing somebody on a horse slaying a dragon. Enrico stood there with dignity, ignoring his guest, but not in an unfriendly way. Various servants came, whispered to Enrico, received whispered instructions in reply, then disappeared.

The young black girl came down a corridor, saluted Enrico and Danilo, and entered Isabella's chambers. A few minutes later, she came out, bowed, winked — winked! — at Enrico and Danilo, and disappeared down a corridor.

"Enrico! Enrico!" It was Isabella's voice.

Enrico disappeared into Isabella's room. He reappeared, and bowed. "You may go in."

Danilo again entered the Marchesa's room. He bowed. "Madonna Isabella."

She looked at him slyly. "Where did we stay in Rome during the troubles? Where were you housed?"

"We stayed in Palazzo Colonna. I was housed under the roof, Madonna, in the servants' quarters. From the roof we could see the fires burning all over Rome."

"How did we leave Rome?"

"We went in a wagon train to Ostia."

"You seem to have your little story down pat!"

"I am the man I claim to be, Marchesa." Danilo bowed his most extravagant courtly bow. In the few months he had spent in the Republic of Venice he had lost the habit of elaborate bowing and using lofty aristocratic titles, but he was quick to adapt.

"Well, let me tell you." She glared at him. "The Venetian ambassador assured us the *Hesperion* had been scuttled and all the passengers lost at sea."

"My mother, Grazia dei Rossi, was buried at sea; that is true." Visions of his mother's death and the disaster of the *Hesperion* surged up, and his heart was sick at the memory and at his own guilt over her fate, but he kept his expression steady.

"Are you telling me the pirates spared only you among all the passengers on the *Hesperion*? Why you? Because you were a child? Did they find pity in their hearts?"

Danilo gazed straight at her. "The pirates did not find pity in their hearts."

"Then why did they spare you?"

"Marchesa, the pirates decided I would be worthless dead — rubbish to be tossed overboard. But they could make money if they held me for ransom, or if they sold me in the Istanbul slave market, perhaps as a eunuch."

Isabella fiddled with her spectacles, sliding them to the end of her nose. "You don't look like a eunuch."

Danilo bowed low, hiding a smile. "I don't believe I am, Marchesa, at least not the last time I checked."

"Brazen fellow!" She adjusted the spectacles and smiled.

"You have concocted an interesting tale, young man. Let us have a look. Come closer. You have blue eyes, cornflower eyes. And blond curls that catch the sunlight and now you have a beard. That too is blond. And the smooth skin . . . and strong features . . . you do remind me . . . well, perhaps you are not dead. And I may have misled that curious fellow from Venice— your friend Hazan, I believe his name was."

"Mordecai Hazan is no friend of mine."

She sighed. "You are impertinent, and amusing, and quite pleasant to look at. You provide welcome relief for these weary eyes." She blinked at him. "For the moment, I shall not exile you from my presence."

"Thank you, Marchesa."

"Thank the gods and not me. I am in a good mood. You have arrived on the eve of a family celebration. Tonight there will be festivities. At such times, you know, one is inclined towards mirth and levity and benevolence. And in that spirit I invite you to join in our merrymaking. By nightfall, the whole city will be given over to revelry and feasting. There will be theatrical performances, and enough singing and dancing and music to turn Mantua into a melodic paradise. Do you have a taste for music, young man?"

"I learned to play the lute many years ago. In fact, I played and sang when I was a page at your winter court in Rome."

"Interesting. I do believe Grazia's son played the lute. Remarkably gifted, as I recall. He could even sing!" She favored him with a skeptical, almost flirtatious glance. "Will you play for me now?"

"It has been a long time since I played any instrument, Marchesa."

"Oh? And what have you been doing all these years, then, young man?"

Danilo took a deep breath. "It's a long story."

"Give me the short version."

"I was kept for ransom by the pirates that killed my mother. And my father ransomed me."

"Your father?"

"My legal father."

"And who, pray tell, is your legal father?

"Judah del Medigo."

"Yes, of course! If you are who you claim to be . . . if you are . . . how could I forget?" She squinted at him, and furrowed her brow. "Judah del Medigo—Grazia's husband—he was personal physician to the Pope, and he treated François I, King of France, and is now personal physician to Suleiman the Magnificent, is he not?"

"That is correct. But there is more." And Danilo told her how he had been enlisted in the Sultan's School for Pages, how he had joined the Sultan's service, how he had gone on the Bagdad campaign, and how—unfortunately—he had made a powerful enemy and had to leave Istanbul, and so now here he was. As a result of these distracting adventures, his musical abilities had almost certainly withered away.

Isabella frowned. "So you are saying you cannot play."

"I no longer even own a lute."

She flashed a crafty smile. "You can use mine."

Danilo bowed. This was not good. His ineptitude with the lute would bring his smidgen of credibility with the Marchesa crashing down. He cleared his throat. "Well, then, madam, I shall attempt to rekindle my musical memory. I apologize in advance. It will be a miserable performance."

"Bravo!" She tilted her head to one side and grinned. "You are a brave fellow." She clapped and called out, "Bring me my lute!" A few seconds later, a servant in livery appeared with the instrument; he bowed, handed it over, and disappeared.

Danilo stared at it. He had not seen a lute for such a long time. He frowned. Had he ever played one of these strange-looking things? It looked rather like a very large pear, but made of wood, and cut in half; it had some indecipherable engravings on it, and it had strings. This was not going to end well.

He closed his eyes and put his fingers to the strings.

A horrible discordant sound emerged.

He opened his eyes.

Isabella stared at him. "It is clear you have no idea how to play. You are supposed to seduce a lute, not murder it!"

"Madonna, I beg you, give me one more chance."

"My ears cannot stand it. What you did to that poor lute is a crime. I have a good mind to call Enrico and have you tossed out into the street or, better, have you stored away down in the dungeon."

Danilo bowed, ready to accept his fate.

"Oh, bowing! You try my patience! You are like my courtiers of old! Always bowing and scraping and making a great fuss with titles and compliments, as if we were in a fairy tale or old-fashioned French romance." Her frown became a smile. "However, I have a forgiving nature—I have often been told so. 'She is a saint!' That's what they say. 'Her patience is legendary!' Try again. Please do not hurt that lute—or my ears!"

Danilo closed his eyes. He concentrated. He tried to put himself back into his younger self, when he was a child, when his mother was still alive, when he was innocent and passionate and did things spontaneously, without thinking about them at all, even less than he did now. He cradled the lute, he caressed the wood, he let his fingers delicately stroke the strings, trying to evoke those long-distant memories; maybe his fingers would be more skilled at remembering than he was.

He began to play.

Magically, his fingers found their way—they leaped from string to string, they stroked, they caressed, they rippled along the cords, delicately they plucked their way, here and there. Out came a melody from the depths of the past. He was shocked and surprised. Words rose up from somewhere equally deep. He began to sing.

"Oh beauteous rose of Judea, oh, my sweet soul, wretch that I am, must I perish for serving well and loving faithfully? See, I am dying for love of this Jewess. Help me in my despair. Do not let me die!"

Isabella stood and stepped forward, limping badly. The light coming from one of the tall windows shone on her face. Her eyes glowed, her mouth was half open. She was entranced.

The song ended. Danilo stood, stunned, holding the lute, wondering what had possessed him. The song brought back a whole world, long walks down avenues lined by poplar trees, a voice, a smile, a quick stride, a steady hand, a loud sympathetic laugh—it brought back, in all his glory, his blood father, Pirro Gonzaga.

"Bravo, my young gallant! You have a fine singing voice! You do know the Mantua Gonzagas have loved music for generations. And so has my family, the d'Este dynasty of Ferrara. My father, Ercole I d'Este, Duke of Ferrara, made a name for himself as a patron of the arts. My husband, Francesco II Gonzaga, Marquis of Mantua, and I continued that tradition here in Mantua. We even founded a theatrical company. Now they tour everywhere. Your singing is marvelous!"

"Thank you."

"Where did you learn that song?"

"Lord Pirro Gonzaga sang it during walks we took when I was a boy at your court."

"Pirro . . ." Isabella's eyes darkened. "He loved Grazia. But we must not mention his name."

"I . . ."

"Tut, do not say a word! The walls have ears, you know. Even the tapestries are spies. You are perhaps still too young to understand what happened to Pirro. When a young man, a gallant beautiful warrior, is in love with a beautiful woman and he cannot have her, feelings can run very high. Desire and love are intensified; obstacles are an aphrodisiac; the two lovers are divided by insurmountable barriers, by those most powerful of forces, family and class and religion. . . . And then, finally, he learns that he can have her; that she will sacrifice family, and history, and religion—everything—just for him. And he learns too that he has a son by her . . . finally, they can

· 294 ·

be united! Finally, he can embrace his love and his son. And then . . ." She waved at the walls and tapestries, as if indicating the fates, and destiny.

"And then . . . ?"

"He is wild with joy. He cannot wait to share his happiness, to greet his newly discovered son, and to openly declare his forbidden love . . . and then . . ."

"And then . . . ?"

"Both the woman he loves and the son he has yet to declare his own, though he already loves the lad . . ." She stopped. She looked away. The sun, entering from one of the tall windows, shone on her eyes—they were wet.

"Then . . ."

"Then he learns they are dead, their bodies lost at sea. They are nothing, not even dust."

"And then?"

"Such a man, full of pent-up passion and high ideals, inspired by a glorious and unbounded love for his woman, goes mad with grief. He does foolish things, he makes important enemies, and he . . ."

Danilo waited.

Isabella looked down, her lashes silver with tears. "He is banished. His name is not to be mentioned, not here in Mantua, not here in his home. Federico, my son, hates him with a passionate hatred . . . and for us, here, he does not exist. But here, between the two of us, I will defy the tapestries and the walls. The song you sang—how well you sang it!—Pirro wrote that song for the woman he loved."

"And?"

"And he told me he sang it for her only, and for one other person—his son."

"Lord Pirro is hiding somewhere," Isabella said. She limped to the window. "Rome, Milan, Florence . . . I don't know where or what he is doing. I don't know if he will ever be able to come home."

"Hiding?"

"If he allows himself to be found, he might recognize you—or he might not. You know how men are! They are as fickle as the breeze, and cruel as the tempest. Even a broken heart can be fickle. Wounds crust over; scars make a man—or a woman—hard, forgetful, and ungrateful. In any case, Pirro did not marry your mother; if you are Grazia's boy, Doctor Judah del Medigo is your legal father."

"Yes, he is," said Danilo, but as he said this, unbidden images of Lord Pirro flashed into his mind: Pirro's laughing eyes, his proud, imperious look, his bright smile, his warrior's stance; and the love with which he spoke of Grazia, his gusto when he explained his plans for her and their future life together. Now, as a man, Danilo realized he was only beginning to understand Lord Pirro's passion. And Grazia herself—how divided she had been! She was fiercely loyal to her family, to the faith of her forefathers, to Judaism, but she loved Lord Pirro with all her heart and yearned to be his wife. She was torn in two.

Isabella looked away. "Your mother was passionately in love with Pirro. I tried to convince her to convert to Christianity, to save her eternal soul, so she could live her love to the fullest, openly, with Pirro; she wavered. In the end, I believe she was not going to abandon the faith of her fathers."

"My mother was passionately loyal."

"I was with Pirro when the Venetian ambassador told us the *Hesperion* had been lost. I have never seen a more grief-stricken soul. He stood as if he had been turned to stone. He kept repeating that it couldn't be, that there must be a mistake! He became a different man. There was no reasoning with him. He made enemies. There was a duel, a death, and Pirro fled. If you are Grazia's son, he did indeed love you."

Danilo took a deep breath. "Thank you, Marchesa!"

"I must be discreet. The Duke would be furious if he learned I was making inquiries about Pirro or trying to find out where he is. I would be in very hot water. But if Pirro recognizes you, I will recognize you too."

"Even though I am a bastard?"

She laughed. "In the Gonzaga tradition, my dear young man, legitimacy counts for little. What matters is blood." She rose to her feet and stepped forward. "The Gonzaga men spawn bastards left, right, and center. It never stops, I'm afraid. Bastards everywhere!"

2 9

AN ENCHANTED

PLACE

"THIS IS MY LITTLE STUDIOLO," ISABELLA SAID, SHOWING Danilo inside.

The space was luminous, all the light coming from windows set high up in the walls. The ceiling was deeply embossed with elaborate wooden intaglios, and it seemed to glow, all in gold, with blue inserts like glimpses of the sky; and the light reflected off the walls, which were covered in paintings and decorated with more wooden intaglios, representing music and musical instruments, among which, of course, was a lute. Golden, single-stemmed candelabra lined the walls. The doors were framed by multicolored marble. The floor was of square terra-cotta tiles, richly patterned in brightly colored designs, representing, among other things, the sun, shining with all its rays. The effect was like stepping into an enchanted place, or onto an enchanted island.

"Extraordinary." Danilo gazed at the room. He was awestruck.

"My little studio was originally up in a tower in Castello di San Giorgio, but after Francesco died, I transferred it down here, to the *Corte Vecchio*, the Old Court. It is where I collect all my beautiful things. It is also my refuge, with my grotto, farther down, where I keep my special collections. I am dangerously greedy for things of beauty."

"Indeed."

"You will, I suppose, have had occasion to appreciate fine examples of female beauty. They say the women of the Sultan's harem are extremely beautiful — and talented!"

"I have not made their acquaintance, Madonna, however much I might have desired to do so."

"They tell me that in the Ghetto Nuovo in Venice there are some very beautiful Jewish girls, and that some of them are cultured and highly intelligent."

"That is quite possible, Madonna," Danilo said, nodding. Did Isabella know about Miriamne? With spies everywhere and spies spying upon spies — as la Zufolina had in an amiable way been spying on him — there was no way to know who might know what.

Isabella waved at two immense paintings. "Now, here are works by Andrea Mantegna! He was such a nice fellow, though grumpy, very demanding and quite snobbish, you know. And such a slow worker, meticulous, a perfectionist! Old-fashioned, he was, and by the time he did these, rather out of date. I had to apply the whip several times. I told him I would throw him into a dungeon. I had to stamp my feet. And Andrea always needed money! You would think, would you not, that artists would not be so greedy!"

"Artists do need to eat, Madonna."

Isabella glanced at him. "You have your mother's sharp tongue, I see. I suppose that is good. Here you see the *Parnassus*, Venus and Apollo, up on the stone arch, and this over here is *Pallas Expelling the Vices from the Garden of Virtue*. I wanted something more modern and dynamic. But I couldn't persuade him. You can't teach an old dog new tricks, or so they say. I wanted him to represent virtues triumphing over vices, a true struggle. The world is a battlefield, is it not, between good and evil?"

"And sometimes it is difficult to know which is which."

"Very clever. Perhaps you have been studying Machiavelli."

"I have glanced at his works." Indeed, he had read a few fascinating chapters and discussed them with Miriamne. He gazed at the painting of *Pallas Expelling the Vices from the Garden of Virtue*. It was a roiling, stormy, seething, cosmic drama, with various creatures being driven away, rough and tumble, through a little lily pond by an armed goddess who looked like Minerva, the Roman goddess of wisdom, whom the Greeks called Athena. Danilo's classical education, which his mother had given him, kept coming back. Cupids fluttered away in terror; a naked, armless woman, representing sloth, was being led away on a leash by a crabby, vicious-looking woman. Animal-like figures, part-human, part-beast, were fleeing from Minerva. It was all very allegorical, Danilo reckoned, everything standing for something else. A beautiful naked woman, with her arms full of half-human babies, was also fleeing. Who was she? What did she represent? She reminded him of someone . . . perhaps Celeste, Titian's favorite model; no, that was not quite right . . . the overflowing, seething, cornucopia of imagery, with all its literary and classical allusions, was so unlike the austere abstract art of Islam! But in real life, unlike this allegorical scramble of panicking, fleeing figures, who was truly virtuous? Who was wicked? It was not always clear. For the Venetians, Suleiman was a dangerous enemy and rival. For Danilo and for the Ottomans, he was a hero. For Saida, he was her father; she loved him, and he loved her.

Isabella limped back and forth in front of the painting. "Life passes so quickly. It is like a dream, Danilo, it is insubstantial." She stopped and put her hand on Danilo's arm. "I married Francesco Gonzaga in 1490. It seems only yesterday. I was fifteen. Our family, the d'Este family, were, as you know, patrons of the arts. My father, Ercole d'Este, ruler of Ferrara, turned the city into a showplace for music."

"Yes, my mother often talked of musical performances in Ferrara. For her they were a pure delight."

"I am rather good at the lyre, if I do say so myself. I brought artists from Ferrara with me." She limped up to the painting, leaning in very close, looking at the texture of brush strokes. "And there I was, fifteen, just turning sixteen, freshly arrived in a city I didn't know, and Mantegna—he was sixty years old by then—arrives back from two years in Rome to find this slip of a girl ruling the roost. He was quite unhappy. He'd been serving the Gonzaga family for thirty years and he was used to being the boss. Here was this snippet of a d'Este teenager bossing him around. I kept him on his toes until he died, poor fellow."

Danilo turned to follow Isabella. The high windows cast a mellow light on the room, as if it were bathed in gold.

"Here are some of the musical instruments I have collected. The viols, the lutes, a clavichord," she said, "and you can see that the engraved wooden panels represent various musical instruments. This little studio reflects all the delights of the senses as trained by the arts."

"You were known for your singing too, were you not?"

"Oh, yes." She looked up at him, as if startled into innocence. Danilo realized what she must have looked like when she arrived in Mantua, a mere girl, suddenly a bride, suddenly an independent patroness of the arts. "In those days, my voice was quite good." Her eyelashes fluttered.

"I am sure it still is." Danilo looked into her eyes, beautiful eyes, but tired, with leaden circles, cheeks that sagged, grayness beneath the rouge, chapped lips that quivered. The vision of the youthful Isabella vanished.

She sighed and took his arm. "Oh, the things I have done! The life I have lived! I was a legend, Danilo. And now what does it come down to? An old woman alone, imprisoned, limping around a few rooms. To think I corresponded with Leonardo da Vinci, with Correggio, with Raphael, with Giovanni Bellini, the most important Venetian painter of this generation, and with Perugino, with all the greatest artists of the age."

"They owe you a great deal."

"We did pay them handsomely and put up with their caprices. Leonardo was always turning to something new, always sketching the most remarkable contraptions— machines that could fly, guns that could fire many bullets at once, all sorts of fantasies. His imagination was on fire. He was an engineer as much as an artist. He just couldn't concentrate; he left things unfinished. He loved flimflam, and putting on a show. He designed the celebrations for my sister's wedding, a huge affair, no expense spared, with spectacular effects. Yes, he loved ephemera—flashy, flamboyant events, and then, poof, all gone! Leonardo really had too many ideas, he was too ambitious sometimes, splashy overreach, you know; and he was left-handed too! Dressed in pink satins, flaunted around, and perfumed his clothes and his body, terribly precious and occasionally quite affected; always surrounded by pretty boys. This put Michelangelo into a rage, for some reason. Leonardo got into trouble, too. He was accused of sodomy, but he got off, I think, by the skin of his teeth. Friends in high places, you know."

"Well, genius . . ."

"Absolutely—genius is wayward and sometimes without discipline. If you are going to break some rules, those chaps think, why not break them all?"

"That is an interesting point—and like Aretino, I suppose."

"Like all of them. I am full of interesting points, Danilo. I may be old, but I am not stupid. I ruled Mantua for more than a decade, I had eight children, I debated the best philosophers, I corresponded with the greatest minds of our time, and I promoted the greatest artists of the age. It is not easy being a woman." She fluttered her lashes again; her eyes, when they came alive, were beautiful. Youth was a ghost. Occasionally it returned.

"You are the opposite of stupid, my Lady; the whole world knows that!"

"It has been said I am the very paragon of womanhood. And I set the style in women's fashion for a decade or two; even French women took note."

"The plunging neckline," said Danilo with a smile, remembering Miriamne being excited by the idea and copying it, in her own modest way.

"I did pioneer that, for the upper classes. Venetian women leaped at the idea. And I believe the courtesan Veronica Libero—she's a splendid poet as well, you know—has taken everything a step further, typical of the Venetians."

"And I believe you designed perfumes." In fact, Veronica had told him about Isabella's experiments with perfumes and her promotion of new combinations of scents.

"I am interested in how to invent new mixtures—roses from Provence; strawberries, melons, and resins of various kinds, amber oil. You can create exotic and sensual, or relaxing, or invigorating and fresh perfumes. It is a whole language. I have a small courtyard garden in the Corte Vecchia where I cultivate fruit and herbs, and experiment with new combinations of odors, strawberries and fennel and rosemary, for example. You are very well-informed for a young gentleman who has spent his time at the Sultan's court. Did you learn all of this from the girls in the harem you claim to have no acquaintance with?"

He laughed. Veronica Libero's salon had been a true education in all things feminine, as rigorous in its own way as the pages' school in Istanbul. "I believe you designed clothing as well, different combinations of silk, and satin, and lace . . ."

"Yes, I am interested in fashion. It is an essential part of being a gentlewoman, or a gentleman for that matter. Men should know what women want, what interests them. But we were talking of genius and talent." She took on a serious and puzzled expression. "I never really understood why Michelangelo couldn't stand the sight of Leonardo until now. I sometimes think we see parts of ourselves we don't like, parts we repress, in other people, don't you? And then we hate that person. They are like an unflattering mirror. Unlike Leonardo, Michelangelo was austere; I don't think he liked his own passions very much. He tucked his desires away, somehow, out of sight. Did you know Leonardo could draw with one hand and, at the same time, write with the other?"

"Perhaps, Marchesa, it was a reflection of Leonardo's divided personality—it could be he was many men or many people in one body." Danilo stepped back to get a better view of *Pallas Expelling the Vices from the Garden of Virtue*. He recalled how Miriamne had diagnosed him as suffering from a split personality—perhaps an indecisive and paralyzed personality—after examining his right and left hands.

"A bit monstrous of Leonardo, I think—a prodigy and a wonder, and rather a show-off. Leonardo did do a sketch of me though, in profile, very simple and classic. It shows me gazing off into space. I was twenty-four." She smiled at Danilo, the smile of a naughty, delighted child. "And Titian painted a portrait of me years ago. I didn't like it. He portrayed me as an old woman. Now, he is doing another—it will show me, I hope, in a better light. He is a proud fellow, Titian, courtly and suave, and he can negotiate as almost an equal with emperors and kings; he knows his own worth. So he holes up in Venice with people like Aretino and does what he wants. I wasn't an old woman, not then, and Titian had the effrontery to make me old. I threw a regular fit." She sighed and took Danilo's arm. "Time is cruel, Danilo. You look into a mirror and you see a stranger. It happens overnight. I feel as young as I felt then. Well, as I said, Titian is painting another portrait of me. I want it to be me as I was, as I remember myself. I don't think that is too much to ask, is it?"

"No, it isn't!" Danilo exclaimed. La Marchesa was leaning heavily, on his arm now.

"Now look, look over here—Mantegna did these two bronze reliefs for me. The man might have been stubborn, but he could turn his hand to anything! It is a small room, so everything has to be intimate. Correggio painted these two additional paintings over here—the *Allegory of Virtue* and the *Allegory of Vice*."

With Isabella still leaning on his arm, Danilo inspected them carefully. They were much more dynamic than the Mantegna paintings, with swirling action springing out of the background, out of the depths, towards the foreground, towards the viewer. And the touch was lighter, more impressionistic, less precision of drawing and line, more emotion, less classical, and more fluid than Mantegna. To his surprise, Danilo realized he was becoming a connoisseur. He was learning to see. Well, that was what *The Book of the Courtier* said. A gentleman should be master of the arts as well as of the dagger, the lance, and the sword; a good horseman, knowledgeable about hounds, a deadly hunter; adept at politics, clever with strategy, gallant with women, and capable of appreciating talent in whatever fields they manifested themselves—horsemanship or perfumes, and the design of cannons or chemises. Miriamne would be proud of him. Her image surged up. A spasm shot through his heart; it was physical, like a stab from a knife.

"Is something wrong?"

"Thank you, Marchesa, it is nothing."

Isabella tilted her head. "Sensitive too . . . ? Did you leave a beautiful Muslim girl behind in Istanbul? Perhaps you left one of the beautiful Jewish girls of the Ghetto all alone, and sad, and pining for you? You are very handsome, you know. Strange to say, some men do not realize how attractive they are."

This was striking too close to home—could Isabella know of Saida and of Miriamne? He looked down at the toes of his boots. "I make few conquests, Madonna. I am a modest fellow, rather cautious, really. Women can be intimidating."

"Women can be dangerous, I should know!" Isabella laughed. "And so can artists. Artists need cultivating. Some of them are quite spoiled. They exaggerate the difficulty of what you've asked them to do; they throw tantrums, make scenes, and invent excuses. And they delay, and delay! Costs run over; it is terrible."

"I imagine it must be." Danilo remembered Grazia telling

him how the Gonzagas and the d'Estes were often reluctant to pay bills. Mantegna was known to be stubborn and proud, and to insist on being paid.

"If he wasn't paid on time, Mantegna would ask for land or something like that. On a valuable bit of land the Gonzagas gave him, he built his own house—a gem, I must say! It is a masterpiece of classical design, resurrecting the style of ancient Rome. The old man knew what he was doing."

Danilo inclined his head. He had vague memories of Mantegna's house and its design, or was it something his mother had told him? He remembered a sober-looking, perfectly square brick house that looked like a cube outside, but had an elegant, circular internal courtyard that seemed strangely reassuring. Was that right? His mother said it was original and a brilliant example of the architectural theories developed by Leon Battista Alberti, and that Mantegna had almost certainly designed the house himself. And it was in that house that Mantegna painted his portrait of Grazia; she was seventeen years old . . . It was strange how these bits and pieces of memory came flooding back. He could see Grazia, turning to him with her brilliant smile.

Isabella was gazing at him. "One must keep one's eyes open. It is important, Danilo, to know as much as you can about everything. You never know when a tidbit of knowledge will come in handy—the average price of olive oil in Naples in September, for example, or who is about to become a cardinal."

"So we are scavengers of information," Danilo said, remembering a conversation with Veronica Libero, "gathering up bits and pieces here and there, and trying to piece them together to make something of them, like the merchants on the Rialto picking up bits of news—prices, weather, crop failures. We are cobblers, cobbling together our own destinies."

Isabella glanced at him sharply. "You have Grazia's intelligence. Your mother was a quick one, but stubborn too. As for me, I learned much from my sister, Beatrice. We shared everything. She was more beautiful than I ever was. Alas, she was wilful, obstinate, and not always discreet. She married Ludovico Sforza. He was overambitious, perhaps crazy. Ludovico brought misfortune on Italy. Perhaps more than any other man, he destroyed the old Italy."

"How did he do that?"

"Ludovico—they called him 'the Moor' because he was very dark—was determined and calculating, but shortsighted. Resentment and thirst for revenge are not good counselors. To settle some scores with his enemies, particularly the Neapolitans, and thinking he was making a clever move, he convinced the French to attack Naples by invading Italy, which they did, in 1494, under Charles VIII. If you invite the Devil into your house, you are making a big mistake. The French had a huge army, lots of cannons, and they massacred everywhere they went. The little Italian states, up to that point, had just played at war, skirmishing with each other for profit and glory and family feuds. But this French invasion was real war, with a real army. And then, once these French had seen Italy, and seen how rich and pleasant and divided and defenseless it was, the news got around, and everybody decided to invade Italy: the French, again and again; the Germans, and Charles V; the Spanish King and Holy Roman Emperor. So we have had nonstop wars, real wars, not fiddly little play wars, and we had the catastrophe of the Sack of Rome, and untold disasters. Italy has never recovered—and we are all still paying for Ludovico's folly. We Italians are all living on borrowed time. The French finally got tired of Ludovico, seized Milan, and threw him in a dungeon in France, where he died."

"And what happened to your sister, Beatrice?"

"She died young, alas, in childbirth. She was only twenty-one. A woman is lucky if she lives beyond her first child." Isabella glanced at one of the Correggios. "Each time I look at this, I see something new. Look and listen and learn. That's what I say. I wish I could go on forever, just to learn and to experience beauty."

"Marchesa?" said a voice behind them.

The young black girl—she was perhaps twelve or thirteen—stepped into the room. She was now wearing a burgundy silk gown, with a necklace and a gold cross on a chain, and sparkling white low-heeled shoes; she moved gracefully, as if she were dancing towards them.

"Ah, my little black treasure!" Isabella smiled at the girl and then turned to Danilo. "Isn't she beautiful?" She turned back to the girl, reached out her hand, and put in on the girl's shoulder, as if displaying her. "What is it, my pearl?"

"The Master of the Hounds wishes to know if he can feed the dogs now, my Lady. Duke Federico left no instructions. I believe he forgot to." The girl bowed, and then stood up, straight as a little soldier, her head tossed back, and a bold and amused look in her eyes, a delighted smile on her lips. She glanced at Danilo, a flirtatious, even insolent gaze.

Isabella put her hand to her forehead. "Oh, bother—decisions, decisions. Tell them they can feed the dogs, but not too much. The dogs should be keen but not ravenous, not hysterical. I believe Federico wants to take them hunting when he gets back from whatever mischief he is presently involved in. If they are full, they will be lazy and not want to hunt. And if they do not behave, if they are not eager, Federico will be in a foul mood. And we will all suffer the consequences!"

"Yes, my Lady. I shall tell them." The girl curtsied, glanced coyly at Danilo, and left.

"She's a beautiful girl," said Danilo. "The way she moves, she's quick and fluid, like a dancer."

"She is as black as night, or anthracite, or ebony, whichever is blackest, I never can tell. The painters know more about color shades than I do. They have lots of splendid words for tints and tones and shades that I can never remember. Several years ago, I told my impresario—a very artistic fellow, Andreas Satti—to buy a black slave in the Venice slave market. I told Andreas I wanted a girl slave, as black as possible—the blackest of black, and the most beautiful creature alive, and young, so that I could train her. He bought her in Venice when she was just a baby. It is so strange, the wonder of nature. I have collected several black slaves, boys and girls, men and women. They fascinate me. I have given her the name Sappho, after the Greek poet. Sappho is exceptionally clever, really, and most delightful. And around here, now that I am no longer in command, and can't move as easily as I used to, Sappho serves as my eyes and ears. She sees and knows and understands everything that goes on, who does what, who's in, who's out."

"She is your intelligence service." Danilo thought of Zarah and la Zufolina, barely out of childhood, extremely pretty, charming, and gathering secrets as easily as breathing.

"Even Venice could not do better. People trust her because she is a slave. And she is a child. She can do no harm, has no power. And she is charming, and very attractive. If I am to give good advice—though I am rarely asked—I need to feel the pulse of the people. Of course I still have my little fief of Solarolo, a small town near the Adriatic coast, which I govern, and my schools for girls, and a few craft workshops I set up; I keep an eye on all of that."

"You are known to be an exceptionally wise ruler."

"You truly are a diplomat! When I stood in for my husband, and later, when I was Regent, yes, I was rather good at it. The people knew I cared for their welfare." She smiled. "My son, Duke Federico, adores Sappho, but sometimes resents her. He is mercurial. I worry about what will happen to her when I am gone." Isabella paused and took a deep breath. "Slaves are expensive. I have had several extraordinary blond slaves too, men and women; beautiful, tall, exotic creatures, with perfect white skin, like ivory, and the most marvellously sculpted and symmetrical features, and wild wilful tempers, from the eastern Slavic countries. I even had several—and these are truly hard to find because of the Ottomans—from the Black Sea, from the Crimean slave markets, untamed blond creatures, and strong too! But they have to come through Istanbul, which of course makes them even more expensive. Middlemen mark up the price of slaves in a shameful way. They truly exploit us.

I believe the Sultan's harem consists largely of women slaves bought near the Black Sea, in the Crimean Khanate slave markets, is that not true?"

"Yes, it is," Danilo said, remembering his own encounters with Hürrem. "The Sultan's wife was a slave. She was from the Slavic tribes far north of the Black Sea, possibly captured by a raiding party of Tartars. The Sultan's mother, Hafsa Sultan, who was herself probably from the Caucasus Mountains, or possibly the Crimea, purchased Hürrem as a present for her son. Even if they are slaves, the women of the harem have, I believe, enormous influence."

"Well, I suppose a harem is one way of dealing with men's appetites. You know, Danilo, we women are just too patient. Sometimes I think we need to take over. Our men are always away making war! Or they are taken prisoner, as my husband, Francesco, was. While he was imprisoned in Venice, I ruled and I had to keep Mantua from being gobbled up. I was good at governing; I refused to ransom Francesco by giving the Venetians my son, Federico, in exchange; my husband never forgave me for that. The Venetians said they would execute Francesco if I didn't do what they wanted. I said, 'Go ahead—execute him!' Of course, I was gambling that they wouldn't do it. Francesco was furious, but I preserved Mantua's independence. My mother, who was originally Eleanor of Naples, and became by marriage Duchess of Ferrara, was very clever, and she took over from her husband—my father, Ercole d'Este—when he was away fighting or getting lost somewhere, as he often did."

Danilo smiled. "My mother told me how your father brought all the best musicians and composers from France and northern Europe to Ferrara, and how this helped change Italian music. Didn't your father try to avoid getting Ferrara involved in wars?"

"Indeed he did. In the end, my father learned his lesson and tried to stay out of wars. Mother never liked wars. You know, my mother told me that when she was on her way from Naples, she stopped off in Rome—this was on her way to get married to my father. When she stopped in Rome, the Romans, Borgia Cardinals, gave her the use of a chamber pot made of silver! Can you imagine? A silver chamber pot! And the feasts and meals, she told me, went on forever! Just like the Borgias, those vulgar Spaniards! Always plotting! Spending other people's money trying to curry favor. Of course, the Borgias are Spanish, so high-handed barbarism is to be expected. In any case, men are often hopeless in administering a state. It is like a household, one must have a sense of measure."

"Indeed, one must." Danilo smiled. Maybe it wasn't such a bad idea, having women in charge. From what he had heard, some of the women in the Sultan's harem intended to do—or had done—just that. Hürrem, for instance.

Isabella laughed and poked him in the chest. "You are a clever young man—you agree with me on almost everything. That is a good sign. A true diplomat."

"That, I presume, is a compliment?"

"Not entirely. You must want something."

"I would like to know more of . . ."

"Do not think of him! Do not mention his name!"

Danilo inclined his head. He must obey. But he was eager to discover all he could about Pirro, and in the end, to find the man. What else was he to do with his life? He could not return to Venice or Istanbul. Perhaps he could join Pirro in his adventures—whatever they were—and make his fortune, and return to Venice and ask for Miriamne's hand!

"Men! Men! Always dreaming!" Isabella sighed, "Now, when I think of *my* husband."

Danilo held Isabella's gaze. When discussing husbands, a non-committal attitude was prudent for the seasoned diplomat he was rapidly becoming.

"Francesco was eight years older than I. He was brilliant, handsome, and strong, a true warrior and a leader of men. Our destinies are often sealed when we are young, Danilo. I was engaged when I was six years old, and Francesco was fourteen. It was politics of course. I was from Ferrara and Ferrara needed an alliance with Mantua. But, you know, necessity can create love. For many years I loved Francesco. He was so brave! He had gusto; he loved hunting and feasting, and he loved women, rather too much. As a soldier, I think he was more enthusiastic than—how shall I put it?—intelligent. Not a great strategist, and a little weak and confused on tactics. And he was impulsive. He became involved with Lucrezia Borgia, my sister-in-law. My brother was married to her and besotted with her—and my husband was obsessed with her! Both men smitten by the same woman! When she discovered Francesco had syphilis, Lucrezia dropped him like a hot stone. I think his heart was broken . . ."

Danilo nodded, but said nothing.

Isabella blinked, wiped away a tear, and turned her gaze away into empty space, lost perhaps in the past. She took a deep breath. "Ah, Lucrezia Borgia. I hated her with a fury, but I had to pretend to like her and I did admire her. She was beautiful and full of mischief, charming and flirtatious, and highly learned. When she was defending herself in her first divorce case she addressed the court in perfect Latin—even the professors were bowled over. No one could resist, but with such wiles and plotting as not even good old Machiavelli could imagine. She was a product of that dreadful family of hers. Her father was Rodrigo Borgia, Pope Alexander VI; his appetites were unlimited. They say Lucrezia slept with her father and with her brother, Cesare, but I really don't believe it—rumors spread by her enemies, I think. Her brother killed everyone who crossed him. It is said the Tiber was awash in cadavers, piling up on the banks of the river or under the bridges. Cesare killed his own brother, too, it was rumored. Lucrezia's father died of poisoning; possibly he accidentally killed himself with poison he meant for a cardinal he didn't like. Pregnancy killed Lucrezia, complications after giving birth, all that beauty and energy and wit, and to die so young!"

"A sad ending," Danilo said softly, feeling he had to say something, but that to express too much sympathy for

Lucrezia would not be astute. Such maneuvering was becoming second nature. He was no longer a bumptious page at the Sultan's court, galloping mindlessly about on his gallant horse, Bucephalus. Would Miriamne be proud of his tact, or would she be disgusted by his calculated praise? Veronica Libero and Zarah would, of course, smile; they were artists in seduction and subtle flattery.

"Francesco had contracted the disease not from Lucrezia, I am certain of this. He caught it from some common prostitute, a lady of the street, not from a courtesan—that would have been respectable. Francesco had a dark side, addicted to risk, to plunges into the darkness, a thirst that had to be slaked. Lucrezia was dangerous, that was part of her charm. But he also sought adventure, stimulation, in lower quarters, among common prostitutes. And so he caught it . . . It is horrible. It hollows out a man, or a woman. They call it the French disease, though I suppose that is a slander. You know how the flesh rots, then it stinks, and the gums bleed and the teeth fall out, and the sores spread. And his hair, so beautiful, all began to fall out, and his skull and scalp were visible, and waxen, as if he were already laid in his grave. People take mercury to try to cure it. But the cure may be worse than the disease; it turns the teeth black, among other things. In spite of all that, Francesco and I did have our love. Before Lucrezia showed up. She was insatiable. Well, she had suffered. She loved her second husband, Alfonso, and when he was wounded, she spent weeks nursing him back to health, but when she was out of the room, his enemies strangled him in his bed. Lucrezia was heartbroken. After that, she had to have everything—sleep with my brother and my husband! She even wanted my friendship! Oh, well. And so Francesco died. And I became Regent of Mantua."

Isabella seemed to waver on her feet. Danilo took her arm and said, "Your court and your patronage of the arts were—and are—famous throughout Europe. Even in Istanbul, people speak of you."

"Really? Well, that is something, then."

With his help, she limped towards a gilded straight-backed wooden armchair, set in one corner of the *studiolo*. She sat down, shifting her weight heavily. "Oh, the times we had! I had a company of dwarfs. They would prance around and play silly tricks. There was one, Catherine she was called, a squat, funny, ridiculous little thing. If I was holding a banquet I would tell her to hitch up her skirts and pee. And she would pee, in front of everyone. In front of the Duke of Milan once! He couldn't stop laughing. Great fun it was."

"I can imagine." Danilo frowned. The Sultan's court had a more austere sense of humor, and a rather strict sense of decorum. Indeed, Suleiman would probably not find a lady dwarf opening her legs and peeing in front of potentates comical.

"I laughed until the tears came! This Catherine was a rascal too—used to steal things, little bibelots and objects, cups, wine glasses, tassels. Anything small enough and not nailed down, she would grab whatever it was and scurry off, lickety-split, waddle-waddle-waddle, and hide her loot in her room. Sometimes I'd send a servant to fetch the things back. She was only this high, always pickled or soused and sozzled, weaving about, this way and that, and falling flat on her face. She's dead now."

"That is sad."

"Everyone is dead, Danilo. You get to a time in life when everybody is dead."

Danilo nodded. Death, they said, was hard to imagine, though in his twenty years he had seen plenty of death—during the Sultan's campaigns; during the avalanche in the Zagros Mountains; during the flight from Rome, when he and his mother and Isabella fled from the city towards Ostia; on the pirate ship, when his mother was murdered—dead with one shot and tossed overboard—and everyone else massacred; on campaign with the Sultan's army. And then of course, he had killed a Man in Black, with a quick thrust of his knife, in Istanbul; he still remembered feeling, under his knife, the man's beating heart, ceasing. That was death.

"Good old Mantegna, he's dead. He was our court painter for decades. He was very slow and meticulous. His paintings had wonderful details, very soothing when you looked at them, even when the subject was disturbing. He considered everything from a lofty, philosophic, Platonic distance, distilled things into their ideal form, their essence, their stillness. I don't think he ever understood the new flamboyant, exciting, dramatic style, which is so full of movement and clashing forces and forms; and I don't think the younger artists understood him either, even when they learned from him. I'm sure Mantegna thought their techniques showy and cheap. Generations are often at war with each other. Giorgione and Carpaccio, both dead. Raphael, he's dead; Leonardo, dead. Giovanni Bellini, dead. Perugino is dead! Why, they are all dead! Nobody is left! And here am I—alive!"

With Danilo's help, she rose, slowly, painfully, from the chair.

The windows, high above, projected light down onto the wooden paneling. Danilo followed as Isabella pointed with her small, plump fingers, and moved forward as if hypnotized by the objects. "This is one of my favorites." She ran her fingers over a sleeping cupid. "Michelangelo created this, and he treated it with acid to make it look like it was an ancient statue. In fact, he made a forgery. He was young; he wanted to prove he was as skilled as the ancients. That was cheating. A stunt to gain attention. It did make him famous. And still, I love it."

Danilo leaned close to inspect the beautiful sleeping cupid. It looked rather like la Zufolina, finely chiseled features, exquisite little nose, and sensuous full lips.

"And now . . ." Isabella wiped away a tear. "Ah, now! Now!" Isabella turned to Danilo. She seemed a bit adrift, a bit lost. "My son and I . . . A mother's lot is not always a happy one."

Danilo nodded.

"My son, Federico, had Giulio Romano—a wonderful artist—build a sort of pleasure pavilion, the Palazzo Tè."

"I heard it was built on the edge of the marshlands," Danilo said, "where the old stables used to be, a sort of island, an image of paradise."

"Precisely, it was where the horses were kept. And now Federico keeps his woman there—Isabella Boschetti. Horses and women, they are specialties of Gonzaga men, and dogs, of course!"

"They are also interested in art and music, so I've been told," Danilo said, hoping to steer Isabella away from sensitive and bitter topics.

"Of course art—only the best! Giulio Romano worked with Raphael, you know. Palazzo Tè is exquisite, but I am not allowed near the place. Federico was furious that I arranged his marriage for him. He has never forgiven me. He has never liked his wife, Margaret Paleologa, Marchesa of Monferrat."

"Ah." Danilo nodded sagely, poker-faced. He did not want to get involved in a civil war between Federico and his mother, or between Isabella and la Boschetti. He had heard from Titian that la Boschetti was exceptionally beautiful, and that Federico was infatuated.

"I'd love to show you the Palazzo Tè. But as I said, I am not allowed to set foot in the place." She sighed, downcast, and then shifted to a flirtatious pout. "A mother does everything for her son and what does she get in return? Rejection, humiliation—cast off like an old rag! Old age is not a happy state, particularly for women."

"You, Marchesa, are ageless. Books have been written about you!"

"There is a book about me. It rather holds me up as a model of womanhood. *De mulieribus, On Women*, by Mario Equicola. He wrote it in Latin almost 36 years ago. The decades fly, Danilo."

She coughed. Suddenly, she was out of breath. She leaned against him, and he felt all her fragility, the mortality of this powerful, exceptional woman, here in the midst of her treasures. The light streaming down from above, the paintings, and the embossed wooden panels, the marble ornamentation, made a little personal utopia and refuge. "I knew them all, you know. Mantegna, Leonardo, Titian, Raphael, Giorgione . . ." She reached out her hand. "I am tired now. I must rest—and I have things to attend to."

"Of course," Danilo said, taking her on his arm.

"I knew them all," she said.

"Yes, Marchesa." And he led her out of her little paradise.

3 0

SAPPHO

WHEN ISABELLA HAD RETIRED TO HER PERSONAL rooms, Danilo was left to roam the Ducal Palace. He went through several reception rooms hung with tapestries and paintings representing various scenes from classical mythology, and with windows looking out on various gardens, and then, in a corridor, he came upon Sappho.

She was talking to a heavyset man holding a big, black, iron skillet. He wore his tunic buttoned to his neck, and a sort of large bib smeared with grease and blood and various savory-looking juices. He had a jovial, clean-shaven face, a triple chin, full bright lips, and red cheeks, and the shadow of his shaved beard went almost up to his twinkling eyes and the curly black hair spilling from under his cap. He was saying, "If that is what they want, that is what they are going to get, but it should be simmered more slowly, which means it would be among the last plates to be served. But there is no accounting for taste."

Sappho inclined her head slightly. "That is indeed so, Master Ansaldo."

"Thank you for warning me!" The cook disappeared through an almost-invisible side door. With a quick, dance-like pivot, Sappho turned to Danilo and, flashing a huge smile said, "What may I do for you, sir?"

"I am just wandering about. I have not been in Mantua since I was a child."

"If you have any questions, you can ask me. I'd be glad to help."

"I do have one question. Where are you from? I mean originally, before you were here."

"I have often asked myself that precise question. In fact, I have no memory of before. Here is where I am. Now is where I am. I know of nothing else." Her smile was bright, but with a tinge of melancholy. "People have told me stories of where I might be from, but it all begins in the Venetian slave market."

"Nothing from before?"

"No. I had a brother once, but he is dead. He was brought here with me. He did caprioles in the court. We were very small. He made la Marchesa laugh! She doesn't like to mention him now. It makes her sad. Showing off for her, he tried to jump over a very high fence—he shouldn't have done it—and he fell and hurt his head. He was unconscious and had a fever; he never woke up. I cried and cried. Perhaps she thinks talking about him would make me sad, or perhaps she has simply forgotten him. Our masters do forget things, you know; their lives are so full."

"I am sorry."

She shrugged.

"How do you occupy your time?"

"I read. I study. Marchesa Isabella wanted me to know how to read and how to write. She wants me to be cultivated. I help la Marchesa when she wants to dictate a letter sometimes. I have had some fine teachers. My calligraphy is excellent. Her eyes get tired and her hands are not as good at writing as they were. I run messages, so I am virtually everywhere in the palace and also in the town. I know everyone; and everyone knows me. And I do sometimes go to Palazzo Tè. I rather like

Federico's friend—his mistress, la Boschetti. La Marchesa cannot go there; but I can. I make pastries, and I dream sometimes. And my dreams are strange. They might, I think, be an entry into . . ."

"Ah, there you are!" Isabella appeared in a doorway. Caught and framed in the daylight streaming in, she looked even older than before, haggard and plump, sagging, with a prominent tummy and withered throat. "I didn't need so much of a rest after all."

Sappho smiled, and sketched a modest curtsy.

"At night, Sappho becomes invisible. I can only see her smile, which is so bright. But I can't see her, she is so black. Aren't you, my pearl?"

"Yes, Marchesa Isabella, I imagine that I am." Sappho curtsied, while giving Isabella a bold and amused smile that seemed to mean "We are playing a game, you and I," and in which Danilo was sure he saw a hint of compassion for the older woman. "I appear, and then—poof—I disappear! And, then, surprise, there I am again!"

Isabella, who was limping, and leaning on a cane, laughed, and then coughed. "I think perhaps I should buy her a companion. You will need a husband one day, will you not, my love?"

"Who would have me?"

"Any man would be honored. But you would need someone intelligent enough to match your wit. Perhaps I can buy the right person." Isabella turned to Danilo. "Let us have a little talk. Here, we can sit over here." Isabella motioned towards a group of chairs.

"I shall leave you, then, Madonna." Sappho curtsied. The light from the tall windows played upon her shoulders, on the curve of her collarbone, on her glossy braids.

"Stay, my pearl, you may find this interesting. Sit down with us." Isabella motioned to a chair. Sappho, waiting until both Isabella and Danilo were seated, sat down.

"Danilo, I fear the end is coming for all our little courts and dukedoms. We will be swept away and gobbled up by monsters—by France, and Spain, and the Germans. We city states and small dukedoms are all in competition. We all want the best artists, architects, musicians, and philosophers, and the artists take advantage, my dear Danilo, they take advantage. The prices go up."

Sappho leaned forward, listening intently, her bright eyes absorbing every nuance, every gesture, as if taking mental notes.

"I was brought up in Ferrara, as you know, with the best in music and poetry . . ." Isabella's words faded; her mind wandered. She looked at Danilo and then at Sappho, but her gaze was far away, as if not seeing them. Her eyes closed, her head wavered, then slumped, and she snored. Danilo stared at her. Could this Isabella, weakened and aged as she was, help him at all in his quest for Pirro? How could she possibly . . .?

Sappho narrowed her eyes and nodded, indicating he should take the initiative, speak, and bring Isabella back to herself.

Danilo coughed. "Music and poetry, indeed!"

"Ah, yes, indeed," Isabella said, almost with disdain, her head jerking up. "As I told you, my sister's husband, Ludovico, invited the Devil—the French—into Italy, and the Devil—the French— swallowed him, and Milan, whole." Isabella paused and drifted.

Sappho nodded at Danilo.

"And Venice?" he said, rather louder than he should have.

"Venice, of course, arrogant and supreme, is so proud, riding on its lagoon, with its wonderful artists and publishers. I do not know how the Venetians do it. Somehow it all works. But, as you know, even Venice is in crisis . . ." Her words slowed down, her attention was fading.

"Yes?"

Isabella suddenly perked up. "Your friends the Turks are taking over the Mediterranean with their new fleet and have cut off Venice from the Orient, from the trade in spices, and fine silks, and so on. Venice used to have a monopoly, could charge monstrous prices, a huge mark-up. Even for slaves, they would charge horribly inflated prices."

"Yes, those days of the Venetian monopoly have faded, partly at least." Danilo glanced at Sappho, thinking what it might be like, as a slave, to hear your price discussed as if you were a bale of cotton.

"But, Madonna," Sappho said brightly, giving her mistress a cue, "it is not only the Ottomans."

"Yes, my pearl, you are quite right. The whole pattern of trade is changing. The Spanish and Portuguese discoveries, with their bold navigators and sleek caravels, have created a huge problem for Venice. The moment the merchants on the Rialto learned that Vasco da Gama had sailed around Africa to India, they understood the implications—the spice trade monopoly was dead, and so there was an immediate banking and credit crisis in Venice. The people on the Rialto are clever; they see the larger import and scope of events. In an instant, they realized what it meant: Venice's power to dominate trade to the East had been smashed. Spices could now be brought directly from India around Africa. Of course the Venetians always find a way to bounce back. And then all of Europe is threatened. Your friend Suleiman has allied himself with the Barbary pirates of North Africa, and they are raiding our coasts and attacking shipping. So we are surrounded by wickedness and plotting on all sides."

It occurred to Danilo that here, safely ensconced in the Ducal Palace, he had forgotten, just briefly, that Hürrem's killers were hot on his trail, and that he was, quite possibly, being pursued as a spy against Venice. He cleared his throat. "Speaking of the Ottomans, Madam, I have a bit of a problem."

Isabella brightened. "I adore problems. Problems are to be solved—a challenge, are they not? Without challenges we would die." Her eyes sparkled.

"I may soon be accused of being a spy for the Ottomans—against Venice. You see, the other day I had a tour of the Arsenal . . ."

"The Arsenal?" Sappho's eyes went wide. "How—?"

Isabella held up her hand. "Tell me no more! I don't want to know."

"Mordecai Hazan, he lured . . ."

"The same Mordecai who asked me if you were dead? He clearly *wanted* you dead."

"Well, he . . ."

"No more. Sappho doesn't want to know. I don't want to know. Knowing such things is dangerous!" She hiccupped and patted her mouth. "What is the other problem?"

"Hürrem, the wife of the Sultan—"

"Remarkable woman . . ."

"So everyone tells me." Danilo frowned. Every mention of that woman was irritating. "In brief, the Grand Vizier, Pargali Ibrahim Pasha, is dead now, but before he died, he put a flea in Hürrem's ear—the idea that I was going to poison Suleiman, and . . ."

Isabella leaned forward. "So they have sent assassins to kill you, the alleged poisoner of the Sultan."

"Yes, and these assassins, two Men in Black, have been seen in Venice."

"Men in Black!" Isabella clapped. "I love high politics, intrigues, and cloak-and-dagger adventures." Her eyes shone.

"And I had a run-in with them, and—"

"Did you hear that, Sappho? This young man fought off the Men in Black, no less!"

Sappho tilted her head, half-closed her eyes, and gazed at Danilo though lowered lids. "You fought them?"

Not knowing what overcame him, Danilo jumped up and began to act it out. "I was alone, except for a torch-boy. Toto was his name, a cute, quick, ingenious little fellow—knows all about sounds and smells and how to feel your way around at night. I told Toto to hide. And I told him to use the torch to distract them, to lure them forward, as if we were still walking ahead, beyond the next corner. It was a dark night, pitch-black, with no moon and no stars visible, and fog coming in. The two killers were tracking me down a path beside a canal. I was unarmed. They had daggers. I found a rake and a shovel. I hid in a doorway."

"An ambush, my pearl!" Isabella leaned forward in her chair. "That takes quick thinking."

"I waited until they were opposite me. I struck one of the dastardly fellows quickly." Danilo leaped forward, imitating the thrust of the rake. "He toppled backwards and fell off the quay, shouting, and—splash—he was in the water, thrashing about, screaming for help. He didn't know how to swim. The other devil turned towards me. He was huge, fierce-looking."

"Was it daylight? You could see his face?"

"No, well. It was . . . anyway, he struck out with the dagger. I sidestepped." Danilo leaped aside, and swung his arm out and sideways. "And I smashed him straight in the face with the sharp edge of the shovel."

"Oh," Sappho put her hand to her cheek. "That must have hurt!"

"The rascal's face opened like a split melon. But he was strong and determined and he came at me again, waving his dagger, half-blinded by blood. He was huge."

"You said that already."

"And fast. We fought, and fought, twirling around each other, he lunging, me jumping aside, until finally I smashed him, and smashed him, and smashed him . . ." Danilo jumped up and down, imitating the action. "And I drove him into the canal."

"Oh, my! Oh, my goodness!"

"They were hollering for help, in Turkish. Neither could swim. Making an ungodly racket, waking the whole neighborhood. So I found my torch-boy, Toto, and we got out of there."

Danilo sat down. What had come over him? He was an idiot. He had been boasting, and, according to the code of the gentleman, as set out in *The Book of the Courtier*, boasting was not done. Braggadocio and boosterism were caddish. Why had he behaved like an ass? Miriamne would cover her mouth and laugh at him and insist on examining his palm for signs of boastfulness! Perhaps somewhere in the mountains of Jupiter . . .

Both Isabella and Sappho were smiling with a mixture of admiration . . . and indulgence. He sighed. Live and learn!

"So that was how it ended. It happened only a few days ago, and if they are alive — and I am pretty sure they are — they will not give up so easily."

"That was a splendid story, Danilo. You have added some spice to the life of an old lady who loved your mother very much."

"Signor Danilo may still be in danger," said Sappho.

"Yes, my pearl. As always, you see the essential point. I, Isabella d'Este, shall devise some diabolically clever plot to save you from these Ottoman Islamist assassins. I delight in plots and ingenious devices, don't I, Sappho? This will be fun!"

Sappho smiled. "Indeed. The more complicated the device, the better!"

"Well, fun . . ." Danilo smiled uneasily. "I'm not sure."

Isabella held up her hand. "I must prepare for tonight's festivities, which will include a marvelous theatrical performance. I want you to have a tour of Mantua. Sappho will guide you. She knows the city as well as I do. You trained as a warrior with Suleiman?"

"I did. The lance, the sword, and the dagger are not unknown to me, Marchesa, and also hand-to-hand combat, and cavalry charges, madam, and gunnery." Danilo stopped. Damn! He was doing that bombastic thing again. He glanced at Sappho. She was leaning back in her chair, her lips showing a suggestion of a smile, and her eyes half-closed. He almost blushed.

"And so, as you have just demonstrated so vividly to us, you can defend yourself."

"I imagine I can," he murmured.

"If you can hack up two assassins and toss them into a canal, I am sure you are equal to anything poor little Mantua can offer."

Danilo shrugged, trying to make a dismissive gesture; his boasting was going to get him into trouble. He could feel it.

"Well, in spite of your undoubted prowess, I shall send two guards along with you and Sappho, just to be doubly sure I do not end up with your blood on my hands."

SAPPHO TOOK DANILO THROUGH the rooms and pavilions of the Ducal Palace. Two guards followed at a discreet distance. "Isabella has her rooms in the oldest part, built about two hundred years ago. The palace has these very beautiful internal courtyards, with arcades, like cloisters, but airy and open, again letting in the light. I like to sit here and read."

"A beautiful and restful place to read, I imagine."

"Yes, and there are some very exciting rooms, particularly up in Castello di San Giorgio, rooms that speak of love." She led Danilo down a corridor. "Of course, this place is bathed in blood too. Some say it makes the earth more fertile and helps the flowers bloom. In 1328 Ludovico Gonzaga murdered his friend Bonacolsi and massacred the Bonacolsi family. That's how the Gonzagas came to rule over Mantua—by killing everybody, including friends and lovers."

"That's a familiar story."

She turned and pointed to two tall windows at the end of a corridor. "The light in Mantua is interesting, perhaps unique, since there is water all around. Mantua sticks out into the three lakes, and there is a canal cutting Mantua off at the neck of the headland. Mantua is like an island. There are reflections everywhere."

As she turned to Danilo, the afternoon light danced over her face. "Mantua is an ancient town. Before it was Roman, it was an Etruscan settlement. The name of the town, people say, comes from the Etruscan god, Mantus; he was a god of the underworld here in the valley of the Po. And, as I'm sure you know, the Roman poet Virgil was born near here, and Petrarch came here on a visit."

"I did know that." Danilo could recite quite a bit of Virgil; Grazia had insisted he acquire knowledge of the classics. Virgil was one of the greatest poets of Rome, and he wrote the epic *Aeneid*, giving Rome its soul, as someone said, and a motto: *Fortune favors the bold.*

Sappho led the way down a corridor. "And did you know Baldassare Castiglione, who wrote *The Book of the Courtier*, the indispensable guide to being a true gentleman, was born near Mantua?"

Danilo smiled. *The Book of the Courtier* was one of the volumes that Miriamne kept on her little shelf, next to Machiavelli and Boccaccio, above her work table.

"And this is the Sala del Pisanello." Sappho gestured towards the walls. "It has these half-finished frescoes by Pisanello. It shows a battle in which Lancelot and Tristan fought before setting off to search for the grail. He worked here for the Gonzaga family about one hundred years ago."

They went along a corridor, out through some gardens, and entered the forbidding Castle, then climbed some steep stairs and came to the famous *Camera degli Sposi*, the Bridal Chamber.

"And here, in the northeast tower of Castello di San Giorgio, is the famous *Camera degli Sposi*, painted by Andrea Mantegna in the 1460s and '70s, it took him about ten years."

They walked into the *Camera degli Sposi*. "Really, this room is just a simple cube." Sappho swung around, pointing. "But, as you can see, Mantegna created a sort of wonderland, with landscapes, and architectural features, and panoramas in many overlapping dimensions, so it seems grandiose and open to space."

"I see lots of dogs and horses . . . and a few family members."

Sappho leaned her head back and gave him her sneaky, insolent little girl smile. "Indeed, Madonna Isabella says that the Gonzagas have always loved their horses and dogs more than their women."

Danilo leaned close and peered at a detail—two men holding firmly collared hounds, right next to the doorway frame. The hounds were silver-gray, eager, strong-looking beasts; ready for the hunt.

"Madonna Isabella says the Gonzagas are very careful breeding their dogs and horses; perhaps more careful than when breeding humans and heirs." Sappho favored him with a sly sideways glance.

Danilo nodded. She was a subtle girl, this Sappho.

"And then there is an open landscape, people in the foreground, roads zigzagging away, echoed by the hills, to give an effect of distance and depth, and far away, a castle on the horizon." Sappho moved to the middle of the room. "And look up above you."

Danilo looked up. There it was — the famous oculus his mother had mentioned in her Secret Book, the round opening above them; a tromp l'oeil, entirely illusory, with fluffy clouds, and a tender blue sky, and putti and cupids looking down on them from a basket-weave fence, and the leaves of a plant tumbling over, showing from a vase. "Very lifelike."

"I think it is one of the first examples of the tromp l'oeil oculus."

"It is impressive."

"Back then, Ludovico Gonzaga and Barbara Brandenburg used to sleep here, or so I imagine it." Sappho was gazing upwards, and she turned and with a gesture indicated the place where the aristocratic bed might have stood. "Ludovico also used it as a reception room."

Danilo gazed at the spot. The love lives of princes and dukes were usually public and highly publicized knowledge; which bed so-and-so had slept in and with whom and when and for how long, that sort of fascinating thing. Of the doings of great ones, especially when it came to fornication and copulation, the little ones would prattle and take infinite delight — it was a new form of bread and circuses. Of course, the sex really did concern high politics — who was conceived and how, and by whom and with whom, was vital knowledge for hereditary dynasties and rulers, and for their peoples and neighbors.

"This is where I like to imagine they made love," Sappho said.

"Really?"

"I should like to make love someday. I'm sure it would be interesting." She ran her fingers wistfully along a wooden panel.

"I'm sure it would," said Danilo, "be interesting, I mean."

She gazed into his eyes dreamily, with that half-asleep look that she wore so well, and then she turned away. "And here we see a family portrait, also by Mantegna. It shows Ludovico and his bride, Barbara. She was the niece of the Holy Roman Emperor. It is a classical image, as you can see, carefully composed, with precise outlines, static poses, often in profile, truly the Mantegna style."

"Yes, carefully posed, very classical." It occurred to Danilo he was beginning to feel at ease with such language. He was not sure this was entirely a good thing; perhaps it was better to remain naive, and just stare and see what one might see. The language of the connoisseur seemed too easy, perhaps deceptively easy, to acquire. If it was easy, did it mean anything? Was it just an expression of facile inauthenticity, of playing a role? One should try, at least once in a while, to be true to oneself. Perhaps tongue-tied honesty was the better path.

"If you look up at the oculus again more closely, you will see Mantegna did have a sense of humor. There are some women—including a black woman like me—peering over the balustrade and down into the bedroom, and they have a bucket of water, or perhaps slops, held up by a broomstick, which they might just dump on the couple as they sleep, or even while they are making love."

Danilo craned his neck. The women up there were all amused, staring down at Sappho's imagined lovers.

"And then there are the two little putti. One is facing us, and looks like he is getting ready to pee on us. And the other has turned his cute little bum in our direction, and looks like he just might drop a turd or two down on the sleeping couple."

Danilo laughed. "So Mantegna was not entirely an old grump."

"I don't think he was, though of course I never met him; he died long before I was born."

"So many Gonzagas were conceived here," said Danilo, staring at the space where the imagined bridal and matrimonial bed had stood, and thinking of his own place in this brilliant and bloody dynasty that reached back into the mists of time.

"Yes," said Sappho, "the Castello di San Giorgio is where the Gonzaga bloodline was preserved." She gazed at him with that all-understanding little smile, this time wistful and sad. Did this young slave girl feel sorry for him, for Danilo del Medigo?

OUTSIDE THE AIR WAS chillier. The early afternoon was darker. Sappho turned to him and pointed back the way they had come. "Castello di San Giorgio is massive, a bit frightening. The walls rise almost straight out of the water. The red brick looks very nice when the sun is setting, and it has overhanging battlements, with four towers at the corners, and a moat with drawbridges. It is right here, at the Castello, that the middle lake meets the lower lake, so the Castello controls the passage between the two."

Danilo eyed the castle. It did look formidable. If he were to attack Mantua . . .

Sappho smiled, as if she had noticed his calculating warrior's glance. "There is a legend about the castle. They say it is haunted by two ghosts. Agnese Visconti of the Milanese Visconti family was married when she was fourteen years old to Francesco Gonzaga, also fourteen. Their marriage was to seal an alliance between Milan and Mantua. But later Francesco, for some obscure, quite possibly dishonest motive, accused his beautiful young wife of adultery with a courtier. The trial was quick and probably rigged. They cut off Agnese's head and hung her young lover by the neck until he was dead."

"That wasn't nice."

"But rather typical of the times."

"And of our times," said Danilo. He wished Miriamne were here to share this. Sappho was good company, and full of tales and information that would be a pure delight for Miriamne.

"It is said now that, to take their revenge as restless souls unjustly murdered, Agnese and her lover return each night to the castle and make wild uninhibited love all night, until dawn breaks over the fields and hills of Mantua. And then they disappear. Sometimes if I'm out very early, or very late, I think I hear them—and I shiver all over and run back home. And Enrico once told me he actually saw them up there on the battlements. But I think he was only trying to scare me."

"Best, then, to stay away from the Castello, at night."

"Precisely."

As Sappho took Danilo on her quick tour of the rest of the city, virtually every spot brought back memories of his childhood and of his mother, Grazia. She had once taken him down to the lake and they had looked out over the water, and two swans had appeared and Grazia had fed them; and then they walked along a street and stopped to gaze at the soaring façade of Mantua's cathedral, which had seemed to Danilo so huge, so high.

When Grazia was alive, Palazzo Tè did not even exist. The building was low, elegant, and absolutely symmetrical, with a line of arcades made of graceful arches, a central entry, and rows of Doric columns that seemed symmetrical but were not; and a central garden surrounded by a curved and open colonnade. In the afternoon light, the building had a light, dreamy quality, but it also presented a balanced, solid impression with its low, long, classical central structure.

"Why is Marchesa Isabella not allowed to enter Palazzo Tè?" Danilo asked.

"The Duke hates her interfering with his life." Sappho gave him that knowing sideways glance. "His mistress, Isabella Boschetti, is charming, I think. Federico had the artist and architect Giulio Romano design Palazzo Tè about ten years ago for la Boschetti. The paintings and frescoes inside are extraordinary, lots of exuberant mythological subjects, and there is also a grotto, a romantic little cave where you can imagine you are a primitive person before the beginning of the world. In Mantua everybody calls Federico's lady 'the Beautiful Boschetti.' Palazzo Tè, as you can see, was built on a little island, right at the edge of the marshes."

"So there is water, water, everywhere . . ."

"This is a watery place. It was here that Francesco, Federico's father, had stables where he used to keep and train his horses. The Gonzaga men do love their dogs and horses!" Sappho laughed, and glanced back at the two guards, who smiled at her. She became more serious. "Duke Federico comes here, to Palazzo Tè, to get away from business. But now, I think, we must get back to the Ducal Palace. There will be a performance this evening. And you must be hungry. It will be quite a while before the evening meal. Would you perhaps like something quick to eat?"

"Indeed, I would," said Danilo.

When they returned to the Ducal Palace, Sappho arranged for Danilo to be fed. Would he mind eating in the kitchens? No, he wouldn't mind at all.

And so a trencher of bread with sliced meats and cheeses was prepared, and a pitcher of wine was set on a wooden table in a corner of the vast kitchen, and Danilo dug in. He was starving.

Sappho set off to see if Donna Isabella was awake and if she wished to see Danilo.

"So Sappho has given you the tour, has she?" Ansaldo, the cook, was busying himself with the stove and giving directions to his assistants, who numbered about fifteen people, mostly men and a few women. "She's a clever girl, that one, and a saint, the things she puts up with, but Donna Isabella loves her as if she were a daughter. And Sappho acts, if I may confide, sir, as a sort of diplomat, soothes hurt feelings, calms ruffled spirits, and acts as a go-between for Isabella and Duke Federico."

"I understand relations are not ideal."

"That would be so, sir! If we tiny folk are allowed to natter about the great ones. Mantua is a small city, sir, and most everybody's business is most everybody's business, if you know what I mean—Watch you don't spill that, you rascal! People are worried that when Isabella dies, and let us hope that it will not be for many years, things will change, and not for the better. Isabella cared for the people. Duke Federico is not a well man, sir, not at all well."

"Oh?"

"He inherited from his father, I fear, the French disease—syphilis. It runs in the blood, so it ruins a man before he can sow his own wild oats. And Federico, I do believe, has never recovered from the fact that his mother was Regent for so long, and so ruled him in all things, and from the fact that she was such a good ruler, saved us from foreign domination, the very model of a princess. So, now that he has power, he will not listen to her on anything. Above all he will not listen as regards Pirro Gonzaga—in Mantua, Pirro has ceased to exist."

"That is really too bad." Danilo hesitated before swallowing. Pirro was a non-person. That would make things doubly difficult. "Do you know anything of him, of Pirro?"

"Almost nothing. No one speaks of him. And Isabella suffers from Federico's hostility, of course, and her isolation. So you coming here and any entertainment are welcome to Isabella and a relief from the pains of age."

Sappho appeared in the doorway.

"But I talk too much, I do," the cook rubbed his hands, "and the lass here knows it, doesn't she?"

"But everything you say, Master Ansaldo, is prepared and spoken with such wisdom, and spiced with such wit, that it is a pleasure to hear whatever you say, and one receives delight and instruction all at once."

Sappho led Danilo out of the kitchen and down several corridors lined with tapestries and paintings with mythological subjects, gods, goddesses, and cupids, and lush landscapes.

Finally they came to Isabella, who was waiting for them in her rooms. "Danilo." Isabella stood up and smiled, "I should like to show you our theatrical company and the theater we have set up for them."

Danilo bowed. "Thank you, Sappho, for a most enlightening tour of Mantua."

Sappho curtsied, favored Danilo with an enormous smile, and vanished out the door.

"You will take my arm, Danilo. Sometimes, when I am with Sappho, I forget how old I am—we have such fun. Then I look at her again, at the way she moves and laughs, and her grace in all things, and I see the contrast and I remember and feel in my bones how old I am."

Danilo and Isabella exited the Ducal Palace and went across a courtyard. They entered the palace again and came out onto a lawn, where a new pavilion was being built. Danilo glanced at the soaring walls and rows of windows and it struck him once again how grandiose this place was. The best architects and artists had been brought to this little city, and had turned it into a jewel, a model for future cities, and a model, for many, of how one should live one's life. And because of his mother and Pirro, he was part of all this.

As if she had read his mind, Isabella leaned closer to Danilo and whispered. "Not a day goes by that I don't think of Pirro!" She hesitated. "You have brought all this back to me—the affection I bore Grazia, the wonderful times we had together, and my love for Pirro."

"I hope it is not too painful."

"Yes, it is painful, but . . . pain can be creative. Suffering is the mother of invention."

"You think so?"

"I do. Duke Federico is against any contact with Pirro, even any mention of his name. But . . . I . . ." She stopped walking and turned her face up to Danilo. "Danilo, it will be difficult, I must be crafty and secretive, but I am going to find Pirro and I will write to him—about you! And if I do find any clues to Pirro's whereabouts, I shall tell you, so that you can seek him out, so you will know how to find him! You do need to see your father. And Pirro must see his son."

31

ORPHEUS

A FEW SECONDS LATER, WITH ISABELLA STILL CLINGING TO his arm, Danilo found himself standing in the middle of a bare central aisle in the newly built pavilion, surrounded by rows of seats painted in vivid colors.

Isabella put her hand on the back of a chair. "My husband and I built this little pavilion as a theater to house the resident acting company that we sponsor here in Mantua."

The space could take perhaps two hundred people. Chairs were set out in rows facing a raised stage, and behind the stage were backdrops and what looked like drawings. The walls rose up, with frescoes and vertical candelabra, and a curtain was hanging on both sides of the stage. Perhaps they could pull the curtains shut and hide what they were doing. This was interesting—a real theater.

"Until recently, as you may know, theater was based on religious themes and usually played in churches. The playwright Angelo Poliziano shattered that tradition with a new drama based on a Greek legend, *The Fable of Orpheus*.

"I know the story." Danilo looked around. Memories flooded back. His mother, when she read to him, was re-enacting her own tragedy, her own emotion, her impossible and forbidden love affair with Pirro, and she transferred her emotion and expressed it in the dramatic and beautiful way she read the stories. The tragic stories of love lost were mirrors reflecting her own story. "My mother told me stories from the old Greek myths to lull me to sleep. Her voice always choked when she read the tale of Orpheus and Eurydice."

"Yes," said Isabella, with a theatrical sigh. "It is a touching story."

"It does not end well." Danilo closed his eyes. He was seeing the scenes as if they were unfolding in front of his eyes: Miriamne was in the role of Eurydice, and behind Miriamne was a ghost, Saida; and behind Saida . . . Grazia. He was Orpheus. He had lost them all, and it was his doing! Out of love, he had lost the ones he loved. He opened his eyes. "The God of the Underworld releases Eurydice from a lifetime in Hades, but he imposes one condition: when Orpheus is leading Eurydice out of Hades, he must not look back. If he did, the God of the Underworld would reclaim Eurydice and she would spend all eternity in Hades, in the Kingdom of Death. But Orpheus cannot resist. He casts a quick glance backwards. Eurydice is condemned, swept back to Hades. Orpheus loses his love for all eternity."

"And a tale that has lived through the centuries," Isabella said, "the instant of loss repeated over and over, like an obsession." Isabella sat down and motioned to Danilo to go closer to the stage, to have a look at the set. As Danilo walked forward, an actor began to recite. The air was dusty with carpentry and the smell of paint, but the man's voice came through, loud and clear.

Oh what song of mine can witness my misfortune, all my suffering and my agony! How shall I find tears enough?

The soaring voice broke off in a sudden explosion of hacking coughs that went on and on.

"This actor is ill," Danilo said, turning to Isabella. "He needs a doctor."

"He's supposed to be sick. This aria comes at the end of the piece, when Orpheus is dying."

"It sounded real to me."

The coughing subsided. The singer resumed Orpheus's Lament.

For so long as the gods shall frame my life, in such a piteous state, shall I never love another!

The singer broke off into a series of gasps. Within seconds, a manager appeared from the wings. "Get the Jew physician. Nico is coughing blood."

Isabella got up and she and Danilo moved towards the stage.

"Perhaps I can help," Danilo said, "I was raised in a doctor's household. I have some knowledge of—"

"Tut, tut! Don't trouble yourself." Isabella laid her hand on Danilo's arm. "He's merely an actor. We have a Jewish doctor in Mantua. I am sure someone can find him in time to save the fellow's life."

Danilo opened his mouth to object, but Isabella pressed on. "What really concerns me is this: My nephew, Ercole II, the Este Duke of Ferrara, is riding in from Ferrara to attend tonight's performance. We must not disappoint him."

The director, a handsome, rather overweight man, with an abundance of curly gray-and-black locks and big, soulful eyes, pushed his way out from behind the curtains.

"Poor Nico is too sick to perform!"

"Surely not," said Isabella.

"I'm afraid so. And we have no understudy for Orpheus. I am too old to play the part, and if you will excuse the indelicacy, Marchesa, also too corpulent, too rich in flesh. Life has been too good to me, my Lady, and I have eaten and drunk deep of it. Pluck the rosebuds, seize the day, and seize it with both hands!" He patted his stomach.

Isabella turned to Danilo. "This is Andreas Satti. He is the manager and director and author and stage designer and impresario of our little theatrical group. He writes, he composes, he plays, he sings, he paints, and he designs the scenery and costumes. He does just about everything. And he eats and drinks like a whole company of soldiers."

Andreas Satti ran his hand through his hair. It was a grand, operatic gesture of pure histrionic anguish. His eyes shone with the liquid light of desperation, as if he were about to burst into tears. "We have no one! We need someone young, strong, and handsome, an ideal hero, like that strapping young fellow at your side, Marchesa. When I look at this young man I see Orpheus. I see our hero! He is Orpheus!"

The woman who had been playing Eurydice, and who was standing like a statue in the shadows, stepped forward into the light. She looked like a goddess portrayed by ancient sculptors and modern painters, a slender blonde with bright blue eyes and white skin high in color at the cheeks. Beautiful, painfully so. Her gaze lingered on Danilo; a smile flickered on her lips, her bright teeth just showing.

Andreas turned to her, his mood suddenly shifting. "Step back, Eurydice darling. Yes, that's it, that is perfect, hieratic and still, as if you have become a pillar of salt, lost forever in the shadowy kingdom of the dead." He fluttered his hands towards her. "Back to Hell you go, back to Hades, under the thumb of the God of Death himself! Just feel, darling, just feel the tragic weight of it."

"Does this work?" She bowed her head, standing absolutely still, statuesque.

"Utterly perfect! Darling, you are an angel!" He blew her a kiss. "This is Angelica, the light of our life, the guiding star of our endeavors, the compass of our ship, the pole star of our little convoy, the soul of our company of players."

She inclined her head in greeting.

Danilo felt he should comment on the beauty of the young actress, but something told him it would be impolitic to do so. If Isabella wanted the beauty of the young woman commented on, she would do it herself, as she had done with Sappho.

Angelica wore a simple, long-sleeved white blouse with a low neckline, a blue bodice with scarlet cross-lacing, and a long, pleated black skirt that went to her ankles and swayed gracefully with a soft alluring swish as she moved. She sighed. "If only this young gentleman could sing the songs of Orpheus."

Andreas struck his forehead with the heel of his hand. "A stroke of genius! Angelica, you have given us the solution to our problem."

"I did? What did I say?" Her blond hair, falling loose, sparkled like gold in the light streaming in from above.

With a sweep of his arm, Andreas indicated Danilo. "This young man has the looks but not the words, while I have the words but not the looks."

"How does that solve our problem?"

"We do the play as a mime."

Danilo frowned. What was going on? This exchange was too fast for him. Worse, it seemed to involve him!

"Oh, I see!" Angelica laughed. "This beautiful young man will mime the part on stage and you, Andreas, will sing from the shadows so the public will think our handsome gentleman here is doing the singing."

Danilo stepped back. "I . . . don't have any experience . . . no training as an actor. I am a fighter, a man of the lance, the sword, and the dagger." He blushed suddenly, wondering why he had once again become so boastful. It must be this blonde. Damnation!

Angelica studied him. "Pity. You would have made a smashing Orpheus to my Eurydice."

"And he still will," Isabella said firmly. Lifting her skirt, she stepped with difficulty onto the stage. "You told me you would like to find a way to repay my hospitality." She gave Danilo her most winning smile.

Danilo bowed. Damn! He had fallen into a trap!

"I will show him the moves myself," Andreas said. "And I will crouch out of sight in the Cave of Hades that Leonardo designed, and speak the words, and Angelica can help guide him. Since he is familiar with lances, daggers, and swords, we may even introduce a little action into the piece. Audiences love duels!"

Isabella smiled at Danilo as if she owned him. "My friend here is a trained duelist. You know how to obey orders, too, do you not?"

"Yes, of course, my Lady." Danilo bowed. What had he gotten himself into? His puerile boasting had catapulted him into this farce. And now he would be forced to make a fool of himself up on stage, playing at being something and somebody he was not, in front of a mob of people who might throw vegetables, rotten eggs, and rubbish while he, strutting and fretting amidst the decor, was a prisoner in his role and could not leap down from the stage and challenge anybody to a real duel. What a . . . !

"Then it is decided!" Isabella clapped her hands in delight

"Poor innocent warrior!" Angelica said, laughing. "He has no idea what he is in for!"

Andreas looked Danilo up and down and turned to one of the stagehands. "He needs to be cleaned up. Get the barber to shave his beard. Get my tailor and have him patch together a hero's outfit. Make it . . . frilly, full of frills."

"Shave my beard? Frilly . . . full of frills!" Danilo shrank back.

"And you actors better start rehearsing. There are only a few hours before the curtain rises!"

"Hours?" said Danilo, stunned.

"I am leaving my friend in your tender care, Angelica," said Isabella. "I am sure you know what to do with him."

Angelica sketched out a theatrical curtsey and shot a look at Danilo. "I certainly do, my Lady."

Isabella turned and limped away, saying over her shoulder, "We expect great things from you, Danilo! A whole new world is opening up, and with it great things!"

SHOUTS ECHOED THROUGH THE theater.

"Bravo, bravo!"

The audience, and first and foremost, Isabella d'Este, and her nephew, Ercole II, Duke of Ferrara, stood and clapped and clapped.

When the applause died down, Isabella presented her nephew, the son of the infamous Lucrezia Borgia, to the players. The Duke had ridden since sunrise to attend the night's performance and was visibly exhausted. But, putting on a gracious front, he took a moment to compliment the director, Andreas Satti. And then, turning to Danilo, he clapped him on the shoulder. "That was a marvelous dueling scene. You are an excellent swordsman!"

Danilo bowed low to hide his grimace. How awful it had been! His beard had been shaved away, he had been unmanned, desexed, dressed up in that flimsy white costume, like a girl's frilly dress. The very thought of it was odious — prancing around like an idiot! "I am not an actor."

"You could have fooled me."

"I merely mimed the part while Maestro Andreas sang it. My appearance tonight I owe to him and to Marchesa Isabella. It was temporary."

"You are a natural." The Duke smiled, and poked him in the chest.

Danilo swallowed his indignation. What had he come to? He, Danilo del Medigo — the leading student, and best lancer, the most accomplished horseman in the Sultan's school, the born fighter, the virtuoso with dagger and spear, the campaigner on the road with the Islamic armies of Suleiman the Magnificent, to be clothed now in this flimsy bit of flimflam, legs bare, exposed for all to see — it was intolerable.

On the other hand, he had been moved by the play. When Orpheus realized he had condemned his great love to death for all eternity, and when Angelica faded from sight as the lights went down, real tears had flooded his eyes.

The Duke moved on to congratulate the other members

of the cast. It was clear that, like everyone else, he was much taken by Angelica's charm. Soon he was telling the actress and others gathered around them stories of his hunting adventures, his dogs, and his horses; and various boars and stags that had been cornered and brought to bay and slain in the most dramatic circumstances. Angelica laughed and encouraged the young duke to tell them more.

Isabella whispered to Danilo, "This is good for my nephew. He needs intellectual stimulation and entertainment."

Sappho appeared and put her hand on Isabella's arm. Her expression was serious. "My Lady," she whispered.

"Yes, my pearl. What is it?"

"The Men in Black," she said.

Isabella frowned. "What of them?"

"They are here, in Mantua."

ISABELLA STEERED SAPPHO AND Danilo towards a corner.

"What have you learned?"

"There are two of them. They have been making inquiries after a young man matching Signor Danilo's description." Sappho glanced at Danilo. "One of them has half his face covered in bandages."

Isabella turned to Danilo. "As you predicted, Danilo, the killers did not drown. So at least you will not go to hell for that! And now they have come to finish the job. The Sultan's assassins are very skilled and very stubborn, I have heard."

"Yes, such is their reputation," said Danilo. It was annoying. Everybody seemed to compliment his enemies—Hürrem was "a very remarkable woman," the Men in Black were "very stubborn and highly skilled."

Sappho lowered her voice. "I took the liberty, my Lady, of arranging to have the two misdirected. Two workmen restoring the castle wall said they believed they had seen a person who looked like Signor Danilo heading towards the Duke's Tavern."

Danilo frowned. "Thank you, but when they—"

"The tavern master, Signor Ciecherella, is a friendly and accommodating person, and he was helpful enough to say he had, in fact, seen a young man corresponding to their description, and that he had bought a frisky five-year-old mare called Lucy to take him to San Agnes in Monte, which is, as you know, many miles and about eight days distant. Signor Ciecherella added some useful details, such as that the young man had seemed in a hurry and had galloped off leaving a great cloud of dust behind him, spurring Lucy to the utmost, and that he looked like he had not slept for several days. He also mentioned that the young man—who had seemed intent on losing some creditors or some such thing—had mentioned he might take the long way around just to fool his pursuers, and go by Rocca di Lonato del Garda, which of course makes the trip twice or even three times as long."

Isabella clapped. "Another fine performance this evening. Thank you, my pearl."

Danilo bowed towards Sappho. He owed this precocious teenager a great deal; she had perhaps saved his life. But what would come next?

"So the killers really are after you, Danilo!" Isabella exclaimed gaily; she seemed to be taking great pleasure in his misadventures.

"It does seem so."

"And Venice too is almost certainly in pursuit of you since your little visit to the Arsenal. The crime of spying on the Arsenal is death, preceded by a lengthy bout of torture and ignominy. Your mutilated body will be strung up on poles close to Piazza San Marco, and after this display you will suffer the additional indignity of being dismembered, perhaps fed to dogs, or pigs—whichever, given your beliefs, would be considered worse—and then whatever miserable remains are left will be buried in unsanctified ground in an unknown spot so that no one can ever mourn you or visit your resting place. Which, in such cases, is not really a resting place, since it is well known that unshriven souls tossed anonymously into unsanctified ground wander and are lost forever."

Danilo bowed. "Thank you, my Lady. You paint a vivid picture."

"The Most Serene Republic takes affairs of security seriously," said Sappho, deadpan.

"So what are we to do with you?" Isabella cast a glance across the room at the Duke, still in animated conversation with Angelica. "My nephew appears to have recovered his energies. The Duke has inherited some of his mother Lucrezia's sexual verve. I wonder if he can be of any use to us in this matter."

She walked over to the Duke and separated him from the actors. They had a brief exchange. The Duke shook his head and grimaced. Isabella nodded, and returned to Danilo and Sappho.

"The Duke tells me he is in difficult negotiations with Venice, which is always trying to bully little Ferrara, and he can't give the Venetians any excuses to interfere in Ferrara's affairs." Isabella paused, out of breath. "The Duke has inherited much of his mother's character, as well as her sexual appetite. He carries, after all, Borgia blood. Ercole can be capricious. If the mood struck him, he'd as soon throw you in one of his dungeons as invite you to dinner. Did you know that two of his uncles are still imprisoned? They have been locked up for decades, in little cells in the Castello Estense, the family castle. His father put them there, and Ercole has kept them there. So he is not to be trusted." She gazed at him. "What shall we do with you, Danilo?"

Sappho grinned. "We could send him off on a ship to America or England, or some other cold, out-of-the-way place where nobody dangerous or of significance ever goes."

Danilo frowned. Was the girl serious? He had no intention of going to America, or even worse, England, where it was reputed the food was terrible, the manners barbaric, and the climate unspeakable. No culture whatsoever. Besides, he'd have to learn the language. And no one who counted spoke English, a useless, bastard, ugly mishmash of an unpronounceable guttural, provincial Germanic tongue. Even worse, England had hardly any army to speak of, let alone a decent navy, no ships worth mentioning.

"A charming idea, my pearl. But, perhaps . . ." Isabella paused and fingered the gold-colored cord that attached her spectacles to her girdle. She lifted the spectacles and turned them this way and that. Finally, she put them on, perching them at the very end of her nose. "You are indeed a handsome specimen, Danilo." She gazed at him through the lenses.

Servants had arrived signaling that the evening feast was about to be served. The whole night, outdoors and indoors, would be spent in revelry, with strolling musicians, dances, and food—roast beef, lamb, and chicken, bread and rice, vegetables of all sorts, and fish too—served in taverns, on the streets, in the squares, and in the Ducal Palace.

"Where do the actors head next, my pearl?"

"To Bologna, I believe, my Lady. They leave at dawn. Then, onward through the mountains to Florence."

Isabella turned to Danilo. "Hunger makes me fidgety. I cannot concentrate. Let us go. The feast awaits! Don't worry, Danilo, there are guards at the gates. No Turks or Venetians will sneak in to slay you, not while we are eating, at least. And in the meantime I will think about my plan. I do not like to make decisions when hungry."

3 2

A FOOL IN MOTLEY

ANILO, AS A GUEST OF ISABELLA, WAS SEATED WITH THE
gentry.

He ate what he could, but he was worried that
Sappho had gotten her information wrong or that the assassins
had seen through her subterfuge and returned. He worried too
that he was putting others at risk; the two workmen who had
misdirected the killers, Signor Ciecherella, the kindly tavern
owner, Sappho herself.

Finally, it was past midnight. Music was coming from every
direction. Shouts and laughter drifted in from the squares and
streets and taverns. Mantua was entertaining itself.

"Well, I think have indeed concocted an ingenious and
entertaining plot to keep you safe, Danilo." Isabella patted her
mouth.

Duke Ercole had gone off to see about his horses. Isabella
had said goodbye to her principal guests, and then, with Danilo
and Sappho standing almost at attention, hanging on her every
word, Isabella pronounced her judgment.

"I have had time to digest your problem, Danilo, and chew it over and wash it down, and I have a plan. It is the very, very best plan."

"Oh?"

"Sometimes it is best . . ."

"Yes?"

"To hide in plain sight."

"Very philosophical, my Lady, but . . ."

"You shall become an actor."

Danilo started back. The woman could not be serious!

"Oh! He will become an actor!" Sappho, who had been listening intently, giggled and clapped, and then covered her mouth and looked down.

Isabella put her hand on Sappho's shoulder and turned to Danilo. "The actors' caravan will afford you a safe refuge from both killers and magistrates."

Danilo was dumbfounded. "Why do you think that?"

"The last place anyone will think to look for you is on stage, gallivanting and prancing about, and wooing a fair maid."

Danilo winced.

"And consider this. You will have access to anything you might ever need to transform yourself! Costumes! Dyes! Makeup! Rouge!"

"Dyes? Makeup? Rouge?"

"A disguise, Danilo!"

"But I am not an actor!"

"Oh?" Isabella said archly. "Really? Do you have no experience pretending to be something or someone you are not?"

Danilo looked at her sharply. What was she implying? How much did she know of his spying in Venice?

"The performance you gave tonight proves the contrary, dear Danilo. As Duke Ercole said, you are a natural actor. And when you told Sappho and me about your adventures with the Men in Black in Venice, why you acted it all out, and so vividly, you transported us right into the action! Didn't he transport us directly into the action, my pearl?"

"Indeed he did!" Sappho said, unable to hide her amusement.

Danilo fumed. He had brought everything that had happened, all the bad things ever, onto himself. It served him right! He was a fool! How could he be such an idiot?

The Duke returned from his horses and sidled over to join them. He greeted Sappho with great warmth, eyeing her up and down. "Look how little Sappho has grown!" He turned to Isabella. "If you wish to sell Sappho, I would be an eager buyer. She would be a great addition to the treasures of Ferrara."

Sappho smiled tightly. Clearly, she was terrified. Danilo held his breath. The girl's life hung in the balance. To be an absolute prisoner of the whims of others! To be bought and sold! It made him ashamed of his anger at his own — privileged — fate.

He bowed and went and stood in a corner of a far room; he stared at the walls and worried about Sappho and brooded: about destiny, about braggadocio, about love lost; about Saida and about Miriamne, her smile, her laughter, her tears. How had he got himself exiled from the ones he loved, and condemned to be a prancing fool garbed in motley?

He could not return to the others. He collected his carpetbag and paced up and down a narrow side corridor, thinking. Perhaps he should just stride off into the night, wander the world, take his chances. But without Isabella, how could he find Pirro? He stroked his chin, now clean-shaven. He felt unmanned and naked. Thank God there was already a hint of stubble. If any of the cadets at the Sultan's school had seen him like this, frolicking about, capering this way and that, their laughter would echo into infinity! And the whole thing had no logic. The duel had been added — just like that, pure caprice — by Andreas to sprinkle some extra spice into the spectacle and exploit Danilo's dexterity with a sword. A fatuous world of make-believe! Was he to become a clown?

Sappho was standing next to him. "Are you ready, Master Danilo?"

She was trembling, her movements slower, and her elegant hands clutched together, but still putting on a brave face.

"Forgive me . . . you are not being sold, I hope."

"No. For the moment I am anchored right here, in Mantua. La Marchesa needs me."

"Yes, she certainly does."

She managed a brighter smile. "You, on the other hand . . ."

Danilo took a deep breath and nodded. What were his trivial tribulations, after all, compared to hers? She was chattel, a piece of furniture; her owners could dispose of her as they wished, the merest caprice could destroy her life. "There is no predicting destiny," he said.

"Let us go!" Sappho lifted her chin proudly and, striding on ahead, she led him back to the theater, where it seemed his destiny was to don motley, to be a fool!

IN THE THEATER, ISABELLA, deep in discussion with Andreas and Angelica, turned and greeted Danilo with the self-satisfied grin of an accomplished conspirator. "Our director, Maestro Andreas, has quite a little bag of tricks—makeup, wigs, costumes of every type, hair dye, and skin dye!"

Danilo nodded. The horrors were piling up faster than he could have imagined.

"I have a dye pot that will turn that mop of golden curls into a flowing dark cloud." Andreas said, gazing at Danilo, eyeing the potential. "You will not recognize yourself!"

Sappho glanced at him, nodded, and blinked her sympathy.

Isabella clapped. "That solves one problem. And Danilo, while you are on tour, you can entrust anything you have of value to me."

"I have only one thing of value: a portrait of my mother painted by Mantegna."

"Ah, yes, I remember that painting. It is exquisite. It captures the true essence of Grazia, so beautiful, and only seventeen years old! It will be safe here. I will hang it along with the other portraits Mantegna made for us." Isabella gave Danilo a wide smile, "One word, Danilo."

And she turned aside, beckoned him to her, and whispered, "While you are on tour, Danilo, I shall—secretly, of course—try to track down Pirro, so you can find him and finally be reunited. This is between us, you understand!"

She patted him on the shoulder and turned back to Angelica. "My dear Angelica, I shall leave our new recruit in your care. Don't let him out of your sight."

"He shall not escape," said Angelica.

"Indeed, I hope you wrap him up tight in your bedroll!" Isabella gave the actress an indulgent smile of complicity.

Danilo turned towards Isabella. What had the woman just said? Parcelling him off like a piece of baggage? He glanced at Sappho. She shrugged. If he understood correctly, Angelica was married to Maestro Andreas, who did not look as if he was the type of man who would easily turn over his belongings, let alone his wife, to another man, though of course he was an actor, and who knew what sorts of immoral mischief such itinerant thespians would put up with.

Angelica yawned, daintily covering her mouth and blinking at Danilo. "He shall be wrapped up tight as tight can be."

LATER THAT NIGHT IN a large, sparsely furnished room in some far wing of the Ducal properties, Angelica stood in a white nightgown that went down to her ankles, looking like Eurydice, a shimmering statue. The windows were covered with thick drapes that reached from the ceiling to the floor. Paintings hung on the wall, with cupids and maidens frolicking, gods and goddesses getting into mischief, and castles and moody mountains lowering suggestively in the background. Candles burned on a table next to the bed. The bed roll—actually a real four-poster bed with a gold-and-crimson silk-damask baldaquin—stood against one wall. The bed stared at Danilo. Danilo stared back.

He cleared his throat. "What will Maestro Andreas say, then, when he realizes you have taken a strange man into your bed, Angelica?"

The actress sat down on the edge of the bed. She blinked at him, yawned, stretched her arms above her head, and ran her fingers through her hair, which was loose and golden and fell well below her shoulders. "Oh, don't worry about Andreas! My husband will not even notice his wife is in another man's bed or that another man is in his wife's. In any case, he already knows what your fate will be." Tilting her head to one side, she favored Danilo with a charming smile. "He cares not a whit. Andreas prefers boys."

Danilo sighed. "That is a rather widespread taste."

"Both modern and ancient. All the best people do it. Socrates and Plato and Alexander the Great . . . Leonardo . . . Virtually anyone of consequence. Andreas is a true gentleman, and my best friend. I owe him everything." She stood up and slipped out of her nightgown, lifting it up over her head. Her body was long, with a slender waist, full breasts catching reflections of the candlelight, and long legs that reminded him of the glimpses he had had of Veronica Libero's justly famous limbs. He drew in his breath. She smiled, folded the nightgown neatly over a chair, and slid into bed.

"Why do you owe him everything?" He tried to look away. Her face, framed in the golden curls, was designed by the gods to attract a man's gaze. And, under the sheets, he imagined her creamy skin, her naked body pressing against the cloth. What would a true gentleman—schooled in the Sultan's Academy and trained by *The Book of the Courtier*—do in such a circumstance? He sighed, and began to pull off his doublet and leggings but kept his underclothes. Surely that counted for something.

"I was a slave." Angelica plumped up the pillows. "Andreas bought me."

"You were a slave?"

"I was captured by Muslim pirates in Dalmatia. The coast is wild, though the Venetians ostensibly control it and they—and occasionally the Ottomans—try to tame it, and send warships and so on, but it's impossible to be everywhere at once. Too many cliffs, islands, mountain passes, forests . . . lots of places for pirates to hide. So even if the Venetians send warships . . ."

"I have heard it is a wild coast. Illyria, it was called."

"That's right. Perhaps I am related to the ancient Illyrians—I often feel I'm a girl from ancient pagan and Greek times. It's a beautiful coast, if you like cliffs and wild frothing seas, and strong north winds, and long balmy summer days perfumed with pine and cedar, with crickets and cicadas making a racket, and high mountains and deep coves, and steep narrow passes, and pebbled and sandy beaches, and forests that seem to reach to the sky. We villagers sometimes don't count as Christians, so, legally, we can be enslaved, even by Christians. Particularly if, not knowing Italian or French, we can't explain who and what we are." She looked him up and down. "You don't need to wear any clothes, Signor Danilo."

"Well . . ." Danilo hesitated.

"Acting requires intimacy."

"I am not an actor."

"I know, dear Danilo del Medigo, you are a warrior. You can do great things with a horse, a lance, a sword, and a dagger. You are probably very good with dogs too. You are a scholar. You read and speak Persian and Turkish and Arabic and Italian and undoubtedly French. You are an aristocrat, probably with Gonzaga blood flowing in your veins. You are a man of many parts!"

"You know a great deal about me."

"Madonna Isabella likes to talk. I think she thinks of you almost as kin, she admired your mother so much. But princes and aristocrats are cautious in bestowing favors, and even callous and forgetful of their servants. Sappho also gave me some details, how you fought off two killers in Venice. Sappho acted it out—she's an excellent mime—'Stab, stab, stab, lunge, lunge, splash! And, poof, he conquered them all,' is what she said. So conquer those underthings too—toss them away and get into bed."

Danilo blushed and looked down. Then, in one quick motion, he pulled off the last of his underthings, folded everything carefully on a trunk, slid under the covers, and lay down next to her. She propped herself up on an elbow. Behind her was the gold-and-crimson baldaquin. Above were the rafters and the arched roof of the room. There was a smell of grain in the air, of stucco and paint, and of open fields.

"The Barbary pirates, you know, the ones from North Africa, from the Barbary shore, the ones who work with Barbarossa—Red Beard, Suleiman's pirate admiral—they came ashore at dawn and raided my village, which was in one of those deep inlets that are so common on the Dalmatian coast. They killed all the old people—most of our young men were away fighting another village, and perhaps raiding cattle. My father, who was gentle but fierce, was away too; he was the leader. I was young, a child really. They killed my mother because she fought the man who tried to rape her, and they killed my older sister, Clara, because she had a limp. She was not valuable. They raped Clara first, and then they killed her. They enjoyed doing it. They laughed. They had big teeth and flashing eyes."

She clenched her fist and closed her eyes. "I can see it as if it were still happening right now, over and over. But it is as if it happened to somebody else, not me. Except that when I think of my sister—and all she had was a little limp, hardly noticeable—and my mother, who was a wild and funny and beautiful woman, then, well, then I want to cry."

Her eyes glistened in the lamplight. Danilo touched her cheek and ran his finger down to her chin.

She sniffled and then smiled a little. "It helps with the acting. If I am to cry, all I have to do is . . . remember. I find the tears within me, they are always there. Perhaps we should all cry more often. People are becoming too hard. Some people know how to find their tears more easily than others."

Danilo half-closed his eyes. He wondered what would summon tears—his forced parting from Saida, his forced parting from Miriamne, Judah del Medigo abandoned in Istanbul and not knowing what had happened to his son, the death of his mother and of all the passengers on the *Hesperion*, and all those who died in wars, or in illness, or who were reduced to slavery . . .

"I was kept in the galley hold of their boat with all the other women and children. My hair was shaved off because of lice. I was naked, or almost, and offered up for inspection. I was skinny then, not even a teenager, and boyish looking. I liked climbing trees and I was excellent with a bow and arrow and spear. A wild little thing."

Danilo brushed a strand of blond hair away from her forehead. He thought: I like touching her. The ghost of Miriamne stood silently by, watching, judging. He shook it away.

"They were North Africans, Muslims, headed towards Tunis to sell us on the slave market. We were about three hundred, I think, mostly women and children, in several ships. I was allowed up on deck once or twice to be soaped down, splashed with water, and checked for lice. The galley's oarsmen—two men to a bench on both sides of the boat, sweating away under the crack of the whip—were Christians the pirates had captured and reduced to slavery. They were practically naked, wearing just loin cloths; chained to their benches, burnt and blistered by the sun, their skin raw with sores, and bleeding—rowing and rowing and rowing. Their muscles bulged, and oil and sweat gleamed on their dirt-streaked skin. They stank. The slave master applied the whip. I remember the slashing sound, and the ripple and snap of the canvas when the sails caught the wind. Then our Muslim pirates—our Saracens— were attacked by Christian pirates, a French crew mostly, and all the Muslims were killed except a few who were enslaved, while we were 'liberated.' But the Christian pirates decided that we would remain slaves, that I and the other girls and boys and women, were valuable booty."

"I thought Christians were not allowed to enslave other Christians."

"In theory, that is so, dear Danilo, but I was a child. We were mostly children, and the women were mainly illiterate peasants, with some pagans, eastern Slavs among them, and these French pirates declared we were filthy pagans, and so could be enslaved and sold. Nobody really spoke French or Italian—there was nobody to speak for us. I had only a few words and I was too terrified and ignorant to protest."

"I see. So . . ."

"So we were unloaded onto another ship and taken to the slave market in Venice—a shipment of Slavs, destined for slavery. When money is involved, people often don't ask too many questions."

"Of course, I have seen that myself. But how did you end up here?"

"It was a lucky coincidence. At the very moment I was put on sale, Andreas had been sent from Mantua to buy some slaves as well as some special silk embroideries and porcelain for Marchesa Isabella. He was looking for a boy or two for himself, to do acrobatic tricks or juggling, and to play pageboys and suchlike in the theater, and perhaps for his own amusement on cold lonely nights. And, then . . . Well, he decided to purchase me."

"But you are not a boy."

"No, I am not a boy. How perceptive of you, Danilo! But I looked like a boy—a beautiful boy, Andreas said. He knew I was a girl, of course. My hair had only begun to grow back, so it was short like stubble. I was between ten and eleven, not yet a woman. No breasts, no hips, a flat little thing. Perhaps that saved me. I could easily have been sold to a rich wicked old man with violent and dirty tastes. I probably would have died. Or I would have murdered my owner and been drawn and quartered or beheaded or hung from a rafter. I had a blinding headache, standing up there on the platform in the glare of the sun. The bidding for the slaves was fierce. I was terrified. I thought I was going to be sick, and be punished for being sick.

"The slave markets are noisy. People shout, and in many languages. All your clothes, if you have any clothes, are taken away. You are shackled together with ankle and wrist chains, sometimes chains around the neck, with a collar. Left out in the sun, naked or almost naked, you can get badly burnt. You are filthy. They shove you around, poke at you. They pull your mouth open to look at your teeth. Often they have dirty fingers. There were women of all ages, and children and teenagers, and of course there were boys. The boys, particularly the young and pretty ones, if sold in eastern markets, would become eunuchs, their testicles and penises cut off. Though sometimes, I've been told, it's just the testicles, and sometimes it's just the penis—different effects for different purposes, I suppose—and unless they do it right, it can be fatal."

"So I've heard." Danilo had heard horrifying whispered accounts of those operations from some of his fellow students at the Sultan's school, and he had seen a number of eunuchs in Istanbul—hairless, plump, sly, calculating creatures with soft voices, neither man nor woman. And he, too, had Judah not ransomed him, would perhaps have suffered a similar fate.

"Andreas was gentle. He was polite. He was clean, even his fingernails. And his shirt was white, and perfect. He circled around me. I could smell his perfume. He touched me gently, stroking my sides and my shoulders. Then he caressed what little hair I had on my head, put his finger under my chin, tilted my face up towards him, asked me to smile, and then he smiled. It seemed to be a very kind and friendly smile—but that made it even more frightening. I thought, 'This man is smiling, that must mean he is very wicked, even more than the others.' He asked me to talk. I spoke only a few words of Italian, so I said hello and asked him how he was, and I said it was a hot sunny day, which was about as much as I could manage, so I apologized and said I didn't know much Italian. And then when there was a brief break in the bidding and haranguing, he spoke very quietly to the slave merchant and handed over a bag of coin. He told me later I was rather expensive, but he had just won quite a bit of money gambling, and he decided to spend his winnings on me. He said he could always buy a boy or two later, but that when he saw me he knew he had to have me. The gods sometimes are kind.

"So, at first, I was his servant. He dressed me often as a pageboy. Perhaps this was rather naughty of him, or wishful thinking. I performed as an extra and as a pageboy in plays. Sometimes I slept with Andreas, and sometimes, he used me as a man can use a boy, but he was gentle and he always made me feel loved and cared for. Men can be executed for this, but I would never wish that on him. He taught me good Italian and arranged for me to learn how to read and write—Italian and French and some dialects. I even had tutors, very good ones too. And then when I filled out and became a woman, he stopped sleeping with me and he taught me more about acting, and how to declaim, and to act in Italian and French and Spanish, and even to use a bit of Latin and Greek. Perhaps it is wrong, but I came to love him in a way, not in a romantic way, but as a mentor and a friend. So he has made me what I am, for better or for worse."

Danilo kissed her. He couldn't resist. He did it slowly, tenderly, and he wondered at himself. Was love so fickle? Was memory so weak?

Angelica drew back. "You do know how to kiss, dear Danilo. I suspect you are a talented lover. You must have had a good teacher. I wager it was an older woman. No, was it a younger woman? Perhaps a harem girl! They are as wise, I believe, in the ways of love as the courtesans of Venice." Angelica laughed. She slid up onto his body, and, looking down, kissed him. Her golden hair fell over his face like a tented veil, perfumed and smelling like sweet lemons. Danilo took her in his arms. The kiss lasted, a deep, exploring kiss; her breasts brushed against his chest, and she pulled back and lifted herself up, slightly arched, the candlelight gleaming on her breasts and golden hair; he seized her at the waist and guided her as she slowly lowered herself down, and he felt himself plunging into her, deeper and deeper and deeper.

Later that night, she whispered, "Do you trust me?"

He wasn't sure that he did, but he said, "Yes." What else could a man say to a woman he was holding in his arms, a woman he had just made love to, a woman whose warm naked body was pressed against his, a woman who was giving him comfort and shelter—for without her and her bed, he would quite possibly be sleeping out under the stars.

"Then I shall do it," she said.

"Do what?"

"Are you ready?" She gazed at him steadily.

"Yes, I'm ready." He stroked the side of her face. A strand of hair tumbled down her cheek and touched the corner of her lips. He brushed it away.

She closed her eyes and recited the lines, delicately, with feeling, *"Here it was, also, that I saw a nation of souls, lost, far more lost than those that exist above . . ."* She stopped and looked at him.

Danilo was stunned. This was what Marco had told him. If someone quoted this verse of Dante's, it meant that person was a spy; it meant that person worked for Venice, for Marco. He held his breath. Spies were everywhere. Venice was everywhere. Marco was everywhere. There was no escape.

She kissed him. It was a sweet and violent kiss, a mix of aggression and possession.

"Do you trust me?" she said.

Danilo took a deep breath. "Yes. Yes, I do."

INTERLUDE

3 3

SONGS OF ABSENCE

M IRIAMNE STEPPED BACK FROM THE WINDOW OF HER
workroom.

Each time she looked, she held her breath and prayed she might see Danilo striding across the Campo in that proud quick way he had, as if he had something important to do and was rushing to do it; sometimes she thought she did see him, his broad shoulders, his strong arms. When she accompanied her father to synagogue and looked down from the women's gallery, she would glimpse Danilo's blond curls under the skull cap. But no, it was always someone else, a stranger, a visitor. Each time, she put on a bright smile and swallowed her grief.

Miriamne continued her life as it had been before Danilo. She looked after her father. She helped and comforted Uncle Isaac in his last illness, and when he died she helped prepare his body and organize the shiva. She sat with his friends and listened to the stories of Old Isaac when he was a young blade and the mischief he got into, and stories from when he was a rich gambler, and the less edifying mischief he got into when his addiction to gambling turned destructive—how once, in one night, by pure bold bluff, he had earned two hundred ducats; how, when escaping from an enemy, he had had to climb over rooftops and then jump into a canal, and had come back home soaking wet, which his wife did not appreciate at all. And Mariamne told them stories about his old age, how Isaac had become Old Uncle Isaac, and how, with infinite kindness and tact, and some humor, he had become, in his last years, a guide and a sage, always warning about disasters to come, but warm and generous and loving to everyone.

When Jessica and Jacob's mother died, Miriamne effectively adopted the children and schooled them, with help from her father. She doggedly resisted the blandishments and threats of her brother, who kept trying to force her to marry Jeremiah. Mordecai, it seemed, always needed money, and Jeremiah was the man who provided it; and Jeremiah wanted his reward—and his reward was to be Miriamne Hazan. Rabbi Hazan backed Miriamne, saying, "She has time, Mordecai, she has time. She has much to do and much to learn, and she wishes to learn and do those things." Unspoken in the rabbi's defense of his daughter was the fact that Miriamne did not have a sufficient dowry for her to make a desirable match, and this was the rabbi's own personal burden of guilt to bear. Beyond that, Rabbi Hazan knew more than he wanted to know about Jeremiah's treatment of his first wife, who had died under rather suspicious circumstances. As if that weren't enough, the rabbi had also heard about some of Jeremiah's less savory, even dangerous, connections, when they were alluded to, perhaps as a warning, by one of Venice's leading book collectors and best-informed citizens, a certain distinguished gentleman everyone called "the Senator."

As the cycles of the Jewish year—with its months based on the lunar cycle—slowly turned and meshed in a complicated and shifting way with the Christian Julian calendar, Miriamne helped with and observed all the Jewish festivals. Each one had for her its own dear meaning: Jewish New Year, Rosh

Hashanah, Yom Kippur, Chanukah, and Purim. She prepared herself for Yom Kippur—the Day of Atonement—by examining her conscience, as tradition required. Had she hurt anyone, or insulted anyone? Had she failed to help someone whom she could have helped? Had she neglected someone to whom she could have given succor? She then tried to right those wrongs before the day of Yom Kippur arrived, before she felt she could atone for her sins. On the day itself, she kept the strictest fast, attended prayers in the synagogue, and abstained from work, though occasionally, when in her workroom, she would cast a longing glance at an unfinished amulet.

She was scrupulous in helping her father prepare for each festival and she knew all the stories behind them; she tended to find the more allegorical, spiritual, and ethical implications most interesting.

Miriamne read deep in Jewish lore, and continued to read the philosophers as well as plunge into secular Italian literature, some of it quite naughty.

Miriamne began to write poetry. At first, just single lines would pop into her head, and images, and then verses, and then whole poems; she did it while she worked on her amulets. The words would sing or talk in her head—as if she were talking to herself or perhaps arguing with Danilo—and she'd stop her work and write the words down. The poems, of course, were love poems, letters of yearning, of desire, directed towards the absent and invisible lover. Her muse, even though she never named him, was Danilo del Medigo. She kept the lines and the poems on scraps of paper in a drawer in her work desk. She began to rearrange the scraps, pulling the lines and verses together.

Finally, she showed her work—twenty-five poems—to her father, leaving the sheaf of pages with him, and going back to her little workroom, her heart beating with trepidation. She tried to concentrate on an amulet, but it was difficult to focus. How would her father judge her? Would he consider the poems blasphemy? Would he condemn them as expressions of worldly passion, earthly desire? Her father appeared in her doorway. He rubbed his eyes. "You are like your mother. She was almost too many things contained in one woman, in one person—too much for this world." His eyes were glossy. He lifted the poems and read a few lines out loud. He repeated several lines. Then he looked up and he said, "My daughter, your words break my heart, and they make my heart soar."

Miriamne asked the publisher Daniel Bomberg about publishing the poems. He said he wasn't printing poetry, not for the moment, but just down the *calle* there was a printer, Giovanni Sabaddin, a Christian, a true Venetian, who did print poems. Miriamne steeled herself and, with Jessica and Jacob in tow, she went to the printer.

He looked up and saw the yellow veil. "What can I do for you, Jewess?"

She explained.

He rubbed his forehead and sighed, "Poetry, eh?" He held out his hand. She passed him the sheaf of loosely bound papers.

"You might as well sit down," he said. "Luca here can show the children how the presses work, that will keep them busy. You are lucky. This is a quiet moment. We are waiting for a manuscript. Here is something to read." He handed her a small book. The place smelled of ink and paper, and old rags and grease and metal. Light came down from windows high up in the walls and two lamps burned on little shelves. Books and sheaves of paper were piled up helter skelter on shelves. The printing press itself was partly visible through a doorway, a large wooden machine with a bulky wooden frame and a screw or lever to press down on the paper. Light came in from someplace above; there was a man toiling away, putting the letters in place, wearing an ink-stained apron and a cap tilted down over his forehead. Jessica and Jacob could be heard in the back of the shop. Young Luca was explaining things. Time passed. Signor Sabaddin turned over the pages. He went back and read some more. Finally, he looked up at her. "You wrote this?"

"Yes, Signor, I wrote it."

"What is your name?"

"Miriamne — Miriamne Hazan."

"Signorina?"

"Yes, Signorina."

"Well, Signorina Miriamne, this is remarkable work — an exquisite expression of yearning for the absent lover. Dante had Beatrice; Petrarch had Laura; and you, obviously, have an ideal of chivalrous manhood. I have rarely seen such intense and true emotion." Signor Sabaddin rubbed his chin.

Miriamne blushed. Was he being ironic? Would he suddenly laugh at her, slap his knee, and exclaim what a joke this was? She ventured, carefully, almost primly, "Thank you, sir."

He was frowning, looking down at the bundle of papers. "It will make a small volume. I will print them and offer them for sale — or my partner, Michelis, a stationer, will. We will take printing costs, overhead, and our own profit out of the sales, and you will get the remainder. I doubt if you will make any money, but people will be able to read them."

"That is all I want, Signor."

And so Miriamne published a slender volume of poetry, *Songs of Absence*.

People remarked on it. People spoke to her about it. Even in the Rialto Market shopkeepers mentioned it. Miriamne felt it was strange, people she did not know reading her words, feeling her feelings, living, for a moment, her thoughts.

One afternoon, she was sitting at her workbench fashioning a particularly intricate emerald amulet when Filippo, Vincenzo's young man, knocked. "Here's a note for you, Signorina Miriamne," he said, with a neat little bow. He handed her an elegant note — expensive paper, perfumed, folded and sealed with wax.

In wonderment, Miriamne gazed at it; she slit the wax seal with a knife.

I have just read your poems, dear Miriamne, and they are exquisite. You reminded me of feelings I have not had in a long time. And you made me feel and see things in a way I had not seen or felt before. You capture the very essence of love, of yearning, of desire—and of absence. Even the great and notorious Aretino—and he is a superb critic, among the many other things he is—praises your work. I hope, Miriamne, that you will accept this compliment from a woman such as I. With all my best wishes, I am your admirer and humble servant, Veronica Libero

Miriamne's heart flipped over. Pain surged up, and memories of that horrible night on the riva degli Schiavoni when she fought with Danilo, after he had bowed towards the beautiful and notorious Veronica Libero. And pleasure surged up too, and shock, at being recognized as a fellow poet, almost as a friend, by a renowned poet who was also a famous courtesan, the greatest in Venice, perhaps in Europe.

Filippo was lingering at the door. "Are you all right, Signorina?"

Miriamne realized she was breathing quickly. Her heart still stung; all her yearning and loneliness welled up. Did she hate Veronica Libero? Could she love the work, and yet hate the woman? She gathered her wits and smiled. "I am quite fine, Filippo. Thank you!"

"Is there an answer, Signorina?"

Miriamne had not thought of an answer and knew that such a compliment did not require one. She imagined briefly she might ask Veronica Libero if she knew anything about Danilo, about what had happened, about why he had disappeared . . . But, no, for many reasons she could not put that into words, it would not be a good idea.

"Yes, there is an answer."

She wrote:

Dear Veronica, thank you for your kind words about my humble little volume. Your poetry is known throughout Italy and Europe and I have read all of your published poems. They have

given me much delight. And they have taught me a great deal. I
accept your kind words, with all my heart and with gratitude
and joy. I remain your constant admirer, Miriamne Hazan.

MIRIAMNE AND VERONICA LIBERO began to exchange little
notes—their thoughts on literature, their observations of life
and art, and their general musings—and Miriamne, though
she did not meet Veronica, felt that she had a true friend, and
strangely, given the life Veronica led, a soul sister. Their notes
grew longer, became mutual confessions of intimate thoughts
and dreams. They sent each other books, Miriamne sometimes relying on advice from her father, who was bemused but
accepting of this strange sisterhood his precocious daughter had
entered into with one of the most notorious women in Europe.
Veronica supplied Miriamne with literary gossip and critical
insights and suggestions for further reading. Miriamne's thirst
for knowledge only intensified. Veronica, who was up to date
on all the latest trends, was helpful with ideas for books to read
or pamphlets to consult. Miriamne read voraciously, about art
and artists as well as about philosophy; she learned French and,
with the help of a French lady, became quite fluent. And whenever she had time, as a distraction from her yearning for that
ideal image she had constructed of Danilo, she explored Venice
and all its marvelous neighborhoods and buildings; and all the
art in the churches and the guilds, and the civic places; and
sometimes, even in the great private houses.

She soon published a second book. This time it was prose,
a series of sketches of life in Venice and life in the Ghetto.
It was a success, and praised by both the famous Veronica
Libero and Pietro Aretino. Even the artist Titian was heard
saying he found it inspiring, "This young woman, this charming and I am told beautiful Jewess, captures the picturesque,
intensely visual side of so much Venetian life. She is a true
Venetian, a person who teaches us to see and feel what it is to
be Venetian."

But there was a void in Mariamne's heart. Its name was Danilo del Medigo. She wondered if she would ever see him again, and she wondered too if in the end she should give in to Mordecai and accept Jeremiah. Now that she had become well-known, he had become even more obsessed and obsequious than before, which made him even more repulsive. Danilo stood in her mind and imagination as the paragon of men. She wondered if in truth she would die an old maid. Perhaps it would not be such a sad destiny after all. Perhaps she would have to live with the memory and the ideal of Danilo—that, and the laughter she had shared with him would have to suffice. Merely the idea of Danilo was . . . an inspiration.

3 4

THE SENATOR AND
THE BANKER

IT WAS A BLUSTERY JANUARY DAY WITH A CHILL WIND WHIST-
ling in the arcades and courtyards of Venice. The Senator
wrapped his cloak close around him and headed for an
inn not usually frequented by such eminent personages as he,
but where he could sit in a small private room, near a cozy fire,
and drink a mug of hot wine and eat a plate of sausage.

He sat down, shivered, and shook himself to get rid of the
drops of water. He didn't like the cold and the wet. He would
have preferred to live in a place visited by balmy breezes and
adorned with a palm tree or two, but what could he do? He was
Venetian! Venice was mostly north of the palm-tree line and
this was not the season for balmy breezes. The Senator had just
taken a first comforting sip of wine when the curtain dividing
his niche from the rest of the inn opened.

The young man who entered was handsome in a dark,
romantic way. The Senator stood and reached out a hand.

"Samuel Mendes, I presume," the Senator said.

"The same, Senator." Mendes smiled, and sketched a slight bow.

The Senator indicated a seat at the small table.

The dark wooden paneling, the heavy wooden tables, and the fire burning merrily in one corner made the little room an ideal refuge from the wet chilly weather. A waitress entered and Samuel Mendes ordered his wine and his food.

"Well," said the Senator, leaning forward, "Signor Mendes, we perhaps have some parallel interests."

"That may well be, Senator." Samuel Mendes leaned back and considered the older man. The Senator's face was marked by war, by the years, and by the sun, but he appeared lean and vigorous. His beard was neatly trimmed; everything about him was meticulous. This was a man who practiced fine-tuned self-control.

The food arrived steaming hot. The Senator tapped his fingers on the tabletop. "You, I believe, are trying to set up a network to save the New Christians and the Jews and move them out of reach of Charles V and the Spanish and Portuguese inquisitions—imprisonment, torture, execution, being burned at the stake—and numerous other vexations."

Samuel hesitated. He had heard the Senator was a man of great integrity and experience. He often played a key role in the deliberations of the Council of Ten. "Yes, we are interested in the safety of all citizens," Samuel pronounced carefully. He took a sip of the wine, which the waitress had just placed next to his plate.

The Senator picked up an olive and began to chew it. "Your bank has a wide network of agents throughout Europe, and your agents are very well-informed."

Samuel soaked a piece of bread in oil. "Bankers need to know what is going on. We need to understand what risks the future might bring. Lending money is a risky business. And so much depends on information—detailed, relevant, timely information."

The Senator sighed, or feigned a sigh. "It is much the same with commerce in general, and with politics and war—timely, trustworthy information can mean the difference between peace and war, victory and defeat, life and death." He drank some wine. "Some months ago—last April, on the Eve of Passover—you made an approach to a young man, a Jew, who had just arrived from Istanbul."

Samuel Mendes said nothing.

The Senator continued to eat. "These olives are excellent, I must say. Well, that young man is a fine fellow. He has made some enemies, unfortunately."

Samuel presumed the Senator was alluding to Danilo del Medigo. And he knew that the Venice spy service, under the direction of the Council of Ten, often used Jews as spies. Jews were vulnerable, they often needed protection, or protection for their families, so they were easy to threaten and easy to purchase or recruit. And Jews were literate, and frequently they were cultured, intelligent, and adaptable; and quite often, having been tossed hither and thither, they spoke a number of languages and had contacts everywhere among the Jewish diaspora. Being outsiders, they were often not noticed—as slaves, servants, and domestic animals are not noticed—and so, while occasionally frequenting the highest levels of society, they overheard things and learned things that insiders, true Christians or true Muslims, paradoxically, would not be privileged to hear.

It was a strange situation being a Jew in such circumstances; it consisted of continual humiliation and incessant vexations, big and small, and yet in some ways it was, for a favored few, a life of privilege and wealth and access to power, or at least closeness to power. But even then it was a perilous existence. Everything could be lost in an instant if the government changed, if a king wanted to cancel his debts or declare bankruptcy; or if the mood changed, a harvest failed, a charismatic friar arrived who hated Jews, or a mob rose up in anger. Then, however rich you were, all could be lost, one's life and the lives of one's children and loved ones, since the real power, the political and military power, was always held by others. Such was the price of eternal exile.

The Senator leaned back and gazed at Samuel. "As I said, that admirable young man—handsome devil, too, and a talented linguist—has made some enemies through no fault of his own." The Senator took a swallow of wine and narrowed his eyes. "And though I cannot for the moment defend the young man, I will tell you this: The allies of his enemies are my enemies. I am, as it were, playing for time."

Samuel nodded.

The Senator lifted a piece of meat, contemplated it, and popped it in his mouth. "I believe you wanted the young man to work for you."

Samuel would, in fact, have liked to recruit Danilo, first as an informer, then as an agent. And then, if it all worked out, as a financier and organizer of the rescue networks his aunt, Beatrice de Luna, was setting up, and eventually as a banker. Danilo's languages, charm, physical and military prowess, and contacts and experience in Istanbul made him a rarity, and an ideal candidate.

The Senator looked Samuel in the eye. "Well, I think it would be helpful—for me, that is—if he did work for you, informally of course, and invisibly, in gathering information."

"Yes, but . . ."

The Senator raised a hand. He refilled Samuel's glass. "The young man is presently part . . . of an acting company."

Samuel feigned surprise and ignorance, and he knew that the Senator knew he was feigning surprise and ignorance, and he knew that the Senator knew he knew. It was a pleasure to deal with such a man.

"Yes, he's an actor!" The Senator laughed. "We never discover what talents we have until we put our hands to something, do we? I once had to fix a wheel on a cart; I had no idea I could do it until I had to do it. Horrible spot we were in, too—mountains, and bandits all around. The carter was too badly hurt to help. Well, that was long ago." The Senator waved the past away. "In any case, this acting career involves visiting various cities in Italy; many of these cities have Jewish communities. And . . ."

"And you would like to know what is going on in those communities."

"That would be helpful, but not exclusively that. As a Jew, our young man will have access to people and information in the Jewish communities. But as an actor, and as part of a troupe of actors, he will have access to social and political circles — the elites — where Jews and bankers do not always have a natural entrée, not in a relaxed, informal way, when people are amusing themselves and drinking and off their guard."

"So you are proposing the Mendes Bank use him as a spy."

The Senator plucked an olive and gazed at it, turning it in his fingers. "Well, 'spy' is a very big word, Samuel, or a very little word, depending on how you look at it, but I think he might be rather like a roving reporter or diplomatic correspondent, and it might be useful for both our interests if he were to share any information that can be of use to both sides. We have some common enemies."

"Yes, but they will not always be your enemies, Senator." Samuel paused. "Nor will we always be your friends, or you ours."

"True, Samuel! That is true, but in the meantime . . ." The Senator smiled benignly and let the thought linger. He filled Samuel's glass.

Samuel lifted the glass. "I must discuss this with my colleagues."

"Take your time. I can facilitate contacts with the young man at any time, if you like. We have our own channels, you see. I rather think it might be useful for both of us. Our young man is an acute observer. He can keep his eyes and ears open and perhaps send a report from time to time both to my organization and to your Mendes Bank."

After the Senator left, Samuel remained sitting at their little table. He ordered another glass of wine. His next appointment was not for two hours, and it was cold outside. It was clear to Samuel from his conversation with the Senator that Danilo del Medigo already was a spy, but a spy for Venice; the Senator had clearly indicated such was the case. The acting company was some sort of cover. Why would the Senator trust Samuel Mendes, and why would he want to add Danilo to the network of the Mendes Bank? Ah, yes, *quid pro quo* . . . If Venice shared information—and agents—with the Mendes Bank, then the Mendes Bank would share information with Venice. Also, the agent would have two avenues of protection, perhaps, and the backup logistics would be more solid. And if there was, as the Senator had hinted, some sort of battle going on inside Venice, and possibly inside the Council of Ten, then this way the Senator could protect his "assets" by providing a backdoor escape. If Danilo were in danger, and if he were somehow betrayed by the hostile faction in Venice, the Mendes Bank could offer a separate network, protection, and perhaps cover, and an escape route for him and whoever was working with him. Poor Danilo del Medigo was trapped on all sides, and the Senator wanted a backup plan for Danilo and for his other agents, as well as to tap into an additional source of information: the bank and its network. Ah, the Senator was a charming old fox!

Samuel left the inn an hour later; by that time, he had made up his mind. But first he would have to consult with Beatrice de Luna or, as she increasingly preferred, Gracia Nasi, who had escaped from Portugal and was now in Antwerp, where, though in less danger than in Lisbon, she was still threatened by Charles V and his Spanish inquisition. It never stopped! Beatrice was clever, but even she could be trapped. Even she could die.

ON THE ROAD

THE ACROBAT

Bologna

D ANILO SWUNG FROM ROPES.
He zipped across the stage. He glided here and
there. Finally, he leaped to the ground and, waving
his sword left and right, drove the poor villains off the stage, into
the billowing waves of the ocean, which, at the very moment,
somehow contrived to whip up a horrendous tempest.

This was in Bologna, and Danilo was once again cast as a
hero—but a different kind of hero. His hair was dyed black,
his complexion darkened to seem that of a Moor. He was the
captain of a pirate ship on the high seas, but—and this was
important—he was a good pirate, willing and able to sink the
ships of his rivals, the Barbary pirates.

And, of course, he saved the demoiselle in distress, Angelica,
scantily clad and tied in most alluring fashion to the mast of a
ship. He slashed through the ropes and set her free and everyone clapped and shouted,

"Bravo!"

"Did you see that?"

"A true acrobat!"

Danilo did not have to speak any lines, which was lucky. He grimaced and danced about and swung his sword this way and that.

After the applause died down, the troupe met some of the leading citizens at a reception. Danilo, with a mop of thick, blackened curls and a thick fake beard, made as few remarks as he could. Luckily, he could fake a Turkish accent.

Instructions from Marco indicated that Danilo and Angelica were to gather as much information as they could from whomever they could, and that they were now working not only for Venice, but also for the Mendes Bank and Beatrice de Luna.

Danilo wondered if there was anyone in Bologna who might have information on the whereabouts of Pirro Gonzaga. But he could not raise the subject without endangering himself, and possibly Pirro. Isabella had promised she would do her own research, and send whatever information she gleaned about Pirro's whereabouts to Danilo. In the meantime, he would see what he could find out on his own.

Angelica showed considerable talent, Danilo observed, in getting people to talk to her, and about serious things — who was plotting against whom, and what the various political personages believed, and what agendas they were pushing. Where had the girl acquired these subtle talents of seduction? People spoke to her as if she were a confessor, or an old and intimate friend.

Bologna was ruled by the Church in conjunction with the nobles and some of the richest merchants. The city was rich, very rich. It was, in many ways, unique. It had been under Papal rule, off and on, for centuries. It had the oldest university in Europe, and perhaps in the world. The various noble families had built brick skyscraper towers as signs of their prestige and power — and as fortresses so they could throw hot pitch and rocks down on their rivals. The towers and the covered brick arcades made Bologna a beautiful and comfortable city. You could walk almost anywhere sheltered from the rain. Bologna had an active Jewish community and many attended the university. Jews had been active in Bologna for a thousand years. There was a chair of Hebrew in the University of Bologna. And Jews could live anywhere they wished in the city.

It was in Bologna that Grazia had met and fallen in love with Pirro Gonzaga. So this was the city where, in a sense, Danilo's own story had begun.

Later, when they were all walking towards their lodgings under a sheltering brick arcade, having eaten a huge meal of minestrone, beef and veal, and thick slabs of gravy-soaked bread, in a tavern just off the main square, Angelica, her arm linked in Danilo's, said, "Bologna is so warm and inviting, even if the climate is damp; all these brick arcades mean you can walk everywhere sheltered from the rain, the sleet, and the snow."

"They certainly know how to eat," said Andreas, herding the troupe along. "Come along, you rascals," he shouted to his two child protégés—nine-year-old twins with dark curly hair and glossy, nut-brown skin. Andreas had bought the two orphans from their "uncle," a very unpleasant and venal and sadistic fellow, in Palermo six months before and named them Achilles and Ajax. "Time for bed!" The boys were precocious. They played pageboys, young girls, and sometimes little clowns or minor servants. On the first day, they had introduced themselves to Danilo.

"I'm Achilles, he's Ajax," said the first, holding out his hand to Danilo.

"I'm Ajax," said the second, "he's Achilles."

"Those are not our real names."

"No."

"No."

"Maestro Andreas decided we need new names."

"Uncle Eduardo sold us."

"I didn't like Uncle Eduardo."

"No, nor did I."

"He was not a real uncle."

"No, he wasn't."

"Maestro Andreas is better."

"He bought both of us, together."

"We come as a pair, or as he said, a set."

"Maestro Andreas shouldn't eat so much, or drink."

"Even master cook Ansaldo said so."

"I worry."

"We worry."

The other members of the troupe included a blond giant, Pietro, who looked after travel and lodgings; and Laura, a cute slip of a girl, supple as an acrobat, pale with a beautiful oval face, who played old women and maids, though she was quite young. Tommaso, a sturdy, handsome, middle-sized fellow, played the small parts; Antonio, a slim fellow with a long pointed nose and a high forehead, played minor villains and court officials; and Clara, a petite, slender, blue-eyed blonde, played perky young maidservants. Nico, who had fallen sick in Mantua, had been left behind. Isabella's Jewish doctor had declared the poor man had only a few weeks to live.

As they entered the vestibule of their lodgings, Danilo and Angelica were discussing some of their latest intelligence gleanings, bits and pieces of gossip they had picked up during a reception after one of their performances. "But if that Gian Pietro Carafa fellow becomes Pope," Danilo was saying, "there will be trouble in all of the Papal territories, at least for the Jews and the New Christians, and that will include Bologna."

Outside in the shadowy street, thick flakes of snow began to fall.

"Oh, look—snow!" Angelica shivered and pressed herself close to Danilo.

"It will be chilly heading through the mountains tomorrow," declared Pietro. He fussed around Angelica, Danilo noticed, and often blushed and turned away when the actress looked at him or joked with him. Angelica had declared that Danilo, in effect, belonged to her, and that she and Danilo must share a room.

"Otherwise, how will I enjoy the man's company?" she asked. Poor Pietro arranged for this, one more complication! He was always fretting about renting horses, mules, wagons, or carts, or finding accommodation on a galley or a river barge, and finding inns or hostels that would be willing to take the troupe, if an aristocratic home or a stable was not available.

"Some of the passes are high and the weather may not be friendly." Andreas grimaced. "I'm going to bed. Good night!" He trundled off up the stairs, followed by Achilles and Ajax.

"I know those roads," Pietro said. "It will be hard tomorrow, and dangerous. Good night! Until tomorrow!"

Alone in their room, Angelica and Danilo looked at each other. "First things first," Angelica said. She sat down at a wobbly little desk. "I would prefer daylight, but I suppose two candles must suffice."

Danilo knelt and put a coin under one leg of the table to steady it. "Does that work?"

Angelica grinned down at him, "A knight in shining armor, armed with two soldi!"

She dipped the point of a quill into the ink pot. "So, for our first joint report, Danilo, let me explain our system. We change it periodically of course, but for the moment this is what we are doing, this is the way we communicate with Marco. We use the words in this 1532 edition of the *Tales of Boccaccio* as our codebook. This number is the page number, this is the number indicating the line, and this number indicates the letter on the line. And then every three letters, we reverse the order of what the numbers indicate. That way we build up the words, sentences, and paragraphs."

"Sounds simple."

"Simple, but tedious. But here is the fun part. We also replace a few important words. Melons are Cardinals, a squid is the Pope."

"Ha!" Daniel said.

Angelica looked at him, amused. "And walnuts are the Jews. So we send what might look like a grocery list. Like this." She lifted the quill out of the ink pot and wrote down three numbers quickly. The ink was quite clear; then, as it dried, it faded and faded until the page looked blank.

"I know that trick," said Danilo. Saida had first taught him about invisible ink, and they had carried on their secret correspondence by using it. He wondered if perhaps invisible ink would provide a way of writing to Miriamne and explaining ... No, he couldn't do that—it was too dangerous! And how could he explain his life now? What of Angelica?

"Lovers and spies have much in common, you know!" Angelica flashed her very best innocent smile. Her bright full lips and eyes and her tumbling blond locks shone in the candlelight.

"What? What do you mean?" Danilo exclaimed. Did she know about Miriamne? Saida?

"Nothing. I only meant that secret affairs are the most exciting affairs."

He narrowed his eyes. "You are the devil herself."

They made two copies of each of their reports—on the political situation, on the influence of the clergy, and on the Jewish community in Bologna—one for Marco and one for Marco to send to Samuel Mendes.

"These go to Pietro. He will deliver them," said Angelica. "He is two rooms down the hallway, just opposite the staircase. He is expecting you."

Holding one of the candles, Danilo went down the corridor and knocked very softly on the door. Pietro, rubbing his eyes and yawning, opened the door, bowed, and without a word, took the four folded pieces of paper. He nodded at Danilo and closed the door.

Back in their room, Danilo took off his clothes and slid into one side of the bed; Angelica slid into the other. The room was very cold. Their bodies were warm. They held each other, they kissed, they made love. It was tender and funny, and slow and intimate and playful. Afterwards, in the peaceful, exhausted moments that followed, Angelica said, "And so, my dear Jewish prince ..."

He gave her a quizzical, amused look. She had never mentioned his Jewishness before.

"Of course I know you are a Jew, we've already made love — remember? And anyway, did you think Isabella would not tell me?"

He shut her mouth with a kiss.

She drew back and gazed at him. "It must be hard for you, living here on the road among us non-Jews, with our strange, uncouth, pagan customs, eating pork and all sorts of unspeakable and unsavory things!"

"I adapt." Danilo said with a laugh.

"In any case, Donna Isabella told me some of your story." She looked at him with bright eyes. "And then I had other sources."

"Really?"

"Yes, really." She let her lips brush against his. "We must help you find your blood father and reclaim your birthright."

"What do you know about that?"

"That you are probably the son of Pirro Gonzaga."

"Probably?"

"Isabella's words. Though she said 'almost certainly.' And Pirro, like you, is a fugitive, pursued by killers or rivals." She yawned. "Pirro has gone mad, has killed people, has incurred debts, has disappeared. Nobody knows where he is, though he might have been seen in Florence, which is our next stop."

"He has?"

"Mm . . . maybe . . ." Her eyes closed; she was asleep.

3 6

THE PILGRIM

"**W**E ARE GOING TO GET CAUGHT IN A BLIZZARD," Pietro nodded towards the mountains, dark shapes looming in the thickening air and dimming light.

The little troupe of actors had left the vast fertile flatness of the Po Valley behind and joined a caravan, a party of merchants and pilgrims heading into the hills of the Apennines on the way from Bologna to Florence. The high crags, deep forests, endless ridges, and narrow ravines and valleys of the Apennines that separated Bologna from Florence looked forbidding.

The road was rutted and icy and narrow, and dense dark clouds gathered in the craggy hills. The long line of carts laden with goods and the mules pulling them disappeared ahead in blinding swirls of snow. Most of the travelers walked, sometimes climbing on board a cart or a wagon if they just couldn't go on.

"We are going to get stuck in this snowstorm."

"There is an inn halfway up the pass."

The mules trudged, hauling their loads of cloth and sacks of rice and grain. The carts rumbled heavily; the snow eddied down, thicker and thicker; large wet flakes and then small, icy, stinging flakes. One of the mules stumbled. The carter helped it to its feet; the mule brayed—a weird sound, lost in the muffled snowy emptiness.

A mile farther on, the same mule collapsed. A leg was broken, and it fell onto its side, twisting the yoke of the cart. The carter swore. He unhooked the mule from the yoke. With the help of two other men, he pushed the mule over the cliff; the body plunged down, bounced off a ledge, shattering, and disappeared into the trees below. Angelica looked away.

"Good mule!" the carter said. "I had it for two years now. Bloody hard for the other mule, left alone like this, but what can a man do?"

"You know, this was an old military road," said one of the pilgrims, staggering up beside Angelica. He was a thin old man with a deeply tanned face; he was shivering terribly. His gait had become unsteady, and he was weaving back and forth.

Angelica had wrapped a thick shawl around her shoulders, and now she lifted it and draped it across the old man. His legs looked awfully thin.

"I can go no farther."

"Of course you can," said Angelica. "We can help you. Come, you must get up on this cart."

Pietro and Danilo stepped forward and helped lift the old man up onto one of the carts, already heaped high with merchandise and two families huddled together beneath heavy coats and blankets.

The children were crying. Ice was forming in their hair, and their ears were red; one little girl was trembling so hard, she couldn't stop.

"The children," said Angelica, "can't go on much longer."

A line of them was straggling along behind, holding one another's hands, making a little chain lest one get lost in the snow.

Pietro and Danilo lifted the children onto the overburdened carts. They perched, looking like they'd topple off. The mules plodded onward. Achilles and Ajax were already seated on a cart, sheltered by a large tent-like cloak and a blanket, and totally absorbed in a game of cards.

Andreas walked along the edge of the little caravan. "Keep moving! Keep moving! If we stop, everyone will freeze! Come on, keep going on!" The wind whipped his cape around him, and as he walked he became a vague silhouette, fading into swirling snow and dusk, and then he was gone, invisible, just swirling snow.

"Danilo, darling, go and see that Andreas doesn't get into trouble."

Danilo put his head down into the wind, pulled his cap close and, blinking against the hard flakes, his eyelashes frozen, his cheeks stinging, he shivered as he strode along beside the line of carts. The snow whirled down, thicker and thicker. The wind rose. The cold penetrated the bones right down to the soul.

He found Andreas standing beside the road, staring at the slowly moving line. "Some of them will not make it, Danilo. Some of the pilgrims are too weak. How far is it to the inn?"

"Pietro says about five miles."

"So another hour or three at least."

"If nothing else happens."

Andreas nodded. His hood and shoulders were covered in snow. He sneezed and wiped his nose with a large white handkerchief. His eyebrows were stiff with ice. Snow swirled down around them.

As the carts went by, Danilo and Andreas looked up. Angelica was now perched on a cart, on top of bales of luggage, holding three children and their mother close. She had put a blanket over them but took none for herself. When she turned her face to Danilo, he saw that she was white and shivering. "Poor things, they are so cold," she shouted. She climbed off the cart to help the old pilgrim who had gotten off, insisting he could walk, in order to make place for the children.

The old pilgrim staggered. "This road has been here since the times of the Caesars. It was the favorite of . . ." He stopped and started to tremble. "I have never felt so cold."

Angelica took his arm. "We just have to get you up onto one of these carts. I'll find a place for you."

"I'm a tailor from Brescia. I worked all my life. My wife is dead now, children all dead too. I've always wanted to see . . . I have yearned . . . always yearned to see . . ." The old man faltered and Angelica steadied him.

"What have you yearned to see?"

"The Holy Land."

The pilgrim ceased speaking then, and he reached out, grasping Angelica's shoulder.

"I think . . ." he muttered, and before she could catch him, he fell straight down at her feet, his head hitting the icy road with a crack.

Danilo was instantly next to Angelica and knelt beside her next to the old man. He felt for a pulse; he looked at Angelica. "He's dead."

The old man's eyes stared up at them, glassy, blue, and empty. Snow swirled down, the wind whistled and roared. Danilo closed the old man's eyes. "We must care for the body," said Angelica. They lifted him onto a cart, finding what space they could. The carter made way for the corpse. "There he is, snug, just behind me! Too bad we don't have a priest."

"We must keep going." Andreas waved the carts ahead. "There is no choice. Perhaps there will be a priest at the inn."

One young woman, sitting on one of the carts between bundles of cloth, tipped forward, her face ashen. She too was dead, but nobody noticed until Danilo tried to wake her. He left her in place; there was nothing to be done.

Pietro and Danilo walked along the edge of the caravan, making sure nobody was left behind and frozen, and that the mules kept moving. Achilles and Ajax had jumped down from their perch to make room for the younger children. They walked along, just behind the second-last cart, laughing and joking about the snow.

"I don't know if they've ever seen snow before," said Pietro to Danilo. "Andreas bought them—well, adopted them—in Sicily."

Just as Andreas was helping an old man to steady himself, one of the wagons veered suddenly towards them, almost pushing Andreas and the old man off the road into the abyss that yawned hundreds of feet straight down. Andreas pushed the old man back. The mule and the wagon were headed towards the precipice. The mule was confused. It brayed. Andreas shouted. The carter, who had fallen asleep, jerked awake and pulled back on the reins. The mule stopped just in time. "Mother of God!" whispered the carter, but his words were swept away by the wind and the snow.

Danilo came up to help guide the mule and the wagon back onto the path. "Thank you!" cried out the carter.

As the swirling wall of snow closed in, Danilo lowered his head. His eyelashes were frozen, and snow had gotten inside his long overcoat. He peered ahead. They had no choice now but to continue forward, ever forward. There was no way back.

3 7

FLORENCE

F OUR DAYS LATER, THEY ROLLED INTO FLORENCE, CLATTERING
over cobblestones and creaking over icy pools of mud,
and were put up at a sprawling coach house not far from
the river Arno. The city still echoed with the effects of the rule of
the mad Dominican friar, Savonarola, and the struggles between
the supporters and enemies of the ruling Medici family.

Danilo's mother had lived through Savonarola's reign. It
had happened during Charles VIII's French invasion of Italy,
the invasion that Isabella d'Este's brother-in-law, Ludovico
Sforza, had triggered by inviting the French into Italy to help
solve a personal quarrel.

With the French army at the gates of the city, a popular revolt
chased the ruling Medici family out. Savonarola took over and
declared that the city would be the New Jerusalem, the world
center of Christianity; he inspired squads of young men and
boys—thugs—to roam the streets and punish immodesty in
dress or behavior. Fashionably dressed women and men were
pursued and beaten by gangs of fanatical ruffians.

In the squares and streets, Savonarola set up "bonfires of the vanities"—burning books, paintings, and sculptures. Grazia had described the events for Danilo in her *Secret Book*. All forms of joy in life were banned and punished. Works by Boccaccio and Dante and Botticelli were burned. Artists, trapped in Florence or caught up in Savonarola's puritanical crusade, submitted and agreed to destroy their own works. Books, scientific instruments, priceless tapestries, sumptuous clothes, all were thrown into the fire. Statues were smashed, buildings defaced.

Danilo and Angelica had received their new instructions. Pietro had brought a folded, sealed envelope containing the instructions written in invisible ink, with an innocuous message—*Good luck on your trip*—in normal ink. Danilo and Angelica were to set about inquiring about the condition of the Jews in Florence. Earlier, the Jews had played an important role as moneylenders and they had been protected by the ruling Medici family. Savonarola had commanded that all Jews be expulsed from the city. But he fell and was tortured and put to death just before his edict could take effect. The Jews had been given a reprieve.

Danilo did not like fanaticism. He had seen firsthand the fiery cruel violence of Brother Bruno Salvo, who was undoubtedly an admirer of Savonarola, and cut from the same cloth. Was Suleiman a fanatic? Some might certainly consider him so. He did intend to lead a Holy War of conquest against the West. What did Saida think? She was so moderate, so practical and fun-loving, but of course she loved her father. And Angelica, what did she think of all the fiery fanaticism that seemed to be spreading?

He realized that for some reason, he didn't consider Angelica to be a Christian, though she always wore a little gold cross on a chain around her neck. When necessary she attended mass; in public, she would cross herself, when appropriate, but in reality she seemed more a pagan spirit. It was as if she had stepped out of that classical world Grazia so admired, the world of pagan delight and wisdom.

That night they were lying in bed, in a tangle of sheets, when there was a discreet knock at the door. Angelica was lying sprawled on her stomach with her arm across Danilo's chest. Without bothering to move, Angelica called, "Come in, Pietro!"

Pietro came in, looking abashed. He looked down, blushed, and held out an envelope.

"Another missive from one of our many masters!" Grabbing a sheet to cover herself, Angelica sprang out of bed, leaped across the room, accepted the envelope, and kissed Pietro on the cheek.

Pietro blushed again, bowed, and closed the door softly behind him.

Angelica opened the envelope and put the paper over a candle that had been slowly smoldering on the table next to the bed. The letters became clear. Danilo leaned over her shoulder. "This one is not even in code," Angelica said. "Marco must have been in a hurry."

Danilo, an edict has been sent out secretly from Venice to track you down, arrest you, and deliver you to the Republic's dungeons, to be imprisoned, then judged, and then, after torture and other inconveniences, to be executed for spying against the Most Serene Republic. Our enemies want to make an example of you. The results of the trial are a foregone conclusion. Your corpse, or parts of it, will be hung on the Piazzetta in the sun and the wind and the rain for people to contemplate. You must continue with the troupe. Our enemies will not think of looking for you up on stage. I am coming to Florence, M.

MARCO AND DANILO RENDEZVOUSED in a low-down tavern. Marco told Danilo, with great regret, that he could not, for the moment, protect him.

"There are factions in Venice, Danilo, hostile factions, and we are doing our best to eliminate them. But it will take time. You must continue to play your role as an actor—and stay away from Venice. It's politics, you know."

"Politics!" Danilo hated the word. He had gone back to reading Machiavelli in his spare time, a small volume of *The Prince* he had purchased in a side street in the Jewish quarter. It was a dirty business, politics. "What about Angelica? Can I share this with her?"

Marco looked him in the eye. "She already knows. She is one of the best. Share everything with her, and consult her, by all means, but only you two. Don't tell Pietro anything he doesn't need to know. It is the best way to protect him. The less people know, the better it is for everyone."

"I understand."

"Now, we are interested in everything. Observation is the key. Find out who is wearing what, who stands next to whom, who smiles at whom, who glances at whom, who is sleeping with whom, who is jealous of whom, which men prefer the love of another man to that of a woman, which women prefer the love of another woman to that of a man, who has invented a new printing press, or other device, and how it works. Get us diagrams when you can, or draw them. Find out whose credit is good and whose credit is less so; what the prices are for clothes, foodstuffs, wool, cotton, pepper, silk, and apples; who prefers Titian to Giorgione, what pamphlets are being published about what subjects, where and by whom. Find out everything you can. No detail is too small," Marco said. "Keep your eyes peeled, and your ears open."

"But . . . why? How are such things useful?"

Marco looked at him steadily. "Information is gold. All information."

"And I am always to work with Angelica?"

"Yes, she has the eye."

"I noticed."

"By the way, Danilo, just to add to your amusement, there is news of the Men in Black. They have been seen in Venice, in Mantua, and in some godforsaken mountain villages looking for you. They seem lost, but they are still hunting."

Danilo smiled; so Sappho's elaborate ruse had actually

worked, sending the men up into the Dolomites or the Alps, or wherever she had sent them.

"One of them wears an eyepatch, and has only half a nose. Villagers call him The Man without a Nose. I suppose that was your doing."

Danilo looked down at the table and studied his wine glass. "Possibly."

Marco smiled. "Well done. But these chaps will not give up. We must continue the charade. The public loves you. Now they want not just your gestures, but your words. You must become a true actor, deploying all your talents. Just being a mime is no longer good enough—the public demands more, so you will become, I am sure, a virtuoso, while continuing to work for us of course, and for our silent partner."

"Samuel Mendes."

"Yes."

Danilo frowned, as if this spying thing were an unpleasant prospect, but in truth, having Angelica as a partner made spying interesting. Playing secret games and sharing secrets with a beautiful, uninhibited, and highly intelligent woman was an attractive prospect. Besides, he was naturally curious, as was Angelica, so it all hung together rather nicely. But the acting thing, well, he had not warmed to it. It was utterly undignified. Then, there was Miriamne . . .

"All of this is a question of life and death," Marco said. "If the wrong people seize power in the Republic—then, perhaps, we can no longer protect anyone. Not you, not Angelica, not the Ghetto, not—"

"Not Miriamne, not Rabbi Hazan?"

"No one will be safe." Marco stood, shook Danilo's hand, and disappeared out the door into the wet, drizzly dusk.

3 8
THE VENTRILOQUIST

Florence

"NO, THIS I CANNOT DO!"

"Yes, you have to do it," said Angelica. "You are too popular. People want to hear you speak, they want to hear your voice. You must learn your lines."

Danilo paced up and down. The large, rather bare room in a semi-abandoned Florentine palazzo had been set aside as the troupe's special space for rehearsals, and it also served as Angelica and Danilo's bedroom and washing room. A large brass tub had been placed behind a curtain in one corner.

"A star cannot be just a mime." Angelica said, beaming at him. "A star must speak, declaim, enunciate, and give orations!" Her grin was bright in the candlelight; the impertinent female was enjoying this!

"Damnation!"

Angelica had a towel wrapped around her head and another around her body; she was sitting on a wooden stool, staring at

him in a sweetly exasperated way. She had just had a bath, in
the big steamy brass tub, which had been filled almost to the
brim with hot water by Pietro. Her body was damp and her
skin sparkled, giving off a sort of soapy, spicy scent that would
have made Danilo drunk with lust were he not so exasperated.
She slipped off the wooden stool and stood up.

She was barefoot, legs slightly apart, standing her ground
on the varnished pine boards of the big empty room that contained their bed and their bath, and where they were, in this
very moment, rehearsing. The play was a tragic-comedic farce
about a puffed-up Spaniard hidalgo who tries to seduce a demoiselle with his bluster and braggadocio, and who ends up . . .

"I just don't know how to do it!" Danilo strutted back and
forth, he gritted his teeth and tore at his hair. "This is beyond me!"

"You can do it. I know you can do it!"

He stared hard at the floorboards. Some of the boards, he
noticed, had big knots in them, but the whole floor had been
waxed and was smooth as silk. Where had they gotten these
planks? Timber was essential. You built galleys with timber.
Timber supplies were a weak point in . . . No, he was trying to
distract himself. The Men in Black loomed in his imagination.
Some night they would come storming in, while he was in
bed with Angelica, and they would slaughter the two of them
before he could grab his dagger. He must remember to keep
it within reach. And then there were those factions in Venice,
they might surprise him any day. Angelica must not sense his
fear; she would worry, she would want to kill somebody. She
could be ferocious.

He looked up and growled, "How can people speak words
that are not their own? I don't understand this acting thing!
Reality is reality. How can one spiral off into make-believe? I
like facts. Facts are facts. I am a down-to-earth, practical fellow,
a man of action, with my feet on the ground."

The towel wrapped tightly around Angelica's head made
her look like a female version of an Ottoman sultan, endowing
her with a priestly hieratic authority.

"You are like a little boy," she said as she favored him with a particularly intense gaze. "A little boy who needs a spanking." Slowly, articulating each syllable, as if to a total idiot, she continued, "You did read, aloud, to your intimate friend, the Sultan, Suleiman the Magnificent, did you not, on that Baghdad campaign you have told me so much about? Those big fat cannons and so forth . . ."

"That was different." Danilo kicked at the floorboards, and looked up at her slyly. She was closing in on him, preparing to leap; he must find a way out of the ambush.

"How, pray tell?"

"I was translating, so the words—in Turkish—were my own."

Angelica twirled abruptly. The towel peeled away from one breast, and she slapped it back into place. "Unreasonable man! Stubborn warrior! Divine idiot! I am going to tear out my hair!"

Her eyes blazed. It looked as if she were about to leap on him. She stopped, took a deep breath, and in a sublimely even voice she enunciated slowly, deadpan: "So, where were we?"

"You were telling me I can easily enunciate and pronounce the words of another fellow who wrote them pretending to be yet another fellow—and this latter fellow, whom I am supposed to play, is a fool, by the way—and as for me, Danilo, I am saying that no, I can't, because I am I, and I am not another. In particular, I am not that pathetic nonsensical buffoon!"

She came up close and looked up at him. He stared into her eyes. How was it that a woman could be so beautiful and so perverse? She stared back. Her lips glowed. Her teeth shone. Her eyes were so blue, so blue, so . . .

Pressing her hand against his chest, she whispered with her perfumed breath, "Now, let us see if there is some way I can plant some tiny little bit of wisdom into that beautiful thick skull of yours! Hmm!"

She stepped away and strode back and forth. She moved, Danilo noticed—not for the first time—like a dancer, with fluid grace, like young Sappho.

Angelica swept the towel from her head, placed it on the back of a chair, shook her hair out, and turned to him with her most sweet, accomplished, and submissive smile. "You speak many tongues and yet you say you cannot master two or three lines?"

Danilo wondered if just possibly he was being perverse. He also suspected—no, he was certain—he was being herded towards a trap. "Yes! I mean, no! I cannot."

"I see. And did you, dear Danilo, invent those words of French or Italian or Arabic or Turkish that you speak? Did you invent the word 'siege' or the word 'bilge' or the word 'war'?"

"Ah, no . . ."

"So . . . you, Danilo del Medigo, did not invent the French or Italian or Turkish or Persian language. Not even Arabic?"

Danilo bit his lip; this was a classic pincer movement, an ambush coming from several sides at once.

"So it follows logically, my dear Danilo, that if you can utter any word at all, you can utter words written by someone else just as easily as you can utter your own words, because your own words, by your own admission, are not your own. They are French or Arabic or Turkish or Italian words, words invented somewhere back in the eons of time far beyond the deepest reaches of memory."

"You are a wicked girl, Angelica."

"Andreas has often told me so. Let's try those lines again."

Danilo tried.

"Say it again! Say it as if you mean it!"

Danilo struck a martial pose. "Sirrah, I am come here, to this place, to run you through! I shall skewer you! I shall impale you! I shall . . ." He stopped. "Strutting and braggadocio are not part of the true knight. A true knight would be decorous and polite and modest. He would be a study in understatement. Or a true villain." He was shouting now. "If that is what I am, I would just run the fellow through the gut, disembowel him, and be done with it."

Angelica sat down on the stool, her knees under her chin; she smiled at him. The towel, which she seemed to have forgotten about, barely covered anything. Her smile had all the patience and irony of a saint dealing with a recalcitrant and idiotic sinner. She sighed. Beatitude has its limits. "Well, darling, you might be onto something there. That is just the point, isn't it?"

"What point?"

"This fellow, unlike you, Danilo, is not a true knight. He is not a gentleman, he is not modest and decorous like you. He is a boaster, a bully, and a fraud. He struts and he puffs. He trumpets his virtues. That's why he doesn't get the girl!"

"So I am to play a cad, am I?"

"Yes, this time you play a cad and a fool!"

"A fool!"

"Now there you are! A pout you can do. You definitely know how to pout. Bravo!"

Danilo frowned, opened his mouth, shut it, and stopped frowning.

"The next time, Danilo, you will be a perfect hero! You will be the best damned hero that was ever seen on this sublunary terrestrial orb, even if I have to write the role myself."

Danilo rubbed his chin and glanced sideways at Angelica, perched there, a semi-naked schoolmarm, the sort of woman that lascivious master artist Giulio Romano or even Titian would die to use as a model. He squared his shoulders, puffed out his chest, and strode back and forth. "Ah, you there, miserable worm! I have come to run you through, I shall spill your guts, I shall open your spleen, I shall split your liver, I shall spray your bile! Your very belly will explode this way, that way, every which way!"

"You are improvising."

"I am what?"

"Making it up."

"Oh."

"That is not bad. That is good. Danilo, this is the way you — ah — worm your way into the role, you become the cad you are meant to be."

He growled. "I am a cad! I am a cad!"

"It's a game, Danilo."

"I shall run you through—villain!" Danilo snarled as he leaped forward, almost impaling Angelica, who stepped deftly aside.

"That is it! Wonderful!"

"Splendid!" Andreas cried; he had just come into the room. "He'll do, won't he, Angelica?"

"He'll certainly do, Andreas. He'll do and he'll do and he'll do! Now try it again, Danilo."

"I shall run you through—villain!"

"Angelica, stand in for the villain!" Andreas waved directions.

Angelica tucked the towel tight and stepped forward, picking up a long wooden rod. She and Danilo dueled, twirling around. Andreas walked around them, at a safe distance so as not to be impaled, rubbing his chin and making a suggestion now and then as to the choreography. Finally, Andreas clapped. "That is good. That is perfect. Enough! You must not wear yourselves out!"

During all the dueling, twirling around barefoot as she was, Angelica's towel had fallen away. She didn't seem to notice.

"She is good," said Danilo. Dueling had worked him into a perfect lather. He wondered if her bath water might still be warm.

Andreas rubbed his hands. "This will be a fine production, a splendid show!"

"I knew he could do it!" said Angelica. And swooping up the towel, she wrapped it around her waist and disappeared behind a curtain to put on some clothes.

"I think we might change your role, Danilo," said Andreas.

"What?" Danilo stared. What was the man saying? That he had to learn new lines? That he had to become somebody else? He had already gone to all these lengths to throw himself into the role of the fool, the braggart, the . . .

"Angelica has trained you so well that I think perhaps I shall rewrite the part about that Spanish chap; you will become Italian, and you will be the hero . . ."

"The hero?"

"Yes! The hero, with several splendid speeches."

"Several?"

"Yes, and a fine duel! I must leave you now! I must write your new lines." With an exaggerated courtly bow, Andreas disappeared out the door.

Danilo fumed. He was in the perfect frame of mind to be a villain, and now . . .

Pietro entered through the open door, looked around, and blushed. "Letter for Signor Danilo," he said, holding it out. Danilo took it, and recognized the handwriting—Isabella d'Este.

Quickly, he slit the wax seal with his dagger.

Dear Danilo,

I understand your acting career is proving a wonderful success. And that, made up and disguised as you are, no wandering Man in Black or Venetian agent would ever realize that you are you. This is as it should be! I have been making, in so far as I can, discreet inquiries as to the whereabouts of our friend Pirro. It seems he may have been in hiding briefly in Florence or on its outskirts, possibly on the left bank, downstream from the Ponte Vecchio, and in Pisa. Perhaps the company can go there so you can explore. I have had my agents set up a few performance dates for you. I knew you would make a wonderful actor. I am, I must admit, delighted with the accuracy of my own insight. I really am a genius! My greetings to dear Angelica; I am sure she is instructing you in all the subtleties of the thespian arts. This note I am now giving to Sappho. She will see it is delivered without anybody being the wiser. She works miracles, that girl!—Isabella d'Este, Marchesa of Mantua.

Danilo stared into space. He folded the letter carefully and slipped it into his pocket. He must of course destroy it; if the wrong eyes were to read it, the contents would put Pirro and

Isabella in danger, not to mention Angelica and the members of the troupe. He walked up and down. He looked out the window. He went back to the fireplace, where a merry fire was burning brightly. Angelica and Andreas and the others would be back soon. Someone could enter at any moment. He took the letter out of his pocket and knelt by the fire. He hesitated just for an instant, and tossed it onto the flames. The paper flared up. He watched Isabella's words burn. Now, at least, he knew what he had to do. And he would have to do it alone. He stood up.

3 9

THE WAGES OF
SUCCESS

Florence

THAT NIGHT DANILO STOOD IN FRONT OF THE AUDIENCE. IT was the first time he was to speak lines. The lights were bright torches, hundreds of candles flickered. It was dazzling, as bright a glare as day. He couldn't see the public at all. How many were they? How were they reacting?

From out of the shadows Angelica appeared, running towards him, her clothes in disorder, fluttering rags, seeking salvation in his arms. He was, after all, the hero. He spoke. And the words came naturally and flowed as if he had invented them himself, as if they were his words, and as if he were really there in the forest, saving Angelica, the fair demoiselle, from all the perils that surrounded them in the darkness out behind the lights, in the eternal darkness that threatened them all, every moment of their lives, the eternal darkness that in the end consumes us all!

Out of the darkness came thunderous applause.

THAT EVENING, THE PLAYERS met some of their public—bourgeois merchants, a few professional people, and university students—and were treated to a fine meal of succulent lamb and beef stew, thick slices of dark crunchy bread, copious mugs of ale, and a very strong red wine in the palazzo of a merchant who was close to the Medici family. The ceiling was high with heavy wooden beams, and the dark panelled walls were lined with tapestries and the long wooden table laden with food and drink. Torches lit the room.

Danilo, nervously looking around for killers and Venetian agents, spoke to a merchant and a priest and a rabbi. He learned a great deal about what was going on in Florence and some of the problems in the Jewish community. The local Jewish moneylenders and pawnbrokers were being threatened by the friars, Franciscans and Dominicans, who accused them of exploiting the poor, being the murderers of Christ, and acting as sources of immorality in Florence. Also, the fate of the Jews depended upon the good graces of the Duke, and the Duke was not in the most solid position.

One of the merchants, a florid, obese, talkative fellow in a richly embroidered emerald-green outfit, was quite forthcoming. "Ah, you know the Duke, Alessandro de' Medici, protects the Jews. He is a dark horse himself. Now, mind you, this is just a rumor, but they say he is not the son of his mother, but of an African servant in the Medici household, a beautiful girl, it is said. Her name was Simonetta da Collevecchio; she died about two or three years ago. So you see, Alessandro may not be the son of his official mother."

"That must have been quite a feat, to keep it hidden, I mean." Danilo raised an eyebrow. The Gonzagas were not unique. What had Isabella said about them? That they spawned bastards right, left, and center? And of course he was one of them.

"And Alessandro may not actually be the son of his official father either—Lorenzo de' Medici—but is probably the illegitimate son of Pope Clement VII and Simonetta, you see, so Alessandro's birth and origins are all a tangled cover-up." The man rubbed his finger against the side of his nose and winked, lifted his mug to his lips, and buried his moustache in it. He wiped his mouth. "In any case, Alessandro has enemies."

"Really?" Danilo said, taking a deep swallow of the brew. Illegitimacy seemed to be an epidemic, at least among aristocrats. This man was a font of information, but Danilo was thinking mainly of the letter from Isabella d'Este. Later that night, or early the next day, he would sneak out and snoop around to see if he could find any traces of Pirro.

"Alessandro may not be long for this world. And if he goes, it is not clear that the Ducal government will resist if the Pope insists on a really serious inquisition targeting the New Christians, or if the Pope insists the city banish its Jews or confine them to a ghetto."

A little bit later, with Danilo trailing just behind her and listening to every word, Angelica managed to corner and charm a distinguished elderly prelate with a round glowing face, narrow crafty eyes, and a large tummy tucked comfortably into his ecclesiastical regalia. Danilo moved in close and watched as the man fingered his belt, patted his belly, and explained his point of view to Angelica, "A new pope, when one arrives—and I hope that will be soon—will be much less understanding of such frivolous and wicked creatures as actors, artists, Jews, writers, pamphleteers, scribblers, poets, and playwrights, and those abominable New Christians. People will burn, my dear, people will burn!"

"The present pope is not rigorous enough, your eminence?" Angelica favored the prelate with one of her most engaging and innocent smiles.

"No, my dear, he is not." The prelate smiled. He patted his stomach again and fingered the medallion hanging around his neck. "Our dear pope, Paul III, is a weakling who really doesn't have the interests the True Faith at heart." The prelate covered his mouth and emitted a mild belch. "The Pope has done nothing to stop the spread of heresy, in particular the Protestant heresy, which some call Lutheranism. It is catching on like wildfire, particularly in northern Europe. The Pope's inaction will condemn millions of souls to burn forever in the fires of Hell."

"How horrible, your eminence!" Angelica cried, and looked up through her eyelashes at the man.

Danilo could see the prelate's cheeks redden as he gave her his best, most benign, most ecclesiastical smile. "But you, my dear young woman, are a true ornament of the finest of the fine thespian arts, as practiced in classical antiquity, in ancient Greece upon the Athenian stage, and in ancient Rome at the height of its power and grandeur," he said, while he eyed Angelica's cleavage.

"Thank you, your Eminence." Angelica curtsied, revealing yet more cleavage, and glancing sideways at Danilo, who of course had caught every word.

LATE THAT NIGHT, BY candlelight, Danilo and Angelica composed their notes. They reported on Jacob Abravanel, a Sephardic Jew from Ferrara, who was working in Florence to convince Alessandro de' Medici to allow Jews and New Christians fleeing from Spain and Portugal to live and work in Florence. The Duke was favorably inclined. But it was tricky. If the Jews became too successful they might stir up resentment, and then the Duke, a calculating opportunist who, if he wished to survive, had to trim his sails to each passing breeze, might, at the first sign of trouble, turn against them. On the question of Venice, the Duke was waiting to see which way the wind would blow. The situation was fluid. If war came, he might side with Venice, or with her enemies.

Angelica and Danilo recorded it all in their special code in invisible ink and consigned the folded paper to Pietro, who sent it on its mysterious way. Later, just as Danilo and Angelica were sliding into bed, Pietro returned with another letter from Isabella.

> *Dear Danilo, This will be just a quick note. I have learned that some bounty hunters have been hired to track down Pirro and do him harm. I am not sure if it is debts he owes, or if it is pure revenge the bounty hunters are bent on—kidnapping or murder, I am not sure which. It is all very obscure. I just wanted to warn you, and also Angelica. If you go looking for Pirro, be very, very careful—other dangerous people are looking for him too.—Isabella d'Este, Marchesa of Mantua*

This time, since she was there, Angelica too read the letter. "Oh, dear! Danilo, don't do anything foolish. Or, if you do something foolish, let me be foolish with you!"

4 0

THE LOWER DEPTHS

Florence

E ARLY THE NEXT MORNING, WHILE ANGELICA WAS BUSY
arranging something with Pietro, Danilo slipped out
alone. He crossed the Ponte Vecchio, where some of the
merchants and moneylenders were just opening their shops,
and following the hint contained in Isabella's letter, he went to
an inn on the left bank. The ramshackle building was perched
right on the bank of the Arno River. It was a disreputable dark
place where riffraff, fugitives, eccentrics of various kinds were
known to gather. Just as he got to the door, a red-faced, angry-
looking woman came out and threw a bucket of slops into the
alleyway. Chickens and a small pig made for the slops, clucking
and grunting. It was freezing cold—how had the chickens not
died? "They roost in there," said the woman with a nod to a
small shack, and she spat onto the paving stones. "Wise creatures, pigs and chickens—wiser than some people I know."
She spat again, and disappeared through a side door.

Danilo sat down by the fire in the dark, gloomy dining room and ordered a mug of ale and a trencher of bread with cheese. He cornered an old-timer, the sort of fellow who looked like he knew everything, and offered the man drinks. After an hour of gossip and meandering talk, Danilo learned that Pirro had been in Florence, but that he was long gone.

"How long?" Danilo asked.

"Months," croaked the old man. "He'd been gambling, and drinking. Made a few enemies, and so he had to flee."

"Do you remember anything else about him?"

"Aye. He was always looking around as if he was haunted. When he was in his cups he sang, always the same song. '*Oh beauteous rose of Judea, oh my sweet soul . . . do not leave me to die . . .*' something, something, something; a sweet melody. Must have been true love, eh?" The old man faked a cough. "My throat is fearsome dry, sir . . ."

Danilo paid for more ale. The old man had gnarled hands, and his long, dirty fingernails scratched at the tabletop nervously, spasmodically. He had an absent look in his eyes and nothing more to offer.

Outside the inn, snow whipped around Danilo's overcoat, and blustery gusts tunnelled down the dirty, crooked, narrow street. No one was about. He walked quickly. He wanted to shed the squalor. The song—spluttering from the old man's lips, spat out like an obscenity from between his broken teeth—had been soiled. The man's slurred words had contaminated the memory of Grazia and her love for Pirro, who was clearly in a bad state and lost or hiding who knew where.

But there was something else. The song had aroused a blossoming yearning, a feeling of tenderness—*Oh, beauteous rose of Judea . . .*

Miriamne would be just getting up, or perhaps she was already working at her amulets, or reading Boccaccio, or preparing Jessica and Jacob for an outing, or helping Rabbi Hazan.

She had a way of turning towards you and tossing her head

back, a way of gazing at you as if you were the most important person in the world.

Her smile, its sudden brightness, would light up the world. *Oh, beauteous rose of Judea* . . .

The wind blew in great gusts down the river Arno, which looked frozen, glowering black in the gray morning air. *Oh, beauteous rose* . . .

He pulled his collar higher and crossed the Ponte Vecchio. When he reached the inn, he looked up to see Angelica watching for him in the window.

41

A CLOSE SHAVE

Pisa

"I T'S DOUBLY DANGEROUS, YOU KNOW. YOU ARE A FUGITIVE
chasing a fugitive."

Sunlight streamed through the tall stained-glass
windows of the refectory. Angelica was preparing Danilo for
his new role in Pisa. He was seated on a stiff-backed, hard-
bottomed wooden chair, his face covered in soap, and Angelica
was wielding a wicked-looking blade. They had already
been out and strolled around, looking at the Leaning Tower,
Cathedral Square, and other sights, including some villas dat-
ing from when the city had been a prosperous port, a rival to
Florence and Genova.

But nowhere was there any sign of Pirro Gonzaga. Danilo
had made inquiries in some of the less-reputable inns. Nope, no
way, were the replies he got—when he got any reply at all—
from several shifty, rough-looking characters.

"This pursuit of Pirro is vain and dangerous." Angelica said as she stood back and contemplated Danilo's foam-covered face. "You will get yourself killed. You will get us all killed. I want you to relax. What is this Pirro to you? What is blood? What is family even? Who needs it?" She stood, arms akimbo, holding the razor, giving him her annoyed schoolmarm stare.

"I need to know. I need to see him face-to-face. I want him to recognize that I am his son. I want him to know that his love for Grazia was not in vain."

"But what good would that do? What does it even mean?"

"I don't know," Danilo said honestly.

"You are a child." Angelica held the razor steady. "Hold still. I said, hold still."

"I can do it myself."

"I want to do it."

"You are a stubborn girl. You will cut off my nose."

"Your nose is far too pretty. I swear I won't. Of course, if you fluff your lines, or if you are really, really annoying, then I might decide to cut it off. But my hand is steady, my eye is keen. Fear not, fair gentleman, your beauty shall remain, under my loving hand, absolutely unsullied. The Men in Black, on the other hand . . ."

"I surrender, Angelica."

"An unvarnished, unlettered, beardless lad, a country bumpkin—that is what you are going to play." She scraped the blade down his cheek. It made a crisp raspy sound. She dipped the blade in the bowl of water. "But really, this pursuit could get you killed, you know."

"You said that already."

"I know I said that already."

"Many things could get me killed. This likely isn't one of them."

"Oh, you are so innocent!" Angelica pointed the razor at Isabella's letter, lying open on the table. "Isabella said that bounty hunters are on Pirro's trail, hired by his enemies, and if they run into you, and if they figure out who you are, then they will take you hostage and try for ransom, and then zip, your throat is cut!" She slipped the blade right under his nostrils, and with a quick sideways swipe, deftly executed, totally denuded his upper lip.

"I'm not an innocent."

"I know that, sweet prince. You are noble and scholarly, a man of war and a man of peace, skilful with dagger, lance, and sword, and a marvel astride a stallion — or an eager and sweaty mare. You are a true son of your father, a true Gonzaga, a condottiere and a warrior, the opposite of innocent! From the moment I first saw you I knew that."

"You are perverse, Angelica, and a poet! And perhaps a courtly flatterer."

"Pietro Aretino has nothing on me! But it is a cut-throat world among those aristocrats. When they are not making love, they are murdering each other. Look at Alessandro de' Medici: lured off, promised a secret assignation with a beautiful lady, a night of wild passion — ambushed and murdered by his own cousin."

"Just weeks after he watched us play," said Danilo. "He stood and applauded. Splendid fellow, I thought."

Angelica stood back and examined her work. "Look at you now! Such sweet precise lips, and oh, the man's chin! Let me ask you, ladies and gentlemen, has there ever been a chin like this chin? And the cheekbones so very fine, such perfection! Never have you, ladies and gentlemen, seen their likes before!" She kissed him. "I am very angry, you know. I may sound peaceful and happy, but I am angry — you are chasing a dangerous illusion. Pirro is not what he was, and not what you think he was; maybe he never was. There are dangers enough — Men in Black, rogue Venetian agents, and now Pirro and the people who may want him dead! Children must grow up someday and cast their mythical fathers aside! At some point you must ask yourself what you are really searching for."

This struck a nerve. What the devil was he searching for?

"Besides," Angelica blinked at him. "I hate sleeping with a man I know is going to die."

"Shut up!" Danilo kissed her, leaving a big clownish dollop of bubbly foam on the end of her nose.

She sneezed.

4 2

HOW TO BE A FOP

Pisa

"WELL, CHILDREN—LET ME TRY TO EXPLAIN. THIS IS a satirical play, scandalous and funny. You do see what I mean?" Andreas paced up and down while Angelica watched and Pietro shifted bits of scenery and backdrop—a full moon in a starry sky and a castle on a cliff side, beetling over the sparkling waves of a stormy sea. Tommaso and Laura, Clara and Antonio, and Achilles and Ajax leaned or sat against the wall of the large rehearsal room, watching.

Andreas stopped in front of Danilo. "So you, Danilo, will play a naive provincial fellow, just turned up in Rome. Rome is decadent, you know. But your character does not realize this. In fact, you probably wouldn't know what 'decadent' means. And you, the naive fellow, yearn to be fashionable, but you don't know how. So you make every mistake in the book. You are a hayseed, out of your depth, but you don't know you are out of your depth. You don't even realize there is such a thing as depth. This is a satire. You understand satire, don't you, darling?"

Danilo glanced peevishly at Angelica, who winked. Achilles and Ajax poked each other and giggled. It was hilarious when Andreas slipped, as he occasionally did, into a scolding and flirtatious mode; he was endearingly condescending,

Andreas paced back and forth, waving his arms. "This is a satire on the manners and pretentions of Rome — Rome on the eve of its great catastrophe, Rome in its splendor, before the Spaniards and Germans of Charles V's army rape and pillage and burn their way through the city, Rome just before the Sack of Rome. You, Danilo, are the naive outsider who, without really understanding what he is seeing, allows us, the audience, to see through his eyes — that is, through your eyes — and thus to see the ridiculous pretention and falseness of Rome, but also the underlying tragedy of it all. You are ridiculous, but in your naiveté, you are a truth-teller, you reveal the ridiculousness of others, of the whole system."

Danilo nodded and stroked his chin.

"Rome's history is a story of glory and catastrophe, darling. In short, you have to play a pretentious fop, totally out of his depth."

Danilo scratched his head: A fop. How to do a fop? He half-closed his eyes. There were those young fellows he had seen one night in gondolas going past Veronica Libero's mansion, trying to be noticed, with their tight bright-scarlet leggings, their flared jackets and extravagant ruffs, their high heels and giggly, high-pitched voices. And the way they wagged their hips, and showed their legs, and swiveled their sword sheaths, and bowed, and blinked their eyes as if a mote of dust had gotten into them! He and Veronica with Zarah and the Senator, were standing in the window. Several fashionable young lads also paraded by on the walkway below and played it up. "Look at those tasty young things," said Veronica. "I doubt they'll come to any good!" The Senator laughed. "I was like that once!"

The scene came alive. Danilo *saw* it. He *heard* the Senator. He *saw* those young men. It was a sketch in his head. It was visual, but even more, it was visceral—he *felt* those fops, their movements, attitudes, gestures; he felt them in his muscles and in his bones. He was possessed.

He bowed to Andreas, then he moved—he pranced, he swiveled on his heel, and he swayed like a tree caught in the fiercest of storms. He stuck out his bottom.

Finally he turned, and stared at Andreas.

Angelica, who had been sitting on a stool, jumped up and clapped. The actors broke out in laughter—even Pietro, who almost never laughed. Achilles and Ajax were rolling on the floor.

Andreas put his hand to his throat. "That was almost too good, Danilo. You are a perfect fop. Now if you could offer your handkerchief to the lady, just so . . . with this sort of bow . . . sticking your bottom out even further, and your right leg just so . . ."

Danilo *was* a fop! Truly, he was possessed. Once he had the image, filched from that scene under Veronica's balcony, it was irresistible. He didn't have to think, he *became* the fop. He frowned. Could it be that he, Danilo del Medigo, virile warrior cadet in service of the Sultan, had become an actor?

For this role he was heavily made up, with rosy red cheeks, false moustaches and a beard, and his fop was a huge success. The moment he appeared onstage, the audience roared with laughter. People were in tears. They pointed—the buffoon, the fool! Danilo pranced, he repeated the strong bits, he swiveled, and he bent low. The audience went into hysterics. So this was what fame was like! Danilo del Medigo had not only become an actor; Danilo del Medigo had become a ham.

Dear Danilo and Angelica,
I have arranged with Andreas for some performances on the Adriatic coast, between Ortona and Pesaro with a stop-over in Urbino. This will involve crossing over the mountains.

So do be careful! The mountains, as you know, are infested by bandits and brigands who do not usually exercise pity when it comes to their victims. The dead cannot appeal for redress. And then there are seasonal storms, as you are aware. Please take care! I meantime busy myself with my work of detection. For the moment, I have nothing to report. Pirro may have been seen in Rome, but that was many, many months ago, and I would not credit the report with any interest. I shall continue. I am confiding this note to Sappho so that I will be sure it gets to you without being intercepted.

    —Isabella d'Este, Marchesa of Mantua

4 3

THE ABYSS

T HEY STARTED THE TREK INTO THE MOUNTAINS AN HOUR
or two before dawn. Twenty wagons and carts, a
few riders on horseback, a train of mules, all headed
towards the coastal city of Ortona, which lay on a little cliffside
peninsula sticking out into the Adriatic Sea.

The weather had been wild. A few days before it had rained,
a pure, blinding silver deluge with thunder such as Danilo
had never heard, and then the temperature dropped, and the
blizzard began. It was blinding and everything was quickly
covered in a layer of ice. Even walking on level ground was
treacherous, but here in the mountains, on a narrow road, it
was suicide. The mules and horses were slipping and sliding.
Danilo strode ahead carefully and climbed onto a cart beside
Angelica, and took the reins. It was like that dreadful time they
had gone across the mountain pass from Bologna to Florence;
but this was worse.

Thicker and thicker, the snow came down around them.
The caravan slowed almost to a stop. The snow made it difficult

to see anything clearly. A dull echoing roar came from some-where ahead of them.

"What is that sound?" Angelica cocked her head, listening. The road was on the side of a cliff, walls of rock going up to the left, and plunging down to the right. "What is that? It sounds like it's getting closer."

"I think it's an avalanche." Danilo, who was holding the reins loosely, peered through the snow. "Somewhere up ahead."

Danilo shivered. He had already lived through an avalanche, the one that had buried Suleiman's army during the Baghdad campaign. He had almost been buried alive. And he had seen many die—so many. "We'd better stop. We'd better head back."

"It won't be easy." Angelica gestured towards the long cara-van of wagons and carts stretching behind them, a blurred line of carts and wagons, mules and people darkly huddled, slowly advancing into the whiteness. "It is so narrow here, it will be almost impossible to turn the carts around. Maybe the ava-lanche won't hit the road. We could just stop, and wait and see."

"Yes, we'd better order them to stop." Danilo could see, ahead of them, Andreas, a stout figure walking along, wrapped and hunched against the blizzard, his hand on the edge of one of the carts. He was peering upwards, while the twins, Achilles and Ajax, were shouting and laughing, cavorting and horsing around just in front of him, vague silhouettes in the thick slant-ing snowfall.

Then, so fast Danilo could scarcely make it out, one of the boys disappeared.

"Something's happened," he shouted to Angelica. "Hold the reins." He jumped down from the cart and ran forward through the blinding blizzard.

"Achilles!" Andreas screamed. The snow raged around them.

The wagons had stopped. Danilo ran up to Andreas.

Achilles was lying wounded on a ledge about fifteen feet down from the edge of the roadway. He must have gone too close to the edge and toppled over the cliff. Andreas began to climb down after him.

Danilo edged out onto the peak of rock behind Andreas as far as he dared, and climbed down. He was almost within reach of Andreas when the ledge cracked with a sound like thunder. It disintegrated, exploding into a million fragments, carrying Achilles and Andreas, as it hurtled down with a roar.

Danilo stared. There was nothing now below him but empty space, swirling snow.

He backed away and climbed back. More land began to slide. He scrambled up to the road just as the bank crumbled beneath him. He stood at the edge and peered down. Nothing . . . Ah, Andreas, Achilles . . .

Behind him, someone grasped his sleeve. He turned. It was little Ajax, his face as white as the snow, not yet taking it in. His nose was running, his lips were blue. Danilo's heart clenched.

Then a sound, a thunderous, rising sound.

"Danilo!" Angelica screamed.

He turned and saw it coming from above—a monstrous wave of rocks and mud heading straight towards him and Ajax.

Danilo grabbed Ajax. "No!" Ajax screamed, lunging for the edge. Danilo lifted him up and ran. Pietro and Angelica had stopped the caravan. All the wagons and horses and carts and people in front of them were swept away in a rush of rocks and water and mud, the vast river of a collapsing mountainside. The roaring went on for a long time. When it stopped they were left on the mountain, with the road swept away.

They all stood staring. Angelica, tears streaming down her face, sheltered Ajax under her cloak. Pietro and Danilo went cautiously to the edge and peered over.

"You did what you could." Pietro said as he pulled his collar closer. The wind was even stronger.

Danilo shook his head. "If I had been only a moment sooner, perhaps . . ."

Pietro looked at him sharply. "It would have made no difference."

They managed to turn what remained of the caravan around and headed back. It took them until well past nightfall to get to the nearest inn.

The next day, Pietro and Danilo went searching for the bodies. They spent five days down in the valley and on the mountainside. It was bitterly cold, but the sky had turned blue, and the sun shone. Andreas and Achilles were never found.

For the first few days Angelica insisted they let Ajax sleep with them. Then Pietro took him to sleep in the room with the rest of the actors. The boy became silent and timid. He stayed as close to Angelica as he could.

At the end of the fifth day, Angelica's face was streaming with tears. She turned away from the window and faced Danilo. "We have to continue, Danilo. It is what Andreas would have wanted. Will you help me and Pietro keep the troupe together?"

Danilo took her in his arms; he would not have abandoned this brave young woman and her friends even if he had not been under obligation to Isabella and to Venice.

THE ACTORS WERE DISPIRITED, but they knew only one life.

Angelica called a meeting of the troupe and insisted that they continue, for Andreas and for themselves. She looked around at them and smiled through her tears. "Tommaso, Laura, Antonio, Clara—and Ajax—you are my protégés, and we are a family, and the idea that you are performing and giving pleasure to so many people keeps me alive. Pietro and Danilo and I will make sure that we all continue. The show," her voice broke, just for a moment, "must go on!"

Dear Danilo and Angelica,

I still have not recovered from the news of Andreas's death and that of poor little Achilles. Andreas, when he was a boy, was the most beautiful of creatures. He was slender, nut-brown, sylphlike, with curly black hair and bright shining eyes. He was always in the sun, always laughing, with the brightest and most charming of smiles. He delighted in swimming and in running.

He was talented, too—he could sing and play the lute, and compose a sonnet or a speech at the drop of a hat. Everybody loved him. Giulio Romano adored him and used him as a model. Andreas was an ancient classic statue of youth come to life. Sometimes the gods bestow too many gifts too soon. And then, at some point, fate takes its revenge. Somewhere, buried in the portly and expansive man and his extravagant gestures, was the slender boy who never grew up. I think, in his love for boys such as Achilles and Ajax, Andreas was, in some part of his heart, looking for himself, that lost little boy. But we can never really recover that lost self, nor the years of yesterday which are truly gone.

I have heard some interesting news of Pirro. It seems he might have sought refuge with Giulia Gonzaga—you will remember that Barbarossa tried to kidnap her and make a gift of her to the Sultan—since they are distant relatives. Giulia, as you probably know, had her young savior, the fellow who slipped her out from Barbarossa's grasp, murdered. Perhaps she put too high a price on her own virtue. But that is neither here nor there.

As for Pirro, it seems that Giulia, who has recently become quite religious and perhaps a bit of a bigot, rebuffed his request for shelter and protection. This is indirect gossip, so who knows if any of it is true.

The story continues. Not finding refuge in Giulia's fief of Fondi, Pirro apparently—according to my informants— headed south to Naples. And there the trail runs cold. This information, if accurate, is several months old. So who knows where Pirro might have hidden himself by now. I too long to see him again and hold him in my arms!

I have offered your services as a theatrical troupe in the Kingdom of Naples; this will allow you to continue your search for Pirro, and also it will take you farther, I believe, from the

Men in Black, and from any Venetian enemies who may be
searching for you. —Isabella d'Este, Marchesa of Mantua.

"She's encouraging you in your dangerous quixotic quest, my dear," said Angelica, making a moue of disgust and tying her hair up in a ponytail. "This Pirro is a mirage! It will draw you into dangerous waters!"

44

INVASION

ONE SIZZLING HOT DAY IN MIDSUMMER, 1537, THE TROUPE, on its way to Naples, had just arrived in a little town on the coast, south of Rome, not far from Fondi, the town where Barbarossa had tried to kidnap Giulia Gonzaga. In frustration when he didn't get her, he massacred everybody he and his men could find. The court of Guilia Gonzaga had also apparently been one of Pirro's stops in his flight from hunters and enemies, and undoubtedly from his own demons.

In this charming town the central square faced the harbor, where little fishing boats bobbed gently against the quay and fishing nets were laid out to dry in the sun. The local castle soared up over the square and served as the bishop's palace. Its walls rose straight up, slanted inward only slightly, the top furnished with battlements and towers and crenellations. The castle looked more like a medieval fortress than the home of a bishop. Modest houses straggled down to the quayside, where, just a bit farther on from the fishing boats, a colorful outdoor market was in full swing.

On one side of the central square, Angelica and Danilo were explaining how they would set up their performance space on the cobblestones, where they would put the stage and the seats, if there were seats, and so on . . . Pietro was unloading the cart and placing some of their materials beside a wall.

Ajax was sitting alone, perched on the lip of a fountain, listening, but distracted by an unhappy-looking mule tethered at the castle gate and wearing a conical scarlet and black fool's hat that somebody had tied on its head as a joke.

A ruckus suddenly arose from the coastal road that entered the square just behind the city wall. They all turned. Four Spanish Neapolitan horsemen, warrior messengers, representatives of the Spanish viceroy who governed Naples, thundered into the piazza, the hooves of their dark horses striking bright sparks on the cobblestones. The horses' bodies, lathered in sweat, shone in the hot sunlight as they swerved, reared up, and came to a halt in front of the bishop's palace. The riders jumped off. People came running. The bishop and his attendants appeared at the doorway. A woman screamed.

"Suleiman's troops have landed! The invasion has begun!"

"WE ARE ALL GOING to die!" someone shouted.

"What's going on?" Angelica turned to Danilo.

"The Ottomans have come ashore and they are sowing panic," he whispered to her. "That's the first aim—to sow panic, destroy morale."

People were rushing forward and gathering around the horsemen. Fishermen ran up from the quay, rubbing their roughened hands, their mouths open, their eyes round with fear. People leaned out of windows. Women with heavily laden baskets—bread, fish, vegetables, and calamari—came running from the market and fell on their knees. People were shouting. A woman held a cross high in front of her and screamed for Christ to save them.

"With this sort of panic," Angelica said, "Suleiman hardly needs to invade. Italy will collapse all by itself."

"What is this about?" Danilo asked the leading horseman.

"The Ottomans!" the man managed to say. The horsemen were breathless, excited, their eyes wild. "Barbarossa, Suleiman's pirate admiral, has landed thousands of troops. He's got cavalry and guns. They've come ashore near Castro. His cavalry and infantry are rampaging up and down the countryside, slaying every person they meet."

"The very soil reeks of blood," said another, his gaunt, bearded face dripping sweat, his horse's flanks stained with what looked like blood. "Limbs chopped off, torsos disembowelled, heads skewered on pikes."

"You saw this?"

"Yes," the horseman nodded. "With these two eyes. Clear as I'm looking at you now. We have been sent to warn the populace — watch out for Ottoman ships, Ottoman raiders."

Danilo glanced at Angelica. "This is what they call a strategy of terror."

"It certainly seems to be working." She looked around at the panicked crowd.

"The Ottomans," a tall skinny rider said. He coughed, took a deep breath, wiped his mouth, and continued, "are laying siege to the fortress of Otranto. They have brought their guns and are battering down the walls. There is no hope. Everyone in Otranto will die."

A handsome thin man, with a scar down the side of his face and a bandage on one arm, said, "They are enslaving everyone they don't kill."

"The Church will have to evacuate Rome," a thickset man, who looked to be one of the town merchants, said. "They will have to evacuate Naples."

Ajax jumped off the lip of the fountain and came running over to Angelica. "Are we going to see a battle, Angelica?"

"I hope not, Ajax, but you stay close to me." She tousled his hair. "We have to decide what we are going to do." She kissed the top of his head; the boy had become like a son to her.

Angelica, Danilo, and Pietro walked away from the rising hysteria. Ajax tagged along, keeping just behind Angelica.

"What do you think, my warrior prince?" she asked.

Danilo put his arm around her shoulders. "I think it is a long way from Otranto to here. I'd say a thirty- or forty-day march, even for lightly armed troops. Those horsemen are reporting things they heard, not things they saw. I am sure of it. So let's say a month-and-a-half, unless they are going to land more troops up this side of the peninsula by ship, which I doubt Suleiman would do. In any case, this is a small town, not of much interest to Suleiman or Barbarossa. I don't imagine Suleiman's main army has landed yet. This may be just a raid to test the defenses. Otranto will probably keep them busy for a time. Let us hold our performance in any case, if we can."

"Are you sure?" said Angelica, "The actors are our responsibility!"

"Running away won't save anybody. And it isn't necessary. Tomorrow we will head north. We will cancel Naples."

"The show must go on," said Pietro. "It is what Andreas would have wanted." He looked around and surveyed the little scene—where the stage could go, where the audience would sit. Clara and Laura were already miming their roles and Tommaso was reading the script to Antonio.

"The show must go on," said Ajax. He stepped forward and took Angelica's hand.

She tousled the boy's hair again and smiled, but her eyes were serious. She knelt and pulled Ajax to her, holding him tight; if anything happened to him she would kill herself.

"I see I am outnumbered," she said. "You gentlemen have ganged up on this lonely girl—the show will go on!"

THE CROWD AT THE performance was small.

They had intended a comical play about pirates, but Danilo decreed, with Angelica's agreement, that they would instead perform the comedy in which he played the provincial fop, arriving in Rome confused and flummoxed by all the pretension and falseness of the city. Even that comedy, though, evoked memories of the Sack of Rome. Attention was fitful. Laughter was rare. Applause was sparse. People were terrified.

Even the performers were nervous. But Danilo, stimulated by the sense of danger, played with brio, not dampened by the muted reaction of the audience. And Angelica responded to his fervor. They were acting for each other. Ajax, who was playing an impertinent pageboy, made his best, most mischievous effort ever.

They ate in the bishop's palace near the kitchens. The bishop—a portly, elaborately dressed, clean-shaven man with narrow suspicious eyes and a bad limp, visited them briefly; he complimented them on the performance, which he had not seen. He was distracted and nervous. Danilo noticed that the bishop's servants were packing valuables in large wicker baskets and wooden cases to be shipped in the morning, probably on the Roman galley which he noted had just slipped into the sleepy little port, and was lying about one hundred yards off shore.

They slept in an inn, fitfully. In the middle of the night, more riders galloped into town with reports that more Ottoman troops had landed along the coast, not far from Naples. Danilo slipped out of bed and questioned the men. They had seen nothing directly, but were reporting rumors.

Danilo went back to bed. "Just rumors," he said, and kissed Angelica on the forehead.

"We surely won't go to Naples now," Angelica said.

"Naples is cancelled. Isabella will understand."

They rose in the dark, packed hurriedly, and headed north with a caravan of wagons carrying people who wanted to get as far away from Otranto and the south as possible.

It had occurred to Danilo that Suleiman's ships might make raids farther up the coast, even reaching as far as where they were.

"War is exciting," said Ajax. He was sitting next to Angelica. She put her arms around the lad's shoulders and held him close.

"No, my boy," said Danilo, "it's not."

By midmorning it was sweltering. The roads were dusty and endless; the palm trees wilted, their fronds covered in dust; the fields were bone-dry, baking in the pitiless blazing sun. Onwards they plodded—the horses, and the mules, and the humans—in the wagons or on foot, taking turns riding and walking. The roads ran close to the coast. Danilo kept his dagger concealed beneath his jacket and Pietro had a truncheon, which he always kept close at hand. Danilo scanned the horizon of the glimmering misty sea, the beautiful turquoise and blue Tyrrhenian, from which death in the guise of Muslim pirates and raiders could come at any time.

Some peasants took the actors' small caravan of rough, unpainted hired wagons for Suleiman's invading army and fled, screaming, through the dusty, shimmering, heat-soaked fields to warn their families, while others loped off to hide in the woods. Still others stood by the roadside, absolutely still, bug-eyed, mouths open, clutching their hats to their chests.

As the afternoon wore on, the heat and humidity built and clouds gathered. The air darkened. "It's going to rain," Danilo observed. Over the hills, thunderheads were piling up, and out to sea, the waves picked up, sharp dark whitecaps, lit with flecks of lowering sunlight. "We'd better look for shelter."

They put the mules and horses in the stables of the next inn. Powerful gusts swept across the road. The palm trees thrashed violently. Just as they were taking shelter, the rain arrived, a pure wall of water.

"Biblical deluge," muttered Danilo, peering out the stable door. Sheets of silver water smashed down onto the roadway, turning everything to mud, pools of water, rivulets running every which way.

The innkeeper was a fat, jovial, red-faced fellow with long curly black hair, ruby lips, and sparkling eyes. "Now what would you like to eat and drink, then? We have more than enough. As long as you have coin, you can eat your fill! Such rumors, eh? People will believe anything! Panic—why, everybody has run away except me and my family, we intend to die right here. I will take my stand! Those fellows don't frighten me! Pirates are always active along this coast, Barbarossa and his Muslims, and renegade Greeks, and Barbary pirates from North Africa, we are used to them. We have our own Saracen tower, you know." He led Danilo to a window and pointed. Peering through the rain and the gathering dusk, Danilo could just make out the round tower, high up on a craggy ridge. The innkeeper cleared his throat. "We are prepared. Those are refuges and lookouts so we can see the pirates and warn people, and people can take refuge in the tower. There are hundreds of these so-called Saracen towers along the coast. We have people up there right now, watching. But, you know," he laid his finger by the side of his nose and looked sly. "I've heard that the richest families in Naples are clamoring to get aboard galleys heading north."

Another of the refugees piped up. "And in the Vatican, Pope Paul III has packed his bags. Prelates first, widows and orphans last! Poor people not at all!"

"They say many cardinals and bishops have already left. Galleys were being called to Rome's port of Ostia to help in the evacuation."

"Aye, aye! The end of Christendom, as has often been foretold, is nigh."

"Where is Ajax?" Angelica looked around, calling his name over and over. He was nowhere in the dining room, nowhere in the inn. "Danilo! I must find him!" She yelled wildly and rushed out into the storm.

Danilo followed. "I'll look for him!"

Danilo and Angelica ran out onto the road that led to the village. Just dimly visible in the downpour and the dusk was a small figure walking in that direction. It was Ajax, shoulders hunched, pelted with rain, and looking very tiny. Danilo and Angelica ran towards him.

"Where are you going?"

Ajax kept walking. "Nowhere! I don't belong to anybody. Someday you are going to leave me behind."

Angelica took his arm and knelt by him in the mud. "No, Ajax. We will never leave you behind. I will never leave you behind! I love you." She pulled the small boy as close to her as she could and kissed him over and over, and finally, sobbing, he buried his face in her shoulder.

45

SPOLETO: POST

MORTEM

D ANILO MANAGED TO SCHEDULE THREE NIGHTS — THEN
several weeks of rehearsal — in the beautiful little
market town of Spoleto, in the foothills of the mountains of Umbria, on the off chance that a hint about Pirro's presence here would turn out to be true. Spoleto had the added
advantage of being near the mountains, far from the sea and
Muslim raiders, and with plenty of places to hide and seek refuge, should Suleiman's army actually land in Italy and get so
far north. Shortly after arriving, Danilo and Angelica received
a note from Marco, summoning them.

In a tavern just down the street and around the corner from
the troupe's inn, Marco was walking up and down in front of a
brightly burning fireplace.

"So, Marco, what news?" Danilo shrugged out of his
overcoat.

"I thought you'd want to know what happened with

Suleiman, and with Venice. As you know, Venice unfortunately has not been able to avoid war with Suleiman."

"Yes, we know that," said Angelica, shaking off the rain that had accumulated on her shoulders. The three of them sat at a table in a curtained niche and Marco ordered wine and cheese.

"Your information about Suleiman's preparations for the invasion corroborated much that we knew. Here is what happened. Early last summer, Suleiman traveled to Valona, just as you predicted he would, Danilo. He had gathered several hundred galleys and 300,000 troops, including cavalry, and siege and field guns."

"Three hundred thousand men," Angelica whispered.

"That's five to ten times larger than the largest European armies," Marco said.

Angelica shivered and gazed into the fire. "I don't even want to think about what that means."

"As you know, Suleiman ordered Barbarossa to land thousands of troops and cavalry at Castro near Otranto, in Southern Italy, and lay siege to the city."

Danilo nodded. "This was certainly a rehearsal for the main invasion. We saw panic in small towns along the coast and in the countryside. Townspeople were loading up what they had and scurrying for the woods and hills, hoping to hide in the mountains. People were taking refuge in the coastal fortifications, those things they call Saracen towers that have been built all along the coast as refuges from pirates. Galleys had come to the ports to pick up the important people and take them north. Everybody was shouting that in Rome the Pope was packing his bags and going to run for it."

Marco filled their glasses. "Panic certainly spread in Rome. All those who could were preparing to leave. Imagine, ten years after the Sack of Rome, the Eternal City was about to be conquered by Islam. Saint Peters would become a mosque. The capital of Christendom doomed."

"It's hard to imagine," said Angelica, lifting her glass, "And yet Constantinople, the capital of the Eastern Empire and

Eastern Christianity fell, and tens of thousands died and were reduced to slavery." Her lips trembled. She hid the trembling by pressing the mug to her mouth and drinking.

Danilo watched her closely. Her hand was shaking. She feared nothing more than slavery. She had told him that if she closed her eyes she could still see her sister, see the man stabbing her in the heart, then chopping off her head with one sweep of an axe; and she could see her mother struggling, fighting, being raped, and then butchered.

Marco's eyes looked weary. "For two weeks, Barbarossa's men raged up and down the countryside in Apulia. They slaughtered everyone they met—tens of thousands died—they burned towns and farms to the ground, destroyed Castro and Otranto, and captured, we estimate, just over 10,000 whom they took away to be sold into slavery. At the end of two weeks Barbarossa withdrew, leaving ruins and mourning behind him."

Angelica stared at the red wine.

"They took young men, women, and children." Marco had a long drink and wiped his mouth with the back of his hand. "Otranto was a small sample of what might have happened had the invasion gone as planned. Terror is an effective weapon. But Suleiman had a couple of problems—and so, in the end, he withdrew his army to Istanbul and put off the invasion. Let us hope it never takes place."

Danilo could see, in his mind's eye, what those problems would have been; he had predicted them.

"The first, as you pointed out, Danilo, was the island of Corfu, controlled by Venice. Part of the problem was the Venetian fleet, lurking in the Adriatic. Both Corfu and the fleet threatened Suleiman's supply lines. In a full invasion, he, and part of his army, could have been cut off and trapped. It takes time to transport 300,000 men, plus horses and cannons."

Danilo half-closed his eyes. He could imagine it, a battle between Venetian and Ottoman galleys at sea, and part of Suleiman's army isolated.

"If you look at a map, Angelica, you will see how Corfu is right across from the heel of the Italian boot." Marco took a piece of paper and sketched a map of the Italian boot, showing Corfu, the Adriatic Sea, Otranto, and the Albanian port of Valona. "Corfu controls the narrow strait between Italy and the Balkans; it controls the entry into and exit from the Adriatic Sea."

Danilo knew the map by heart. Once he had seen a similar one in Suleiman's tent, laid out on a low table, and Suleiman leaning over it, with his hand moving along the Albanian coast and stopping at the island of Corfu.

"So, Corfu was a thorn in the side of Suleiman's invasion plans. If Venice controlled Corfu, it might just possibly intercept Suleiman's invading fleet . . ."

"And break off his supplies and communications, and interrupt the invasion," Angelica said, staring at Marco's drawing.

"Then came the second of Suleiman's problems: His ally, François I, who is often skittish and unpredictable, had not yet begun his invasion of northern Italy. François had run into trouble and had been delayed. So Suleiman decided he had time to attack and take Corfu. He withdrew Barbarossa from Otranto. The rehearsal had been a success. Nothing was able to resist Barbarossa's guns, cavalry, and artillery. And so Suleiman turned to Corfu, only sixty miles from the Italian coast. He would grab Corfu."

Danilo nodded. "It would be an ideal base from which to launch a future invasion."

"That is precisely right, Danilo. If you control Corfu, you control the Adriatic, and if you control the Adriatic, you control the whole of the east coast of Italy. You can invade anywhere anytime."

Angelica was studying the map. She pointed at the island of Corfu. "So—Suleiman attacked Corfu, which belongs to Venice, and Venice found itself at war with Suleiman."

"Yes, that is how Venice was drawn into war with the Ottomans. Suleiman mobilized 325 ships, 25,000 troops, and some very efficient artillery batteries. The island was occupied by Suleiman's army. But the Venetian citadel had been especially designed with thick low earthworks to absorb a heavy bombardment and to resist Suleiman's guns. It held out by the skin of its teeth. Thus Venice and the Corfu garrison blocked Suleiman's grandiose project."

"Conquering Italy and Rome, the capital of Christendom for Islam . . ." Angelica looked at Marco.

"Exactly."

"And then?"

"Then the plague came to our rescue."

"Ah."

"A huge army in temporary, crowded encampments is, as you know, Danilo, extremely vulnerable to disease. And plague appeared among his men. So Suleiman wisely withdrew from the island. The siege of Corfu lasted only twelve days. With him, though, Suleiman took some 20,000 men, women, and children from the island to be sold into slavery. He led his army back towards Istanbul. The invasion and the immediate threat of invasion was over—is over."

Angelica said not a word, just stared at Marco. He held her gaze, then looked down. "Twenty thousand taken into slavery. I know, Angelica, I know."

Danilo put his arm around her; she pressed against him, picked up her mug, and took a long slow drink.

"Now that we Venetians are at war with him, Suleiman will turn to other, more vulnerable Venetian colonies and trading posts in the Aegean Sea, and we are sure he will pick them off, one by one. For the moment, there is little we can do."

Angelica tapped her carefully cut fingernails on the table. "I would dearly love to kill every single pirate in the world," she said in a calm, even voice. "I would be absolutely without pity. I would execute them all."

Danilo pulled her close to him, held her, and kissed her hair.

Marco waited a moment, then, looking into Angelica's eyes, he said. "There is one positive development. The threat woke the Pope—he had been criminally complacent, blind to the approaching threat. Now, at last, he is terrified of Suleiman and has finally realized the extent of the danger. So he is begging François I and Charles V to make peace, nudging them towards a so-called 'Holy League' to oppose Suleiman's conquest of Europe. Only if Europe pulls together can we resist the Ottomans, that's the idea. This might be helpful. We shall see. We Venetians will probably join, if the thing comes about. But as you know, we don't like to be tied down—and for the moment, the danger to Italy and to Christendom has passed."

Danilo sighed. "So Islam's conquest of Italy has been put off; it will be for another time."

"Exactly. Suleiman has withdrawn his fleet and marched his army back to camps close to the Ottoman capital. So for the moment it is over. Europe has had yet another reprieve. But sooner or later Suleiman, or the next Turkish sultan, or the next, will try; and then they will try again, and again. Islam, after all, believes it is the final and true word of God."

"So does Christianity," said Angelica, perking up. "It claims it is the final and true word of God. Remember the crusades! Christian knights went off and massacred Muslims and— along the way—Jews. And since I was considered a pagan, the Christians were quite happy to sell me into slavery."

"Yes. That is true." Marco nodded.

"Now Christians fight among themselves, Protestants and Catholics, as to what Christianity really means, and they massacre each other over the question." Angelica fingered the golden cross that hung from her neck. "And while they squabble, they are looking for scapegoats, and among the scapegoats will always be the Jews."

Marco nodded. "That too is a tragedy, and it is a tragedy that has only just begun."

"But we are here, and the show must go on," said Angelica, suddenly smiling, and raising her glass.

And the three of them, clinking glasses grimly, repeated, "The show must go on!"

Dear Danilo and Angelica,

You have never been far from my heart, particularly after the horrible tragedy which claimed the life of Maestro Andreas and of sweet Achilles. Even here, far away, the thought that they are no longer with us leaves a void in my heart. And then there is the horrible tragedy of Otranto—the second time the city has been sacked by the Ottomans and its inhabitants massacred and carried off into slavery. That last time, in 1480, I was six years old, and I remember the tales of horror that we children were told, and even the survivors who turned up at the d'Este court in Ferrara, refugees and one priest—I remember him vividly—who had seen much and had somehow, only God knows how, escaped with his life, poor man. And then we have seen the attack on Corfu. Terrible slaughter and so many poor souls taken into slavery, but the garrison and fortress held. Good old Venetians! Well, this time, it appears the Ottomans have failed, Suleiman has taken his 300,000 men back to their camps near Istanbul. Good riddance, I say. I do hope it will be a long time before they try again.

Well, let us move on! I have arranged for you to be welcomed in Rome just before the Christmas season. I do realize, Danilo, that Rome may bring back painful memories of the last weeks we all spent together—you, your mother, and I, and so many others, virtual prisoners in Palazzo Colonna—and of the dreadful sea voyage which claimed Grazia's life.

However, Rome will allow you to meet some important people, and to perform before some impressive personages.

Also, I have received information that my dear Pirro may be living under an assumed name, hiding from his pursuers in Rome, not far from via Giulia or near the Pantheon, or down towards the Tiber, in the Jewish quarter. That is all I know. It is not much, and it is very vague. But you perhaps can ferret out more information than I have at present been able to glean. I must smuggle this letter out, as Federico is extremely suspicious and indeed, he might, if he knew where Pirro was to be found, send killers to hunt him down. Some people do bear

grudges a long time. Sappho will see that this letter is deliv-
ered into safe hands so it can reach you without interference.
—Isabella d'Este, Marchesa of Mantua

4 6

R U I N S

Rome

D ANILO PULLED UP HIS COLLAR. IT WAS BITTERLY COLD in Rome.

He could see his breath mingling with Angelica's. He remembered that Pirro Gonzaga had tried to prevent the Sack of Rome, had tried to negotiate with the leaders of the Imperial Army, to direct them away from the Eternal City, but to no avail. Perhaps that failure too had broken Pirro's heart, since it had led to the death of the woman he loved, and — as far as he knew — to the death of his only son. Maybe it was guilt that was crushing Pirro, causing him to flee. Maybe more than anything, Pirro was a fugitive from himself, from his own guilt. That comment of Angelica's came back: you have to figure out who or what you are really searching for.

Pietro was unloading their luggage from a cart. Tommaso and Ajax were helping. The boy had become much more cheerful and independent. And though he wanted always to be close to Angelica, and to know that she was close by, he no longer clung to her. Clara, a sweet young thing, was carrying baskets inside. Laura, who had complained of a headache, was already inside the building, wandering around somewhere, probably being attended to by Antonio, who was, truth be told, smitten with her.

It was deep winter. Even now, more than a decade after Charles V's troops had gone wild, Rome was a shattered city, and the recent narrow escape from Suleiman added to the atmosphere of doom and a sense of the end of times.

Many buildings were charred ruins and many were empty. The Spanish and German troops of Charles V's army, who had run amok pillaging, raping, murdering, and burning their way through the Eternal City, had left their mark everywhere. Monuments and works of art had been destroyed. Almost all the artists and architects and engineers—the glory and ornament of the city—had fled; only a few had returned. Some of the streets were piled with rubbish, broken and smashed and burnt furniture, tapestries that had been scorched, and stony rubble from walls that had fallen down. But people were trying to pick up the pieces and put their lives together.

On the way to their lodgings they had passed in front of Palazzo Farnese. Alessandro Farnese, who had become Pope Paul III, had ordered the building of the Palazzo—which had been interrupted by the Sack of Rome—accelerated. It was an enormous building in the midst of expansion. The partly built and hugely imposing four-story façade towered up over Piazza Farnese and projected a sense of power, consisting as it did of rows of giant windows looming down, and deep overhanging, intimidating cornices. The façade had been designed and construction was being overseen by Michelangelo. Danilo glanced back at it as they left the piazza. What wealth! What immense, showy, even overweening, talent!

The acting troupe set up their theater inside a very large room in a semi-abandoned palazzo a few streets and alleyways from Palazzo Farnese. It was just off the new via Giulia, which had been commissioned by the late pope Julius II, and was being built as a prestigious street to cut across part of ancient Rome and run parallel to the Tiber.

It was a pleasure to be inside. Danilo rubbed his hands and shook the cold dampness from his shoulders. The winter wind whistled outside the tall windows of the large reception room. A fire burned in a gigantic fireplace. Logs were piled up on the floor. Some of the tapestries on the walls had been charred in fires set by the looters. Two or three paintings in large gilded frames leaned against the walls, and pieces of furniture were placed here and there. It all looked improvised, like a nomadic encampment.

The servant who seemed to rule the roost in this half-ruined kingdom was a tall, thin, older man, his back bent as if he were carrying the weight of the woes of the world upon his shoulders.

"That was a little over ten years ago," he told them. "Yes, they came in here, and they raped all the servants, and then they killed them. I was at the country estate, though my wife was here. She died, along with my children."

Carrying a torch aloft, he led Danilo, Angelica, and the others along a corridor.

"And they only let the young countess go because she was pregnant — she was twenty-one years old — and she gave them her jewels to buy her life. She begged for the others — her servants, her dependants — but in vain. They were Spaniards and Germans, drunk and hungry, filthy and cold, Charles V's troops. They hadn't been paid in months. So they killed, and raped, and pillaged their way through the city."

"How dreadful," Angelica whispered.

Danilo knew words were useless, but he knew too that Angelica felt she had to say something, and that at the mention of rape and pillage she was back in the past, witnessing what had happened to her sister and her mother.

"You and your companions can sleep here, in these rooms," said the servant. "It is a trifle primitive, I'm afraid. We have many rooms that are empty. As I said, we are still rebuilding." He pulled aside a curtain. "See, that palazzo across the way is entirely burnt out, just a shell of itself. Many buildings need to be entirely rebuilt. Vagabonds and thieves camp in the ruins."

Danilo had his own memories of those dreadful days. He remembered the excitement; he remembered that Grazia did not want to abandon her home in the Jewish quarter, in the Portico of Octavia, but how as the dangers grew, she decided she must. He remembered being taken by Pirro to see the imperial camp, to witness the German troops, the mercenary pikesmen, the Landsknechts, in revolt against their generals, and he remembered being treated like a little soldier. It was all a grand show! And then began the horror. What illusions he had had as a boy!

The servant rubbed his chilly hands together. "They stripped and speared the nuns, and impaled some of them, sometimes still alive, on those long pikes the German foot soldiers carry. Sometimes they raped the nuns before they killed them, sometimes after. Some men have a taste for freshly killed flesh, and others have a taste for inflicting pain on one who is still alive. They impaled the poor women upright on pikes outside St. Peter's, a sort of parody, I believe, of the crucifixion. They were German Lutherans. It was meant as blasphemy, as profanation."

Angelica pulled her coat collar closer.

The old man swung open two tall, gilded doors, and led them into a particularly large room, designed to hold hundreds of people.

"You can perform in this room, can you not?"

The room was splendid, with beautiful proportions, and it was bare, without any furniture at all. It did have, however, a large, roaring fire in a monumental marble fireplace. "This will do very well," Danilo said. "This will be excellent."

Angelica pulled Ajax to her. "Go warm yourself by the fire, darling! And you, Laura, go and rest, you need it. Clara, maybe you could help Laura. She's not feeling well. Tommaso, you look frozen, and you too, Antonio—stay by the fire!"

"We will bring in chairs." The old servant said, then paused as if lost, as if groping for words. "There are many rooms in this mansion, but they are not very well-furnished, I'm afraid. Everything, all the furniture, was torn out and wrecked. But there are rooms in which you can camp. The kitchens are working. There will be food. And as you can see, some of the rooms have fires lit for warmth."

"Is it possible to have hot water for bathing?" Angelica whispered, leaning towards the old man.

He smiled. "Ah, my Lady has a special request?" He smiled a conspiratorial smile. "Yes, Signora, I am sure that we can provide water. There are fires in the kitchens, and buckets. It will depend how many people I can have on duty."

"Thank you!"

"You know the population of Rome shrank to less than half what it was before the Sack." Perhaps only 10,000 people were left.

"Is that true?"

"Yes, it is now perhaps back up . . . to 30,000, a bit more possibly. But under Pope Julius II, in those ten years, from 1503 to 1513, Rome was glorious. It had a population of about 50,000 or even more. Of course, during the Sack, the artists and writers almost all fled. The glory and glamor and talent are gone, I'm afraid." He gazed at them. "It is delightful to have you here — you bring life, you bring laughter. I can almost imagine my wife alive again. She was a favorite of the young countess, and they both delighted in theater."

"THE JEWS MUST PAY!"

The players were mingling with the members of the audience in another large reception room, where a buffet of bubbling-hot roast lamb and pork, thick minestrone and cream soups, and an assortment of cheeses and breads had been set out close to a roaring fire. In the midst of the surrounding desolation and poverty, this was an island of luxury and warmth, privilege and power.

"The Jews must pay," repeated the Cardinal.

The Cardinal, surrounded by a group of admirers, was pushing for a new and vigorous inquisition in Venice and Rome—and throughout Italy. He was a tall, thin, slightly bent old man with an unruly graying beard and wet lips, and he wore the long gown of an ecclesiastic. He had received his cardinal's hat, Danilo had heard, because he had been the lover of the influential sister of an earlier pope. He also had, so it was rumored, several current lovers and a string of illegitimate children. He was widely touted as a probable future pope. The Cardinal had an eye for female beauty, so at a nod from Danilo, Angelica cornered the man for herself.

The Cardinal's eyes sparkled as he leaned over the young woman. Danilo sidled in and hovered nearby, casually inspecting books on a shelf, and listened as the Cardinal focused all his attention on Angelica. The other guests, seeing the Cardinal's interest in the actress, drifted discreetly away, leaving him and Angelica in an intimate tête-à-tête.

"We must purify Christianity of all that taints it—Jews, Muslims, and those so-called New Christians. I call them False Christians. *Marranos*, swine, as some people prefer to name them. And above all, we must vanquish this new heresy called Protestantism!" The Cardinal favored Angelica with a benign, unctuous smile. Her blond hair and blue eyes as well as the gold cross dangling in her cleavage, assured him that she was a pure-blooded Catholic.

Angelica gave him her warmest smile. "Your Eminence, what of Rome?"

"God works in mysterious ways," said the Cardinal, leaning closer. "The punishment was sublime. The troops of Charles V's army were instruments of Divine Will."

"Really?"

"Yes, my dear. Rome was punished because it was too pagan, too rich, too indulgent, and too forgiving. And the popes were corrupt. They frequented artists and writers and poets—riff-raff, individuals with unchristian tastes and ideas. The popes

accumulated wealth and power. They gave riches and sine-
cures to their lovers, their families, their loose women, their
catamites—and the children they slept with. They exploited
and neglected the poor. They forgot—or worse, ignored—the
lessons of Christ. Humility, humility is the thing, and charity!
So punishment came upon Rome, just as punishment came on
ancient Israel. And the plague came to Rome, and even drought
came to Rome, and destruction, just as it rained down on Sodom
and Gomorrah. The punishment took many forms. Charles V's
troops killed and raped and burned their way through the city,
and when the looting and burning and killing had stopped, the
city starved. Famine struck—grain reserves had been exhausted
and destroyed; deliveries from the countryside ceased. After the
drought came the floods. The Tiber rose up and engulfed the
poorest parts of town, punishing the poor for the sins of the
rich—and the sins of the Church. God's hand was visible."

"Will Rome rise again? After this divine chastisement, what
can be done?"

Danilo, listening to all this, knew there were glimmers
of reconstruction happening. Pope Paul III, in power for the
last three years, was determined to rebuild the city. Outside,
around the corner, via Giulia was being built, the first modern
street to be pushed through the old center of Rome. So perhaps, out of the ashes of humiliation and devastation, a new,
more glorious Rome would rise, like the Rome his mother
had known, the cultured and dynamic Rome of Julius II, and
the banker Agostino Chigi and his famous Venetian mistress,
Francesca Ordeaschi.

The Cardinal smiled. "Purity! We must purify everything,
my dear. We must cut out and hunt down corruption and heresy. We must burn away the wicked. We must re-establish
the standards of the old days, the greatness of the Church.
Slaves that have been freed must be returned to their masters.
Freedom breeds license."

Danilo saw that even at the mention of slavery, Angelica
kept her gaze and smile steady. The Cardinal curled his hand

into a fist. "We must delve deep into souls, into the deepest, most intimate nooks and crannies of consciousness, and seek out impurity wherever it lurks, and extirpate it! And then, with purifying and cleansing fire, we must cauterize the wounds. Jews, Muslims, New Christians, *Marranos*, Protestants, heretics, they must all be cast out!"

"An ambitious program, your Eminence." Angelica smiled.

"The survival of Christianity depends on it! A great wave of purification must sweep Europe until all corruption and all the rubbish are swept away. A new inquisition, grander and greater and more rigorous than any before, will soon be declared, and it shall sweep them all away—the heretics, the New Christians, and those so-called Protestants who infest the North, running naked through the streets and performing other abominations." The Cardinal smiled amiably. "Come with me for just a moment," he said, and he turned and led Angelica away. Angelica cast a backward glance at Danilo, and he lost sight of them as they disappeared into a curtained alcove. He drifted in that direction but didn't dare go too close. He waited anxiously.

Finally, Angelica emerged, followed by the Cardinal, who bowed towards her, then drifted off and was immediately surrounded by a group of admirers and supplicants.

Angelica beckoned to Danilo. She moved to a window, pulled aside a thick curtain, and peeked out at the snow.

"You were very successful with the Cardinal," said Danilo, a slight edge to his voice.

"You think so?" She turned to him, a strange light in her eyes. "Truth be told, I don't really believe any of it."

"Don't believe what?"

"I don't believe in the priests and all their nonsense—but if I confess this, you can denounce me and have them burn me at the stake, should the fancy strike you." She wrinkled her brow, and twisted her lips, a parody of thoughtfulness.

He laughed. "I will never denounce you."

"People change, Danilo." She smiled. It was a sad smile. "If you think about it, if the priests knew what they claim to know, they would be the wisest and the best of men, or so it seems to me, and they are, most of them, far from that. Some of them are fine, judicious, upstanding, generous people, but many are dull and wicked creatures, and their priesthood gives them the power to deploy their wickedness and stupidity to the fullest and most cruel extent. Just think of the Spanish and Portuguese Inquisitions! Just think of the massacres and the corruption!" She took a deep drink of wine and smiled again. "'Here I stand. I can do no other.'"

Danilo gazed at her and, still smiling, she held his gaze. She was quoting Martin Luther, the arch-Protestant, the deadliest enemy of the Church. She was truly remarkable. And was she, just possibly, a heretic, or even a Protestant?

The Governor of Spoleto joined them at the window and rubbed his chin. "Rome is truly a ruin. Pope Clement VIII was a fool not to bribe the Imperial Army, and Charles V was a criminal to let his troops run wild. He should have paid them. But he had trouble raising loans. The bankers were exhausted— they had no more credit to extend."

"That would be a problem," said Danilo, "unpaid troops are dangerous." He was only nine years old when he had seen the troops of Charles V in revolt against their own officers. He had seen it with his own eyes, Pirro Gonzaga standing beside him, his hand on his shoulder.

"Indeed they are," said the Governor. "The leaderless riff-raff wanted to destroy Rome—thousands of troops, Germans and Spaniards. Most of the Germans were Lutherans, so they considered Rome the whore of Babylon. About 20,000 died, we think, though it is difficult to get an accurate count. Rome was reduced to a shadow of itself. This has become a gloomy place. The streets are full of orphans who rob and steal. They will even kill if they are hungry enough; the children have become animals. And if a man wants a boy or a girl, for carnal pleasure or as a servant or a slave, then he can have them. All he needs is a few coins, or a bit of cheese, or a hunk of bread. That will buy a man a night of sex, or a week, or a lifetime."

"Terrible times," Angelica said.

"Terrible?" the Governor said, raising his eyebrows. "Times worse than terrible! Even the little children are killers."

4 7

EVEN LITTLE
CHILDREN KILL

Rome

I T WAS LATE, LONG AFTER THE RECEPTION, LONG AFTER THE
others had gone to bed.

"I'm going out," Danilo said as he pulled on his overcoat.

"I'm coming with you." Angelica put aside the book she was
reading; the candle flame flickered from her sudden movement.

"No. It will be dangerous."

"Ah. You are going looking for your father, for Pirro. I see. I
don't care. If you are going to be crazy, I am determined to be
crazy with you."

"It's the only time I have to look."

"Yes, my dear, let us look for this will-o'-the-wisp blood
father of yours. Isabella gave us our hints, and her blessing. But
I doubt we will find him prowling out of doors on a dark frozen
Roman night like this."

"One never knows. Stranger things have happened."

Two guards stood just inside the massive doors of the palazzo. "You should not wander out like this, certainly not so late. Not in Rome," one of them said.

The other nodded. "Beggars and bandits and whores, and God knows what other rabble and riffraff, are out tonight. They are cold and they are hungry. They will kill for a piece of bread."

"We will be careful," said Danilo, with a polite bow.

"Yes, thank you," said Angelica.

"So be it, then," said the taller of the two guards. "Good luck!"

Warmly bundled, Danilo and Angelica stepped outside. The tall heavy doors thudded shut behind them. A few sparse flakes of snow were falling.

"You know, part of me doesn't care at all." Angelica took his arm.

"About what?"

"Whether I live or die. Since Andreas and Achilles are gone, I'm not sure about myself—who I am, what I am, why I am, what purpose I serve."

"You are life itself, Angelica. You have me, and Ajax, and Pietro, who love you; the whole troupe depends on you!" Danilo pulled her close and kissed her. Her lips were warm. Their breath made a white intermingled cloud in the ice-cold air. He gazed into her eyes, so blue, with little silver drops on the jet-black lashes.

They headed towards via Giulia. Danilo peered through the falling snow. Via Giulia was a straight line stretching away into the moonlit distance. It looked like an abandoned construction site: many buildings half-finished, the street itself not fully completed, part of an urban renewal scheme begun before the catastrophe.

"Well, there are some very chic buildings here," said Angelica, huddling close, "But most of them are unfinished— refuges for squatters or gamblers. I believe the Florentines intend to take it over and make their own Roman neighborhood, and thus it will become very fashionable. But that will take time."

There was not a soul to be seen on the long, half-finished street.

Angelica shivered. "I doubt Pirro will be out on a night like this." Snowflakes drifted down. She turned her face up and caught some with her tongue.

Danilo watched her. "Let's head to the Portico of Octavia, near the river. It's where the Jews live, where my mother and her husband—my legal father, Judah del Medigo—lived."

"And it's where Pirro might also be found, at least according to Isabella's letter." Angelica favored Danilo with a roguish, indulgent smile.

The narrow alleys were lit only by the moon, a contrast of bright silvery light and knife-sharp black shadows. Some streets were cobblestoned, others consisted of mud and frozen puddles that reflected the moonlight; the buildings loomed up, their walls ghostly. Lying in the streets—under archways, in alcoves, under ledges—were dark bundles of rags: the homeless beggars, many of whom were children.

"Pleasure, do you wish for pleasure?" An old woman surged up out of an alleyway and held out her trembling hand. Her face was caved in on one side. Her nails, lit by the moon, were long and filthy, her hands crooked and twisted like claws. Her skin was marked with running sores that looked black in the moonlight. Danilo bowed slightly, "No thank you, madam."

"I can give pleasure. I am an expert, an expert in the arts of the skin."

"Arts of the skin?"

"Special caresses, like nothing you have ever known."

"She means she can give you pleasure with a sensual massage, combined with sex. Or that is what she did once, I suppose," said Angelica, tightening her grip on Danilo's arm.

The old woman grinned. Her teeth on one side were gone. There was a deep scar across the collapsed side of her face.

Angelica stared at it. The old woman laughed. "It was a man, dearie, a sailor. Said I charged too much. I was pretty. They called me la Bella. Hello Bella. Greetings Bella! I was renowned. So many kisses I knew. Sweet kisses. He broke my face and crushed my hands, each finger, one at a time. Men are not to be trusted. This one, your fair boy here, is he to be trusted?"

"He is indeed to be trusted," said Angelica, smiling kindly.

Danilo laid two coins in the old woman's hand. As he and Angelica turned away, she cried after them. "Goodbye, dear hearts. Take care. The world is a dangerous place!"

They walked to the Tiber, near the arches and columns and pediment that made up the Portico of Octavia. Their breath formed white clouds in the moonlight. Nearby, the river was low and muddy, partly frozen. Danilo remembered that Pirro had thought the Tiber, at full flood, could protect Rome from the marauding army; now, it would protect from nothing. You might even be able to walk across it.

Dark silhouettes crouched and scavenged along the riverbank. A man was standing on a jutting triangle of broken masonry, looking down at the river. He turned at their approach. "It floods. Particularly down there, where the poor live; that's where the river turns. They get flooded out, down by the Ponte Sisto and the Portico of Octavia. And then they fall sick."

"It's too cold to be sick," said Angelica. "You'd die."

"And they do die." The man nodded towards the Portico. "That's where the fish market is. That's the smell. You can taste it, even on a frozen night like this. The Jews live in those houses there. Nobody else wants to be next to the stench of fish."

Danilo looked at the man, an honest enough fellow, one who liked to talk; you ran into them everywhere. "Did you ever hear of Pirro Gonzaga? People told me he stayed here."

"Ah, Pirro Gonzaga . . ." The man glanced sideways, checking for eavesdroppers. "A great man! But, alas, or so I've heard . . ."

"What have you heard?"

"Heartbroken, gambling, you know, dueling, not stable, not anymore. Madness has gripped his heart, they say, and grief."

"Do you know where he might be?"

The man was suddenly cautious. He looked sideways again. The moonlight caught the whites of his eyes, fleeting bright flashes. "No, I don't. It seems he owes people money. Not the sort of people you want to owe money to."

"Do you have names?"

"Does he owe you money?"

"No."

"If you have coin, perhaps I have names."

Danilo placed coins in the man's hand.

"There's a Colonna and there's a moneylender, a sort of pawnbroker, I think his name is Abramo Falcon, and I do believe Gonzaga gambled with one of the Borgia boys. Not wise, you know, not wise at all. Those Borgia are Spaniards; they settle their debts with a dagger. But I've not heard of Pirro Gonzaga for months now. Maybe he's gone. Maybe he's dead. In this place, people disappear all the time."

"Thank you, good sir."

"Be careful who you mix with," the man warned. "This is a dangerous place in dangerous times."

"Let's go back," said Angelica. "We won't find anything tonight."

"But you wanted to explore near the Pantheon." Danilo pulled Angelica closer, breathing in her perfume. "We can double back through Piazza Navona."

"Well, my gallant friend, if you insist." She kissed him.

And so they wandered, looking left and right, Danilo, as ever, aware that danger could come from any direction; the Men in Black might surge up out of the past, or agents from Venice might suddenly dash out of a side alley.

They came out in front of the Pantheon. The ancient temple, now a church, loomed up in front of them, and the dome above, intact through the centuries. It was strange, this ancient magnificence in the midst of modern desolation. The doors were open.

A few snowflakes swirled down. Angelica licked some from her lips. Danilo held her close. She pressed against him. He sensed something in the air, something not right. Then he saw her.

It was a little girl, all bundled in rags. She was maybe ten or twelve years old. She was dancing on an overturned block of white marble. "Hello pretty lady, hello pretty gentleman, look at me! Give me coin! Give me coin!" She opened the rags to display her pale white body—a decoy and a distraction, it glistened like ivory in the moonlight.

Danilo tightened his grip on Angelica. He glanced around. The child was meant to draw his attention while the mob closed in. Yes, there they were! Out of the shadows came small figures, ten of them, perhaps fifteen, all children, all ragged, bundled up splotches of darkness.

They would stab, and rob, and strip, and leave him and Angelica, or any strangers they met, dead in the street. Danilo saw it as clearly as if it had already happened.

Angelica, sensing something was wrong, had tightened her hold on his arm.

"Run," he whispered. "The doors are still open—run!"

"And you?"

"I'll distract them." Danilo didn't want to kill a child, but if he had to . . .

Angelica ran, and dark shapes galloped after her. She had long legs, she was fast, but the small flock was gaining on her. Danilo charged at the children, aiming to cut them off, and attacking them from behind. Others, he could sense them, were galloping in behind him. He seized one—probably a boy—picked him up and hurled him away, and then another, and another.

Little hands were grabbing at his coat, little figures—miniature bandits—were swarming in front of him. He took out his knife and slashed wildly, running as fast as he could, kicking them away. If one of them had a knife and got him in an artery, it wouldn't matter how skilful or strong he was.

Then he was under the Portico of the Pantheon. The great doors were swinging shut, two guards were pushing them. Angelica, surrounded by a swirl of small figures, was only a few yards away; she turned and struck out with her bag. The guards stopped closing the giant doors. Danilo, rushing to her side, heard a guard say, "You can't come in! The church is closed."

Danilo pushed Angelica through the doors and slipped in behind her. A guard lunged at the children who, seeing the guards were armed with long-handled axes, fell back.

They screamed, "We see you, pretty lady! You won't be so pretty, pretty lady! We see you, you gentleman, we will have you."

The two guards pushed the doors shut with a great echoing thud.

Danilo held Angelica close. "Did they hurt you?"

"No, not at all. I think I hurt some of them. One of them tried to bite me. She was beautiful, but an animal!"

The vast circular domed space, with its giant oculus open to the sky letting the moonlight enter, smelled of incense and candles and was silent and muted. Candles burned at the altar and in front of a number of tombs. Everything was made of marble.

Angelica genuflected and made the sign of the cross.

The moonlight shone obliquely on one of the walls.

An old priest came towards them—a thin, bent man with narrow eyes and on his breath the cold, rancid, bittersweet bouquet of wine. "We were just closing for the night," he said.

"I do apologize, Father." Angelica gave the priest her best smile. "We were attacked by a gang of children. My companion would have had to kill them or they would have killed us."

"Yes, they are a scourge. Wild things, orphans and gangs, they scavenge for food, prostitute and sell themselves, and strike down travelers and laggards—it's no good being out at night."

"Thank you, Father, for giving us sanctuary."

The priest nodded with a palsied shake of his head. "My blessings upon you, my dears. It is a cold night. Are you visitors to Rome?"

"Yes, from Mantua and from Venice."

The priest nodded and laughed. "Ah, you wicked Venetians, and out on a night like this! I do hope you have a warm place to sleep tonight."

"We are just about to go there now."

"I knew a man from Mantua, a warrior. Now a shadow of what he might once have been, alas. Love and death will do that to a man."

"Yes," Danilo said distractedly. He was wondering how they would get back to their lodgings.

"Familiar story: lost the love of his life and his son. A Jewess, she was."

Angelica, who had been listening, put a hand on Danilo's arm. "His wife and son?" she said.

"Both killed by pirates. Awful thing, pirates. The Jewess was going to convert, you know, and marry him. But alas, her soul was lost, and that of their son too, and . . . Well, this man, too, now he is lost." The priest waved his hands at the cross that caught reflections of the moonlight. Clouds moved in the open oculus above them. Rare snowflakes swirled down, sparkling briefly in the smoky, incensed air.

Danilo leaned forward. "Do you recall his name?"

The priest pursed his lips. "Related to the Gonzagas, in fact, he is a Gonzaga. I can't recall a name, I'm sorry."

"And do you know where he is now, Father?"

"Ah, well . . . you know, the strange thing is . . ."

"Yes?"

"I think he may have taken refuge among the Jews. But it is merely a rumor, you know."

"The Jews live mostly down by the Portico of Octavia?"

"Indeed, it is a smelly place, close by the fish market. You know, in ancient times the Portico of Octavia, which is a sort of colonnade, sheltered the entries to two pagan temples— Octavia was the elder sister of the Emperor Augustus, hence the name. Now there is a church in the Portico, the Holy Angel of the Fish Market. And I believe the warrior—he is not so young now—may have gone there. Perhaps he is searching for the ghost of his beautiful Jewess, or even of his son." He put his finger next to his nose and rubbed it. "And then, I did also hear that he had left for Naples. I do believe that was what I heard. But an old man's mind wanders, you know."

The two guards approached. "The child rabble will have moved on to other prey, Father. We must close."

"Ah yes, people must sleep. People have families to get to. You are right, Giovanni, you are right, Mario. You are married men; you have warm arms and warm beds eager to welcome you!" He turned to Danilo. "We must close this sacred space. I am sorry."

"You have been very kind." Danilo bowed.

"My blessings are with you, my children." The priest raised his hand and then turned from them and wandered off shakily, his hand wavering in the air.

The guards cautiously opened the doors. "It's clear."

Danilo and Angelica slipped out and the giant doors closed heavily behind them. They scanned the portico, looking for any sign of the urchins. All was silent. The moonlit columns of the portico cast giant shadows.

Angelica took Danilo's arm. "We are living dangerously being out here."

"We are warriors, you and I; we will prevail, even against the children." He smiled.

"Even against the least among these," said Angelica, her wistful smile lit up by a sudden slash of moonlight coming down between two darkened buildings. "It's a dreadful choice—kill or be killed." Angelica tightened her grip on his arm. "And we are being quite sinful, you and I, walking unchaperoned, the Jew and the pagan slave, searching for a man who is lost and does not want to be found."

"But if he knew I was alive, then . . ."

"Yes, my warrior prince, if he discovers you are alive, then perhaps he will find meaning in life, fatherhood and joy. Perhaps he will return to being the gallant, dashing, lighthearted but amorous young aristocrat you remember. But if you reveal yourself, publicly, to be who you are, then you attract the attention of the Men in Black, not to mention the enemy faction in Venice."

"Ah, problems, problems . . ."

"I adore being with a hunted man—it makes things so exciting!" She snuggled closer and kissed him on the nose.

There were huts in the alleys and in some of the streets and ruins, and huddled underneath the ancient buildings people had set up tents and built campfires. Dark anonymous heaps—people—lay in the shadows. A woman was crouched over a small fire, yellow flames reflecting in her face. "Want some food, darlings?" She looked up, her gravelly voice heavy with phlegm. "Have you come to look at us, the poor people? Have you come to stare at misery?" She spat in their direction, a splash of sputum, bright silver in the moonlight.

They returned to the palazzo and knocked at the door.

After a few moments, a guard opened the door and peeked out. "You have survived," he said. He ushered them in and then crossbolted the door behind them.

Danilo and Angelica headed to their room in the vast, half-ruined, half-deserted palace. A large fire was still burning in the giant fireplace.

"This is luxury."

"No bed."

Their bedrolls were laid out next to each other on the parquet floor.

"And there is not much possibility of washing. It's too late to get that special order of hot water the Master of the House kindly promised."

"I am going to wash anyway," said Angelica. "There is a fountain in the courtyard. I saw it. It was actually gushing water!"

"It will be cold."

"Of course it will be cold."

They went down the long, wide marble staircase, passing by shattered busts and statues in dark niches. "This is like a ghost city, truly. It's like a desert. It is amazing how fast civilization can become desolation."

They came to the ground floor and an enormous empty, unlit vestibule. They found a doorway and made their way into the interior courtyard. The pavement was a mixture of cobblestones and frozen mud. The fountain was running. Angelica glanced around. "Well, I don't care. She lifted off her coat and her chemise and turned to Danilo. "Splash me. And wash me. Here's the soap."

"Soap?"

"Yes, soap."

"Is soap healthy?" Danilo made a comic face. Angelica was quite aware that Danilo was addicted to soap and water. Both of them, stripping in turn, washed. The water was icy. Angelica's skin, covered in goosebumps, was blue in the light of the stars. Danilo washed her down. He was not shy.

"This is very intimate." Angelica's teeth chattered.

"It is very cold, dear Angelica."

"This will be the death of us."

"Quite possibly." He scrubbed harder.

They shivered as they ran back up the marble stairs to their room and dried themselves by the fire, then pulled their bedrolls close to the flames and each other to make it seem they were in one bedroll. Then, fully dressed, they put on their cloaks and overcoats and lay down, two parallel mummies.

"I can see my breath," Angelica said.

They stared at the ceiling. It was very high, and vaulted, just visible in the reflections of the moonlight and firelight. Curtains had not yet been provided for the room. The tall windows looked out on a ruined street.

"How many people do you think died in the Sack of Rome?" Angelica asked.

"The Governor of Spoleto said about 20,000. My mother was one of them. She was killed while we were escaping, murdered by pirates."

"Danilo, I remember. You told me the story. I'm so sorry." Angelica put her hand to his face and caressed it. "Pirates have intervened in our lives in so many ways." The flames of the fireplace projected a golden glow over both of them.

"Yes, pirates have touched us both tragically." He kissed her. She was the best of friends; yet strangely, he did not love her. Love, however foolish and unrealistic, was still reserved for Miriamne.

"I have a gift for you!" Angelica reached into a secret pocket in her cloak and pulled out a small velvet sack. She handed it to him. "Open it!"

He untied the braided cord. Inside, he found a sparkling gold coin. He held it up to the light. It was Roman, struck more than 1,500 years ago, when Augustus Caesar ruled. It looked like new.

"The Cardinal gave it to me!"

"He gave it to you?"

"In the alcove, he wanted a kiss. He insisted." Angelica licked her lips and looked naughty. "So I gave him the kiss, a quick little peck. He seemed pleased. He gave me the coin. He said it was to reward us for our performance, you and I. I want you to have it. It will protect you and bring good luck."

"Like an amulet?"

"Yes, an amulet—it will protect you, always."

"This is too much, really! An amulet!" He thought of Miriamne and her amulets, and of the love and passion with which she spoke of them. And he thought how callous and callow he had been—and still was—having left one woman behind without a word of explanation, without even a good-bye, and having fallen so easily and so naturally it seemed, into the arms of another. What was Miriamne doing now? What was she thinking?

"I insist you take it, Danilo. I want nothing bad to happen to you—ever." Angelica kissed him and he returned the kiss. In the cold room, her lips were warm and her hand was soft.

"I shall keep it with me always," he said.

4 8

FOREBODINGS

Rome

DANILO HAD ARRANGED TO MEET SOME MEMBERS OF THE Roman Jewish community. He wanted to get information about Jewish life in Rome and to learn anything he could about Pirro Gonzaga. Had Pirro taken refuge in the Jewish community? That would be a dangerous thing to do. Had he borrowed money from the Jews? That would be dangerous too, both for Pirro and for the lenders.

Danilo took Angelica with him; he wanted her intelligence, her distance from the problems of the Jews, her detachment as a gentile, and the extra eyes and ears she provided. She would have insisted on coming anyway.

They met at night in the home of Rabbi Elia Alamano. A fire burned and many gathered around, all wanting to speak. The conversation was a chorus of lamentations. The men crowded around Danilo and some of the women crowded around Angelica. Then, as the conversation became intense, they all gathered together. It was difficult in that dark room, with just the light of the fire and candles, to distinguish who was who; what Angelica and Danilo took away from the experience was just a collection of images and voices . . . all mingling into one.

"There are perhaps two thousand Jews in the city. We have been here since Imperial Rome, since Republican Rome, before Julius Caesar," said Rabbi Alamano. He glanced at Danilo and brushed at his vest.

"And now they treat us as strangers, as enemies," said a much shorter man, gazing up at Angelica. His name was Zacheria and he was a goldsmith; Angelica had gathered that much. Catching the candlelight, his eyes were deep brown and glossy, as if about to overflow with tears

"They want to move us into one district, like the walled Ghetto Nuovo in Venice," said Esther, a dark-haired woman with lively eyes, glancing at her husband, a tall stooped gentleman named Saul.

"Hatred for us Jews is not new, but it is getting stronger," said a younger man with sharp, crafty eyes, who examined Danilo and Angelica very carefully. His name, Danilo remembered, was Gershom.

"The Spanish and the Portuguese are pushing for punishment of the Jews," said Saul, fingering his long gray-and-white beard. "And Charles V has become, everywhere, the enemy of us Jews, though he often depends on the Jewish banks — the banks of New Christians — for financing."

"If you lend money to somebody, that is a sure way of turning that person into an enemy." Gershom said with a laugh.

"If they put us in a ghetto and put walls around it, there will be certain advantages," Saul said. He coughed and glanced at his wife. She nodded darkly.

"What advantages? It will be like we are in a prison." Gershom glanced at Saul and Zacheria and Esther, and snorted.

"Or a fortress. It will be easier for us to defend ourselves," said the Rabbi. He sighed and stroked his beard. His sad eyes gazed for a moment at Angelica's cross, dangling between her breasts. He cleared his throat. "And if we are confined to a ghetto it will be harder for the young to assimilate, to lose themselves in the Christian world and abandon Judaism. We will remain ourselves, within our own community. We will be able to practice our religion and our traditions, and we will keep our history."

"It will not be easy at all. They will degrade and humiliate us," said Saul. "They will let us do only the most shameful work. They will brand us—make us wear yellow. Make our women wear a yellow veil."

"Like prostitutes," Esther said, her gaze fixed on Angelica.

"Yes, exactly—like prostitutes. They want to reduce us to buffoons and clowns and whores for their amusement." Gershom declared.

"They will let us be pawnbrokers, of that I am sure."

"And so people will hate us that much more."

"And they will ask why we remain Jewish." This was another man speaking; he was younger than Saul, and sprightly, and had a mischievous sparkle in his eyes. "Why do we remain Jewish, by the way?"

"You know the answer, Aaron! We are proud, we are the chosen people. Our suffering is proof that God has chosen us. Our trials are the mark of His solicitude and interest. We are chosen, therefore we suffer; we suffer, therefore we are chosen. That is the interpretation the rabbis have put upon it."

"Clever rabbis!" Aaron laughed.

"And we will not be able to own property."

"No, that is true," Aaron said, more sober now, and he glanced at Angelica, the only gentile in the room. "We are the people without land, condemned to be in exile everywhere, rootless forever."

No one wished to talk about Pirro. But at the end, Rabbi Alamano took Danilo aside. "I believe Pirro Gonzaga has gone to Naples. It may be he wishes to join some Spanish adventurers and embark for the New World, try his hand at exploration to gain a fortune in gold—or in the slave trade."

WHEN DANILO AND ANGELICA returned to their lodgings, another note from Isabella was waiting for them. Danilo handed it to Angelica; she slit it open using a knife and unfolded the paper.

Danilo, Angelica,

These are melancholy times. Even if Suleiman has given up his plan of conquering Italy, and even if his army has returned to Istanbul, I fear that the old easy-going ways, the insouciance and creativity, the self-assured bravado and brilliance, are everywhere giving way to fear and suspicion and hatred. The division in the Church is much to blame.

Fear of heresy and Protestantism is spreading. In Ferrara, my nephew Ercole's wife, Renée of France, is suspected of the Protestant heresy. So, all is confusion! My school for girls is one small thing I am doing to try to keep the flame of creativity and brilliance alive. And the ceramic workshops I set up are still, I understand, doing well. And I am experimenting with new ways of governance in the little town of Solarolo in Romagna, which is my private fief; it is small enough that I can experiment with theories in good governance.

Danilo, I have again heard a rumor that Pirro, fleeing creditors in Rome, has been seen in Naples. It is just a rumor. Pirro does not want to be found, and I begin to fear I sent you on a wild goose chase. But we must work with what we have. My mother was a princess of Naples, and though our family connection was broken by war, I still have many contacts. I am told Pirro is perhaps about to embark for Spain and then for the New World. These are just hints I have gleaned from talking to my occasional visitors. I feel more and more alone.

I have arranged for you to perform in Naples, so you can see what you will see. Naples is — was — wonderful!

After Naples, I wish you to do a short tour in the North, ending in Milan, and then to return directly to Mantua. This is an order. Back to Mantua! My son, Duke Federico, sees your troupe of actors as, in some ways, a projection of me and of my influence. He was not enthusiastic about your return; in fact,

for these three years since you joined the troupe, Danilo, he for-
bade it. But he has finally relented and given his permission.
And so now at last I can see you, my good friends, and together
we can mourn for Andreas and for sweet young Achilles.

How the years fly! You have been away too long. I am
eager to see you, all of you, and I do have some news which I
hope will be useful to you, Danilo. Sappho will see this letter
is delivered into the right hands so it will reach you without
tampering or interference. There are spies everywhere, as you
know. I don't know how the girl works these miracles, but
somehow she does!

—Isabella, Marchesa of Mantua.

(Oh, and I enclose for both of you a small book of poems. It is
rather remarkable. It was written by a Jewess who lives in the
Ghetto Nuovo—Miriamne Hazan. For you, Danilo, it may
bring back some memories. She has become rather celebrated.
Even Titian, I am told, speaks highly of her.)

4 9

TROUBLE AT SEA

"THERE IT IS — NAPLES WILL BE JUST AROUND THAT POINT of land," said Angelica, pointing. Ajax had come to stand next to her. She held the boy tight. "Naples is an exciting place, Ajax! You will love it!"

There were just the four of them — Danilo, Angelica, Pietro, and little Ajax. They had been traveling all day and were exhausted. The other actors had gone ahead on an earlier galley, and were undoubtedly already settled in.

"That is the island of Ischia off to our left. And that shadow over there to the south is Capri, where the Emperor Tiberius built a splendid home, Villa Jovis."

They were on a light, fast galley that they had boarded in Ostia, Rome's port. The oars rose and fell in a regular rhythm, and the large lateen sail billowed lazily out, pushing them onward over the thumping waves.

Ajax pointed. "Is that the volcano? That shadow in the sky."

"Yes, my darling. That is Vesuvius. Perhaps the most famous volcano in the world. It destroyed a Roman city called Pompeii in 79 AD, almost 1,500 years ago, and buried the whole place and all the people in ash."

"What is that?" Danilo stiffened and pointed behind them.

A fast-moving galley was following them, approaching quickly; there was something about it that did not look friendly.

A shout went up: "Pirates!" The oarsmen rowed harder, the oars rising and falling faster and faster.

"Barbary pirates! North Africans! They are Muslims!"

Screams rose on every side. People fell to their knees, imploring God to save them. Men reached towards the sky, invoking the powers of the Almighty, praying for protection. One woman tore at her clothes, baring one breast; she wailed to heaven and the Virgin Mary to save her.

Angelica seized Danilo's arm and looked into his eyes. Her voice was calm and quiet. "I must not be taken, Danilo. If we are taken, you have your dagger. Promise me you will use it." Her eyes shone, and her lips were bright.

Ajax looked up at her. "Will we be taken?"

"We will not be taken, I promise." Danilo winked at the boy.

"If Danilo says we will not be taken, Ajax, we will not be taken," said Angelica, wiping her eyes, giving both Danilo and Ajax a radiant smile.

Danilo kissed Angelica. "Stay here. I'll be back."

He strode forward up to the harried captain, who was urging the oarsmen on. The captain turned to him. "What the hell do you want?"

"You have cannons, don't you, Captain?"

"Several light cannons in the bow; two, less effective, in the stern. What of it?" The captain glanced back at their pursuers. The pirate galley — with two sails and more oarsmen — was gaining on them.

Danilo said, "Swing around and face the pirates, and fire off a salvo or two. That may give them pause."

"It will slow us down."

"I know. But . . ."

"Yes, you're right." The captain lifted his cap and scratched his head. Sweat pearled on his brow. "We are too slow. We won't escape in any case." He narrowed his eyes, and squinted at the pirate ship. "Well, let us be bold, then." He shouted his orders. The oarsmen on one side of the galley stopped rowing; the oarsmen on the other side kept rowing, the lateen sail swung around, and the men manning the rudder shoved it hard to one side.

The galley began to turn. To Danilo it seemed an agonizingly slow movement. For a moment he doubted the wisdom of his suggestion. Had he condemned them all to a bloody death or lifelong servitude? He went back to join Angelica and Ajax. Pietro was standing protectively next to them.

Danilo shielded his eyes and squinted through the glare towards the pirates. The sun was low in the west. Finally, their galley, facing into the breeze, was heading straight towards the pirates. This turnaround seemed to surprise the pirates. Sometimes heavily armed Italian warships were disguised as innocent merchant galleys to lure pirates into a fight.

The pirate ship began to turn slowly, as if hesitating to come closer. It briefly offered its side, a tempting target for cannon.

"I'm going forward. I know how to handle a cannon," Danilo shouted against the wind, and he ran towards the bow.

Angelica stayed behind with Pietro and the other passengers. Ajax had taken shelter next to her. "Will we fight them, Angelica?"

"We will fight them, Ajax!" Pietro clenched his fists. "We will fight them!"

Angelica put her hands on the boy's shoulders. Ajax was still young, small for his age, and far too pretty. If he were captured, a horrible fate awaited him.

Sailors were handing out weapons, swords and pikes and daggers. Pietro had taken a sword. "I think I remember how to use this," he said.

"I will take one too," said Angelica to the sailor.

He raised an eyebrow.

"She knows how to use a sword," Pietro said. "She has vanquished many a pirate!"

"I would like such a woman by my side!" The sailor smiled, and handed Angelica a sword. "The more the merrier!" He went on to hand out weaponry to the other passengers.

"On the stage, I can vanquish anyone!" Angelica said, and winked at Ajax. Then she turned to Pietro and whispered, "Ajax must not fall into the hands of those barbarians. You know what that would mean. You know what to do."

"I understand."

Ajax was excited, watching the pirate ship come closer. "It's going to be a battle! It's going to be a fight!" he shouted, eager to see blood.

A boom echoed and a splash of water went up next to the pirate ship. Then another boom and a puff of smoke rose off the pirate's deck. Another boom and the mast of the pirate ship began to lean to one side, and then slowly collapsed.

"My god, that was a lucky shot," whispered Angelica.

"That was a rare one!" Pietro's eyes were shining. "That was one chance in a hundred."

The passengers, some of them still on their knees, watched as if hypnotized. The pirate ship slowly began to turn away.

"A miracle! A miracle!" people shouted. Those who had been standing fell to their knees.

A puff of smoke plumed from the pirate ship, and a boom echoed.

Ajax went running to the gunnel. "Look, Angelica! Look!"

"Get down, Ajax!" Angelica ran to push him down to the deck.

Another puff of smoke plumed from the pirate ship. There was a huge crash, and bits of flaming cloth and splinters of wood sprayed over the deck. People screamed. Many dropped flat to the deck.

The smoke cleared. The breeze was rising.

Another boom echoed, but there was no impact this time. Smoke rose from the pirate ship.

"It just hit the cargo. I think everybody is fine." Angelica glanced at the flaming mass of crates and wicker baskets. She brushed hair from her face, her hairnet had slipped back. She looked around. Ajax was shouting, his eyes bright. Another puff of smoke and a distant roar rose from the pirate ship. She shouted, "Get down, Ajax! Lie down on the deck!"

"I want to watch!"

Angelica looked around to see if there were any wounded. Sailors were clambering over the stacks of goods, using buckets of water and sand to put out the flames.

Up at the prow, Danilo crouched next to one of the cannons. He was in his element. His blood raced. He knew precisely what he was doing. "A little to the left," he shouted. The sailor shifted the aim of the gun, "Good! That's right! Now!"

A second later, the cannon lurched back, flames roared, and the cannon ball shot off, arcing through the air. Flames shot up on the pirate's deck. "Good!" shouted Danilo.

He glanced back. Angelica was standing bravely on deck sheltering the boy. She was holding a sword. The wind was in her hair. She waved and then reached for Ajax, who was cavorting and celebrating what seemed like victory. Danilo waved back, and then he saw, behind her, several galleys, warships, coming out from the Bay of Naples and headed towards them.

Shouts went up. "The Lord be Praised!"

"The Madonna! The Madonna!"

"Help is coming," the captain shouted.

Another boom and flash from the pirate ship.

And then there was a shattering crack, in midships, just next to the mast; Danilo glanced back, but there was smoke and flame everywhere, he couldn't see anything. He couldn't see Angelica, or Pietro, or Ajax.

"The wind is up. We can run for it!"

The captain shouted out orders, the lateen sail swung around, and the oarsmen began to pull on the oars. Catching the sunlight, the oars rose and fell, rose and fell. The two steersmen at the stern hauled the lever of the rudder; the galley swung around, the sail billowed out. Two more booms and huge splashes fell next to her prow as the galley picked up speed.

The pirate ship was falling behind. Now it was turning away, its oars flashing, its shattered mast sticking up, the fallen sail covering much of the deck.

The captain was shouting. "Put out those fires! Get the sand! Get the buckets!" He turned to Danilo. "They must have been desperate to attack alone like that, and so close to harbor." He put his hand on Danilo's shoulder. "I have to see how badly we have been damaged. But in the meantime, thank you, sir, you have been a great help. Now you'd better go and check that your people have not been hurt. The smoke makes it impossible to see. There may be dead, there may be wounded." He turned away, waving. "Keep the sail clear! Swing her, swing her around."

Danilo looked through the smoke as it cleared—no Angelica.

He ran back to where she had been.

The deck was covered in blood. Crates and wicker baskets were shattered; two goats lay dead, and there were chicken feathers everywhere. The woman who had stripped off her clothes to pray to the Madonna was sitting against a railing, splattered with blood, cradling a wounded child. A merchant, wiping his forehead, was leaning towards her, trying to comfort her. Sailors were up on the cargo deck trying to smother the flames. Bodies and bits of bodies were scattered here and there. Danilo pushed through it all, his eyes running.

And there she was, Pietro and Ajax kneeling over her. Ajax looked up at Danilo. "She was trying to save me, Signor Danilo. She was pushing me down so I wouldn't get hurt."

Angelica was lying sprawled face-up on the deck, covered in blood. Danilo knelt next to Pietro and Ajax. Her arm was stretched out, still clutching the sword. Her eyes were open and unblinking, blue like the sky. The breeze rose, stirring her long flowing hair, partly plastered to the deck by blood.

Her lips moved. "Danilo . . ."

50

DEATH AND NAPLES

I N NAPLES, THERE WAS A LETTER FROM ISABELLA. DANILO
opened it.

Dear Danilo and Angelica,

*I worry about you, Danilo, my dear friend. Some Venetian
agents have been asking about you and I have feigned ignorance.
Sappho, who always has her ear to the ground, tells me there is
some sort of struggle going on inside the Venetian government
and that this may be militating against establishing your innocence. It is all very mysterious. I shall do what I can, my friend.*

*Meantime, Danilo, with this letter I wish to attest to all
who may read my words that I, Isabella d'Este, Marchesa of
Mantua, accept and acknowledge you, Danilo del Medigo,
as the son of Pirro Gonzaga and therefore as a member of the
Gonzaga family, albeit an informal member. This may help
should the need for such a document ever arise.*

—Isabella d'Este, Marchesa of Mantua

"AND WHO ARE YOU, dear sir?" Angelica said, blinking up at Danilo.

"I am Danilo, your friend." Danilo leaned close.

"And I am Pietro," said Pietro.

Angelica was lying on a bed in the palazzo that had been assigned to them, just off the port, with a view over the Bay of Naples. Her hair was spread out around her head like a shimmering representation of the sun. Only a few streaks of blood were visible.

"Now, the funny thing is, you know, and this is very strange—I don't remember my own name. Who am I?"

"You are Angelica Satti, widow of Andreas Satti, and you are an actress."

"Angelica Satti? An actress? Hmm. I think I'd rather be a princess. And you are Pietro?" Angelica gazed up at the blond giant. "You said you are Pietro."

"I am Pietro. I am here to serve you, Angelica."

It took almost a week for Angelica to recover, during which their lives—and that of the troupe—hung in suspense. Angelica was not badly wounded, just a blow to her head that left a small scar above the hairline that was soon virtually invisible. Her appetite was unchanged, as vigorous as ever. And she insisted she did not want to rest. "I may not know who I am, but I do not want to lie around. I want to move. I want to look at things." So Danilo and Pietro took her out into the city of Naples, and she was curious about everything—markets, churches, street performers, shops, and monuments—and, strangely, she seemed not very troubled by not having any personal memories or any idea of who she was. When asked to recite a role, she remembered the lines. "Now that is strange, isn't it?" She glanced at Danilo and at Pietro. "I don't remember when I learned the lines, but I remember them perfectly, and I even know how to play them."

Angelica was like a child possessed of too much energy, infinitely curious and never content to sit still. Both Danilo and Pietro tried to moderate her enthusiasms, but Naples was too much of a temptation. She had to see everything and touch everything.

It was a bustling crowded city, huddled up against cliffs and mountains, and under the shadow of the volcano Vesuvius. All of Southern Italy, Sicily, and the island of Sardinia were now part of the Spanish Empire and came under the rule of Charles V, the Holy Roman Emperor, under his command of the Kingdom of Spain. Almost all the Jews—many of whom had been living in Naples and Sicily for five hundred years or more—had slowly been driven out. Oppressed by Spanish orthodoxy and the Inquisition, the splendor of Neapolitan culture died, and the agony lasted decades, then centuries.

Late one evening . . .

"You and I sleep together?" Angelica said, gazing at Danilo. She was holding in her hand the slim volume of poetry Isabella had sent them, *Songs of Absence* by Miriamne Hazan.

"Well, yes, we do."

"That's awfully nice. I really do like that idea." She put the volume of poems down on the bedside table. "These poems are beautiful," she said. "It is as if . . . as if she were describing you, Danilo, precisely you . . . and at the same time . . . it is as if she were describing the love any woman can feel for any man . . . or any man for any woman . . . They are universal, those poems, eternal, the feelings they express. She must be a remarkable person, this Miriamne Hazan . . ."

"Yes, I imagine she is," Danilo said softly, taking Angelica by the hand and pulling her—his wounded friend, his heroic, generous, wounded lover—gently to him. He embraced her and caressed her hair. He had read the poems himself, many times. Would he ever see Miriamne again? Would he ever see her smile, or hear her laughter? He knew each poem by heart. Yes, they were beautiful, so beautiful, Miriamne Hazan's *Songs of Absence*.

That night Danilo and Angelica slept together for the first time since Angelica had been wounded. At first, she lay quietly next to him, running her hand over his chest and shoulders.

Then she kissed him, and next she slid slowly, an inch at a time, on top of him, kissing and caressing her way teasingly forward. Then suddenly, in one swift move, she was astraddle him, and from within the cascade of perfumed blond hair lit up by the candlelight, she gazed down at him.

He was about to say something. She closed his lips with her lips, with a kiss that was at first delicate, a tiny tentative nibble, and then with her full lips, and then with her tongue, and then it seemed with her whole body.

They made love. It was a tempest of bodily contact and bodily hunger. And then they both collapsed back and lay there, holding hands, staring at the dancing patterns the candlelight made on the embossed ceiling.

"I remember. Suddenly, I remember everything." Angelica propped herself up on one elbow and looked down at Danilo. She pushed the blond strands back from her eyes and forehead and played with his beard and stroked his forehead. "I remember it all—I remember Isabella, and Andreas, and little Achilles, and the dreadful avalanche. I remember Marco—and I remember how you and I and Pietro work for Venice, and for the Mendes Bank. I remember the codes we use. I remember the Men in Black, and Pirro Gonzaga, and your quest for your blood father, your quest to redeem the last days of your mother's life by telling Pirro how she loved him and how she gave him a son . . . Oh, dear friend, I am so glad you have come into my life—and that you are my friend."

The next morning, she declared that they would go ahead on schedule and that they would perform as planned. "We owe it to Isabella. She promised Naples that we would perform, so we will perform."

"But . . ." said Danilo.

"But . . ." said Pietro.

"I do not need to rest," Angelica said, gazing at them both. "Kind gentlemen and friends, I am perfectly capable of doing anything I have to do. I am perfectly capable of performing! We are here to do a job. Let's do it!"

"Pietro and I think . . . you should get some rest."

"Tut, tut! The best thing for me is to be busy." Angelica's eyes were bright. "I remember it now, I even remember the fight with the pirates! Brave little Ajax was so excited. He was shouting 'We're winning! We're winning!' And he was proud of you too, both of you—Pietro, you with your sword, and Danilo, you commanding the cannons. He was almost delirious with joy! And then there was the explosion. I couldn't see anything. I thought he was dead! There was a child that looked just like him that had been cut into two . . ."

"Ajax is fine. You saved him. You pushed him down. The man who was standing next to Ajax—hardly anything was left of that chap!"

"Yes, I remember. I was strutting around, playing with that sword—Then I threw myself on Ajax, and then I don't remember anything. I guess that piece of metal must have hit me . . ."

"Ajax is fine. In fact, here he is, coming in the door."

Ajax entered. He was indeed a beautiful boy, his teeth bright in a glorious smile. He gave a perfect pageboy bow and offered Angelica a bouquet of flowers. "Here, my Lady, you are my savior. I picked these up in the market—and got a bargain too!"

"My dear Ajax, you are truly a knight, just like Danilo and Pietro!" Angelica embraced the boy. He was not shy about accepting her embrace, leaning his head on her shoulder. "You are the true knight, my Lady!" he said, borrowing a line from one of the plays in their repertoire, and declaiming it with panache.

Fifteen days after their arrival in Naples, Angelica was back on stage, just as if nothing had happened, throwing herself with gusto into her roles. And of course, she and they were a hit—the applause was loud and long.

ANGELICA WAS DINING LATE with Danilo. The scar, he noticed, was not at all visible. "You know, Danilo, Ajax needs a companion, and I think I have found one."

"Yes?"

"You remember when you and Pietro were guiding me around Naples—it was part of my cure, I suppose, and you two were humoring me. I was wild to see the world. It seemed to be new. I was like a child, it was so exciting, and I was afraid that it was a dream and I would blink and it would all disappear. There was that little girl who was doing handstands and walking on her hands. She also played the flute, and excellently. She was begging. Under that colonnade."

"I remember—a beautiful child, perhaps ten or eleven."

"Well, her name is Martina and she is an orphan. She knows how to read. I went to investigate. Her guardian is not very much interested in her—too busy with his duties and with his own children. And his wife has too many cares and worries to look after Martina. She is an exquisite little girl, and she would be a great addition to our troupe. And she is Ajax's age, just a bit younger. I think she would be happy to come with us—she has already caught Ajax's eye."

"It's a responsibility . . ."

"We already have responsibilities, dear Danilo!" She stood up and kissed the crown of his head and ruffled his hair. She replaced his cap, and then sat down and lifted up a trencher of bread that was dripping gravy. "I noticed Ajax gazing at her, and she at him. And they talked. And they were soon laughing like idiots. I think it will work. In any case, everybody has responsibilities, my dear Danilo." Her eyes twinkled, and she ate.

And so little Martina, the Neapolitan orphan with acrobatic and musical talents and sharp Neapolitan wit, joined their troupe. She had nut-brown skin, mischievous dark eyes, and glossy jet-black curls. As for Ajax, it was indeed love at first sight.

ON THEIR LAST NIGHT in Naples, there was a reception for the troupe after the play.

Angelica, eyeing a very important prelate, said, "I need to know what the Cardinal is thinking . . . Maybe I can . . ."

Danilo gave her a stern look. The Cardinal, a Neapolitan, was known to be a dangerous man. He had a vile temper, was known to have killed at least two gentlemen, and had mistreated an unknown number of women. He had much influence, it was said, in the Roman Curia, but he was rumored to be extremely misogynous. He almost certainly would not want to talk to an actress; after all, the actors were considered barely human and were here on sufferance. "No, I think trying to seduce another cardinal is not a good idea. Haven't you had your fill of cardinals? And isn't life risky enough? If you have pirates, do you need cardinals too?"

"Me? I? Not go there? I can go anywhere. I am a former slave girl, a wandering player, an actress—why, I am almost a gypsy. I have no responsibilities, and nothing to lose. I can seduce a cardinal just like that! Just you watch me!" She tossed her head and snapped her fingers, a toreadora about to tackle a formidable bull.

Danilo watched her approach the man, and when the Cardinal smiled and they started talking, Danilo saw that, for the moment at least, Angelica's charm had worked its usual magic. He turned away and looked out the window at the sea that glittered in the distance, the Bay of Naples. Then he went to another window and looked at the extraordinary moonlit silhouette of the volcano Vesuvius.

"Beautiful, but dangerous," said a voice close behind his shoulder. Danilo turned to find an officer of the Armies of the Empire of Spain—the Empire of Charles V—standing next to him. Danilo raised a quizzical eyebrow. The officer nodded at Vesuvius. "The beautiful volcano." Then he turned and nodded towards Angelica, who was deep in conversation with the infamous Cardinal. "And the beautiful lady!"

"Yes." Danilo laughed.

"Beauty is dangerous," said the officer, "and when beauty and brains are united in one, doubly dangerous. Love, too, is dangerous. A friend of mine—wonderful fellow, but suffering the pangs of love—once said ... ah, but he is a Gonzaga, so ..."

"So?"

"You people are from Mantua, so perhaps you know him, though he is old enough to be your father. Well, his great love, a beautiful Jewess for whom he wrote a song, died, and their son died with her, and so my friend has never recovered, I fear, even though it happened many years ago. One should be made of sterner stuff."

"Where is he now?"

"He's disappeared very mysteriously, I have no idea what has happened to him. I rather liked him, though he is a broken man." The officer put his hand on Danilo's shoulder. "In any case, that was a splendid performance tonight, my friend. You and your colleagues gave me and my men a great deal of pleasure. But your beautiful fellow player is in dangerous waters there with the Cardinal. The man murders his enemies, or those he suspects of being his enemies, even one woman—it is said he slit her throat." The officer bowed to Danilo and went across the room, beckoned by an assistant to the Spanish viceroy, the man who ruled Naples and Southern Italy for Charles V.

Angelica returned to Danilo. He handed her a glass of wine.

"The Cardinal said he thinks the split in the Church— that's the way he described it, 'the split in the Church,' the split between Protestants and Catholics—will lead to a hundred years of war. 'Millions will die,' is what he said."

"Millions will die?"

"Yes."

At that moment, Pietro appeared in the doorway, holding a note. He motioned to them. Angelica followed Danilo. All around them, people were laughing. It appeared the Viceroy had just told a joke—something involving a monkey, a prostitute, and a priest.

Pietro handed the note to Danilo, and the three of them went out onto the terrace, which overlooked the Bay of Naples on one side and the volcano Vesuvius on the other.

"It's from Mantua. It must be from Isabella. She wants us to return, to come back to her, so possibly this letter will contain the details." Danilo took out his dagger and slit the seal. He glanced up. Moonlight shone in silver streaks on the flanks of Vesuvius. Low down on one side of the volcano a storm was brewing, a thick dark pile-up of clouds lit by the moon, and below the clouds were flashes of lightning. Thunder rolled in, angry, prolonged, and muffled by the distance. Moonlight sparkled like a million diamonds on the Bay of Naples.

There was more uproarious laughter from inside.

"They will be telling more dirty stories," said Angelica, laughing, "We are probably missing all the juicy bits."

"I am sure Ajax and Martina or Laura will give us the details," said Danilo, as he unfolded the thick, luxurious paper. "They are the experts."

There was more laughter, and a few people came wandering out onto the terrace, chattering. Somebody cried out, "Oh, what a splendid night! See, look at Vesuvius, all lit up so brilliantly, and underneath the mountain, a storm. How sublime!"

More thunder echoed, closer this time.

"I think it will rain, and soon," someone said. People, dark silhouettes, had gathered on the terrace.

Danilo gazed at the letter. He put his hand to his heart and looked at Angelica and Pietro.

"What is it, darling? Why are you so pale?"

"What is it, Danilo?" Even Pietro was suddenly worried.

Danilo stared at them. "I don't know how to say this."

"Say it, darling."

Danilo took a deep breath. He had difficulty pronouncing the words. "Our patroness, our friend, Isabella d'Este . . . is dead."

TWO WOMEN

Venice

MIRIAMNE AND JESSICA WERE OUT SHOPPING. MIRIAMNE laid her hand on a bolt of cloth. The weave was fine, the pattern gorgeous—too gorgeous, really. "What do you think of this, Jessica?"

Jessica glanced at the cloth. "It is glorious, Miriamne," she said. "It is positively sumptuous, almost too much. It's the sort of thing some Catholic priests love to wear."

Then Jessica drifted away, exploring. She was now almost sixteen years old, a real lady, and she adored going about the city with Miriamne. Everybody loved Miriamne and everybody spoke to her—fishmongers, moneylenders, clothes merchants, fruit and vegetable sellers, artists in ateliers, workers on construction sites—even one of the priests of the Chiesa di San Giacometto near the Rialto Market. He was a nice old man who liked to gossip with Miriamne, and now with Jessica too, since she was, as he said, "a real grown-up lady and so beautiful," and he always inquired after Rabbi Hazan and asked Miriamne to pass on his greetings to the rabbi.

Miriamne gazed at the velvet with its rich, shifting reflections of red, violet, and green. Light came down from skylights and flooded in from an open door. All around her were rolls of velvet and silk and cotton and damask, and even some woolen products from Flanders. A cornucopia of sensations, colors, patterns, and textures. The materials had different scents too, each its specific, particular perfume. She lifted up a sample of velvet, rubbed it between her fingers, and sniffed at it. It smelled of sandalwood, and suggested distant exotic lands. It made her imagination soar. She glanced up. Jessica was on the other side of the shop talking with the merchant's wife, Signora Valentina.

Sensing someone behind her, Miriamne turned. A startlingly beautiful woman, only a few feet away, was staring at her. They were separated only by two bolts of cloth leaning against the wall. Miriamne lifted her yellow veil and pushed it back. The woman had milk-white skin, red hair, fine features, and large sympathetic eyes. She smiled, a tentative, marvellously beautiful smile. Miriamne glanced again at Jessica, busy talking with Signora Valentina and a curly haired, beautiful young boy who seemed to be another customer. Miriamne dared—she smiled and moved forward. She reached out her hand.

"Veronica," she said.

"Miriamne!" Veronica took the hand and inclined her head in salutation. "Miriamne."

"So, at last, we meet," said Miriamne. "I feel we are already the closest of friends."

"You are very kind and generous, Miriamne, to one such as I. You do know of course what I am."

Miriamne laughed. "How could I not know? Oh, my dear friend, you have been my companion, in my thoughts, directing my reading, sharing your passions—your literary passions—with me."

Veronica laughed. She put her hand on Miriamne's arm. "You, my dear, have all the passions that one could ever conceive. Your poems, and even your two new books about Venice, have taught me new things about love, and I thought I knew everything!" Veronica paused, and then spoke more seriously. "I suspect that, once, I hurt you, without meaning to."

Miriamne raised an eyebrow.

Veronica hesitated and then explained, "The night of the fireworks, on the riva degli Schiavoni, I smiled at your friend."

Miriamne looked down. She blushed.

"I smiled at that very handsome man—if I may be so bold."

"Be bold." Miriamne looked up, her heart beating stronger. This woman, this stranger whom she had never met before, had, through their exchanged letters and confidences, become in many ways her closest friend.

"He is a wonderful, intelligent, and sensitive man, Miriamne, and he is fully worthy of your love. Your poems capture him perfectly."

Miriamne was blushing again. She looked up and gazed into Veronica's eyes, an unspoken question quivering there, in the golden dusky air between them.

Veronica hesitated. "In my life, I have to be very discreet. But ever since that night, I have wanted to tell you, Miriamne, that your friend fully deserves your love. He loves you. I saw it in his eyes; I saw it in his heart. He did speak to me, alluding to you, and it could only have been you. And no, Miriamne, he and I never made love. We were never lovers. We were friends. That is all, and we were forced to be friends—and this you must not mention to anyone, it is absolutely essential for your safety, for his, and for mine—we were forced to be friends and colleagues because of some work we had to do for Venice."

"For Venice . . ." Miriamne nodded. So Danilo, on his mysterious evenings, he had been . . . She would not ask.

"No, do not ask!" Veronica smiled.

Miriamne nodded.

"Your friend, the man who loves you, has disappeared from our lives. But if I understand anything about passion, he will almost certainly return—and he will be yours. Such love cannot be denied."

Jessica was suddenly there, and the curly haired boy was with her; but it turned out it was not a boy at all, but a beautiful young woman with dark golden skin, jet-black hair, and large soulful eyes lit up with a mischievous twinkle—wearing a subtly androgynous costume.

"This is Zarah," said Jessica, enthusiastic at having met a new friend.

"And this is Veronica," said Miriamne, wondering what sort of wonderful whirling abyss she, a modest Jewish girl from the Ghetto, had jumped into, dragging poor innocent Jessica with her.

The next half hour they spent, the four of them, guided by Signora Valentina, exploring the treasures of the shop. Velvet brocaded damasks; colored silks woven in patterns of parrots, monkeys, and flowers; silk velvets from Lyon; satins with patterns of castles, landscapes, dragons, and distant mountain tops.

Outside the shop, the sun streamed down and, only a few paces away, the vibrant life of Venice went on in a fever of commerce, gossiping, money changing, buying and selling, haggling and arguing. Finally, with regret, they parted, as if the four of them were the oldest friends.

"They are beautiful," said Jessica, as she and Miriamne headed back towards the Ghetto, "and Zarah is so funny! For her, everything is amusing. She has a very intelligent cat called Phoebe, who catches all the rats and mice she can find."

"Yes, they are beautiful."

"Miriamne," Jessica took Miriamne's arm, "you really don't realize how beautiful *you* are. You know what Zarah said? When we were watching the two of you, she said, 'Those are the two most beautiful women in Venice, they are both writers, they are both beautiful, and they are *friends!*' And Zarah poked me in the ribs and laughed and said, 'And that is the *real* miracle!' She is so funny!"

"Perhaps we'd better not mention . . ."

"Oh yes, I know. I understand. Zarah told me! I know who Veronica is and what she and Zarah do." Jessica tightened her hold on Miriamne's arm. "This is our secret! Silence is golden."

5 2

THE INQUISITOR

Milan

"I WILL SQUEEZE THEM DRY, THOSE JEWS, THOSE SO-CALLED New Christians, every last one!" Jean Vuysting crushed the glass; it shattered, making a loud cracking sound, like the shot of a musket. Vuysting looked at it, as if surprised at what he had done. His hand was dripping red wine, and blood ran from the tips of his fingers.

From Naples—where they had learned of Isabella d'Este's death—the troupe had been ordered by the Duke of Mantua to continue their tour as it had been planned, traveling north to Rome, and then to a variety of provincial cities, passing through Florence and Pisa and others, and finally they arrived, not really having had time to mourn for Isabella, in Milan, the rich city that is the gateway to the Alps and northern Europe, or, if you are traveling south, the gateway to Italy and all its wealth and freedoms.

Danilo was at a reception after the first performance in

Milan. Milan was now ruled by Emperor Charles V, and Danilo was standing face-to-face with the man who, as Emperor Charles V's representative in Milan, was charged with capturing Jews and New Christians as they tried to escape south to Venice, Ferrara, and Mantua, city states that still served as relatively safe refuges for them. Vuysting was the effective head of the Milanese Inquisition. But it was not only an inquisition, it was a large-scale extortion racket. Vuysting and his agents robbed everyone they seized.

"They are pouring over the Alps, through the passes, these so-called refugees, these New Christians. Jewish vermin! That is what they are!" Vuysting stared at Danilo. "But you players, you actors, you are frivolous, you understand nothing." Vuysting glanced at his hand, dripping blood and still holding the broken glass—a hand that had tortured and killed many a poor helpless soul.

"We see, we listen," said Danilo, daring to be frank. In their roles as spies, as agents of Venice and of the Mendes Bank, he and Angelica were, of course, always observing, watching for even the smallest details, as Marco had insisted, and they were always acting too, even when off stage. It was exhilarating wearing a mask, all day every day—like tiptoeing along a high wire, at risk of falling at any moment to your death, but it was also exhausting.

"You see, you listen . . . So just what do you players see, and what do you hear?" Staring into Danilo's eyes, Vuysting licked and sucked the blood and the wine from his fingers. Every gesture the man made was a threat. A servant rushed forward with a new glass, brimming with fine red Tuscan wine.

"We see that people everywhere are afraid," said Danilo, with an even voice.

Vuysting took the glass and nodded at the servant. "And so they should be. Heresy gains ground everywhere, the so-called Protestants infect the Empire and push us to civil war. And the Jews and New Christians—those secret Jews—undermine society and the Church. Christendom is collapsing, divided and betrayed from within. It will be an easy prey for Suleiman and his Muslim hordes when they next invade us. But in the end, we shall be victorious. As for the New Christians and the Jews, we shall crush them like the vermin they are, and we shall seize their lifeblood—gold, money, coins, ducats . . ."

Danilo held the man's defiant gaze.

The high-ceilinged room, with rich tapestries, embossed coffered ceilings, parquet floors, a roaring fireplace, and tall windows, was in a rather grandiose building just next to the grand palazzo, where the man who ruled Milan had his offices.

The performance, a light but scandalous comedy of Roman manners before the 1527 Sack of Rome, starred Danilo as the clownish provincial, one of his most popular roles, one he had been playing now for a number of years, a hayseed trying to look sophisticated and getting everything wrong.

"A brilliant performance. Stupidity has never been so well portrayed." And with those words, Jean Vuysting, one of the Emperor's most ruthless and corrupt anti-Semitic agents, lifted his glass and toasted with Danilo del Medigo. Their glasses touched. They drank.

"Actors are often Jews, sad to say," said Vuysting, wiping his mouth and staring at Danilo.

"Really?" Danilo raised an eyebrow.

"Yes, the Gonzagas or the d'Este family had some Jewish jugglers, I believe. Along with their dwarfs, and fools, and black servants, and other rubbish. Ridiculous, clownish, low fellows, they were. Silly, frivolous aristocrats are so decadent they will laugh at anything."

Yes, the audience had roared with laughter. Danilo still had his magic touch, even if his heart was not in it. An air of gloom hung over the whole troupe; the ghosts of Andreas and Achilles and above all, the ghost of Isabella d'Este, their dead patron, the person who had brought them all together, strode among them, even in the most hilarious moments.

"We are cursed," Pietro had said that afternoon, well before the performance.

"Shush, Pietro," Angelica laid her hand on his wrist. "You'll frighten the youngsters."

Tommaso and Laura and the others laughed. "Now we are youngsters!"

Ajax seemed sad, and turned way. "I loved Aunt Isabella. She was so kind, and she loved Achilles and Andreas, and I loved them."

Little Martina glanced at him. "Let's play cards!"

Ajax immediately brightened. "I am very good, you know! I will beat you! I always beat you!"

"We shall see. You may be from Palermo, which you told me about. But I am from Naples, and nobody ever beats us at anything." Martina led him off into an alcove where they spent the next hour dueling with all their wits.

WHEN DANILO AND ANGELICA were alone, and she was preparing his makeup, she burst out, "I don't want to be here. I hate Milan! We should be heading to Mantua. We should be going home to Mantua. We should be going home to mourn and to pay tribute to Isabella. But of course, the Duke does not want us there!"

"No, we can't go to Mantua. For now, being on tour, and being in Milan is where we must be. Federico refused permission for us to return to Mantua, and he ordered us to come to Milan."

"I know! But dear Danilo, it makes me furious!"

"I don't think the Duke likes to be reminded of Isabella. And we are part of Isabella's heritage."

"Yes, we are still living that heritage." Angelica wiped her eyes. "All the stops since Naples, Isabella set them up; she even scheduled us for Milan, and arranged for us to meet the leaders here—even including that dreadful Jean Vuysting. Soon we shall have to plan our own tours. I don't think we can depend on Duke Federico for help."

Danilo knew the contents of Federico's letter by heart. It was burned into his soul. He really didn't trust the Duke at all.

From what he had heard and been able to understand, the Duke was a difficult, irascible, and scheming man, and of course he had made life difficult for his mother, Isabella.

> *Danilo and Angelica:*
>
> *Mother is dead. Isabella had a long and brilliant life. I know she would want you to continue your work entertaining and enlightening the good people of our various Italian states. I have arranged that you continue your tour, as planned by Isabella, going from Naples to Rome, Florence, Pisa, and so forth, and then to Milan.*
>
> *The situation here in Mantua is delicate. I forbid you to return to our city. The time is not now ripe or appropriate for light frivolous entertainments or distractions of any kind. So to Rome, Florence, Pisa, etc., and to Milan you go. Other orders will follow.*
>
> *—Federico II Gonzaga, Duke of Mantua and Marquis of Montferrat*

THE EVENING AFTER THE reception with Jean Vuysting, the troupe gathered to pay tribute to their friend Isabella. They were finally ready, Angelica thought, to celebrate the formidable Isabella d'Este. The room was an unused one in the semi-abandoned Quattrocento palazzo, Palazzo Agnello, where they had been assigned one wing that was not presently being used. The lofty windows had thick curtains, a fire burned in the fireplace, and reflections of the flames and candles glittered off the high, coffered, and gilded ceiling.

Danilo turned to Angelica. "Well, the time has come to pay homage to our patroness and to all that she did for all of us, and for so many other people as well."

"Yes," said Angelica. "We have waited too long."

A few moments later, all the actors entered the room, gathering together. It was the first time in the rushed and chaotic tour that followed Naples that they were able and ready, after the shock, to pay homage to their illustrious patroness.

Angelica, smiling as befits a hostess and master of ceremonies, had set out several bottles on a table. Ajax and Little Martina acted as her assistants.

"Let us drink to Isabella then," said Angelica. "If she were alive we would be at her side, in Mantua. She wanted us to come home. And she had finally convinced the Duke to let us return. She would be scolding us, making us surpass ourselves. She would insist we do our best."

Danilo raised his glass. He looked around at the troupe, the survivors—Pietro, Laura, Clara, Tommaso, and Antonio; and Ajax and his companion, the charming Little Martina. In recent years, while he was constantly on the move, Isabella had been the pole star in his life, a fixed element protecting him, and always underpinning and guiding his search for his father, for Pirro.

And now Isabella—beautiful, mischievous, celebrated, talented, imperious Isabella—was dead.

Isabella had recognized him as the son of Pirro Gonzaga. He put his hand to his chest, where he kept Isabella's letter attesting to his status; it was always close to his heart.

"She was one of the greatest, perhaps the greatest, women of the age," Angelica was saying. "Isabella commissioned and bought from all the most brilliant and renowned artists of our time—Raphael, Leonardo da Vinci, Perugino, Giorgione, Giovanni Bellini, Giulio Romano, Correggio, and Titian. She encouraged Andrea Mantegna to do his finest and most subtle work. She knew what she wanted and she didn't hesitate to ask for it. She often annoyed artists by giving specific, very specific, instructions! Bellini complained to her that he wanted to let his fancy run free and not be tied down by a specific recipe. She got mad at Titian because in a portrait he made her look her age. And when Perugino painted Athena naked instead of clothed, as Isabella had requested, she told him he just wanted to show off that he could still do an excellent nude, even though he was quite old. Isabella loved pagan and classical themes wedded to a moral lesson, and she insisted on putting women at the center of art. Beyond her genius as a collector and patroness and con-noisseur, Isabella was herself a creator of perfumes, a pioneer of fashion and design, and above all she was a wise, compassion-ate, and careful ruler, defending and saving the independence of Mantua and its people when it was most threatened. She cre-ated a wonderful school for girls and set up craft workshops so that people could learn skills and earn a livelihood. She believed in women and in the future of women. And to us, her actors, she was loyal, demanding, generous—and inspiring!" Angelica raised her glass. "Let us drink to Madonna Isabella d'Este. May her soul be at peace and may she be rewarded for all the great and princely things she accomplished in her life."

"To Isabella!" Danilo drank deeply, emptying his glass. Isabella had been part of his life from before he was born; Isabella's family had given Grazia a step up into the aristocratic world, and the Gonzagas had protected Grazia's father when he fell into trouble because of gambling debts.

Danilo himself would not exist except for Isabella and the Gonzagas; from this moment on he felt unanchored, and even more than before a stranger even to himself.

But, Angelica reminded him with a quick glance and a nod, there was work to do: a tragedy was taking place, and it was not a theatrical tragedy, and it was not in the past; it was real and it was happening now. She leaned towards him and whispered, "We have work to do."

IN MILAN, IN FACT, under Jean Vuysting the Inquisition was in full force.

Milan and the narrow Alpine valleys leading to Milan were bottlenecks for all the Jews and New Christians, refugees escaping from Portugal and northern Europe. Here they could be ambushed and trapped, their children and their treasures taken from them, and sometimes, their lives.

In spite of Beatrice de Luna's efforts to delay it, the Portuguese Inquisition had begun back in 1536, and it was now gathering steam everywhere, with a Roman Inquisition threatening Italy, too. Thousands were being persecuted. Hundreds would soon die, burned alive at the stake, in a multitude of *autos da fé* Acts of Faith.

As the Inquisition spread, thousands of New Christians, threatened with expropriation and death, fled Portugal and all the territories ruled by Charles V. The refugees had to evade police, border controls, criminals, smugglers, pirates, and kidnappers. They had to get themselves and their families to safety, crossing frontiers, sneaking through woods and swamps, and fording rivers in the middle of the night.

If they had wealth and property, they had to dispose of it or find a way to transfer it onwards, so they could arrive at their final destination not entirely destitute. Fishing boats were used, and merchant galleys. Captains were bribed and customs officials bought off; the whole enterprise was vast, expensive, and dangerous.

Many of the Portuguese refugees went first to Bristol, in England, where there was an important New Christian and Jewish community. Then they would transfer to Antwerp, the great port and banking center, where New Christians such as Beatrice de Luna — Gracia Nasi, to use her Jewish name — controlled the Mendes Bank and the escape networks that led towards Italy and freedom.

The refugees would be put up in safe houses and then they would move on, through France or Burgundy or Southern Germany, towards Switzerland and the Alpine passes, constantly harassed and pursued by the authorities, making the perilous passage in small groups or single families through the Alps, often with little food or water, and without adequate clothing to protect them from the freezing temperatures and massive storms in the narrow and perilous mountain passes.

But Milan and Jean Vuysting stood at the foot of the mountain passes and controlled the roads running north and south from the Germanic countries into Italy. And after the misadventures and miscalculations of Isabella d'Este's brother-in-law,

Ludovico Sforza, Milan and its territory had fallen under the domain of Emperor Charles V.

THE THEATER COMPANY'S TEMPORARY home in Milan, the large, semi-abandoned Quattrocento palace, Palazzo Agnello, was fascinating. The place had endless corridors, giant windows and fireplaces, huge reception rooms, and bits of elegant furniture scattered here and there.

Danilo and Angelica were camping in one of the huge empty rooms. They had just retired from their celebration of Isabella d'Este's life, and they were still recovering from the dubious honor of meeting, the evening before, the Devil himself—Jean Vuysting.

"What a difference between two people!" Angelica ripped off her hairnet and shook out her hair. "Isabella—a representative of all that is enlightened, all that is cultivated, all that is curious about the world, open to new experiences and generous with friends and enemies—and that . . . that . . . that abominable creature, that Jean Vuysting!"

"He is . . . well, he is what he is," said Danilo, unbuttoning his jacket.

"I am furious!" Angelica picked up a piece of paper and paced up and down. She stopped in front of the fireplace. The flames reflected in her hair and rippled on her emerald gown.

She turned to Danilo. Her narrow-waisted bodice, laced tightly with golden cords, set off her figure admirably. She looked like Eurydice, the doomed heroine, the first time he had caught a glimpse of her. She resembled a statue, a heroic goddess about to go to war. "I don't hate easily, but I do hate this fellow. Jean Vuysting is not only a cruel fanatic, he is corrupt. He is taking most of the loot for himself. He is not even passing it to the Emperor."

"Yes, he betrays everybody, even his imperial master," said Danilo, gazing at her. She really was remarkable. Danilo went to the wobbly little desk that served as their office, sat down, and got out the pot of invisible ink, a quill, and a sheet of paper.

"Vuysting has lookouts on most of the paths through the Alps." Angelica began to pace again. "The paths are already horribly difficult for these poor people, chased hither and thither and hounded by Charles V and his underlings. How many cases have we heard of children and old and weak people dying up there in the Alpine passes from exposure and starvation? And they must leave the bodies. Just like we had to leave Andreas and poor little Achilles, buried God knows where! It is heartbreaking! Vuysting should be drawn and quartered."

She swung around, strode over, and sat next to Danilo at the unsteady wooden table, and they began by candlelight to compose their weekly intelligence reports, one to Marco and one to Samuel Mendes.

"This has to get to Samuel Mendes quickly." Danilo uncapped the ink pot. "They have to warn the refugees to avoid Milan or make sure that, if they have to come through Milan, they have no valuables with them, and no servants or hangers-on who might betray them. And if their children can be sent separately, by a safe route, even better."

Angelica dipped the quill into the ink pot.

Danilo pondered. "One way is to have all their valuables shipped separately to Venice or Ferrara. One man who can do that is the Venetian merchant Federico Montalvo. He is as Christian as they come. He has a brother who is angling to be a cardinal—though that does not put one beyond suspicion of being a secret Jew. And he has correspondents in Antwerp and Amsterdam and Munich. So he could ship goods. And the Fuggers are Christian bankers who work with the Mendes Bank; they can arrange for some shipments. It helps if the merchant or banker is impeccably Christian so there is no suspicion of collusion. If the funds arrive in Ferrara or Venice they may be taxed, but the taxes and charges will be legal and above board, and any misuse can be appealed."

Angelica turned halfway around in her chair. "Another way is to liquidate the assets in Antwerp or Amsterdam, and then have a bill of exchange drawn on a merchant or a bank in Venice or Ferrara. That means you only carry a piece of paper. We often use a bill of exchange so we can get credit when we arrive in a town. Andreas taught me and Pietro how to do that."

"That's an excellent idea. I bet the Mendes Bank is already doing that. It is even better if the piece of paper travels with someone else, someone above or below suspicion."

Danilo and Angelica spent several intense hours hunched over *Tales of Boccaccio* and Dante's *Inferno*, coding the information about Jean Vuysting and his network of agents. Thanks to Angelica's charms—she had served some very strong wine to one of Vuysting's assistants after their second performance—they had the names and locations of many of the agents. This would allow the refugees to make detours and avoid capture.

While flipping through the pages of Boccaccio and Dante, Danilo couldn't resist thinking of Miriamne—how she would read her favorite quotes out loud, how precise her understanding of each phrase was . . . And now she was well-known poet and—as Marco had told him in a letter—an intimate friend of Veronica Libero! In his mind, he recited several of Miriamne's poems.

"You are distracted, dear Danilo. It looked like you had stumbled into paradise. I was rather jealous! I do believe you were conversing with an angel."

"Sorry. Let's see, where were we . . . ?"

"I'll bet it was a woman! A very poetical creature."

"How could you think . . . ?" Danilo put on his most innocent expression.

Angelica gave him a wicked smile.

PIETRO, WHO HAD BEEN out scouting in the city, appeared at the door and loomed up in the flickering candlelight.

"You look tired!" Angelica jumped up and put her hand on the giant's chest.

Pietro cleared his throat. "It has been a long day, that's all."

He took the little sack she gave him containing the secret messages, hidden in its lining, bowed low before Angelica, and left.

53

SECRET DREAMS

"**P**IETRO WORSHIPS YOU, YOU KNOW," DANILO SAID.
Angelica stretched and yawned, "Oh, to sleep,
to sleep, perchance to dream." They slid, naked,
under the covers. "Oh, that is nice!" she purred. "Your body
is warm!"

"And yours, Angelica . . . ." Danilo ran his hand along her
side, and up over her shoulders and breasts. He was feeling
weirdly divided, with two women on his mind—one here,
warm, perfumed; and the other, talking and joking and reciting poetry in his head. "Your body, well, my Lady, it is . . ."

Angelica shut him up with a kiss.

"By the way . . ." Danilo kissed her back, and got lost in the
kiss, which continued for a long time, and he forgot what he
was going to say.

Angelica snuggled close to him and put her arm across his
chest. "What were you going to say?"

"What?"

"What is *by the way* . . . ? Where was the *by the way* leading?"

"*By the way?* Oh, yes, I meant to ask, *by the way* — do I snore?"

"No, my idiot lover, you do not snore. But you do dream."

"I dream?"

"Yes."

"Do I talk in my sleep?"

"Sometimes. Mostly it's whimpering, growling, and crying, and once or twice shouting. You shouted, 'No, no, no!' The next time you speak in your dream I shall take note and I shall tell you anything I discover. You mumbled something once about palm-reading and the mountains of the moon, and about reading Boccaccio being very naughty. Then you did, in fact, snore." After giving him a last kiss, Angelica buried her face in his shoulder and fell fast asleep.

Danilo stared at the ceiling, listening to her breathing. Had he dreamed of Miriamne? He must not utter her name. He must not endanger her. Much later, he too fell asleep.

His sleep was a dozen voyages.

He was fleeing across Istanbul, with the Men in Black in hot pursuit. In a glowing doorway, ghostly and abstract like no doorway that had ever existed, he swung around and plunged his dagger into the chest of his pursuer. The killer billowed back, just an empty cape with no body in it,

He was in a dark, narrow, dead-end alley. Toto was holding up a smoky torch that was twice as tall as he was. He whispered into Danilo's ear. "Listen to the sounds. You can tell anything, sir, from the sounds. Just listen!"

He was standing with Miriamne on a beach. It was night, with a full moon all alone in the silk-black sky. The little waves were bright with sparkling phosphorescence. They were holding hands. The beach was white under the moonlight with sharp shadows from the palm trees and a beached fishing boat. He seized Miriamne around the waist, pulled her to him, and kissed her, and she sighed and whispered, holding his face in her hands, 'I love you, Danilo! I love you!'

There was a splashing sound. Veronica Libero, her gold-red hair loose and flowing down to her waist, naked except for a transparent veil that was soaking wet, stepped out of the waves. She opened her arms, 'Oh, my children! Venice is like Aphrodite, the Goddess of Love, and she deserves all our care, all our solicitude.'

In his arms, Miriamne dissolved into a swirl of black fragments. 'Oh, Danilo, how could you!' she cried out, and then Miriamne was lost like Lot's wife, turned to a pillar of salt, lost like Eurydice, cast back forever into Hades.

THE SUN STREAMED THROUGH the tall windows of the great empty room in the Palazzo Agnello. When Danilo woke, he found himself looking into Angelica's eyes. She was lying on her side next to him, already wide awake, propped on an elbow, staring down at him. She pursed her lips, narrowed her eyes, and asked, "Who is Bucephalus?"

"Bucephalus? Why?"

"I lay awake all night, waiting for you to speak. And just when I'd given up, off you went, saying things like, 'Dear Bucephalus, adored Bucephalus. Bucephalus, do you have enough to eat? Let me give you a good brushing, Bucephalus. Forgive me, fair Bucephalus!' I was mad with jealousy. I almost woke you up. You went on and on: 'Oh, Bucephalus! Bucephalus!' Tossing this way and that. Is Bucephalus some beautiful Ottoman woman—or some Arab boy?"

"It's . . ."

"It's?"

"A horse."

"A horse?"

"Yes, a horse."

Angelica struggled to suppress the smile quivering on her lips. She put her hand over her mouth and rolled her eyes. "You, Danilo, are a true man!"

Danilo put on his most stern expression. "Bucephalus is the bravest, the strongest, the quickest, and the most loyal horse in the world! Just a touch of my thighs, a slight tightening of my muscles, and Bucephalus obeys. He has the quickest and most sensitive reflexes, and can help me with my lance in the most extraordinary ways. With Bucephalus my every thought is instantly translated into action. Bucephalus understands my every mood, and when I am sad, he consoles me, and . . ." Danilo went into a detailed, animated description of the many contests and races and acrobatic lance-throwing competitions he and Bucephalus had entered into. They had won every damned one of them too!

"I do hope your command of poetic passion extends to the worship of women."

"Well . . ."

"I know, I know. You have had one great love. I have intuited this. She rises like a ghost from your dreams. She is brave and beautiful and very, very clever. Don't worry, my lips are sealed." She kissed him. "Dear Danilo, you must be careful. Do not dream where other people can hear. With me, you are safe. But there are forces around us much greater than we are, and they are insidious and dangerous, even more dangerous than we can imagine."

"I can imagine," said Danilo.

"Good." Angelica sprang up from the bedroll. She splashed her face, under her arms, and between her legs with water from the washing bowl and then began to pull on her clothes. "We must hurry or we will be late. Perhaps we can find time to seriously bathe somewhere after if we are very clever, and if Pietro can identify a good source of water and find a tub worthy of the name." She began to do up her hair. Then she stopped. "Darling Danilo, while you were dreaming, you did mention another name . . ."

"What?"

"Not just Bucephalus, but another name — it's on the tip of my tongue."

"Tell me."

"Let me see. Can I remember? Hmm! Yes, I can. You will be angry and I will be jealous."

Danilo held his breath. He must not reveal Miriamne's name. But he had just now remembered dreaming of Miriamne. He had been dreaming of Miriamne often. She was haunting him. She was in his bones and in his flesh and in his dreams. Had anything happened to her? He didn't believe in dreams telling the truth, in all these ghostly shadows, but . . .

"Was she your first love?" She slipped into her white chemise, little pleats and frills framing the plunging neckline, and gazed at him with an expression between true love and comradely friendship. She finished dressing and went to open the door. "We really should go."

"What was the name?"

"The name," she said, "was Saida."

Danilo grabbed Angelica by the arm and swung her around to face him.

"You must never mention that name—not ever. It is a secret, a matter of life and death."

"I see."

"Do you?"

"Yes, I understand. Now, darling Danilo, let go of my arm. You are hurting me."

He let her go. Her eyes were wet. She opened the door, and without looking back, closed it behind her.

YOU HURT THE MOST
THE ONES YOU LOVE

NGELICA WAS UPSET. AND DANILO WAS UPSET BECAUSE SHE was upset and because he had upset her. Long before the afternoon performance, in fact much too early, she put on her makeup. It was extra bright, the scarlet lips drawn large, almost clown-like, and bright splotches of rouge on her cheeks. She looked like a parody of herself.

When Danilo looked at her and tried to hold her gaze, she gave him a smile, a metallic caricature. Eyes glittering as if wet, she turned away and bent over a sheaf of papers, pretending to be consulting with Pietro or Laura about something terribly important.

So it continued until the afternoon, when she began to apply makeup to Danilo for his role as a romantic, buccaneering Algerian pirate, who falls in love with the beautiful French girl he acquired as a slave when he captured a storm-crippled Christian pilgrim ship on its way to the Holy Land.

Angelica stepped back and surveyed her work. "I see deep into your heart, you know. It is an essential skill for women—particularly a woman like me—to see into a man's heart. A woman's survival depends on it."

Danilo was pleased; at least she was talking. "Really?" he asked, inviting her to say more.

"Of course, dear idiot, you are too much of a gentleman to realize it, but for women, men are dangerous. Men stab us in our hearts, all the time, every day! Men are the greatest danger a woman faces—greater than lions and wolves and wild boars, all put together!"

Danilo scowled. He was wrapped in a big bib so that the makeup would not soil his costume. "Are men really that dangerous?"

She kissed him on the very end of his nose, carefully, so as not to muss the makeup. "Men are bigger and stronger and usually faster than we are. Men's passions are violent and quick; but sex, the actual act, means less to a man than it does to a woman. We fall in love, and too easily. Men loom over us, they make us feel small; they have big deep voices, to command attention and appear intelligent—and all that extra hair!" She stroked his beard lightly and played with some of the curls, now dyed jet-black with the latest magic potion from France that Pietro and Angelica had acquired in a little apothecary shop in Milan. "Sex, violence, and power go together for men, much more than for women. Men have the money, they have the Church, they have the weapons, and some of them even have their wits about them!"

"It must be awful to be a woman." Danilo looked up at her. "And what do you see, dear Angelica, when you plunge deep into my heart?"

"Ah, my dear man! You really do want to know about you?"

"Yes, I do."

"That is our role, for us women, to hold up a flattering mirror."

"Really, I . . ."

"You have had two great loves in your past life—your mother and then a mysterious woman, the woman who is an impossible love, the love whose name we cannot utter. You have lost those two great loves. Your mother died saving you, so you feel guilty for causing her death, which you shouldn't feel, I must say. You were a boy, and she chose to leap in front of you. More importantly, the wicked pirate chose to shoot, which he didn't have to. He could have spared her, he could have just torn the two of you off the pile of Isabella's artistic treasures. These pirates are nasty, cruel, unprincipled folk who delight in the suffering they can inflict. And the second love, the one who must not be named! She is unattainable. You can-not have her. And so you are in mourning for that lost love, too. But . . ."

"But what?"

"But there is a new love, a third, more recent one. You are in love with this woman, and for some reason you have been separated from her. She is the perfect woman for you. Even I would like her. You believe you can never have her. But you are wrong. She will be the woman for you."

"And what about you, Angelica?"

Angelica blushed and looked down. She fiddled with the brushes in her hands. "Ah, cruel man! For me, you are a gift. You are a friend, a gallant gentleman, and a partner." She looked away, turned her back, put the two brushes in their box. "But I cannot keep you. And you cannot keep me. You must move on . . . You have a destiny!"

"A destiny," Danilo muttered.

She turned to face him. "I am an actor. I shall always be an actor, flirting with shadows on the stage in a land of frivolous make-believe, with Pietro as my guardian. I have a destiny too, Danilo." She made a clownish and then a tragic face, both exag-gerated by the bright makeup, then bowed from the waist, a low, mocking, courtier's act of tribute to a superior being. She straightened up, put the back of her hand to her forehead, and declaimed, "Fate is a goddess, remember! She commands us all! You are destined for more serious and exalted things. I am a mere shadow, a ghost, a player. I am never what I seem." Her eyes were bright with tears, her smile brilliant with defiance.

Danilo stared at her. This wonderful woman, his friend, was suffering, and she was suffering because of him. He began to say something, but . . .

"There is nothing you can say." She put her finger against his chest, like an accusation. "Don't pout! Don't be a little boy! You are an idealist, even if you deny it. You just need to find the right cause. Then your divided self will be unified in one constant flame of action and love. With love you will find purpose."

She took out a brush again and added a few brush strokes to his cheeks, then stepped back and contemplated her work. "There! You are perfect! The most fearful Algerian pirate that ever was! Youth is a passing fancy, you know, Danilo. It doesn't last."

Danilo wanted to seize Angelica in his arms and declare his undying love for her, but he knew it would be a lie, and that she would know it was a lie, and that instead of comforting her, such a lie would be a double betrayal that would redouble her unhappiness.

"My dearest Danilo, you will marry some beautiful Jewess, and you will have children, and you will become a patriarch. And you will be rich and content and have a long happy life. You will help many people, and save many lives. In old age you will be venerated for your wisdom. Such is my prophecy!"

"You prophesize?"

"I am a witch, Danilo—I cast spells!" Suddenly she twinkled with mischief.

Danilo saw once again, for just an instant, the girl Angelica must have been not so long ago—before she had seen her mother and sister murdered, before she had been kidnapped and sold into slavery, before she had been bought by Andreas, before she had learned to play so many roles so well. Once, this wonderful young woman had been a child, dazzling, spontaneous, and innocent. He and Saida, too, had been children when they played in their island paradise, when Saida read to him and he read to her, and when they shared their most intimate secrets and hopes and fears. He moved to kiss Angelica.

"No, no!" She moved away and giggled like a very young girl, covering her mouth with her hand. She twirled around. Then she looked up at him and blinked away what might or might not have been tears. "You'd muss your makeup! As for love, your destiny is that third woman. From your dreams, I know her too—her name is Miriamne!"

A BRIEF ENCOUNTER

Venice

T HEY WERE STAYING IN A LITTLE INN OUTSIDE LUCCA IN western Tuscany when a letter arrived from Mantua. Federico II, Duke of Mantua, Isabella's son and their patron, was dead.

"Francesco is dead!"

"Francesco is dead?"

"What does that mean?"

"Francesco's son is only six years old. There is a power vacuum. It says here that three Regents will govern in his place. And the Regents order us to head to Venice right away."

"Venice!" Danilo went pale.

Angelica stared at the letter. "The Regents who run Mantua now that Federico II is gone say they are in some complicated negotiations with Venice, and one of the tidbits—or bribes— they have offered to the Most Serene Republic consists of four nights of performances by us. And so, my darlings, we are ordered to Venice."

As Angelica read the letter and explained what it meant, Danilo stood there, in the midst of the others, without saying a word.

"We can't refuse," said Angelica, glancing at Danilo. "We must go. Without Mantua's protection we can do nothing—we would cease to exist." She curled her fist, and looked down at it.

"No, we can't refuse," said Pietro.

"Venice—how exciting! How wonderful!" Clara and Laura clapped, and Tommaso and Antonio made jokes about Venetian women. Ajax made a smart remark about Venetian girls, and Little Martina pushed him, and blushed, and they both giggled.

Danilo followed Angelica out of the inn to the garden, which was rather wild and sloped down to a small stream that sparkled and glittered in the sunlight.

"Venice—we can't go to Venice!"

"We must go, darling. We have very specific instructions. Here, look at the letter. We will be performing twice, in a little piazza near Saint Mark's Square, and then in the Campo of the Ghetto Nuovo. The Campo is an ideal space."

"The Campo of the Ghetto Nuovo!"

"Yes."

"If I am seen there it will put everybody in danger. As you know, there is a faction in Venice that wants me dead. They claim I spied on the Arsenal, that I delivered ship-building plans and secrets to the Sultan!"

"Don't worry, darling, you will be disguised. I am a master of makeup and camouflage. No one will have any idea who or what you are."

"It is too big a risk!"

"Oh, dear Danilo, you are the bravest and cleverest of men, you will get through this! I know it is dangerous. But we have survived so many adventures, we will surely survive this!" She looked thoughtful for a moment. "This may well be a blessing in disguise. Sometimes, Danilo, demons must be faced if they are to be vanquished."

THE APPLAUSE ECHOED IN the Campo of the Ghetto Nuovo.

It was a balmy, beautiful Venetian evening. The last glimmerings of day had just died. The light of torches reflected on the towering blocks of flats, on the trees and their layers of leaves, on the faces of the audience.

Danilo was hideously made up as a ridiculous and villainous Moor, a North African pirate menacing orphans and widows on a ship heading out of Naples. It was an elaborate play, partly a tragedy and partly a comedy. The audience, Christians and Jews, loved it. After the applause died down, Danilo refused to mingle with the public, so Angelica stayed with him, peeking out from behind the curtain. Danilo took one look at the crowd and started back, pale under his makeup—he had seen Miriamne.

Miriamne was there, in the midst of the crowd, and just behind her was Mordecai. Miriamne had not changed. She shone, with her high color, dark flashing eyes, and jet-black hair spilling down over her shoulders. She was glancing around, sparkling with intelligence and curiosity, elegantly but modestly dressed as was suitable for a young Jewish woman who was also a well-known, even celebrated, Venetian poet.

"What did you see?" Angelica leaned forward and peered out. "Who is that gorgeous Jewess over there?" Angelica turned to him. "If that woman is free, she is definitely the one for you."

"That is . . . that is Miriamne." His heart soared and sank at the same time. He couldn't face Miriamne—the dangers were too many, the emotions too strong after dreaming of her these last months. Maybe the dreams had been a warning, not a promise.

Angelica looked again. "So that is Miriamne! The exquisite poet, the famous writer . . . !"

"Yes, that is Miriamne, and that is her brother, Mordecai, behind her—the handsome, dark, evil-looking fellow talking to the pretty blond waitress.

"Your dreams do not lie, nor does my witchcraft!" Angelica turned to Danilo. "Somehow I knew it! Well, she is perfect. Exactly like my idea of an Old Testament heroine, and absolutely every woman's worst nightmare of a rival—talented, intelligent, poetical, and beautiful. Even if she doesn't want to, that girl throws everybody else into the shade. I am going to die of jealousy! You must talk to her."

"I can't. It's too dangerous."

"You might be missing your unique and only chance, darling. I am a fiery girl, you know, but I do try not to be jealous. I love my vagabond life. And I want you to have a future, a serious future. I want you to be happy."

"No, we can't risk it! You can't—"

"Stay here, I am going to speak to her."

"Wait!"

But Angelica, still in costume—a long scarlet robe slit up one side, a tight bodice with emerald green shoulders laced up with golden cords, her hair flowing down over her shoulders—had already slipped through the curtains.

MIRIAMNE HAD BEEN SHEPHERDING Jessica and Jacob; they had wandered off with some of the other younger people. Now she was looking for her father; he must be somewhere in the crowd, though he had hinted to her that theater was not one of his favorite things and that he might retreat to his studio to read.

She turned away from Mordecai, who was hovering darkly, monopolized by blond Mika, one of Vincenzo's nieces. Mika was serving as a waitress, but she didn't seem to mind neglecting her patrons to express her interest in Mordecai.

Miriamne nodded at several people. She felt a bit lost. Strangely, she wished Veronica Libero were here. She fancied the two of them could sit down and take apart the play bit by bit, laugh at it, and compare it to work by Aretino, and to other plays and tales they had discussed.

Mika was suddenly at her elbow, offering her a glass of wine. Miriamne nodded, smiled, and accepted with thanks. Mika and Melania had become quite attentive over the months, always inquiring as to her health, and eager like Filippo, Vincenzo's messenger boy, to run errands for her or accompany her if she needed to go shopping and didn't have anyone to help. Sometimes she felt as if she had a little army of guardian angels.

The evening was sublime, lingering slowly into twilight. A gentle breeze rustled in the trees, and the apartment buildings, with candles shining in some windows, soared up around them. It had been a funny play. The villainous Moor had been particularly ridiculous and athletic, prancing around and threatening the heroine with all sorts of dire fates. She smiled at the memory. But there had been something else about that Moor . . .

Just as she was thinking—what *was* it about the Moor that gave her a funny feeling in her tummy?—she turned and saw the actress who had played the heroine, the damsel in distress, making her way through the crowd, accepting compliments, flashing a smile, looking left and right, and exchanging a word here and there. And then the actress was there, right in front of her, armed with that extraordinary and glorious smile.

Miriamne complimented the woman on her performance. The actress bowed, and said, "My name is Angelica. And you are the famous poet Miriamne Hazan. Finally I meet you! And I have someone I'd like you to meet. A fellow actor you will find interesting. He is an admirer of yours."

Miriamne glanced back. Mordecai was still distracted. Mika was listening to him, blinking her big blue eyes as if she were hypnotized by his charm. Mordecai liked to talk, and Mika was delightful and attentive. Miriamne followed Angelica through the crowd and slipped with her behind the curtain set up to protect the back of the stage and all its strange theatrical mechanisms and devices.

The ridiculous Moor, the pirate, was standing there, tall, broad-shouldered, his back towards them. He reminded her of . . . He turned towards her. It was . . . it was . . .

"Danilo . . . ?"

Miriamne's heart leapt. She was breathless; was it a trap? What sort of trap was it? "Oh!" She covered her mouth with her hand and stepped back. She wanted to run, then she remembered what Veronica Libero had said—that Danilo was . . .

"Miriamne . . ."

"I'll leave you two." Angelica squeezed Miriamne's arm, then retreated to the curtain, where she turned her back on them and peered out at the crowd again.

Miriamne stared at Danilo. "Is it you?"

The wicked pirate looked down at his feet. "It is me, Miriamne."

"Oh, I don't know what . . ."

"Miriamne . . ."

"What are you, Danilo? Who are you? Where did you go? Why did you leave me? You didn't say a word! My father was heartbroken. He trusted you! And so did I!"

"I . . ."

"Everything you said was a lie! Whatever else I am, Danilo, I am not a dirty old rag to be tossed away and forgotten." Her eyes filled with tears. "Seeing you, seeing you, well, it . . . I don't know what to say!"

Danilo stood there, appalled, trapped in his ridiculous costume. If he declared his love he would put Miriamne in danger, and he would not be able to follow up his declaration with . . .

"Goodbye, Danilo, goodbye . . ." Miriamne turned and strode away, skirt swirling, but just as she was about to step out from behind the curtain, Angelica took her by the arm and swung her around so the two women faced each other.

"Miriamne—may I call you Miriamne?"

"Yes." Miriamne dabbed at her eyes. "This man walked out on my family and has no excuse. Why can't this man explain why he disappeared?"

"He is too honorable."

"Too honorable?"

"Miriamne . . ." Danilo began, coming up behind them. Miriamne looked so beautiful, so unhappy, so angry, and he loved her desperately, but if he confessed his love, he would put them all in danger.

"Honorable?" Miriamne stared at Angelica, then turned and stared at Danilo. "He isn't even the person he said he was. He said he was Danilo del Medigo . . ." Miriamne had dozens of thoughts all at once. Veronica Libero had hinted that Danilo was honorable, that what he had done was for the safety of all, and for Venice, but she had not explained why or how he was honorable. She had hinted that she could not explain, and the mystery was . . .

"He *is* Danilo del Medigo," said Angelica.

He sneaked away in the middle of the night!"

"To protect you and your father," Angelica said

"From what?"

"From your brother."

Danilo stepped forward. "Angelica, don't do this!"

Angelica put her hand on Miriamne's arm. "Danilo will not say this, but I will."

"Say what?"

"Your brother threatened Danilo."

"How?"

"He took Danilo on a visit to the Arsenal. For various reasons, Danilo couldn't refuse."

"It's impossible. People are hanged for just peeping in!"

Danilo stepped forward. He cleared his throat. "Mordecai laid a trap for me."

"Yes," said Angelica, "Mordecai set a trap. He was going to report Danilo as a spy. In fact, he did report Danilo as a spy."

"A spy?" The full import of Veronica Libero's words settled upon her. "That would mean death."

"Death, yes. If Danilo were living with you and your father, that would have put both of you in mortal danger.

That would put everybody in the Ghetto in danger. So Danilo disappeared."

Danilo laid his hand on Miriamne's arm. "In one way, Mordecai was trying to protect you from an imposter, but on another level, he wanted me out of the way because he wanted you to marry Jeremiah. Because Mordecai needed money. He owed Jeremiah and Jeremiah owed other people favors . . . powerful people who can put everybody in danger . . ."

Miriamne stared at Danilo. All her feelings, bottled up for so long and expressed only in her poetry, surged up. She hesitated. She could sense the intimacy and friendship between Danilo and this beautiful blonde, but for some reason she trusted Angelica, she seemed utterly without guile. She was, Miriamne understood, a good person, and she too was in love with Danilo. Their physical ease with each other indicated such a level of intimacy.

"Have you and Danilo . . . are you . . . ?" Miriamne asked before she realized she was going to utter the question.

Angelica looked straight into Miriamne's eyes. "Yes, we have . . . Yes, we are."

Miriamne gazed at the two of them, Danilo and Angelica. Danilo held her gaze but then looked down, something like shame appearing under his grotesque makeup. Miriamne was quite aware of what went on out there, in the big wide world beyond the Ghetto Nuovo. And having been in correspondence with Veronica Libero, she had a pretty clear idea of the sorts of mischief men and women could get into. And actors and actresses on the road, playing passionate and funny roles, thrust into each other's arms, into each other's souls, night after night . . .

Miriamne frowned. "Well, what do we do?"

"You two are destined for each other, so we keep in contact," said Angelica. "We have a recipe for invisible ink, do we not?"

"Invisible ink . . . ?"

Angelica turned away and peeked out through the curtains once more. "Uh-oh, your handsome brother is looking around.

He may be wondering where you are. Come, Miriamne! You and I will reappear and I shall deliver you back to Mordecai."

Miriamne put her hand on Danilo's chest—that old familiar gesture that dated from the first night she met him and came so naturally. He put his hands on her shoulders. It felt, oh, so good—to be touched, to be touched, finally, by Danilo.

Angelica led Miriamne away, saying, "Danilo is yours, dear Miriamne, and we will find a solution, I promise you!"

56

MISTAKEN IDENTITY

Venice

LATER THAT EVENING THERE WAS A RECEPTION FOR THE
actors at Pietro Aretino's mansion. Danilo remembered
the room well. The glass dome overhead shone like a
great jewel, reflecting the candlelight; the tapestries and divans
scattered here and there gave the place an exotic and opulent
air of the Orient, something between a nomadic encampment
and a pagan temple.

Aretino was in his usual form. "You are very beautiful, all
of you."

All the actors bowed and curtsied and then made for the
buffet.

"Well, Daniel, it has been a long time," said Aretino, shaking hands with Danilo.

Angelica looked at him sharply.

"An alias," Danilo whispered.

"Well, my dears," Aretino said, as he spread his arms wide,

"what is mine is yours, for the moment at least, so please serve yourselves. Venice gives us the joy of freedom and it allows us to partake of the earthly pleasures as well, the fine wines, these grapes, these olives, these apples, and then the fish, the wonderful fish. They arrive from everywhere, practically on my doorstep. Tomorrow, at dawn, the world will be renewed with the overflowing cornucopia and primeval chaos of the Rialto Market."

La Zufolina, youthfully, stunningly androgynous, was dressed as a naughty young gentleman; she bowed gallantly towards Danilo, kissed his hand, and whispered, "Greetings, dear colleague!" and then drifted off and spent much of the evening playing an obsessed young suitor with Angelica. She was keeping a careful eye on Ajax and Little Martina, who were obviously in paradise gobbling up things at the buffet, giggling nonstop, and ogling the interesting crowd. It included a half-naked young girl who was serving wine, an exotic, dark-skinned girl in what looked like Moorish costume, a gaggle of handsome young men, and also, as Ajax informed Martina, some very famous people, though he didn't know who they were.

"Did you hear about the terrible incident in Bologna?" asked Aretino. "Apparently a tall blond fellow named Giovanni Da Pisa, who was in the Jewish quarter to do some business, had just come out of the banker Anselmo's house when he was set upon by two Turkish killers, specialized assassins."

"They were Men in Black . . ." la Zufolina said, glancing at Danilo.

"Yes, that's it, darling," Aretino nodded towards her, "Men in Black."

Angelica rolled her eyes. The last thing she needed now was more complications and Ottoman killers on the loose, pursuing poor Danilo.

"Well, these two Men in Black apparently thought Da Pisa was someone else. They stabbed him seven times—through the chest, in the gut, in the back, in the groin, everywhere. He was strong, and tried to fight them off. But he bled to death.

Anselmo came out and guards came running. The two devils tried to escape, but they were trapped and jumped into the Reno Canal. They were fished out and set upon by a mob. One of them was an absolute brute. He had only one eye and half a nose. It is said they were out for revenge against someone, and had orders from Istanbul."

"Orders from Istanbul?" said Angelica, glancing at Danilo. "That's a long way to come to kill someone."

Danilo struggled to maintain a smile. Those stab wounds had been undoubtedly meant for him. So even after more than five years, the Men in Black were still looking for him. And if these chaps failed, and if Hürrem realized they had failed, then she would send other killers. If you had the budget—and the Ottoman Empire was immensely rich—there was an endless supply of assassins. And in the meantime, some poor innocent fellow had died because of him!

Titian was standing in a corner with his favorite model, Celeste Volpe. They were the center of a small circle. Danilo wandered over to join them.

"Ah, Daniel, it is wonderful to see you."

Celeste nodded. "It has been some time, Signor Daniel, we have missed you. On the road all the time, I suppose."

Titian leaned forward. "We were just speaking of Mantua. I have several contracts—or I did—to do work for Mantua. But the Regents have cancelled some of them. Rather annoying, really. Strange things are happening—I hear that much of Isabella's heritage is being squandered."

"I am very sad to hear that." Danilo knew that Titian was very well-informed about what was happening in Mantua; he just had to listen and he would learn.

The conversation continued naturally, on a multitude of subjects, as if the two men had just separated the night before. They discussed painting, the Venetian school, happenings in Rome, and Charles V. And the Gonzaga family and their tastes in art, and the remarkable young Jewish poet and writer Miriamne Hazan, whose books had been praised by Veronica Libero and Aretino, among others. "I have read everything she's published," said Celeste. "I can't wait for her next book."

And, finally, everyone headed off, leaving Aretino to deal with his harem, which included several new waifs, two sick and lost Germans, and a doe-eyed fifteen-year-old girl from Morocco who had unaccountably washed up alone in Venice and had made her way to Aretino's salon, as if by fate.

Angelica took Danilo's arm. "Tomorrow we go to Padua. It's not too far. You will be close to Miriamne, and you can write to her, and she can write to you."

Danilo turned to her. "You are a strange and wonderful woman, you know."

"I know, Danilo. I am absolutely marvelous!" She let go of his hand and did an improvised dance step in front of him." The moon lit her up as if she were on a stage; her eyes sparkled.

"I know now what I have to do," said Danilo, and when she moved towards him, he opened his arms, and she laid her head on his shoulder. Danilo kissed her on the forehead and said again, "I know now what I have to do."

57

INVISIBLE INK

Venice

MIRIAMNE WAS GAZING OUT THE WINDOW OF HER LIT-
tle studio workshop, thinking she must concentrate
and get back to working on the amulets. Literary
fame had greatly added to her business. She had a backlog of
commissions, and the little precious stones and settings were
lined up on her work table. But she couldn't stop thinking about
the night before. It seemed an illusion. Had it really happened?
Was Danilo real? Was that strange creature, Angelica, real?

There was a knock on the door.

"Come in!" Miriamne said as she turned around.

It was Angelica. She was certainly real enough. She swept
into the little room, looked around, and flashed her glorious
smile, and before Miriamne could react, put her hands on
Miriamne's waist and kissed her on both cheeks. "Miriamne,
you are even more exquisite here in your secret little lair than
out in the Campo!"

Miriamne wanted to return the compliment, but somehow she didn't dare, and so she just said, "Here, sit down! Welcome to my modest kingdom."

"These are wonderful!" Angelica picked up one of the amulets.

Miriamne explained the amulets, how she made them, and the symbolism and magic properties attributed to each gem and each stone. "Of course, it may be just superstition; Danilo rather thinks so. But, you know, if people believe in these properties, then, in some way, it will help them, it changes their attitude — and that can be everything! Besides, I like them, just for themselves, for their beauty."

"That is fascinating," said Angelica. "I couldn't agree more." She scanned the bookshelf. "Ah, we share some literary tastes too! Dante, Boccaccio, Aretino, Veronica Libero, French romances, Plato, and your own poetry, too, the second volume, I see . . ." And Angelica, who had received from Marco a copy of *Songs of Sun and Water*, Miriamne's second collection of poems, picked up the volume and, without opening it, recited two of the poems by heart.

"You have conquered me, dear Angelica!" Miriamne laughed and leaned forward and kissed the actress on the cheek.

"Now, let us get to work." Out of her purse, Angelica took a glass pot, which was sealed with a cork, and set it down on the table.

"What is that — poison?"

Angelica laughed. "It is invisible ink. You write your letter on normal, good-quality paper. The letters will look normal. You allow the ink to dry, and the letters disappear. Danilo knows how to make them reappear at the other end. We have been ordered to Padua. We leave later today. Look. You seal your letter with wax, with this little seal, and you slip the letter to Vincenzo. And Vincenzo will see that it is delivered to Danilo. When you receive your letters, again through Vincenzo, they will appear to be blank sheets of paper. Hold a candle under the paper to heat it up, and in less than thirty seconds the writing will appear."

"I see." Miriamne leaned close.

Angelica dipped her quill. "It works like this . . ."

THAT VERY NIGHT, MIRIAMNE wrote her first letter with invisible ink.

She dipped the quill in the little pot of ink, writing easily in an elegant script. She wrote a number of lines; the letters appeared, but once she had gone on a line or two and the ink dried, the earlier letters and words disappeared. Where she had written the first sentences, the paper looked entirely blank. This was rather unsettling, but she continued to write, and write. And then she ended. After a few seconds, her letter, with all its feeling, disappeared. She was holding what looked like a virgin piece of paper. Perhaps it was a metaphor of some kind. Her heart was broken, but it was her heart, and she had decided to let it break.

Danilo, dearest . . . I think of you always and of your generous friend Angelica. It was so strange to see you, finally, after all this time, and to see you in that ridiculous outfit and makeup. When I think of it I don't know whether I want to laugh or cry. I am writing you from the very depth of my heart. My brother Mordecai—and I know he has offended you and endangered you in the most terrible of ways—has done things which are unforgivable, but he is my brother, and very sick, and he is in trouble. He is once again pressing me to marry Jeremiah. He says he will lose everything—even his life—if I do not obey. Jeremiah is at our home for supper almost every evening—leering at me in the most horrible way. Even my father is beginning to give in. And among the elders, I have very few allies. I am in a terrible fix. I don't know what to do. I am strong. But time is running out. I fear—perhaps I exaggerate—that they may do something foolish, even kidnap me! Love, from your friend, Miriamne.

KIDNAPPED

5 8

A FLUTTERING BIRD

Padua

I N PADUA, THE TROUPE NEEDED SEVERAL WEEKS OF REHEARSAL.
Since Angelica had met Miriamne, she and Danilo
continued to share the same room, and the same bed, but
by mutual unspoken accord, they no longer made love, though
Angelica often lay against Danilo, or let her arm rest across his
chest.

Miriamne's letters were beautiful; she and Danilo had
exchanged as many as two letters a day since he had left
Venice — and, yes, he now knew what he had to do. Just a few
bits of business to clear out of the way.

At Angelica's insistence, the troupe opened its season in
Padua with a scandalous play by Aretino, *Il Marescalco*. The duke
of a small dukedom — quite clearly it is Mantua — decides to
punish his woman-hating stable master by marrying the fellow
to a woman who is really a boy in disguise. But the Duke does
not know that the stable master prefers men to women, so the

punishment turns out to be, for the stable master, a delightful surprise, a true gift. Thus the Duke's plot backfires in a most spectacular manner.

The applause was frenetic. The audience consisted of university students, many of whom were from Venice, and a fair number of them Jews. All of them loved the scandal and the performances.

Afterward, Angelica was surrounded by a buzzing flurry of excited young men. Ajax and Martina kept busy helping the servants serve wine and food by conveying glasses and mugs back and forth and filling people's glasses. They were also making smart little remarks to the students; Ajax and Martina were skilled at charming anyone they met, male or female. And when they wanted to, they knew how to ham it up and get laughs.

Danilo, still in his disguise, pushed his way through the crowd, saying nice things in response to the extravagant compliments he received.

He opened a side door, saluted the porters, and went out into the fresh air. They had been traveling and performing nonstop for weeks. This performance, which involved lots of witty and complicated dialogue, and quite a few action scenes, had been exhausting. He needed to clear his head. He was covered in sweat and dizzy. He wanted to sit down and write a letter to Miriamne and share his latest adventures with her. He was expecting to hear from her, but no letter had yet arrived that day. He had asked Angelica that morning what would become of them—of him and Angelica—now that he was, it seemed, betrothed to Miriamne.

"Oh, I shall always be your friend, and Miriamne's too. In any case, I shall survive whatever comes to pass." She kissed him on the lips. "Don't you worry your pretty little head about me!"

Now, after the performance, standing outside by the back door to the theater, Danilo glanced up and down the street. The moon was full. The walls gleamed silver, the cobblestones shone, the shadows were sharp and deep. It felt like autumn.

The breeze was balmy, but something about the smells and the quality of the light suggested the coming of winter. Soon the snow would fall.

Inside, Angelica would still be entertaining the students and the public. Angelica seemed to be busier these days, buzzing with projects and plans. Maybe she was trying to keep herself distracted. She knew she was losing Danilo, had already lost him, and probably did not want to dwell on that thought. She was lighter, more ironic and distracted, and sometimes she laughed too easily. Her acting and her choice of plays had become less restrained, more daring. She had insisted on giving special lessons to Ajax and Martina, turning both mischievous youngsters into little scholars. Tonight the actors were invited to a real meal—not buffet crumbs—in a tavern with some students. There were Jews among the students, mostly studying law and medicine. Some of the students were from Venice, and many were foreign, from England, France, Germany, and Holland, so it would be an opportunity to gather more information—tidbits for the Council of Ten in Venice and the Mendes Bank.

Just as he was ready to go back inside, Danilo's attention was caught by a bird. It fluttered away from the edge of a building and whirled upwards into the sky, a dark arrow-like shadow, making a great racket—perhaps its nesting place had been attacked or disturbed by a rat or a mouse or a rival bird. The sounds and the darkness reminded him of Toto in Venice, and the boy's exceptional ear for sound on the darkest and foggiest of nights, and that thought reminded him of the Men in Black who had been shadowing him ever since. Remembering how he had tossed the two of them into the canal, he smiled. Yes, he must go in.

A dark string of cloud collided with the moon, making a long silver scribble in the sky. Danilo took out the velvet pouch in which he kept the gold coin, with its profile of Caesar Augustus, that Angelica had given him after their performance at the Cardinal's palace in Rome. It would protect him and bring him luck, she had said, like an amulet. He thought of Miriamne, bent over her amulets, a true artist. He wanted to feel the coin between his fingers, just the comfort of it, the feeling of being close to someone who believed in him, who loved him and was really more marvelous than she realized. Miriamne loved like a saint, and she had no idea how exceptional she was.

He was about to slip the coin out of its pouch when a shadow surged up out of nowhere. Danilo was about to turn when there was a thud and he felt a sharp pain on the side of his head. He crumpled, and the cobblestones rushed up, bright silver in the moonlight. Then there was nothing.

ANGELICA'S
MISSION

"YOU SAY THE QUICKEST WAY TO VENICE IS BY BARGE?"
Angelica had, for some ridiculous reason, seen
herself leaping on a horse and riding across the
lagoon and straight into Saint Mark's Square, saving Danilo
from whatever dreadful fate had overtaken him. "Yes," Pietro
said. "The quickest—the only—way to Venice right now and
at this time is by barge."

And so it was they were on a barge.

Angelica walked up and down on the deck. She wanted to
gnaw at her knuckles. She glanced at her hands, chewed her
lip, and growled. She had the little gold coin, in its black velvet
pouch, in her pocket. She took it out and gazed at it. When she
left the party and went to look for Danilo, there was no sign
of him. She called out. No answer. It was not like him to disappear. Then she looked down and there it was, the little black
pouch, lying on the cobblestones. And inside was the coin.

Since she had pressed it into his hand, he had never been parted from it. If the Men in Black assassins had overtaken him, they would have left his body there. And so it must have been the Venetians. But which Venetians?

Pietro stood next to her, massive, his arms folded across his chest. "I know."

"What do you know, Pietro?" Angelica turned to him. He was loyal, strong as an ox, and with as good a heart as any she had ever known.

"What I know, Signorina Angelica, is that when great events are afoot and the lives of ones we love hang in the balance, and when we are in ignorance as to how such events will end, then time crawls slowly. And there must be anguish in your soul."

Angelica had never in all the time she had known Pietro heard him make such a long speech or express such a complicated thought. "Yes, Pietro, you are right. I am worried. And time is passing slowly."

"So it is for both of us, Signorina Angelica. Signor Danilo is a fine gentleman. He is even a fine actor." Pietro smiled. This, too, was rare. He always looked so grim. It was a beautiful smile, innocent and fresh, sweet as a cherub's.

"We shall save him, Pietro, I am sure of that. Nothing bad can come to him as long as we are loyal to him."

Pietro nodded, but said nothing.

Angelica steeled herself; she had to believe that Danilo was still alive, but the chances of that were . . . perhaps slim . . .

She had not slept all night. Now, the sun was just rising over the marshes. Fields of reeds stretched away, tinted with radiant splashes of gold. A heron lifted off slowly from near the trembling wall of green. The sky was blue, without a single cloud. Beyond the reeds, the silver line of the lagoon shimmered, as if it were made of pure air and not water, as if it were not the lagoon, but part of the sky itself. And as the barge entered the lagoon, faint in the distance, in a gold and silver haze, was the silhouette of the city of Venice, the Most Serene Republic, with its tall bell tower, its domes and steeples and palaces, all floating on the water as if they were made of dreams and not of brick and timber and stone.

As they got nearer, a galley entered the Giudecca canal. And behind it, approaching San Marco, came a rather heavy-looking round ship or galleon. Behind their own barge on the canal were other boats and barges and light galleys, all moving towards or away from Venice. Whenever Angelica thought about it, the city seemed like a marvelous machine of almost alchemical powers, taking spices, metals, textiles, timber, precious stones, foodstuffs, even people — slaves and workers and merchants and craftsmen — and turning it all into pure gold, into a flow of ducats, from which great fortunes were made and great palaces and churches and towers were built.

Angelica sighed. Where, in the midst of all this, was Danilo? However clever he was, and however strong and quick, Danilo was still mortal. She gripped the wooden railing. She would not let herself think it. He could not be dead.

Behind them, some chickens that were being transported in coops had begun to cluck, pigs in cages had begun to squeal.

"Do you think, Angelica," Pietro said, "they have just realized they are headed for somebody's dinner table?"

"I imagine they have." She squinted against the dazzling light of the lagoon. Wherever Danilo was, she knew he was still alive, she just knew it! "But listen, Pietro. Soon we will land; we must have a plan."

"Yes, Angelica, we must have a plan." He smiled again. "Tell me the plan."

ANGELICA STRODE DOWN THE narrow Venetian street, skirts swishing along the uneven paving stones, Pietro looming at her side. Men and women turned to glance at them, the determined striding woman and the hulking giant.

Saint Mark's Square thronged with crowds — merchants, money changers, politicians. Everywhere people had set up stalls and little booths. Hawkers shouted, builders hammered, carpenters sawed; overpowering smells came from every direction—vegetables, tar, sawdust, pine, and cedar; fresh fish and frying fish, and roasting lamb and pork.

"Lots of building going on," Angelica remarked, just to say something. Talking was better than thinking. If she thought at all, she would think terrible thoughts—prison, torture, death. She glanced at the scaffolding and the workers. After the Sack of Rome, architects and artists had fled the Eternal City and come to Venice. She had heard the stories. She knew some of the refugees. The Florentine architect Jacopo Sansovino, who had escaped from Rome, had been given the job of modernizing Saint Mark's Square. He was building and rebuilding the Mint and the Library and designing decorations to go next to the Bell Tower, and some extra decorations for the façade of the Basilica of Saint Mark's.

Angelica and Pietro turned into the Piazzetta that opened out onto the lagoon. On their left, the Doge's Palace loomed up—its gothic filigree façade making it look almost insubstantial—and the two tall granite columns in the Piazzetta. On top of one, Saint Theodor carried a spear and slayed a crocodile; on the other, the winged lion, the symbol of Saint Mark, stood proud. Framed by these two columns, glittering in the sunlight, was the vista over Saint Mark's Basin, with all the ships and galleys and galleons coming and going, and gondolas everywhere, bobbing in the ripples and gentle waves of the vast expanse of the lagoon.

Angelica turned towards Saint Mark's, a glittering, crouching monster of a building, a Byzantine relic and a crucial symbol of the power and pride of Venice. The first time she had been inside it had reminded her of a dark cave in the hills behind her home in Dalmatia, with stalactites and stalagmites, all those strange golden images, and candles everywhere. For some reason, the claustrophobic candlelit gloom and shimmering gold had made her weak at the knees.

Squatting at the foot of one of the granite columns was a boy, an urchin she knew and had often used as a messenger in her communications with Marco. She strode straight up to him.

"Well, Tommaso, how are you, then?"

The boy, who had been crouching on his heels gossiping with other boys, bounced up, sketched a courtly bow, and said, "Signorina Angelica! It has been a long time!"

"It has been a long time, Tommaso! I need to speak to our mutual friend. It is urgent and important."

"Yes, Signorina! I shall see if I can find him. You wish to meet him at the usual place?"

"Yes, Tommaso, the usual place!" She dropped some coin into his open palm.

"Thank you, Signorina! May God bless your every action, and the Madonna look over you all your life!" Tommaso sprinted off, disappearing into the crowd.

"Well, Pietro, let us go then, and we shall see what we shall see."

They left the Piazzetta, crossed Saint Mark's Square, and headed to the clock tower just opposite the *Campanile*. They plunged into the jostling crowd on *le Mercerie*, the main shopping street of the city, which linked Saint Mark's Square, the government and religious center, to the Rialto, the business center and main market.

Five minutes later, after checking behind her, Angelica slipped into a crooked shady alleyway. Pietro remained behind at the corner to make sure no one had been following them down *le Mercerie*. Inside the alleyway, the storefronts were dilapidated and boarded up. Dead geraniums, rust-colored, stood in chipped flower pots. A one-eyed, toothless old woman with long gray hair looked out of a doorway. She stared and muttered, "Witch," and spat at Angelica as she went past. Angelica turned, flashed a dazzling smile, and watched the woman, terrified, scurry inside, slamming the door behind her. Forty seconds later, Pietro left *le Mercerie* and followed Angelica down the twisting alleyway, catching up with her just as she went round a tight little bend. Coming up behind, he loomed over her. Pietro—and she knew this—would die to defend her.

"So far so good, Pietro." She put her hand on his arm. "Now we go through this little doorway, down this little corridor, and through this second door into a courtyard; there is also an entry out back, so we can slip away if we have to."

They went through the low wooden doorway and came into the tiny, enclosed courtyard. There they sat down on a stone bench and waited. There was a vine growing up the wall opposite the bench, attaching itself to a wooden trellis, and a single barred window. A small stone step led to a narrow corridor that ended at a leather shop. The smell of tanning fluid, oil and varnish, and fresh leather drifted into the courtyard. And mingling with those was a smell of roasting lamb and pork from a tavern just around the corner. Far above, in the small space between the buildings, was a square of blue sky. Angelica took a deep breath. All the sensations, for some reason, were startlingly intense.

She closed her eyes. How awful death must be! Not to smell the air, or see the sky, or feel the breeze. But then, in death, probably one felt nothing at all. It would be neither good nor bad; it would just not be—not be anything.

Pietro got up and stood against the wall opposite Angelica, his arms crossed, his eyes shifting left and right, attentive to any dangers that might spring up from any direction.

Time passed. Angelica felt she was dissolving. The tension melted away. Lack of sleep was catching up with her. She opened her eyes and blinked to keep herself awake. Pietro, leaning against the wall, was clearly wide awake, alert to everything. He nodded at her. He was her guardian angel. Someone somewhere was singing a sweet melody; somebody somewhere else was whistling a tune. Angelica covered her mouth and yawned. Workers were hammering on something—wooden planks probably. It was a hollow sound, redolent of sunlight, smelling of cedar, a sleepy, hypnotic sound. She blinked, she nodded. She hadn't slept for so long, she'd been operating on pure nervous energy, she must stay awake. Her head jerked up, and then . . . It was so warm, so dreamy, so vague . . .

Then suddenly, standing above her, looking down, his face in shadow, his head and cap dark against the brilliant splotch of blue sky, was Marco.

"Tommaso brought your message. I came as quickly as I could." Marco was visibly out of breath.

Pietro nodded at Marco and Marco nodded back.

He sat down on the bench next to her.

"So, what is so urgent, Angelica?"

She explained what had happened. "Danilo has been kidnapped and perhaps . . ." she hesitated.

"Don't say it." Marco put his hand on hers. "From what you have just told me, we have, I believe, a private plot on our hands, a scheme involving a hostile faction in the Council of Ten and some of our agents who have gone rogue."

"Rogue?"

"There is a person who hates Danilo. I believe false accusations have been concocted, and to carry out the kidnapping itself, private thugs—not Venetian agents—were used. The person I suspect, the blackmailer, is a desperate man, but he is not brave or ruthless enough, I think, to be an outright killer— not yet, anyway."

"So there is hope? Danilo might still be alive."

"Yes. He might be."

"Thank you, Marco, thank you!" Angelica breathed a sigh of relief.

"If my theory is correct, Danilo's enemy is working with a powerful group that is hostile to us, our work, and our allies, and to what you and I and Pietro and Danilo are doing. Danilo's accuser is a pawn in a game bigger than he understands."

Angelica looked up at Pietro, leaning against the wall, keeping watch for anyone who might appear in the small alleyway. He nodded. As long as he was there, she should not worry about anything; he would keep her safe, and they would save Danilo—that's what he was saying.

"The accuser," she said, "is it Mordecai Hazan?"

"Yes. If Danilo has been kidnapped, Mordecai Hazan would be involved."

"What do we do now?"

"We first find out if Danilo is alive and if he is in custody. If he is in custody, we must persuade the Council of Ten to deal with this business, to expedite matters and not turn this over to the Jewish community as an internal affair. If that happened, we might lose control of the situation. It could get complicated."

"And it could be dangerous for other Jews, and for the community itself."

"Yes, it would be dangerous if it were considered a Jewish matter," Marco said, "for Miriamne and Rabbi Hazan in particular. Incidentally, you might warn Miriamne of what has happened." Marco smiled at Angelica. She felt a little frisson of fear and pleasure that Marco seemed to know so well what she feared. Strangely, it made her feel less alone.

Marco stood up. "I shall do my best to find him. You and Pietro meet me back here just before sunset," he said.

And then he was gone.

6 0

THERE ARE MANY
WAYS TO DIE

Venice

D ANILO WOKE WITH A HORRIBLE HEADACHE AND HE
couldn't see a thing. Leather pressed against his nose
and forehead and mouth. His head was in a hood, or
a bag. He had chaotic memories of being pulled this way and
that. He shook his head. Images began to return. He remembered being tied up, wrists behind his back and legs bound
together, and then tossed into a sack. He feared he was going to
be dumped into a canal and drown. But he was thrown down,
like a sack of potatoes, onto some sort of softer surface. After a
few minutes, he realized from the smooth sense of motion and
the sounds—ropes, oars, splashes, the flutter and snapping of a
sail and the creak of masts and rigging—that he was on a boat.

Then the sack had been torn open. It was still night. He saw
stars above, and a sweep of canvas—the sail. He was given

something to drink, the liquid forced down his throat. It tasted bitter. It didn't taste like water. It was probably a drug of some kind—or poison. He tried to spit it out. Then everything went black again.

Now, slowly coming back to himself, he realized that time had passed. He was no longer on the boat. He was blindfolded. His arms were chained, pinioned behind his back, and his ankles and legs were also bound. He was lying on his side on what felt like straw. Through the hemp smell of the rough sackcloth, the place smelled like sweat and piss and shit and vomit.

Should he shout or just wait and see what happened? He would wait. Who had done this? Had the Men in Black finally caught up with him? But surely they would have just slit his throat. Unless they wanted to ship him back to Istanbul for execution, so that Hürrem could be sure her order had been carried out. No, that seemed improbable, unless they were going to sell him into slavery on a galley; that would be a fate worse than death. Could it be the Venetians? Had Mordecai's vendetta finally caught up with him, and now. . . Then all at once, the blindfold was ripped away.

He blinked. It was dark. The sweat on his face suddenly felt cool. As his eyes cleared, he began to distinguish things. He was in a cell with stone walls and a door with a small window with metal bars. Smoky torches were burning outside the cell. Turning, he looked up into the face of a thickset, unshaven fellow wearing a simple black jerkin and a small cap.

"Well, my fine lad, you are in trouble." The fellow licked his lips, leaving a slick of saliva. "They have yet to judge you, but I'm sure it will be quick and harsh!" The accent was Venetian.

"I . . ." Danilo croaked; his voice was raw. He looked down at himself—he was naked, filthy, with just a soiled loincloth for clothing.

The man put his finger to his lips. "Silence is golden. I don't want to hear any nonsense about your being innocent, about this all being a terrible mistake and other such rubbish. Don't talk until you are told to talk. There will be time for talking, yes, yes! They will make you talk. I am sure. They will establish your guilt sure as brimstone. And once your guilt is established, well, then . . ." And with a big grin, the fellow drew his forefinger across his throat.

Danilo stared at the man. He had thick jowls and a prominent Adam's apple, and a scraggly wispy beard where the hair had not been shaved away.

A man in another cell was hollering that he should not be in prison. Danilo bit his lip. The walls were thick and stone; the jailer's accent was Venetian. The air, however stifling and stinking, had that dampness he always associated with Venice. The walls were sweating, little beads of liquid sparkling in the torchlight.

He must be in Venice in the prison of the Doge's Palace. Why would he be in the Doge's prison? Had Mordecai really carried out his threat, and had the accusation landed him here? But that was an old story. The Venetian secret service must have let the case grow cold, as factions fought inside the mysterious world of Venetian politics. Also, the Venetians usually arrested you, they didn't kidnap you . . . But then, of course, if Mordecai had intercepted any of the letters Danilo had sent to Miriamne or she had sent to him, he might have decided to destroy him. But to do such a thing, Mordecai must have had help.

"If you don't confess to everything and denounce all your accomplices they will test out a little persuasion on you. You know—a little gentle help." The jailer licked his thick wet lips again. Beads of sweat gleamed in the dark gray stubble of his sallow cheeks. "Now, you may know, or you may not know, that Venice generally does not approve of torture. But we do make an exception, now and then, for particularly heinous crimes such as spying, and we have a few methods. For example, we have the *strappado*, and you probably know what that involves."

Danilo stared at the man. Torture had occurred to Danilo. Would he have the strength of character, the pure guts and stubbornness, to resist? What could they ask him? What did he know? Of course, he knew about Marco's network, he knew about Angelica, he knew about the Mendes Bank and Beatrice de Luna's project to rescue the Jews and the New Christians from the Inquisition, he knew about Rabbi Hazan's business trading in forbidden books . . .

"We tie your hands behind your back, you see." The fellow bared his uneven, dirty teeth in what was meant, apparently, to be a grin. "And then we hoist you up by your wrists, so you are hanging. This will pull your shoulders out of their sockets, and if done long enough it will break some bones." He bent down and brought his face to within an inch of Danilo's, took a deep breath, and exhaled a mixture of onions, garlic, and something rancid—perhaps mussels—that Danilo could not identify.

"Here, have some water." The jailer straightened up, picked up a bucket, and pushed it against Danilo's lips. Danilo drank, awkwardly, water spilling and splashing down his chin.

"Mind you, my friend, I don't think the *strappado* works, or any type of torture. People just lie and tell you what you want to hear. Or they get stubborn and shut up and let you kill them or wreck their bodies—every muscle and ligament and tendon torn—until they are just a lump of howling flesh and can't even earn a living by begging. People turn away in disgust."

He paused and lifted the bucket away from Danilo. "So the *strappado* is not one of my favorites. Now, the thumb screw, that's an ugly one, let me tell you! You insert a man's thumbs— rarely a woman's—in the vice, and then you screw the vice tighter and tighter until you crush them. It makes a man's hands pretty useless if you do it well." He stroked his chin and nodded thoughtfully. "You can use it to crush toes too, and all the bones of the foot. It will give a man a painful limp, make him walk bowlegged or not walk at all. Turns a sparky young blade into a drooling, doddering old duffer in a few days. You'd be amazed!"

The jailer's eyes took on a faraway look. He held the bucket limply and it swayed back and forth in his hand. "And they can pluck or pinch bits of flesh out of your body or face with red hot pliers. That is something I have seen more than once! There is an art to all of this. It leaves a man much less pretty than he once was. And you are a handsome lad, and still young, so I reckon you would like to hang onto your looks. The ladies like a smooth-skinned, blue-eyed, blond-haired gentleman. And you are built like a true Frank, with fine muscles—a horseman, I reckon, looking at your thighs, if I may be so bold and truthful and forgiven for making such intimate insinuations."

The jailer stood back, set the bucket down, rubbed his scraggly beard, and looked squarely at Danilo. "Yes, yes, you are a comely gentleman. A true epitome of masculine pulchritude! I am sure the ladies eat you up!" He paused, a mischievous gleam lighting up his eye. "Then there's the rack. Well, you and I know all about the rack—they lay you out on this frame, see, and slowly turn the rollers so the rack stretches and stretches. Then they really crank them around, and—pop, pop, pop—your limbs separate at the joints, knees, hips, elbows, shoulders, ankles, wrists. You never get the use of your joints back. Limbs just dangle there, useless, and you are a broken puppet. You lie in the sun or in the darkness paralyzed and useless, hardly even able to crawl. Ah, the ingenuity of man, it is truly without limit."

The jailer paused for breath and pulled an evil-looking something out of the sack that hung from his belt. "Here's some bread. You will need your strength. I'm hoping they don't do any of this to you. Mind you, I have no idea what the charges are. So I don't know what they will ask you to confess to. But if you ended up in here, my dear fellow, then you must have done something, or displeased somebody important enough to cast you down. I'll let you up later so you can do your business in that big pot over there. They empty it every couple of days to keep the place sweet as a meadow in springtime. Now, before I go, a bit of advice. The rules here are strict—no visits, no meetings, no friends, no messages, no women. No one has ever escaped from this place."

"I have no intention of escaping." Danilo's throat was raw, his tongue heavy. The dull light from the torches and the windows high above hurt his eyes.

"Good, that's good. You are a quick learner." The jailer's broken teeth beamed, displaying his pleasure. The man a few cells away screamed.

Danilo coughed. "I just want to get a few words out to a friend. Let her know how I am."

"I told you: no meetings, no friends, no visitors, no messages."

"I understand." Danilo realized he would have to wait for his chance, or for destiny to strike. As Angelica often reminded him, destiny was a capricious goddess. The fates were furies, or they could be, and sometimes the best advice, even in the most desperate situations, was to sit tight and wait to see what happened. Opportunities might present themselves. But he couldn't wait, not really, since others might be in danger—Angelica, Miriamne, Marco, Rabbi Hazan, the whole troupe of actors . . . If the Men in Black were behind the kidnapping, he would not be alive. They would have killed him and dumped his body in the lagoon. They would not have thrown him in the prison of the Doge's Palace! If Mordecai was behind this little caper, and if Mordecai's plot went awry, then Miriamne would certainly be in danger. A hopeless gambler—if that was what Mordecai was—would often sell his soul, and his family, for money. He had to get a message out.

"And as I said," the jailer went on, picking his teeth with a long pointed fingernail, "no one has ever escaped."

"But I just want to get a message out. It could be worth your while."

"My dear lad! Now, I thought you were cleverer than that. I am not to be bought. I do not sell my soul. Besides, it would be dangerous. I might find myself where you are now."

"What would it take?"

"You couldn't afford it."

"What if I could?"

"I do not accept bribes." The jailer hitched up his trousers and adjusted his collar. "But I am not without heart. I might be able to send out a message of some kind. Let me think about it. Probably I can't. But I might, you get my meaning?"

"Thank you."

"In the meantime, there is no need for you to spend the last days of your life chained to a wall. Hold out your feet. I'll let you move around a bit. Give you time to prepare your soul for its next voyage, to heaven or hell, depending, I suppose, on the state of your soul at the time of departure and whether you have been shriven or not, and whether you truly repent and so on and so forth. All of which requires wisdom and humility, and time to contemplate and consider all that must be considered, if you follow my meaning."

"I believe I do."

The jailer struck off the chains. The air resonated with a metallic clang as if one of the gods had come down with a cleaver. "Now, my lad, you are free to leap, to dance and caper if you so desire." The jailer went to the cell door, opened it, and stepped out. He stood there for a moment, gazing at his prisoner.

Danilo rubbed his arms and legs. They were numb and tingling. He flexed his fingers. He was hungry and he needed to pee. He rose and approached the bucket and peed. It was full, almost overflowing with excrement and piss.

The cell door clanged shut behind him. The man from the next cell screamed again.

"Why is he screaming," Danilo asked, "that old man?"

"Old man?" the jailer shouted through the slit in the door, "That lad is younger than you are."

And he turned the key in the lock.

6 1

YOU DID WHAT?

Venice

"YOU DID WHAT?" MIRIAMNE CLENCHED HER FISTS AND turned to face her brother.

"It was to protect you." Mordecai stood next to what used to be Danilo's work table, pale, trembling. "I denounced the traitor, the spy, the imposter," Mordecai stuttered. His lips were wet with spittle. His handsome face was gaunt, glistening with thick sticky sweat. His smooth tanned skin had turned to translucent wax. His eyes were bloodshot and wet, as if he were about to cry; maybe he was about to cry. Good, Miriamne thought, let him cry! Then she relented a little.

"You are sick." She stepped closer. "Mordecai. You are sick. You would not have done what you did if you were not sick. You convinced father that Danilo was a fraud and an imposter. You almost convinced me. But I couldn't believe it. I never believed it. And now . . . you may have murdered him. You may have murdered us all. Venice will not forgive such an evil trick—accusing an innocent man of spying! They will take us all for spies. And you know what happens to spies!"

Mordecai collapsed onto the work stool that Danilo had used when he was translating Agrippa.

"I have made mistakes, Miriamne, but everything I do, I do for you. I think only of your happiness. You must marry Jeremiah."

"I will not marry Jeremiah. I refuse to marry Jeremiah. I won't even contemplate marrying Jeremiah. And you cannot make me."

"He is a holy man, a learned man."

"He is not a holy man and his learning is—excuse me, but I do not respect his learning. He is merely prejudiced. He dresses up his ignorance in false rabbinic wisdom, gnomic little twisted fables, and long tangled disquisitions. He is clever, but he is a fraud and a parasite on that wisdom; he exploits the scriptures and misuses them. He is a charlatan."

"But he is . . . He is rich as Croesus. Think of the ducats!" Mordecai looked up at her, his eyes pleading.

"Ducats! Ducats! Ducats! Yes, I know. You have told me a thousand times how rich he is. I do not want to be rich; I do not care to be rich. I want to be honest. And tell me, Mordecai, why are you so desperate for money? Why? For in truth, you just want to sell me for a handful of ducats, is that not so?"

"I . . . I have made some debts."

"From gambling?"

He looked down. His hands—long, slender, beautiful hands—dangled between his legs, the veins showing, glowing with sweat, as if he had just dipped them in water. "Yes. Gambling."

"Oh, Mordecai! Why can you not resist?"

"And I am ill. I think, dear Miriamne, I am dying."

"Oh, Mordecai!" She stepped forward, knelt in front of him, and looked up at his face. How haggard it was! His beard, once so fine and full, was now gray, scraggly, and thin. And his eyes, his beautiful eyes, hollowed out and sad, infinitely sad.

"I have poisoned myself." Mordecai blinked at her. "I have poisoned myself in my experiments. I do not know how to cure myself."

"I will help you." She stood up. "And Danilo? You must withdraw your charges and insinuations. He is blameless."

"How do you know?"

"I know," she said, and looked away. Her secret correspondence with Danilo was — and must be — kept a secret.

Something changed in his face. "How do you know?" He stood and, suddenly violent, suddenly strong, seized her by both wrists, pulling her to him. "Tell me, what do you know about this man, this so-called Danilo del Medigo? He should be gone, dead! Perhaps he already is! Yes, I hope he is dead!"

"Let go of me! You are hurting me! Let go, Mordecai!"

Mordecai pushed her against the wall. His face pressed close to hers. His breath was bitter, coppery. Her bookshelf toppled and the books tumbled to the floor. Mordecai's breath was fetid, his hands slippery with sweat. He twisted her wrists. "You have been keeping secrets, Miriamne. You have been writing to that evil wretch!"

She cried out, "You spy!" Mordecai let go of her wrists and staggered back, covering his mouth as he coughed violently. A splash of blood appeared between his fingers.

Miriamne lunged for the door, pausing there, horrified. "Stay right there, Mordecai," she said, "You need help. Don't move."

Mordecai stood there, haggard, half-crazy, blood dripping from his lips.

62

AN AFFAIR OF STATE

Venice

ON THE RIVA DEGLI SCHIAVONI, NOT FAR FROM SAINT Mark's Square, Marco clasped his hands behind his back and walked slowly, thoughtfully. Beside him strolled a tall elderly man dressed in the black cap and long black robe of a patrician. The Senator was a member of one of the ruling families of Venice, among the first merchant families who had built the city and who were able to prove that, even before the year 1297, they had been among the founders of Venice. The Senator frequented Veronica Libero's; he was reputed to know virtually everything that happened in Venice, and he was the one who had suggested to Marco they recruit Danilo for service to the Council of Ten.

The Senator leaned towards Marco. "So you say our young man, Danilo del Medigo, is still valuable, that he has been doing good work."

"Yes, he has been very useful, Senator. And he has been

working very well with our agent, the young . . ."

"The young actress Angelica, yes, and the late, much lamented impresario, Andreas."

"Genius is often odd, Senator."

"Indeed, that is true. The actress, I met her once, I believe at Aretino's. It was an interesting evening. She is a lovely woman, high-spirited, intelligent, and quick—she sees things."

"Yes, she does. And she can attest to the fact that our young man has been with the acting troupe all this time, and not spying against Venice."

"Well, that is good. It adds to the credibility of our case for the defense, and it might be exactly what we need to tip things in our favor with the Council of Ten. But it would be best that you do not expose yourself directly."

"Exactly. I would prefer not to be seen to be involved in this affair."

"Well, good! And the accuser, what about him? He arranged this violent kidnapping, did he not? And he is an ally, in fact, of our enemies in the Council."

"Yes, he set the men onto Danilo. Rogue elements in a way, thugs, people who used to work for us and now work for the opposite faction, for our political enemies."

"Ah, rogue elements." The Senator turned his gaze upon Marco. "We do not like rogue elements. People full of initiative, grit, and gumption, yes; but rogue, no. Otherwise . . ." He swung his arm out as if to encompass the whole city, the Basin of Saint Mark, the ships, the gondolas, the galleys, the galleons . . .

"Otherwise decline, collapse, disaster," said Marco, completing the Senator's thought.

"Precisely." The Senator turned to Marco. "So you say this del Medigo has relatives at the Court of the Sultan."

"Yes, now this is complicated." Marco was quite aware the Senator often feigned ignorance of things he knew quite well. In fact, it was the Senator who had suggested they recruit Danilo in the first place; it was not forgetfulness, it was . . . indirection.

"Explain," said the Senator. "I adore complicated."

"Well, del Medigo is the son, the legal son, of Judah del Medigo."

"Personal physician to Suleiman."

"Yes, precisely. A man who has the absolute trust of the Sultan and who, I am told, would die before betraying that trust."

"The Sultan is a lucky man." The Senator sighed. "This Judah del Medigo was personal physician to the Pope, was he not?"

"Yes, and close to the Chigi banking family."

"Ah, really? Hmm! Oh, well, yes, now I remember—del Medigo was one of the best doctors in Italy, and Jewish of course."

"Yes, well, to complicate matters . . ."

"Yes?"

Marco leaned forward. "To complicate matters, Danilo is quite possibly not the blood son of Judah del Medigo."

"Oh, now that is juicy." The Senator turned his amused, detached gaze on Marco.

"He is probably the blood son of one of the Gonzagas."

"Well, then . . ."

"Isabella d'Este had an assistant, a well-known writer and scholar, Grazia dei Rossi."

"Hmm." The Senator rubbed his chin. "She wrote a book about remarkable women. She knew Agostino Chigi. He helped publish her book, I believe. Yes, yes, she was killed, was she not, in the Sack of Rome . . . ?"

"Not in Rome itself. She was murdered, so it is said—accounts are incomplete and contradictory—by pirates."

"Pirates?" the Senator sighed. "They are a scourge."

"In any case, Grazia dei Rossi was Jewish, which means that, according to Jewish law and tradition, her son, Danilo, is Jewish, whoever his father might be, and the father is probably Pirro Gonzaga."

"Ah, Pirro Gonzaga! The bright star who became a black sheep. Pirro disappeared, I believe."

"Yes. Pirro was in exile, then a fugitive, and now—who knows? But there is another complication."

"Boxes within boxes within boxes!"

"A few years ago, Danilo del Medigo apparently saved the Sultan's life."

"I am not sure that was a service to Venice or to the West!"

"Danilo spiked a wild boar or something like that."

"A brave fellow."

"In any case, this made the Grand Vizier, Ibrahim Pasha, jealous. So, apparently—it's rather obscure—the Grand Vizier accused Danilo del Medigo of planning to assassinate Suleiman."

"Ah, that's more like it, murder! But this was pure concoction?"

"I am certain of it."

"Our friend the Grand Vizier came to a bad end, did he not?"

"Yes, Ibrahim had just returned from signing Suleiman's treaty with France. He was at the height of his powers. He was Greek, exceptionally handsome, very close to Suleiman, almost Suleiman's equal in power. The two were like brothers. Sometime in the night of 16 March, 1536, Ibrahim was attacked in his apartment in Topkapi Palace, where his bedroom was next to the bedroom of the Sultan. Ibrahim was strangled. When his body was discovered the next morning, the walls of his bedroom were covered in blood. Apparently, Ibrahim fought, and fought hard, for his life."

"What, I wonder, was the cause of his downfall?"

"We don't know." Marco wondered if the Senator knew something, but the man's face betrayed nothing, only the amused curiosity of a lofty and detached observer of human folly and the lamentable onrush of events. "Various theories were put forward—that Ibrahim had betrayed Suleiman in some way, making a deal with Suleiman's enemies, principally Charles V of the Spanish Empire, or the Shah of Persia. But there was no motive. Ibrahim had everything: power and money. The most likely explanation is that Ibrahim had run afoul of Hürrem."

"Ah, the Sultan's slave-girl wife, the famous Hürrem!" The Senator smiled, as if savoring a particularly delicious display of irony.

"Yes. The theory is that Hürrem wished—wishes—to control Suleiman, to rule his mind completely, and, after the death of his mother, the only obstacle to her power over Suleiman was his great servant and friend, Ibrahim. So she managed to poison Suleiman's mind against Ibrahim."

"And so Suleiman had his beautiful friend and faithful slave, his favorite, killed. All the man's power—poof! Gone!"

"Exactly. Ibrahim had become arrogant, tactless, and very rich, and so had made a lot of enemies. He didn't disguise the fact that he despised Islam."

"Despised Islam! Oh, dear. That would get one in trouble! And arrogant! Let us be modest, then!" The Senator smiled. "Now what are we to do about young del Medigo? Do you think he might still—in spite of the Grand Vizier's accusation—have some influence with the Sultan?"

"Yes, I think he well might," said Marco. He was not going to share information about Princess Saida and her relationship with Danilo with anyone, not even the Senator, not even a member of the Council of Ten. It was too explosive and too dangerous. Marco was, in his own way, protective of his flock. He did not want any harm to come to Angelica, Pietro, or Danilo—or, since she was a possible asset, to Princess Saida. He was also sure that once the Grand Vizier's story had been put to rest, and Hürrem, hopefully, had lost interest in pursuing Danilo, then Danilo would have access to the Princess, and through her—or through his father, Judah—to Suleiman. How best to use that influence would be the next question to ask.

"And Danilo has in fact continued to provide you with useful information?" The Senator saw the summaries, and he knew what information had been gathered, but he liked to feign ignorance; it was a tactic which over many long decades had become second nature. He knew as much as Marco did about Danilo and Angelica, almost certainly much more.

"As I said, Angelica and he have been a fine team."

"And he has relations with the Mendes Bank, that little agreement we set up with Samuel Mendes. It has functioned well?"

"Yes."

"I thought it would. Mendes is a good man. And Danilo is loyal to the Jewish community?"

"I would say he is, certainly, yes."

"Well, it would be good to keep an eye on that, too. Let us try to pluck Danilo del Medigo out of his present difficulties. I shall talk to my colleagues. I will need Angelica as a testimony to Danilo's activities and so on. Could you have Angelica appear before us, here? Well disguised, so no one sees her face, and no one can tell whether it is a man or a woman, or of what age or condition."

"I certainly can do that."

"Towards sunset? At eight o'clock?"

"Of course."

"Good, good. It is always a great pleasure, very entertaining, speaking with you, Marco. Oh, one other thing. What about the accuser? Who is he?"

"Mordecai Hazan, a Jew, lives in the Ghetto with his father and sister."

"Rabbi Hazan?

"Yes."

"The rabbi is a fine fellow if a bit up in the clouds, a bit of a mystic, and very good at curing people with herbs and such like. Good, I believe, at finding rare editions, forbidden books, that sort of thing. I have used his services myself more than once — Hush-hush, and turn-a-blind-eye sort of thing. And the daughter. She is a prize, too bad . . ."

"Too bad?"

"Too bad she's a Jewess and . . ."

". . . And there is not much money."

"Yes, quite. You really are terribly clever, Marco. She does deserve a rich match. She is splendidly talented, a poet and a fine writer. Even Aretino praises her, and Veronica Libero, no less, has become one of her friends. I spoke to Miriamne once or twice. I may be old, Marco, but I still have the eye, even now."

"Well, Senator, you are one of the great patrons of the arts, are you not?"

"How very kind of you to say so, Marco! Well, what then is going to be done about this Mordecai?"

"He has debts."

"Ah."

"Gambling debts."

"Damnation—gambling is the ruination of many a good man. If even the Jews can't resist, well then, we are all doomed. And I believe Mordecai is in league with that clever but shifty banker—what is his name?"

"Jeremiah Levy. Mordecai Hazan owes him money."

"Ah, yes, Jeremiah. Articulate, clever, very full of himself. A talented fellow, with, alas, a cruel side, and Jeremiah is in league with our very dear Venetian enemies, quite clever but rather unprincipled people, who fancy themselves Machiavellian puppeteers pulling strings this way and that. This del Medigo affair may be just what we need to rout and defeat these fellows. Sometimes a small event can shift the balance and turn the tide. If we prove del Medigo's innocence, we discredit our enemies, and then, with luck, we obtain the swing votes on the Council. So, this Mordecai . . ."

"He's an alchemist. He is ill. He might have poisoned himself with some metal or chemical concoction. And there is another possibility . . ."

"Yes?"

"The French disease, syphilis."

"Ah, God preserve us! Are we going to look after him?"

"Yes sir, I shall see he is looked after."

"With delicacy, Marco. Choose the time. Make it invisible. We would not want to upset Rabbi Hazan or the beautiful and talented Miriamne."

"Of course not, Senator."

"Till later, then."

"Yes."

The Senator watched Marco disappear through the crowd. Of course he knew everything about Marco, including his real name and where he slept and what woman he slept with—the admirable Letizia. He knew Marco's wife, who also worked for the service and was, like Marco, almost excessively clever and in the Senator's opinion, like Marco, totally trustworthy. And he knew that Marco knew that he knew. Well, that was the way of the world.

The Senator left the Piazzetta and entered the Doge's Palace through the main entry. He went directly to the archives of the Council of Ten and asked for files regarding several subjects: one concerned a certain Judah del Medigo, another concerned a certain Danilo del Medigo, and a third was a file on the late Isabella d'Este, a file in which a certain beautiful and talented Jewess, Grazia dei Rossi, figured prominently, particularly in the years just before the catastrophe of 1527.

He didn't need to consult the file on Angelica, which was cross-referenced with the contributions she had made to a great many other files—files on the Turks, on the Papacy, on powerful merchants, on Jewish communities everywhere, and on the banks and financiers throughout Europe. Angelica was almost as valuable a source as Veronica Libero, who was a wonder.

The Senator knew Angelica's story by heart. He had first spotted her at the slave auction more than a decade ago. She was at that time, he imagined, about eleven years old, perhaps a bit younger or a bit older, a little sliver of a thing, her hair shorn to her skull. She was shivering in fear and holding herself, trying to protect and cover herself. They had just taken off the chains and shackles so that she could be fully displayed. Ah, he had thought, ah, she is a marvel, this poor shivering naked creature.

And so he had whispered to Andreas Satti that Andreas must purchase a girl that was about to be sold. "We shall find a use for her. Even from here I can sense her intelligence." Andreas looked aghast. "But the money . . . for a girl!" The Senator had smiled. "Don't worry about the money, Andreas. I shall look after the money. And Andreas, she looks rather like a boy, I think." Andreas took one look at the girl, and the Senator could see that in his own way Andreas was smitten. "No harm must come to her, Andreas." "No, I swear." Andreas put his hand to his heart. "And Andreas, if she proves as intelligent as I wager she is, then you—we—will give her the best education possible, the very best. No expense spared. You understand? And Andreas, I shall remain invisible. She must never suspect I exist or have anything to do with her. Understood?" "I understand, Senator." And Andreas had been true to his word. Angelica had become a magnificent and talented young woman—a fine actress, an extraordinary beauty—and a considerable asset to the Most Serene Republic of Venice. The Senator climbed the stairs. Sometimes he imagined making himself known to Angelica as her secret benefactor, but that would be breaking the rules. There were times when he regretted the rules.

He entered the vast Council of Ten meeting room and glanced at the high windows and the embossed gilded ceiling. It was all, he thought, an ostentatious display of wealth and power if there ever was one. However, it did serve its purpose—it was intimidating.

"Gentlemen," he said, "we have a small problem, and perhaps, a fine opportunity." Old Gritti looked up. Old Foscari leaned back in his seat. Young Greco pretended to be scribbling something, but then he looked up too. Zeno, who was arranging some papers, glanced up and smiled; he was as wily as a fox, and one of the Senator's key allies. Together they had maneuvered through any number of crises. Establishing Danilo del Medigo's innocence would be extremely useful to the upcoming power play. It quite probably could tip the balance of power in their favor, and both the Senator and Zeno knew it.

The men gathered at the table were friends and enemies and among the wisest men of the Republic, and they were all eager to know what case the Senator had brought them. These little individual cases were the most amusing, and a welcome distraction from the great affairs of state. Peace with the Sultan or not? And what to do about threats from the Emperor, Charles V, and what in the world was one to make of French policy? François I was brilliant, but he was unstable and erratic. And then there was the Papacy, now holding together an anti-Ottoman pact, but always wanting to interfere in the affairs of Venice. The Papacy was always falling into the hands of some robber-baron family and it was always unpredictable and capricious, but it had, alas, considerable moral sway everywhere. And now the Papacy was feeling extra vulnerable and threatened on many sides, struggling against radical mystical friars—Dominicans and Franciscans—and northern heretics who called themselves Protestants. They were designated Protestants, since they protested against everything, or Lutherans, as they were also known, after Martin Luther, the priest who had apparently triggered the whole massive revolt. It was a revolt that was spreading like wildfire, even with episodes of naked prophets running about in the streets in the Low Countries and Germany, and declaring the Second Coming and Apocalypse as imminent. And then there was the Mendes Bank, a very powerful group, run by New Christians, secret Jews. Frankly, the Senator did not care if Jews were open or secret, as long as they were useful. He wished them no harm; indeed he rather liked them, hence his—useful—alliance with Samuel Mendes.

"This is a small case, gentlemen, but you might find it amusing. And perhaps, if we are in the right mood, we might even do a good deed or two!"

63

ENCOUNTER IN THE
GHETTO

Venice

MIRIAMNE FLEW OUT THE FRONT DOOR INTO A GLORI-
ous day, her wrists still stinging from where
Mordecai had grabbed her. The façades of the
towering apartment blocks of the Ghetto shone brightly in the
sunlight. The Campo was crowded with Jews and Christians,
Venetians and strangers, people in robes, people in turbans,
people in caps, all colors—black, red, yellow, blue, turquoise—
all mingled together doing business, shouting, gesticulat-
ing. The water-seller was bellowing something at somebody.
People accosted her, of course they did! They always did! "Ah,
Miriamne, have you a moment?" "Ah, Miriamne, I want to
show you my little girl's new dress, isn't it a marvel?" "Ah,
Miriamne . . ." "Ah, Miriamne . . ." People on all sides, eager to
speak to her, eager to gossip, hungry for her advice, wanting

to show her something—a new chemise, a pair of shoes, a necklace, and even, occasionally, a book . . . It was brilliant and warm, and the voices were friendly, but Miriamne, pushing through the crowds, was plunged into inner darkness—her brother was insane, and her beloved Danilo was probably dead.

Just then, she noticed a hulking blond man with a simple peasant's face, broad shoulders, and huge muscles, and she recognized him as a member of Danilo's theater group. Beside him she saw a flash of blond hair, barely restrained by a hairnet, and a shimmering red-and-gold dress—Angelica.

Miriamne moved to call out to them, grew dizzy, stumbled.

Suddenly Angelica was by her side, had taken her by the arm, and lifted her up, saying, "Miriamne, darling!"

Miriamne was pulled out of the darkness and into the light. Angelica was so direct, so abrupt, and so intimate; instinctively, Miriamne knew she was her ally, and that she could be trusted.

"It's about Danilo," Angelica whispered as soon as she and Miriamne—and Angelica's guardian, whose name it turned out was Pietro—had managed to get out of the crowd and find refuge in a far corner of the Campo.

"I know," said Miriamne, "and I'm afraid . . ."

"You are afraid it's your brother."

"It *is* my brother," Miriamne said, feeling that the confession was not dangerous, since Angelica already seemed to know everything. "He may have killed Danilo!" Miriamne put her hand to her mouth. She could hardly breathe.

Angelica's gaze steadied her. "We are trying to find out if Danilo is alive," she said, in an even, calm voice.

But Angelica's eyes were glossy with tears. Miriamne glanced at Pietro. He stood over them like a protecting angel. She took a deep breath. "What can we do?"

"I think for the moment the best thing is to do nothing, but just make sure your brother—"

"Mordecai . . ."

"Yes. Just make sure Mordecai doesn't do anything foolish."

"What could he do?"

"I don't know, but . . . I think he's mixed up with some very dangerous people."

"He's ill, very ill, I think, and he is in debt."

"Gambling?"

"Yes. And, now . . ." Miriamne stared at Angelica. "I think Mordecai just struck out at Danilo now, because . . . because of me. His idea is . . ."

"Yes, go on." Angelica smiled encouragingly.

"Well, the fact is this: I am partly to blame."

"No, you aren't."

Miriamne waved the objection aside. "I refused to marry Jeremiah. He is old, nasty, very cruel, and he despises women."

"Not unusual."

"In any case, he is Mordecai's only hope."

"This Jeremiah is rich."

"Very rich."

"I see."

"And Mordecai must have discovered some of Danilo's letters. And he realized that . . ." Miriamne stopped. She was so furious with everything—with herself, with Mordecai, with the situation! She found it impossible to go on.

Angelica put her hand on Miriamne's shoulder. "Mordecai realized that Danilo and your love for him was still an obstacle to the marriage with Jeremiah and all his money. So Danilo was an impediment, an enemy."

"Yes."

"And he decided to get rid of Danilo."

"I think so."

"Or perhaps he wanted to use Danilo as leverage."

"How? How could he do that?"

"I'm not sure, but he might think he has the power—through friends—to have Danilo released, and the price for that . . ."

"Would be me agreeing to marry Jeremiah."

"Yes. Possibly. Mordecai is part of something much bigger, I suspect, and I am not sure he understands this himself."

Miriamne frowned. "I feel like I am a piece of cheese being bargained over."

"We've all felt like that sometimes, Miriamne, we women. What I have come to tell you is this: do not give in, do not agree to marry Jeremiah." Angelica glanced up at Pietro.

Pietro nodded.

"But also," Angelica went on, "I can assure you, Miriamne, that friends—powerful friends—are working to find Danilo and, if he is alive, to have him released from wherever he is being held. They will find him." The two women stared at each other.

"Yes." Miriamne nodded. "We shall assume that is true. Danilo is alive." Her eyes brightened. "And yes, your friends will find him."

JESSICA CLIMBED THE NARROW, dark stairs to Miriamne's rooms. She wanted to ask Miriamne if they could go to the Rialto Market tomorrow, and if they could take Jacob with them. Jacob was not really very mature; he could be petulant, and he sometimes got tired and had to be coaxed to keep moving. Uncle Goldman had said he would come. But he was too old to take them alone. And he was deaf, and often got lost like Old Uncle Isaac, so they would need Miriamne.

Jessica came to Miriamne's door, which was open. This was unusual. She hesitated just a second, and then called out, "Miriamne? It's Jessica!" She waited. And then, since there was no answer, she went straight in.

Mordecai was slumped in Miriamne's chair. Miriamne was not there. Two candles burned, and the light from the little window with its iron bars fell across Mordecai's face. It was covered in sweat, his eyes stared at her. Jessica loved Mordecai, although he was rarely in Venice. He was always traveling, always collecting metals and instruments for his experiments. Since her mother died, Miriamne and Mordecai had become like her own family, and most days she and Jacob ate at Rabbi

Hazan's table. Mordecai, when she was younger, always liked to play games, and he liked to teach her things. He talked about the big wide world and all the stars and constellations; he seemed to know a great many truly interesting things.

"Uncle Mordecai," she said. He was not seeing her. Sweat dripped from his chin. There was a black-and-red sore on his cheek and flecks of red in his beard — blood, maybe it was blood.

"Uncle Mordecai?" Jessica bit her lip. This was not right.

Foam bubbled from the corner of his mouth. Jessica backed away towards the doorway. "You bitch," Mordecai muttered. Then suddenly, getting up, he screamed, "You bitch! You have destroyed me!"

Jessica backed farther away.

"Bitch! Bitch! Bitch!" he screamed. He lunged for her.

Jessica stepped aside. Now he was in the doorway, blocking her way out. He growled, the foaming snarl of a mad dog, saliva dripping from the corners of his mouth. Jessica swiveled back towards the workbench, where Miriamne's tools and the little necklace she was working on were all neatly laid out. Jessica pushed her back against the workbench; she reached behind her for one of Miriamne's tools — the sharp little chisel which had always looked so dangerous. Her fingers closed around it. With the light falling straight on Mordecai's face, he looked even worse. He looked really sick. And he looked as if he were asleep, not seeing her at all. He was having a nightmare, but he was awake, standing up and with his eyes wide open.

He lunged, and as she stepped aside she let go of the chisel; he slapped her. It was a mighty slap, and it sent her reeling against the wall. She cried and fell down.

Mordecai loomed over her. "You will pay!" He picked up the chisel and stared at it; then he plunged it down with all his might, with all the weight of his body.

Jessica swiveled aside. Her dress was caught, pinned down by the chisel. She tugged to get it free. It ripped.

She jumped to her feet as Mordecai stumbled blindly and fell to his knees. The chisel bit into the floor again and again.

Wood chips flew. Mordecai coughed and made a horrible sound. Blood spurted from his mouth. It had a sickening, horrible stench.

Jessica crawled and scrambled through the door and leaped down the stairs coming out onto the Campo, breathless. She had to find Miriamne. She had to find Rabbi Hazan. People were everywhere, as usual.

Melania was standing close by, holding a basket of vegetables and talking to Abel, the tailor. She turned and reached out. "Why Jessica, you look like you . . . Your face is all red. One side of your face is all red. What happened?"

"I'm looking for Miriamne."

"Ah, Miriamne! She is over there with the rabbi, talking to some outsiders, the actress from the Mantua troupe, I think."

"Thank you, Melania," Jessica said, and started towards Miriamne. She put her fingers to her lips. Blood! He had hit her so hard! It was like a devil or a shedim had gotten into Mordecai, carried off his soul, and left only a demonic spirit lurking darkly inside behind his empty eyes. The Mordecai she knew, who played games and told funny jokes and always looked so handsome and dashing, was dead.

6 4

THE MASK

"SOMETIMES I WISH I WERE A JEW," SAID PIETRO.

"What? Why? Whatever for?" Angelica took his arm. "I wouldn't wish that on anybody!"

"Did you see how they are all together? Did you see how close the families are? The rabbi, Miriamne, Jessica . . . Their love is total. Whereas . . ."

"Whereas?"

"Whereas we are wanderers, vagabonds. We don't have a family. We don't have a history."

"We are our family, Pietro. I am your family. Our friendship is our history! And as for the Jews, they are wanderers too. They are always in exile. Their only home is in Palestine and it is a home most of them have never known."

"I suppose we are all in the hands of God."

"Oh, Pietro!" She leaned against him, then reached up and kissed him on the cheek. "You are the best and the wisest of men. Come, we don't want to be late for Marco."

They shoved their way along *le Mercerie* through the

shopping crowds, the multitude and variety that was Venice.

Marco was waiting in the little courtyard, pacing up and down, his hands behind his back, his fingers twisting and untwisting. "Well, my children, welcome back. You warned the Jewess, did you not?"

"Yes, we did."

"Good."

"I think Mordecai Hazan is very sick," Angelica said, "perhaps going insane. He attacked a young woman, Jessica, and . . ."

". . . attacked a young woman . . . ?"

"She is fine. I mean, shocked, but fine. She's a girl, still a child really. Mordecai attacked her with a chisel; he had some sort of fit—foaming at the mouth. He is mad, I think, insane."

"Well, that may make things easier." Marco rubbed his chin. "You, Angelica, must appear before the Council of Ten without delay."

"What?" Angelica started back. "The Council of Ten—me?" The Council of Ten, the secretive committee protecting Venice's internal and external security and in charge of intelligence gathering, had a fearsome reputation. Her heart plummeted. She saw herself rotting for decades in a dungeon in the depths of the Doge's Palace. "I am to appear now?"

"Yes, Pietro and I must stay out of sight. And you will be wearing this." Marco bent over. Out of a large sack he pulled a full-face carnival mask and a shapeless tan-colored garment that looked like a monk's habit, including long loose sleeves, a full hood, and gloves.

"A disguise?"

"Yes, you are a spy. No one must see who you are, not even the members of the Council of Ten."

"It looks like I'm being sent to a nunnery, or worse, a monastery."

"Think of it as a performance."

"A performance!" Angelica squared her shoulders and nodded. "All right, that's what it will be—a performance."

"This will fit over everything you are wearing. For obvious

reasons—as you are one of our best secret agents—your identity must not be revealed."

With Pietro's help, Angelica slipped into the garment. She disappeared, except for her face, which was framed by the hood. She picked up the mask. "I put this on now?"

"Yes. Now."

She flipped back the hood and fitted the highly decorated, androgynously beautiful black-and-white mask. Pietro tied and tightened the leather bands. The mask fit like a second skin, covering her whole face. She pulled the hood back into place. She disappeared. Angelica no longer existed.

"Well?" Her voice, muffled by the mask, was deeper, almost masculine.

"Perfect. Now, outside, down this little side alley, there will be two gentlemen dressed as you are. They will accompany you to the Doge's Palace. Then they will bring you back here. You will not speak to them. Not a single word! Stay in the costume until you return here. Only one person is to hear your voice: the Senator. Only him. No one else. You will recognize him when you see him. We have enemies who would destroy me, you, Pietro, Danilo, and our whole network. You understand?"

"I understand."

"Good. You will be brought before a committee. You are to answer questions about Danilo del Medigo. And if you can, you must avoid anything that can reveal your own identity. Just follow the script you and I prepared precisely for such an occasion."

"I am your obedient servant."

"Good luck. Pietro and I will await your return, here."

She hesitated. "I'm not sure I see the point of this, the Council and so on."

"The point? Why, to free Danilo!"

"Free him?"

"Yes. Did I not tell you? Danilo del Medigo is alive!"

DANILO WAS ALIVE! SHE'D known it in her heart all along. Alive! She could hardly keep the grin from her face as she was escorted across the city by two anonymous monk-like creatures who spoke not a word. They were equally tall, head and shoulders above her; they strode quickly, their habits swishing against the pavement. Their masks and hoods hid their faces and, like her, they wore gloves. People turned and stared, then looked away; something untoward and dangerous was happening. Perhaps a spy was being accompanied to the Doge's prison for torture, and eventually, execution.

They arrived at the Doge's Palace. Angelica's two unknown guardians bowed and disappeared. A servant was waiting for her. He motioned that she was to follow him. It was hot and sticky inside the rough cloth habit and behind the thick mask. Her face was beaded in sweat. In the thick gloves her hands felt clumsy. The servant bowed, pointed, and left her. Waiting at the top of a staircase was a tall, thin old man. She recognized him as Senator Vittorio Altebrando, the leader of one of the city's greatest patrician families; she'd seen him standing on a platform in several of the civic ceremonies Venice loved to put on. And once, passing in the street, he had nodded to her, which she had found surprising. He was one of the richest and most powerful men in Venice.

"My dear," he said, "I know who you are, and you know who I am, but your identity shall remain our secret."

Angelica bowed her head to indicate that she understood.

"I shall be your advocate, should anything go wrong, but I am sure nothing will. Let us go."

They entered a lofty monumental room with high ceilings and paintings on all the walls. The Senator indicated that Angelica was to sit down and he sat next to her. Opposite, across a broad table, sat a row of gentlemen whom she knew must be the most powerful in Venice: the Council of Ten.

One of the men looked up, "Senator Altebrando, can you testify to the honor and trustworthiness of the witness? The witness is disguised. We have no idea who this person is."

"Yes, absolutely, the witness is trustworthy," the Senator answered. "Not only that, but I can say—and I have a rather complete knowledge of these affairs—that the witness has provided great services to Venice, secret services, and continues to do so, which is why the witness is appearing before you in disguise. The witness has demonstrated extreme courage, often in dangerous situations, and brilliant initiative in serving the Republic, and I am sure the witness will provide equally valuable services in the future. Such services, as you know, require the utmost secrecy."

"Thank you, Senator. Let us proceed."

They asked Angelica if she knew the prisoner Danilo del Medigo; if he was a credit to Venice; if he had done service for Venice; if he had been in Venice on certain dates, and so on. Sometimes Angelica had to evoke moments in her memory. She bent close and whispered her answers to the Senator, who then repeated them in a loud voice to the committee. "The witness says . . ." The questions, Angelica quickly realized, were designed to ascertain Danilo's innocence of certain charges, and she could answer them all with negatives—no, he was not in Venice on August 3, 1537; no, he was not in Milan on January 18, 1538—and without indicating where Danilo had, in fact, been on the given dates. Then finally, after whispered discussions among the members, the chair bowed towards the Senator. "We shall now deliberate, and I believe we will provide an answer within a few hours."

Angelica and the Senator exited the room. "Now, you will go back to your rendezvous point. I will send someone with news. Keep your disguise handy. You may need it."

"What if they decide Danilo is guilty of whatever he is supposed to be guilty of?"

"Let us not dwell on that unpleasant possibility, my dear. Your testimony has been essential. And I believe I carry some weight with the Council. But we all have enemies. And some of them would like to—how shall I put it—to compromise our efforts, to sabotage our networks. And, in that case . . ."

"Danilo would be a victim."

"Yes, as is so often the case with innocents, he would be a victim of affairs having nothing to do with him, crushed by plots and counter-plots concerning others. Not to mention the fact that he has gotten in the way of a rather sick and confused fellow who has struck out against him—very unadvisedly, I must say. Ah, here are your two amiable escorts." He bowed. "I do hope we shall meet again, you and I, and in better circumstances."

DANILO PACED. IT MUST be Mordecai. He could think of nobody else, except Hürrem, who wished him such ill, and Hürrem's Men in Black would not have tossed him into a Venetian prison. He leaned against the wall and wiped his brow. If he were declared guilty of whatever the charge was, what would happen to Miriamne? What would happen to Angelica, or even to Pietro? Mordecai might have put the whole network in danger, and even the links to the Mendes Bank and to Samuel Mendes himself. Mordecai was a shortsighted fool with a narrow horizon. He might have set off an avalanche without having the least idea of the powers he had unleashed. Damn! Danilo smashed his fist against the wall. The worst thing of all was being trapped, unable to act, unable to do anything.

The guard appeared at the door of the cell and looked in through the tiny barred window. "Well, sir, how are we doing? I believe your case is being heard at this very moment. For the dreadful type of crime of which you are accused, sir—and I have just discovered the heinous nature of said crime, it is too ghastly for words—the punishment is usually swift and total."

"What dreadful crime have I been accused of, then?"

"I'm not at liberty to say, sir. But it will mean death, sure as I am standing here. That message you wanted to send. Perhaps it could be arranged, now that I have thought it over; for a consideration, of course. And I'd gladly accept any bits of gold you might have stashed away in or around your body somewhere. A poor man such as I can use anything he can lay his hands on, sir. I have a wife and six children, seven hungry mouths, not counting my own, and you wouldn't believe, sir, how much it costs to keep such creatures in food, and clothed with a few rags, and with a roof over their heads. Ah, well, if you are not in a chatty mood, I quite understand, sir. It has been decreed that you not see a priest, not for the moment at least. They want to keep you isolated, I believe. But I have a priest handy, sir, if the moment comes."

"I will not need a priest, thank you, jailer. But it is very kind of you to offer one." Danilo gave him his most gracious smile.

"Perhaps you are a Jew."

"Indeed I am."

"That makes it doubly sad, sir."

"Oh? And why is that?"

"If you are executed, then I suppose you must go to Hell, for the Jews, I have heard, are in league with the Devil."

"I'm not sure the Devil would have me, jailer. I have not been a very good Jew."

"Then perhaps you will end up in limbo or in purgatory. I am not very conversant with theology, sir, so I am not sure what your destiny will be, but I do hope it will be a happy one. Perhaps they will not condemn you, sir. There is always that possibility."

"I suppose there is, jailer. It is very kind of you to think of it."

"Well, I must be off on my rounds. Always pleasant chatting with you."

"And with you, jailer. I wish you well."

"Ah, one thing, sir—I have been told that a young woman is in great danger because of your misdeeds. It's a terrible weight to have on a man's shoulders, destroying some innocent maiden. Just gossip, of course."

"What woman, what danger? Jailer!"

But he was gone. His torch cast wavering shadows outside the cell door, and then once again there was blackness.

≫╼

AT MIDNIGHT, ANGELICA WAS ordered to make her way back to the Doge's Palace with her two anonymous guardians. She was again draped in the monk's costume, with heavy hood, ornate mask, and gloves. Marco, looking worried, had come to inform her of the orders: she was to return immediately to the Doge's Palace. He had not told her anything more. When she asked, he said that no one would tell him anything.

Angelica could see that Marco feared it had all somehow gone terribly wrong. She trembled. She must have failed Danilo. He was going to die. And she was to be arrested, she would find herself in the dungeon, and be left there to rot. Had Senator Altebrando betrayed them? Had he been unable to save them?

If she were to die or be left incommunicado in a dungeon, the worst thing would be knowing she had failed to save Danilo. And he, going to his death, would never even know she had tried; and poor Miriamne would once again be abandoned, feeling everyone had betrayed her. God only knew what would happen to her! Angelica yearned to ask her two guardians—one of whom was holding a flaming torch high above his head—what had happened, but she was forbidden to speak. As they made their way through the dimly lit alleyways, the rare nocturnal passersby averted their faces.

When they arrived at the Doge's Palace, the two monk-like creatures led her down narrow stairs into a dank cellar. Her heart thumped against her chest, sweat trickled between her breasts: it was the prison of the Doge's Palace. So this was her destination. Would she ever again see the light of day? She took a deep breath.

One of the guardians handed her a folded note sealed with a thick red insignia and pointed downwards into what looked like an entry to Hell. Then they left, disappearing back up the way they'd come.

Angelica swallowed, squared her shoulders, and went on alone, down and down. The walls leaned inwards, sweating and filthy; she must be below the waterline. At the bottom, she went along a narrow corridor towards a dim light, and came to a tiny room lit by one candle. A guard was sitting there, snoozing.

She stood in the doorway, waiting. She coughed.

The guard started up. "Mother of God! What masked specter is this?"

With her gloved hand, she handed him the sealed document from beneath her cloak. He shot her a look, then took a small knife, slit the seal, and unfolded the document. He stared at it, then pushed back his cap and scratched his head. Under the thick monk's habit, Angelica was trembling and coated in sweat. Did the note decree her death? Did it indicate which tortures she was to endure? The guard looked up at her, a puzzled expression on his face. He called out. Another guard appeared, a thickset man with sallow jowls and bad teeth. The second guard blinked at the document, rubbed his chin, and licked his thick lips. Then he shrugged and turned to Angelica. "Follow me," he said.

Sweat trickled down her back. Her lips trembled. She was going to be sick. She must not be sick. She followed the man down another narrow corridor. It was a filthy, fetid place—urine, shit, sweat, rotten food . . . Somebody somewhere screamed. A madman? Someone being tortured? The voice sounded infinitely old, high-pitched, and clogged with phlegm. Was it a man or a woman? Impossible to tell. The voice was hardly human. Angelica shivered. What would she become if she were locked forever in such a place, never to see any of her loved ones again, never to see the sun, never to breathe fresh air, never to walk free? She would go mad.

The guard stopped and took out his keys. He unlocked a thick door.

"Here," he said.

Angelica went to the doorway. Was she to enter? Was this to be her new home? No, she could not accept this! She would live, she would fight! She turned and shoved the jailer, trying to push past him and run. But the corridor was too narrow and he was bulky and strong. He grabbed her arms and held her like a vise. His face close to her mask, his breath smelled of garlic and rancid wine. "No choice, not down here! In you go!" He pushed her through the doorway. She stumbled and almost fell. Behind her, the door slammed shut; the key turned.

ANGELICA STARED INTO THE darkness, only a dim halo of light falling from a torch set high on the opposite wall . . . onto a man. Slowly her eyes adjusted.

Standing there, in the middle of the cell, was Danilo. Oh, thank God! He was alive. Danilo really was alive! He was naked except for a skimpy loincloth. It didn't look like he'd been tortured. She opened her mouth to speak, shut it. What was she to do? Was she allowed to speak? Were they to be tortured together, and die together?

She heard the guard approach and raised a gloved finger to the lips painted on her mask.

Danilo, tense, watched her closely. Obviously he had no idea who or what she was. She could see what he was thinking— she was an assassin, disguised, sent to kill him anonymously.

The lock clicked; the cell door opened again. The guard threw a sack on the floor beside her. "Get dressed," he said, nodding towards Danilo.

Angelica took the sack and held it out to Danilo. He hesitated, and then took it. In the bag were a mask and a monk's habit. That had to be a good sign. Were they allowing him to leave with her? She held her breath.

The guard disappeared. The door slammed shut.

"Who are you?"

She put her finger again to the painted mouth.

"I shall assume you mean me no harm."

She nodded.

Danilo dressed, but he was careful not to look away from her. He was all nervous muscle, glistening with sweat, ready to spring into action, ready to defend himself if she were to pull a dagger from her cloak. He looked like one of those paintings of

Saint Sebastian, naked and muscular and pierced with arrows. Not for the first time, she thought how he would only need a split second to change from gallant gentleman to ferocious animal. His body, she had always known, was not just the body of a lover; it was a weapon. In spite of her fear, she felt a ripple of sensual pleasure, and a quick flood of delicious memories.

After a moment, the guard returned, swung the door wide, and stepped back. Danilo and Angelica exchanged a glance. Angelica led him out. At the foot of the stairs, the guard gave his broken-toothed smile. "I was told to give you this." He handed a sealed note to Angelica, and said to Danilo. "It has been a pleasure, sir. We had some fine conversations while you were our guest."

"I assure you the pleasure was all mine, jailer," said Danilo, his voice muffled by the mask.

THEY MET IN A small alleyway that led off the riva degli Schiavoni. The waters of Saint Mark's Basin sparkled in the moonlight at the end of the alley, framed by two high walls. The Senator sat down on a small stone bench, partly illuminated by moonlight, and he patted the stone. Marco sat down next to him.

"Are you satisfied, Senator?" Marco was exhausted. It had been a long, tense day. In the background there had been fierce and complex negotiations, and until the last moment the whole affair—and Danilo's destiny—had hung in the balance. But finally, the majority of the Council of Ten had clearly pronounced for Danilo del Medigo's innocence; this was a vindication of their position, and a crushing defeat for their enemies. Jeremiah Levy had been declared persona non grata in Venice. Punishment of exile had been pronounced against several minor Venetian personalities; the Machiavellian puppeteers' puppets had had their strings cut. And the Jewish community had escaped any sanction or blame.

"Yes, I am. One thing at a time, you know. Now that we have our hands free, we may be able to negotiate a new bargain with Suleiman, though I fear we will sacrifice quite a bit in doing so. Del Medigo may eventually be useful if this new peace with the Ottomans is maintained, or even if war begins again, for after that war there will again be peace, and then war, and then peace. And so it goes."

"And what about that Jew, Mordecai . . . He caused a great deal of trouble."

The Senator sighed. "Sometimes I hate this job."

Marco nodded. "Mordecai is more or less insane and he will soon be dead, perhaps within a few days."

"Not our affair then. Time heals all."

"Yes," said Marco.

"As for his fellow conspirators, the thugs he used to capture our young friend, and some of their low-level backers, they should be dealt with."

"Yes, Senator."

"They are not Jews. They are Venetians. They belong to us and we cannot have rogue elements on the loose. We don't know what else they may do. So they must be looked after, cleanly, discreetly, and forever."

"I understand. It will be done."

6 5

DANILO'S CRUSADE

PROTECTED BY THE CURTAINS OF THE SMALL PRIVATE CABIN in the middle of a gondola heading down the Grand Canal, Danilo shed his mask and turned to the strange monk. "And you, what are you?"

Angelica, who had just finished reading the note the guard had given her, took off her mask and flipped back her hood.

"Angelica! But how . . . ?"

"Shush! We have been ordered to disappear, to lie low, to return to our tour, and stay away from Venice, at least for a few weeks or months."

"And . . . ?"

"And . . . We make a plan."

"But — what about Miriamne?"

"I have talked to Miriamne. Marco will watch over her. Pietro is staying in Venice for a few days to make sure Miriamne is protected. There are others close to her who will watch over her — Vincenzo, his boy Filippo, and I believe his nieces too, Melania and Mika, who are always in the Ghetto.

If I understand correctly, they all work for Marco, and they all work through Marco, for the Council of Ten. Later, we can arrange a discreet rendezvous for you and Miriamne. And of course, you can correspond. Invisible ink still works wonders!"

"How did you get me out of there?"

"Friends in high places, very high places. Marco knows how to pull strings. We were part of a much larger battle — a fight between two factions in the Council of Ten and in the Senate. I have no idea of the details. But our friends won, that I do know."

"What about Mordecai?"

"Mordecai is ill. He will be dead soon."

"Poor Miriamne. I must see her."

"Patience, my friend; it will be arranged."

"Where do we go now?"

"Pietro will join us in a day or two with news once he is assured Miriamne is in good hands. The troupe will stay in Padua for a month or two to rehearse and get ready for the next season. You and I will rehearse with the rest and lie low until you can go back to Venice."

"Now I need some clothes, real clothes."

"True," Angelica laughed. "But you did look very attractive naked."

A WEEK LATER, IN PADUA, rehearsals were proceeding well and all the actors were in fine form. Late one night, Angelica was alone in her room taking stock. She was pleased. Ajax and Martina made a splendid pair. They could both play naughty pageboys, and they could both play girls, although that stage would soon end for Ajax. Martina was a virtuoso on the flute, and Ajax was excellent on the lute, so together they could put on a wonderful interlude, or play strolling musicians and mingle with the public. Still, there was a bit of spice lacking — she needed another female lead to complement her own performances. Tommaso was developing a talent for leading roles — he might replace Danilo when the moment came, which it surely would, and soon. Danilo was restless, eager to get back to Miriamne, scribbling notes to her every night, ready finally to settle on his destiny.

It had been a long day.

Angelica intended to plunge into a hot bath before collapsing into bed. She stood, indecisive, for a moment.

Things were moving very fast. A note had arrived that afternoon from the banker Samuel Mendes saying he was coming to Padua to meet with Danilo. Mendes was in Rome and would be in Padua in about ten days, he reckoned. Would the troupe still be there? "Yes, we will still be here, and I am eager to see you," Danilo had written back, as Angelica leaned over his shoulder.

Now, contemplating the bath, Angelica sighed, in an imitation of one of dear lamented Andreas's more operatic expressions, put her hand to her forehead, and rolled her eyes. "Oh, what a fool am I! Oh, foolish wench, tossing away all that you love and desire!" She paused, and shrugged. "Well, that's that, then. What's done is done."

She removed her velvet jacket, her chemise, and the net that disciplined her hair, and slipped out of her skirt and underthings. She stepped into the tub of hot water and lowered herself down.

It was not easy to obtain water—let alone hot water. But somehow she had charmed her way into the hearts of the water boys and the servants at the palazzo where the troupe was staying. A handful of coin had helped too; charm can only go so far.

Ah, the water was piping hot, and the soap perfumed! She sank into the steamy liquid. She closed her eyes. Samuel Mendes was going to offer Danilo work, or a mission, she was sure of it. And Danilo, though he might want to resist, wouldn't in the end, and so . . .

And so, Danilo's acting career was about to come to an end.

And so, everything between Danilo and Angelica would be over.

She opened her eyes. The candles made patterns on the high walls of the room. On the ceiling, nymphs and cupids cavorted, doing complicated things, bucolic flirtations and amours, in some pastoral or mythological scene. Her life had been one long adventure. Soon she would be too old to be the heroine of the romantic and comic plays. She should perhaps think of her future. But the future seemed so far away! Today was magical! Each day, each moment, was a new challenge, a new possibility. Eternity was now. *Carpe diem* — seize life with both hands!

What she did want was Danilo's happiness. She and Danilo had had a very good run, and of course she had to admit, at least to herself, that she was in love with him — deeply, foolishly, head-over-heels in love — but some things were not meant to be.

Miriamne was the woman for Danilo, and almost certainly, Samuel Mendes was the man to make it all happen. Danilo might, quite possibly, become rich. Angelica sighed. She must make notes on the Mendes Bank and its accelerating rescue plans — alluded to in Samuel's note. Also, a few notes on Beatrice de Luna, the power behind the Mendes Bank, would be useful. Marco would be pleased. Things were on the move and Venice needed to know. She reached for the bottle of shampoo and began to wash her hair. Some of the soap got in her eyes. That stung! And what were those unfamiliar things she felt, streaming down her cheeks?

Were they, by any chance, tears?

WHEN DANILO ENTERED, ANGELICA was in bed, reading a book by candlelight.

"The water is still warm," she said, indicating the tub in the adjoining room, "if you wish to take advantage of it."

"Yes," he said. He undressed slowly.

Angelica watched him. "So what do you think of this upcoming meeting with Signor Mendes? He said it is very important."

"He will offer me a job — a mission of some kind."

"And will you accept?"

"I'll think about it."

"*He'll think about it!* Ah, Danilo, you are a marvellously indecisive man, a true artist of procrastination! You are still a boy, an adolescent, flitting about from flower to flower! It's part of what makes you so beautiful but so frustrating! Miriamne will have her hands full!" She put the book on the bedside table. "Shall I scrub your back?"

"Hmm."

"*Hmm*. The man says *Hmm. Hmm* is excellent. *Hmm* is admirable!" She climbed out of the bed, walked towards the tub, and lifted off her chemise. "I don't want to get it wet."

Danilo lowered himself into the water.

"They heated it especially for us in the kitchens."

Angelica knelt next to the tub and scrubbed Danilo's back and his shoulders, and then she scrubbed his chest. "Well, darling, now your chest is all sparkling clean. I do believe I am rather talented at this sort of personal care and grooming. I belong in a harem, giving luxurious pleasure to some fat old pasha or sultan or pirate, or in a stable, looking after your good steed, Bucephalus. I would be very talented with a brush and I would be a wonderful stable boy, or girl, carrying manure to-and-fro, I'm sure. Maybe it would have been for the best if I had been sold off to Cairo or Tunis or even Istanbul." She vigorously massaged his head and face.

"You are not meant for a harem, Angelica."

"Oh? I'm not so sure. I believe I'd be excellent in a harem." She leaned back and studied his face. "What's going on? You're very quiet."

"I've been thinking."

"Thinking—how painful!"

"Before I see Samuel, I'm going to Mantua to reclaim my heritage and to settle things. And I need to find out about Pirro—where he is and what he is doing. I will present Isabella's letter to the Regents. It confirms my status as Pirro's son. I must clarify this. It's for my mother, really. I must." He frowned and repeated, "I must."

"You're going to Mantua? To confront the Regents? Well, my chivalrous knight in shining armor, if you are going to be foolish and do something crazy, then I will come with you. The troupe can look after itself here in Padua. They have lots to do. Ajax and Martina and the others have learned most of their parts. Tommaso has been training to be your understudy. Pietro will keep them in hand. The sooner we put this Pirro Gonzaga thing to bed, the better. He has haunted you for too long, that's what I think! It is time to turn the page—the future and Miriamne await you!"

66

MANTUA

D ANILO AND ANGELICA ARRIVED IN MANTUA TOWARDS
dusk.

The low sun turned the walls and towers and churches a glowing amber, as if the whole city were made of gold. The various pavilions of the Ducal Palace, the Palazzo del Capitano, the Domus Nova and the Corte Vecchia, shone in the twilight, and Castello di San Giorgio stood tall, forbidding, with its blank walls, battlements, and towers.

They settled into the pleasant old inn of Signor Ciecherella. But the atmosphere seemed rather chilly, people less friendly than they used to be.

"Maybe it's us." Angelica stretched, wiggling her shoulders, and yawned. "Maybe we are just tired. When I'm exhausted I think everybody is grumpy."

"Maybe," said Danilo. He left Angelica and set off alone for the Ducal Palace.

The massive façade of the palace and its labyrinth of buildings always gave him a special thrill, and they brought back so many happy and sad memories.

In the reception room, Enrico—the gloomy yet distinguished Master of the House, who had greeted him that first time when he sought an audience with Isabella—looked at him strangely, as if he had never seen him before.

"Who did you say you were, sir?"

Danilo was taken aback. "But you know who I am, man!"

"Perhaps my memory is failing, sir."

"Very well, then, Enrico. If we are playing games, my name is Danilo del Medigo, and I am expected by the Regents."

"Very well, sir. I shall announce your presence to the Regent. Only one of the three Regents is present at the moment." Enrico turned on his heel and disappeared.

Danilo stood alone in the entry hall. It had huge doors, large windows, and a few tapestries. It was sparsely furnished and spooky. Several servants he knew walked past. No one looked at him. No one acknowledged his presence. It was as if he didn't exist; this was very strange and did not bode well. Perhaps the feeling Angelica had noted at the inn was not just an effect of their fatigue. Maybe people had been warned to shun them. He walked up and down. He glanced out a window. Snowflakes had begun to fall. He walked out onto the terrace. He glanced at the Castello di San Giorgio. It loomed darkly, protecting the passage between the middle and the lower lakes. He recalled the story Sappho had told him of the doomed lovers who returned to the castle each night to make love from dusk to dawn. What had happened to Sappho? Had she survived in Mantua after Isabella died?

Across the terrace was the Old Court. Isabella had been so proud, giving him the tour. How lonely and isolated she had become! Then there were all his mother's stories of life in Mantua, of her life with Isabella, of Isabella's capricious but generous nature and brilliant mind. It saddened him to think of them—Grazia and Isabella.

He went back inside.

One of the maidservants came down the corridor; Danilo

smiled at her. "Hello, Lucia! How are you? What news of Sappho?"

She stared at him as if she had never seen him before. "Sappho? I know no Sappho." And she disappeared down another corridor. Danilo frowned. Perhaps he had gone mad. Maybe he had never been in Mantua at all. Maybe it was all a dream—or a nightmare. Maybe his whole life was a dream, an illusion.

Enrico returned. He stood there, a stony look on his face. His eyes were distant.

"Well?"

"You may enter, sir, but by the servants' entrance, as befits a player and a vagabond."

Danilo felt the color drain from his face. That he should be insulted like this, in Mantua, in the palace that was the home of Isabella, and with Gonzaga blood running in his veins, was intolerable. His muscles tensed. But no, patience and forbearance were best. "Very well, then! Show me."

Enrico gestured to a snotty young man. This servant, an unshaven fellow in the simplest, lowest-rank livery, led Danilo down several long corridors to the servants' entrance. Trying to make conversation, Danilo asked, "How is Sappho doing? What news of her?"

Without turning, the young man said, "I have never heard that name. Here you are then, the servants' entrance." The man nodded and disappeared.

Danilo entered, proceeded down another corridor, and was shown by another young manservant into a large reception room.

"A player is come to see you, your Excellency," the servant said, and disappeared.

The Regent, one of three governing in the name of Isabella's grandson, ten-year-old Francesco Gonzaga III, was standing alone by the large fireplace, where a fire, piled high with cut logs, roared and sparkled, casting a golden light over the ornate tables and chairs, and the arched ceilings with their paintings and frescoes. Two large steel-gray Neapolitan mastiffs lying by the fire got up, came over, and sniffed at Danilo.

"So what is this about, then?" said the Regent, a heavy-set man with a thick broken nose that was twisted sideways, and straight black hair. Without waiting for an answer, the man turned his back to Danilo and faced the fire. "I suppose you've come to discuss the troupe's plans. That can be discussed with the stable master. I have nothing to do with that sort of thing."

"I am not . . ." Danilo began, "I am not an actor."

The Regent turned and leveled his cold dark gaze at him.

Danilo hesitated. What had happened? Was the man in his dotage? "Sir, I am Danilo del Medigo. I am the son of Pirro Gonzaga."

"I have heard rumors that someone was making that ridiculous claim. It is nonsense. Repeat it, sirrah, and I shall have you thrown in the dungeon. The dungeon is not comfortable these cold autumn nights. We might forget you are there. The walls are thick. No one ever hears a thing. People disappear, you know." The Regent sighed and smiled, almost wistfully.

"Forgive me, but Marchesa Isabella confirmed the fact, and . . ."

The Regent's expression hardened. "Isabella is dead."

"I know." Danilo pulled the precious letter from his vest and held it out. "Here it is, written in Isabella's own hand."

The Regent took the letter, glanced at it, shrugged, and tossed it into the fire.

"But . . ." Danilo started forward, then thought better of it; he watched the letter crumple up, break into flame, and turn black. Whole lives—his, Grazia's, Pirro's—all reduced in an instant to ashes.

"That paper is of no importance." The Regent smiled. "Isabella was not herself in her last years, she was not entirely . . ." He knocked his index finger against his temple. "She was not entirely there. Anything Isabella said, or wrote, meant nothing." The Regent waved away the existence of the formidable Isabella d'Este, as if she were an illusion who had never existed at all. The dogs growled menacingly.

"But Federico . . ."

"He's dead too." The Regent once again turned his back to Danilo, then picked up an iron poker and stirred the fire. The flames roared higher, lighting up the room.

"So," Danilo hesitated to repeat it, "what Isabella and Federico said means nothing."

"Promises, promises! They mean nothing. I presume, sirrah, you are bright enough to know that."

"I'm beginning to believe it." Danilo gazed at the man's thick back and broad shoulders.

The Regent turned again to face him. He was a rough-hewn mercenary warrior. His small eyes sparkled; the firelight deepened the shadows on both sides of his broken nose. To challenge the man directly would endanger all Danilo's friends, Angelica, and the members of the troupe. Their livelihood depended on Mantua, on a friendly Regent. But there was one thing he would not leave without. "I left Mantegna's portrait of my mother, Grazia dei Rossi, with Madonna Isabella. I would like . . ."

"That is Gonzaga property. We intend to sell it and some of the other ridiculous things Isabella collected. Cash is better than trinkets." He shrugged. "Difficult times."

"It belongs to me."

"I am beginning to lose patience, young man!" The Regent waved the poker in front of him. The point glowed red-hot. "Have you any proof of ownership?"

Danilo hesitated. He didn't have any proof. He could see what the man was thinking: what would be just punishment for this impertinent vagabond, this piece of itinerant scum?

"Lord Pirro can testify for me. He knows that Isabella gave the portrait to Grazia."

"Ha!" The Regent snorted. "Lord Pirro, what a fellow! He was totally irresponsible! And then the man fell into an endless funk. Killed a man, he did, your Lord Pirro, became a fugitive.

Always in mourning, always mooning about! Gambling! Debts! Made dangerous enemies! Useless! A silly romantic, sowing his seed to the four winds, he had no thought for tomorrow, no consideration for family, no dignity!"

Danilo was about to speak. Then something struck him. ". . . Lord Pirro . . . *was?*"

The Regent looked up sharply.

"Are you deaf, man?"

"But . . ."

"I said *was*.

"But . . ."

"Pirro is dead!"

DANILO WANDERED THE CORRIDORS, STUNNED.

The Regent had been clear. "I don't even know where the body is, in some damned wilderness. Brazil, or somewhere. Lost up some creek or river. Natives speared him to death and ate him, for all I know. The Spanish or Portuguese Viceroy, or whatever he is called, sent us back a few of his belongings. The dead don't speak, the dead can't speak, and the dead have no rights."

Danilo wandered, aimless, past busts and tapestries and frescoes. There were no servants in view. It was a cold place and a frigid parting.

Lord Pirro, that gallant young man, dead . . . But he would not have been young. Not anymore. But he would be forever young for Danilo, who knew him no other way. Pirro had been so full of energy and self-confidence, so generous and gallant to Danilo. So Pirro had probably never learned the truth, never learned his son was alive.

The song Pirro had written for Grazia came back to Danilo now. He hummed a few bars. He could still see Pirro's smile and hear his voice. Danilo stood, staring into space. He knew what Angelica would say: "Lord Pirro is not really dead, Danilo; he lives on in his son, he lives on in you."

The sky was gray, snow drifted down from above. The wind was rising, the walls of the palace seemed barren and hostile, the windows blank and forbidding. Whatever the cost, he must find a way to reclaim—or purchase—his mother's portrait. It was the only thing he had that belonged to her, aside from her *Secret Book*. The snow fell harder. He was not fond of snow, particularly after barely surviving the avalanche that had almost destroyed the Sultan's army; and worse, the avalanche that had claimed poor Andreas and little Achilles. Snow was a bad omen. Then he noticed a slender figure, a woman with her hood up; she had come out of a doorway and was headed towards him.

Sappho.

"SIGNOR DANILO, I HEARD you were here." She smiled the familiar warm rich smile; her features had sharpened, her black skin was lustrous, her teeth bright. Her figure had grown tall and willowy; she was even more beautiful than before.

"Sappho. It is good to see you."

"I heard the Regent was going to send you away."

"For them, I am nobody and nothing."

"I am sorry. I know how much Isabella wanted to have you as part of the family."

"Well, my dear Sappho, that is part of the past now. Some things are best given up."

"Perhaps . . ." She paused. "I apologize, Signor Danilo, but I have a question for you."

"What is it?"

They began to walk, side by side. He offered his arm. She took it.

"The Duke has freed me, well, the Regent arranged it—notarized my freedom."

"He didn't sell you?"

"No, he just said they didn't want me."

"Ah, so . . ."

"So I am cast out, on my own, and . . ."

"You don't know what to do."

"No."

"We are a fine pair, aren't we?"

"I shouldn't have bothered you."

Danilo looked down at the ground. He was being utterly insensitive. How horrible it must be for her. His own problems were trivial. What must she feel? Purchased in the slave market of Venice when just a child, she had no memory of where she was born or who her parents were; transported to Mantua, and trained by Isabella to be a toy, a pet, a performer, and now . . . He turned to her. "I have an idea."

Sappho looked at him doubtfully.

"Why do you not come with us? I'm not sure it will come to anything, but perhaps—perhaps we can find you work."

"Work?"

"You would earn your keep, have friends, and a family."

She hesitated. She looked up at the sky. "It is getting cold."

"Will you come?"

She gazed up at the castle walls and shivered. "This has been my home since, well, since I can remember. But now I have no friends here. They have all been sent away. I still have some friends outside—Ansaldo and Signor Ciecherella—but they can't show their favor too openly lest they offend the Regents. Everywhere in Mantua there are averted faces, and nervous glances, or people—nice people—crossing the street to avoid greeting me lest the Regents get angry with them. I remind the Regents of Isabella, which is not a good thing."

"And so?"

"I'm thinking . . ."

"You're thinking!" Danilo laughed. "Look, Angelica is here with me, the actors are in Padua; you can join them there. You have many talents, do you not?"

"I can sing, dance, recite . . ."

"Well, then?"

She smiled. "Yes. I will come."

6 7

DUTY CALLS

Venice

MIRIAMNE KNELT BY THE BED AND PUT A COLD CLOTH on her brother's forehead. Mordecai gasped for breath. He was covered in sores and bleeding from the mouth. He had lost some of his teeth; much of his hair had fallen out. He was dying. He had been such a beautiful young man, such a wit, so playful and generous and funny, and he was her brother. Up until a few years ago she had adored him, without any reservation. But now . . .

Death was close.

But somehow Mordecai lingered on . . .

Miriamne had to look after him. Her duty was here, with her family. Danilo was a dream. Seeing him in his ridiculous makeup and costume had been like an illusion, a hallucination of happiness, a parody. Exchanging letters with him had been a delight, once again sharing thoughts, little jokes, passing fancies. But . . . Danilo was life as it *could* be, not as it *should* be.

She must be loyal to her roots, to her duty, however painful it was. She would write to Angelica: *"He is yours. I must stay here. Sometimes one must abandon one's dreams!"*

She stood up and glanced out the window. Frost had touched the trees. The leaves spiraled down, out of sight. Winter had come so quickly. Only weeks ago it had been like midsummer. Tonight would be bitterly cold. She must make sure everyone was warm, had enough to eat, and was comfortable. She had to see to Jessica and to Jacob. They were growing up, but they still needed care and love. She had to see to her father. Everyone needed care—even Mordecai. Duty, after all, was duty, and her duty was clear.

68

SAPPHO

Mantua

ANGELICA PICKED UP HER FORK. "WELL, IF THAT IS THE WAY these stupid Gonzagas are going to behave, then there is no place for you here. Don't fret about it—with Isabella and Pirro gone, the Gonzagas don't deserve you!"

She cut into her roast lamb with gusto.

"I'm not fretting. I am angry. I feel betrayed." Danilo pushed food around his plate.

"I understand. But my dear, life must continue. Now your way is clear. You have Miriamne, and you have Samuel Mendes and the Mendes Bank. Come, eat your supper, and we shall decide what to do."

"As always, you are the voice of wisdom." Danilo touched her hand. He stared at his food.

She chewed, then sighed. "No appetite?"

"I am a fool." He poked at a hunk of delicious-looking crusty bread. It was soaked with warm, steaming gravy.

"Where then, dearest, is your dunce's cap?"

He mimed a mournful smile. "I lost it." He made a face.

"Impossible child!" Angelica tapped her fingers on the table. Melancholy was not part of her repertoire. "Well, darling," she said as she raised another slice of lamb to her mouth, "we need a plan."

"A plan . . . a plan . . ." He speared a hunk of lamb with his knife and gazed at it. "This was once a living thing."

"Yes, it was."

"Probably only hours ago."

"Yes, if it's fresh."

"Now, it is just meat."

"Yes, Danilo. Life is brief. Life is cruel. Life is not necessarily just. The predators prey upon their prey and then the predators become prey to other predators, and so on."

Carefully, daintily, she leaned forward, bit into the meat dangling from the end of his knife, and slid it into her mouth. She swallowed, and licked her lips. "Eat, dear Danilo, eat. You will need your strength." She piled more vegetables onto her plate, and another hunk of lamb, then growled and ordered him to eat, piece by piece. "Eat that! And now that piece! Now that! Good boy!"

THAT NIGHT, DANILO AND Angelica slept at the inn in a room with an empty fireplace and windows that had turned to shimmering crystal because of the frost. Angelica had piled furs and blankets over the bed.

"Cold," she said as she slid, still wearing a shift and furs, into the bed.

Danilo followed her. He had not undressed. They huddled against each other for warmth, both of them wearing woolen caps.

"This is strangely intimate, Danilo, but I do prefer it when we are wearing no clothes at all."

"So do I."

"And I love it when it is so warm that we melt into the air and the air melts into us, and every breath we take is pure pleasure, and when the flowers spill all of their perfumes into the air. And we can run about like nymphs and satyrs, and do marvelous, mischievous, naked things without a thought for tomorrow."

"Yes."

"And what does it smell like now?"

"It smells like cold ash, wet wood, old greasepaint, and . . . and stale human sweat."

"Yes, stale human sweat, grown cold."

"And cow dung and horse dung because we are next to the stables."

"Oh, that is so romantic! I know, Danilo, that I will lose you, and that I must lose you. But I do not want to lose you."

The two of them were silent, clinging to each other like the chaste orphans they were.

Danilo told Angelica he had seen Sappho.

"Of course, I know her. She is superb. Isabella had her trained by the best teachers. Talented . . . Danilo! She is exactly what the troupe needs—exotic, beautiful, and funny."

"That had occurred to me too," said Danilo.

Angelica drew back. "This was your intention all along! You are becoming devious and even calculating, my dear innocent, wide-eyed Danilo." She kissed him on the cheek. "We actors have robbed you of your virginity."

IN THE MORNING, SNOW was falling. Angelica looked out the window and up at the sky, shuddered, and exclaimed, "How gloomy, how dreadful!"

They were in the midst of breakfast, mugs of dark ale, a sort of minestrone soup, and thick chunks of bread, when Sappho entered. She was stylishly dressed, standing as straight as a guardsman. She shook the snow from her shoulders. "Signor Danilo, I have come, as you suggested I should."

Danilo stood, went to her, and took her by the hand. "You remember Angelica."

Angelica stood and reached out her arms.

The two women embraced, then Angelica stepped back. "Let me look at you, marvelous Sappho. It has been too long since we played and sang together.

"Yes, far too long, Signora Angelica." Her eyes sparkled, her bright lips shone.

"Call me Angelica, Sappho. The 'signora' makes me feel too important and too old; and you are free now, no longer a servant, and no longer a slave."

"Thank you, Angelica."

"So, you will come to Padua with us, and you will join the troupe, and you and I will be acting and singing and dancing together. Is that a good idea?"

"That is an excellent idea!"

"Let us show Danilo what we can do, shall we? He doubts, sometimes, that I have any talent at all."

"That's outrageous, Angelica! I never said or thought any such thing!" Danilo snorted. "You have been my teacher and my guiding star!"

Angelica winked at Sappho. "Start us off, will you?"

Sappho sang an exquisite rendering of Jacopo da Fogliano's "The Love, my Lady, I bear for you." After a few verses, Angelica put her arm around Sappho's waist and joined her in singing. The two women sang so well, and harmonized so perfectly, looking into each other's eyes, it seemed as if they had spent years practicing this very song.

Angelica laughed and took Sappho by the arm. "We are leaving in a few hours. Do you have much in the way of baggage?"

"Just a carpetbag, mostly clothes and a few books, because I was told I had to leave, but I had no idea where I was to leave for."

"Padua! Is that agreeable? Good, but let me warn you, Sappho, life on the road is not like life at court."

"I am quite aware of that, Angelica!" Sappho laughed.

Danilo watched with fascination. The warmth between Angelica and Sappho made him, for some reason, especially happy. And then he thought about the Little Duke. He and his Regents were liquidating everything that reminded them of Isabella d'Este, the Little Duke's grandmother. She was being erased from history. Strange were the ways of men — and of children and of aristocrats and rulers. Danilo wanted to remember his family, or families; the child-Duke wanted to forget his.

Or, at least, the Regents wanted him to forget.

69

DESTINY

Padua

AFTER A THREE-DAY TRIP, ANGELICA, DANILO, AND SAPPHO arrived in Padua to join the other actors.

Angelica and Danilo were in their room unpacking when Danilo received a letter from Miriamne. She announced she must give him up. Duty called. She had to look after her father and her brother and all the other people she felt responsible for in the Ghetto. Danilo turned ash-gray and sat down. He held out the letter as if it were a dangerous weapon; he stared at it.

Angelica exploded. She strode up and down. "This is nonsense! Miriamne has no right to sacrifice herself like this! Danilo, you write right back to her and tell her you are not going to accept this, that you are going to be hers, and she is going to be yours. And that we are going to arrange this as quickly as possible. No delays, no excuses, no shillyshally! You hear me?!"

"Yes, I shall write to her now."

"Even better, why don't you go straight to Venice and talk to her yourself."

"Is there time?"

"Of course there's time. We are not performing for two weeks, so this is the best of times. From Padua to Venice is no distance at all!"

Danilo held her and kissed her. It was very strange to be embracing and thanking a woman who had been his lover and whom he loved, and who was pushing him into the arms of another woman.

"Yes, yes! I know. I'm an angel. While you are reassuring Miriamne, I shall introduce Sappho to our routines and our scripts. She and I will develop some material designed just for her, perhaps something about damsels in distress and pirates and crusades and dragons or something. Meantime, we are all going to have dinner. I am starving!"

Pietro entered the room, "Danilo, here is a note from Samuel Mendes. He is waiting for you in the dining room."

Angelica grinned. "You see! The fates are conspiring against you! No more dithering, no more ratiocination! See, Danilo, I told you, it is the time for action and for love. You must now seize your destiny!"

Danilo left Angelica and Sappho and the others in the main dining room and stepped off into a curtained side alcove, where he knew Samuel Mendes was waiting.

Samuel was seated at an oak table with two mugs of wine and plates of boiled eggs, smoked fish, bread, and cheese.

Samuel stood up and embraced Danilo, then they sat down. Samuel pushed a plate of food and a mug of wine towards Danilo. "We need you now. We cannot wait any longer. The only truly safe place for Jews is in the Ottoman Empire. The Muslims, for the moment, are our only sure allies and our only recourse."

"What is involved?" Danilo took a deep drink of wine. He had been just about to ride off to claim Miriamne, and now a new stage in his life was about to begin; an abyss was opening under his feet. "If this job involves going back to Istanbul, I'd be putting not only myself at risk, but my father and . . ."

"I know all that." Samuel took a long drink of wine. "You go in disguise. You face the dangers. The Men in Black are not magicians. You are cleverer than they are. You clarify things with your father."

Through the curtain they could hear Angelica and Sappho singing a delicate romantic song, while someone—probably Ajax—accompanied them on the lute. "Who is that singing with Angelica?"

"Sappho."

"They sing like angels."

"Sappho was trained by Isabella d'Este. She believes she may be Ethiopian, but she really has no idea who or what she is. She was taken by pirates when very young, and bought on the slave market. The d'Este family has an eye for beauty and talent."

"That is true. The d'Este family, since it has ruled Ferrara, has also, as you know, been a great friend to the Jews and the New Christians. But now nowhere is safe, not even Ferrara."

"I realize that."

Samuel picked up a piece of bread and broke it into pieces. "Recently, when Jews were driven out of the Spanish Empire, and when the Inquisition burned secret Jews—New Christians like me—like firewood in the squares of Spain and Portugal, the Sultan allowed those who escaped to find refuge in the Ottoman Empire."

"I know. I attended the Ahrida Synagogue in Istanbul. There are many Sephardic communities in Istanbul."

"Well, as you know, in the Sultan's eyes there is no difference between Christians and Jews; all are non-Muslims, therefore inferior. Though we Jews and Christians, unlike pagans, are for Muslims 'People of the Book,' which gives us some status." Samuel took another deep swallow of wine, and worked on the bread and cheese. "Right now, we need somebody who has direct access to Suleiman. We have to set up the headquarters of the Mendes Bank in Istanbul, beyond the reach of the Inquisition and blackmail. It's urgent—we have no time to lose."

"You want me to approach the Sultan?" Danilo laughed. "He probably thinks I planned to poison him."

"No. We don't want you to approach the Sultan. I am thinking of your father." Samuel paused. "Doctor del Medigo has direct access to the Sultan."

"I'm sure my father hates me. I am sure he doesn't understand why I left him without a word."

"He might understand."

"No, no. He must believe that I was—that I am—a traitor." Danilo hesitated, then lifted the mug to his lips. "It's the only way to protect him. He must have nothing to do with me."

"I think it's time you and your father made up. Reconciliation is overdue."

"How?"

"As I said, you travel secretly to Istanbul. You have learned how to disguise yourself, have you not?"

"Life isn't theater."

"I'm not so sure, Danilo. Life is often theater. I never stop playing a role, nor does my aunt. She plays at being Beatrice de Luna when in reality she is Grazia Nasi."

Danilo leaned back. He toyed with a piece of bread. He tapped his fingers on the table. Raucous sounds came from next door. Angelica and Sappho had moved on to reciting naughty verse, taking turns with the lines, probably acting them out. The other actors and customers at the inn were laughing uproariously. Danilo thought of Miriamne. She should be here, she needed to be saved from sacrificing herself to her brother, to her father, to her sense of duty . . .

"You have to face your past sometime, Danilo. You can't keep running forever. And if you carry out this mission for us, there will be many advantages."

"Which are?"

"You will have exciting work! You will have money, lots of it. You will be able to buy the portrait of your mother you told me about. In fact, I can acquire it for the Mendes Bank and hold it for you."

"That's very kind."

"And then there is Miriamne."

Danilo leaned back. Miriamne was in Venice, but her presence here in this room was palpable. He could hear her voice as she fiercely confronted him and argued a point, feel the delicate softness of her hands when she touched him, see the bright gloss of her lips and her brilliant smile . . . No, he must not let her throw herself away out of a sense of duty. He had to save her. He must leave for Venice immediately.

"Establishing the bank in Istanbul with the Sultan's protection is worth a great deal to us. Your work with Angelica has already been extraordinary. It is amazing the access you actors have. And it's a very different access from that of merchants and bankers—or even diplomats."

Danilo laughed. "Cardinals and even popes are less guarded when they are talking to actors, particularly to an actress like Angelica."

"You see!" Samuel smiled and leaned back. "If you work for the Mendes Bank you can rescue Miriamne and marry her, and even make sure the troupe has some security, and that Angelica and the others are not risking starvation or worse." Samuel paused. "In fact, I will do this: whatever happens, Miriamne's future will be assured, brilliantly assured. I personally shall see to it. We at the Mendes Bank have many friends, powerful friends. And I think you know that. So, what is it to be? Are you with us?"

Danilo picked up a trencher. "I need to chew on this."

"Chew."

Angelica stuck her head around the corner. "Signor Mendes, have you finished torturing our dear Danilo?"

Samuel laughed. "Yes, I do believe I have." He rose.

Danilo laid a hand on Samuel's sleeve. "I'll do it," he said.

7 0

LINGERING AT
TWILIGHT

Venice

THE SENATOR WAS SITTING ON A STONE BENCH IN THE lowering sun on the riva degli Schiavoni, just off the Piazzetta of San Marco. The stone was warm, and from here he could gaze out on Saint Mark's Basin and watch the warships and merchantmen and gondolas as they passed by. It was one of his favorite places.

"Sit with me, Marco." The Senator patted the space next to him. "Old men, like lizards, love to sit in the sun." He closed his eyes. "You want to feel a little warmth, even if it's only skin-deep."

Marco sat down.

The Senator gazed at the ships and, just beyond the crowded shipping lane, at the *Isola San Giorgio*—the Island of Saint George—and its immense monastery. He sighed. "So . . .

How long has it taken for Venice to build its empire? One thousand years?" He paused, and then answered his own question. "Maybe more. You know, Marco, an old man wants something to remain of himself, of what he has done, of what he has built."

Marco contemplated the old man. With his sun-burnished skin, the Senator looked as if he had been sculpted out of mahogany. His thin, handsome face, marked by many battles and many decades, was beautiful—yes, there was no other word for it—beautiful. It was impossible to think that the Senator might die one day. He seemed immortal.

"Look around you, Marco. Venice is still building. Piazza San Marco is far from finished. And the Arsenal is in the middle of a massive construction program, building more and more warships. We have recovered from our recent wars. We still have much to do, much that we must do. But I sometimes wonder what is to become of us." The Senator nodded towards three fashionable, brightly painted gondolas passing by. "I wonder if we are becoming decadent. Look at that: rich people showing off, displaying their wealth, sometimes even with Black African gondoliers because they are exotic and handsome and fashionable. And then we have patrician women traipsing around in platform shoes so high they can hardly stand up. And they have parties galore, and furniture and furnishings more luxurious every year." The Senator laughed.

Marco nodded. "The poor are not so happy seeing all this display of wealth and arrogance."

"Ostentation by the rich is bad for the Republic. People must feel they are part of the Republic, that in some sense we are all equal, all part of a family. I have in mind to introduce a sumptuary law stipulating that all gondolas must be painted black. That would put an end to this competitive flashiness." The Senator chuckled. "And weddings, the cost of weddings has become outrageous! Just to show off! And then you have women lounging in the sun, using the sunlight to bleach their hair blond. My granddaughter does it. Well, fashions come and go."

Marco nodded. "Perhaps the patrician women are bored, sequestered at home. It is a sterile life—servants and slaves do all the work and look after the children. Little is left for the lady of the house. And many of them are well-educated, highly intelligent, and curious about life. They are restless, they need to do something."

"If I had my way, Marco, upper-class women would be free to work. The only women who can do anything are lower-class women, who work, often at very hard jobs with long hours; or courtesans, who, if they are successful and protected, can do what they like and hold salons and write poetry. Perhaps a woman like Veronica Libero is in the best position of all."

"She is exceptional."

"Veronica is an admirable woman, an asset to the Republic. She keeps her finger on the pulse. She knows what's what. You know, Marco, when the elite get out of touch, ordinary folk wonder who the Republic is for, and that is dangerous. And we fob them off with heroes and saints, tales of derring-do, religious processions, marvelous paintings and architecture, and so on. If the truth were known, many of our forefathers were thugs . . . we looted and stole our way through the East. Those horses up there on Saint Mark's, they were robbed from Constantinople. And the winged lion, the beautiful bronze statue, the symbol of Venice itself, it was carried off from somewhere in Turkey, so they say. We Venetians are busy magpies. We steal from everybody's nest. Even our architecture is a wild mix of borrowings—Medieval, Romanesque, Gothic, Byzantine, and Classical. The body of Saint Mark himself was purloined from Alexandria under the nose of the Egyptians. Amusing story, that—hidden under a shipment of pork so the Muslims held their noses and refused to inspect the cargo. We like to tell ourselves how clever we are."

"People need myths and fairy tales."

"Indeed. And frauds are not frauds if people believe in them—then they are myths and religions!" The Senator pointed at a passing war galley—the rhythm of the gleaming oars smoothly rising and falling; the big, triangular, lateen sail just beginning to billow out. It was a low, sleek ship armed with cannon fore and aft, with a metal prow that could ram and sink virtually any conceivable enemy galley. "We used to row our own war galleys, fight our own battles. Now we rely on slaves or mercenaries."

"You have fought, haven't you, Senator? You don't talk about it much."

The Senator laughed. "I'll babble at home, with the family. Play the garrulous old man, if I've had a glass or two too many, or for my great-grandchildren. Children these days love guts and gore and scary, bloody things. I tell them about eyes gouged out, arms hacked off, legs blown away, villains drawn-and-quartered or beheaded, and boys and girls in chains and sold into slavery. It puts them to sleep."

"They will make good warriors."

The Senator laughed. "Yes, Livia, the little girl, would make a wonderful warrior. She is nine years old and as blood-thirsty as they come. Beautiful too."

Marco nodded. Crowds of people were passing by. Farther down, on the quay, vendors shouted out the virtues of their wares. Women and servants—blond men and women, slaves from the eastern steppes—were shopping. Some haggled over prices, weights, quality. People stopped to gossip. Two distinguished gentlemen nodded discreetly to the Senator.

"The populace are like children, Marco. They need entertainment, spectacle, and heroes. So we give them Evil versus Good, simplified fairy tales. Venice is a republic, not a monarchy. We need entertainment to keep people distracted, to give them a sense of belonging. But you must excuse me. I am rattling on. Old men like to talk about when, once upon a time, they were important, or thought they were."

"You are still a power in the Republic, Senator, perhaps one of the greatest."

"That is very kind of you, Marco. I do worry about the future. Suleiman will nibble away at us. He will lop off bits and pieces: a colony, an island, a naval base. He didn't get Corfu, which was a godsend, and in part, thanks to some good intelligence, we were prepared. If he had taken Corfu, Italy, the Papacy, and quite possibly Venice would have been doomed. We are on the defensive here. We are not the only clever ones, Marco, not by a long shot."

"I would prefer it if we were."

The Senator laughed. "So would I, Marco, so would I! Well, I must leave you. Veronica Libero has some interesting guests this evening, some German and Egyptian merchants, a Spaniard, and even an Englishman. The English King, Henry VIII, is building a navy, and spending a lot of gold on it. I'm curious to have the latest news on that, particularly the shipbuilding technologies they are developing. The Atlantic is the future, Marco, the Atlantic—mark my words!"

The Senator stood and put a hand on Marco's shoulder. "Now that young Danilo del Medigo is setting off on his own for the Mendes Bank, we must be sure the Jewess, Miriamne, is looked after and protected, and ready for him on his return. We don't want any untoward incidents, do we?"

"We are keeping a close watch on Miriamne and her unhappy brother." Marco knew the Senator knew about Vincenzo and his two clever nieces, Melania and Mika, and Vincenzo's messenger boy, Filippo, and how they kept an eye on the Ghetto for the Service, reporting every movement, every day.

"And Marco, we must make sure Angelica is safe now that Danilo will no longer be at her side. She is, as you have said yourself, an important—what is the word?—an important *asset.*"

"Yes, Senator, I shall watch over her. And she has Pietro."

"I do want the young woman to be happy. Happiness makes for stability. Has she a new love interest? She does deserve some human warmth."

Marco bit his lip, looked down, and nodded.

"Ah, so she has a new friend. Already? Let us see!" The Senator closed his eyes. "No, don't tell me, let me guess. Rather dark, and quite beautiful, exotic. Curious, always knows every-thing about everything. Tall, willowy, a talented entertainer, trained by Isabella d'Este. This new friend was once a slave, like Angelica, and bought, like Angelica, on the slave market in Venice. Am I right? This new friend is a young woman, and she is one of your, shall I say, contacts?"

Marco sighed, looked up, and nodded.

"Ah well, we shall not tell the priests and the good friars about this particular friendship; some of them have little patience for the natural diversity of human desire, which is strange, when you think of it."

"Why strange?"

"The founder of their religion was rather understanding of the vagaries of desire. And certainly he was not as obsessed with sex as his followers, hardly ever talked about it, in fact." The Senator bowed. "Well, Marco, we shall meet again soon. It is always a pleasure. And thank you for listening to the ramb-lings of an old man." The Senator saluted and headed off down the riva degli Schiavoni.

Marco watched the Senator until he was lost in the crowd. A light dawned: the Senator had arranged for Andreas Satti to purchase Angelica so many years ago; and she had been edu-cated and trained, without ever knowing the source, through the Senator, and prepared for her mission. And then Sappho, an exquisite child, had been purchased in Venice, also through the offices of Andreas Satti. Sappho had been trained by Isabella d'Este and private tutors, in calligraphy, languages, and the arts of charm and seduction. She was famous for always know-ing everything that was going on in Mantua, everything about the Gonzaga and the d'Este dynasties, and she had been a very useful asset indeed. Why hadn't he thought of it before? Marco laughed. The Senator had arranged the purchase and education of both Angelica and Sappho—and then for their liberation! Marco nodded, chuckling. He looked up. A child, her finger in her mouth, was staring at him, wide-eyed, visibly wondering: who is that crazy man who is talking to himself? Well, perhaps he was crazy. His life, in a sense, had been an illusion. He'd always thought *he* was the recruiter, the puppet master, but . . . It had always been the Senator.

The little girl had taken her finger out of her mouth. She smiled at him and turned away, skipping down the riva degli Schiavoni following her mother, who turned and called, "Come on, Grazia! Don't dawdle!" Marco nodded to himself. Life was strange.

The war galley that had just passed in front of the riva degli Schiavoni had swung around and come to a stop, banners flying, oars up, sails folded. Now it fired off all its cannons in a salute. The salvoes boomed across the Basin of Saint Mark, echoed off the Doge's Palace, and down the Grand Canal. Flags and streamers and pennants waved from other boats, merchantmen, and warships, and a flotilla of bright gondolas was gathering in homage to the glory that was the Most Serene Republic—*la Serenissima*—to the magnificence and grandeur of the myth, known to all throughout the world, as Venice.

ISTANBUL

7 1

LA DONZELLA

C LAD IN THE BILLOWING TROUSERS AND BROCADE KAFTAN
of a silk merchant, with his hair dyed black, his skin
stained walnut, and his beard tinted a pepper-and-
salt mix, Danilo del Medigo—now known as Bekir Ahmed—
watched Venice recede as the merchant galley *La Donzella*—The
Damsel—headed towards the passage through the Lido that
would take it out of the Venetian lagoon and into the open,
sparkling Adriatic Sea. In the offing, in the direction of distant
Dalmatia and the Balkans, a storm was visible moving across
the glittering sunlit water, and heading towards *La Donzella*.

Danilo leaned against the railing. It was 300 miles from Venice
to the Dalmatian port of Ragusa. In normal times, the voyage
should take seven to ten days, depending on the weather. He
glanced westward and shaded his eyes from the lowering sun.
Silhouetted against the light, people moved about on deck, merchants, pilgrims, and a few families voyaging to visit relatives.

The galley was carrying about 250 passengers, one of the
seamen had informed him, and was freighted mainly with

· 615 ·

textiles—specialized woven-silk products, bales of wool, brocades—and some furniture and art, Venetian glassware, and barrels of wine. They were bound for Ragusa, a rich and independent trading city halfway down the east shore of the Adriatic, and which had once been a Venetian possession and now kept its independence by paying a tribute to Suleiman and his Ottoman Empire. The ship was about 160 feet long, Danilo had estimated as he paced the deck, and about 40 feet wide where the beam was broadest. It rode low in the water, heavily laden with merchandise and people, and ballasted with sand, gravel, and weaponry—cannons, wheels, and shells, ordinance for the defense of Ragusa.

His leave-taking had been emotional. Sappho held Danilo's hands and stared into his eyes. "You saved my life, Signor Danilo, you really did!" She rose up on her tiptoes and kissed him on both cheeks.

Angelica, strangely, seemed to be the person least moved by his imminent departure. She had helped him pack, as she had so often done before. "Now Danilo, you must begin to prepare for your new life!" She said this with a bright smile, though Danilo did notice a catch in her voice when she pronounced the word "new." "You must not take any excessive risks. It will be cold; you must take that jacket I bought you."

When she was helping him pack, Angelica had insisted he see Miriamne in Venice. "Yes, I am going to do that. I have arranged everything," he said. Angelica put her hands on her hips. "You must keep your word to her, Danilo."

"It is sacred." He smiled. "You two women, or should I say you three women—you, Sappho, and Miriamne—it's like you are sisters, and all ganging up on me."

"Sisters? We are the furies!" Angelica laughed that fresh and youthful laugh that made Danilo realize, yet again, how much beauty and goodness there still was in the world.

She insisted on seeing him off when he got into the coach that would take him to the barge stop for Venice. Sappho came with her. They had become inseparable. As the coach raced away, with Danilo riding on top, he glanced back, straining to keep them in view. The two women became smaller and smaller, shrinking away. Angelica waved. Sappho waved. The coach turned a corner into a lane of shimmering white poplars, and they were gone—in all of their lives a page had been turned.

The wake of *La Donzella* was a triangle of rippling silver spreading out behind the stern, catching the sunlight in a vibrant shimmering net that fanned out towards the horizon. The lateen sail snapped in the breeze and swung slowly around; the oars rose and fell. The even, unchanging rhythms, the unbroken pulse, could make a man fall asleep. The sunlight, the warm breeze, the dazzling movement, and the crisscrossing glittering patterns—Danilo shaded his eyes against the brilliance. He went to a bench and sat down, blinking at the brightness of it all.

The Lido, the great sandbank that protected Venice's lagoon from the sea, approached. Danilo could make out the buildings and the fishing villages, the gardens and trees.

La Donzella slipped through a channel between two ridges of sand, and it was out in the Adriatic. Suddenly, the waves were crisper and higher; they drummed rhythmically, crashing, splashing thuds, as the galley rode over and cut through them, white spray flashing past the bow.

Venice disappeared, and behind Venice, the great flat valley of the Po had long vanished, with all its canals and rivers, and its vast, rich farmlands and huge industrial and trading wealth. Its brilliant and varied cultures and cities—Mantua, Ferrara, Verona, Padua, Milan—with all their cathedrals, palaces, statues, castles, ramparts, and winding little streets, disappeared.

The wind was up. Danilo turned his face to it. It was stronger now, whipping up foamy, striated whitecaps. To the northwest, he glimpsed the mountains—the snow-capped Alps. They hung dreamily in the air like a great stone wall, towering far beyond the low green-and-gold sandbank of the Lido. The lowering sun lit up the white peaks like some vast backdrop for a magical stage production. Yes, those were the Alps!

And beyond the Alps lay another world—northern Europe and Austria and all the ancient cities of Germany, the center of the Holy Roman Empire, which was ruled by the very Catholic Charles V.

Charles V was proving himself everywhere the enemy of Jews and New Christians. Danilo could understand: Charles was a worried man, fighting desperately for supremacy on three fronts; against Suleiman and the Ottoman Empire to the east, King François I of France to the west, and the growing Protestant revolt within his vast empire to the north.

The Jews and New Christians, and the small independent city states of Italy, were caught in the middle of this struggle between the great powers, between Christendom and Islam, Catholics and Protestants, François I and Charles V. In this world in turmoil, the Jews and the New Christians were easy prey and tempting scapegoats.

What was it that Samuel Mendes had said? All the world was theater? Was it a theater of the mad?

In this great drama, everyone was playing his or her part: Samuel Mendes, Beatrice de Luna, Angelica, the spymaster Marco, the mysterious Senator for whom Marco apparently worked, Pietro the messenger, Sappho with her multiple talents. And then there was Pietro Aretino, the playwright, polemicist, and libertine; and la Zufolina; and Titian and Celeste Volpe; and Veronica Libero and Zarah; and the courtesans who worked for Veronica, spying for the Most Serene Republic of Venice as it fought for survival among new, giant, and hungry world powers with more wealth, vastly bigger armies, and rapidly expanding navies. All the currents of commerce and wealth were shifting away from Venice. And yet *la Serenissima* refused to give in, refused to cede. She was determined to survive.

And then, the Jews . . . struggling everywhere just to live . . . hemmed in, exploited, hated, vilified, murdered, despoiled of everything, burned at the stake, expelled from cities that had been their homes for hundreds of years. The great disaster of the Inquisition was spreading like a plague, and with it, hatred of Jews was also spreading like a plague. Danilo and Angelica, in their travels, had seen the hatred and fear growing. The brave, creative, licentious world of Aretino, la Zufolina, Veronica Libero and Zarah, Titian and Leonardo, and Isabella d'Este was doomed. Fear and hate were overwhelming tolerance and freedom.

Danilo closed his eyes and let himself melt into the rippling wind and the sun and the thump, thump, thump of *La Donzella* striking the waves. This was the very sea across which Suleiman and his Muslim army had attempted to invade Italy, and they would attempt perhaps again, and again, and again. It would not end well; none of it would end well. Fear would reign in Europe. The Inquisition would burn books; it would burn men, women, and children at the stake. It would poison hearts and minds, urging everyone to spy on everyone else; sister would turn against sister, brother against brother, son against father, wife against husband. The Inquisition would pry into the deepest recesses of consciousness. Nothing would be private, nothing would be sacred. The hatred, once freed from all limits of civilization and decorum, would know no limits. What had that cardinal told Angelica in Naples? He had said that there would be religious war for one hundred years?

The sea squall was closer. The waves were higher, splashing the deck, spray breaking, silver sparkles in the light. The sails snapped tightly as *La Donzella* raced to outrun the rain and wind and flashes of lightning.

Then there was Miriamne.

Miriamne was dark and deep, a stormy passionate beauty, even if good-humored. She was rooted in a community, in a particular place. Everyone in the Ghetto knew Miriamne and everyone admired and loved her, though some of the more conservative thought she was too free and easy, too eager to experience the delights of Venice — too Venetian, too intellectual and poetic, and too well-known and celebrated, famous even, for a modest Jewish girl. But even as a poet and writer, Miriamne was rooted in a time and a place.

In contrast, Angelica, the girl from a village in Illyria, was a vagabond, always on the move, always smiling, hardly ever stormy, and her family, the company of actors, was on the move too, nomads trekking through sun and rain, mountain and plain. Angelica moved fluidly, like a dancer and, when she wished, she strode like a warrior or cavorted like a boy. Angelica was like the breeze—and as far as religious beliefs went she didn't seem to have time for them, though she did wear that little golden cross, went to mass, and confessed regularly. When once they had discussed it, she had said she preferred the ancient philosophers to the Biblical prophets; that she'd seen too much of religion, and of priests, to take any of it seriously; that she'd seen too much of men—and people in general—to take them seriously either.

Miriamne was proud to be a Jewess, defiant, never hesitating to look someone in the eye and challenge them if she detected the slightest hint of disdain or hatred for her Judaism. And she was, as she had affirmed to him more than once, a Venetian. "I am Venetian to the core, Danilo. I adore Venice. I love listening to the dialects; each *sestiere* or neighbourhood of the city has its own way of speaking. Did you know that? And I adore the paintings and the buildings, and walking the *calles* and the *fondamenti* and the alleyways and the canal-side walkways; I love Piazza San Marco, and the Piazzetta, and the sight of all the ships coming and going. Do you know, I actually get a little shiver when I hear the bells of the *Campanile* of San Marco? I feel in my blood and in my flesh and bones all the people hurrying to work, the apprentices, the craftsmen, the bricklayers, the seamstresses, the merchants, the bankers, the pawnbrokers and moneylenders, the fishmongers . . . It is a whole world, and it is my world!"

When he had gone to the Ghetto, he had told Miriamne that the time had come, that if she wanted him he was hers. He had to leave on a secret mission, but he would return soon, to her, this time without fail. He would happily live with her in the Ghetto, and he would help her care for her father and for Mordecai, for Jessica and Jacob.

"But . . ."

He silenced her with a kiss.

It was the first time he had kissed her. Her eyes were wide and glossy. A single tear ran down her cheek; it caught the light.

She leaned in and kissed him back—a deep, passionate, true kiss, a covenant. "But Danilo, what will you do for money?"

"I am going to be working."

She drew back, just a bit, and returned to her pert skeptical manner. "Acting?"

"No, not acting. Though acting may be involved."

"Really?"

"I am, it seems, to become a banker."

"A banker! Oh, how horrible!" She laughed. "I suppose bankers are actors."

"They are indeed!" He put his hands around her waist— her beautiful, supple, slender waist. "I wish to marry you—if you agree, that is."

"Let me think."

"You have to think?"

"As I told you, as I wrote to you, I have my father to look after, and my brother. As you know, Mordecai is ill and . . ."

"Well, I offer my services to help you look after your father, and even Mordecai. I shall be at your side."

"You will help?"

"Yes, I will—you will not be alone. Your father, in fact . . ."

"I know—father adores you. Once he learned what you had sacrificed to protect us, how you had to become a fugitive, and an actor, and . . ."

Danilo brushed his lips against hers. "He has given his consent . . ."

Miriamne gazed at him for a long time. "Well, if father agrees, I must say that, after much due consideration," she looked up at him through her eyelashes, "and having looked at the problem from all possible angles, I do believe I am ready to accept."

Danilo laughed. "So is that a yes?"

"That is a yes." She gazed at him. "Kiss me."

He did. It lasted for quite a while. A kiss, Danilo had learned, could be a conversation, a long, loving, challenging, wonderfully sensual conversation. Who needed words when you had this?

Danilo took a deep breath. "Tomorrow then, at the morning service, we shall become man and wife. I have spoken to your father. The contracts are ready to be signed. And your father has the witnesses, elders from the synagogue, who are eager to be part of it."

"Really? You men all got together—even the elders—and planned this ambush, this pincer movement, this surprise attack without me!"

"Well, I . . . I mean, we . . ."

"Men!" She put on an adorable pout, gazed at him, and laughed. "This is madness, you know! This is a cavalry charge, my young warrior. Well, I will allow you this one unilateral decision. But be it understood, from now on I intend to have an equal say in everything. I am quite used to being independent! Is that understood?"

"It is indeed, my Lady!" Danilo bowed an exaggerated courtly bow. Then he straightened up, she offered her lips, and they kissed.

"So it is sealed and settled, then," she said, her head cocked to one side, giving him her best ironic, mischievous smile.

"It is!"

And so the next day, during the morning service in the Ashkenazi Synagogue in the Ghetto Nuovo, Danilo del Medigo and Miriamne Hazan became man and wife. The requisite quorum of ten men—indeed there were many more—was present to make the marriage religiously watertight. The wedding canopy was the one used by Rabbi Hazan and his wife, Miriamne's mother, when they married, so many years before.

It was a quiet but joyous ceremony. Everyone was delighted, it was clear, to see Miriamne so happy; and everyone too, particularly Jessica and Jacob, was delighted to have Danilo back among them. Jeremiah had been banished, mysteriously, from Venice, and Mordecai was sunk in the last stages of delirium. Two days later, he died. Danilo was able to sit shiva, but then a week later, he embarked for Istanbul.

STANDING NOW ON THE deck of *La Donzella*, Danilo recalled not the sad moments, when Mordecai passed away, but Miriamne's delightful laugh and the wonderful hours, days, and nights they had spent together. Miriamne was as artful, and as funny, and as sensual as it was possible for a woman to be. Being with her was ecstasy, like being a child again. And they knew what sort of a life would face them; it would be an adventure — yes, it certainly would.

He turned his face into the wind once more. A slanting curtain of slate-black rain caught the rays of the sun; the clouds above the oblique veil were lit with a golden halo, their undersides black.

He glanced at his fellow passengers, a few merchants and pilgrims hoping to travel to the Holy Land, to Jerusalem and other cities in what had once, oh so long ago, been Israel — the eternal Promised Land dreamed of by Jews scattered throughout the world.

In a sudden burst, the rain swept across the deck. It slashed down on wooden benches and railings, on tightly packed bales of goods strapped down on a special wooden deck that extended all around the ship. *La Donzella* plowed valiantly through the waves — thump, thump, thump — as foam splashed over the railings.

Danilo sheltered with the others in the cabin. The space, soaked with humidity and crowded with passengers and crew, smelled of wet wool, cotton, and perfumes of various kinds. Soon, food was served. Danilo discovered he had a fine appetite. He had fresh roasted lamb, strong red wine, an assortment of cheeses and breads. He thought of Miriamne: in his mind, he touched her, he kissed her, his hands moved over her hair, her shoulders; they lay together, they whispered, they made love . . .

The rain pattered and thundered on the decks. It was a deluge, silver rivulets ran every which way.

Then, just as the sun was setting, the storm passed. Suddenly, it was night. Under a mass of stars and the great arc of the Milky Way, the passengers stood on deck. They stretched and walked up and down, smelling the humidity, talking in low tones, with bursts of laughter here and there,. The air was cooler. Danilo lingered in a doorway. The constellations shone overhead, and a myriad of stars, and a few planets too—Jupiter and Mars. Venus had already set. Perhaps Miriamne was in the Campo, looking up at these same stars, reading into them a whole world of human emotion and symbolism. She had told him how she and Veronica Libero—her intimate friend, it turned out—had discussed the constellations, and the planets, and the symbolism of the skies, and how through all those external wonders, poets and ordinary people had found through the ages a way of talking of their inner worlds and all their fears, hopes, yearnings, and passions. He felt, in his mind, Miriamne pressing against him, her body curving into his, her lips touching his, her breath mingling with his breath.

A man came out of the doorway and stopped next to him. He was a pilgrim from Marseilles, a Christian. In heavily accented French, he told Danilo about his hopes of seeing Jerusalem, and traveling to Bethlehem and to the River Jordan. "The Pope has just declared an inquisition in Italy," said the man. "It will be terrible—people forced to confess, children torn from their parents, people burned at the stake—as it was in Spain and in Portugal. They call it an Act of Faith."

"So the new Inquisition has begun," said Danilo, with a trembling sense of foreboding in his heart. Finally the net was closing. Perhaps, if he was successful in Istanbul, it would be just in time. Perhaps the Mendes Bank could save those thousands—tens of thousands—of people Samuel Mendes had spoken about. What would become of them all—of Samuel, and Rabbi Hazan, and Miriamne? What would become of Beatrice de Luna, and Pietro Aretino, and Veronica Libero? What would become of freedom?

"I want none of it. It is an evil thing, I say." The pilgrim paused and looked up at the stars. "I want to model my life on Christ," the man said, making the sign of the cross.

"That is not at all a bad idea," said Danilo. He wondered at it—at all the sublime and all the horrendous things that had been done in the name of the Jewish rabbi the Christians called Christ the Savior, the man who had walked in Galilee, succored prostitutes, preached to the poor, and declared that one should "Do unto others as you would have them do unto you."

Danilo looked up at the stars. Yes, perhaps Miriamne—*his wife*, Miriamne, his companion for the rest of his life—was gazing at those same stars, and thinking the same thoughts.

7 2

R O X A N A

NINE DAYS LATER, DANILO GAZED UP AT THE WALLS OF Ragusa, with watchtowers looming over the harbor. Behind the city were steep hills and behind the hills were mountains, and beyond the mountains lay the frontier of Suleiman's Ottoman Empire. As *La Donzella* entered the harbor, banners fluttered from the battlements, cannons boomed, and trumpets announced the ship's arrival.

Danilo spent his first day exploring the streets. He needed to loosen his limbs. Ragusa was a beautiful city, a port on its own little peninsula sticking out into the Adriatic, Italian in design, with pomegranate and orange trees in the public squares. It was a rich city that had been ruled by Venice for 150 years back before becoming an independent republic; the atmosphere reminded Danilo of Venice. Venice had left its mark, as it had in so many places around the Adriatic and the Aegean. Many of the inhabitants spoke Italian. This little republic was a trading nation, with its own navy and merchant fleet modeled on Venice's, trading up and down the Adriatic and towards Italy and the East. It would soon fall completely under Ottoman suzerainty, Danilo was sure of this. It was only a matter of time before Suleiman's writ extended to this stretch of the coast of the Adriatic Sea.

After sleeping two nights in a comfortable inn, Danilo joined a caravan of traders and pilgrims heading down the coast and then inland. He had bought a horse, a frisky but patient and understanding mare called Roxana. He was delighted by the fact that "Roxana" was Persian for "Dawn." It was a good omen, and having Roxana as his companion was more than congenial. It had been a long time since Danilo had ridden freely along an open road.

After several days on the highway, camping out, the caravan crossed a ford near the bubbling torrent of a river; then it turned inland, and went through a mountain pass, leaving the sparkling, balmy Adriatic behind. The weather turned. Snow blew out of a fierce black sky. The wind was freezing. Suddenly it was winter, a blizzard in a mountain pass, exactly like that horrible day Andreas and Achilles had died.

Danilo rode with the wagon train along a gravel trail, then on a narrow path of frozen mud, with deep ruts that the wagons navigated slowly and carefully, bumping and jolting along. Heading ever higher, their route wound through a succession of landscapes: ravines, valleys, uplands, mountain passes, forests, half-wild pasture, and river valleys again.

Danilo looked up at the mountains, studying them as a general would study a landscape: the ridges ran parallel, he noted, to the Adriatic coast; it was as if the ripples and surges of rock had been pushed up by the Adriatic itself. Danilo sketched a map in his mind. Cities like Ragusa, along the coast, had a wall of rock behind them that separated them from the interior; that was why they had been able to defend their independence for so long from whatever armies and kingdoms, surging up beyond the mountains, dominated the inland valleys and flatlands.

The mountain ridges were a formidable barrier, walling off invaders from the east; this wall of mountains explained how Venice, using sea power alone, had been able to dominate parts of this eastern shore of the Adriatic for hundreds of years. Because of the mountains, invading from the land was much harder than invading from the sea. Then too, the coast was so ragged and jagged, with so many islands, inlets, and bays, it was ideal for pirates. If you were a pirate, there were so many places to hide, so many places to dodge away and avoid the Venetian and Ottoman navies. Fate was capricious. It was on this coast, but far to the north, that Angelica had been captured and sold into servitude. Danilo spurred his horse onwards. It was remarkable how chance, pure chance, determined so much in everyone's life.

Late one afternoon they were in the midst of crossing a ford in a river, yet another river, yet another ford. The water was up to the axles, swirling around the wheels of the wagons. The last wagon was struggling in midstream, the horses heaving, the spars creaking, the driver shouting and applying the whip. It was slow, desperate, and painful. Danilo heard a crashing roar from upstream. A wall of water, crested with foam and debris, was rushing between the banks, carrying everything with it, coming straight at them. A flash flood!

The wave slammed into the struggling wagon; the water rose, swirling around, ready to carry away everything. The wagon groaned and was lifted up, carried sideways, twisting, as if breaking in two. With a great crack, an axle split. A wheel came off. The wagon flipped over on its side, came crashing down, and was swept downstream, spilling out passengers and goods. Two women, two children, and bales of silk were swept away. The horses, released from the broken staves, clambered to shore. The driver, who had been tossed off, was lying in a pool, bloodied. He stood up, dazed, and clambered after the horses.

Danilo leaped off Roxana, ripped off his clothes, and waded into the water. It was frigid. He took a deep breath and plunged under, swimming desperately, pushing his way frantically through the foaming, swirling flood. He splashed up to the surface. He was in a pool of still water just below the rapids.

One of the children was nearby, a little girl, screaming and swallowing water; she sank out of sight. Danilo dove down, then came up next to the child. She was on the surface, wild-eyed, spluttering. He shouted in Italian, "Hold on!"

Danilo dragged her to shallow water, she stumbled; he held her up. Her pale oval face, eyes wide, lips purple with cold, looked up at him. One of the merchants had come down to help.

Danilo handed off the girl and plunged back into the water; this time he brought back a little boy. Next he swam towards one of the women. She was shouting for help and floundering in the foaming, swirling water. She was hysterical and fought him like ten devils, but he managed to subdue her and drag her to the edge of the pond. But he knew that getting her out of the water had taken too much time.

With a sinking heart, he plunged back. He found the body of the other woman, floating just under the water, her face turned upwards. Her eyes were open as if she were staring at the sky; the oval face had a saintly quality, something one might see in a painting in Veronica Libero's salon. Danilo carried the body to shore. It was heavy, a dead weight. The clothes were running water. She had a gash on her forehead, just at the hairline, but that was not what had killed her. If only the other woman hadn't panicked!

The dead woman, it turned out, was the children's mother. The woman who had panicked and fought was the children's aunt; she was weeping, and wailing, and making such a fuss everyone was standing around in a circle, paying attention to her.

It was deadly cold. The bales of silk were bouncing back and forth farther down the stream, heading for a waterfall. They had not sunk, strangely, but they would. Danilo stood watching in a sort of stunned and shocked paralysis.

The silk merchant stood with his hands on his hips. "Who will recover the silk? That silk is worth so many ducats, so many ducats! I am ruined. I am a poor man. I am not a rich man. I cannot afford such a loss."

The two children were huddled up, shivering, at the roadside. Someone had put blankets over their shoulders. Danilo glanced at his arms — goosebumps. He was freezing.

"Here, take this," someone said. It was an old man with a wizened face tanned to the consistency of leather. "What?" Danilo blinked. And then he realized the man was offering a flask of wine.

"Thanks." Danilo gulped down the wine and handed the flask back to the old man.

Danilo realized he was shivering horribly, trembling as if stricken by Saint Vitus's dance. He managed — it was a tussle — to pull on his jacket and trousers. His teeth were chattering. He couldn't stop them. He sat down on a log and pulled on his boots. It was not easy; he had to struggle mightily to steady his hands. The sky was a cold white blank of fog closing in. Snow was coming. Who would look after the children? The other wagons of the caravan had stopped in a line. People stood on the edge of the road in small groups; they were in shock, talking, pointing. Danilo's horse, his faithful Roxana, stood patiently waiting for him. How far was it to the next stop, to the next resting place? Some men had gone downstream to try to retrieve the bales of silk. But it seemed they were too late. The bales had gone over the waterfall and disappeared. The caravan still had a long way to go, about 600 miles. Danilo stood. "I'll ride ahead and see if they can prepare a big fire at the next stop to warm everybody up."

Danilo goaded Roxana to a gallop. She seemed happy to race along the ancient road, free now to go much faster than the plodding caravan, where the slowest wagons set the pace. Soon Danilo came to the big sprawling compound that was to be their stopover for the night. He took Roxana to the stables — this was also where the humans would sleep.

The innkeeper, who spoke Italian and some Turkish, was not at first very friendly, but he warmed up. "You should see some of the caravans that come through here. They don't prepare. They know nothing of travel. They are often poor ignorant people—pilgrims—convinced by some charlatan to set off on a long dangerous voyage they don't understand. Many die, believe you me." He served Danilo wine and told him to sit by the fire.

"I will take the wine, but I am going out to see if the others are coming."

"Be careful, sir, there are bandits out there, too. These hills are full of hiding places. If they see a man alone, with a good horse, he and the horse are fair game."

"I'll be careful." Danilo wrapped himself in the blanket the inn master had given him, swallowed the mug of wine, and went out into the dusk. To the east the jagged ridge of a mountain range reached up to the sky. Out of the east, too, came a glacial wind. He left Roxana in the stable, walked down the road, and waited. If the caravan didn't appear soon he would get Roxana and ride out in search of them. Snow swirled around. It wrapped him close, like a shroud. Thicker and thicker it came. Danilo shivered. Snow stuck to his eyelashes, got in his eyes. He could hardly see anything. Night was coming on. Finally, the caravan appeared; slowly, it advanced out of the veil of swirling snow.

Danilo walked forward to meet them. He helped the children and the hysterical woman, who was still moaning and shouting. By now everybody had decided to ignore her. The children said nothing; they shivered, wrapped in the blankets.

The innkeeper turned out to be more amiable than he'd seemed. His wife and four women servants fussed over the children. Mulled wine was served, and steaming hot food laid out on trenchers with large slices of bread.

Danilo looked in a mirror and realized that, as a result of his plunge into the river, his makeup was streaking and coming off. He decided that this must be a sign from fate, so he got out the special soap and washed it all away—the dark skin, the black beard and hair. It took a good hour, and several buckets of water, but by the end Danilo was a new man—himself. He was once again the fair-haired, northern-looking young man his father would remember. He was no longer Bekir Ahmed; once again he was, in appearance at least, Danilo del Medigo. The other passengers, when they saw the new Danilo, seemed hardly to notice. They were preoccupied with other things.

That night in the stables, Danilo slept soundly, lying on a bedroll under several layers of blankets, on a wooden platform. The horses were tied up below, breathing heavily, their warmth rising to envelop the sleeping humans. His own horse, dear Roxana, was just below him. It was reassuring. At one point in the night, he thought he was coming down with a fever. Chills rippled along his body. But by morning he felt better. Everyone was readying to depart. The two pale children were with their aunt, who had finally calmed down. Guilt, Danilo knew very well, would come later.

73

JUDAH DEL MEDIGO

T HE SUN WAS RISING OVER ISTANBUL; IT ILLUMINATED THE
city's bone-white buildings and set their tiled rooftops
ablaze. The dawn call to prayer rang out, interspersed
with the calls of milkmen and yogurt sellers, as citizens began
to go about their daily business in the vast sprawling capital of
the huge empire of Suleiman the Magnificent.

Danilo sold Roxana at the caravan terminal. He patted and
stroked her. She whinnied and neighed and looked at him with
her big dark-brown eyes. She had been a patient, loyal, and
high-spirited companion. He was leaving behind a friend. She
would probably soon be making the return trip along the same
roads. He wondered if he too would be making the same trip.
Then again, there was still the risk that he would never leave
Istanbul, not alive.

No. He wouldn't allow himself to think it. Come what
may, he would return to Miriamne. He would embrace her,
he would protect her, and they would have children and
grandchildren, and their home would be full of laughter and

light. And he would return to the fight to save Jews and New Christians. Samuel Mendes and Gracia Nasi's struggle had become his struggle.

He crossed the sparkling waters of the Golden Horn on the ferry. Out of the morning mist, the walls of Topkapi Palace emerged, towers and domes just showing above the trees. He would soon be standing before his father's house. What must his father think of him after all these years? He must be extraordinarily bitter after being so rudely abandoned by his only son.

Danilo glanced around, inspecting each of the passengers pacing the deck. Had anyone recognized him? Spies were everywhere. Had he been spotted by the Sultan's spies or the Men in Black?

Coming ashore at the quayside, he climbed the slope, entered the Topkapi Palace grounds, and presented himself at the door to his father's house, his childhood home. Memories of all the days spent in this house suddenly surged up. His father was always worried about him. He was young and foolish and just a boy, enamored of war, of horses, and of adventures, and paid little attention to his father's wisdom and caution. He always wanted to sneak out and have an escapade. Oh, what a thoughtless young fellow he had been!

The servant who opened the door stood in shock for a moment. "Master Danilo! Oh, it has been so long!"

"Yes it has, Fazil." Danilo shook the man's hand. "How is father? Will he see me?"

"Oh, Master Danilo, that is the greatest wish of your father's heart. He has missed you terribly. But he is sleeping right now."

"I don't want to wake him."

"Here, let me help you with your things."

Danilo entered the vestibule. Nothing had changed. Time stood still. More than six years of his life evaporated. There they were—the same rugs and the same heavy mahogany furniture, the same colors on the walls, the same paintings and drawings. The same smell of books from his father's studio, just like the smell of books in Rabbi Hazan's studio; the same shadowy rooms perfumed with the same smell of herbs and medicines, the same curtains tightly drawn. No time had passed at all. He waited nervously.

"You will want to eat, Master Danilo; you must be exhausted. Have you come from far?"

"I've come from Venice."

"Ah, Venice, I would so like to visit! They say it is beautiful."

"Yes, it is."

"We have been waiting for you to return. Your father never gave up hope that you were alive. He was sure you would appear someday. I hesitate to wake him. He has just now fallen asleep; it was a restless night. May we give him an hour of rest before we wake him with the good news?"

"Of course." Danilo bowed.

"The Doctor was so certain you would return that he has not allowed us to touch anything in your rooms. Everything has remained just as you left it."

"Thank you, Fazil. I'll just go and sit down for a bit."

"Certainly, Master Danilo."

Danilo climbed the stairs to his old quarters. He stood in the middle of the room. He opened a wardrobe. His clothes were hanging just as he had left them. His page uniforms, and some books he had picked up, and a pebble and a shell that Saida had given him. The whole past welled up from some place deep inside him. He was, for an instant, a boy again. He took a deep breath. No, he was no longer a boy. He was a man, with a man's destiny. He was a married man, with a beautiful wife! He spent some time poking into cupboards and examining shelves, his old books, his notebooks, his notes from school, his drawings, feeling transported back in time.

Fazil appeared in the doorway. "Your father is awake."

"Good! Will he see me?"

"Master Danilo, we have not yet told your father that you are here. We thought it would be a wonderful surprise for him to open his eyes and see for himself that his hopes have been fulfilled."

Fazil opened the door to Judah's room and stepped aside.

Nothing could have prepared Danilo for the pale, palsied figure he saw huddled up in the corner of the bed. Judah was a skeletal ruin.

HIS FATHER'S EYES OPENED. Slowly, they focused. His cheekbones stood out, dark leaden shadows circled his eyes. His neck was withered and scrawny, his beard a sparse white shadow of what it once had been. His Adam's apple moved when he swallowed. His nightgown was open on his sunken chest, the hairs stark white against yellow, waxen skin. His chest rose and fell with his quick shallow breaths. He reached out a gaunt, bony hand.

"I am dreaming, Fazil."

"No, sir," said the servant, who was standing by the doorway, "you are not dreaming. It is your son. It is truly your son, come back to us."

"Danilo?"

"Yes, father, I am here. I have come back."

"Ah, at last! Let me touch you."

Danilo moved forward. Judah reached out and ran his hand over Danilo's face, just touching it with his fingertips, sculpting and sensing Danilo's features, as if he were blind. "I cannot believe it."

"You are ill, father. I am sorry. I had no idea. Fazil, why did you not tell me?"

"I am sorry, Master, I thought you knew!"

"Ah, it is nothing!" Judah coughed. "Age catches up with a man. It is ironic, is it not? The physician cannot cure himself! The Sultan is a wonderful man, but he is rather demanding; he does not accept excuses. Wherever he went, he wanted me with him, and . . ." Judah stopped, overcome by a fit of coughing.

Fazil handed Danilo a serviette and Danilo handed it to his father. Judah put it to his mouth. He was coughing up blood. "Ah," Judah sighed. "For some things, Danilo, there is no cure." He leaned back, propped up on the pillows. The flickering candlelight deepened the shadows, made Judah seem even gaunter. "Now . . . Danilo . . ." Judah breathed with difficulty.

Danilo took his father's hand and held it. "I have been in Italy, Father. In Venice, and Ferrara, and Mantua, and Rome, and Naples, and Milan . . ."

Judah's eyes brightened. "I miss Italy so much. When I think of Italy, I think of your mother . . ." His voice faded. His eyes closed. The wheezing rhythm of his shallow breathing and the flickering of the candle flame were the only sounds in the room.

Danilo tightened his grip on his father's hand and turned, in desperation, to the servant. Fazil nodded. "He'll come back. This happens more and more often."

After a few moments Judah's eyes opened. He blinked, focusing on Danilo. "Ah, I feared I had dreamt it. But you are here." He smiled weakly. "Now, Danilo, I have a question — it is not a reproach. Why did you disappear so suddenly, without a word, and without ever getting in touch with me?" He patted Danilo's hand. "It is not a reprimand. I am curious, because I have heard some things that I find difficult . . ."

"Father, remember during the Baghdad campaign I . . . well . . . I saved the Sultan's life."

"Of course I remember. You also read to him, the adventures of Alexander the Great. He has spoken of it to me. He learned a great deal, he says, from Alexander's adventures; and from his misadventures; from his tactics, but also from his mistakes — his overreach, and not knowing when to stop."

"Well, the Grand Vizier, Ibrahim Pasha . . ."

"A proud and vain fellow. He didn't end so well, did he?"

"No, he didn't."

Judah put out his hand and stroked the side of his son's face. "It was a miserable way to die, strangled to death in his bedroom. He fought, you know. Blood everywhere, up and down the walls; it was terrible."

"Yes, a miserable death." Danilo hesitated. "It seems that Ibrahim Pasha was jealous of my closeness to the Sultan."

"That would be natural. All of his power and wealth came from being the closest person to Suleiman. You are a handsome and charming young man, and talented. You had become very close to the Sultan."

"Ibrahim sent a message to the Sultan's wife, to Hürrem . . ."

"Hürrem, a clever and dangerous woman."

"Yes. Ibrahim's message convinced Hürrem I was going to poison the Sultan."

"You—poison the Sultan? Ridiculous!" Judah closed his eyes. He paused for a labored breath. "But if anything would rouse the tiger in Hürrem it would be a threat to the Sultan's life. I suspect it was her enmity that led to the death of Ibrahim. He was greedy and uppity, and hungry for glory, casting a shadow even over the Sultan. And Ibrahim was not Muslim; he was, particularly towards the end, openly contemptuous of Islam. And then too, he still had influence with Suleiman, and I think Hürrem wanted to have all the influence for herself."

"Hürrem sent the Men in Black after me with the order to kill me on sight and dump my body into the Bosphorus, so I would simply disappear and no one would ever know what had happened to me."

"And so you fled. And you didn't tell me or anyone, in order to protect us."

Danilo looked down. "Yes."

"Remarkable!"

"But now I am back, but just for a brief time."

"If the Men in Black are still looking for you, then . . ."

"Yes. And I have also come with a mission."

"So you are truly a man now. You have a mission! Your main mission in life, Danilo, was to ride a horse, win a contest, throw a lance! Any talk of a larger cause, a noble cause, and you would turn your back and scowl." Judah smiled at the memory. "You were so young! You lived in the present! No thought for tomorrow! So, what is this mission?"

"My mission is to get official approval from the Sultan for the Mendes Bank to open its head office here, in Istanbul."

"And why, in particular, have you been given this mission?"

"Because of you, father."

"Because I have access to the Sultan." Judah nodded and coughed. He laughed and spread his arms; it was a feeble gesture that clearly left him exhausted. "I am not sure I am of any use to the Sultan now, or to anyone else for that matter. And I am not sure I have that kind of influence. But if I can help you, I shall." He coughed again.

"He is getting tired," whispered Fazil. Rachel, the maidservant, came in with fresh cloths and towels, bowed, and disappeared. Danilo stood.

Judah opened his eyes. "No, no, stay! There are many things we must discuss! You are going to ask me . . . I can see a question in your eyes."

Danilo hesitated; he did not want to hurt his father, but he had to know. So much had happened that depended on this question—the decline of Pirro Gonzaga, and his death, and Danilo's rejection by the House of Gonzaga. "Did you not write to Isabella d'Este and tell her I had survived the shipwreck of the *Hyperion*? They all thought I was dead. Lord Pirro thought I was dead. He left for America and he died there."

"Oh, Pirro is dead. I am sorry to hear that . . . It adds to the burden of my guilt. He was a fine man. Your mother loved him very much. So you missed a chance to unite with your . . . your blood father." Judah closed his eyes. "The truth is I wrote many letters to Isabella, and many versions of the same letter, all telling her you had survived and were safe with me." His breath became ragged and wheezy. His chest heaved. His long yellow fingers clutched at the blanket. He opened his eyes again. "But I never sent any of them..."

"You never sent any of them?" Danilo bit his lip. Suddenly, so many things were clear, and he finally understood why so many things had happened.

Judah gazed at him. "No. I didn't send any of them. You see, my son, I . . . I did not have the courage. I . . . I love you so much . . . and I loved your mother so much . . . And . . . well,

I didn't want to share you with another father. Even the thought of it was too painful. I was terrified that Pirro and Isabella would take you away from me. I couldn't contemplate even the slightest chance that I might lose you. Can you forgive me?"

"Yes, of course, Father." Danilo leaned forward and hugged him. "All of that means nothing now that we are together, finally together." And in fact, now it all did seem strangely insignificant and unreal—searching for Pirro, and dreaming of being accepted, for his mother's sake, as one of the Gonzagas. What had Angelica called it, a will-o'-the-wisp pursuit? She had said, 'You are a fugitive pursuing a ghostly fugitive who does not want to be found.' She was right. Here, looking at his father, his real father, the man who had raised him, none of it seemed to matter.

"So you want me to use my influence with the Sultan to help the Mendes Bank."

"If you agree, yes."

"I hope you realize that in all the years I have been with the Sultan I have never used my influence for private gain or for business."

"I know that, Father."

"Well, then, perhaps you can explain to me why the Mendes Bank is so important to you, and why it is so important for the bank to have its headquarters in Istanbul."

Danilo explained how the situation for Jews and New Christians was getting worse and worse, how the Inquisition was extending its reach, possibly over all of Italy and even Venice, and how the Mendes Bank had created an escape route for those trapped by the Inquisition or exploited or expelled. "There is no place—or little place—for Jews or New Christians in European Christendom, Father." Danilo paused. "The only refuge for the moment is the Ottoman Empire. Jews are welcome here in a way they are no longer tolerated in the Christian states of Europe."

"It is strange, now, how intolerance has spread through Europe." Judah coughed and covered his mouth. His fingers came away stained with bright flecks of blood. "Once upon a time, I thought the world was becoming more reasonable—then we had the Sack of Rome, and massacres everywhere. And fear and intolerance are spreading. At the time, even before the Sack of Rome, I foresaw a holocaust—no one listened!"

"You were right, Father. The Inquisition is being set up in more and more countries. Some priests and friars want the Inquisition to be imposed everywhere, even in Ferrara and Venice and Mantua."

"So the Mendes Bank is at the heart of a rescue plan." Judah gazed at Danilo. "You may deny it, my son, but you have much of your mother's idealism in you. You have become a man with a cause."

Danilo looked down. He had long ago compromised his position as a detached outsider. Now he was a husband; soon perhaps he would be a father.

"I shall do it, Danilo. If I have the strength, I will intercede with the Sultan in favor of the bank. Have you any documents explaining the nature of the bank, and its main officers?"

"I do."

"Good. Tomorrow I shall study the documents, and then I shall speak to the Sultan."

"I also want to reclaim Mantegna's portrait of Mother."

"What happened to the portrait? I thought you took it with you."

"I gave it to Isabella d'Este when I went on the road with the acting company . . ."

"On the road . . . with an acting company?"

"It's a long story. It was my way of escaping from the Men in Black."

"More and more surprises. My son has become an actor! And you met some beautiful actresses, I suppose."

Danilo looked down. "I met one beautiful actress—and a true friend."

"Not Jewish, I imagine."

"No. She's a gentile. But she knew and accepted that she and I would not stay together, and that I would not marry her."

"That is quite amazing. You are lucky. She is obviously an enlightened young woman—very modern, and very pagan, as I hear some such people are. Carpe diem!" Judah smiled. "All my life I have been a serious and scholarly man. I have often averted my eyes from even a glimpse of the less licit pleasures of this world. But I would have liked to meet this young woman. It sounds as if she has been a friend to you."

"Angelica is enlightened and loyal. She can be fierce and has a wonderful sense of humor. She is an ally. She helped me . . . is helping me . . ."

"She helped you . . . is helping you . . . Ah, Danilo, I have missed you so much, not only as my son, but also as an entertaining—and unpredictable—companion and friend. You used to come back from the Sultan's school full of tales of jousting and races, and talked endlessly of your horse, Bucephalus! And now—women! My boy is truly a man. I am not blind, you know, however much it might seem that I am! Old men have eyes and feelings too. So, what is this good gentile helping you with?"

"Angelica helped me to stay in touch with the woman I have married, Miriamne."

"Married?"

"Yes, father, married. I am married."

"This Miriamne is a nice Jewish girl, I hope."

"Yes, father, she is marvelous, an exceptional woman. Her father is Rabbi Hazan, in Venice, in the Ghetto. Miriamne is beautiful . . . she is . . . she is intelligent, talented, a published poet and writer, known in Venice and Italy; she is high-spirited, independent of mind, and kind and generous and brave."

"She sounds wonderful. I wish I could meet her . . . Rabbi Hazan, yes . . . of the Ghetto Nuovo . . . Ah, women! Often I think we don't deserve them!" Judah's hand was on the blanket. It curled in a spasm, his fingers plucked at the fabric. "I really didn't deserve Grazia, you know. Your mother was a marvel! Beyond extraordinary! You were telling me about Mantegna's portrait. Did Isabella lose it? How can we get it back?"

"The new rulers of Mantua—the Regents for Duke Francesco III, who is only a child—refuse to acknowledge my claim to it. They say that since Mantegna was their court painter when he painted the portrait, it belongs to the Gonzaga family. One of the Regents told me they plan to sell their Mantegna collection at an auction. I may be wrong, but they seem to want to get rid of anything that reminds them of Isabella."

"If you have connections with the Mendes Bank, then surely you can buy the painting." Judah laughed. "And perhaps you could buy the whole Gonzaga collection as well! You might even buy Mantua itself!"

Judah collapsed into a choking fit. It shook his whole skeletal frame.

Fazil moved forward. "Here is medicine for the cough. But it will make him sleepy. I think that is enough for now."

Danilo helped his father swallow the thick amber-colored liquid. It was sweet and smelled of some herb Danilo couldn't identify.

After a few minutes, the cough ceased. Judah raised his gnarled, emaciated hand, seized Danilo's, and held on. Judah's grip was strong, but so very cold. Then his grip faded and his eyes closed. He lay back against the pillows; his breathing slowed and became more regular.

"He will sleep now." Fazil tucked the blanket closer around Judah's chin.

"I will stay with him and sleep here," said Danilo.

"As you wish, Master Danilo." Fazil bowed. "I shall be close by if you need me."

"Thank you, Fazil."

Danilo lay down on the covers next to his father. For a long time he listened to his father's breathing. Just as Danilo was dozing off, he noticed the breathing slowed. And then it ceased.

Danilo sat up abruptly and called Fazil. They tried to revive Judah. They tried long and hard, using smelling salts, rubbing and pumping on his chest, but to no avail.

Danilo's father, Judah del Medigo, the most famous doctor of his generation, the man whose learning was legendary, whose touch was reputed to be magical, who had ministered to popes and potentates, to the King of France—and to the most powerful man in the world, Suleiman the Magnificent—was dead.

FOR DANILO THE TRANSITION from living flesh to inert dead flesh had been so sudden and absolute, it was terrifying. The dead body had nothing to do with the living person who had been with him and joking just a few hours before. Danilo had seen people die, of course; he had even killed people. But, for the first time, the instantaneous irredeemable nature of death struck him. The body, as a vessel of the soul, was sacred, and it would be treated according to the Jewish rituals.

Within a few hours, Judah's mortal remains had been washed and purified, and placed in the casket with candles lit nearby. Danilo was left alone with the body and he gazed upon his father—no sooner gained than lost. Judah looked distinguished and at peace, even angelic, in the white funeral linen shroud, his kippah on his head and his *tallit*, or fringed prayer shawl, wrapped around his shoulders.

At Danilo's request, only Fazil and Rachel accompanied him to the cemetery. After a rabbi had said the prayers and left them, Danilo stood with the two servants next to the grave. He gazed down at the shovelfuls of earth on his father's casket, deep in the shadows of the grave. In the distance, the waters of the Bosphorus sparkled in the sunlight, a gentle breeze wafted over the ground, and the sky overhead was deep, pure blue and magnificent.

The tranquil immensity and beauty of the day contrasted with the darkness within Danilo's soul. Judah was so much more important to him than he had realized. How could he have been so ignorant of his own heart? How could he have been so blind to his own love and need for love?

Staring at the earth, he realized that because of his father's death his mission to Istanbul was doomed. He no longer had access to the Sultan. There would be no time to sit shiva or to mourn; he must, for his own safety and the safety of others, take care of his father's affairs and leave Istanbul as quickly as possible. He would return to Italy, empty-handed. He had failed. He had failed in everything. What would become of Miriamne? What would become of Angelica and all the others? What about Samuel Mendes, Gracia Nasi, and the Mendes Bank? What about all the nameless refugees who now would find no refuge?

He heard the pounding of horses' hooves and the rattling of a carriage. Danilo turned. Surging up into the cemetery was a magnificent carriage, the imperial Ottoman insignia emblazoned on its doors.

FAZIL AND RACHEL SHRANK back and bowed low. It was the Sultan himself—Suleiman the Magnificent. This was exceptional. The Sultan was not in the habit of attending ordinary people's funerals.

The Sultan, gloriously attired, stepped out of the carriage. A moment later, he was followed by his daughter, the incomparably beautiful, the sublimely powerful princess Saida.

Fazil whispered, "That is Princess Saida, the most beautiful woman in the Empire! She is said to be more powerful, even, than the Grand Vizier."

Danilo stared. Was he going to be arrested for planning to poison the Sultan? Would he be accused of being Saida's secret lover? Or was the Sultan here to honor his long-time personal physician, the Jewish doctor who had served him loyally, effectively, and with utter devotion for many long years?

As Danilo and the servants moved back to a respectable distance, the Sultan, accompanied by Saida and four janissary officers, approached the graveside. The Sultan nodded at Danilo, but his expression was deadpan. He did not approach, nor did he indicate that Danilo should approach him. Suleiman stopped and stood at the edge of the grave, alone—the ruler of the greatest empire in the world. He seemed to be talking to himself; perhaps he was uttering a prayer, or maybe he was addressing his old friend, Judah del Medigo, the doctor who had traveled with him on many of his most difficult campaigns.

Saida, in a neat little cap and veil, embroidered satin jacket, and long flowing dress, followed her father at a respectful distance and then turned to acknowledge Danilo's presence.

Danilo bowed and approached her.

"My condolences, sir." The Princess held out a hand. "Your father's attentions to my father over the years were much appreciated. Doctor Judah del Medigo will be remembered and sorely missed." Saida's bearing was regal, proud, and distant; she behaved as if she and Danilo were strangers. A great gap had opened between them.

Then she whispered quickly, "Call on me this afternoon at home in the third court." She inclined her head slightly. "Again, sir, my condolences. Your loss, I must add, is also our loss—my father's and mine."

And with that, Princess Saida returned to the waiting coach, followed by her father. The janissaries saluted. A servant opened the coach door, and as they entered the Sultan's carriage, it struck Danilo that Saida was living the life she had warned him she was destined to live.

THE PRINCESS

TOPKAPI PALACE STOOD ON THE HIGH GROUND OF SERAGLIO Point, the airy and breezy peninsula surrounded by water on three sides. The warm, sweet breeze moved in the trees, making a rustling sound. The palace was a sprawling collection of halls and pavilions, with vast courtyards open to the sky and the sun, with light airy gazebos. It had once been familiar to Danilo; but now it seemed exotic and strange. It occurred to him that the very lightness of the place was an expression of the imperial self-confidence of the Ottomans— *we are invincible, nobody can touch us*, the openness said.

The Third Courtyard was so large, so airy, so open to the vast blue sky above, and so natural—with trees and grass and walkways, and light slender columns, and high luminous windows—that it evoked the nomad encampments of the Turks as they galloped in from the steppes and created their vast sprawling empire, which now reached from Hungary to Egypt, along the coasts of North Africa, and from the Black Sea and the Mediterranean to the Persian Gulf and the Arabian Sea.

The fountains splashed water that sparkled silver in the sunlight; the trees, casting dappled shadows on the grass, reached gracefully for the heavens. There was such self-confidence in the delicacy of the architecture, it reminded Danilo of the frothy gothic tracery of the Doge's Palace in Venice. Here in Topkapi, behind the delicacy, of course, was the high, blank-faced wall that protected the harem, the female kingdom where the Sultan's slaves and eunuchs and concubines lived in a labyrinth of highly decorated rooms, a mystery within a mystery. Everywhere were the abstract patterns, the bright colors, and the elaborate geometric designs of Islamic and Turkish art. It was truly grand. And once he had been a part of it.

Danilo faced no impediment in entering the house. He was escorted into a marvelous room—high ceilings, lamps burning here and there, brocade divans and sofas, hanging tapestries and luxurious rugs, all laid out with impeccable taste.

"Danilo del Medigo." Saida rose from a bank of fluffy pillows to greet him. She was magnificent in a long flowing gown, strings of pearls and jewels in her hair, a richly patterned bustier that emphasized her narrow waist, and an open flowing skirt, dazzlingly bright with swirling patterns, that went down to her ankles. Brilliant jewels shone at her wrists. Her delicate high-heeled shoes were covered in sparkling gems. Her eyes were bright. Her smile was that wonderful, frank smile he had never forgotten. Each movement was subtle and graceful. "I feared I might never see you again. What brings you back to Istanbul?"

He bowed. "I'm here on a rather delicate mission."

She nodded to her servants. "You may leave us. Danilo is an old and trusted friend, the son of the late Doctor Judah del Medigo."

When the servants had disappeared, Saida tilted her head back and looked at him with that old imperious and amused gaze. A smile hovered on her lips. "Well, what sort of mission?"

"The Mendes Bank has hired me to use my father's influence with the Sultan. The bank needs permission to establish its headquarters in Istanbul."

Saida gazed at him. She hesitated. "He was a great man, your father, wise and compassionate. He was patient and brave, and he suffered much, and he suffered, I think, alone. My father drove him too hard, I'm afraid. Judah del Medigo did honor to his people. My father loved him. Hürrem came to love him. I of course loved him. Judah missed you greatly. He was stoic, always in good humor. He never revealed his suffering or his loneliness."

"I know."

She took a deep breath and turned her back on him, her long skirt billowing around her, the lamplight sparkling in her hair. Then she turned to face him, her expression suddenly naked. "I think of you always, Danilo."

"I . . . I never stopped thinking of you, Saida."

"We were too much for each other, we were too close; we were too many things for each other. We meant too much . . . We dared . . . We . . ." She stopped. "You were my teacher."

"And you mine."

"We were children. Our imaginations ran wild."

"Our childhood was paradise."

"It was innocence, yes." She held his gaze. "And innocence is soon lost. Our island paradise is no more." Saida smiled wistfully. "All of this is very grand." She motioned towards the room—the divans, the tapestries, the chandeliers, the gilt-and-scarlet satin. "I have a good life. My husband loves me."

"He would be a fool not to."

"Flattery!" Her eyes flashed with the old humor, the old irony. "Ah, Danilo, you were a boy once, a golden-haired boy, with the bluest of eyes."

"And you . . ."

"I was a girl."

"A naughty girl. You scolded and teased."

"And you teased me! And you taught me about knights in shining armor and fair damsels in distress, and great deeds and chivalrous acts."

"And you taught me Persian. . ."

She put her finger to her lips. He must not say it.

"Some things we taught each other." She smiled. It was the wicked smile that appeared when she was about to tease him. "You and Bucephalus and your lance . . . you were so proud!"

"I was a boy."

"No, Danilo, you were a man already, the best of men. The best of men, after all, are but children—chasing baubles, bubbles, dreams, fame, and fortune . . . But then . . ." She spread her arms. The light rippled off the sleeves of her blouse, the jewels at her wrists.

"Two worlds . . ."

"*Many* worlds . . ." Saida's eyes sparkled. ". . . divide us."

"Yes."

He was reminded of her quicksilver changes of mood, the shimmering range of her feelings, the vastness of her intelligence; she was always challenging, always adventuring, never predictable. He glimpsed in her eyes the glossy sparkle of tears. "Tell me about the bank! Tell me about your mission."

"You may have heard of the Mendes Bank."

"My husband has mentioned it. It is a bank run by New Christians. They are rich, and they are persecuted. The Mendes Bank provides finance for the Portuguese and Spanish monarchies, and Charles V, and even the English King, Henry VIII, is that right?"

"Yes."

She was totally businesslike now. "I have heard that these New Christians are often accused of—how do they put it—of backsliding, of secretly remaining Jewish. And they are punished for that, for being secret Jews or for proselytizing, secretly, for Judaism. Their children are taken away from them, and all their wealth, and sometimes, if they refuse to recant and to submit to their inquisitors, they are punished, tortured, and often burned at the stake."

"Yes."

"Why aren't they allowed to just remain Jewish? They pay a tax for the privilege, and they can . . ."

"It is complicated. The Christians are afraid of the Jews."

"Afraid—why?"

"Preachers claim that the Jews murdered Christ, who for Christians is the Messiah. Christianity, the Christians argue, has replaced Judaism, so it is no longer a valid religion, and the Jews are wicked, and in league with the Devil, because they refuse to see the light. They refuse to see that Christ is the Messiah, that Christ has brought salvation and has replaced the laws of Judaism with the redemption offered by Christianity. So they want the Jews to renounce their religion and become Christians."

"That's logical, I suppose, if you accept the premise."

"If the Jews do not submit and accept conversion to Christianity, they are often expelled from the country. At best, they are not allowed to work, so they are reduced to poverty. In 1492, they were expelled from Spain and forced to convert to Christianity in Portugal in 1497. But even if they do convert to become "New Christians," they are often accused of continuing to practice Judaism, and are imprisoned, tortured, and frequently executed. Many New Christians were massacred in 1505 in Lisbon. And so it goes. It is getting worse. The Inquisition is spreading."

"That is appalling and barbaric. There should be no compulsion in religion, so says the Prophet. If a person does not choose to believe, then they do not believe. And pretending to believe, or being forced to believe, is not really belief, is it? But that is enough theology. Let's get back to the bank. Why is it useful for Istanbul and the Sultan that its headquarters be set up here?"

"It will bring talented financiers to Istanbul, it will be good for commerce, and . . ."

" . . . and . . ."

"And it will help protect Jews and New Christians who are threatened in Europe."

"How?"

"It will allow a way to escape from danger, a network of agents, routes to travel, and safe houses and refuges. And it will provide a way to move wealth to safety."

"Move Jewish and New Christian wealth to safety—here?"

"Yes."

Saida tilted her face upwards and wrinkled her nose the way she used to when they were playmates. "Things have changed in the Sultan's court since you've been away."

"Oh?"

"Hürrem is older, not as high-spirited as she was. She depends on me, trusts me. I am now my father's trusted confidante."

"He has made a wise choice."

Saida waved the compliment aside. "You have become a diplomat. That is a frightful development. I imagine some beautiful women and clever fellows have been your tutors."

Danilo almost blushed.

Saida took a deep breath. "Well, well . . . I see I have struck home." She cleared her throat. "Father trusts me. He knows I have his best interests at heart. If I advise him to authorize the opening of the headquarters of your bank in Istanbul, I am sure he will do so. The Ottomans were horsemen, as you know, warriors from the steppes, not particularly sophisticated. They need help building the Empire."

"Yes."

"So we have Greeks, Italians, Jews, Venetians, Neapolitans, Spaniards, even some Englishmen, working here, living here—bankers, craftsmen, shipbuilders, architects, goldsmiths. . . This bank of yours will be a splendid addition to Istanbul and the Empire. And if more Jews come, well, that is all the better, I think. They will bring their money, energy, skills, intelligence, and contacts. We need to learn fast, and learn as much as we can."

"That's what the Venetians say."

"Ah, the Venetians! They are dangerous people. Spies everywhere, true merchants, always calculating profit and loss. They are our traditional enemies and our major trading partners. I admire them. It is love and hate, I suppose. They have their own district here in Istanbul—merchants mostly. I have met a few of them. I would dearly love to visit Venice, but I fear I never shall."

Danilo imagined Saida meeting Angelica and Miriamne. What a force they would be.

"Do you have documents describing the bank and its structure, the businesses it is involved in, balance sheets, investments, and so on?"

"Yes." Danilo handed her the package of documents.

She walked around, examining the pages. "Conveniently translated into Turkish. That is good." She turned more pages, scanning them intently.

Finally she looked up and favored him with a magnificent smile. "This looks rather impressive. They have a large network, lots of capital, and what looks like a solid financial position. I see a woman is the chief owner and officer of the bank.

"Beatrice de Luna, by her Christian name, but Gracia Nasi by her Jewish name, which is the name she prefers. She comes from a Spanish-Portuguese New Christian family. She is the mind behind the bank—and its rescue operations."

"I rather like that. I would love to meet her."

"I am sure you will."

Saida gazed at him with that amused, imperious smile. "Well, Danilo del Medigo, you shall receive permission to set up your bank, I guarantee it. You can put your mind at ease on that score. You have my word. Now . . ." She sat down and patted the pillows beside her invitingly. "Come sit by me, and let us take a moment to relive the happy days of our youth."

And so they talked about the games they played as children. About their picnics on the island of Kinali, where they found caves ideal for the imprisonment of kidnapped princesses, and even a battered, dried up fountain—but a fountain nevertheless—of the sort likely to be encountered by any Christian princess escaping the clutches of a villainous Saracen, or by a Muslim princess escaping the clutches of a rapacious Crusader.

That was the place where, long ago, they had re-enacted

Ariosto's *Orlando Furioso*, playing the roles of Isabella and Zerbino, a name that resonated sharply in Danilo's memory.

"Then suddenly," Danilo said, "I was accepted into the Sultan's School for Pages. Our games were over, and you were locked away in your father's harem, like a princess in a tower, to await the marriage he had chosen for you."

"I never promised you the future. I never promised happiness. My destiny was predetermined. It was written in the stars; from childhood, I knew it was so."

"I was the one living in a dream." He smiled, abashed. "And I thought the dream was dead. Then out of nowhere, I received a note, telling me to expect a surprise at the Grand Vizier's dock. I never burned that note. I have it still. It was wrapped around a cinnamon stick and tied with a silk ribbon. And then I discovered a side of you that in all our games I had never seen. I remember every moment of that first cruise we took in your father's caïque on the Bosphorus. To this day I dream of you, spread out on a bed of leaves in the royal caïque, dressed in that diaphanous stuff that made you look like you were floating in a cloud. For me, the magic never ceased. In my dreams, I nurtured the hope that I might somehow find a way to persuade your father to grant me your hand."

"I married the man my father chose. Our eldest son was born nine months to the day after our wedding and is his father's pride and joy."

"I see," Danilo whispered. He realized how huge the gap that separated them had become. He had a wife; she had a husband, a son!

Saida called out to a waiting attendant, "Bring in Zerbino."

"Zerbino? That is . . . an unusual name."

"It is a name I picked out of our reading of *Orlando Furioso* by Ariosto. Remember you read it to me so that I would learn some Italian? I have never forgotten the beautiful words and the music of your voice as you read them."

Danilo blinked. She gazed straight at him, and not even a flicker of her eyelashes admitted to any special meaning in the choice of this strange name — when she was teasing him, it was one of the pet names she gave him.

"Ah," she said, looking up, "there you are. Come."

Out of the shadows and into the lamplight stepped a boy with a mop of golden curls and a striking pair of blue eyes.

SAIDA BECKONED TO THE boy, "Come! Don't be shy. Shake hands with a dear friend, whom I have known since I was your age."

The boy came forward. Danilo, in shock, was barely able to reach out to shake the small hand being held out to him.

"I am delighted to meet you," said Danilo in Turkish, bowing slightly.

"The honor is all mine, sir," said the boy.

"You are a warrior, I suppose," said Danilo.

"I have my lance, and a pony, and a little dagger with jewels that sparkle."

"That sounds splendid." Danilo bowed again. He opened his mouth to say something more, closed it. Saida watched him closely.

"Now run along." Saida waved the boy away.

When the lad was safely out of earshot, she turned to Danilo. "I want you to know he is a fine young man, carefully reared . . . and much loved by his father."

"Saida . . ."

She raised a hand. "Not a word! Now that you have seen him, you understand. There is a resemblance, markedly pronounced when you are side by side. If it were to be noticed, it would put me, my child, and all of us in peril."

"I understand . . ." Danilo bowed his head. He was still reeling. He was a father!

"So you can see you must leave Istanbul at once and never return. There can be no delay. As my parting gift, I have commandeered one of the galleys in my father's fleet. It will sail by the Grand Vizier's Dock at sunrise and take you on board. It will ensure you a safe and comfortable journey across the

Mediterranean, back to Venice and your life in Italy. The captain will be expecting you. He will extend you every courtesy."

"Thank you," Danilo whispered, still trying to take it all in. He turned to leave, then remembered. "There is one small thing," he said, "Hürrem's order to the Men in Black to kill me..."

"Oh, that!" She waved the concern aside. "I cancelled that order years ago."

75

IN MANY WORLDS
AT ONCE

SON!

His hand on the galley railing, Danilo gazed at the sparkling waves. He could still see the little boy, and the dignified, proud way he shook hands. How strange life was! How circular.

Back in Venice, Miriamne, his bride, his wife, was awaiting him, and almost certainly they would soon have children of their own. But out here, always, would be this boy. And he was leaving him behind. There was no other choice.

As the galley moved away from shore and out into the middle of the Bosphorus, Danilo gazed at Istanbul as the city in all its glory, the capital of the immense Ottoman Empire, glided past. The domes and spires of the Hagia Sophia, the minarets and domes of other mosques, the great riverside homes and mansions. The shipyards, where shipwrights worked day and night and around the year to build the Ottoman fleet that would challenge Venice's and Charles V's dominion over the Mediterranean.

They were now heading towards the Sea of Marmara. The wind rose—a fresh, sweet sea breeze. He had sailed along this very stretch of water in Princess Saida's caïque. She had explained to him how, seen from this angle, the shape of the city looked like the head of a dog. Its nose was Seraglio Point, the promontory where the channel of the Golden Horn connects with the Bosphorus and the Bosphorus enters the Sea of Marmara, and the land walls are slung across its chest like a necklace.

So much of the great imperial city—once Constantinople and now Istanbul—now fading from view, he had learned to see through Saida's eyes, to describe and think about using her words. He would never see it again. He would never see Saida, or their son.

Seraglio Point, shimmering above him in the burgeoning light of the new day, was the site of so many of his memories in Topkapi Palace, with its vast gardens and defensive walls. It was where three waters met: the Bosphorus, which led to the Black Sea, the Crimea, and the vast steppes of the East and Asia; and the Golden Horn inlet, which divided the city and gave Seraglio Point its impregnable setting. And here he was, in a galley in the Bosphorus channel, which opened into the Sea of Marmara, leading to the Dardanelle Passage and the Mediterranean—to Venice, to Italy, to Europe and all the wealth of Christendom.

When Danilo glanced towards the southern shore opposite Seraglio Point, he was gazing at Asia; when he looked back at the northern shore and Seraglio Point, he was staring at Europe. This truly was an imperial crossroads, spanning continents, where his own destiny had crossed so many other destinies.

After leaving Saida, Danilo had returned to Judah's house. Judah had not been a rich man. Aside from a shelf full of books regarding medical practice and a few volumes of the classics—Marcus Aurelius, Plato, and some Aristotle—and of Jewish learning, he did not have much in the way of physical possessions. As proof that Judah had continued to count on his son's return, he had long ago named Danilo the executor of his estate. All Judah's instructions were meticulously clear, just like Judah himself, so there was not much for Danilo to do except make sure that they were carried out.

The house was part of the Sultan's domain, so it reverted to the Sultan. Danilo consulted with the leaders of the Jewish community. They told him that in addition to the provisions in Judah's will, they would make sure that Judah's servants were well looked after and that the books and instruments and his collection of herbs and remedies would find useful new homes. A number of young Jewish doctors had been taught and coached by Judah, and they told Danilo they would continue to honor Judah's work.

Danilo realized how little he had appreciated or known his father when he was alive. "I have been ungenerous, insensitive, and inconsiderate," he had said to Rachel.

"Not at all, Master Danilo," she said. "You were young and you had to go away. It is a man's fate to travel."

And now he was sailing forth towards his wife, and a new life.

The wake of the galley was now spreading wider, glittering silver. It was a luxurious vessel with several first-class cabins; good food, the captain assured him, was guaranteed. They carried animals on board for slaughter; the meat would be fresh. This was one of the Sultan's very own crafts. It bore the Imperial Insignia and flew the Imperial flag, declaring that the vessel and its occupants sailed under the protection of the Ottoman Sultan.

The sail snapped in the wind. They rounded a point, and there, spread out on the waters, were dozens, perhaps hundreds of ships, a vast armada of small and large galleys and large round-bottomed galleons. It was the Ottoman fleet, the great instrument of war that Suleiman was building to challenge Venice and Spain, to conquer the Mediterranean, to sweep along the shores of North Africa, and perhaps to make another try at invading Italy and conquering Rome, the heart of Christendom.

Angelica, if she had been with him, would have taken detailed notes, later transcribing them into code, quill in hand, licking her lips and concentrating so hard that her blue eyes tended, just for a second, to become adorably cross-eyed. A strand of hair would fall across her nose, and she'd impatiently brush it or blow it away.

Bits and pieces of experience and love and friendship scattered among three women and many worlds! There was the Ottoman world of the Sultan, his military training, and Saida—and his son. He had a son! Yes, he had a son!

And then there was the world of Venice and all its beautiful worldliness and suave, strangely principled cynicism. And the world of the Christian aristocrats, the world of Pietro Aretino, Titian, and Veronica Libero. And the brilliant, violent city states, the world of Raphael and Mantegna and Leonardo, of Michelangelo, of Isabella d'Este. And the world of his mother, Grazia, and Pirro Gonzaga, his mother's great passion and his blood father, a hero and an adventurer, dead in a distant forest in the New World.

And there was the world of Judah, his legal father, the world of Jewish and Western science, the world of doctors, and the synagogue; and the world of the Venetian Ghetto, the world of Miriamne and Rabbi Hazan.

Danger lurked everywhere. And he would protect them all, everyone he loved. And he loved the whole world. He was a product of Christianity and its old-fashioned, romantic warrior ideal of chivalry. And he was a product of the Ottoman Empire and its grand Islamic warrior culture. And he was also a Jew, the son of Grazia dei Rossi and Judah del Medigo, and all their scholarly love and passion for ideas. His world had come full circle, taking him back to the Ghetto where he was born. And he was the husband of Miriamne . . .

To the two of them, the whole world beckoned . . .

Anything was possible.

And what of his son? Where would fate take the boy? He felt, somehow, that he would see the boy again, somewhere, sometime, his son, this other son of two fathers who, like him, would live in, and love in, many worlds at once.

CODA

THE ROMAN INQUISITION BEGAN IN 1542 AND QUICKLY spread throughout Italy. Jews were confined, in one city after another, to ghettos. The Spanish and Portuguese Inquisitions spread to the New World, reaping thousands of victims.

Using networks set up by the Mendes Bank, thousands of Jews and New Christians escaped persecution and death in Europe and made their way to the Ottoman Empire, which became, under the rule of the Sultans for 400 years, a center of Jewish and Sephardic culture. As for the Mendes Bank, it would, for many generations, dominate Ottoman finance and the Empire's trade with Europe.

Gracia Nasi—alias Beatrice de Luna—moved to Istanbul. She set up many Jewish charitable institutions and established a Jewish settlement in Palestine, near the town of Tiberius. She hoped to live her last years in Palestine, but died before she could make the voyage.

The d'Este family's city state of Ferrara was absorbed into the Papal States in 1597, and its long centuries of brilliance were extinguished.

The Gonzaga family's city state of Mantua was smashed by war, devastated by plague, and finally incorporated into the Austrian Empire in 1708.

What the world would later call the Italian Renaissance had come to an end; it was buried under the ideology of the Counter-Reformation, as the Catholic Church and the Papacy mobilized all their energies in a pitiless war against heresy and Protestantism.

By saving Corfu in 1537, Venice, the Most Serene Republic, probably saved Italy, and possibly Europe, from Islamic and Ottoman conquest. Three decades later, in 1571, in alliance with Spain, Venice defeated the Ottoman Empire in a great naval battle at Lepanto. This ended the Ottoman effort to dominate the Mediterranean, invade Italy, and conquer Rome.

The Republic of Venice survived for another two-and-a-half centuries. Increasingly, it became a shadow and a mockery of itself, a byword for luxury, excess, and hedonistic decadence. In 1797, an ambitious young French general, Napoleon Bonaparte, abolished the Republic of Venice, ending its 1400 years of independence.

The Catholic-Protestant wars that began in the 1530s and 1540s lasted, as one cardinal had predicted to Angelica, more than one hundred years.

During those wars, between 6 and 10 million people died.

ACKNOWLEDGEMENTS

THEY SAY IT TAKES a whole village to raise a child, and *Son of Two Fathers* would not have been possible without the help of many, many people. So, on my behalf and on behalf of Jacqueline — "Jackie" — Park, I would like to mention a few of the helpers, friends, colleagues, and experts who provided insight and advice, and who also helped Jackie through some difficult — but very creative — years. Dr. Carol Kitai, Dr. Alan Berger, Sandra Rabinovitch, Uri Sagman, Michael Manzi, Doreen Sears, Dr. Russell Westkirk, Bernadette — "Bernie" — Sulgit, Ann Petrie, Jasu Mistry, Gillian McDermott, and Kirsten Scollie — all were close to Jackie and all provided inspiration for her. Howard Cohen and Ron Soskolne were continuously there to support Jackie. M. E. Dunbar, Jeannyfer Reglos, Jeneth Pabularcon, Sharon Agbunag, and Vivian Andrion were tireless in helping Jackie do her best and be her best, helping her to keep the creative energies flowing.

Jonathan Coutts, Alpesh Mistry, and Joseph Ramochland worked closely with Jackie on the book, doing research, taking notes, and acting when necessary as very skilled, critical-minded amanuenses. In Italy, Elena Solari, Laura Sabbadin,

Roberta Curiel, and Tamara Andruszkiewicz opened doors and provided invaluable background information and contacts for both Jackie and myself. Rabbi Eliezer Zalmanov, Christine Eberle, Robin Roger, Kenneth Bartlett, Ionna Iordanou, Julian and Anna Porter, and Chuck Shamata checked facts and came up with priceless suggestions and insights, making the book much richer for them.

Researching the book meant consulting dozens—perhaps hundreds—of publications, but one book stands out: Andrée Aelion Brooks's *The Woman Who Defied Kings*, which tells the extraordinary, true, and little-known story of Beatrice de Luna, or Gracia Nasi, her underground rescue networks, and her powerful Mendes Bank.

I want to express a particular thanks, from Jackie and myself, to the extraordinary publishing team at House of Anansi, including Jacqueline Baker, Maria Golikova, Michelle MacAleese, and Janie Yoon, and to the president and publisher of Anansi, Sarah MacLachlan. And, on my own behalf, I would like to thank my friend and agent, John Pearce, of Westwood Creative Artists, for his generous advice and skilled support.

JACQUELINE PARK (1925–2018) was the bestselling author of the Grazia dei Rossi Trilogy (*The Secret Book of Grazia dei Rossi: Book 1*, *The Legacy of Grazia dei Rossi: Book 2*, and *Son of Two Fathers: Book 3*). She was also the founding chairman of the Dramatic Writing Program and professor emerita at New York University's Tisch School of the Arts.

GILBERT REID is a veteran television and radio producer and writer who lived and worked for thirty years in Europe. He was nominated for a Gemini Award for Best Documentary Writing for *Storming the Ridge*, and for eleven years he was the director of the Canadian Cultural Center in Rome. He has written for the *Globe and Mail*, the *Times Literary Supplement*, and many other publications, and he has interviewed such personalities as Robert Altman, Marguerite Duras, Sergio Leone, and Northrop Frye. He is the author of the critically acclaimed story collection *So This Is Love*. His short story "Pavilion 24" was nominated for Best Fiction by the Canadian Magazine Awards. He lives in Toronto.